Herman Melville

was born in New York City in 1819. When his father died, he was forced to leave school and find work. After passing through some minor clerical jobs, the eighteen-year-old young man shipped out to sea, first on a short cargo trip, then, at twenty-one, on a three-year South Sea whaling venture. From the experiences accumulated on this voyage would come the material for his early books, *Typee* (1846) and *Omoo* (1847), as well as for such masterpieces as *Moby-Dick* (1851), *Pierre,* (1852), *The Piazza Tales* (1856) and *Billy Budd, Sailor* (posthumous, 1924).

Though the first two novels—popular romantic adventures—sold well, Melville's more serious writing failed to attract a large audience, perhaps because it attacked the current philosophy of transcendentalism and its espoused "self-reliance." (As he made clear in the savagely comic *The Confidence Man* (1857), Melville thought very little of Emersonian philosophy.) He spent his later years working as a customs inspector on the New York docks, writing only the poems comprising *Battle-Pieces* (1866). He died in 1891, leaving *Billy Budd, Sailor* unpublished.

This edition of *Moby-Dick*, edited with an introduction by Charles Child Walcutt, contains the complete text of the novel; a brief life of the author; selections from his letters (including the brilliant exchanges with Nathaniel Hawthorne); a sampling of reviews by Melville's contemporaries; six moden essays (including D.H. Lawrence's famous critique); and a short bibliography.

Bantam Classics
Ask your bookseller for these other American classics

THE ADVENTURES OF HUCKLEBERRY FINN, Mark Twain
THE ADVENTURES OF TOM SAWYER, Mark Twain
LIFE ON THE MISSISSIPPI, Mark Twain
A CONNECTICUT YANKEE IN KING ARTHUR'S COURT,
  Mark Twain
PUDD'NHEAD WILSON, Mark Twain
THE CALL OF THE WILD and WHITE FANG, Jack London
THE SEA WOLF, Jack London
MOBY-DICK, Herman Melville
BILLY BUDD and OTHER STORIES, Herman Melville
THE SCARLET LETTER, Nathaniel Hawthorne
THE HOUSE OF THE SEVEN GABLES, Nathaniel Hawthorne
THE RED BADGE OF COURAGE, Stephen Crane
WALDEN and OTHER WRITINGS, Henry David Thoreau

Moby-Dick
by Herman Melville

Edited and with an Introduction by Charles Child Walcutt

BANTAM BOOKS
TORONTO · NEW YORK · LONDON

MOBY-DICK
A Bantam Book

PRINTING HISTORY
Moby-Dick *was first published in 1851*
First Bantam publication / February 1967
Bantam Classic edition / March 1981

ISBN 0-553-21007-6

Published simultaneously in the United States and Canada

Bantam Books are published by Bantam Books, Inc. Its trade-
mark, consisting of the words "Bantam Books" and the por-
trayal of a bantam, is Registered in U.S. Patent and Trademark
Office and in other countries. Marca Registrada. Bantam
Books, Inc., 666 Fifth Avenue, New York, New York 10103.

PRINTED IN THE UNITED STATES OF AMERICA

0 9 8 7 6 5 4 3 2

CONTENTS

CRITICISM AND CONTEXT

What Coleridge's ancient mariner said about his ill-fated voyage—

> We were the first that ever burst
> Into that silent sea.

might well have been said of Melville's *Moby-Dick*. Its first readers were shocked and startled by the strange world it revealed to them. It was greeted by most English and American reviewers with respect but also with impatience and bewilderment. More than half the leading periodicals ignored it. The reactions of the rest ranged from glowing praise for its lively and vigorous style to severe censures for its bombast and its unnovelistic form. The consensus of reviewers described it as a wild mixture of philosophy, blasphemy, fancy, wit, exuberance, and adventure.

Initially, Melville seems to have started writing it as a sea adventure in the tradition of *Mardi* and *White Jacket*. On June 27, 1850, he offered the partly completed manuscript to an English publisher describing it as "a romance of adventure, founded upon certain wild legends in the Southern Sperm Whale Fisheries, and illustrated by the author's own personal experience, of two years and more, as a harpooner." The change in his conception of the novel seems to have dated from July of the same year when he read Nathaniel Hawthorne's *Mosses from an Old Manse*. In August, Melville met Hawthorne and the two joined in deep kinship over problems which they profoundly and almost uniquely shared. Later Melville spent several days with Hawthorne at Lenox and they engaged in long sympathetic exchanges. In Hawthorne, Melville found a man who understood his most deeply-suppressed intimations—a man who had written about them already, although in a manner that was so restrained and evasive that no one except perhaps Melville himself had understood their implications. He told Hawthorne what he may not have dared tell any other man: "The reason the mass of men fear God, and *at bottom dislike* Him, is because they rather distrust His heart, and fancy Him all brain like a watch."

Influenced by Hawthorne, Melville produced a new and different book from the one he had begun. Published in October, 1851, a year late, *Moby-Dick* was dedicated to Hawthorne "In Token of my Appreciation for his Genius." Hawthorne's letter to Melville about *Moby-Dick* is lost. Melville received it about November 15, 1851, and replied, "A sense of unspeakable security is in me this moment, on account of your having understood the book. I have written a wicked book, and feel spotless as a lamb." He went on to express his astonishment at Hawthorne's so exactly sharing his deepest thoughts and fully sensing what Melville had despaired of ever being able to communicate.

Not only was *Moby-Dick* changed, it was also vastly enlarged. What Melville in June, 1850, described as half of it was probably only a small quarter of the finished work. As Melville's symbols generated meanings and further meanings, the book grew in size and complexity. What began with Calvinism reached out into Zoroastrianism; what began as a symbol of nature became a symbol of God and then of Man.

Stylistically, Melville was influenced by Sir Thomas Browne, the seventeenth-century writer whose prose impressed many American authors of the nineteenth century. Melville also drew heavily on Shakespeare both for style and character. Pip, for example, seems to be modeled after the Fool in *King Lear*. Ahab defying the fire in Chapter CXIX recalls Lear out in the storm on the heath, challenging the gods in their ultimate injustice. In the great Chapter XXXVI where Ahab declares his purpose to the crew, he does so in creditable Shakespearean blank verse, which Melville printed as prose.

> *Take off thine eye! More intolerable*
> *Than fiends' glarings is a doltish stare!*
> *So, so; thou reddenest and palest;*
> *My heat has melted thee to anger-glow.*
> *But look ye, Starbuck, what is said in heat,*
> *That thing unsays itself. These are men*
> *From whom warm words are small indignity.*
> *I meant not to incense thee. Let it go.*
> *Look! see yonder Turkish cheeks of spotted tawn—*
> *Living, breathing pictures painted by the sun.*
> *The Pagan leopards—the unrecking and*
> *Unworshipping things, that live; and seek, and give*
> *No reasons for the torrid life they feel!*
> *The crew, man, the crew! Are they not one and all*
> *With Ahab, in this matter of the whale?*

The more one rereads this passage, the more strikingly it reproduces the movement of the verse in Shakespeare's great tragedies, especially in *King Lear*. Even the slight irregularities that appear in the first three lines above are characteristic of Shakespeare.

In the fervor and jubilation of the act of creation, Melville wrote to Duyckinck, "Can you send me about fifty fast-writing youths, with an easy style & not averse to polishing their labors?" With such a staff he might have been able to stay abreast of his inspiration. Without it, he was bound to feel that his creature grew faster than he could control it. "God keep me from ever completing anything," he wrote when he came to understand that this condition was inevitable to a conception like his. "This whole book is but a draught—nay, but a draught of a draught. Oh, Time, Strength, Cash, and Patience!"

A second reason for the greater size of the rewritten book is that its thesis cannot be simply, or even clearly stated. It has to be "rendered," to use Henry James's famous word, and the rendering involves indirections and ambiguities that carry the reader more and more deeply into the maze of Truth. At the same time, what Melville had to say was in some aspects so blasphemous, so utterly shocking to the religious sensibilities of his contemporaries that he dared not come out with it directly. On top of his proliferating symbols, he imposed a style of jocular evasion, of double and triple talk, of sly hints and impudent ironies, which made it difficult to hold him directly responsible for his most audacious statements and the impieties they express. Not only was he uneasy about speaking out directly; he was also oppressed by the realization that no artistic communication is more than a fraction of what the artist intends.

His book is difficult and complex because Melville does not reduce the dilemmas of the world and of life to childish simplicities. In *Moby-Dick* he is dealing with matters of profound mystery. Melville himself was concerned because he was unable to express all he meant, or even to bare all of his deepest thoughts.

Moby-Dick is a story contrived to explore and exemplify an idea. The journey in quest of Moby-Dick is an intellectual journey in quest of a truth. The novel therefore does not take the traditional dramatic form of problem-conflict-choice (climax)-and dénouement. Ahab is pitted against an antagonist he does not understand. The action of the book is, physically, the pursuit of the white whale; but spiritually it is the story of Ahab's developing idea of what his antagonist represents and what he plans to *do* as his understanding of his antagonist develops. By the end of the story Ahab has knowledge, warnings, and portents. He has the loving appeals of Pip, the noble eloquence of Starbuck, and the warmth of home to draw him away from a final confrontation he knows to be hopeless. Yet he must go on. His decision to go on is not the result of a clear-cut choice, but of his fatal compulsion. "What is it, what nameless, inscrutable, unearthly thing is it; what cozening hidden lord and master, and cruel, remorseless emperor commands me; that against all natural lovings and longings, so keep I pushing, and crowding, and jamming myself on all the time?" Ahab asks, and he has no answer. The Idea is in command and the characterization of Ahab is somewhat baffling because his intellectual development is at cross-purposes with his drive for revenge.

Melville allows us to consider various possibilities in his conceptions of the nature of evil and of the universe:

1. That the universe and God are all-good, essentially spiritual. This is the transcendental view that unites God, man, and nature in mutual perfection.

2. That the universe is controlled by an omnipotent and benevolent God who permits evil in man and nature. This is Christian dualism, which carries an enormous range of dogma, interpretation, and philosophy.

3. That good and evil are independent, equally powerful principles perpetually at war for control of the universe. This is Zoroastrian or Manichaean.

4. That the universe or God is essentially evil.

5. That the universe is chaotic.

6. That the universe is orderly but godless, therefore indifferent.

All, or almost all, critics have agreed on the special importance of the whale as a symbol. The extraordinary range of concepts and possibilities which the whale is made to suggest gives *Moby-Dick* its great richness. At first, the whale is Nature, a source of oil, meat, whalebone, and the valuable spermaceti oil. It is also the largest and the most powerful of all creatures, capable of sudden and incredible feats of destruction. It is impossible, as Ishmael discovers, to picture or describe the whale because it does not keep its shape unless it is in the water, and it is impossible to get close enough to it without being in the direst danger. Legends have grown up around the White Whale among mariners, until he has come to be thought both immortal and ubiquitous.

The whalers, then, become seekers of an ultimate truth,

which retreats farther and farther into the forbidden depths of
the remotest seas. They discover "that mortally intolerable
truth, that all deep, earnest thinking is but the intrepid effort
of the soul to keep the open independence of her sea; while
the wildest winds of heaven and earth conspire to cast her on
the treacherous, slavish shore." (XXIII) From such tropes,
generated by an exploration of his great symbol, Melville con-
structs some of the most extraordinary sentences in American
literature, sentences that derive their concreteness and vitality,
their wonderful poetic qualities, directly from the powers that
he releases in his symbol. Trying to get close enough to know
Moby-Dick, his pursuers come to the ultimate inseparable
and incomprehensible juxtaposition of Good and Evil. "Judge,
then, to what pitches of inflamed, distracted fury the minds of
his more desperate hunters were impelled, when amid the chips
of chewed boats, and the sinking limbs of torn comrades,
they swam out of the white curds of the whale's direful wrath
into the serene, exasperating sunlight, that smiled on, as if at a
birth or a bridal." (XLI) From this graphic image of horror
and frustration, Melville goes on to even more terrifyingly
mysterious suggestions: "But not yet have we solved the incantation of this whiteness, and learned why it appeals with
such power to the soul; and more strange and far more portentous—why, as we have seen, it is at once the most meaning
symbol of spiritual things, nay, the very veil of the Christian's
Deity; and yet should be as it is, the intensifying agent in
things the most appalling to mankind." (XLII) In abstracting
and exploring one quality of the whale—its whiteness—Melville generates whole worlds of suggestions and new meanings
beyond Christianity, beyond the various religions of the East,
which are invoked in his search into the unknown, beyond
good and evil, almost beyond the possibility of meaning, till
"the palsied universe lies before us a leper; and like wilful
travellers in Lapland, who refuse to wear colored and coloring
glasses upon their eyes, so the wretched infidel gazes himself
blind at the monumental white shroud that wraps all the prospect around him. And of all these things the Albino whale
was the symbol. Wonder ye then at the fiery hunt?"

In *Moby-Dick*, his great "draught of a draught," Melville
went farther into the mystery of man's deathbound plight than
any other American writer has done before or since.

In Token
of my admiration for his genius,
This book is inscribed
to
NATHANIEL HAWTHORNE.

ETYMOLOGY

(SUPPLIED BY A LATE CONSUMPTIVE
USHER TO A GRAMMAR SCHOOL.)

THE pale Usher—threadbare in coat, heart, body, and brain; I see him now. He was ever dusting his old lexicons and grammars, with a queer handkerchief, mockingly embellished with all the gay flags of all the known nations of the world. He loved to dust his old grammars; it somehow mildly reminded him of his mortality.

"While you take in hand to school others, and to teach them by what name a whale-fish is to be called in our tongue, leaving out, through ignorance, the letter H, which almost alone maketh up the signification of the word, you deliver that which is not true."

Hackluyt.

*"WHALE. * * * Sw. and Dan.* hval. *This animal is named from roundness or rolling; for in Dan.* hvalt *is arched or vaulted."*

Webster's Dictionary.

*"WHALE. * * * It is more immediately from the Dut. and Ger.* Wallen; A.S. Walw-ian, *to roll, to wallow."*

Richardson's Dictionary.

ח	*Hebrew.*
χητος,	*Greek.*
CETUS,	*Latin.*
WHŒL,	*Anglo-Saxon.*
HVALT,	*Danish.*
WAL,	*Dutch.*
HWAL,	*Swedish.*
WHALE,	*Icelandic.*
WHALE,	*English.*
BALEINE,	*French.*
BALLENA,	*Spanish.*
PEKEE-NUEE-NUEE,	*Fegee.*
PEHEE-NUEE-NUEE,	*Erromangoan.*

EXTRACTS

(SUPPLIED BY A SUB-SUB-LIBRARIAN.)

IT will be seen that this mere painstaking burrower and grub-worm of a poor devil of a Sub-Sub appears to have gone through the long Vaticans and street-stalls of the earth, picking up whatever random allusions to whales he could anyways find in any book whatsoever, sacred or profane. Therefore you must not, in every case at least, take the higgledy-piggledy whale statements, however authentic, in these extracts, for veritable gospel cetology. Far from it. As touching the ancient authors generally, as well as the poets here appearing, these extracts are solely valuable or entertaining, as affording a glancing bird's eye view of what has been promiscuously said, thought, fancied, and sung of Leviathan, by many nations and generations, including our own.

So fare thee well, poor devil of a Sub-Sub, whose commentator I am. Thou belongest to that hopeless, sallow tribe which no wine of this world will ever warm; and for whom even Pale Sherry would be too rosy-strong; but with whom one sometimes loves to sit, and feel poor-devilish, too; and grow convivial upon tears; and say to them bluntly, with full eyes and empty glasses, and in not altogether unpleasant sadness—Give it up, Sub-Subs! For by how much the more pains ye take to please the world, by so much the more shall ye for ever go thankless! Would that I could clear out Hampton Court and the Tuileries for ye! But gulp down your tears and hie aloft to the royal-mast with your hearts; for your friends who have gone before are clearing out the seven-storied heavens, and making refugees of long-pampered Gabriel, Michael, and Raphael, against your coming. Here ye strike but splintered hearts together—there, ye shall strike unsplinterable glasses!

"And God created great whales."
Genesis.

"Leviathan maketh a path to shine after him;
One would think the deep to be hoary."
Job.

"Now the Lord had prepared a great fish to swallow up Jonah."
Jonah.

"There go the ships; there is that Leviathan whom thou hast
made to play therein."   *Psalms.*

"In that day, the Lord with his sore, and great, and strong
sword, shall punish Leviathan the piercing serpent, even Leviathan
that crooked serpent; and he shall slay the dragon that is in the
sea."   *Isaiah.*

"And what thing soever besides cometh within the chaos of this
monster's mouth, be it beast, boat, or stone, down it goes all
incontinently that foul great swallow of his, and perisheth in the
bottomless gulf of his paunch."   *Holland's Plutarch's Morals.*

"The Indian Sea breedeth the most and the biggest fishes that
are: among which the Whales and Whirlpooles called Balæne,
take up as much in length as four acres or arpens of land."
Holland's Pliny.

"Scarcely had we proceeded two days on the sea, when about
sunrise a great many Whales and other monsters of the sea, appeared. Among the former, one was of a most monstrous size.
* * This came towards us, open-mouthed, raising the waves on
all sides, and beating the sea before him into a foam."
Tooke's Lucian. "The True History."

"He visited this country also with a view of catching horse-
whales, which had bones of very great value for their teeth, of
which he brought some to the king. * * * The best whales
were catched in his own country, of which some were forty-eight,
some fifty yards long. He said that he was one of six who had
killed sixty in two days."
*Other or Octher's verbal narrative taken down
from his mouth by King Alfred. A.D.* 890.

"And whereas all the other things, whether beast or vessel, that
enter into the dreadful gulf of this monster's (whale's) mouth, are
immediately lost and swallowed up, the sea-gudgeon retires into it
in great security, and there sleeps."
Montaigne.—Apology for Raimond Sebond.

"Let us fly, let us fly! Old Nick take me if it is not Leviathan
described by the noble prophet Moses in the life of patient Job."
Rabelais.

"This whale's liver was two cart-loads."   *Stowe's Annals.*

"The great Leviathan that maketh the seas to seethe like boiling pan." *Lord Bacon's Version of the Psalms.*

"Touching that monstrous bulk of the whale or ork we have received nothing certain. They grow exceeding fat, insomuch that an incredible quantity of oil will be extracted out of one whale." *Ibid. "History of Life and Death."*

"The sovereignest thing on earth is parmacetti for an inward bruise." *King Henry.*

"Very like a whale." *Hamlet.*

"Which to secure, no skill of leach's art
Mote him availle, but to returne againe
To his wound's worker, that with lowly dart,
Dinting his breast, had bred his restless paine,
Like as the wounded whale to shore flies thro' the maine." *The Fairie Queen.*

"Immense as whales, the motion of whose vast bodies can in a peaceful calm trouble the ocean till it boil." *Sir William Davenport. Preface to Gondibert.*

"What spermacetti is, men might justly doubt, since the learned Hosmannus in his work of thirty years, saith plainly, *Nescio quid sit.*" *Sir T. Browne. Of Sperma Ceti and the Sperma Ceti Whale. Vide his V. E.*

"Like Spencer's Talus with his modern flail
He threatens ruin with his ponderous tail.

*   *   *   *   *

Their fixed jav'lins in his side he wears,
And on his back a grove of pikes appears." *Waller's Battle of the Summer Islands.*

"By art is created that great Leviathan, called a Commonwealth or State—(in Latin, Civitas) which is but an artificial man." *Opening sentence of Hobbes's Leviathan.*

"Silly Mansoul swallowed it without chewing, as if it had been a sprat in the mouth of a whale." *Pilgrim's Progress.*

"That sea beast
Leviathan, which God of all his works
Created hugest that swim the ocean stream." *Paradise Lost.*

—————— "There Leviathan,
Hugest of living creatures, in the deep
Stretched like a promontory sleeps or swims.
And seems a moving land; and at his gills
Draws in, and at his breath spouts out a sea."

Ibid.

"The mighty whales which swim in a sea of water, and have a
sea of oil swimming in them."

Fuller's Profane and Holy State.

"So close behind some promontory lie
The huge Leviathans to attend their prey,
And give no chace, but swallow in the fry,
Which through their gaping jaws mistake the way."

Dryden's Annus Mirabilis.

"While the whale is floating at the stern of the ship, they cut off
his head, and tow it with a boat as near the shore as it will
come; but it will be aground in twelve or thirteen feet water."

Thomas Edge's Ten Voyages to Spitzbergen, in Purchass.

"In their way they saw many whales sporting in the ocean, and
in wantonness fuzzing up the water through their pipes and vents,
which nature has placed on their shoulders."

Sir T. Herbert's Voyages into Asia and Africa. Harris Coll.

"Here they saw such huge troops of whales, that they were
forced to proceed with a great deal of caution for fear they
should run their ship upon them."

Schouten's Sixth Circumnavigation.

"We set sail from the Elbe, wind N. E. in the ship called The
Jonas-in-the-Whale. * * *
Some say the whale can't open his mouth, but that is a
fable. * * *
They frequently climb up the masts to see whether they can see
a whale, for the first discoverer has a ducat for his pains. * * *
I was told of a whale taken near Shetland, that had above a
barrel of herrings in his belly. * * *
One of our harpooners told me that he caught once a whale
in Spitzbergen that was white all over."

A Voyage to Greenland, A.D. 1671. Harris Coll.

"Several whales have come in upon this coast (Fife). Anno
1652, one eighty feet in length of the whale-bone kind came in,
which, (as I was informed) besides a vast quantity of oil, did

afford 500 weight of baleen. The jaws of it stand for a gate in the garden of Pitferren." *Sibbald's Fife and Kinross.*

"Myself have agreed to try whether I can master and kill this Sperma-ceti whale, for I could never hear of any of that sort that was killed by any man, such is his fierceness and swiftness."
Richard Strafford's Letter from the Bermudas.
Phil. Trans. A.D. 1668.

"Whales in the sea
God's voice obey."

N. E. Primer.

"We saw also abundance of large whales, there being more in those southern seas, as I may say, by a hundred to one; than we have to the northward of us."
Captain Cowley's Voyage round the Globe. A.D. 1729.

* * * * * "and the breath of the whale is frequently attended with such an insupportable smell, as to bring on a disorder of the brain." *Ulloa's South America.*

"To fifty chosen sylphs of special note,
We trust the important charge, the petticoat.
Oft have we known that seven-fold fence to fail,
Tho' stuffed with hoops and armed with ribs of whale."
Rape of the Lock.

"If we compare land animals in respect to magnitude, with those that take up their abode in the deep, we shall find they will appear contemptible in the comparison. The whale is doubtless the largest animal in creation." *Goldsmith, Nat. His.*

"If you should write a fable for little fishes, you would make them speak like great whales." *Goldsmith to Johnson.*

"In the afternoon we saw what was supposed to be a rock, but it was found to be a dead whale, which some Asiatics had killed, and were then towing ashore. They seemed to endeavor to conceal themselves behind the whale, in order to avoid being seen by us."
Cook's Voyages.

"The larger whales, they seldom venture to attack. They stand in so great dread of some of them, that when out at sea they are afraid to mention even their names, and carry dung, limestone, juniper-wood, and some other articles of the same nature in their boats, in order to terrify and prevent their too near approach."
Uno Von Troil's Letters on Banks's and
Solander's Voyage to Iceland in 1772.

"The Spermacetti Whale found by the Nantuckois, is an active, fierce animal, and requires vast address and boldness in the fishermen."

> *Thomas Jefferson's Whale Memorial to the French minister in 1778.*

"And pray, sir, what in the world is equal to it?"

> *Edmund Burke's reference in Parliament to the Nantucket Whale-Fishery.*

"Spain——a great whale stranded on the shores of Europe."

> *Edmund Burke. (somewhere.)*

"A tenth branch of the king's ordinary revenue, said to be grounded on the consideration of his guarding and protecting the seas from pirates and robbers, is the right to *royal* fish, which are whale and sturgeon. And these, when either thrown ashore or caught near the coast, are the property of the king."

> *Blackstone.*

"Soon to the sport of death the crews repair:
Rodmond unerring o'er his head suspends
The barbed steel, and every turn attends."

> *Falconer's Shipwreck.*

"Bright shone the roofs, the domes, the spires,
    And rockets blew self driven,
To hang their momentary fire
    Around the vault of heaven.

"So fire with water to compare,
    The ocean serves on high,
Up-spouted by a whale in air,
    To express unwieldy joy."

> *Cowper, on the Queen's Visit to London.*

"Ten or fifteen gallons of blood are thrown out of the heart at a stroke, with immense velocity."

> *John Hunter's account of the dissection of a whale. (A small sized one.)*

"The aorta of a whale is larger in the bore than the main pipe of the water-works at London Bridge, and the water roaring in its passage through that pipe is inferior in impetus and velocity to the blood gushing from the whale's heart."   *Paley's Theology.*

"The whale is a mammiferous animal without hind feet."

> *Baron Cuvier.*

"In 40 degrees south, we saw Spermacetti Whales, but did not take any till the first of May, the sea being then covered with them."

> *Colnett's Voyage for the Purpose of*
> *Extending the Spermacetti Whale Fishery.*

"In the free element beneath me swam,
  Floundered and dived, in play, in chace, in battle,
  Fishes of every color, form, and kind;
  Which language cannot paint, and mariner
  Had never seen; from dread Leviathan
  To insect millions peopling every wave:
  Gather'd in shoals immense, like floating islands,
  Led by mysterious instincts through that waste
  And trackless region, though on every side
  Assaulted by voracious enemies,
  Whales, sharks, and monsters, arm'd in front or jaw,
  With swords, saws, spiral horns, or hooked fangs."

> *Montgomery's World before the Flood.*

"Io! Pæan! Io! sing,
  To the finny people's king.
  Not a mightier whale than this
  In the vast Atlantic is;
  Not a fatter fish than he,
  Flounders round the Polar Sea."

> *Charles Lamb's Triumph of the Whale.*

"In the year 1690 some persons were on a high hill observing the whales spouting and sporting with each other, when one observed; there—pointing to the sea—is a green pasture where our children's grand-children will go for bread."

> *Obed Macy's History of Nantucket.*

"I built a cottage for Susan and myself and made a gateway in the form of a Gothic Arch, by setting up a whale's jaw bones."

> *Hawthorne's Twice Told Tales.*

"She came to bespeak a monument for her first love, who had been killed by a whale in the Pacific Ocean, no less than forty years ago."

> *Ibid.*

"No, Sir, 'tis a Right Whale," answered Tom; "I saw his spout; he threw up a pair of as pretty rainbows as a Christian would wish to look at. He's a raal oil-butt, that fellow!"

> *Cooper's Pilot.*

"The papers were brought in, and we saw in the Berlin Gazette that whales had been introduced on the stage there."

Eckermann's Conversations with Goethe.

"My God! Mr. Chace, what is the matter?" I answered, "we have been stove by a whale."

"Narrative of the Shipwreck of the Whale Ship Essex of Nantucket, which was attacked and finally destroyed by a large Sperm Whale in the Pacific Ocean." By Owen Chace of Nantucket, first mate of said vessel. New York. 1821.

"A mariner sat in the shrouds one night,
 The wind was piping free;
Now bright, now dimmed, was the moonlight pale,
And the phospher gleamed in the wake of the whale,
 As it floundered in the sea."

Elizabeth Oakes Smith.

"The quantity of line withdrawn from the different boats engaged in the capture of this one whale, amounted altogether to 10,440 yards or nearly six English miles." * * *

"Sometimes the whale shakes its tremendous tail in the air, which, cracking like a whip, resounds to the distance of three or four miles." *Scoresby.*

"Mad with the agonies he endures from these fresh attacks, the infuriated Sperm Whale rolls over and over; he rears his enormous head, and with wide expanded jaws snaps at everything around him; he rushes at the boats with his head; they are propelled before him with vast swiftness, and sometimes utterly destroyed.

* * * It is a matter of great astonishment that the consideration of the habits of so interesting, and, in a commercial point of view, of so important an animal (as the Sperm Whale) should have been so entirely neglected, or should have excited so little curiosity among the numerous, and many of them competent observers, that of late years must have possessed the most abundant and the most convenient opportunities of witnessing their habitudes." *Thomas Beale's History of the Sperm Whale*, 1839.

"The Cachalot" (Sperm Whale) "is not only better armed than the True Whale" (Greenland or Right Whale) "in possessing a formidable weapon at either extremity of its body, but also more frequently displays a disposition to employ these weapons offensively, and in a manner at once so artful, bold, and mischievous, as to lead to its being regarded as the most dangerous to attack of all the known species of the whale tribe."

Frederick Debell Bennett's Whaling Voyage Round the Globe. 1840.

October 13. "There she blows," was sung out from the mast-head.
"Where away?" demanded the captain.
"Three points off the lee bow, sir."
"Raise up your wheel. Steady!"
"Steady, sir."
"Mast-head ahoy! Do you see that whale now?"
"Ay ay, sir! A shoal of Sperm Whales! There she blows! There she breaches!"
"Sing out! sing out every time!"
"Ay ay, sir! There she blows! there—there—*thar* she blows—bowes—bo-o-o-s!"
"How far off?"
"Two miles and a half."
"Thunder and lightning! so near! Call all hands!"
J. Ross Browne's Etchings of a Whaling Cruize. 1846.

"The Whale-ship Globe, on board of which vessel occurred the horrid transactions we are about to relate, belonged to the island of Nantucket."

*Narrative of the Globe Mutiny, by
Lay and Hussey survivors. AD.* 1828.

"Being once pursued by a whale which he had wounded, he parried the assault for some time with a lance; but the furious monster at length rushed on the boat; himself and comrades only being preserved by leaping into the water when they saw the onset was inevitable."

Missionary Journal of Tyerman and Bennett.

"Nantucket itself," said Mr. Webster, "is a very striking and peculiar portion of the National interest. There is a population of eight or nine thousand persons, living here in the sea, adding largely every year to the National wealth by the boldest and most persevering industry."

*Report of Daniel Webster's Speech in the U. S.
Senate, on the application for the Erection
of a Breakwater at Nantucket.* 1828.

"The whale fell directly over him, and probably killed him in a moment."

*"The Whale and his Captors, or The Whaleman's
Adventures and the Whale's Biography, gathered
on the Homeward Cruise of the Commodore
Preble." By Rev. Henry T. Cheever.*

"If you make the least damn bit of noise," replied Samuel, "I will send you to hell."

> *Life of Samuel Comstock (the mutineer), by his brother, William Comstock. Another Version of the whale-ship Globe narrative.*

"The voyages of the Dutch and English to the Northern Ocean, in order, if possible, to discover a passage through it to India, though they failed of their main object, laid open the haunts of the whale." *McCulloch's Commercial Dictionary.*

"These things are reciprocal; the ball rebounds, only to bound forward again; for now in laying open the haunts of the whale, the whalemen seem to have indirectly hit upon new clews to that same mystic North-West Passage."

> *From "Something" unpublished.*

"It is impossible to meet a whale-ship on the ocean without being struck by her near appearance. The vessel under short sail, with look-outs at the mast-heads, eagerly scanning the wide expanse around them, has a totally different air from those engaged in a regular voyage." *Currents and Whaling. U. S. Ex. Ex.*

"Pedestrians in the vicinity of London and elsewhere may recollect having seen large curved bones set upright in the earth, either to form arches over gateways, or entrances to alcoves, and they may perhaps have been told that these were the ribs of whales."

> *Tales of a Whale Voyager to the Arctic Ocean.*

"It was not till the boats returned from the pursuit of these whales, that the whites saw their ship in bloody possession of the savages enrolled among the crew."

> *Newspaper Account of the Taking and Retaking of the Whale-ship Hobomack.*

"It is generally well known that out of the crews of Whaling vessels (American) few ever return in the ships on board of which they departed." *Cruise in a Whale Boat.*

"Suddenly a mighty mass emerged from the water, and shot up perpendicularly into the air. It was the whale."

> *Miriam Coffin or the Whale Fisherman.*

"The Whale is harpooned to be sure; but bethink you, how you would manage a powerful unbroken colt, with the mere appliance of a rope tied to the root of his tail."

> *A Chapter on Whaling in Ribs and Trucks.*

"On one occasion I saw two of these monsters (whales) probably male and female, slowly swimming, one after the other, within less than a stone's throw of the shore" (Terra Del Fuego), "over which the beech tree extended its branches."

Darwin's Voyage of a Naturalist.

" 'Stern all!' exclaimed the mate, as upon turning his head, he saw the distended jaws of a large Sperm Whale close to the head of the boat, threatening it with instant destruction;—'Stern all, for your lives!' "

Wharton the Whale Killer.

"So be cheery, my lads, let your hearts never fail,
While the bold harpooner is striking the whale!"

Nantucket Song.

"Oh, the rare old Whale, mid storm and gale
In his ocean home will be
A giant in might, where might is right,
And King of the boundless sea."

Whale Song.

LOOMINGS I

CALL me Ishmael. Some years ago—never mind how long precisely—having little or no money in my purse, and nothing particular to interest me on shore, I thought I would sail about a little and see the watery part of the world. It is a way I have of driving off the spleen, and regulating the circulation. Whenever I find myself growing grim about the mouth; whenever it is a damp, drizzly November in my soul; whenever I find myself involuntarily pausing before coffin warehouses, and bringing up the rear of every funeral I meet; and especially whenever my hypos get such an upper hand of me, that it requires a strong moral principle to prevent me from deliberately stepping into the street, and methodically knocking people's hats off—then, I account it high time to get to sea as soon as I can. This is my substitute for pistol and ball. With a philosophical flourish Cato throws himself upon his sword; I quietly take to the ship. There is nothing surprising in this. If they but knew it, almost all men in their degree, some time or other, cherish very nearly the same feelings towards the ocean with me.

There now is your insular city of the Manhattoes, belted round by wharves as Indian isles by coral reefs—commerce surrounds it with her surf. Right and left, the streets take you waterward. Its extreme down-town is the battery, where that noble mole is washed by waves, and cooled by breezes, which a few hours previous were out of sight of land. Look at the crowds of water-gazers there.

Circumambulate the city of a dreamy Sabbath afternoon. Go from Corlears Hook to Coenties Slip, and from thence, by Whitehall, northward. What do you see?—Posted like silent sentinels all around the town, stand thousands upon thousands of mortal men fixed in ocean reveries. Some leaning against the spiles; some seated upon the pier-heads; some looking over the bulwarks of ships from China; some high aloft in the rigging, as if striving to get a still better seaward peep. But these are all landsmen; of week days pent up in lath and plaster—tied to counters, nailed to benches, clinched to desks. How then is this? Are the green fields gone? What do they here?

But look! here come more crowds, pacing straight for the water, and seemingly bound for a dive. Strange! Nothing will content them but the extremest limit of the land; loitering under the shady lee of yonder warehouses will not suffice. No. They must get just as nigh the water as they possibly can without falling in. And there they stand—miles of them—leagues. Inlanders all, they come from lanes and alleys, streets and avenues—north, east, south, and west. Yet here they all unite. Tell me, does the magnetic virtue of the needles of the compasses of all those ships attract them thither?

Once more. Say, you are in the country; in some high land of lakes. Take almost any path you please, and ten to one it carries you down in a dale, and leaves you there by a pool in the stream. There is magic in it. Let the most absent-minded of men be plunged in his deepest reveries—stand that man on his legs, set his feet a-going, and he will infallibly lead you to water, if water there be in all that region. Should you ever be athirst in the great American desert, try this experiment, if your caravan happen to be supplied with a metaphysical professor. Yes, as every one knows, meditation and water are wedded for ever.

But here is an artist. He desires to paint you the dreamiest, shadiest, quietest, most enchanting bit of romantic landscape in all the valley of the Saco. What is the chief element he employs? There stand his trees, each with a hollow trunk, as if a hermit and a crucifix were within; and here sleeps his meadow, and there sleep his cattle; and up from yonder cottage goes a sleepy smoke. Deep into distant woodlands winds a mazy way, reaching to overlapping spurs of mountains bathed in their hill-side blue. But though the picture lies thus tranced, and though this pine-tree shakes down its sighs like leaves upon this shepherd's head, yet all were vain, unless the shepherd's eye were fixed upon the magic stream before him. Go visit the Prairies in June, when for scores on scores of miles you wade knee-deep among Tiger-lilies—what is the one charm wanting?—Water—there is not a drop of water there! Were Niagara but a cataract of sand, would you travel your thousand miles to see it? Why did the poor poet of Tennessee, upon suddenly receiving two handfuls of silver, deliberate whether to buy him a coat, which he sadly needed, or invest his money in a pedestrian trip to Rockaway Beach? Why is almost every robust healthy boy with a robust healthy soul in him, at some time or other crazy to go to sea? Why upon your first voyage as a passenger, did you yourself feel such a mystical vibration, when first told that you and your ship were now out of sight of land? Why did the old Persians hold the sea holy? Why did the Greeks give it a separate deity, and own brother of Jove? Surely all this is not without meaning. And still deeper the meaning of that story of Narcissus, who because he could not grasp the tormenting, mild image he saw in the fountain, plunged into it and was drowned. But that same image, we ourselves see in all rivers and oceans. It is the image of the ungraspable phantom of life; and this is the key to it all.

Now, when I say that I am in the habit of going to sea whenever I begin to grow hazy about the eyes, and begin to be over conscious of my lungs, I do not mean to have it inferred that I ever go to sea as a passenger. For to go as a passenger you must needs have a purse, and a purse is but a rag unless you have something in it. Besides, passengers get sea-sick—grow quarrelsome—don't sleep of nights—do not enjoy themselves much, as a general thing;—no, I never go as a passenger; nor, though I am something of a salt, do I ever go to sea as a Commodore, or a Captain, or a Cook. I abandon the glory and distinction of such offices to those who like them. For my part, I abominate all honorable respectable toils, trials, and tribulations of every kind whatsoever. It is quite as much as I can do to take care of myself, without taking care of ships, barques, brigs, schooners, and what not. And as for going as cook,—though I confess there is considerable glory in that, a cook being a sort of officer on ship-board—yet, somehow, I never fancied broiling fowls;—though once broiled, judiciously buttered, and judgmatically salted and peppered, there is no one who will speak more respectfully, not to say reverentially, of a broiled fowl than I will. It is out of the idolatrous dotings of the old Egyptians upon broiled ibis and roasted river horse, that you see the mummies of those creatures in their huge bake-houses the pyramids.

No, when I go to sea, I go as a simple sailor, right before the mast, plumb down into the forecastle, aloft there to the royal mast-head. True, they rather order me about some, and make me jump from spar to spar, like a grasshopper in a May meadow. And at first, this sort of thing is unpleasant enough. It touches one's sense of honor, particularly if you come of an old established family in the land, the Van Rensselaers, or Randolphs, or Hardicanutes. And more than all, if just previous to putting your hand into the tar-pot, you have been lording it as a country schoolmaster, making the tallest boys stand in awe of you. The transition is a keen one, I assure you, from a schoolmaster to a sailor, and requires a strong decoction of Seneca and the Stoics to enable you to grin and bear it. But even this wears off in time.

What of it, if some old hunks of a sea-captain orders me to get a broom and sweep down the decks? What does that indignity amount to, weighed, I mean, in the scales of the New Testament? Do you think the archangel Gabriel thinks anything the less of me, because I promptly and respectfully obey that old hunks in that particular instance? Who aint a slave? Tell me that. Well, then, however the old sea-captains may order me about—however they may thump and punch me about, I have the satisfaction of knowing that it is all right; that everybody else is one way or other served in much the same way—either in a physical or metaphysical point of view, that is; and so the universal thump is passed round, and all hands should rub each other's shoulder-blades, and be content.

Again, I always go to sea as a sailor, because they make a point of paying me for my trouble, whereas they never pay passengers a single penny that I ever heard of. On the contrary, passengers themselves must pay. And there is all the difference in the world between paying and being paid. The act of paying is perhaps the most uncomfortable infliction that the two orchard thieves entailed upon us. But *being paid,*—what will compare with it? The urbane activity with which a man receives money is really marvellous, considering that we so earnestly believe money to be the root of all earthly ills, and that on no account can a monied man enter heaven. Ah! how cheerfully we consign ourselves to perdition!

Finally, I always go to sea as a sailor, because of the wholesome exercise and pure air of the forecastle deck. For as in this world, head winds are far more prevalent than winds from astern (that is, if you never violate the Pythagorean maxim), so for the most part the Commodore on the quarter-deck gets his atmosphere at second hand from the sailors on the forecastle. He thinks he breathes it first; but not so. In much the same way do the commonalty lead their leaders in many other things, at the same time that the leaders little suspect it. But wherefore it was that after having repeatedly smelt the sea as a merchant sailor, I should now take it into my head to go on a whaling voyage; this the invisible police officer of the Fates, who has the constant surveillance of me, and secretly dogs me, and influences me in some unaccountable way—he can better answer than any one else. And, doubtless, my going on this whaling voyage, formed part of the grand programme of Providence that was drawn up a long time ago. It came in as a sort of brief interlude and solo between more extensive performances. I take it that this part of the bill must have run something like this:

*"Grand Contested Election for the Presidency of the
United States.*
"WHALING VOYAGE BY ONE ISHMAEL.
"BLOODY BATTLE IN AFFGHANISTAN."

Though I cannot tell why it was exactly that those stage managers, the Fates, put me down for this shabby part of a whaling voyage, when others were set down for magnificent parts in high tragedies, and short and easy parts in genteel comedies, and jolly parts in farces—though I cannot tell why this was exactly; yet, now that I recall all the circumstances, I think I can see a little into the springs and motives which being cunningly presented to me under various disguises, induced me to set about performing the part I did, besides cajoling me into the delusion that it was a choice resulting from my own unbiased freewill and discriminating judgment.

Chief among these motives was the overwhelming idea of the great whale himself. Such a portentous and mysterious monster roused all my curiosity. Then the wild and distant seas where he rolled his island bulk; the undeliverable, nameless perils of the whale; these, with all the attending marvels of a thousand Patagonian sights and sounds, helped to sway me to my wish. With other men, perhaps, such things would not have been inducements; but as for me, I am tormented with an everlasting itch for things remote. I love to sail forbidden seas, and land on barbarous coasts. Not ignoring what is good, I am quick to perceive a horror, and could still be social with it—would they let me—since it is but well to be on friendly terms with all the inmates of the place one lodges in.

By reason of these things, then, the whaling voyage was welcome; the great flood-gates of the wonder-world swung open, and in the wild conceits that swayed me to my purpose, two and two there floated into my inmost soul, endless processions of the whale, and, mid most of them all, one grand hooded phantom, like a snow hill in the air.

THE CARPET-BAG   II

I STUFFED a shirt or two into my old carpet-bag, tucked it under my arm, and started for Cape Horn and the Pacific. Quitting the good city of old Manhatto, I duly arrived in New Bedford. It was on a Saturday night in December. Much was I disappointed upon learning that the little packet for Nantucket had already sailed, and that no way of reaching that place would offer, till the following Monday.

As most young candidates for the pains and penalties of whaling stop at this same New Bedford, thence to embark on their voyage, it may as well be related that I, for one, had no idea of so doing. For my mind was made up to sail in no other than a Nantucket craft, because there was a fine, boisterous something about everything connected with that famous old island, which amazingly pleased me. Besides though New Bedford has of late been gradually monopolizing the business of whaling, and though in this matter poor old Nantucket is now much behind her, yet Nantucket was her great original—the Tyre of this Carthage;—the place where the first dead American whale was stranded. Where else but from Nantucket did those aboriginal whalemen, the Red-Men, first sally out in canoes to give chase to the Leviathan? And where but from Nantucket, too, did that first adventurous little sloop put forth, partly laden with imported cobble-stones—so goes the story—to throw at the whales, in order to discover when they were nigh enough to risk a harpoon from the bowsprit?

Now having a night, a day, and still another night following before me in New Bedford, ere I could embark for my destined port, it became a matter of concernment where I was to eat and sleep meanwhile. It was a very dubious-looking, nay, a very dark and dismal night, bitingly cold and cheerless. I knew no one in the place. With anxious grapnels I had sounded my pocket, and only brought up a few pieces of silver,—So, wherever you go, Ishmael, said I to myself, as I stood in the middle of a dreary street shouldering my bag, and comparing the gloom towards the north with the darkness towards the south—wherever in your wisdom you may conclude to lodge for the night, my dear Ishmael, be sure to inquire the price, and don't be too particular.

With halting steps I paced the streets, and passed the sign of "The Crossed Harpoons"—but it looked too expensive and jolly there. Further on, from the bright red windows of the "Sword-Fish Inn," there came such fervent rays, that it seemed to have melted the packed snow and ice from before the house, for everywhere else the congealed frost lay ten inches thick in a hard, asphaltic pavement,—rather weary for me, when I struck my foot against the flinty projections, because from hard, remorseless service the soles of my boots were in a most miserable plight. Too expensive and jolly, again thought I, pausing one moment to watch the broad glare in the street, and hear the sounds of the tinkling glasses within. But go on, Ishmael, said I at last; don't you hear? get away from before the door; your patched boots are stopping the way. So on I went. I now by instinct followed the streets that took me waterward, for there, doubtless, were the cheapest, if not the cheeriest inns.

Such dreary streets! blocks of blackness, not houses, on either hand, and here and there a candle, like a candle mov-

ing about in a tomb. At this hour of the night, of the last
day of the week, that quarter of the town proved all but
deserted. But presently I came to a smoky light proceeding
from a low, wide building, the door of which stood in-
vitingly open. It had a careless look, as if it were meant for
the uses of the public; so, entering, the first thing I did was
to stumble over an ash-box in the porch. Ha! thought I, ha,
as the flying particles almost choked me, are these ashes
from that destroyed city, Gomorrah? But "The Crossed Harpoons," and "The Sword-Fish?"—this, then, must needs be
the sign of "The Trap." However, I picked myself up and
hearing a loud voice within, pushed on and opened a second,
interior door.

It seemed the great Black Parliament sitting in Tophet. A
hundred black faces turned round in their rows to peer; and
beyond, a black Angel of Doom was beating a book in a
pulpit. It was a negro church; and the preacher's text was
about the blackness of darkness, and the weeping and wail-
ing and teeth-gnashing there. Ha, Ishmael, muttered I, backing out, Wretched entertainment at the sign of "The Trap!"

Moving on, I at last came to a dim sort of light not far
from the docks, and heard a forlorn creaking in the air;
and looking up, saw a swinging sign over the door with a
white painting upon it, faintly representing a tall straight jet
of misty spray, and these words underneath—"The Spouter-
Inn:—Peter Coffin."

Coffin?—Spouter?—Rather ominous in that particular connexion, thought I. But it is a common name in Nantucket,
they say, and I suppose this Peter here is an emigrant from
there. As the light looked so dim, and the place, for the
time, looked quiet enough, and the dilapidated little wooden
house itself looked as if it might have been carted here from
the ruins of some burnt district, and as the swinging sign
had a poverty-stricken sort of creak to it, I thought that here
was the very spot for cheap lodgings, and the best of pea
coffee.

It was a queer sort of place—a gable-ended old house, one
side palsied as it were, and leaning over sadly. It stood on a
sharp bleak corner, where that tempestuous wind Euroclydon
kept up a worse howling than ever it did about poor Paul's
tossed craft. Euroclydon, nevertheless, is a mighty pleasant zephyr to any one in-doors, with his feet on the hob
quietly toasting for bed. "In judging of that tempestuous
wind called Euroclydon," says an old writer—of whose works

I possess the only copy extant—"it maketh a marvellous difference, whether thou lookest out at it from a glass window where the frost is all on the outside, or whether thou observest it from that sashless window, where the frost is on both sides, and of which the wight Death is the only glazier." True enough, thought I, as this passage occurred to my mind—old black-letter, thou reasonest well. Yes, these eyes are windows, and this body of mine is the house. What a pity they didn't stop up the chinks and the crannies though, and thrust in a little lint here and there. But it's too late to make any improvements now. The universe is finished; the copestone is on, and the chips were carted off a million years ago. Poor Lazarus there, chattering his teeth against the curbstone for his pillow, and shaking off his tatters with his shiverings, he might plug up both ears with rags, and put a corncob into his mouth, and yet that would not keep out the tempestuous Euroclydon. Euroclydon! says old Dives, in his red silken wrapper—(he had a redder one afterwards) pooh, pooh! What a fine frosty night; how Orion glitters; what northern lights! Let them talk of their oriental summer climes of everlasting conservatories; give me the privilege of making my own summer with my own coals.

But what thinks Lazarus? Can he warm his blue hands by holding them up to the grand northern lights? Would not Lazarus rather be in Sumatra than here? Would he not far rather lay him down lengthwise along the line of the equator; yea, ye gods! go down to the fiery pit itself, in order to keep out this frost?

Now, that Lazarus should lie stranded there on the curbstone before the door of Dives, this is more wonderful than that an iceberg should be moored to one of the Moluccas. Yet Dives himself, he too lives like a Czar in an ice palace made of frozen sighs, and being a president of a temperance society, he only drinks the tepid tears of orphans.

But no more of this blubbering now, we are going a-whaling, and there is plenty of that yet to come. Let us scrape the ice from our frosted feet, and see what sort of a place this "Spouter" may be.

THE SPOUTER-INN   **III**

ENTERING that gable-ended Spouter-Inn, you found yourself in a wide, low, straggling entry with old-fashioned wain-
scots, reminding one of the bulwarks of some condemned old
craft. On one side hung a very large oil-painting so thoroughly besmoked, and every way defaced, that in the un-
equal cross-lights by which you viewed it, it was only by
diligent study and a series of systematic visits to it, and
careful inquiry of the neighbors, that you could any way
arrive at an understanding of its purpose. Such unaccountable
masses of shades and shadows, that at first you almost
thought some ambitious young artist, in the time of the New
England hags, had endeavored to delineate chaos be-
witched. But by dint of much and earnest contemplation,
and oft repeated ponderings, and especially by throwing
open the little window towards the back of the entry, you at
last come to the conclusion that such an idea, however wild,
might not be altogether unwarranted.

But what most puzzled and confounded you was a long,
limber, portentous, black mass of something hovering in the
centre of the picture over three blue, dim, perpendicular lines
floating in a nameless yeast. A boggy, soggy, squitchy picture truly, enough to drive a nervous man distracted. Yet
was there a sort of indefinite, half-attained, unimaginable
sublimity about it that fairly froze you to it, till you involuntarily took an oath with yourself to find out what that
marvellous painting meant. Ever and anon a bright but,
alas, deceptive idea would dart you through.—It's the Black
Sea in a midnight gale.—It's the unnatural combat of the
four primal elements.—It's a blasted heath.—It's a Hyperborean winter scene.—It's the breaking-up of the ice-bound
stream of Time. But at last all these fancies yielded to that
one portentous something in the picture's midst. *That* once
found out, and all the rest were plain. But stop; does it not
bear a faint resemblance to a gigantic fish? even the great
leviathan himself?

In fact, the artist's design seemed this: a final theory of
my own, partly based upon the aggregated opinions of many
aged persons with whom I conversed upon the subject. The

picture represents a Cape-Horner in a great hurricane; the half-foundered ship weltering there with its three dismantled masts alone visible; and an exasperated whale, purposing to spring clean over the craft, is in the enormous act of impaling himself upon the three mast-heads.

The opposite wall of this entry was hung all over with a heathenish array of monstrous clubs and spears. Some were thickly set with glittering teeth resembling ivory saws; others were tufted with knots of human hair; and one was sickle-shaped, with a vast handle sweeping round like the segment made in the new-mown grass by a long-armed mower. You shuddered as you gazed, and wondered what monstrous cannibal and savage could ever have gone a death-harvesting with such a hacking, horrifying implement. Mixed with these were rusty old whaling lances and harpoons all broken and deformed. Some were storied weapons. With this once long lance, now wildly elbowed, fifty years ago did Nathan Swain kill fifteen whales between a sunrise and a sunset. And that harpoon—so like a corkscrew now—was flung in Javan seas, and run away with by a whale, years afterward slain off the Cape of Blanco. The original iron entered nigh the tail, and, like a restless needle sojourning in the body of a man, travelled full forty feet, and at last was found imbedded in the hump.

Crossing this dusky entry, and on through yon low-arched way—cut through what in old times must have been a great central chimney with fire-places all round—you enter the public room. A still duskier place is this, with such low ponderous beams above, and such old wrinkled planks beneath, that you would almost fancy you trod some old craft's cockpits, especially of such a howling night, when this corner-anchored old ark rocked so furiously. On one side stood a long, low, shelf-like table covered with cracked glass cases, filled with dusty rarities gathered from this wide world's remotest nooks. Projecting from the further angle of the room stands a dark-looking den—the bar—a rude attempt at a right whale's head. Be that how it may, there stands the vast arched bone of the whale's jaw, so wide, a coach might almost drive beneath it. Within are shabby shelves, ranged round with old decanters, bottles, flasks; and in those jaws of swift destruction, like another cursed Jonah (by which name indeed they called him), bustles a little withered old man, who, for their money, dearly sells the sailors deliriums and death.

Abominable are the tumblers into which he pours his poison. Though true cylinders without—within, the villanous green goggling glasses deceitfully tapered downwards to a cheating bottom. Parallel meridians rudely pecked into the glass, surround these footpads' goblets. Fill to *this* mark, and your charge is but a penny; to *this* a penny more; and so on to the full glass—the Cape Horn measure, which you may gulp down for a shilling.

Upon entering the place I found a number of young seamen gathered about a table, examining by a dim light divers specimens of *skrimshander*. I sought the landlord, and telling him I desired to be accommodated with a room, received for answer that his house was full—not a bed unoccupied. "But avast," he added, tapping his forehead, "you haint no objections to sharing a harpooneer's blanket, have ye? I 'spose you are goin' a whalin', so you'd better get used to that sort of thing."

I told him that I never liked to sleep two in a bed; that if I should ever do so, it would depend upon who the harpooneer might be, and that if he (the landlord) really had no other place for me, and the harpooneer was not decidedly objectionable, why rather than wander further about a strange town on so bitter a night, I would put up with the half of any decent man's blanket.

"I thought so. All right; take a seat. Supper?—you want supper? Supper'll be ready directly."

I sat down on an old wooden settle, carved all over like a bench on the Battery. At one end a ruminating tar was still further adorning it with his jack-knife, stooping over and diligently working away at the space between his legs. He was trying his hand at a ship under full sail, but he didn't make much headway, I thought.

At last some four or five of us were summoned to our meal in an adjoining room. It was cold as Iceland—no fire at all —the landlord said he couldn't afford it. Nothing but two dismal tallow candles, each in a winding sheet. We were fain to button up our monkey jackets, and hold to our lips cups of scalding tea with our half frozen fingers. But the fare was of the most substantial kind—not only meat and potatoes, but dumplings; good heavens! dumplings for supper! One young fellow in a green box coat, addressed himself to these dumplings in a most direful manner.

"My boy," said the landlord, "you'll have the nightmare to a dead sartainty."

"Landlord," I whispered, "that aint the harpooneer, is it?"

"Oh, no," said he, looking a sort of diabolically funny, "the harpooneer is a dark complexioned chap. He never eats dumplings, he don't—he eats nothing but steaks, and likes 'em rare."

"The devil he does," says I. "Where is that harpooneer? Is he here?"

"He'll be here afore long," was the answer.

I could not help it, but I began to feel suspicious of this "dark complexioned" harpooneer. At any rate, I made up my mind that if it so turned out that we should sleep together, he must undress and get into bed before I did.

Supper over, the company went back to the bar-room, when, knowing not what else to do with myself, I resolved to spend the rest of the evening as a looker on.

Presently a rioting noise was heard without. Starting up, the landlord cried, "That's the Grampus's crew. I seed her reported in the offing this morning; a three years' voyage, and a full ship. Hurrah, boys; now we'll have the latest news from the Feegees."

A tramping of sea boots was heard in the entry; the door was flung open, and in rolled a wild set of mariners enough. Enveloped in their shaggy watch coats, and with their heads muffled in woolen comforters, all bedarned and ragged, and their beards stiff with icicles, they seemed an eruption of bears from Labrador. They had just landed from their boat, and this was the first house they entered. No wonder, then, that they made a straight wake for the whale's mouth—the bar—when the wrinkled little old Jonah, there officiating, soon poured them out brimmers all round. One complained of a bad cold in his head, upon which Jonah mixed him a pitch-like potion of gin and molasses, which he swore was a sovereign cure for all colds and catarrhs whatsoever, never mind of how long standing, or whether caught off the coast of Labrador, or on the weather side of an ice-island.

The liquor soon mounted into their heads, as it generally does even with the arrantest topers newly landed from sea, and they began capering about most obstreperously.

I observed, however, that one of them held somewhat aloof, and though he seemed desirous not to spoil the hilarity of his shipmates by his own sober face, yet upon the whole he refrained from making as much noise as the rest. This man interested me at once; and since the sea-gods had or-

dained that he should soon become my shipmate (though but
a sleeping-partner one, so far as this narrative is concerned),
I will here venture upon a little description of him. He
stood full six feet in height, with noble shoulders, and a chest
like a coffer-dam. I have seldom seen such brawn in a man.
His face was deeply brown and burnt, making his white teeth
dazzling by the contrast; while in the deep shadows of his
eyes floated some reminiscences that did not seem to give
him much joy. His voice at once announced that he was a
Southerner, and from his fine stature, I thought he must be
one of those tall mountaineers from the Alleganian Ridge in
Virginia. When the revelry of his companions had mounted
to its height, this man slipped away unobserved, and I
saw no more of him till he became my comrade on the sea.
In a few minutes, however, he was missed by his shipmates,
and being, it seems, for some reason a huge favorite with
them, they raised a cry of "Bulkington! Bulkington! where's
Bulkington?" and darted out of the house in pursuit of him.

It was now about nine o'clock, and the room seeming almost supernaturally quiet after these orgies, I began to con-
gratulate myself upon a little plan that had occurred to me
just previous to the entrance of the seamen.

No man prefers to sleep two in a bed. In fact, you would
a good deal rather not sleep with your own brother. I don't
know how it is, but people like to be private when they are
sleeping. And when it comes to sleeping with an unknown
stranger, in a strange inn, in a strange town, and that
stranger a harpooneer, then your objections indefinitely
multiply. Nor was there any earthly reason why I as a sailor
should sleep two in a bed, more than anybody else; for
sailors no more sleep two in a bed at sea, than bachelor Kings
do ashore. To be sure they all sleep together in one apartment, but you have your own hammock, and cover yourself
with your own blanket, and sleep in your own skin.

The more I pondered over this harpooneer, the more I
abominated the thought of sleeping with him. It was fair to
presume that being a harpooneer, his linen or woolen, as the
case might be, would not be of the tidiest, certainly none
of the finest. I began to twitch all over. Besides, it was
getting late, and my decent harpooneer ought to be home
and going bedwards. Suppose now, he should tumble in upon
me at midnight—how could I tell from what vile hole he
had been coming?

"Landlord! I've changed my mind about that harpooneer.
—I shan't sleep with him. I'll try the bench here."

"Just as you please; I'm sorry I cant spare ye a table-
cloth for a mattress, and it's a plaguy rough board here"
—feeling of the knots and notches. "But wait a bit, Skrimshander; I've got a carpenter's plane there in the bar—wait,
I say, and I'll make ye snug enough." So saying he procured the plane; and with his old silk handkerchief first
dusting the bench, vigorously set to planing away at my bed,
the while grinning like an ape. The shavings flew right and
left; till at last the plane-iron came bump against an indestructible knot. The landlord was near spraining his wrist,
and I told him for heaven's sake to quit—the bed was soft
enough to suit me, and I did not know how all the planing
in the world could make eider down of a pine plank. So
gathering up the shavings with another grin, and throwing
them into the great stove in the middle of the room, he went
about his business, and left me in a brown study.

I now took the measure of the bench, and found that it
was a foot too short; but that could be mended with a chair.
But it was a foot too narrow, and the other bench in the
room was about four inches higher than the planed one—so
there was no yoking them. I then placed the first bench lengthwise along the only clear space against the wall, leaving a
little interval between, for my back to settle down in. But
I soon found that there came such a draught of cold air
over me from under the sill of the window, that this plan
would never do at all, especially as another current from
the rickety door met the one from the window, and both
together formed a series of small whirlwinds in the immediate vicinity of the spot where I had thought to spend the
night.

The devil fetch that harpooneer, thought I, but stop,
couldn't I steal a march on him—bolt his door inside, and
jump into his bed, not to be wakened by the most violent
knockings? It seemed no bad idea; but upon second thoughts
I dismissed it. For who could tell but what the next morning,
so soon as I popped out of the room, the harpooneer might
be standing in the entry, all ready to knock me down!

Still, looking around me again, and seeing no possible
chance of spending a sufferable night unless in some other
person's bed, I began to think that after all I might be
cherishing unwarrantable prejudices against this unknown

harpooneer. Thinks I, I'll wait awhile; he must be dropping in before long. I'll have a good look at him then, and perhaps we may become jolly good bedfellows after all—there's no telling.

But though the other boarders kept coming in by ones, twos, and threes, and going to bed, yet no sign of my harpooneer.

"Landlord!" said I, "what sort of a chap is he—does he always keep such late hours?" It was now hard upon twelve o'clock.

The landlord chuckled again with his lean chuckle, and seemed to be mightily tickled at something beyond my comprehension. "No," he answered, "generally he's an early bird—airley to bed and airley to rise—yes, he's the bird what catches the worm.—But to-night he went out a peddling, you see, and I don't see what on airth keeps him so late, unless, may be, he can't sell his head."

"Can't sell his head?—What sort of a bamboozingly story is this you are telling me?" getting into a towering rage. "Do you pretend to say, landlord, that this harpooneer is actually engaged this blessed Saturday night, or rather Sunday morning, in peddling his head around this town?"

"That's precisely it," said the landlord, "and I told him he couldn't sell it here, the market's overstocked."

"With what?" shouted I.

"With heads to be sure; ain't there too many heads in the world?"

"I tell you what it is, landlord," said I, quite calmly, "you'd better stop spinning that yarn to me—I'm not green."

"May be not," taking out a stick and whittling a toothpick, "but I rayther guess you'll be done *brown* if that ere harpooneer hears you a slanderin' his head."

"I'll break it for him," said I, now flying into a passion again at this unaccountable farrago of the landlord's.

"It's broke a'ready," said he.

"Broke," said I—"*broke*, do you mean?"

"Sartain, and that's the very reason he can't sell it, I guess."

"Landlord," said I, going up to him as cool as Mt. Hecla in a snow storm,—"landlord, stop whittling. You and I must understand one another, and that too without delay. I come to your house and want a bed; you tell me you can only give me half a one; that the other half belongs to a certain harpooneer. And about this harpooneer, whom I have not yet seen, you persist in telling me the most mystifying and exasperating stories, tending to beget in me an uncomfortable feeling towards the man whom you design for my bedfellow—a sort of connexion, landlord, which is an intimate and confidential one in the highest degree. I now demand of you to speak out and tell me who and what this harpooneer is, and whether I shall be in all respects safe to spend the night with him. And in the first place, you will be so good as to unsay that story about selling his head, which if true I take to be good evidence that this harpooneer is stark mad, and I've no idea of sleeping with a madman; and you, sir, *you* I mean, landlord, *you*, sir, by trying to induce me to do so knowingly, would thereby render yourself liable to a criminal prosecution."

"Wall," said the landlord, fetching a long breath, "that's a purty long sarmon for a chap that rips a little now and then. But be easy, be easy, this here harpooneer I have been tellin' you of has just arrived from the south seas, where he bought up a lot of 'balmed New Zealand heads (great curios, you know), and he's sold all on 'em but one, and that one he's trying to sell to-night, cause to-morrow's Sunday, and it would not do to be sellin' human heads about the streets when folks is goin' to churches. He wanted to, last Sunday, but I stopped him just as he was goin' out of the door with four heads strung on a string, for all the airth like a string of inions."

This account cleared up the otherwise unaccountable mystery, and showed that the landlord, after all, had had no idea of fooling me—but at the same time what could I think of a harpooneer who stayed out of a Saturday night clean into the holy Sabbath, engaged in such a cannibal business as selling the heads of dead idolators?

"Depend upon it, landlord, that harpooneer is a dangerous man."

"He pays reg'lar," was the rejoinder. "But come, it's getting dreadful late, you had better be turning flukes—it's a nice bed: Sal and me slept in that ere bed the night we were spliced. There's plenty of room for two to kick about in that bed; it an almighty big bed that. Why, afore we give it up, Sal used to put our Sam and little Johnny in the foot of it. But I got a dreaming and sprawling about one night, and somehow, Sam got pitched on the floor, and came near breaking his arm. Arter that, Sal said it wouldn't do. Come along here, I'll give ye a glim in a jiffy;" and so saying he lighted a candle and held it towards me, offering to lead the way. But I stood irresolute; when looking at a clock in the corner, he exclaimed "I vum it's Sunday—you won't see that harpooneer to-night; he's come to anchor somewhere—come along then; *do* come; *won't* ye come?" ,

I considered the matter a moment, and then up stairs we went, and I was ushered into a small room, cold as a clam, and furnished, sure enough, with a prodigious bed, almost big enough indeed for any four harpooneers to sleep abreast.

"There," said the landlord, placing the candle on a crazy old sea chest that did double duty as a wash-stand and centre table; "there, make yourself comfortable now, and good night to ye." I turned round from eyeing the bed, but he had disappeared.

Folding back the counterpane, I stooped over the bed. Though none of the most elegant, it yet stood the scrutiny tolerably well. I then glanced round the room; and besides the bedstead and centre table, could see no other furniture belonging to the place, but a rude shelf, the four walls, and a papered fireboard representing a man striking a whale. Of things not properly belonging to the room, there was a hammock lashed up, and thrown upon the floor in one corner; also a large seaman's bag, containing the harpooneer's wardrobe, no doubt in lieu of a land trunk. Likewise, there was a parcel of outlandish bone fish hooks on the shelf over the fire-place, and a tall harpoon standing at the head of the bed.

But what is this on the chest? I took it up, and held it close to the light, and felt it, and smelt it, and tried every way possible to arrive at some satisfactory conclusion concerning it. I can compare it to nothing but a large door mat, ornamented at the edges with little tinkling tags something like the stained porcupine quills round an Indian moccasin. There was a hole or slit in the middle of this mat, as you see the same in South American ponchos. But could it be possible that any sober harpooneer would get into a door mat, and parade the streets of any Christian town in that sort of guise? I put it on, to try it, and it weighed me down like a hamper, being uncommonly shaggy and thick, and I thought a little damp, as though this mysterious harpooneer had been wearing it of a rainy day. I went up in it to a bit of glass stuck against the wall, and I never saw such a sight in my life. I tore myself out of it in such a hurry that I gave myself a kink in the neck.

I sat down on the side of the bed, and commenced thinking

about this head-peddling harpooneer, and his door mat. After thinking some time on the bed-side, I got up and took off my monkey jacket, and then stood in the middle of the room thinking. I then took off my coat, and thought a little more in my shirt sleeves. But beginning to feel very cold now, half undressed as I was, and remembering what the landlord said about the harpooneer's not coming home at all that night, it being so very late, I made no more ado, but jumped out of my pantaloons and boots, and then blowing out the light tumbled into bed, and commended myself to the care of heaven.

Whether that mattress was stuffed with corn-cobs or broken crockery, there is no telling, but I rolled about a good deal, and could not sleep for a long time. At last I slid off into a light doze, and had pretty nearly made a good offing towards the land of Nod, when I heard a heavy footfall in the passage, and saw a glimmer of light come into the room from under the door.

Lord save me, thinks I, that must be the harpooneer, the infernal head-peddler. But I lay perfectly still, and resolved not to say a word till spoken to. Holding a light in one hand, and that identical New Zealand head in the other, the stranger entered the room, and without looking towards the bed, placed his candle a good way off from me on the floor in one corner, and then began working away at the knotted cords of the large bag I before spoke of as being in the room. I was all eagerness to see his face, but he kept it averted for some time while employed in unlacing the bag's mouth. This accomplished, however, he turned round—when, good heavens! what a sight! Such a face! It was of a dark, purplish, yellow color, here and there stuck over with large, blackish looking squares. Yes, it's just as I thought, he's a terrible bedfellow; he's been in a fight, got dreadfully cut, and here he is, just from the surgeon. But at that moment he chanced to turn his face so towards the light, that I plainly saw they could not be sticking-plasters at all, those black squares on his cheeks. They were stains of some sort or other. At first I knew not what to make of this; but soon an inkling of the truth occurred to me. I remembered a story of a white man—a whaleman too—who, falling among the cannibals, had been tattooed by them. I concluded that this harpooneer, in the course of his distant voyages, must have met with a similar adventure. And what is it, thought I, after all! It's only his outside; a man can be honest in

any sort of skin. But then, what to make of his unearthly
complexion, that part of it, I mean, lying round about, and
completely independent of the squares of tattooing. To be
sure, it might be nothing but a good coat of tropical tanning;
but I never heard of a hot sun's tanning a white man into a
purplish yellow one. However, I had never been in the South
Seas; and perhaps the sun there produced these extraordinary effects upon the skin. Now, while all these ideas
were passing through me like lightning, this harpooneer never
noticed me at all. But, after some difficulty having opened
his bag, he commenced fumbling in it, and presently pulled
out a sort of tomahawk, and a seal-skin wallet with the hair
on. Placing these on the old chest in the middle of the room,
he then took the New Zealand head—a ghastly thing enough
—and crammed it down into the bag. He now took off his
hat—a new beaver hat—when I came nigh singing out with
fresh surprise. There was no hair on his head—none to speak
of at least—nothing but a small scalp-knot twisted up on
his forehead. His bald purplish head now looked for all the
world like a mildewed skull. Had not the stranger stood
between me and the door, I would have bolted out of it quicker than ever I bolted a dinner.

Even as it was, I thought something of slipping out of
the window, but it was the second floor back. I am no
coward, but what to make of this head-peddling purple rascal
altogether passed my comprehension. Ignorance is the parent
of fear, and being completely nonplussed and confounded
about the stranger, I confess I was now as much afraid of
him as if it was the devil himself who had thus broken
into my room at the dead of night. In fact, I was so afraid
of him that I was not game enough just then to address
him, and demand a satisfactory answer concerning what
seemed inexplicable in him.

Meanwhile, he continued the business of undressing, and
at last showed his chest and arms. As I live, these covered
parts of him were checkered with the same squares as his
face; his back, too, was all over the same dark squares; he
seemed to have been in a Thirty Years' War, and just
escaped from it with a sticking-plaster shirt. Still more, his
very legs were marked, as if a parcel of dark green frogs
were running up the trunks of young palms. It was now
quite plain that he must be some abominable savage or other
shipped aboard of a whaleman in the South Seas, and so
landed in this Christian country. I quaked to think of it.

A peddler of heads too—perhaps the heads of his own brothers. He might take a fancy to mine—heavens! look at that tomahawk!

But there was no time for shuddering, for now the savage went about something that completely fascinated my attention, and convinced me that he must indeed be a heathen. Going to his heavy grego, or wrapall, or dreadnaught, which he had previously hung on a chair, he fumbled in the pockets, and produced at length a curious little deformed image with a hunch on its back, and exactly the color of a three days' old Congo baby. Remembering the embalmed head, at first I almost thought that this black manikin was a real baby preserved in some similar manner. But seeing that it was not at all limber, and that it glistened a good deal like polished ebony, I concluded that it must be nothing but a wooden idol, which indeed it proved to be. For now the savage goes up to the empty fire-place, and removing the papered fire-board, sets up this little hunchbacked image, like a tenpin, between the andirons. The chimney jambs and all the bricks inside were very sooty, so that I thought this fire-place made a very appropriate little shrine or Chapel for his Congo idol.

I now screwed my eyes hard towards the half hidden image, feeling but ill at ease meantime—to see what was next to follow. First he takes about a double handful of shavings out of his grego pocket, and places them carefully before the idol; then laying a bit of ship biscuit on top and applying the flame from the lamp, he kindled the shavings into a sacrificial blaze. Presently, after many hasty snatches into the fire, and still hastier withdrawals of his fingers (whereby he seemed to be scorching them badly), he at last succeeded in drawing out the biscuit; then blowing off the heat and ashes a little, he made a polite offer of it to the little negro. But the little devil did not seem to fancy such dry sort of fare at all; he never moved his lips. All these strange antics were accompanied by still stranger guttural noises from the devotee, who seemed to be praying in a sing-song or else singing some pagan psalmody or other, during which his face twitched about in the most unnatural manner. At last extinguishing the fire, he took the idol up very unceremoniously, and bagged it again in his grego pocket as carelessly as if he were a sportsman bagging a dead woodcock.

All these queer proceedings increased my uncomfortable-

ness, and seeing him now exhibiting strong symptoms of concluding his business operations, and jumping into bed with
me, I thought it was high time, now or never, before the
light was put out, to break the spell in which I had so long
been bound.

But the interval I spent in deliberating what to say, was
a fatal one. Taking up his tomahawk from the table, he examined the head of it for an instant, and then holding it
to the light, with his mouth at the handle, he puffed out
great clouds of tobacco smoke. The next moment the light
was extinguished, and this wild cannibal, tomahawk between
his teeth, sprang into bed with me. I sang out, I could not
help it now; and giving a sudden grunt of astonishment he
began feeling me.

Stammering out something, I knew not what, I rolled
away from him against the wall, and then conjured him,
whoever or whatever he might be, to keep quiet, and let me
get up and light the lamp again. But his guttural responses
satisfied me at once that he but ill comprehended my meaning.

"Who-e debel you?"—he at last said—"you no speak-e,
dam-me, I kill-e." And so saying the lighted tomahawk began
flourishing about me in the dark.

"Landlord, for God's sake, Peter Coffin!" shouted I.
"Landlord! Watch! Coffin! Angels! save me!"

"Speak-e! tell-ee me who-ee be, or dam-me, I kill-e!"
again growled the cannibal, while his horrid flourishings of
the tomahawk scattered the hot tobacco ashes about me till I
thought my linen would get on fire. But thank heaven, at
that moment the landlord came into the room light in hand,
and leaping from the bed I ran up to him.

"Don't be afraid now," said he, grinning again. "Queequeg
here wouldn't harm a hair of your head."

"Stop your grinning," shouted I, "and why didn't you tell
me that that infernal harpooneer was a cannibal?"

"I thought ye know'd it;—didn't I tell ye, he was a peddlin'
heads around town?—but turn flukes again and go to sleep.
Queequeg, look here—you sabbee me, I sabbee you—this
man sleepe you—you sabbee?"—

"Me sabbee plenty"—grunted Queequeg, puffing away at
his pipe and sitting up in bed.

"You gettee in," he added, motioning to me with his
tomahawk, and throwing the clothes to one side. He really
did this in not only a civil but a really kind and charitable

way. I stood looking at him a moment. For all his tattooings
he was on the whole a clean, comely looking cannibal. What's
all this fuss I have been making about, thought I to myself—
the man's a human being just as I am: he has just as much
reason to fear me, as I have to be afraid of him. Better sleep
with a sober cannibal than a drunken Christian.

"Landlord," said I, "tell him to stash his tomahawk there,
or pipe, or whatever you call it; tell him to stop smoking,
in short, and I will turn in with him. But I don't fancy having
a man smoking in bed with me. It's dangerous. Besides, I
aint insured."

This being told to Queequeg, he at once complied, and
again politely motioned me to get into bed—rolling over to
one side as much as to say—I wont touch a leg of ye.

"Good night, landlord," said I, "you may go."

I turned in, and never slept better in my life.

THE COUNTERPANE   **IV**

UPON waking next morning about daylight, I found
Queequeg's arm thrown over me in the most loving and
affectionate manner. You had almost thought I had been
his wife. The counterpane was of patchwork, full of odd
little parti-colored squares and triangles; and this arm of
his tattooed all over with an interminable Cretan labyrinth of
a figure, no two parts of which were of one precise shade
—owing I suppose to his keeping his arm at sea unmethodically in sun and shade, his shirt sleeves irregularly rolled
up at various times—this same arm of his, I say, looked
for all the world like a strip of that same patchwork quilt.
Indeed, partly lying on it as the arm did when I first awoke,
I could hardly tell it from the quilt, they so blended their
hues together; and it was only by the sense of weight and
pressure that I could tell that Queequeg was hugging me.

My sensations were strange. Let me try to explain them.
When I was a child, I well remember a somewhat similar
circumstance that befell me; whether it was a reality or a
dream, I never could entirely settle. The circumstance was
this. I had been cutting up some caper or other—I think it
was trying to crawl up the chimney, as I had seen a little
sweep do a few days previous; and my stepmother who,

somehow or other, was all the time whipping me, or sending me to bed supperless,—my mother dragged me by the legs out of the chimney and packed me off to bed; though it was only two o'clock in the afternoon of the 21st June, the longest day in the year in our hemisphere. I felt dreadfully. But there was no help for it, so up stairs I went to my little room in the third floor, undressed myself as slowly as possible so as to kill time, and with a bitter sigh got between the sheets.

I lay there dismally calculating that sixteen entire hours must elapse before I could hope for a resurrection. Sixteen hours in bed! the small of my back ached to think of it. And it was so light too; the sun shining in at the window, and a great rattling of coaches in the streets, and the sound of gay voices all over the house. I felt worse and worse— at last I got up, dressed, and softly going down in my stockinged feet, sought out my stepmother, and suddenly threw myself at her feet, beseeching her as a particular favor to give me a good slippering for my misbehavior; anything indeed but condemning me to lie abed such an unendurable length of time. But she was the best and most conscientious of stepmothers, and back I had to go to my room. For several hours I lay there broad awake, feeling a great deal worse than I have ever done since, even from the greatest subsequent misfortunes. At last I must have fallen into a troubled nightmare of a doze; and slowly waking from it— half steeped in dreams—I opened my eyes, and the before sun-lit room was now wrapped in outer darkness. Instantly I felt a shock running through all my frame; nothing was to be seen, and nothing was to be heard; but a supernatural hand seemed placed in mine. My arm hung over the counterpane, and the nameless, unimaginable, silent form or phantom, to which the hand belonged, seemed closely seated by my bedside. For what seemed ages piled on ages, I lay there, frozen with the most awful fears, not daring to drag away my hand; yet ever thinking that if I could but stir it one single inch, the horrid spell would be broken. I knew not how this consciousness at last glided away from me; but waking in the morning, I shudderingly remembered it all; and for days and weeks and months afterwards I lost myself in confounding attempts to explain the mystery. Nay, to this very hour, I often puzzle myself with it.

Now, take away the awful fear, and my sensations at feeling the supernatural hand in mine were very similar, in

their strangeness, to those which I experienced on waking
up and seeing Queequeg's pagan arm thrown round me. But
at length all the past night's events soberly recurred, one by
one, in fixed reality, and then I lay only alive to the comical
predicament. For though I tried to move his arm—unlock
his bridegroom clasp—yet, sleeping as he was, he still
hugged me tightly, as though naught but death should part
us twain. I now strove to rouse him—"Queequeg!"—but his
only answer was a snore. I then rolled over, my neck feeling
as if it were in a horse-collar; and suddenly felt a slight
scratch. Throwing aside the counterpane, there lay the
tomahawk sleeping by the savage's side, as if it were a
hatchet-faĉed baby. A pretty pickle, truly, thought I; abed
here in a strange house in the broad day, with a cannibal
and a tomahawk! "Queequeg!—in the name of goodness,
Queequeg, wake!" At length, by dint of much wriggling, and
loud and incessant expostulations upon the unbecomingness
of his hugging a fellow male in that matrimonial sort of
style, I succeeded in extracting a grunt; and presently, he
drew back his arm, shook himself all over like a Newfoundland dog just from the water, and sat up in bed, stiff as a
pike-staff, looking at me, and rubbing his eyes as if he did
not altogether remember how I came to be there, though a
dim consciousness of knowing something about me seemed
slowly dawning over him. Meanwhile, I lay quietly eyeing
him, having no serious misgivings now, and bent upon narrowly observing so curious a creature. When, at last, his
mind seemed made up touching the character of his bedfellow, and he became, as it were, reconciled to the fact; he
jumped out upon the floor, and by certain signs and sounds
gave me to understand that, if it pleased me, he would dress
first and then leave me to dress afterwards, leaving the
whole apartment to myself. Thinks I, Queequeg, under the
circumstances, this is a very civilized overture; but, the truth
is, these savages have an innate sense of delicacy, say what
you will; it is marvellous how essentially polite they are. I
pay this particùlar compliment to Queequeg, because he
treated me with so much civility and consideration, while I
was guilty of great rudeness; staring at him from the bed,
and watching all his toilette motions; for the time my curiosity getting the better of my breeding. Nevertheless, a man
like Queequeg you don't see every day, he and his ways were
well worth unusual regarding.

He commenced dressing at top by donning his beaver hat, a

very tall one, by the by, and then—still minus his trowsers—
he hunted up his boots. What under the heavens he did it
for, I cannot tell, but his next movement was to crush himself
—boots in hand, and hat on—under the bed; when, from
sundry violent gaspings and strainings, I inferred he was hard
at work booting himself; though by no law of propriety that
I ever heard of, is any man required to be private when putting on his boots. But Queequeg, do you see, was a creature
in the transition state—neither caterpillar nor butterfly. He
was just enough civilized to show off his outlandishness in the
strangest possible manner. His education was not yet completed. He was an undergraduate. If he had not been a small
degree civilized, he very probably would not have troubled
himself with boots at all; but then, if he had not been still
a savage, he never would have dreamt of getting under the
bed to put them on. At last, he emerged with his hat very
much dented and crushed down over his eyes, and began
creaking and limping about the room, as if, not being much
accustomed to boots, his pair of damp, wrinkled cowhide ones
—probably not made to order either—rather pinched and
tormented him at the first go off of a bitter cold morning.

Seeing, now, that there were no curtains to the window, and
that the street being very narrow, the house opposite commanded a plain view into the room, and observing more and
more the indecorous figure that Queequeg made, staving about
with little else but his hat and boots on; I begged him as
well as I could, to accelerate his toilet somewhat, and particularly to get into his pantaloons as soon as possible. He
complied, and then proceeded to wash himself. At that time
in the morning any Christian would have washed his face;
but Queequeg, to my amazement, contented himself with
restricting his ablutions to his chest, arms, and hands. He
then donned his waistcoat, and taking up a piece of hard
soap on the wash-stand centre-table, dipped it into water and
commenced lathering his face. I was watching to see where
he kept his razor, when lo and behold, he takes the harpoon
from the bed corner, slips out the long wooden stock, un-
sheathes the head, whets it a little on his boot, and striding
up to the bit of mirror against the wall, begins a vigorous
scraping, or rather harpooning of his cheeks. Thinks I, Queequeg, this is using Roger's best cutlery with a vengeance.
Afterwards I wondered the less at this operation when I
came to know of what fine steel the head of a harpoon is

made, and how exceedingly sharp the long straight edges are always kept.

The rest of his toilet was soon achieved, and he proudly marched out of the room, wrapped up in his great pilot monkey jacket, and sporting his harpoon like a marshal's baton.

BREAKFAST V

I QUICKLY followed suit, and descending into the barroom accosted the grinning landlord very pleasantly. I cherished no malice towards him, though he had been skylarking with me not a little in the matter of my bedfellow.

However, a good laugh is a mighty good thing, and rather too scarce a good thing; the more's the pity. So, if any one man, in his own proper person, afford stuff for a good joke to anybody, let him not be backward, but let him cheerfully allow himself to spend and be spent in that way. And the man that has anything bountifully laughable about him, be sure there is more in that man than you perhaps think for.

The bar-room was now full of the boarders who had been dropping in the night previous, and whom I had not as yet had a good look at. They were nearly all whalemen; chief mates, and second mates, and third mates, and sea carpenters, and sea coopers, and sea blacksmiths, and harpooneers, and ship keepers; a brown and brawny company, with bosky beards; an unshorn, shaggy set, all wearing monkey jackets for morning gowns.

You could pretty plainly tell how long each one had been ashore. This young fellow's healthy cheek is like a suntoasted pear in hue, and would seem to smell almost as musky; he cannot have been three days landed from his Indian voyage. That man next him looks a few shades lighter; you might say a touch of satin wood is in him. In the complexion of a third still lingers a tropic tawn, but slightly bleached withal; *he* doubtless has tarried whole weeks ashore. But who could show a cheek like Queequeg? which, barred with various tints, seemed like the Andes' western slope, to show forth in one array, contrasting climates, zone by zone.

"Grub, ho!" now cried the landlord, flinging open a door, and in we went to breakfast.

They say that men who have seen the world, thereby become quite at ease in manner, quite self-possessed in company. Not always, though: Ledyard, the great New England traveller, and Mungo Park, the Scotch one; of all men, they possessed the least assurance in the parlor. But perhaps the mere crossing of Siberia in a sledge drawn by dogs as Ledyard did, or the taking a long solitary walk on an empty stomach, in the negro heart of Africa, which was the sum of poor Mungo's performances—this kind of travel, I say, may not be the very best mode of attaining a high social polish. Still, for the most part, that sort of thing is to be had anywhere.

These reflections just here are occasioned by the circumstance that after we were all seated at the table, and I was preparing to hear some good stories about whaling; to my no small surprise, nearly every man maintained a profound silence. And not only that, but they looked embarrassed. Yes, here were a set of sea-dogs, many of whom without the slightest bashfulness had boarded great whales on the high seas—entire strangers to them—and duelled them dead without winking; and yet, here they sat at a social breakfast table—all of the same calling, all of kindred tastes—looking round as sheepishly at each other as though they had never been out of sight of some sheepfold among the Green Mountains. A curious sight; these bashful bears, these timid warrior whalemen!

But as for Queequeg—why, Queequeg sat there among them—at the head of the table, too, it so chanced; as cool as an icicle. To be sure I cannot say much for his breeding. His greatest admirer could not have cordially justified his bringing his harpoon into breakfast with him, and using it there without ceremony; reaching over the table with it, to the imminent jeopardy of many heads, and grappling the beefsteaks towards him. But *that* was certainly very coolly done by him, and every one knows that in most people's estimation, to do anything coolly is to do it genteelly.

We will not speak of all Queequeg's peculiarities here; how he eschewed coffee and hot rolls, and applied his undivided attention to beefsteaks, done rare. Enough, that when breakfast was over he withdrew like the rest into the public room, lighted his tomahawk-pipe, and was sitting there quietly digesting and smoking with his inseparable hat on, when I sallied out for a stroll.

THE STREET VI

IF I had been astonished at first catching a glimpse of so outlandish an individual as Queequeg circulating among the polite society of a civilized town, that astonishment soon departed upon taking my first daylight stroll through the streets of New Bedford.

In thoroughfares nigh the docks, any considerable seaport will frequently offer to view the queerest looking nondescripts from foreign parts. Even in Broadway and Chestnut streets, Mediterranean mariners will sometimes jostle the affrighted ladies. Regent street is not unknown to Lascars and Malays; and at Bombay, in the Apollo Green, live Yankees have often scared the natives. But New Bedford beats all Water street and Wapping. In these last-mentioned haunts you see only sailors; but in New Bedford, actual cannibals stand chatting at street corners; savages outright; many of whom yet carry on their bones unholy flesh. It makes a stranger stare.

But, besides the Feegeeans, Tongatabooarrs, Erromanggoans, Pannangians, and Brighggians, and, besides the wild specimens of the whaling-craft which unheeded reel about the streets, you will see other sights still more curious, certainly more comical. There weekly arrive in this town scores of green Vermonters and New Hampshire men, all athirst for gain and glory in the fishery. They are mostly young, of stalwart frames; fellows who have felled forests, and now seek to drop the axe and snatch the whale-lance. Many are as green as the Green Mountains whence they came. In some things you would think them but a few hours old. Look there! that chap strutting round the corner. He wears a beaver hat and swallow-tailed coat, girdled with a sailor-belt and sheath-knife. Here comes another with a sou'-wester and a bombazine cloak.

No town-bred dandy will compare with a country-bred one —I mean a downright bumpkin dandy—a fellow that, in the dogdays, will mow his two acres in buckskin gloves for fear of tanning his hands. Now when a country dandy like this takes it into his head to make a distinguished reputation, and

joins the great whale-fishery, you should see the comical
things he does upon reaching the seaport. In bespeaking his
sea-outfit, he orders bell-buttons to his waistcoats; straps to
his canvas trowsers. Ah, poor Hay-Seed! how bitterly will
burst those straps in the first howling gale, when thou art
driven, straps, buttons, and all, down the throat of the
tempest.

But think not that this famous town has only harpooneers,
cannibals, and bumpkins to show her visitors. Not at all. Still
New Bedford is a queer place. Had it not been for us whalemen, that tract of land would this day perhaps have been in
as howling condition as the coast of Labrador. As it is,
parts of her back country are enough to frighten one, they
look so bony. The town itself is perhaps the dearest place
to live in, in all New England. It is a land of oil, true enough:
but not like Canaan; a land, also, of corn and wine. The
streets do not run with milk; nor in the spring-time do they
pave them with fresh eggs. Yet, in spite of this, nowhere in
all America will you find more patrician-like houses; parks
and gardens more opulent, than in New Bedford. Whence
came they? how planted upon this once scraggy scoria of a
country?

Go and gaze upon the iron emblematical harpoons round
yonder lofty mansion, and your question will be answered.
Yes; all these brave houses and flowery gardens came from
the Atlantic, Pacific, and Indian oceans. One and all, they
were harpooned and dragged up hither from the bottom of
the sea. Can Herr Alexander perform a feat like that?

In New Bedford, fathers, they say, give whales for
dowers to their daughters, and portion off their nieces with a
few porpoises a-piece. You must go to New Bedford to see
a brilliant wedding; for, they say, they have reservoirs of
oil in every house, and every night recklessly burn their
lengths in spermaceti candles.

In summer time, the town is sweet to see; full of fine
maples—long avenues of green and gold. And in August,
high in air, the beautiful and bountiful horse-chestnuts, can-
delabra-wise, proffer the passer-by their tapering upright
cones of congregated blossoms. So omnipotent is art; which
in many a district of New Bedford has superinduced bright
terraces of flowers upon the barren refuse rocks thrown aside
at creation's final day.

And the women of New Bedford, they bloom like their
own red roses. But roses only bloom in summer; whereas

the fine carnation of their cheeks is perennial as sunlight in the seventh heavens. Elsewhere match that bloom of theirs, ye cannot, save in Salem, where they tell me the young girls breathe such musk, their sailor sweethearts smell them miles off shore, as though they were drawing nigh the odorous Moluccas instead of the Puritanic sands.

THE CHAPEL   **VII**

IN this same New Bedford there stands a Whaleman's Chapel, and few are the moody fishermen, shortly bound for the Indian Ocean or Pacific, who fail to make a Sunday visit to the spot. I am sure that I did not.

Returning from my first morning stroll, I again sallied out upon this special errand. The sky had changed from clear, sunny cold, to driving sleet and mist. Wrapping myself in my shaggy jacket of cloth called bearskin, I fought my way against the stubborn storm. Entering, I found a small scattered congregation of sailors, and sailors' wives and widows. A muffled silence reigned, only broken at times by the shrieks of the storm. Each silent worshipper seemed purposely sitting apart from the other, as if each silent grief were insular and incommunicable. The chaplain had not yet arrived; and there these silent islands of men and women sat steadfastly eyeing several marble tablets, with black borders, masoned into the wall on either side the pulpit. Three of them ran something like the following, but I do not pretend to quote:

SACRED

TO THE MEMORY

OF

JOHN TALBOT,

Who, at the age of eighteen, was lost overboard,
Near the Isle of Desolation, off Patagonia,
November 1st, 1836.

THIS TABLET

Is erected to his Memory

BY HIS SISTER.

SACRED
To the Memory
OF
ROBERT LONG, WILLIS ELLERY,
NATHAN COLEMAN, WALTER CANNY, SETH MACY,
AND SAMUEL GLEIG,
Forming one of the boats' crews
OF
The Ship Eliza,
Who were towed out of sight by a Whale,
On the Off-shore Ground in the
PACIFIC,
December 31st, 1839.
THIS MARBLE
Is here placed by their surviving
SHIPMATES.

SACRED
To the Memory
OF
The late
CAPTAIN EZEKIEL HARDY,
Who in the bows of his boat was killed by a
Sperm Whale on the coast of Japan,
August 3d, 1833.
THIS TABLET
Is erected to his Memory
BY
HIS WIDOW.

Shaking off the sleet from my ice-glazed hat and jacket, I seated myself near the door, and turning sideways was surprised to see Queequeg near me. Affected by the solemnity of the scene, there was a wondering gaze of incredulous curiosity in his countenance. This savage was the only person present who seemed to notice my entrance; because he was the only one who could not read, and, therefore, was not reading those frigid inscriptions on the wall. Whether any of the relatives of the seamen whose names appeared there were now among the congregation, I knew not; but so many are the unrecorded accidents in the fishery, and so plainly did several women present wear the countenance if not the trappings of some unceasing grief, that I feel sure that here before me were assembled those, in whose unhealing hearts the sight of those bleak tablets sympathetically caused the old wounds to bleed afresh.

Oh! ye whose dead lie buried beneath the green grass; who standing among flowers can say—here, *here* lies my beloved; ye know not the desolation that broods in bosoms like these. What bitter blanks in those black-bordered marbles which cover no ashes! What despair in those immovable inscriptions! What deadly voids and unbidden infidelities in the lines that seem to gnaw upon all Faith, and refuse resurrections to the beings who have placelessly perished without a grave. As well might those tablets stand in the cave of Elephanta as here.

In what census of living creatures, the dead of mankind are included; why it is that a universal proverb says of them, that they tell no tales, though containing more secrets than the Goodwin Sands; how it is that to his name who yesterday departed for the other world, we prefix so significant and infidel a word, and yet do not thus entitle him, if he but embarks for the remotest Indies of this living earth; why the Life Insurance Companies pay death-forfeitures upon immortals; in what eternal, unstirring paralysis, and deadly, hopeless trance, yet lies antique Adam who died sixty round centuries ago; how it is that we still refuse to be comforted for those who we nevertheless maintain are dwelling in unspeakable bliss; why all the living so strive to hush all the dead; wherefore but the rumor of a knocking in a tomb will terrify a whole city. All these things are not without their meanings.

But Faith, like a jackal, feeds among the tombs, and even from these dead doubts she gathers her most vital hope.

It needs scarcely to be told, with what feelings, on the eve of a Nantucket voyage, I regarded those marble tablets, and by the murky light of that darkened, doleful day read the fate of the whalemen who had gone before me. Yes, Ishmael, the same fate may be thine. But somehow I grew merry again. Delightful inducements to embark, fine chance for promotion, it seems—aye, a stove boat will make me an immortal by brevet. Yes, there is death in this business of whaling—a speechlessly quick chaotic bundling of a man into Eternity. But what then? Methinks we have hugely mistaken this matter of Life and Death. Methinks that what they call my shadow here on earth is my true substance. Methinks that in looking at things spiritual, we are too much like oysters observing the sun through the water, and thinking that thick water the thinnest of air. Methinks my body is but the less of my better being. In fact take my body who will, take it I say, it is not me. And therefore three cheers for Nantucket; and come a stove boat and stove body when they will, for stave my soul, Jove himself cannot.

THE PULPIT   VIII

I HAD not been seated very long ere a man of a certain venerable robustness entered; immediately as the storm-pelted door flew back upon admitting him, a quick regardful eyeing of him by all the congregation, sufficiently attested that this fine old man was the chaplain. Yes, it was the famous Father Mapple, so called by the whalemen, among whom he was a very great favorite. He had been a sailor and a harpooneer in his youth, but for many years past had dedicated his life to the ministry. At the time I now write of, Father Mapple was in the hardy winter of a healthy old age; that sort of old age which seems merging into a second flowering youth, for among all the fissures of his wrinkles, there shone certain mild gleams of a newly developing bloom —the spring verdure peeping forth even beneath February's snow. No one having previously heard his history, could for the first time behold Father Mapple without the utmost interest, because there were certain engrafted clerical peculiarities about him, imputable to that adventurous maritime life he had led. When he entered I observed that he carried no umbrella, and certainly had not come in his carriage, for his tarpaulin hat ran down with melting sleet, and his great pilot cloth jacket seemed almost to drag him to the floor with the weight of the water it had absorbed. However, hat and coat and overshoes were one by one removed, and hung up in a little space in an adjacent corner; when, arrayed in a decent suit, he quietly approached the pulpit.

Like most old fashioned pulpits, it was a very lofty one, and since a regular stairs to such a height would, by its long angle with the floor, seriously contract the already small area of the chapel, the architect, it seemed, had acted upon the hint of Father Mapple, and finished the pulpit without a stairs, substituting a perpendicular side ladder, like those used in mounting a ship from a boat at sea. The wife of a whaling captain had provided the chapel with a handsome pair of red worsted man-ropes for this ladder, which, being itself nicely headed, and stained with a mahogany color, the whole contrivance, considering what manner of chapel it was, seemed by no means in bad taste. Halting for an instant at the foot of the ladder, and with both hands grasping the ornamental knobs of the man-ropes, Father Mapple cast a look upwards, and then with a truly sailor-like but still reverential dexterity, hand over hand, mounted the steps as if ascending the main-top of his vessel.

The perpendicular parts of this side ladder, as is usually the case with swinging ones, were of cloth-covered rope, only the rounds were of wood, so that at every step there was a joint. At my first glimpse of the pulpit, it had not escaped me that however convenient for a ship, these joints in the present instance seemed unnecessary. For I was not prepared to see Father Mapple after gaining the height, slowly turn round, and stooping over the pulpit, deliberately drag up the ladder step by step, till the whole was deposited within, leaving him impregnable in his little Quebec.

I pondered some time without fully comprehending the reason for this. Father Mapple enjoyed such a wide reputation for sincerity and sanctity, that I could not suspect him of courting notoriety by any mere tricks of the stage. No, thought I, there must be some sober reason for this thing; furthermore, it must symbolize something unseen. Can it be, then, that by that act of physical isolation, he signifies his spiritual withdrawal for the time, from all outward worldly ties and connexions? Yes, for replenished with the meat and wine of the word, to the faithful man of God, this pulpit, I see, is a self-containing stronghold—a lofty Ehrenbreitstein, with a perennial well of water within the walls.

But the side ladder was not the only strange feature of the place, borrowed from the chaplain's former sea-farings. Between the marble cenotaphs on either hand of the pulpit, the wall which formed its back was adorned with a large painting representing a gallant ship beating against a terrible storm off a lee coast of black rocks and snowy breakers. But high above the flying scud and dark-rolling clouds, there floated a little isle of sunlight, from which beamed forth an angel's face; and this bright face shed a distinct spot of radiance upon the ship's tossed deck, something like that silver plate now inserted into the Victory's plank where

Nelson fell. "Ah, noble ship," the angel seemed to say, "beat on, beat on, thou noble ship, and bear a hardy helm; for lo! the sun is breaking through; the clouds are rolling off —serenest azure is at hand."

Nor was the pulpit itself without a trace of the same sea-taste that had achieved the ladder and the picture. Its panelled front was in the likeness of a ship's bluff bows, and the Holy Bible rested on a projecting piece of scroll work, fashioned after a ship's fiddle-headed beak.

What could be more full of meaning?—for the pulpit is ever this earth's foremost part; all the rest comes in its rear; the pulpit leads the world. From thence it is the storm of God's quick wrath is first descried, and the bow must bear the earliest brunt. From thence it is the God of breezes fair or foul is first invoked for favorable winds. Yes, the world's a ship on its passage out, and not a voyage complete; and the pulpit is its prow.

THE SERMON   IX

FATHER MAPPLE rose, and in a mild voice of unassuming authority ordered the scattered people to condense. "Starboard gangway, there! side away to larboard—larboard gangway to starboard! Midships! midships!"

There was a low rumbling of heavy sea-boots among the benches, and a still slighter shuffling of women's shoes, and all was quiet again, and every eye on the preacher.

He paused a little; then kneeling in the pulpit's bows, folded his large brown hands across his chest, uplifted his closed eyes, and offered a prayer so deeply devout that he seemed kneeling and praying at the bottom of the sea.

This ended, in prolonged solemn tones, like the continual tolling of a bell in a ship that is foundering at sea in a fog— in such tones he commenced reading the following hymn; but changing his manner towards the concluding stanzas, burst forth with a pealing exultation and joy—

> "The ribs and terrors in the whale,
>   Arched over me a dismal gloom,
> While all God's sun-lit waves rolled by,
>   And lift me deepening down to doom.

"I saw the opening maw of hell,
 With endless pains and sorrows there;
Which none but they that feel can tell—
 Oh, I was plunging to despair.

"In black distress, I called my God,
 When I could scarce believe him mine,
He bowed his ear to my complaints—
 No more the whale did me confine.

"With speed he flew to my relief,
 As on a radiant dolphin borne;
Awful, yet bright, as lightning shone
 The face of my Deliverer God.

"My song for ever shall record
 That terrible, that joyful hour;
I give the glory to my God,
 His all the mercy and the power."

Nearly all joined in singing this hymn, which swelled high above the howling of the storm. A brief pause ensued; the preacher slowly turned over the leaves of the Bible, and at last, folding his hand down upon the proper page, said: "Beloved shipmates, clinch the last verse of the first chapter of Jonah—'And God had prepared a great fish to swallow up Jonah.'

"Shipmates, this book, containing only four chapters—four yarns—is one of the smallest strands in the mighty cable of the Scriptures. Yet what depths of the soul does Jonah's deep sealine sound! what a pregnant lesson to us is this prophet! What a noble thing is that canticle in the fish's belly! How billow-like and boisterously grand! We feel the floods surging over us; we sound with him to the kelpy bottom of the waters; sea-weed and all the slime of the sea is about us! But *what* is this lesson that the book of Jonah teaches? Shipmates, it is a two-stranded lesson; a lesson to us all as sinful men, and a lesson to me as a pilot of the living God. As sinful men, it is a lesson to us all, because it is a story of the sin, hard-heartedness, suddenly awakened fears, the swift punishment, repentance, prayers, and finally the deliverance and joy of Jonah. As with all sinners among men, the sin of this son of Amittai was in his wilful disobedience of the command of God—never mind now what that command was, or how conveyed—which he found a hard command. But all the things that God would have us do are hard for us to do—remember that—and hence, he oftener commands us than endeavors to persuade. And if we obey God, we must disobey ourselves; and it is in this disobeying ourselves, wherein the hardness of obeying God consists.

"With this sin of disobedience in him, Jonah still further flouts at God, by seeking to flee from Him. He thinks that a ship made by men, will carry him into countries where God does not reign, but only the Captains of this earth. He skulks about the wharves of Joppa, and seeks a ship that's bound for Tarshish. There lurks, perhaps, a hitherto unheeded meaning here. By all accounts Tarshish could have been no other city than the modern Cadiz. That's the opinion of learned men. And where is Cadiz, shipmates? Cadiz is in Spain; as far by water, from Joppa, as Jonah could possibly have sailed in those ancient days, when the Atlantic was an almost unknown sea. Because Joppa, the modern Jaffa, shipmates, is on the most easterly coast of the Mediterranean, the Syrian; and Tarshish or Cadiz more than two thousand miles to the westward from that, just outside the Straits of Gibraltar. See ye not then, shipmates, that Jonah sought to flee world-wide from God? Miserable man! Oh! most contemtible and worthy of all scorn; with slouched hat and guilty eye, skulking from his God; prowling among the shipping like a vile burglar hastening to cross the seas. So disordered, self-condemning is his look, that had there been policemen in those days, Jonah, on the mere suspicion of something wrong, had been arrested ere he touched a deck. How plainly he's a fugitive! no baggage, not a hat-box, valise, or carpet-bag,—no friends accompany him to the wharf with their adieux. At last, after much dodging search, he finds the Tarshish ship receiving the last items of her cargo; and as he steps on board to see its Captain in the cabin, all the sailors for the moment desist from hoisting in the goods, to mark the stranger's evil eye. Jonah sees this; but in vain he tries to look all ease and confidence; in vain essays his wretched smile. Strong intuitions of the man assure the mariners he can be no innocent. In their gamesome but still serious way, one whispers to the other— 'Jack, he's robbed a widow;' or, 'Joe, do you mark him; he's a bigamist;' or 'Harry lad, I guess he's the adulterer that broke jail in old Gomorrah, or belike, one of the missing murderers from Sodom.' Another runs to read the bill that's stuck against the spile upon the wharf to which the ship is moored, offering five hundred gold coins for the apprehension of a parricide, and containing a description of his person. He reads, and looks from Jonah to the bill; while all his sympathetic shipmates now crowd round Jonah, prepared to lay their hands upon him. Frighted Jonah trembles, and summoning all his boldness to his face, only looks so much the more a coward. He will not confess himself suspected; but that itself is strong suspicion. So he makes the best of it; and when the sailors find him not to be the man that is advertised, they let him pass, and he descends into the cabin.

" 'Who's there?' cries the Captain at his busy desk, hurriedly making out his papers for the Customs—'Who's there?' Oh! how that harmless question mangles Jonah! For the instant he almost turns to flee again. But he rallies. 'I seek a passage in this ship to Tarshish; how soon sail ye, sir?' Thus far the busy Captain had not looked up to Jonah, though the man now stands before him; but no sooner does he hear that hollow voice, than he darts a scrutinizing glance. 'We sail with the next coming tide,' at last he slowly answered, still intently eyeing him. 'No sooner, sir?'—'Soon enough for any honest man that goes a passenger.' Ha! Jonah, that's another stab. But he swiftly calls away the Captain from that scent. 'I'll sail with ye,'—he says,—'the passage money, how much is that?—I'll pay now.' For it is particularly written, shipmates, as if it were a thing not to be overlooked in this history, 'that he paid the fare thereof' ere the craft did sail. And taken with the context, this is full of meaning.

"Now Jonah's Captain, shipmates, was one whose discernment detects crime in any, but whose cupidity exposes it only in the penniless. In this world, shipmates, sin that pays its way can travel freely, and without a passport; whereas Virtue, if a pauper, is stopped at all frontiers. So Jonah's Captain prepares to test the length of Jonah's purse, ere he judge him openly. He charges him thrice the usual sum; and it's assented to. Then the Captain knows that Jonah is a fugitive; but at the same time resolves to help a flight that paves its rear with gold. Yet when Jonah fairly takes out his purse, prudent suspicions still molest the Captain. He rings every coin to find a counterfeit. Not a forger, any way, he mutters; and Jonah is put down for his passage. 'Point out my state-room, Sir,' says Jonah now, 'I'm travel-weary; I need sleep.' 'Thou look'st like it,' says the

Captain, 'there's thy room.' Jonah enters, and would lock the door, but the lock contains no key. Hearing him foolishly fumbling there, the Captain laughs lowly to himself, and mutters something about the doors of convicts' cells being never allowed to be locked within. All dressed and dusty as he is, Jonah throws himself into his berth, and finds the little state-room ceiling almost resting on his forehead. The air is close, and Jonah gasps. Then, in that contracted hole, sunk, too, beneath the ship's water-line, Jonah feels the heralding presentiment of that stifling hour, when the whale shall hold him in the smallest of his bowel's wards.

"Screwed at its axis against the side, a swinging lamp slightly oscillates in Jonah's room; and the ship, heeling over towards the wharf with the weight of the last bales received, the lamp, flame and all, though in slight motion, still maintains a permanent obliquity with reference to the room; though, in truth, infallibly straight itself, it but made obvious the false, lying levels among which it hung. The lamp alarms and frightens Jonah; as lying in his berth his tormented eyes roll round the place, and this thus far successful fugitive finds no refuge for his restless glance. But that contradiction in the lamp more and more appals him. The floor, the ceiling, and the side, are all awry. 'Oh! so my conscience hangs in me!' he groans, 'straight upward, so it burns; but the chambers of my soul are all in crookedness!'

"Like one who after a night of drunken revelry hies to his bed, still reeling, but with conscience yet pricking him, as the plungings of the Roman race-horse but so much the more strike his steel tags into him; as one who in that miserable plight still turns and turns in giddy anguish, praying God for annihilation until the fit be passed; and at last amid the whirl of woe he feels, a deep stupor steals over him, as over the man who bleeds to death, for conscience is the wound, and there's naught to staunch it; so, after sore wrestlings in his berth, Jonah's prodigy of ponderous misery drags him drowning down to sleep.

"And now the time of tide has come; the ship casts off her cables; and from the deserted wharf the uncheered ship for Tarshish, all careening, glides to sea. That ship, my friends, was the first of recorded smugglers! the contraband was Jonah. But the sea rebels; he will not bear the wicked burden. A dreadful storm comes on, the ship is like to break. But now when the boatswain calls all hands to lighten her; when boxes, bales, and jars are clattering overboard; when the wind is shrieking, and the men are yelling, and every plank thunders with trampling feet right over Jonah's head; in all this raging tumult, Jonah sleeps his hideous sleep. He sees no black sky and raging sea, feels not the reeling timbers, and little hears he or heeds he the far rush of the mighty whale, which even now with open mouth is cleaving the seas after him. Aye, shipmates, Jonah was gone down into the sides of the ship—a berth in the cabin as I have taken it, and was fast asleep. But the frightened master comes to him, and shrieks in his dead ear, 'What meanest thou, O sleeper! arise!' Startled from his lethargy by that direful cry, Jonah staggers to his feet, and stumbling to the deck, grasps a shroud, to look out upon the sea. But at that moment he is sprung upon by a panther billow leaping over the bulwarks. Wave after wave thus leaps into the ship, and finding no speedy vent runs roaring fore and aft, till the mariners come nigh to drowning while yet afloat. And ever, as the white moon shows her affrighted face from the steep gullies in the blackness overhead, aghast Jonah sees the rearing bowsprit pointing high upward, but soon beat downward again towards the tormented deep.

"Terrors upon terrors run shouting through his soul. In all his cringing attitudes, the God-fugitive is now too plainly known. The sailors mark him; more and more certain grow their suspicions of him, and at last, fully to test the truth, by referring the whole matter to high Heaven, they fall to casting lots, to see for whose cause this great tempest was upon them. The lot is Jonah's; that discovered, then how furiously they mob him with their questions. 'What is thine occupation? Whence comest thou? Thy country? What people?' But mark now, my shipmates, the behavior of poor Jonah. The eager mariners but ask him who he is, and where from; whereas, they not only receive an answer to those questions, but likewise another answer to a question not put by them, but the unsolicited answer is forced from Jonah by the hard hand of God that is upon him.

"'I am a Hebrew,' he cries—and then—'I fear the Lord the God of Heaven who hath made the sea and the dry land!' Fear him, O Jonah? Aye, well mightest thou fear the Lord God *then!* Straightway, he now goes on to make a full confession; whereupon the mariners became more and more appalled, but still are pitiful. For when Jonah, not yet supplicating God for mercy, since he but too well knew the darkness of his deserts,—when wretched Jonah cries out to

them to take him and cast him forth into the sea, for he
knew that for *his* sake this great tempest was upon them;
they mercifully turn from him, and seek by other means to
save the ship. But all in vain; the indignant gale howls
louder; then, with one hand raised invokingly to God, with
the other they not unreluctantly lay hold of Jonah.

"And now behold Jonah taken up as an anchor and dropped
into the sea; when instantly an oily calmness floats out from
the east, and the sea is still, as Jonah carries down the gale
with him, leaving smooth water behind. He goes down in
the whirling heart of such a masterless commotion that he
scarce heeds the moment when he drops seething into the
yawning jaws awaiting him; and the whale shoots-to all his
ivory teeth, like so many white bolts, upon his prison. Then
Jonah prayed unto the Lord out of the fish's belly. But observe his prayer, and learn a weighty lesson. For sinful as he
is, Jonah does not weep and wail for direct deliverance.
He feels that his dreadful punishment is just. He leaves all
his deliverance to God, contenting himself with this, that
spite of all his pains and pangs, he will still look towards
His holy temple. And here, shipmates, is true and faithful
repentance; not clamorous for pardon, but grateful for punishment. And how pleasing to God was this conduct in
Jonah, is shown in the eventual deliverance of him from
the sea and the whale. Shipmates, I do not place Jonah
before you to be copied for his sin but I do place him before you as a model for repentance. Sin not; but if you do,
take heed to repent of it like Jonah."

While he was speaking these words, the howling of the
shrieking, slanting storm without seemed to add new power
to the preacher, who, when describing Jonah's sea-storm,
seemed tossed by a storm himself. His deep chest heaved
as with a ground-swell; his tossed arms seemed the warring
elements at work; and the thunders that rolled away from
off his swarthy brow, and the light leaping from his eye,
made all his simple hearers look on him with a quick fear
that was strange to them.

There now came a lull in his look, as he silently turned
over the leaves of the Book once more; and, at last, standing
motionless, with closed eyes, for the moment, seemed com-
muning with God and himself.

But again he leaned over towards the people, and bowing
his head lowly, with an aspect of the deepest yet manliest
humility, he spake these words:

"Shipmates, God has laid but one hand upon you; both his hands press upon me. I have read ye by what murky light may be mine the lesson that Jonah teaches to all sinners; and therefore to ye, and still more to me, for I am a greater sinner than ye. And now how gladly would I come down from this mast-head and sit on the hatches there where you sit, and listen as you listen, while some one of you reads *me* that other and more awful lesson which Jonah teaches to *me*, as a pilot of the living God. How being an anointed pilot-prophet, or speaker of true things, and bidden by the Lord to sound those unwelcome truths in the ears of a wicked Nineveh, Jonah, appalled at the hostility he should raise, fled from his mission, and sought to escape his duty and his God by taking ship at Joppa. But God is everywhere; Tarshish he never reached. As we have seen, God came upon him in the whale, and swallowed him down to living gulfs of doom, and with swift slantings tore him along 'into the midst of the seas,' where the eddying depths sucked him ten thousand fathoms down, and 'the weeds were wrapped about his head,' and all the watery world of woe bowled over him. Yet even then beyond the reach of any plummet—'out of the belly of hell'—when the whale grounded upon the ocean's utmost bones, even then, God heard the engulphed, repenting prophet when he cried. Then God spake unto the fish; and from the shuddering cold and blackness of the sea, the whale came breeching up towards the warm and pleasant sun, and all the delights of air and earth; and 'vomited out Jonah upon the dry land;' when the word of the Lord came a second time; and Jonah, bruised and beaten—his ears, like two sea-shells, still multitudinously murmuring of the ocean—Jonah did the Almighty's bidding. And what was that, shipmates? To preach the Truth to the face of Falsehood! That was it!

"This, shipmates, this is that other lesson; and woe to that pilot of the living God who slights it. Woe to him whom this world charms from Gospel duty! Woe to him who seeks to pour oil upon the waters when God has brewed them into a gale! Woe to him who seeks to please rather than to appal! Woe to him whose good name is more to him than goodness! Woe to him who, in this world, courts not dishonor! Woe to him who would not be true, even though to be false were salvation! Yea, woe to him who, as the great Pilot Paul has it, while preaching to others is himself a castaway!"

He drooped and fell away from himself for a moment;

then lifting his face to them again, showed a deep joy in his eyes, as he cried out with a heavenly enthusiasm,—"But oh! shipmates! on the starboard hand of every woe, there is a sure delight; and higher the top of that delight, than the bottom of the woe is deep. Is not the main-truck higher than the kelson is low? Delight is to him—a far, far upward, and inward delight—who against the proud gods and commodores of this earth, ever stands forth his own inexorable self. Delight is to him whose strong arms yet support him, when the ship of this base treacherous world has gone down beneath him. Delight is to him, who gives no quarter in the truth, and kills, burns, and destroys all sin though he pluck it out from under the robes of Senators and Judges. Delight,—top-gallant delight is to him, who acknowledges no law or lord, but the Lord his God, and is only a patriot to heaven. Delight is to him, whom all the waves of the billows of the seas of the boisterous mob can never shake from this sure Keel of the Ages. And eternal delight and deliciousness will be his, who coming to lay him down, can say with his final breath—O Father!—chiefly known to me by Thy rod—mortal or immortal, here I die. I have striven to be Thine, more than to be this world's, or mine own. Yet this is nothing; I leave eternity to Thee; for what is man that he should live out the lifetime of his God?"

He said no more, but slowly waving a benediction, covered his face with his hands, and so remained kneeling, till all the people had departed, and he was left alone in the place.

A BOSOM FRIEND   **X**

RETURNING to the Spouter-Inn from the Chapel, I found Queequeg there quite alone; he having left the Chapel before the benediction some time. He was sitting on a bench before the fire, with his feet on the stove hearth, and in one hand was holding close up to his face that little negro idol of his; peering hard into its face, and with a jack-knife gently whittling away at its nose, meanwhile humming to himself in his heathenish way.

But being now interrupted, he put up the image; and pretty soon, going to the table, took up a large book there, and placing it on his lap began counting the pages with deliberate regularity; at every fiftieth page—as I fancied—stopping a moment, looking vacantly around him, and giving utterance to a long-drawn gurgling whistle of astonishment. He would then begin again at the next fifty; seeming to commence at number one each time, as though he could not count more than fifty, and it was only by such a large number of fifties being found together, that his astonishment at the multitude of pages was excited.

With much interest I sat watching him. Savage though he was, and hideously marred about the face—at least to my taste—his countenance yet had a something in it which was by no means disagreeable. You cannot hide the soul. Through all his unearthly tattooings, I thought I saw the traces of a simple honest heart; and in his large, deep eyes, fiery black and bold, there seemed tokens of a spirit that would dare a thousand devils. And besides all this, there was a certain lofty bearing about the Pagan, which even his uncouthness could not altogether maim. He looked like a man who had never cringed and never had had a creditor. Whether it was, too, that his head being shaved, his forehead was drawn out in freer and brighter relief, and looked more expansive than it otherwise would, this I will not venture to decide; but certain it was his head was phrenologically an excellent one. It may seem ridiculous, but it reminded me of General Washington's head, as seen in the popular busts of him. It had the same long regularly graded retreating slope from above the brows, which were likewise very projecting, like two long promontories thickly wooded on top. Queequeg was George Washington cannibalistically developed.

Whilst I was thus closely scanning him, half-pretending meanwhile to be looking out at the storm from the casement, he never heeded my presence, never troubled himself with so much as a single glance; but appeared wholly occupied with counting the pages of the marvellous book. Considering how sociably we had been sleeping together the night previous, and especially considering the affectionate arm I had found thrown over me upon waking in the morning, I thought this indifference of his very strange. But savages are strange beings; at times you do not know exactly how to take them. At first they are overawing; their calm self-collectedness of simplicity seems a Socratic wisdom. I had noticed also that Queequeg never consorted at all, or

but very little, with the other seamen in the inn. He made
no advances whatever; appeared to have no desire to enlarge
the circle of his acquaintances. All this struck me as mighty
singular; yet, upon second thoughts, there was something
almost sublime in it. Here was a man some twenty thousand
miles from home, by the way of Cape Horn, that is—which
was the only way he could get there—thrown among people
as strange to him as though he were in the planet Jupiter;
and yet he seemed entirely at his ease; preserving the utmost serenity; content with his own companionship; always
equal to himself. Surely this was a touch of fine philosophy;
though no doubt he had never heard there was such a thing
as that. But, perhaps, to be true philosophers, we mortals
should not be conscious of so living or so striving. So soon
as I hear that such or such a man gives himself out for a
philosopher, I conclude that, like the dyspeptic old woman,
he must have "broken his digester."

As I sat there in that now lonely room; the fire burning
low, in that mild stage when, after its first intensity has
warmed the air, it then only glows to be looked at; the
evening shades and phantoms gathering round the casements,
and peering in upon us silent, solitary twain; the storm booming without in solemn swells; I began to be sensible of
strange feelings. I felt a melting in me. No more my splintered heart and maddened hand were turned against the
wolfish world. This soothing savage had redeemed it. There
he sat, his very indifference speaking a nature in which there
lurked no civilized hypocrisies and bland deceits. Wild he
was; a very sight of sights to see; yet I began to feel myself
mysteriously drawn towards him. And those same things
that would have repelled most others, they were the very
magnets that thus drew me. I'll try a pagan friend, thought
I, since Christian kindness has proved but hollow courtesy.
I drew my bench near him, and made some friendly signs
and hints, doing my best to talk with him meanwhile. At
first he little noticed these advances; but presently, upon my
referring to his last night's hospitalities, he made out to ask
me whether we were again to be bedfellows. I told him yes;
whereat I thought he looked pleased, perhaps a little complimented.

We then turned over the book together, and I endeavored
to explain to him the purpose of the printing, and the meaning of the few pictures that were in it. Thus I soon engaged his interest; and from that we went to jabbering the

best we could about the various outer sights to be seen in this famous town. Soon I proposed a social smoke; and, producing his pouch and tomahawk, he quietly offered me a puff. And then we sat exchanging puffs from that wild pipe of his, and keeping it regularly passing between us.

If there yet lurked any ice of indifference towards me in the Pagan's breast, this pleasant, genial smoke we had, soon thawed it out, and left us cronies. He seemed to take to me quite as naturally and unbiddenly as I to him; and when our smoke was over, he pressed his forehead against mine, clasped me round the waist, and said that henceforth we were married; meaning, in his country's phrase, that we were bosom friends; he would gladly die for me, if need should be. In a countryman, this sudden flame of friendship would have seemed far too premature, a thing to be much distrusted; but in this simple savage those old rules would not apply.

After supper, and another social chat and smoke, we went to our room together. He made me a present of his embalmed head; took out his enormous tobacco wallet, and groping under the tobacco, drew out some thirty dollars in silver, then spreading them on the table, and mechanically dividing them into two equal portions, pushed one of them towards me, and said it was mine. I was going to remonstrate; but he silenced me by pouring them into my trowsers' pockets. I let them stay. He then went about his evening prayers, took out his idol, and removed the paper fireboard. By certain signs and symptoms, I thought he seemed anxious for me to join him; but well knowing what was to follow, I deliberated a moment whether, in case he invited me, I would comply or otherwise.

I was a good Christian; born and bred in the bosom of the infallible Presbyterian Church. How then could I unite with this wild idolator in worshipping his piece of wood? But what is worship? thought I. Do you suppose now, Ishmael, that the magnanimous God of heaven and earth—pagans and all included—can possibly be jealous of an insignificant bit of black wood? Impossible! But what is worship?—to do the will of God—*that* is worship. And what is the will of God?—to do to my fellow man what I would have my fellow man to do to me—*that* is the will of God. Now, Queequeg is my fellow man. And what do I wish that this Queequeg would do to me? Why, unite with me in my particular Presbyterian form of worship. Consequently,

I must then unite with him in his; ergo, I must turn idolator.
So I kindled the shavings; helped prop up the innocent little
idol; offered him burnt biscuit with Queequeg; salaamed before him twice or thrice; kissed his nose; and that done,
we undressed and went to bed, at peace with our own consciences and all the world. But we did not go to sleep
without some little chat.

How it is I know not; but there is no place like a bed
for confidential disclosures between friends. Man and wife,
they say, there open the very bottom of their souls to each
other; and some old couples often lie and chat over old
times till nearly morning. Thus, then, in our hearts' honeymoon, lay I and Queequeg—a cosy, loving pair.

NIGHTGOWN   XI

WE had lain thus in bed, chatting and napping at short
intervals, and Queequeg now and then affectionately throwing his brown tattooed legs over mine, and then drawing
them back; so entirely sociable and free and easy were we;
when, at last, by reason of our confabulations, what little
nappishness remained in us altogether departed, and we felt
like getting up again, though day-break was yet some way
down the future.

Yes, we became very wakeful; so much so that our recumbent position began to grow wearisome, and by little
and little we found ourselves sitting up; the clothes well
tucked around us, leaning against the head-board with our
four knees drawn up close together, and our two noses bending over them, as if our knee-pans were warming-pans. We
felt very nice and snug, the more so since it was so chilly
out of doors; indeed out of bed-clothes too, seeing that
there was no fire in the room. The more so, I say, because
truly to enjoy bodily warmth, some small part of you must
be cold, for there is no quality in this world that is not what
it is merely by contrast. Nothing exists in itself. If you
flatter yourself that you are all over comfortable, and have
been so a long time, then you cannot be said to be comfortable any more. But if, like Queequeg and me in the bed,
the tip of your nose or the crown of your head be slightly

chilled, why then, indeed, in the general consciousness you feel most delightfully and unmistakably warm. For this reason a sleeping apartment should never be furnished with a fire, which is one of the luxurious discomforts of the rich. For the height of this sort of deliciousness is to have nothing but the blanket between you and your snugness and the cold of the outer air. Then there you lie like the one warm spark in the heart of an arctic crystal.

We had been sitting in this crouching manner for some time, when all at once I thought I would open my eyes; for when between sheets, whether by day or by night, and whether asleep or awake, I have a way of always keeping my eyes shut, in order the more to concentrate the snugness of being in bed. Because no man can ever feel his own identity aright except his eyes be closed; as if darkness were indeed the proper element of our essences, though light be more congenial to our clayey part. Upon opening my eyes then, and coming out of my own pleasant and self-created darkness into the imposed and coarse outer gloom of the unilluminated twelve-o'clock-at-night, I experienced a disagreeable revulsion. Nor did I at all object to the hint from Queequeg that perhaps it were best to strike a light, seeing that we were so wide awake; and besides he felt a strong desire to have a few quiet puffs from his Tomahawk. Be it said, that though I had felt such a strong repugnance to his smoking in the bed the night before, yet see how elastic our stiff prejudices grow when love once comes to bend them. For now I liked nothing better than to have Queequeg smoking by me, even in bed, because he seemed to be full of such serene household joy then. I no more felt unduly concerned for the landlord's policy of insurance. I was only alive to the condensed confidential comfortableness of sharing a pipe and a blanket with a real friend. With our shaggy jackets drawn about our shoulders, we now passed the Tomahawk from one to the other, till slowly there grew over us a blue hanging tester of smoke, illuminated by the flames of the new-lit lamp.

Whether it was that this undulating tester rolled the savage away to far distant scenes, I know not, but he now spoke of his native island; and, eager to hear his history, I begged him to go on and tell it. He gladly complied. Though at the time I but ill comprehended not a few of his words, yet subsequent disclosures, when I had become more familiar with his broken phraseology, now enable me to present the whole story such as it may prove in the mere skeleton I give.

BIOGRAPHICAL   XII

QUEEQUEG was a native of Kokovoko, an island far away to the West and South. It is not down in any map; true places never are.

When a new-hatched savage running wild about his native woodlands in a grass clout, followed by the nibbling goats, as if he were a green sapling; even then, in Queequeg's ambitious soul, lurked a strong desire to see something more of Christendom than a specimen whaler or two. His father was a High Chief, a King; his uncle a High Priest; and on the maternal side he boasted aunts who were the wives of unconquerable warriors. There was excellent blood in his veins—royal stuff; though sadly vitiated, I fear, by the cannibal propensity he nourished in his untutored youth.

A Sag Harbor ship visited his father's bay, and Queequeg sought a passage to Christian lands. But the ship, having her full complement of seamen, spurned his suit; and not all the King and his father's influence could prevail. But Queequeg vowed a vow. Alone in his canoe, he paddled off to a distant strait, which he knew the ship must pass through when she quitted the island. On one side was a coral reef; on the other a low tongue of land, covered with mangrove thickets that grew out into the water. Hiding his canoe, still afloat, among these thickets, with its prow seaward, he sat down in the stern, paddle low in hand; and when the ship was gliding by, like a flash he darted out; gained her side; with one backward dash of his foot capsized and sank his canoe; climbed up the chains; and throwing himself at full length upon the deck, grappled a ring-bolt there, and swore not to let it go, though hacked in pieces.

In vain the captain threatened to throw him overboard; suspended a cutlass over his naked wrists; Queequeg was the son of a King, and Queequeg budged not. Struck by his desperate dauntlessness, and his wild desire to visit Christendom, the captain at last relented, and told him he might make himself at home. But this fine young savage—this

sea Prince of Wales, never saw the captain's cabin. They put
him down among the sailors, and made a whaleman of him.
But like Czar Peter content to toil in the shipyards of
foreign cities, Queequeg disdained no seeming ignominy, if
thereby he might happily gain the power of enlightening his
untutored countrymen. For at bottom—so he told me—he
was actuated by a profound desire to learn among the
Christians, the arts whereby to make his people still happier
than they were; and more than that, still better than they
were. But, alas! the practices of whalemen soon convinced
him that even Christians could be both miserable and wicked;
infinitely more so, than all his father's heathens. Arrived at
last in old Sag Harbor; and seeing what the sailors did
there; and then going on to Nantucket, and seeing how they
spent their wages in *that* place also, poor Queequeg gave it
up for lost. Thought he, it's a wicked world in all meridians;
I'll die a pagan.

And thus an old idolator at heart, he yet lived among these
Christians, wore their clothes, and tried to talk their gibberish. Hence the queer ways about him, though now some
time from home.

By hints, I asked him whether he did not propose going
back, and having a coronation; since he might now consider
his father dead and gone, he being very old and feeble at
the last accounts. He answered no, not yet; and added that
he was fearful Christianity, or rather Christians, had un-
fitted him for ascending the pure and undefiled throne of
thirty pagan Kings before him. But by and by, he said, he
would return,—as soon as he felt himself baptized again.
For the nonce, however, he proposed to sail about, and sow
his wild oats in all four oceans. They had made a harpooneer
of him, and that barbed iron was in lieu of a sceptre now.

I asked him what might be his immediate purpose, touching his future movements. He answered, to go to sea again,
in his old vocation. Upon this, I told him that whaling
was my own design, and informed him of my intention to
sail out of Nantucket, as being the most promising port
for an adventurous whaleman to embark from. He at once
resolved to accompany me to that island, ship aboard the
same vessel, get into the same watch, the same boat, the
same mess with me, in short to share my every hap;
with both my hands in his, boldly dip into the Potluck of
both worlds. To all this I joyously assented; for besides the
affection I now felt for Queequeg, he was an experienced

harpooneer, and as such, could not fail to be of great use-
fulness to one, who, like me, was wholly ignorant of the
mysteries of whaling, though well acquainted with the sea,
as known to merchant seamen.

His story being ended with his pipe's last dying puff, Queequeg embraced me, pressed his forehead against mine, and
blowing out the light, we rolled over from each other, this
way and that, and very soon were sleeping.

WHEELBARROW   XIII

NEXT morning, Monday, after disposing of the embalmed head to a barber, for a block, I settled my own
and comrade's bill; using, however, my comrade's money.
The grinning landlord, as well as the boarders, seemed
amazingly tickled at the sudden friendship which had sprung
up between me and Queequeg—especially as Peter Coffin's
cock and bull stories about him had previously so much
alarmed me concerning the very person whom I now com-
panied with.

We borrowed a wheelbarrow, and embarking our things,
including my own poor carpet-bag, and Queequeg's canvas
sack and hammock, away we went down to "the Moss,"
the little Nantucket packet schooner moored at the wharf.
As we were going along the people stared; not at Queequeg
so much—for they were used to seeing cannibals like him
in their streets,—but at seeing him and me upon such confidential terms. But we heeded them not, going along wheeling the barrow by turns, and Queequeg now and then
stopping to adjust the sheath on his harpoon barbs. I asked
him why he carried such a troublesome thing with him
ashore, and whether all whaling ships did not find their
own harpoons. To this, in substance, he replied, that though
what I hinted was true enough, yet he had a particular affection for his own harpoon, because it was of assured stuff,
well tried in many a mortal combat, and deeply intimate with
the hearts of whales. In short, like many inland reapers
and mowers, who go into the farmers' meadows armed with
their own scythes—though in no wise obliged to furnish
them—even so, Queequeg, for his own private reasons, pre-
ferred his own harpoon.

Shifting the barrow from my hand to his, he told me a funny story about the first wheelbarrow he had ever seen. It was in Sag Harbor. The owners of his ship, it seems, had lent him one, in which to carry his heavy chest to his boarding house. Not to seem ignorant about the thing—though in truth he was entirely so, concerning the precise way in which to manage the barrow—Queequeg puts his chest upon it; lashes it fast; and then shoulders the barrow and marches up the wharf. "Why," said I, "Queequeg, you might have known better than that, one would think. Didn't the people laugh?"

Upon this, he told me another story. The people of his island of Rokovoko, it seems, at their wedding feasts express the fragrant water of young cocoanuts into a large stained calabash like a punchbowl; and this punchbowl always forms the great central ornament on the braided mat where the feast is held. Now a certain grand merchant ship once touched at Rokovoko, and its commander—from all accounts, a very stately punctilious gentleman, at least for a sea captain—this commander was invited to the wedding feast of Queequeg's sister, a pretty young princess just turned of ten. Well; when all the wedding guests were assembled at the bride's bamboo cottage, this Captain marches in, and being assigned the post of honor, placed himself over against the punchbowl, and between the High Priest and his majesty the King, Queequeg's father. Grace being said,—for those people have their grace as well as we—though Queequeg told me that unlike us, who at such times look downwards to our platters, they, on the contrary, copying the ducks, glance upwards to the great Giver of all feasts—Grace, I say, being said, the High Priest opens the banquet by the immemorial ceremony of the island; that is, dipping his consecrated and consecrating fingers into the bowl before the blessed beverage circulates. Seeing himself placed next the Priest, and noting the ceremony, and thinking himself—being Captain of a ship—as having plain precedence over a mere island King, especially in the King's own house—the Captain coolly proceeds to wash his hands in the punch bowl;—taking it I suppose for a huge finger-glass. "Now," said Queequeg, "what you tink now?—Didn't our people laugh?"

At last, passage paid, and luggage safe, we stood on board the schooner. Hoisting sail, it glided down the Acushnet river. On one side, New Bedford rose in terraces of streets, their ice-covered trees all glittering in the clean, cold air.

Huge hills and mountains of casks on casks were piled upon her wharves, and side by side the world-wandering whale ships lay silent and safely moored at last; while from others came a sound of carpenters and coopers, with blended noises of fires and forges to melt the pitch, all betokening that new cruises were on the start; that one most perilous and long voyage ended, only begins a second; and a second ended, only begins a third, and so on, for ever and for aye. Such is the endlessness, yea, the intolerableness of all earthly effort.

Gaining the more open water, the bracing breeze waxed fresh; the little Moss tossed the quick foam from her bows, as a young colt his snortings. How I snuffed that Tartar air! —how I spurned that turnpike earth!—that common highway all over dented with the marks of slavish heels and hoofs; and turned me to admire the magnanimity of the sea which will permit no records.

At the same foam-fountain, Queequeg seemed to drink and reel with me. His dusky nostrils swelled apart; he showed his filed and pointed teeth. On, on we flew; and our offing gained, the Moss did homage to the blast; ducked and dived her brows as a slave before the Sultan. Sideways leaning, we sideways darted; every ropeyarn tingling like a wire; the two tall masts buckling like Indian canes in land tornadoes. So full of this reeling scene were we, as we stood by the plunging bowsprit, that for some time we did not notice the jeering glances of the passengers, a lubber-like assembly, who marvelled that two fellow beings should be so companionable; as though a white man were anything more dignified than a white-washed negro. But there were some boobies and bumpkins there, who, by their intense greenness, must have come from the heart and centre of all verdure. Queequeg caught one of these young saplings mimicking him behind his back. I thought the bumpkin's hour of doom was come. Dropping his harpoon, the brawny savage caught him in his arms, and by an almost miraculous dexterity and strength, sent him high up bodily into the air; then slightly tapping his stern in mid-somerset, the fellow landed with bursting lungs upon his feet, while Queequeg, turning his back upon him, lighted his tomahawk pipe and passed it to me for a puff.

"Capting! Capting!" yelled the bumpkin, running towards that officer; "Capting, Capting, here's the devil."

"Hallo, _you_ sir," cried the Captain, a gaunt rib of the sea, stalking up to Queequeg, "what in thunder do you mean by that? Don't you know you might have killed that chap?"

"What him say?" said Queequeg, as he mildly turned to me.

"He say," said I, "that you came near kill-e that man there," pointing to the still shivering greenhorn.

"Kill-e," cried Queequeg, twisting his tattooed face into an unearthly expression of disdain, "ah! him bevy small-e fish-e; Queequeg no kill-e so small-e fish-e; Queequeg kill-e big whale!"

"Look you," roared the Captain, "I'll kill-e *you*, you cannibal, if you try any more of your tricks aboard here; so mind your eye."

But it so happened just then, that it was high time for the Captain to mind his own eye. The prodigious strain upon the main-sail had parted the weather-sheet, and the tremendous boom was now flying from side to side, completely sweeping the entire after part of the deck. The poor fellow whom Queequeg had handled so roughly, was swept overboard; all hands were in a panic; and to attempt snatching at the boom to stay it, seemed madness. It flew from right to left, and back again, almost in one ticking of a watch, and every instant seemed on the point of snapping into splinters. Nothing was done, and nothing seemed capable of being done; those on deck rushed towards the bows, and stood eyeing the boom as if it were the lower jaw of an exasperated whale. In the midst of this consternation, Queequeg dropped deftly to his knees, and crawling under the path of the boom, whipped hold of a rope, secured one end to the bulwarks, and then flinging the other like a lasso, caught it round the boom as it swept over his head, and at the next jerk, the spar was that way trapped, and all was safe. The schooner was run into the wind, and while the hands were clearing away the stern boat, Queequeg, stripped to the waist, darted from the side with a long living arc of a leap. For three minutes or more he was seen swimming like a dog, throwing his long arms straight out before him, and by turns revealing his brawny shoulders through the freezing foam. I looked at the grand and glorious fellow, but saw no one to be saved. The greenhorn had gone down. Shooting himself perpendicularly from the water, Queequeg now took an instant's glance around him, and seeming to see just how matters were, dived down and disappeared. A few minutes more, and he rose again, one arm still striking out, and with the other dragging a lifeless form. The boat soon picked them up. The poor bumpkin was restored. All hands voted Queequeg a noble trump; the captain begged his pardon. From that hour I clove to Queequeg like a barnacle; yea, till poor Queequeg took his last long dive.

Was there ever such unconsciousness? He did not seem to think that he at all deserved a medal from the Humane and Magnanimous Societies. He only asked for water—fresh water—something to wipe the brine off; that done, he put on dry clothes, lighted his pipe, and leaning against the bulwarks, and mildly eyeing those around him, seemed to be saying to himself—"It's a mutual, joint-stock world, in all meridians. We cannibals must help these Christians."

NANTUCKET   **XIV**

NOTHING more happened on the passage worthy the mentioning; so, after a fine run, we safely arrived in Nantucket.

Nantucket! Take out your map and look at it. See what a real corner of the world it occupies; how it stands there, away off shore, more lonely than the Eddystone lighthouse. Look at it—a mere hillock, and elbow of sand; all beach, without a background. There is more sand there than you would use in twenty years as a substitute for blotting paper. Some gamesome wights will tell you that they have to plant weeds there, they don't grow naturally; that they import Canada thistles; that they have to send beyond seas for a spile to stop a leak in an oil cask; that pieces of wood in Nantucket are carried about like bits of the true cross in Rome; that people there plant toadstools before their houses, to get under the shade in summer time; that one blade of grass makes an oasis, three blades in a day's walk a prairie; that they wear quicksand shoes, something like Laplander snowshoes; that they are so shut up, belted about, every way inclosed, surrounded, and made an utter island of by the ocean, that to their very chairs and tables small clams will sometimes be found adhering, as to the backs of sea turtles. But these extravaganzas only show that Nantucket is no Illinois.

Look now at the wondrous traditional story of how this island was settled by the red-men. Thus goes the legend. In olden times an eagle swooped down upon the New England coast, and carried off an infant Indian in his talons. With loud lament the parents saw their child borne out of sight over the wide waters. They resolved to follow in the same direction. Setting out in their canoes, after a perilous passage they discovered the island, and there they found an empty ivory casket,—the poor little Indian's skeleton.

What wonder, then, that these Nantucketers, born on a beach, should take to the sea for a livelihood! They first caught crabs and quohogs in the sand; grown bolder, they waded out with nets for mackerel; more experienced, they pushed off in boats and captured cod; and at last, launching a navy of great ships on the sea, explored this watery world; put an incessant belt of circumnavigations round it; peeped in at Behring's Straits; and in all seasons and all oceans declared everlasting war with the mightiest animated mass that has survived the flood; most monstrous and most mountainous! That Himmalehan, salt-sea Mastodon, clothed with such portentousness of unconscious power, that his very panics are more to be dreaded than his most fearless and malicious assaults!

And thus have these naked Nantucketers, these sea hermits, issuing from their ant-hill in the sea, overrun and conquered the watery world like so many Alexanders; parcelling out among them the Atlantic, Pacific, and Indian oceans, as the three pirate powers did Poland. Let America add Mexico to Texas, and pile Cuba upon Canada; let the English overswarm all India, and hang out their blazing banner from the sun; two thirds of this terraqueous globe are the Nantucketer's. For the sea is his; he owns it, as Emperors own empires; other seamen having but a right of way through it. Merchant ships are but extension bridges; armed ones but floating forts; even pirates and privateers, though following the sea as highwaymen the road, they but plunder other ships, other fragments of the land like themselves, without seeking to draw their living from the bottomless deep itself. The Nantucketer, he alone resides and riots on the sea; he alone, in Bible language, goes down to it in ships; to and fro ploughing it as his own special plantation. *There* is his home; *there* lies his business, which a Noah's flood would not interrupt, though it overwhelmed all the millions in China. He lives on the sea, as prairie cocks in the prairie; he hides among the waves, he climbs them as chamois hunters climb the Alps. For years he knows not the land; so that when he comes to it at last, it smells like another world, more strangely than the moon would to an Earthsman. With the landless gull, that at sunset folds her wings and is rocked to sleep

between billows; so at nightfall, the Nantucketer, out of sight
of land, furls his sails, and lays him to his rest, while under
his very pillow rush herds of walruses and whales.

CHOWDER   XV

IT was quite late in the evening when the little Moss
came snugly to anchor, and Queequeg and I went ashore; so
we could attend to no business that day, at least none but a
supper and a bed. The landlord of the Spouter-Inn had recommended us to his cousin Hosea Hussey of the Try Pots,
whom he asserted to be the proprietor of one of the best kept
hotels in all Nantucket, and moreover he had assured us that
cousin Hosea, as he called him, was famous for his chowders.
In short, he plainly hinted that we could not possibly do
better than try pot-luck at the Try Pots. But the directions he
had given us about keeping a yellow warehouse on our starboard hand till we opened a white church to the larboard, and
then keeping that on the larboard hand till we made a corner
three points to the starboard, and that done, then ask the
first man we met where the place was: these crooked directions of his very much puzzled us at first, especially as, at the
outset, Queequeg insisted that the yellow warehouse—our
first point of departure—must be left on the larboard hand,
whereas I had understood Peter Coffin to say it was on the
starboard. However, by dint of beating about a little in the
dark, and now and then knocking up a peaceable inhabitant
to inquire the way, we at last came to something which there
was no mistaking.

Two enormous wooden pots painted black, and suspended
by asses' ears, swung from the cross-trees of an old top-
mast, planted in front of an old doorway. The horns of the
cross-trees were sawed off on the other side, so that this old
top-mast looked not a little like a gallows. Perhaps I was over
sensitive to such impressions at the time, but I could not help
staring at this gallows with a vague misgiving. A sort of crick
was in my neck as I gazed up to the two remaining horns;
yes, *two* of them, one for Queequeg, and one for me. It's
ominous, thinks I. A. Coffin my Innkeeper upon landing in
my first whaling port; tombstones staring at me in the whale-
mens' chapel; and here a gallows! and a pair of prodigious

black pots too! Are these last throwing out oblique hints touching Tophet?

I was called from these reflections by the sight of a freckled woman with yellow hair and a yellow gown, standing in the porch of the inn, under a dull red lamp swinging there, that looked much like an injured eye, and carrying on a brisk scolding with a man in a purple woollen shirt.

"Get along with ye," said she to the man, "or I'll be combing ye!"

"Come on, Queequeg," said I, "all right. There's Mrs. Hussey."

And so it turned out; Mr. Hosea Hussey being from home, but leaving Mrs. Hussey entirely competent to attend to all his affairs. Upon making known our desires for a supper and a bed, Mrs. Hussey, postponing further scolding for the present, ushered us into a little room, and seating us at a table spread with the relics of a recently concluded repast, turned round to us and said—"Clam or Cod?"

"What's that about Cods, ma'am?" said I, with much politeness.

"Clam or Cod?" she repeated.

"A clam for supper? a cold clam; is *that* what you mean, Mrs. Hussey?" says I; "but that's a rather cold and clammy reception in the winter time, ain't it, Mrs. Hussey?"

But being in a great hurry to resume scolding the man in the purple shirt, who was waiting for it in the entry, and seeming to hear nothing but the word "clam," Mrs. Hussey hurried towards an open door leading to the kitchen, and bawling out "clam for two," disappeared.

"Queequeg," said I, "do you think that we can make out a supper for us both on one clam?"

However, a warm savory steam from the kitchen served to belie the apparently cheerless prospect before us. But when that smoking chowder came in, the mystery was delightfully explained. Oh, sweet friends! hearken to me. It was made of small juicy clams, scarcely bigger than hazel nuts, mixed with pounded ship biscuit, and salted pork cut up into little flakes; the whole enriched with butter, and plentifully seasoned with pepper and salt. Our appetites being sharpened by the frosty voyage, and in particular, Queequeg seeing his favorite fishing food before him, and the chowder being surpassing excellent, we despatched it with great expedition: when leaning back a moment and bethinking me of Mrs. Hussey's clam and cod announcement, I thought I would try a little experiment. Stepping to the kitchen door, I uttered the word "cod" with great emphasis, and resumed my seat. In a few moments the savory steam came forth again, but with a different flavor, and in good time a fine cod-chowder was placed before us.

We resumed business; and while plying our spoons in the bowl, thinks I to myself, I wonder now if this here has any effect on the head? What's that stultifying saying about chowder-headed people? "But look, Queequeg, ain't that a live eel in your bowl? Where's your harpoon?"

Fishiest of all fishy places was the Try Pots, which well deserved its name; for the pots there were always boiling chowders. Chowder for breakfast, and chowder for dinner, and chowder for supper, till you began to look for fish-bones coming through your clothes. The area before the house was paved with clamshells. Mrs. Hussey wore a polished necklace of codfish vertebra; and Hosea Hussey had his account books bound in superior old shark-skin. There was a fishy flavor to the milk, too, which I could not at all account for, till one morning happening to take a stroll along the beach among some fishermen's boats, I saw Hosea's brindled cow feeding on fish remnants, and marching along the sand with each foot in a cod's decapitated head, looking very slip-shod, I assure ye.

Supper concluded, we received a lamp, and directions from Mrs. Hussey concerning the nearest way to bed; but, as Queequeg was about to precede me up the stairs, the lady reached forth her arm, and demanded his harpoon; she allowed no harpoon in her chambers. "Why not?" said I; "every true whaleman sleeps with his harpoon—but why not?" "Because it's dangerous," says she. "Ever since young Stiggs coming from that unfort'nt v'y'ge of his, when he was gone four years and a half, with only three barrels of *ile*, was found dead in my first floor back, with his harpoon in his side; ever since then I allow no boarders to take sich dangerous weapons in their rooms at night. So, Mr. Queequeg" (for she had learned his name), "I will just take this here iron, and keep it for you till morning. But the chowder; clam or cod to-morrow for breakfast, men?"

"Both," says I; "and let's have a couple of smoked herring by way of variety."

THE SHIP   XVI

IN bed we concocted our plans for the morrow. But to my surprise and no small concern, Queequeg now gave me to understand, that he had been diligently consulting Yojo —the name of his black little god—and Yojo had told him two or three times over, and strongly insisted upon it every-way, that instead of our going together among the whaling-fleet in harbor, and in concert selecting our craft; instead of this, I say, Yojo earnestly enjoined that the selection of the ship should rest wholly with me, inasmuch as Yojo pur-posed befriending us; and, in order to do so, had already pitched upon a vessel, which, if left to myself, I, Ishmael, should infallibly light upon, for all the world as though it had turned out by chance; and in that vessel I must im-mediately ship myself, for the present irrespective of Quee-queg.

I have forgotten to mention that, in many things, Quee-queg placed great confidence in the excellence of Yojo's judgment and surprising forecast of things; and cherished Yojo with considerable esteem, as a rather good sort of god, who perhaps meant well enough upon the whole, but in all cases did not succeed in his benevolent designs.

Now, this plan of Queequeg's, or rather Yojo's, touching the selection of our craft; I did not like that plan at all. I had not a little relied upon Queequeg's sagacity to point out the whaler best fitted to carry us and our fortunes securely. But as all my remonstrances produced no effect upon Quee-queg, I was obliged to acquiesce; and accordingly prepared to set about this business with a determined rushing sort of energy and vigor, that should quickly settle that trifling little affair. Next morning early, leaving Queequeg shut up with Yojo in our little bedroom—for it seemed that it was some sort of Lent or Ramadan, or day of fasting, humiliation, and prayer with Queequeg and Yojo that day; *how* it was I never could find out, for, though I applied myself to it several times, I never could master his liturgies and XXXIX Articles—leaving Queequeg, then, fasting on his tomahawk pipe, and Yojo warming himself at his sacrificial fire of shavings, I sallied out among the shipping. After much pro-

longed sauntering and many random inquiries, I learnt that
there were three ships up for three-years' voyages—The Devil-
dam, the Tit-bit, and the Pequod. *Devil-Dam,* I do not know
the origin of; *Tit-bit* is obvious; *Pequod,* you will no doubt
remember, was the name of a celebrated tribe of Massachusetts Indians, now extinct as the ancient Medes. I peered and
pryed about the Devil-Dam; from her, hopped over to the Tit-
bit; and, finally, going on board the Pequod, looked around
her for a moment, and then decided that this was the very
ship for us.

You may have seen many a quaint craft in your day, for
aught I know;—squared-toed luggers, mountainous Japanese
junks; butter-box galliots, and what not; but take my word
for it, you never saw such a rare old craft as this same
rare old Pequod. She was a ship of the old school, rather small
if anything; with an old fashioned claw-footed look about her.
Long seasoned and weather-stained in the typhoons and calms
of all four oceans, her old hull's complexion was darkened like
a French grenadier's, who has alike fought in Egypt and
Siberia. Her venerable bows looked bearded. Her masts—
cut somewhere on the coast of Japan, where her original
ones were lost overboard in a gale—her masts stood stiffly
up like the spines of the three old kings of Cologne. Her
ancient decks were worn and wrinkled, like the pilgrim-
worshipped flag-stone in Canterbury Cathedral where Beckett
bled. But to all these her old antiquities, were added new
and marvellous features, pertaining to the wild business that
for more than half a century she had followed. Old Captain Peleg, many years her chief-mate, before he commanded
another vessel of his own, and now a retired seaman, and one
of the principal owners of the Pequod,—this old Peleg, during
the term of his chief-mateship, had built upon her original
grotesqueness, and inlaid it, all over, with a quaintness both
of material and device, unmatched by anything except it be
Thorkill-Hake's carved buckler or bedstead. She was apparelled like any barbaric Ethiopian emperor, his neck heavy
with pendants of polished ivory. She was a thing of trophies.
A cannibal of a craft, tricking herself forth in the chased
bones of her enemies. All round, her unpanelled, open bulwarks were garnished like one continuous jaw, with the long
sharp teeth of the sperm whale, inserted there for pins, to
fasten her old hempen thews and tendons to. Those ran not
through base blocks of land wood, but deftly travelled over
sheaves of sea-ivory. Scorning a turnstile wheel at her rever-

end helm, she sported there a tiller; and that tiller was in one mass, curiously carved from the long narrow lower jaw of her hereditary foe. The helmsman who steered by that tiller in a tempest, felt like the Tartar, when he holds back his fiery steed by clutching its jaw. A noble craft, but somehow a most melancholy! All noble things are touched with that.

Now when I looked about the quarter-deck, for some one having authority, in order to propose myself as a candidate for the voyage, at first I saw nobody; but I could not well overlook a strange sort of tent, or rather wigwam, pitched a little behind the main-mast. It seemed only a temporary erection used in port. It was of a conical shape, some ten feet high; consisting of the long, huge slabs of limber black bone taken from the middle and highest part of the jaws of the right-whale. Planted with their broad ends on the deck, a circle of these slabs laced together, mutually sloped towards each other, and at the apex united in a tufted point, where the loose hairy fibres waved to and fro like the top-knot on some old Pottowottamie Sachem's head. A triangular opening faced towards the bows of the ship, so that the insider commanded a complete view forward.

And half concealed in this queer tenement, I at length found one who by his aspect seemed to have authority; and who, it being noon, and the ship's work suspended, was now enjoying respite from the burden of command. He was seated on an old-fashioned oaken chair, wriggling all over with curious carving; and the bottom of which was formed of a stout interlacing of the same elastic stuff of which the wigwam was constructed.

There was nothing so very particular, perhaps, about the appearance of the elderly man I saw; he was brown and brawny, like most old seamen, and heavily rolled up in blue pilot-cloth, cut in the Quaker style; only there was a fine and almost microscopic net-work of the minutest wrinkles interlacing round his eyes, which must have arisen from his continual sailings in many hard gales, and always looking to windward;—for this causes the muscles about the eyes to become pursed together. Such eye-wrinkles are very effectual in a scowl.

"Is this the Captain of the Pequod?" said I, advancing to the door of the tent.

"Supposing it be the Captain of the Pequod, what dost thou want of him?" he demanded.

"I was thinking of shipping."

"Thou wast, wast thou? I see thou art no Nantucketer—ever been in a stove boat?"

"No, Sir, I never have."

"Dost know nothing at all about whaling, I dare say—eh?"

"Nothing, Sir; but I have no doubt I shall soon learn. I've been several voyages in the merchant service, and I think that——"

"Merchant service be damned. Talk not that lingo to me. Dost see that leg?—I'll take that leg away from thy stern, if ever thou talkest of the marchant service to me again. Marchant service indeed! I suppose now ye feel considerable proud of having served in those marchant ships. But flukes! man, what makes thee want to go a whaling, eh?—it looks a little suspicious, don't it, eh?—Hast not been a pirate, hast thou?—Didst not rob thy last Captain, didst thou?—Dost not think of murdering the officers when thou gettest to sea?"

I protested my innocence of these things. I saw that under the mask of these half humorous inuendoes, this old seaman, as an insulated Quakerish Nantucketer, was full of his insular prejudices, and rather distrustful of all aliens, unless they hailed from Cape Cod or the Vineyard.

"But what takes thee a-whaling? I want to know that before I think of shipping ye."

"Well, sir, I want to see what whaling is. I want to see the world."

"Want to see what whaling is, eh? Have ye clapped eye on Captain Ahab?"

"Who is Captain Ahab, sir?"

"Aye, aye, I thought so. Captain Ahab is the Captain of this ship."

"I am mistaken then. I thought I was speaking to the Captain himself."

"Thou art speaking to Captain Peleg—that's who ye are speaking to, young man. It belongs to me and Captain Bildad to see the Pequod fitted out for the voyage, and supplied with all her needs, including crew. We are part owners and agents. But as I was going to say, if thou wantest to know what whaling is, as thou tellest ye do, I can put ye in a way of finding it out before ye bind yourself to it, past backing out. Clap eye on Captain Ahab, young man, and thou wilt find that he has only one leg."

"What do you mean, sir? Was the other one lost by a whale?"

"Lost by a whale! Young man, come nearer to me: it was

devoured, chewed up, crunched by the monstrousest parmacetty that ever chipped a boat!—ah, ah!"

I was a little alarmed by his energy, perhaps also a little
touched at the hearty grief in his concluding exclamation,
but said as calmly as I could, "What you say is no doubt
true enough sir; but how could I know there was any peculiar ferocity in that particular whale, though indeed I might
have inferred as much from the simple fact of the accident."

"Look ye now, young man, thy lungs are a sort of soft,
d'ye see; thou dost not talk shark a bit. *Sure,* ye've been to
sea before now; sure of that?"

"Sir," said I, "I thought I told you that I had been four
voyages in the merchant——"

"Hard down out of that! Mind what I said about the
marchant service—don't aggravate me—I won't have it. But
let us understand each other. I have given thee a hint about
what whaling is; do ye yet feel inclined for it?"

"I do, sir."

"Very good. Now, art thou the man to pitch a harpoon
down a live whale's throat, and then jump after it? Answer,
quick!"

"I am, sir, if it should be positively indispensable to do so;
not to be got rid of, that is; which I don't take to be the
fact."

"Good again. Now then, thou not only wantest to go a-
whaling, to find out by experience what whaling is, but ye
also want to go in order to see the world? Was not that
what ye said? I thought so. Well then, just step forward
there, and take a peep over the weatherbow, and then back
to me and tell me what ye see there."

For a moment I stood a little puzzled by this curious request, not knowing exactly how to take it, whether humorously or in earnest. But concentrating all his crow's feet into
one scowl, Captain Peleg started me on the errand.

Going forward and glancing over the weather bow, I perceived that the ship swinging to her anchor with the flood-
tide, was now obliquely pointed towards the open ocean. The
prospect was unlimited, but exceedingly monotonous and forbidding; not the slightest variety that I could see.

"Well, what's the report?" said Peleg when I came back;
"what did ye see?"

"Not much," I replied—"nothing but water; considerable
horizon though, and there's a squall coming up, I think."

"Well, what dost thou think of seeing the world? Do ye

wish to go round Cape Horn to see any more of it, eh?
Can't ye see the world where you stand?"

I was a little staggered, but go a-whaling I must, and I
would; and the Pequod was as good a ship as any—I thought
the best—and all this I now repeated to Peleg. Seeing me so
determined, he expressed his willingness to ship me.

"And thou mayest as well sign the papers right off," he
added—"come along with ye." And so saying, he led the
way below deck into the cabin.

Seated on the transom was what seemed to me a most uncommon and surprising figure. It turned out to be Captain
Bildad, who along with Captain Peleg was one of the largest
owners of the vessel; the other shares, as is sometimes the
case in these ports, being held by a crowd of old annuitants;
widows, fatherless children, and chancery wards; each owning
about the value of a timber head, or a foot of plank, or a
nail or two in the ship. People in Nantucket invest their
money in whaling vessels, the same way that you do yours
in approved state stocks bringing in good interest.

Now, Bildad, like Peleg, and indeed many other Nantucketers, was a Quaker, the island having been originally
settled by that sect; and to this day its inhabitants in general
retain in an uncommon measure the peculiarities of the
Quaker, only variously and anomalously modified by things
altogether alien and heterogeneous. For some of these same
Quakers are the most sanguinary of all sailors and whale-
hunters. They are fighting Quakers; they are Quakers with a
vengeance.

So that there are instances among them of men, who,
named with Scripture names—a singularly common fashion
on the island—and in childhood naturally imbibing the
stately dramatic thee and thou of the Quaker idiom; still,
from the audacious, daring, and boundless adventure of their
subsequent lives, strangely blend with these un-outgrown peculiarities, a thousand bold dashes of character, not unworthy
a Scandinavian sea-king, or a poetical Pagan Roman. And
when these things unite in a man of greatly superior natural
force, with a globular brain and a ponderous heart; who
has also by the stillness and seclusion of many long night-
watches in the remotest waters, and beneath constellations
never seen here at the north, been led to think untraditionally
and independently; receiving all nature's sweet or savage
impressions fresh from her own virgin voluntary and con-
fiding breast, and thereby chiefly, but with some help from

accidental advantages, to learn a bold and nervous lofty language—that man makes one in a whole nation's census—a mighty pageant creature, formed for noble tragedies. Nor will it at all detract from him, dramatically regarded, if either by birth or other circumstances, he have what seems a half wilful overruling morbidness at the bottom of his nature. For all men tragically great are made so through a certain morbidness. Be sure of this, O young ambition, all mortal greatness is but disease. But, as yet we have not to do with such an one, but with quite another; and still a man, who, if indeed peculiar, it only results again from another phase of the Quaker, modified by individual circumstances.

Like Captain Peleg, Captain Bildad was a well-to-do, retired whaleman. But unlike Captain Peleg—who cared not a rush for what are called serious things, and indeed deemed those self-same serious things the veriest of all trifles—Captain Bildad had not only been originally educated according to the strictest sect of Nantucket Quakerism, but all his subsequent ocean life, and the sight of many unclad, lovely island creatures, round the Horn—all that had not moved this native born Quaker one single jot, had not so much as altered one angle of his vest. Still, for all this immutableness, was there some lack of common consistency about worthy Captain Bildad. Though refusing, from conscientious scruples, to bear arms against land invaders, yet himself had illimitably invaded the Atlantic and Pacific; and though a sworn foe to human bloodshed, yet had he in his straight-bodied coat, spilled tuns upon tuns of leviathan gore. How now in the contemplative evening of his days, the pious Bildad reconciled these things in the reminiscence, I do not know; but it did not seem to concern him much, and very probably he had long since come to the sage and sensible conclusion that a man's religion is one thing, and this practical world quite another. This world pays dividends. Rising from a little cabinboy in short clothes of the drabbest drab, to a harpooneer in a broad shad-bellied waistcoat; from that becoming boat-header, chief-mate, and captain, and finally a shipowner; Bildad, as I hinted before, had concluded his adventurous career by wholly retiring from active life at the goodly age of sixty, and dedicating his remaining days to the quiet receiving of his well-earned income.

Now Bildad, I am sorry to say, had the reputation of being an incorrigible old hunks, and in his sea-going days, a bitter, hard taskmaster. They told me in Nantucket, though

it certainly seems a curious story, that when he sailed the old
Categut whaleman, his crew, upon arriving home, were mostly
all carried ashore to the hospital, sore exhausted and worn
out. For a pious man, especially for a Quaker, he was certainly rather hard-hearted, to say the least. He never used
to swear, though, at his men, they said; but somehow he
got an inordinate quantity of cruel, unmitigated hard work
out of them. When Bildad was a chief-mate, to have his
drab-colored eye intently looking at you, made you feel completely nervous, till you could clutch something—a hammer
or a marling-spike, and go to work like mad, at something
or other, never mind what. Indolence and idleness perished
from before him. His own person was the exact embodiment
of his utilitarian character. On his long, gaunt body, he
carried no spare flesh, no superfluous beard, his chin having
a soft, economical nap to it, like the worn nap of his
broad-brimmed hat.

Such, then, was the person that I saw seated on the transom when I followed Captain Peleg down into the cabin. The
space between the decks was small; and there, bolt-upright,
sat old Bildad, who always sat so, and never leaned, and this
to save his coat tails. His broad-brim was placed beside him;
his legs were stiffly crossed; his drab vesture was buttoned
up to his chin; and spectacles on nose, he seemed absorbed in
reading from a ponderous volume.

"Bildad," cried Captain Peleg, "at it again, Bildad, eh? Ye
have been studying those Scriptures, now, for the last thirty
years, to my certain knowledge. How far ye got, Bildad?"

As if long habituated to such profane talk from his old
shipmate, Bildad, without noticing his present irreverence,
quietly looked up, and seeing me, glanced again inquiringly
towards Peleg.

"He says he's our man, Bildad," said Peleg, "he wants to
ship."

"Dost thee?" said Bildad, in a hollow tone, and turning
round to me.

"I *dost*," said I unconsciously, he was so intense a Quaker.

"What do ye think of him, Bildad?" said Peleg.

"He'll do," said Bildad, eyeing me, and then went on
spelling away at his book in a mumbling tone quite audible.

I thought him the queerest old Quaker I ever saw,
especially as Peleg, his friend and old shipmate, seemed such
a blusterer. But I said nothing, only looking round me
sharply. Peleg now threw open a chest, and drawing forth

the ship's articles, placed pen and ink before him, and seated himself at a little table. I began to think it was high time to settle with myself at what terms I would be willing to engage for the voyage. I was already aware that in the whaling business they paid no wages; but all hands, including the captain, received certain shares of the profits called *lays,* and that these lays were proportioned to the degree of importance pertaining to the respective duties of the ship's company. I was also aware that being a green hand at whaling, my own lay would not be very large; but considering that I was used to the sea, could steer a ship, splice a rope, and all that, I made no doubt that from all I had heard I should be offered at least the 275th lay—that is, the 275th part of the clear net proceeds of the voyage, whatever that might eventually amount to. And though the 275th lay was what they call a rather *long lay,* yet it was better than nothing; and if we had a lucky voyage, might pretty nearly pay for the clothing I would wear out on it, not to speak of my three years' beef and board, for which I would not have to pay one stiver.

It might be thought that this was a poor way to accumulate a princely fortune—and so it was, a very poor way indeed. But I am one of those that never take on about princely fortunes, and am quite content if the world is ready to board and lodge me, while I am putting up at this grim sign of the Thunder Cloud. Upon the whole, I thought that the 275th lay would be about the fair thing, but would not have been surprised had I been offered the 200th, considering I was of a broad-shouldered make.

But one thing, nevertheless, that made me a little distrustful about receiving a generous share of the profits was this: Ashore, I had heard something of both Captain Peleg and his unaccountable old crony Bildad; how that they being the principal proprietors of the Pequod, therefore the other and more inconsiderable and scattered owners, left nearly the whole management of the ship's affairs to these two. And I did not know but what the stingy old Bildad might have a mighty deal to say about shipping hands, especially as I now found him on board the Pequod, quite at home there in the cabin, and reading his Bible as if at his own fireside. Now while Peleg was vainly trying to mend a pen with his jack-knife, old Bildad, to my no small surprise, considering that he was such an interested party in these proceedings; Bildad never heeded us, but went on mumbling to himself out of his book, *"Lay* not up for yourselves treasures upon earth, where moth—"

"Well, Captain Bildad," interrupted Peleg, "what d'ye say, what lay shall we give this young man?"

"Thou knowest best," was the sepulchral reply, "the seven hundred and seventh-seventh wouldn't be too much, would it?—'where moth and rust do corrupt, but *lay*—'"

Lay, indeed, thought I, and such a lay! the seven hundred and seventy-seventh! Well, old Bildad, you are determined that I, for one, shall not *lay* up many *lays* here below, where moth and rust do corrupt. It was an exceedingly *long lay* that, indeed; and though from the magnitude of the figure it might at first deceive a landsman, yet the slightest consideration will show that though seven hundred and seventy-seven is a pretty large number, yet when you come to make a *teenth* of it, you will then see, I say, that the seven hundred and seventy-seventh part of a farthing is a good deal less than seven hundred and seventy-seven gold doubloons; and so I thought at the time.

"Why, blast your eyes, Bildad," cried Peleg, "thou dost not want to swindle this young man! he must have more than that."

"Seven hundred and seventy-seventh," again said Bildad, without lifting his eyes; and then went on mumbling—"for where your treasure is, there will your heart be also."

"I am going to put him down for the three hundredth," said Peleg, "do ye hear that, Bildad! The three hundredth lay, I say."

Bildad laid down his book, and turning solemnly towards him said, "Captain Peleg, thou hast a generous heart; but thou must consider the duty thou owest to the other owners of this ship—widows and orphans, many of them—and that if we too abundantly reward the labors of this young man, we may be taking the bread from those widows and those orphans. The seven hundred and seventy-seventh lay, Captain Peleg."

"Thou Bildad!" roared Peleg, starting up and clattering about the cabin. "Blast ye, Captain Bildad, if I had followed thy advice in these matters, I would afore now had a conscience to lug about that would be heavy enough to founder the largest ship that ever sailed round Cape Horn."

"Captain Peleg," said Bildad steadily, "thy conscience may be drawing ten inches of water, or ten fathoms, I can't tell; but as thou art still an impenitent man, Captain Peleg, I greatly fear lest thy conscience be but a leaky one; and will in the end sink thee foundering down to the fiery pit, Captain Peleg."

"Fiery pit! fiery pit! ye insult me, man; past all natural bearing, ye insult me. It's an all-fired outrage to tell any human creature that he's bound to hell. Flukes and flames! Bildad, say that again to me, and start my soul-bolts, but I'll —I'll—yes, I'll swallow a live goat with all his hair and horns on. Out of the cabin, ye canting, drab-colored son of a wooden gun—a straight wake with ye!"

As he thundered out this he made a rush at Bildad, but with a marvellous oblique, sliding celerity, Bildad for that time eluded him.

Alarmed at this terrible outburst between the two principal and responsible owners of the ship, and feeling half a mind to give up all idea of sailing in a vessel so questionably owned and temporarily commanded, I stepped aside from the door to give egress to Bildad, who, I made no doubt, was all eagerness to vanish from before the awakened wrath of Peleg. But to my astonishment, he sat down again on the transom very quietly, and seemed to have not the slightest intention of withdrawing. He seemed quite used to impenitent Peleg and his ways. As for Peleg, after letting off his rage as he had, there seemed no more left in him, and he, too, sat down like a lamb, though he twitched a little as if still nervously agitated. "Whew!" he whistled at last—"the squall's gone off to leeward, I think. Bildad, thou used to be good at sharpening a lance, mend that pen, will ye. My jackknife here needs the grindstone. That's he; thank ye, Bildad. Now then, my young man, Ishmael's thy name, didn't ye say? Well then, down ye go here, Ishmael, for the three hundredth lay."

"Captain Peleg," said I, "I have a friend with me who wants to ship too—shall I bring him down to-morrow?"

"To be sure," said Peleg. "Fetch him along, and we'll look at him."

"What lay does he want?" groaned Bildad, glancing up from the book in which he had again been burying himself.

"Oh! never thee mind about that, Bildad," said Peleg. "Has he ever whaled it any?" turning to me.

"Killed more whales than I can count, Captain Peleg."

"Well, bring him along then."

And, after signing the papers, off I went; nothing doubting but that I had done a good morning's work, and that the

Pequod was the identical ship that Yojo had provided to carry Queequeg and me round the Cape.

But I had not proceeded far, when I began to bethink me that the captain with whom I was to sail yet remained unseen by me; though, indeed, in many cases, a whale-ship will be completely fitted out, and receive all her crew on board, ere the captain makes himself visible by arriving to take command; for sometimes these voyages are so prolonged, and the shore intervals at home so exceedingly brief, that if the captain have a family, or any absorbing concernment of that sort, he does not trouble himself much about his ship in port, but leaves her to the owners till all is ready for sea. However, it is always as well to have a look at him before irrevocably committing yourself into his hands. Turning back I accosted Captain Peleg, inquiring where Captain Ahab was to be found.

"And what dost thou want of Captain Ahab? It's all right enough; thou art shipped."

"Yes, but I should like to see him."

"But I don't think thou wilt be able to at present. I don't know exactly what's the matter with him; but he keeps close inside the house; a sort of sick, and yet he don't look so. In fact, he ain't sick; but no, he isn't well either. Any how, young man, he won't always see me, so I don't suppose he will thee. He's a queer man, Captain Ahab—so some think —but a good one. Oh, thou'lt like him well enough; no fear, no fear. He's a grand, ungodly, god-like man, Captain Ahab; doesn't speak much; but, when he does speak, then you may well listen. Mark ye, be forewarned; Ahab's above the common; Ahab's been in colleges, as well as 'mong the cannibals; been used to deeper wonders than the waves; fixed his fiery lance in mightier, stranger foes than whales. His lance! aye, the keenest and the surest that out of all our isle! Oh! he ain't Captain Bildad; no, and he ain't Captain Peleg; *he's Ahab,* boy; and Ahab of old, thou knowest, was a crowned king!"

"And a very vile one. When that wicked king was slain, the dogs, did they not lick his blood?"

"Come hither to me—hither, hither," said Peleg, with a significance in his eye that almost startled me. "Look ye, lad; never say that name on board the Pequod. Never say it anywhere. Captain Ahab did not name himself. 'Twas a foolish, ignorant whim of his crazy, widowed mother, who died when he was only a twelvemonth old. And yet the old squaw Tistig, at Gayhead, said that the name would somehow prove prophetic. And, perhaps, other fools like her may tell thee the same. I wish to warn thee. It's a lie. I know Captain Ahab well; I've sailed with him as mate years ago; I know what he is—a good man—not a pious, good man, like Bildad, but a swearing good man—something like me —only there's a good deal more of him. Aye, aye, I know that he was never very jolly; and I know that on the passage home, he was a little out of his mind for a spell; but it was the sharp shooting pains in his bleeding stump that brought that about, as any one might see. I know, too, that ever since he lost his leg last voyage by that accursed whale, he's been a kind of moody—desperate moody, and savage sometimes; but that will all pass off. And once for all, let me tell thee and assure thee, young man, it's better to sail with a moody good captain than a laughing bad one. So good-bye to thee—and wrong not Captain Ahab, because he happens to have a wicked name. Besides, my boy, he has a wife—not three voyages wedded—a sweet, resigned girl. Think of that; by that sweet girl that old man has a child: hold ye then there can be any utter, hopeless harm in Ahab? No, no, my lad; stricken, blasted, if he be, Ahab has his humanities!"

As I walked away, I was full of thoughtfulness; what had been incidentally revealed to me of Captain Ahab, filled me with a certain wild vagueness of painfulness concerning him. And somehow, at the time, I felt a sympathy and a sorrow for him, but for I don't know what, unless it was the cruel loss of his leg. And yet I also felt a strange awe of him; but that sort of awe, which I cannot at all describe, was not exactly awe; I do not know what it was. But I felt it; and it did not disincline me towards him; though I felt impatience at what seemed like mystery in him, so imperfectly as he was known to me then. However, my thoughts were at length carried in other directions, so that for the present dark Ahab slipped my mind.

THE RAMADAN   **XVII**

As Queequeg's Ramadan, or Fasting and Humiliation, was to continue all day, I did not choose to disturb him till towards night-fall; for I cherish the greatest respect towards everybody's religious obligations, never mind how comical, and could not find it in my heart to undervalue even a congregation of ants worshipping a toadstool; or those other creatures in certain parts of our earth, who with a degree of footmanism quite unprecedented in other planets, bow down before the torso of a deceased landed proprietor merely on account of the inordinate possessions yet owned and rented in his name.

I say, we good Presbyterian Christians should be charitable in these things, and not fancy ourselves so vastly superior to other mortals, pagans and what not, because of their half-crazy conceits on these subjects. There was Queequeg, now, certainly entertaining the most absurd notions about Yojo and his Ramadan;—but what of that? Queequeg thought he knew what he was about, I suppose; he seemed to be content: and there let him rest. All our arguing with him would not avail; let him be, I say: and Heaven have mercy on us all—Presbyterians and Pagans alike—for we are all somehow dreadfully cracked about the head, and sadly need mending.

Towards evening, when I felt assured that all his performances and rituals must be over, I went up to his room and knocked at the door; but no answer. I tried to open it, but it was fastened inside. "Queequeg," said I softly through the key-hole:—all silent. "I say, Queequeg! why don't you speak? It's I—Ishmael." But all remained still as before. I began to grow alarmed. I had allowed him such abundant time; I thought he might have had an apoplectic fit. I looked through the key-hole; but the door opening into an odd corner of the room, the key-hole prospect was but a crooked and sinister one. I could only see part of the foot-board of the bed and a line of the wall, but nothing more. I was surprised to behold resting against the wall the wooden shaft of Queequeg's harpoon, which the landlady the evening previous had taken from him, before our mounting to the chamber. That's strange, thought I; but at any rate, since the harpoon stands yonder, and he seldom or never goes abroad without it, therefore he must be inside here, and no possible mistake.

"Queequeg!—Queequeg!"—all still. Something must have happened. Apoplexy! I tried to burst open the door; but it stubbornly resisted. Running down stairs, I quickly stated my suspicions to the first person I met—the chambermaid. "La! La!" she cried, "I thought something must be the matter. I went to make the bed after breakfast, and the door was locked; and not a mouse to be heard; and it's been just so silent ever since. But I thought, may be, you had both gone off and locked your baggage in for safe keeping. La! La, ma'am!—Mistress! murder! Mrs. Hussey! apoplexy!"—and with these cries, she ran towards the kitchen, I following.

Mrs. Hussey soon appeared, with a mustard-pot in one hand and a vinegar-cruet in the other, having just broken away from the occupation of attending to the castors, and scolding her little black boy meantime.

"Wood-house!" cried I, "which way to it? Run for God's sake, and fetch something to pry open the door—the axe! the axe!—he's had a stroke; depend upon it!"—and so saying I was unmethodically rushing up stairs again empty-handed, when Mrs. Hussey interposed the mustard-pot and vinegar-cruet, and the entire castor of her countenance.

"What's the matter with you, young man?"

"Get the axe! For God's sake, run for the doctor, some one, while I pry it open!"

"Look here," said the landlady, quickly putting down the vinegar-cruet, so as to have one hand free; "look here; are you talking about prying open any of my doors?"—and with that she seized my arm. "What's the matter with you? What's the matter with you, shipmate?"

In as calm, but rapid a manner as possible, I gave her to understand the whole case. Unconsciously clapping the vinegar cruet to one side of her nose, she ruminated for an instant; then exclaimed—"No! I haven't seen it since I put it there." Running to a little closet under the landing of the stairs, she glanced in, and returning, told me that Queequeg's harpoon was missing. "He's killed himself," she cried. "It's unfort'nate Stiggs done over again—there goes another counterpane—God pity his poor mother!—it will be the ruin of my house. Has the poor lad a sister? Where's that girl?—there, Betty, go to Snarles the Painter, and tell him to paint me a sign, with—'no suicides permitted here, and no smoking in the parlor;'—might as well kill both birds at once. Kill? The Lord be merciful to his ghost! What's that noise there? You, young man, avast there!"

And running up after me, she caught me as I was again trying to force open the door.

"I won't allow it; I won't have my premises spoiled. Go for the locksmith, there's one about a mile from here. But avast!" putting her hand in her side-pocket, "here's a key that'll fit, I guess; let's see." And with that, she turned it

in the lock; but, alas! Queequeg's supplemental bolt remained
unwithdrawn within.

"Have to burst it open," said I, and was running down
the entry a little, for a good start, when the landlady caught
at me, again vowing I should not break down her premises; but I tore from her, and with a sudden bodily rush
dashed myself full against the mark.

With a prodigious noise the door flew open, and the knob
slamming against the wall, sent the plaster to the ceiling;
and there, good heavens! there sat Queequeg, altogether cool
and self-collected; right in the middle of the room; squat-
ting on his hams, and holding Yojo on top of his head. He
looked neither one way nor the other way, but sat like a
carved image with scarce a sign of active life.

"Queequeg," said I, going up to him, "Queequeg, what's
the matter with you?"

"He hain't been a sittin' so all day, has he?" said the landlady.

But all we said, not a word could we drag out of him; I
almost felt like pushing him over, so as to change his position, for it was almost intolerable, it seemed so painfully
and unnaturally constrained; especially, as in all probability he had been sitting so for upwards of eight or ten hours,
going too without his regular meals.

"Mrs. Hussey," said I, "he's *alive* at all events; so leave
us, if you please, and I will see to this strange affair myself."

Closing the door upon the landlady, I endeavored to prevail upon Queequeg to take a chair; but in vain. There he
sat; and all he could do—for all my polite arts and blandishments—he would not move a peg, nor say a single word, nor
even look at me, nor notice my presence in any the slightest
way.

I wonder, thought I, if this can possibly be a part of his
Ramadan; do they fast on their hams that way in his native
island. It must be so; yes, it's part of his creed, I suppose;
well, then, let him rest; he'll get up sooner or later, no doubt.
It can't last for ever, thank God, and his Ramadan only
comes once a year; and I don't believe it's very punctual
then.

I went down to supper. After sitting a long time listening
to the long stories of some sailors who had just come from
a plum-pudding voyage, as they called it (that is, a short
whaling-voyage in a schooner or brig, confined to the north
of the line, in the Atlantic Ocean only); after listening to

these plum-puddingers till nearly eleven o'clock, I went up stairs to go to bed, feeling quite sure by this time Queequeg must certainly have brought his Ramadan to a termination. But no; there he was just where I had left him; he had not stirred an inch. I began to grow vexed with him; it seemed so downright senseless and insane to be sitting there all day and half the night on his hams in a cold room, holding a piece of wood on his head.

"For heaven's sake, Queequeg, get up and shake yourself; get up and have some supper. You'll starve; you'll kill yourself, Queequeg." But not a word did he reply.

Despairing of him, therefore, I determined to go to bed and to sleep; and no doubt, before a great while, he would follow me. But previous to turning in, I took my heavy bearskin jacket, and threw it over him, as it promised to be a very cold night; and he had nothing but his ordinary round jacket on. For some time, do all I would, I could not get into the faintest doze. I had blown out the candle; and the mere thought of Queequeg—not four feet off—sitting there in that uneasy position, stark alone in the cold and dark; this made me really wretched. Think of it; sleeping all night in the same room with a wide awake pagan on his hams in this dreary, unaccountable Ramadan!

But somehow I dropped off at last, and knew nothing more till break of day; when, looking over the bedside, there squatted Queequeg, as if he had been screwed down to the floor. But as soon as the first glimpse of sun entered the window, up he got, with stiff and grating joints, but with a cheerful look; limped towards me where I lay; pressed his forehead again against mine; and said his Ramadan was over.

Now, as I before hinted, I have no objection to any person's religion, be it what it may, so long as that person does not kill or insult any other person, because that other person don't believe it also. But when a man's religion becomes really frantic; when it is a positive torment to him; and, in fine, makes this earth of ours an uncomfortable inn to lodge in; then I think it high time to take that individual aside and argue the point with him.

And just so I now did with Queequeg. "Queequeg," said I, "get into bed now, and lie and listen to me." I then went on, beginning with the rise and progress of the primitive religions, and coming down to the various religions of the present time, during which time I labored to show Queequeg

that all these Lents, Ramadans, and prolonged ham-squat-
tings in cold, cheerless rooms were stark nonsense; bad for
the health; useless for the soul; opposed, in short, to the obvious laws of Hygiene and common sense. I told him, too,
that he being in other things such an extremely sensible
and sagacious savage, it pained me, very badly pained me,
to see him now so deplorably foolish about this ridiculous
Ramadan of his. Besides, argued I, fasting makes the body
cave in; hence the spirit caves in; and all thoughts born of a
fast must necessarily be half-starved. This is the reason why
most dyspeptic religionists cherish such melancholy notions
about their hereafters. In one word, Queequeg, said I, rather digressively; hell is an idea first born on an undigested
apple-dumpling; and since then perpetuated through the hereditary dyspepsias nurtured by Ramadans.

I then asked Queequeg whether he himself was ever troubled with dyspepsia; expressing the idea very plainly, so that
he could take it in. He said no; only upon one memorable occasion. It was after a great feast given by his father the king,
on the gaining of a great battle wherein fifty of the enemy had
been killed by about two o'clock in the afternoon, and all
cooked and eaten that very evening.

"No more, Queequeg," said I, shuddering; "that will do;"
for I knew the inferences without his further hinting them. I
had seen a sailor who had visited that very island, and he
told me that it was the custom, when a great battle had been
gained there, to barbecue all the slain in the yard or garden
of the victor; and then, one by one, they were placed in
great wooden trenches, and garnished round like a pilau, with
breadfruit and cocoanuts; and with some parsley in their
mouths, were sent round with the victor's compliments to all
his friends, just as though these presents were so many Christmas turkeys.

After all, I do not think that my remarks about religion
made much impression upon Queequeg. Because, in the first
place, he somehow seemed dull of hearing on that important
subject, unless considered from his own point of view; and, in
the second place, he did not more than one third understand me, couch my ideas simply as I would; and, finally, he
no doubt thought he knew a good deal more about the true
religion than I did. He looked at me with a sort of con-
descending concern and compassion, as though he thought it
a great pity that such a sensible young man should be so
hopelessly lost to evangelical pagan piety.

At last we rose and dressed; and Queequeg, taking a prodigiously hearty breakfast of chowders of all sorts, so that the landlady should not make much profit by reason of his Ramadan, we sallied out to board the Pequod, sauntering along, and picking our teeth with halibut bones.

HIS MARK   **XVIII**

AS we were walking down the end of the wharf towards the ship, Queequeg carrying his harpoon, Captain Peleg in his gruff voice loudly hailed us from his wigwam, saying he had not suspected my friend was a cannibal, and furthermore announcing that he let no cannibals on board that craft, unless they previously produced their papers.

"What do you mean by that, Captain Peleg?" said I, now jumping on the bulwarks, and leaving my comrade standing on the wharf.

"I mean," he replied, "he must show his papers."

"Yea," said Captain Bildad in his hollow voice, sticking his head from behind Peleg's, out of the wigwam. "He must show that he's converted. Son of darkness," he added, turning to Queequeg, "art thou at present in communion with any christian church?"

"Why," said I, "he's a member of the first Congregational Church." Here be it said, that many tattooed savages sailing in Nantucket ships at last come to be converted into the churches.

"First Congregation Church," cried Bildad, "what! that worships in Deacon Deuteronomy Coleman's meeting-house?" and so saying, taking out his spectacles, he rubbed them on his great yellow bandana handkerchief, and putting them on very carefully, came out of the wigwam, and leaning stiffly over the bulwarks, took a good long look at Queequeg.

"How long hath he been a member?" he then said, turning to me; "not very long, I rather guess, young man."

"No," said Peleg, "and he hasn't been baptized right either, or it would have washed some of that devil's blue off his face."

"Do tell, now," cried Bildad, "is this Philistine a regular member of Deacon Deuteronomy's meeting? I never saw him going there, and I pass it every Lord's day."

"I don't know anything about Deacon Deuteronomy or his meeting," said I, "all I know is, that Queequeg here is a born member of the First Congregational Church. He is a deacon himself, Queequeg is."

"Young man," said Bildad sternly, "thou art skylarking with me—explain thyself, thou young Hittite. What church dost thee mean? answer me."

Finding myself thus hard pushed, I replied. "I mean, sir, the same ancient Catholic Church to which you and I, and Captain Peleg there, and Queequeg here, and all of us, and every mother's son and soul of us belong; the great and everlasting First Congregation of this whole worshipping world; we all belong to that; only some of us cherish some queer crotchets noways touching the grand belief; in *that* we all join hands."

"Splice, thou mean'st *splice* hands," cried Peleg, drawing nearer. "Young man, you'd better ship for a missionary, instead of a foremast hand; I never heard a better sermon. Deacon Deuteronomy—why Father Mapple himself couldn't beat it, and he's reckoned something. Come aboard, come aboard; never mind about the papers. I say, tell Quohog there—what's that you call him? tell Quohog to step along. By the great anchor, what a harpoon he's got there! looks like good stuff that; and he handles it about right. I say, Quohog, or whatever your name is, did you ever stand in the head of a whale-boat? did you ever strike a fish?"

Without saying a word, Queequeg, in his wild sort of way, jumped upon the bulwarks, from thence into the bows of one of the whaleboats hanging to the side; and then bracing his left knee, and poising his harpoon, cried out in some such way as this:—

"Cap'ain, you see him small drop tar on water dere? You see him? well, spose him one whale eye, well, den!" and taking sharp aim at it, he darted the iron right over old Bildad's broad brim, clean across the ship's decks, and struck the glistening tar spot out of sight.

"Now," said Queequeg, quietly hauling in the line, "spos-ee him whale-e eye; why, dad whale dead."

"Quick, Bildad," said Peleg, his partner, who, aghast at the close vicinity of the flying harpoon, had retreated towards the cabin gangway. "Quick, I say, you Bildad, and get the ship's papers. We must have Hedgehog there, I mean Quohog, in one of our boats. Look ye, Quohog, we'll give ye the ninetieth lay, and that's more than ever was given a harpooner yet out of Nantucket."

So down we went into the cabin, and to my great joy Queequeg was soon enrolled among the same ship's company to which I myself belonged.

When all preliminaries were over and Peleg had got everything ready for signing, he turned to me and said, "I guess, Quohog there don't know how to write, does he? I say, Quohog, blast ye! dost thou sign thy name or make thy mark?"

But at this question, Queequeg, who had twice or thrice before taken part in similar ceremonies, looked no ways abashed; but taking the offered pen, copied upon the paper, in the proper place, an exact counterpart of a queer round figure which was tattooed upon his arm; so that through Captain Peleg's obstinate mistake touching his appellative, it stood something like this:

> Quohog.
> his ✠ mark.

Meanwhile Captain Bildad sat earnestly and steadfastly eyeing Queequeg, and at last rising solemnly and fumbling in the huge pockets of his broad-skirted drab coat, took out a bundle of tracts, and selecting one entitled "The Latter Day Coming; or No Time to Lose," placed it in Queequeg's hands, and then grasping them and the book with both his, looked earnestly into his eyes, and said, "Son of darkness, I must do my duty by thee; I am part owner of this ship, and feel concerned for the souls of all its crew; if thou still clingest to thy Pagan ways, which I sadly fear, · I beseech thee, remain not for aye a Belial bondsman. Spurn the idol Bell, and the hideous dragon; turn from the wrath to come; mind thine eye, I say; oh! goodness gracious! steer clear of the fiery pit!"

Something of the salt sea yet lingered in old Bildad's language, heterogeneously mixed with Scriptural and domestic phrases.

"Avast there, avast there, Bildad, avast now spoiling our harpooneer," cried Peleg. "Pious harpooneers never make good voyagers—it takes the shark out of 'em; no harpooner is worth a straw who ain't pretty sharkish. There was young Nat Swaine, once the bravest boat-header out of all Nantucket and the Vineyard; he joined the meeting, and never came to good. He got so frightened about his plaguy soul, that he shrinked and sheered away from whales, for fear of after-claps in case he got stove and went to Davy Jones."

"Peleg! Peleg!" said Bildad, lifting his eyes and hands, "thou thyself, as I myself, hast seen many a perilous time; thou knowest, Peleg, what it is to have the fear of death; how, then, can'st thou prate in this ungodly guise. Thou beliest thine own heart, Peleg. Tell me, when this same Pequod here had her three masts overboard in that typhoon on Japan, that same voyage when thou went mate with Captain Ahab, did'st thou not think of Death and the Judgment then?"

"Hear him, hear him now," cried Peleg, marching across the cabin, and thrusting his hands far down into his pockets, —"hear him, all of ye. Think of that! When every moment we thought the ship would sink! Death and the Judgment then? What? With all three masts making such an everlasting thundering against the side; and every sea breaking over us, fore and aft. Think of Death and the Judgment then? No! no time to think about Death then. Life was what Captain Ahab and I was thinking of; and how to save all hands—how to rig jury-masts—how to get into the nearest port; that was what I was thinking of."

Bildad said no more, but buttoning up his coat, stalked on deck, where we followed him. There he stood, very quietly overlooking some sail-makers who were mending a top-sail in the waist. Now and then he stooped to pick up a patch, or save an end of the tarred twine, which otherwise might have been wasted.

THE PROPHET   XIX

"SHIPMATES, have ye shipped in that ship?"

Queequeg and I had just left the Pequod, and were sauntering away from the water, for the moment each occupied with his own thoughts, when the above words were put to us by a stranger, who, pausing before us, levelled his massive forefinger at the vessel in question. He was but shabbily apparelled in faded jacket and patched trowsers; a rag of a black handkerchief investing his neck. A confluent small-pox had in all directions flowed over his face, and left it like the complicated ribbed bed of a torrent, when the rushing waters have been dried up.

"Have ye shipped in her?" he repeated.

"You mean the ship Pequod, I suppose," said I, trying to gain a little more time for an uninterrupted look at him.

"Aye, the Pequod—that ship there," he said, drawing back his whole arm, and then rapidly shoving it straight out from him, with the fixed bayonet of his pointed finger darted full at the object.

"Yes," said I, "we have just signed the articles."

"Anything down there about your souls?"

"About what?"

"Oh, perhaps you hav'n't got any," he said quickly. "No matter though, I know many chaps that hav'n't got any,— good luck to 'em; and they are all the better off for it. A soul's a sort of a fifth wheel to a wagon."

"What are you jabbering about, shipmate?" said I.

"*He's* got enough, though, to make up for all deficiencies of that sort in other chaps," abruptly said the stranger, placing a nervous emphasis upon the word *he*.

"Queequeg," said I, "let's go; this fellow has broken loose from somewhere; he's talking about something and somebody we don't know."

"Stop!" cried the stranger. "Ye said true—ye hav'n't seen Old Thunder yet, have ye?"

"Who's Old Thunder?" said I, again riveted with the insane earnestness of his manner.

"Captain Ahab."

"What! the captain of our ship, the Pequod?"

"Aye, among some of us old sailor chaps, he goes by that name. Ye hav'n't seen him yet, have ye?"

"No, we hav'n't. He's sick they say, but is getting better, and will be all right again before long."

"All right again before long!" laughed the stranger, with a solemnly derisive sort of laugh. "Look ye; when captain Ahab is all right, then this left arm of mine will be all right; not before."

"What do you know about him?"

"What did they *tell* you about him? Say that!"

"They didn't tell much of anything about him; only I've heard that he's a good whale-hunter, and a good captain to his crew."

"That's true, that's true—yes, both true enough. But you

must jump when he gives an order. Step and growl; growl and go—that's the word with Captain Ahab. But nothing about that thing that happened to him off Cape Horn, long ago, when he lay like dead for three days and nights; nothing about that deadly skrimmage with the Spaniard afore the altar in Santa?—heard nothing about that, eh? Nothing about the silver calabash he spat into? And nothing about his losing his leg last voyage, according to the prophecy. Didn't ye hear a word about them matters and something more, eh? No, I didn't think ye did; how could ye? Who knows it? Not all Nantucket, I guess. But hows'ever, mayhap, ye've heard tell about the leg, and how he lost it; aye, ye have heard of that, I dare say. Oh yes, *that* every one knows a'most—I mean they know he's only one leg; and that a parmacetti took the other off."

"My friend," said I, "what all this gibberish is about, I don't know, and I don't much care; for it seems to me that you must be a little damaged in the head. But if you are speaking of Captain Ahab, of that ship there, the Pequod, then let me tell you, that I know all about the loss of his leg."

"*All* about it, eh—sure you do?—all?"

"Pretty sure."

With finger pointed and eye levelled at the Pequod, the beggarlike stranger stood a moment, as if in a troubled reverie; then starting a little, turned and said:—"Ye've shipped, have ye? Names down on the papers? Well, well, what's signed, is signed; and what's to be, will be; and then again, perhaps it won't be, after all. Any how, it's all fixed and arranged a'ready; and some sailors or other must go with him, I suppose; as well these as any other men, God pity 'em! Morning to ye, shipmates, morning; the ineffable heavens bless ye; I'm sorry I stopped ye."

"Look here, friend," said I, "if you have anything important to tell us, out with it; but if you are only trying to bamboozle us, you are mistaken in your game; that's all I have to say."

"And it's said very well, and I like to hear a chap talk up that way; you are just the man for him—the likes of ye. Morning to ye, shipmates, morning! Oh! when ye get there, tell 'em I've concluded not to make one of 'em."

"Ah, my dear fellow, you can't fool us that way—you can't fool us. It is the easiest thing in the world for a man to look as if he had a great secret in him."

"Morning to ye, shipmates, morning."

"Morning it is," said I. "Come along, Queequeg, let's leave this crazy man. But stop, tell me your name, will you?"

"Elijah."

Elijah! thought I, and we walked away, both commenting, after each other's fashion, upon this ragged old sailor; and agreed that he was nothing but a humbug, trying to be a bugbear. But we had not gone perhaps above a hundred yards, when chancing to turn a corner, and looking back as I did so, who should be seen but Elijah following us, though at a distance. Somehow, the sight of him struck me so, that I said nothing to Queequeg of his being behind, but passed on with my comrade, anxious to see whether the stranger would turn the same corner that we did. He did; and then it seemed to me that he was dogging us, but with what intent I could not for the life of me imagine. This circumstance, coupled with his ambiguous, half-hinting, half-revealing, shrouded sort of talk, now begat in me all kinds of vague wonderments and half-apprehensions, and all connected with the Pequod; and Captain Ahab; and the leg he had lost; and the Cape Horn fit; and the silver calabash; and what Captain Peleg had said of him, when I left the ship the day previous; and the prediction of the squaw Tistig; and the voyage we had bound ourselves to sail; and a hundred other shadowy things.

I was resolved to satisfy myself whether this ragged Elijah was really dogging us or not, and with that intent crossed the way with Queequeg, and on that side of it retraced our steps. But Elijah passed on, without seeming to notice us. This relieved me; and once more, and finally as it seemed to me, I pronounced him in my heart, a humbug.

ALL ASTIR   XX

A DAY or two passed, and there was great activity aboard the Pequod. Not only were the old sails being mended, but new sails were coming on board, and bolts of canvas, and coils of rigging; in short, everything betokened that the ship's preparations were hurrying to a close. Captain Peleg seldom or never went ashore, but sat in his wigwam keeping a sharp look-out upon the hands: Bildad did all the purchasing and providing at the stores; and the men employed in the hold and on the rigging were working till long after night-fall.

On the day following Queequeg's signing the articles, word was given at all the inns where the ship's company were stopping, that their chests must be on board before night, for there was no telling how soon the vessel might be sailing. So Queequeg and I got down our traps, resolving, however, to sleep ashore till the last. But it seems they always give very long notices in these cases, and the ship did not sail for several days. But no wonder; there was a good deal to be done, and there is no telling how many things to be thought of, before the Pequod was fully equipped.

Every one knows what a multitude of things—beds, saucepans, knives and forks, shovels and tongs, napkins, nut-crackers, and what not, are indispensable to the business of housekeeping. Just so with whaling, which necessitates a three-years' housekeeping upon the wide ocean, far from all grocers, costermongers, doctors, bakers, and bankers. And though this also holds true of merchant vessels, yet not by any means to the same extent as with whalemen. For besides the great length of the whaling voyage, the numerous articles peculiar to the prosecution of the fishery, and the impossibility of replacing them at the remote harbors usually frequented, it must be remembered, that of all ships, whaling vessels are the most exposed to accidents of all kinds, and especially to the destruction and loss of the very things upon which the success of the voyage most depends. Hence, the spare boats, spare spars, and spare lines and harpoons, and spare everything, almost, but a spare Captain and duplicate ship.

At the period of our arrival at the Island, the heaviest storage of the Pequod had been almost completed; comprising her beef, bread, water, fuel, and iron hoops and staves. But, as before hinted, for some time there was a continual fetching and carrying on board of divers odds and ends, both large and small.

Chief among those who did this fetching and carrying was Captain Bildad's sister, a lean old lady of a most determined and indefatigable spirit, but withal very kindhearted, who seemed resolved that, if *she* could help it, nothing should be found wanting in the Pequod, after once fairly getting to sea. At one time she would come on board with a jar of pickles for the steward's pantry; another time with a bunch of quills for the chief mate's desk, where he kept his log; a third time with a roll of flannel for the small of some one's rheumatic back. Never did any woman better deserve her name, which was Charity—Aunt Charity, as everybody called her. And like a sister of charity did this charitable Aunt Charity bustle about hither and thither, ready to turn her hand and heart to anything that promised to yield safety, comfort, and consolation to all on board a ship in which her beloved brother Bildad was concerned, and in which she herself owned a score or two of well-saved dollars.

But it was startling to see this excellent hearted Quakeress coming on board, as she did the last day, with a long oil-ladle in one hand, and a still longer whaling lance in the other. Nor was Bildad himself nor Captain Peleg at all backward. As for Bildad, he carried about with him a long list of the articles needed, and at every fresh arrival, down went his mark opposite that article upon the paper. Every once and a while Peleg came hobbling out of his whalebone den, roaring at the men down the hatchways, roaring up to the riggers at the mast-head, and then concluded by roaring back into his wigwam.

During these days of preparation, Queequeg and I often visited the craft, and as often I asked about Captain Ahab, and how he was, and when he was going to come on board his ship. To these questions they would answer, that he was getting better and better, and was expected aboard every day; meantime, the two Captains, Peleg and Bildad, could attend to everything necessary to fit the vessel for the voyage. If I had been downright honest with myself, I would have seen very plainly in my heart that I did but half fancy being committed this way to so long a voyage, without once laying my eyes on the man who was to be the absolute dictator of it, so soon as the ship sailed out upon the open sea. But when a man suspects any wrong, it sometimes happens that if he be already involved in the matter, he insensibly strives to cover up his suspicions even from himself. And much this way it was with me. I said nothing, and tried to think nothing.

At last it was given out that some time next day the ship would certainly sail. So next morning, Queequeg and I took a very early start.

GOING ABOARD   XXI

IT was nearly six o'clock, but only grey imperfect misty dawn, when we drew nigh the wharf.

"There are some sailors running ahead there, if I see right," said I to Queequeg, "it can't be shadows; she's off by sunrise, I guess; come on!"

"Avast!" cried a voice, whose owner at the same time coming close behind us, laid a hand upon both our shoulders, and then insinuating himself between us, stood stooping forward a little, in the uncertain twilight, strangely peering from Queequeg to me. It was Elijah.

"Going aboard?"

"Hands off, will you," said I.

"Lookee here," said Queequeg, shaking himself, "go 'way!"

"Aint going aboard, then?"

"Yes, we are," said I, "but what business is that of yours? Do you know, Mr. Elijah, that I consider you a little impertinent?"

"No, no, no; I wasn't aware of that," said Elijah, slowly and wonderingly looking from me to Queequeg, with the most unaccountable glances.

"Elijah," said I, "you will oblige my friend and me by withdrawing. We are going to the Indian and Pacific Oceans, and would prefer not to be detained."

"Ye be, be ye? Coming back afore breakfast?"

"He's cracked, Queequeg," said I, "come on."

"Holloa!" cried stationary Elijah, hailing us when we had removed a few paces.

"Never mind him," said I, "Queequeg, come on."

But he stole up to us again, and suddenly clapping his hand on my shoulder, said—"Did ye see anything looking like men going towards that ship a while ago?"

Struck by this plain matter-of-fact question, I answered, saying, "Yes, I thought I did see four or five men; but it was too dim to be sure."

"Very dim, very dim," said Elijah. "Morning to ye."

Once more we quitted him; but once more he came softly after us; and touching my shoulder again, said, "See if you can find 'em, will ye?"

"Find who?"

"Morning to ye! morning to ye!" he rejoined, again moving off. "Oh! I was going to warn ye against—but never mind, never mind—it's all one, all in the family too;—sharp frost this morning, ain't it? Good bye to ye. Shan't see ye again very soon, I guess; unless it's before the Grand Jury." And with these cracked words he finally departed, leaving me, for the moment, in no small wonderment at his frantic impudence.

At last, stepping on board the Pequod, we found everything in profound quiet, not a soul moving. The cabin entrance was locked within; the hatches were all on, and lumbered with coils of rigging. Going forward to the forecastle, we found the slide of the scuttle open. Seeing a light, we went down, and found only an old rigger there, wrapped in a tattered pea-jacket. He was thrown at whole length upon two chests, his face downwards and inclosed in his folded arms. The profoundest slumber slept upon him.

"Those sailors we saw, Queequeg, where can they have gone to?" said I, looking dubiously at the sleeper. But it seemed that, when on the wharf, Queequeg had not at all noticed what I now alluded to; hence I would have thought myself to have been optically deceived in that matter, were it not for Elijah's otherwise inexplicable question. But I beat the thing down; and again marking the sleeper, jocularly hinted to Queequeg that perhaps we had best sit up with the body; telling him to establish himself accordingly. He put his hand upon the sleeper's rear, as though feeling if it were soft enough; and then, without more ado, sat quietly down there.

"Gracious! Queequeg, don't sit there," said I.

"Oh! perry dood seat," said Queequeg, "my country way; won't hurt him face."

"Face!" said I, "call that his face? very benevolent countenance then; but how hard he breathes, he's heaving himself; get off, Queequeg, you are heavy, it's grinding the face of the poor. Get off, Queequeg! Look, he'll twitch you off soon. I wonder he don't wake."

Queequeg removed himself to just beyond the head of the sleeper, and lighted his tomahawk pipe. I sat at the feet. We kept the pipe passing over the sleeper, from one to the other. Meanwhile, upon questioning him in his broken fashion, Queequeg gave me to understand that, in his land, owing to the absence of settees and sofas of all sorts, the king, chiefs, and great people generally, were in the custom of fattening some of the lower orders for ottomans; and to furnish a house comfortably in that respect, you had only to buy up eight or ten lazy fellows, and lay them round in the piers and alcoves. Besides, it was very convenient on an excursion; much better than those garden-chairs which are convertible into walking-sticks; upon occasion, a chief calling his attendant, and desiring him to make a settee of himself under a spreading tree, perhaps in some damp marshy place.

While narrating these things, every time Queequeg received the tomahawk from me, he flourished the hatchet-side of it over the sleeper's head.

"What's that for, Queequeg?"

"Perry easy, kill-e; oh! perry easy!"

He was going on with some wild reminiscences about his tomahawk pipe, which, it seemed, had in its two uses both brained his foes and soothed his soul, when we were directly attracted to the sleeping rigger. The strong vapor now completely filling the contracted hole, it began to tell upon him. He breathed with a sort of muffledness; then seemed troubled in the nose; then revolved over once or twice; then sat up and rubbed his eyes.

"Holloa!" he breathed at last, "who be ye smokers?"

"Shipped men," answered I, "when does she sail?"

"Aye, aye, ye are going in her, be ye? She sails to-day. The Captain came aboard last night."

"What Captain?—Ahab?"

"Who but him indeed?"

I was going to ask him some further questions concerning Ahab, when we heard a noise on deck.

"Halloa! Starbuck's astir," said the rigger. "He's a lively chief mate, that; good man, and a pious; but all alive now, I must turn to." And so saying he went on deck, and we followed.

It was now clear sunrise. Soon the crew came on board in twos and threes; the riggers bestirred themselves; the mates were actively engaged; and several of the shore people were busy in bringing various last things on board. Meanwhile Captain Ahab remained invisibly enshrined within his cabin.

MERRY CHRISTMAS   XXII

AT length, towards noon, upon the final dismissal of the
ship's riggers, and after the Pequod had been hauled out
from the wharf, and after the ever-thoughtful Charity had
come off in a whaleboat, with her last gift—a night-cap for
Stubb, the second mate, her brother-in-law, and a spare Bible
for the steward—after all this, the two captains, Peleg and
Bildad, issued from the cabin, and turning to the chief mate,
Peleg said:

"Now, Mr. Starbuck, are you sure everything is right? Captain Ahab is all ready—just spoke to him—nothing more to
be got from shore, eh? Well, call all hands, then. Muster 'em
aft here—blast 'em!"

"No need of profane words, however great the hurry,
Peleg," said Bildad, "but away with thee, friend Starbuck,
and do our bidding."

How now! Here upon the very point of starting for the
voyage. Captain Peleg and Captain Bildad were going it with
a high hand on the quarter-deck, just as if they were to be
joint-commanders at sea, as well as to all appearances in
port. And, as for Captain Ahab, no sign of him was yet to
be seen; only, they said he was in the cabin. But then, the
idea was, that his presence was by no means necessary in getting the ship under weigh, and steering her well out to sea. Indeed, as that was not at all his proper business, but the
pilot's; and as he was not yet completely recovered—so they
said—therefore, Captain Ahab stayed below. And all this
seemed natural enough; especially as in the merchant service
many captains never show themselves on deck for a considerable time after heaving up the anchor, but remain over
the cabin table, having a farewell merry-making with their
shore friends, before they quit the ship for good with the
pilot.

But there was not much chance to think over the matter,
for Captain Peleg was now alive. He seemed to do most of
the talking and commanding, and not Bildad.

"Aft here, ye sons of bachelors," he cried, as the sailors
lingered at the main-mast. "Mr. Starbuck, drive 'em aft."

"Strike the tent there!"—was the next order. As I hinted

before, this whalebone marquee was never pitched except in
port; and on board the Pequod, for thirty years, the order
to strike the tent was well known to be the next thing to
heaving up the anchor.

"Man the capstan! Blood and thunder!—jump!"—was the
next command, and the crew sprang for the handspikes.

Now, in getting under weigh, the station generally occupied by the pilot is the forward part of the ship. And here
Bildad, who, with Peleg, be it known, in addition to his other
offices, was one of the licensed pilots of the port—he being
suspected to have got himself made a pilot in order to save
the Nantucket pilot-fee to all the ships he was concerned
in, for he never piloted any other craft—Bildad, I say, might
now be seen actively engaged in looking over the bows for
the approaching anchor, and at intervals singing what seemed
a dismal stave of psalmody, to cheer the hands at the windlass, who roared forth some sort of a chorus about the girls
in Booble Alley, with hearty good will. Nevertheless, not
three days previous. Bildad had told them that no profane
songs would be allowed on board the Pequod, particularly in
getting under weigh; and Charity, his sister, had placed a
small choice copy of Watts in each seaman's berth.

Meantime, overseeing the other part of the ship, Captain
Peleg ripped and swore astern in the most frightful manner.
I almost thought he would sink the ship before the anchor
could be got up; involuntarily I paused on my handspike,
and told Queequeg to do the same, thinking of the perils we
both ran, in starting on the voyage with such a devil for a
pilot. I was comforting myself, however, with the thought that
in pious Bildad might be found some salvation, spite of his
seven hundred and seventy-seventh lay; when I felt a sudden sharp poke in my rear, and turning around, was horri-
fied at the apparition of Captain Peleg in the act of withdrawing his leg from my immediate vicinity. That was my first
kick.

"Is that the way they heave in the marchant service?" he
roared. "Spring, thou sheep-head; spring, and break thy back-
bone! Why don't ye spring, I say, all of ye—spring! Quo-
hag! spring, thou chap with the red whiskers; spring there,
Scotchcap; spring, thou green pants. Spring, I say, all of ye,
and spring your eyes out!" And so saying, he moved along
the windlass, here and there using his leg very freely, while
imperturbable Bildad kept leading off with his psalmody.

Thinks I, Captain Peleg must have been drinking something to-day.

At last the anchor was up, the sails were set, and off we glided. It was a short, cold Christmas; and as the short northern day merged into night, we found ourselves almost broad upon the wintry ocean, whose freezing spray cased us in ice, as in polished armor. The long rows of teeth on the bulwarks glistened in the moonlight; and like the white ivory tusks of some huge elephant, vast curving icicles depended from the bows.

Lank Bildad, as pilot, headed the first watch, and ever and anon, as the old craft dived into the green seas, and sent the shivering frost all over her, and the winds howled, and the cordage rang, his steady notes were heard,—

> "Sweet fields beyond the swelling flood,
>   Stand dressed in living green.
> So to the Jews old Canaan stood,
>   While Jordan rolled between."

Never did those sweet words sound more sweetly to me than then. They were full of hope and fruition. Spite of this frigid winter night in the boisterous Atlantic, spite of my wet feet and wetter jacket, there was yet, it then seemed to me, many a pleasant haven in store; and meads and glades so eternally vernal, that the grass shot up by the spring, untrodden, unwilted, remains at midsummer.

At last we gained such an offing, that the two pilots were needed no longer. The stout sail-boat that had accompanied us began ranging alongside.

It was curious and not unpleasing, how Peleg and Bildad were affected at this juncture, especially Captain Bildad. For loath to depart, yet; very loath to leave, for good, a ship bound on so long and perilous a voyage—beyond both stormy Capes; a ship in which some thousands of his hard earned dollars were invested; a ship, in which an old shipmate sailed as captain; a man almost as old as he, once more starting to encounter all the terrors of the pitiless jaw; loath to say good-bye to a thing so every way brimful of every interest to him,—poor old Bildad lingered long; paced the deck with anxious strides; ran down into the cabin to speak another farewell word there; again came on deck, and looked to windward; looked towards the wide and endless waters, only bounded by the far-off unseen Eastern Continents; looked towards the land; looked aloft; looked right and left; looked everywhere and nowhere; and at last, mechanically coiling a rope upon its pin, convulsively grasped stout Peleg by the hand, and holding up a lantern, for a moment stood gazing heroically in his face, as much as to say, "Nevertheless, friend Peleg, I can stand it; yes, I can."

As for Peleg himself, he took it more like a philosopher; but for all his philosophy, there was a tear twinkling in his eye, when the lantern came too near. And he, too, did not a little run from cabin to deck—now a word below, and now a word with Starbuck, the chief mate.

But, at last, he turned to his comrade, with a final sort of look about him,—"Captain Bildad—come, old shipmate, we must go. Back the main-yard there! Boat ahoy! Stand by to come close alongside, now! Careful, careful!—come, Bildad, boy—say your last. Luck to ye, Starbuck—luck to ye, Mr. Stubb—luck to ye, Mr. Flask—good-bye, and good luck to ye all—and this day three years I'll have a hot supper smoking for ye in old Nantucket. Hurrah and away!"

"God bless ye, and have ye in His holy keeping, men," murmured old Bildad, almost incoherently. "I hope ye'll have fine weather now, so that Captain Ahab may soon be moving among ye—a pleasant sun is all he needs, and ye'll have plenty of them in the tropic voyage ye go. Be careful in the hunt, ye mates. Don't stave the boats needlessly, ye harpooneers; good white cedar plank is raised full three per cent. within the year. Don't forget your prayers, either. Mr. Starbuck, mind that cooper don't waste the spare staves. Oh! the sail-needles are in the green locker! Don't whale it too much a' Lord's days, men; but don't miss a fair chance either, that's rejecting Heaven's good gifts. Have an eye to the molasses tierce, Mr. Stubb; it was a little leaky, I thought. If ye touch at the islands, Mr. Flask, beware of fornication. Good-bye, good-bye! Don't keep that cheese too long down in the hold, Mr. Starbuck; it'll spoil. Be careful with the butter—twenty cents the pound it was, and mind ye, if—"

"Come, come, Captain Bildad; stop palavering,—away!" and with that, Peleg hurried him over the side, and both dropt into the boat.

Ship and boat diverged; the cold, damp night breeze blew between; a screaming gull flew overhead; the two hulls wildly rolled; we gave three heavy-hearted cheers, and blindly plunged like fate into the lone Atlantic.

THE LEE SHORE   XXIII

SOME chapters back, one Bulkington was spoken of, a tall, new-landed mariner, encountered in New Bedford at the inn.

When on that shivering winter's night, the Pequod thrust her vindictive bows into the cold malicious waves, who should I see standing at her helm but Bulkington! I looked with sympathetic awe and fearfulness upon the man, who in midwinter just landed from a four years' dangerous voyage, could so unrestingly push off again for still another tempestuous term. The land seemed scorching to his feet. Wonderfullest things are ever the unmentionable; deep memories yield no epitaphs; this six-inch chapter is the stoneless grave of Bulkington. Let me only say that it fared with him as with the storm-tossed ship, that miserably drives along the leeward land. The port would fain give succor; the port is pitiful; in the port is safety, comfort, hearthstone, supper, warm blankets, friends, all that's kind to our mortalities. But in that gale, the port, the land, is that ship's direst jeopardy; she must fly all hospitality; one touch of land, though it but graze the keel, would make her shudder through and through. With all her might she crowds all sail off shore; in so doing, fights 'gainst the very winds that fain would blow her homeward; seeks all the lashed sea's landlessness again; for refuge's sake forlornly rushing into peril; her only friend her bitterest foe!

Know ye, now, Bulkington? Glimpses do ye seem to see of that mortally intolerable truth; that all deep, earnest thinking is but the intrepid effort of the soul to keep the open independence of her sea; while the wildest winds of heaven and earth conspire to cast her on the treacherous, slavish shore?

But as in landlessness alone resides the highest truth, shoreless, indefinite as God—so, better is it to perish in that howling infinite, than be ingloriously dashed upon the lee, even if that were safety! For worm-like, then, oh! who would craven crawl to land! Terrors of the terrible! is all this agony so vain? Take heart, take heart, O Bulkington! Bear thee grimly, demigod! Up from the spray of thy ocean-perishing— straight up, leaps thy apotheosis!

THE ADVOCATE   XXIV

AS Queequeg and I are now fairly embarked in this business of whaling; and as this business of whaling has somehow come to be regarded among landsmen as a rather unpoetical and disreputable pursuit; therefore, I am all anxiety to convince ye, ye landsmen, of the injustice hereby done to us hunters of whales.

In the first place, it may be deemed almost superfluous to establish the fact, that among people at large, the business of whaling is not accounted on a level with what are called the liberal professions. If a stranger were introduced into any miscellaneous metropolitan society, it would but slightly advance the general opinion of his merits, were he presented to the company as a harpooneer, say; and if in emulation of the naval officers he should append the initials S.W.F. (Sperm Whale Fishery) to his visiting card, such a procedure would be deemed pre-eminently presuming and ridiculous.

Doubtless one leading reason why the world declines honoring us whalemen, is this: they think that, at best, our vocation amounts to a butchering sort of business; and that when actively engaged therein, we are surrounded by all manner of defilements. Butchers we are, that is true. But butchers, also, and butchers of the bloodiest badge have been all Martial Commanders whom the world invariably delights to honor. And as for the matter of the alleged uncleanliness of our business, ye shall soon be initiated into certain facts hitherto pretty generally unknown, and which, upon the whole, will triumphantly plant the sperm whale-ship at least among the cleanliest things of this tidy earth. But even granting the charge in question to be true; what disordered slippery decks of a whale-ship are comparable to the unspeakable carrion of those battle-fields from which so many soldiers return to drink in all ladies' plaudits? And if the idea of peril so much enhances the popular conceit of the soldier's profession; let me assure ye that many a veteran who has freely marched up to a battery, would quickly recoil at the apparition of the sperm whale's vast tail, fanning into eddies the air over his head. For what are the comprehensible terrors of man compared with the interlinked terrors and wonders of God!

But, though the world scouts at us whale hunters, yet does it unwittingly pay us the profoundest homage; yea, an all-abounding adoration! for almost all the tapers, lamps, and candles that burn round the globe, burn, as before so many shrines, to our glory!

But look at this matter in other lights; weigh it in all sorts of scales; see what we whalemen are, and have been.

Why did the Dutch in DeWitt's time have admirals of their whaling fleets? Why did Louis XVI. of France, at his own personal expense, fit out whaling ships from Dunkirk, and politely invite to that town some score or two of families from our own island of Nantucket? Why did Britain between the years 1750 and 1788 pay to her whalemen in bounties upwards of £1,000,000? And lastly, how comes it that we whalemen of America now outnumber all the rest of the banded whalemen in the world; sail a navy of upwards of seven hundred vessels; manned by eighteen thousand men; yearly consuming 4,000,000 of dollars; the ships worth, at the time of sailing, $20,000,000; and every year importing into our harbors a well reaped harvest of $7,000,000. How comes all this, if there be not something puissant in whaling?

But this is not the half; look again.

I freely assert, that the cosmopolite philosopher cannot, for his life, point out one single peaceful influence, which within the last sixty years has operated more potentially upon the whole broad world, taken in one aggregate, than the high and mighty business of whaling. One way and another, it has begotten events so remarkable in themselves, and so continuously momentous in their sequential issues, that whaling may well be regarded as that Egyptian mother, who bore offspring themselves pregnant from her womb. It would be a hopeless, endless task to catalogue all these things. Let a handful suffice. For many years past the whale-ship has been the pioneer in ferreting out the remotest and least known parts of the earth. She has explored seas and archipelagoes which had no chart, where no Cook or Vancouver had ever sailed. If American and European men-of-war now peacefully ride in once savage harbors, let them fire salutes to the honor and the glory of the whale-ship, which originally showed them the way, and first interpreted between them and the savages. They may celebrate as they will the heroes of Exploring Expeditions, your Cookes, your Krusensterns; but I say that scores of anonymous Captains have sailed out of Nantucket, that were as great, and greater than your Cooke and your Krusenstern. For in their succorless empty-handedness, they, in the heathenish sharked waters, and by the beaches of unrecorded, javelin islands, battled with virgin wonders and terrors that Cooke with all his marines and muskets would not willingly have dared. All that is made such a flourish of in the old South Sea Voyages, those things were but the lifetime commonplaces of our heroic Nantucketers. Often, adventures which Vancouver dedicates three chapters to, these men accounted unworthy of being set down in the ship's common log. Ah, the world! Oh, the world!

Until the whale fishery rounded Cape Horn, no commerce but colonial, scarcely any intercourse but colonial, was carried on between Europe and the long line of the opulent Spanish provinces on the Pacific coast. It was the whalemen who first broke through the jealous policy of the Spanish crown, touching those colonies; and, if space permitted, it might be distinctly shown how from those whalemen at last eventuated the liberation of Peru, Chili, and Bolivia from the yoke of Old Spain, and the establishment of the eternal democracy in those parts.

That great America on the other side of the sphere, Australia, was given to the enlightened world by the whalemen. After its first blunder-born discovery by a Dutchman, all other ships long shunned those shores as pestiferously barbarous; but the whale-ship touched there. The whale-ship is the true mother of that now mighty colony. Moreover, in the infancy of the first Australian settlement, the emigrants were several times saved from starvation by the benevolent biscuit of the whale-ship luckily dropping an anchor in their waters. The uncounted isles of all Polynesia confess the same truth, and do commercial homage to the whale-ship, that cleared the way for the missionary and the merchant, and in many cases carried the primitive missionaries to their first destinations. If that double-bolted land, Japan, is ever to become hospitable, it is the whale-ship alone to whom the credit will be due; for already she is on the threshold.

But if, in the face of all this, you still declare that whaling has no aesthetically noble associations connected with it, then am I ready to shiver fifty lances with you there, and unhorse you with a split helmet every time.

The whale has no famous author, and whaling no famous chronicler, you will say.

The whale no famous author, and whaling no famous chronicler? Who wrote the first account of our Leviathan? Who but mighty Job! And who composed the first narrative of a whaling-voyage? Who, but no less a prince than Alfred the Great, who, with his own royal pen, took down the words from Other, the Norwegian whale-hunter of those times! And who pronounced our glowing eulogy in Parliament? Who, but Edmund Burke!

True enough, but then whalemen themselves are poor devils; they have no good blood in their veins.

No good blood in their veins? They have something better than royal blood there. The grandmother of Benjamin Franklin was Mary Morrel; afterwards, by marriage, Mary Folger, one of the old settlers of Nantucket, and the ancestress to a long line of Folgers and harpooners—all kith and kin to noble Benjamin—this day darting the barbed iron from one side of the world to the other.

Good again; but then all confess that somehow whaling is not respectable.

Whaling not respectable? Whaling is imperial! By old English statutory law, the whale is declared "a royal fish."*

Oh, that's only nominal! The whale himself has never figured in any grand imposing way.

The whale never figured in any grand imposing way? In one of the mighty triumphs given to a Roman general upon his entering the world's capital, the bones of a whale, brought all the way from the Syrian coast, were the most conspicuous object in the cymballed procession.*

Grant it, since you cite it; but, say what you will, there is no real dignity in whaling.

No dignity in whaling? The dignity of our calling the very heavens attest. Cetus is a constellation in the South! No more! Drive down your hat in presence of the Czar, and take it off to Queequeg! No more! I know a man that, in his lifetime, has taken three hundred and fifty whales. I account that man more honorable than that great captain of antiquity who boasted of taking as many walled towns.

And, as for me, if, by any possibility, there be any as yet

---

* See subsequent chapters for something more on this head.

undiscovered prime thing in me; if I shall ever deserve any
real repute in that small but high hushed world which I
might not be unreasonably ambitious of; if hereafter I shall
do anything that, upon the whole, a man might rather have
done than to have left undone; if, at my death, my executors, or more properly my creditors, find any precious MSS.
in my desk, then here I prospectively ascribe all the honor
and the glory to whaling; for a whale-ship was my Yale College and my Harvard.

POSTSCRIPT   XXV

IN behalf of the dignity of whaling, I would fain advance
naught but substantiated facts. But after embattling his facts,
an advocate who should wholly suppress a not unreasonable
surmise, which might tell eloquently upon his cause—such
an advocate, would he not be blameworthy?

It is well known that at the coronation of kings and
queens, even modern ones, a certain curious process of sea-
soning them for their functions is gone through. There is a
saltcellar of state, so called, and there may be a caster of
state. How they use the salt, precisely—who knows? Certain I am, however, that a king's head is solemnly oiled at
his coronation, even as a head of salad. Can it be, though,
that they anoint it with a view of making its interior run
well, as they anoint machinery? Much might be ruminated
here, concerning the essential dignity of this regal process, because in common life we esteem but meanly and con-
temptibly a fellow who anoints his hair, and palpably smells
of that anointing. In truth, a mature man who uses hair-oil,
unless medicinally, that man has probably got a quoggy spot
in him somewhere. As a general rule, he can't amount to
much in his totality.

But the only thing to be considered here, is this—what
kind of oil is used at coronations? Certainly it cannot be
olive oil, nor macassar oil, nor castor oil, nor bear's oil,
nor train oil, nor cod-liver oil. What then can it possibly
be, but sperm oil in its unmanufactured, unpolluted state,
the sweetest of all oils?

Think of that, ye loyal Britons! we whalemen supply your
kings and queens with coronation stuff!

KNIGHTS AND SQUIRES   XXVI

THE chief mate of the Pequod was Starbuck, a native of Nantucket, and a Quaker by descent. He was a long, earnest man, and though born on an icy coast, seemed well adapted to endure hot latitudes, his flesh being hard as twice-baked biscuit. Transported to the Indies, his live blood would not spoil like bottled ale. He must have been born in some time of general drought and famine, or upon one of those fast days for which his state is famous. Only some thirty arid summers he had seen; those summers had dried up all his physical superfluousness. But this, his thinness, so to speak, seemed no more the token of wasting anxieties and cares, than it seemed the indication of any bodily blight. It was merely the condensation of the man. He was by no means ill-looking; quite the contrary. His pure tight skin was an excellent fit; and closely wrapped up in it, and embalmed with inner health and strength, like a revivified Egyptian, this Starbuck seemed prepared to endure for long ages to come, and to endure always, as now; for be it Polar snow or torrid sun, like a patent chronometer, his interior vitality was warranted to do well in all climates. Looking into his eyes, you seemed to see there the yet lingering images of those thousand-fold perils he had calmly confronted through life. A staid, steadfast man, whose life for the most part was a telling pantomime of action, and not a tame chapter of sounds. Yet, for all his hardy sobriety and fortitude, there were certain qualities in him which at times affected, and in some cases seemed well nigh to overbalance all the rest. Uncommonly conscientious for a seaman, and endued with a deep natural reverence, the wild watery loneliness of his life did therefore strongly incline him to superstition; but to that sort of superstition, which in some organizations seems rather to spring, somehow, from intelligence than from ignorance. Outward portents and inward presentiments were his. And if at times these things bent the welded iron of his soul, much more did his far-away domestic memories of his young Cape wife and child, tend to bend him still more from the original ruggedness of his nature, and open him still further to those latent influences which, in some honest-hearted men, restrain the gush of dare-devil daring, so often evinced by others in the more perilous vicissitudes of the fishery. "I will have no man in my boat," said Starbuck, "who is not afraid of a whale." By this, he seemed to mean, not only that the most reliable and useful courage was that which arises from the fair estimation of the encountered peril, but that an utterly fearless man is a far more dangerous comrade than a coward.

"Aye, aye," said Stubb, the second mate, "Starbuck, there, is as careful a man as you'll find anywhere in this fishery." But we shall ere long see what that word "careful" precisely means when used by a man like Stubb, or almost any other whale hunter.

Starbuck was no crusader after perils; in him courage was not a sentiment; but a thing simply useful to him, and always at hand upon all mortally practical occasions. Besides, he thought, perhaps, that in this business of whaling, courage was one of the great staple outfits of the ship, like her beef and her bread, and not to be foolishly wasted. Wherefore he had no fancy for lowering for whales after sun-down; nor for persisting in fighting a fish that too much persisted in fighting him. For, thought Starbuck, I am here in this critical ocean to kill whales for my living, and not to be killed by them for theirs; and that hundreds of men had been so killed Starbuck well knew. What doom was his own father's? Where, in the bottomless deeps, could he find the torn limbs of his brother?

With memories like these in him, and moreover, given to a certain superstitiousness, as has been said; the courage of this Starbuck which could, nevertheless, still flourish, must indeed have been extreme. But it was not in reasonable nature that a man so organized, and with such terrible experiences and remembrances as he had; it was not in nature that these things should fail in latently engendering an element in him, which, under suitable circumstances, would break out from its confinement, and burn all his courage up. And brave as he might be, it was that sort of bravery chiefly, visible in some intrepid men, which, while generally abiding firm in the conflict with seas, or winds, or whales, or any of the ordinary irrational horrors of the world, yet cannot withstand those more terrific, because more spiritual terrors, which sometimes menace you from the concentrating brow of an enraged and mighty man.

But were the coming narrative to reveal, in any instance,

the complete abasement of poor Starbuck's fortitude, scarce might I have the heart to write it; for it is a thing most sorrowful, nay shocking, to expose the fall of valor in the soul. Men may seem detestable as joint stock-companies and nations; knaves, fools, and murderers there may be; men may have mean and meagre faces; but man, in the ideal, is so noble and so sparkling, such a grand and glowing creature, that over any ignominious blemish in him all his fellows should run to throw their costliest robes. That immaculate manliness we feel within ourselves, so far within us, that it remains intact though all the outer character seem gone; bleeds with keenest anguish at the undraped spectacle of a valor-ruined man. Nor can piety itself, at such a shameful sight, completely stifle her upbraidings against the permitting stars. But this august dignity I treat of, is not the dignity of kings and robes, but that abounding dignity which has no robed investiture. Thou shalt see it shining in the arm that wields a pick or drives a spike; that democratic dignity which, on all hands, radiates without end from God; Himself! The great God absolute! The centre and circumference of all democracy! His omnipresence, our divine equality!

If, then, to meanest mariners, and renegades and castaways, I shall hereafter ascribe high qualities, though dark; weave round them tragic graces; if even the most mournful, perchance the most abased, among them all, shall at times lift himself to the exalted mounts; if I shall touch that workman's arm with some ethereal light; if I shall spread a rainbow over his disastrous set of sun; then against all mortal critics bear me out in it, thou just Spirit of Equality, which hast spread one royal mantle of humanity over all my kind! Bear me out in it, thou great democratic God! who didst not refuse to the swart convict, Bunyan, the pale, poetic pearl; Thou who didst clothe with doubly hammered leaves of finest gold, the stumped and paupered arm of old Cervantes; Thou who didst pick up Andrew Jackson from the pebbles; who didst hurl him upon a war-horse; who didst thunder him higher than a throne! Thou who, in all Thy mighty, earthly marchings, ever cullest Thy selectest champions from the kingly commons; bear me out in it, O God!

KNIGHTS AND SQUIRES   **XXVII**

STUBB was the second mate. He was a native of Cape Cod; and hence, according to local usage, was called a Cape-Cod-man. A happy-go-lucky; neither craven nor valiant; taking perils as they came with an indifferent air; and while engaged in the most imminent crisis of the chase, toiling away, calm and collected as a journey-man joiner engaged for the year. Good-humored, easy, and careless, he presided over his whale-boat as if the most deadly encounter were but a dinner, and his crew all invited guests. He was as particular about the comfortable arrangement of his part of the boat, as an old stage-driver is about the snugness of his box. When close to the whale, in the very death-lock of the fight, he handled his unpitying lance coolly and off-handedly, as a whistling tinker his hammer. He would hum over his old rigadig tunes while flank and flank with the most exasperated monster. Long usage had, for this Stubb, converted the jaws of death into an easy chair. What he thought of death itself, there is no telling. Whether he ever thought of it at all, might be a question; but, if he ever did chance to cast his mind that way after a comfortable dinner, no doubt, like a good sailor, he took it to be a sort of call of the watch to tumble aloft, and bestir themselves there, about something which he would find out when he obeyed the order, and not sooner.

What, perhaps, with other things, made Stubb such an easy-going, unfearing man, so cheerily trudging off with the burden of life in a world full of grave peddlers, all bowed to the ground with their packs; what helped to bring about that almost impious good-humor of his; that thing must have been his pipe. For, like his nose, his short, black little pipe was one of the regular features of his face. You would almost as soon have expected him to turn out of his bunk without his nose as without his pipe. He kept a whole row of pipes there ready loaded, stuck in a rack, within easy reach of his hand; and, whenever he turned in, he smoked them all out in succession, lighting one from the other to the end of the chapter; then loading them again to be in readiness anew. For, when Stubb dressed, instead of first putting his legs into his trowsers, he put his pipe into his mouth.

I say this continual smoking must have been one cause, at least, of his peculiar disposition; for every one knows that this earthly air, whether ashore or afloat, is terribly infected with the nameless miseries of the numberless mortals who have died exhaling it; and as in time of the cholera, some people go about with a camphorated handkerchief to their mouths; so, likewise, against all mortal tribulations, Stubb's tobacco smoke might have operated as a sort of disinfecting agent.

The third mate was Flask, a native of Tisbury, in Martha's Vineyard. A short, stout, ruddy young fellow, very pugnacious concerning whales, who somehow seemed to think that the great Leviathans had personally and hereditarily affronted him; and therefore it was a sort of point of honor with him, to destroy them whenever encountered. So utterly lost was he to all sense of reverence for the many marvels of their majestic bulk and mystic ways; and so dead to anything like an apprehension of any possible danger from encountering them; that in his poor opinion, the wondrous whale was but a species of magnified mouse, or at least water-rat, requiring only a little circumvention and some small application of time and trouble in order to kill and boil. This ignorant, unconscious fearlessness of his made him a little waggish in the matter of whales; he followed these fish for the fun of it; and a three years' voyage round Cape Horn was only a jolly joke that lasted that length of time. As a carpenter's nails are divided into wrought nails and cut nails; so mankind may be similarly divided. Little Flask was one of the wrought ones; made to clinch tight and last long. They called him King-Post on board of the Pequod; because, in form, he could be well likened to the short, square timber known by that name in Arctic whalers; and which by the means of many radiating side timbers inserted into it, serves to brace the ship against the icy concussions of those battering seas.

Now these three mates—Starbuck, Stubb, and Flask, were momentous men. They it was who by universal prescription commanded three of the Pequod's boats as headsmen. In that grand order of battle in which Captain Ahab would probably marshal his forces to descend on the whales, these three headsmen were as captains of companies. Or, being armed with their long keen whaling spears, they were as a picked

trio of lancers; even as the harpooners were flingers of javelins.

And since in this famous fishery, each mate or headsman,
like a Gothic Knight of old, is always accompanied by his
boatsteerer or harpooneer, who in certain conjunctures provides him with a fresh lance, when the former one has been
badly twisted, or elbowed in the assault; and moreover, as
there generally subsists between the two, a close intimacy
and friendliness; it is therefore but meet, that in this place
we set down who the Pequod's harpooneers were, and to
what headsman each of them belonged.

First of all was Queequeg, whom Starbuck, the chief mate,
had selected for his squire. But Queequeg is already known.

Next was Tashtego, an unmixed Indian from Gay Head, the
most westerly promontory of Martha's Vineyard, where
there still exists the last remnant of a village of red men,
which has long supplied the neighboring island of Nantucket
with many of her most daring harpooneers. In the fishery,
they usually go by the generic name of Gay-Headers. Tashtego's long, lean, sable hair, his high cheek bones, and
black rounding eyes—for an Indian, Oriental in their largeness, but Antarctic in their glittering expression—all this sufficiently proclaimed him an inheritor of the unvitiated blood
of those proud warrior hunters, who, in quest of the great
New England moose, had scoured, bow in hand, the aboriginal forest of the main. But no longer snuffing in the trail
of the wild beasts of the woodland, Tashtego now hunted in
the wake of the great whales of the sea; the unerring harpoon of the son fitly replacing the infallible arrow of the
sires. To look at the tawny brawn of his lithe snaky limbs,
you would almost have credited the superstitions of some
of the earlier Puritans, and half believed this wild Indian
to be a son of the Prince of the Powers of the Air. Tashtego
was Stubb the second mate's squire.

Third among the harpooneers was Daggoo, a gigantic, coal-
black negro-savage, with a lion-like tread—an Ahasuerus to
behold. Suspended from his ears were two golden hoops,
so large that the sailors called them ring-bolts, and would
talk of securing the top-sail halyards to them. In his youth
Daggoo had voluntarily shipped on board of a whaler, lying
in a lonely bay on his native coast. And never having been
anywhere in the world but in Africa, Nantucket, and the pagan harbors most frequented by whalemen; and having now
led for many years the bold life of the fishery in the ships of

owners uncommonly heedful of what manner of men they shipped; Daggoo retained all his barbaric virtues, and erect as a giraffe, moved about the decks in all the pomp of six feet five in his socks. There was a corporeal humility in looking up at him; and a white man standing before him seemed a white flag come to beg truce of a fortress. Curious to tell, this imperial negro, Ahasuerus Daggoo, was the Squire of little Flask, who looked like a chess-man beside him. As for the residue of the Pequod's company, be it said, that at the present day not one in two of the many thousand men before the mast employed in the American whale fishery, are Americans born, though pretty nearly all the officers are. Herein it is the same with the American whale fishery as with the American army and military and merchant navies, and the engineering forces employed in the construction of the American Canals and Railroads. The same, I say, because in all these cases the native American liberally provides the brains, the rest of the world as generously supplying the muscles. No small number of these whaling seamen belong to the Azores, where the outward bound Nantucket whalers frequently touch to augment their crews from the hardy peasants of those rocky shores. In like manner, the Greenland whalers sailing out of Hull or London, put in at the Shetland Islands, to receive the full complement of their crew. Upon the passage homewards, they drop them there again. How it is, there is no telling, but Islanders seem to make the best whalemen. They were nearly all Islanders in the Pequod, *Isolatoes* too, I call such; not acknowledging the common continent of men, but each *Isolato* living on a separate continent of his own. Yet now, federated along one keel, what a set these Isolatoes were! An Anacharsis Clootz deputation from all the isles of the sea, and all the ends of the earth, accompanying Old Ahab in the Pequod to lay the world's grievances before that bar from which not very many of them ever come back. Black Little Pip—he never did—oh, no! he went before. Poor Alabama boy! On the grim Pequod's forecastle, ye shall ere long see him, beating his tambourine; prelusive of the eternal time, when sent for, to the great quarter-deck on high, he was bid strike in with angels, and beat his tambourine in glory; called a coward here, hailed a hero there!

AHAB   XXVIII

FOR several days after leaving Nantucket, nothing above
hatches was seen of Captain Ahab. The mates regularly relieved each other at the watches, and for aught that could
be seen to the contrary, they seemed to be the only commanders of the ship; only they sometimes issued from the
cabin with orders so sudden and peremptory, that after all it
was plain they but commanded vicariously. Yes, their supreme
lord and dictator was there, though hitherto unseen by any
eyes not permitted to penetrate into the now sacred retreat
of the cabin.

Every time I ascended to the deck from my watches below, I instantly gazed aft to mark if any strange face were
visible; for my first vague disquietude touching the unknown
captain, now in the seclusion of the sea, became almost a
perturbation. This was strangely heightened at times by the
ragged Elijah's diabolical incoherences uninvitedly recurring to me, with a subtle energy I could not have before conceived of. But poorly could I withstand them, much as in
other moods I was almost ready to smile at the solemn
whimsicalities of that outlandish prophet of the wharves. But
whatever it was of apprehensiveness or uneasiness—to call
it so—which I felt, yet whenever I came to look about me
in the ship, it seemed against all warrantry to cherish such
emotions. For though the harpooneers, with the great body
of the crew, were a far more barbaric, heathenish, and
motley set than any of the tame merchant-ship companies
which my previous experiences had made me acquainted with,
still I ascribed this—and rightly ascribed it—to the fierce
uniqueness of the very nature of that wild Scandinavian vocation in which I had so abandonedly embarked. But it was
especially the aspect of the three chief officers of the ship,
the mates, which was most forcibly calculated to allay these
colorless misgivings, and induce confidence and cheerfulness
in every presentment of the voyage. Three better, more likely
sea-officers and men, each in his own different way, could
not readily be found, and they were every one of them
Americans; a Nantucketer, a Vineyarder, a Cape man. Now,
it being Christmas when the ship shot from out her harbor,

for a space we had biting Polar weather, though all the time running away from it to the southward; and by every degree and minute of latitude which we sailed, gradually leaving that merciless winter, and all its intolerable weather behind us. It was one of those less lowering, but still grey and gloomy enough mornings of the transition, when with a fair wind the ship was rushing through the water with a vindictive sort of leaping and melancholy rapidity, that as I mounted to the deck at the call of the forenoon watch, so soon as I levelled my glance towards the taffrail, foreboding shivers ran over me. Reality outran apprehension; Captain Ahab stood upon his quarter-deck.

There seemed no sign of common bodily illness about him, nor of the recovery from any. He looked like a man cut away from the stake, when the fire has overrunningly wasted all the limbs without consuming them, or taking away one particle from their compacted aged robustness. His whole high, broad form, seemed made of solid bronze, and shaped in an unalterable mould, like Cellini's cast Perseus. Threading its way out from among his grey hairs, and continuing right down one side of his tawny scorched face and neck, till it disappeared in his clothing, you saw a slender rod-like mark, lividly whitish. It resembled that perpendicular seam sometimes made in the straight, lofty trunk of a great tree, when the upper lightning tearingly darts down it, and without wrenching a single twig, peels and grooves out the bark from top to bottom, ere running off into the soil, leaving the tree still greenly alive, but branded. Whether that mark was born with him, or whether it was the scar left by some desperate wound, no one could certainly say. By some tacit consent, throughout the voyage little or no allusion was made to it, especially by the mates. But once Tashtego's senior, an old Gay-Head Indian among the crew, superstitiously asserted that not till he was full forty years old did Ahab become that way branded, and then it came upon him, not in the fury of any mortal fray, but in an elemental strife at sea. Yet, this wild hint seemed inferentially negatived, by what a grey Manxman insinuated, an old sepulchral man, who, having never before sailed out of Nantucket, had never ere this laid eye upon wild Ahab. Nevertheless, the old sea-traditions, the immemorial credulities, popularly invested this old Manxman with preternatural powers of discernment. So that no white sailor seriously contradicted him when he said that if ever Captain Ahab should

be tranquilly laid out—which might hardly come to pass,
so he muttered—then, whoever should do that last office for
the dead, would find a birth-mark on him from crown to
sole.

So powerfully did the whole grim aspect of Ahab affect
me, and the livid brand which streaked it, that for the first
few moments I hardly noted that not a little of this overbearing grimness was owing to the barbaric white leg upon
which he partly stood. It had previously come to me that
this ivory leg had at sea been fashioned from the polished
bone of the sperm whale's jaw. "Aye, he was dismasted off
Japan," said the old Gay-Head Indian once; "but like his
dismasted craft, he shipped another mast without coming
home for it. He has a quiver of 'em."

I was struck with the singular posture he maintained.
Upon each side of the Pequod's quarter-deck, and pretty close
to the mizzen shrouds, there was an auger hole, bored about
half an inch or so, into the plank. His bone leg steadied in
that hole; one arm elevated, and holding by a shroud;
Captain Ahab stood erect, looking straight out beyond the
ship's ever-pitching prow. There was an infinity of firmest
fortitude, a determinate, unsurrenderable wilfulness, in the
fixed and fearless, forward dedication of that glance. Not a
word he spoke; nor did his officers say aught to him; though
by all their minutest gestures and expressions, they plainly
showed the uneasy, if not painful, consciousness of being
under a troubled master-eye. And not only that, but moody
stricken Ahab stood before them with a crucifixion in his
face; in all the nameless regal overbearing dignity of some
mighty woe.

Ere long, from his first visit in the air, he withdrew into
his cabin. But after that morning, he was every day visible
to the crew; either standing in his pivot-hole, or seated upon
an ivory stool he had; or heavily walking the deck. As the
sky grew less gloomy; indeed, began to grow a little genial,
he became still less and less a recluse; as if, when the ship
had sailed from home, nothing but the dead wintry bleak-
ness of the sea had then kept him so secluded. And, by and
by, it came to pass, that he was almost continually in the
air; but, as yet, for all that he said, or perceptibly did, on
the at last sunny deck, he seemed as unnecessary there as
another mast. But the Pequod was only making a passage
now; not regularly cruising; nearly all whaling preparatives
needing supervision the mates were fully competent to, so

that there was little or nothing, out of himself, to employ
or excite Ahab, now; and thus chase away, for that one interval, the clouds that layer upon layer were piled upon his
brow, as ever all clouds choose the loftiest peaks to pile
themselves upon.

Nevertheless, ere long, the warm, warbling persuasiveness
of the pleasant, holiday weather we came to, seemed gradually to charm him from his mood. For, as when the red-
cheeked, dancing girls, April and May, trip home to the
wintry, misanthropic woods; even the barest, ruggedest,
most thunder-cloven old oak will at least send forth some
few green sprouts, to welcome such glad-hearted visitants;
so Ahab did, in the end, a little respond to the playful al-
lurings of that girlish air. More than once did he put forth
the faint blossom of a look, which, in any other man, would
have soon flowered out in a smile.

ENTER AHAB; TO HIM, STUBB   **XXIX**

SOME days elapsed, and ice and icebergs all astern, the
Pequod now went rolling through the bright Quito spring,
which, at sea, almost perpetually reigns on the threshold of
the eternal August of the Tropic. The warmly cool, clear,
ringing, perfumed, overflowing, redundant days, were as crystal goblets of Persian sherbet, heaped up—flaked up, with
rose-water snow. The starred and stately nights seemed
haughty dames in jewelled velvets, nursing at home in lonely
pride, the memory of their absent conquering Earls, the gold-
en helmeted suns! For sleeping man, 'twas hard to choose
between such winsome days and such seducing nights. But
all the witcheries of that unwaning weather did not merely
lend new spells and potencies to the outward world. Inward
they turned upon the soul, especially when the still mild
hours of eve came on; then, memory shot her crystals as
the clear ice most forms of noiseless twilights. And all these
subtle agencies, more and more they wrought on Ahab's
texture.

Old age is always wakeful; as if, the longer linked with
life, the less man has to do with aught that looks like death.
Among sea-commanders, the old greybeards will oftenest
leave their berths to visit the night-cloaked deck. It was so

with Ahab; only that now, of late, he seemed so much to live in the open air, that truly speaking, his visits were more to the cabin, than from the cabin to the planks. "It feels like going down into one's tomb,"—he would mutter to himself,—"for an old captain like me to be descending this narrow scuttle, to go to my grave-dug berth."

So, almost every twenty-four hours, when the watches of the night were set, and the band on deck sentinelled the slumbers of the band below; and when if a rope was to be hauled upon the forecastle, the sailors flung it not rudely down, as by day, but with some cautiousness dropt it to its place, for fear of disturbing their slumbering shipmates; when this sort of steady quietude would begin to prevail, habitually, the silent steersman would watch the cabin-scuttle; and ere long the old man would emerge, gripping at the iron banister, to help his crippled way. Some considerating touch of humanity was in him; for at times like these, he usually abstained from patrolling the quarter-deck; because to his wearied mates, seeking repose within six inches of his ivory heel, such would have been the reverberating crack and din of that bony step, that their dreams would have been of the crunching teeth of sharks. But once, the mood was on him too deep for common regardings; and as with heavy, lumber-like pace he was measuring the ship from taffrail to mainmast, Stubb, the odd second mate, came up from below, and with a certain unassured, deprecating humorousness, hinted that if Captain Ahab was pleased to walk the planks, then, no one could say nay; but there might be some way of muffling the noise; hinting something indistinctly and hesitatingly about a globe of tow, and the insertion into it, of the ivory heel. Ah! Stubb, thou did'st not know Ahab then.

"Am I a cannon-ball, Stubb," said Ahab, "that thou wouldst wad me that fashion? But go thy ways; I had forgot. Below to thy nightly grave; where such as ye sleep between shrouds, to use ye to the filling one at last.—Down, dog, and kennel!"

Starting at the unforeseen concluding exclamation of the so suddenly scornful old man, Stubb was speechless a moment; then said excitedly, "I am not used to be spoken to that way, sir; I do but less than half like it, sir."

"Avast!" gritted Ahab between his set teeth, and violently moving away, as if to avoid some passionate temptation.

"No, sir; not yet," said Stubb, emboldened, "I will not tamely be called a dog, sir."

"Then be called ten times a donkey, and a mule, and an ass, and begone, or I'll clear the world of thee!"

As he said this, Ahab advanced upon him with such overbearing terrors in his aspect, that Stubb involuntarily retreated.

"I was never served so before without giving a hard blow for it," muttered Stubb, as he found himself descending the cabin-scuttle. "It's very queer. Stop, Stubb; somehow, now, I don't well know whether to go back and strike him, or—what's that?—down here on my knees and pray for him? Yes, that was the thought coming up in me; but it would be the first time I ever *did* pray. It's queer; very queer; and he's queer too; aye, take him fore and aft, he's about the queerest old man Stubb ever sailed with. How he flashed at me!—his eyes like powder-pans! is he mad? Anyway there's something on his mind, as sure as there must be something on a deck when it cracks. He aint in his bed now, either, more than three hours out of the twenty-four; and he don't sleep then. Didn't that Dough-Boy, the steward, tell me that of a morning he always finds the old man's hammock clothes all rumpled and tumbled, and the sheets down at the foot, and the coverlid almost tied into knots, and the pillow a sort of frightful hot, as though a baked brick had been on it? A hot old man! I guess he's got what some folks ashore call a conscience; it's a kind of Tic-Dolly-row they say—worse nor a toothache. Well, well; I don't know what it is, but the Lord keep me from catching it. He's full of riddles; I wonder what he goes into the after hold for, every night, as Dough-Boy tells me he suspects; what's that for, I should like to know? Who's made appointments with him in the hold? Ain't that queer, now? But there's no telling, it's the old game—Here goes for a snooze. Damn me, it's worth a fellow's while to be born into the world, if only to fall right asleep. And now that I think of it, that's about the first thing babies do, and that's a sort of queer, too. Damn me, but all things are queer, come to think of 'em. But that's against my principles. Think not, is my eleventh commandment; and sleep when you can, is my twelfth—So here goes again. But how's that? Didn't he call me a dog? blazes! he called me ten times a donkey, and piled a lot of jackasses on top of *that!* He might as well have kicked me, and done with it. Maybe he *did* kick me, and I didn't observe it, I was so taken all aback with his brow, somehow. It flashed like a bleached bone. What the devil's the matter with me? I don't stand right on my legs. Coming afoul of that old man has a sort of turned me wrong side out. By the Lord, I must have been dreaming, though—How? how? how?—but the only way's to stash it; so here goes to hammock again; and in the morning, I'll see how this plaguey juggling thinks over by day-light."

THE PIPE   **XXX**

WHEN Stubb had departed, Ahab stood for a while leaning over the bulwarks; and then, as had been usual with him of late, calling a sailor of the watch, he sent him below for his ivory stool, and also his pipe. Lighting the pipe at the binnacle lamp and planting the stool on the weather side of the deck, he sat and smoked.

In old Norse times, the thrones of the sea-loving Danish kings were fabricated, saith tradition, of the tusks of the narwhale. How could one look at Ahab then, seated on that tripod of bones, without bethinking him of the royalty it symbolized? For a Khan of the plank, and a king of the sea, and a great lord of Leviathans was Ahab.

Some moments passed, during which the thick vapor came from his mouth in quick and constant puffs, which blew back again into his face. "How now," he soliloquized at last, withdrawing the tube, "this smoking no longer soothes. Oh, my pipe! hard must it go with me if thy charm be gone! Here have I been unconsciously toiling, not pleasuring,— aye, and ignorantly smoking to windward all the while; to windward, and with such nervous whiffs, as if, like the dying whale, my final jets were the strongest and fullest of trouble. What business have I with this pipe? This thing that is meant for sereneness, to send up mild white vapors among mild white hairs, not among torn iron-grey locks like mine. I'll smoke no more—"

He tossed the still lighted pipe into the sea. The fire hissed in the waves; the same instant the ship shot by the bubble the sinking pipe made. With slouched hat, Ahab lurchingly paced the planks.

QUEEN MAB   XXXI

NEXT morning Stubb accosted Flask.

"Such a queer dream, King-Post, I never had. You know
the old man's ivory leg, well I dreamed he kicked me with
it; and when I tried to kick back, upon my soul, my little
man, I kicked my leg right off! And then, presto! Ahab
seemed a pyramid, and I, like a blazing fool, kept kicking at it. But what was still more curious, Flask—you know
how curious all dreams are—through all this rage that I was
in, I somehow seemed to be thinking to myself, that after
all, it was not much of an insult, that kick from Ahab.
'Why,' thinks I, 'what's the row? It's not a real leg, only a
false leg.' And there's a mighty difference between a living
thump and a dead thump. That's what makes a blow from
the hand, Flask, fifty times more savage to bear than a blow
from a cane. The living member—that makes the living insult, my little man. And thinks I to myself all the while,
mind, while I was stubbing my silly toes against that cursed
pyramid—so confoundedly contradictory was it all, all the
while, I say, I was thinking of myself, 'what's his leg now,
but a cane—a whalebone cane. Yes,' thinks I, 'it was only
a playful cudgelling—in fact, only a whaleboning that he
gave me—not a base kick. Besides' thinks I, 'look at it once;
why, the end of it—the foot part—what a small sort of
end it is; whereas, if a broad footed farmer kicked me,
there's a devilish broad insult. But this insult is whittled
down to a point only.' But now comes the greatest joke of
the dream, Flask. While I was battering away at the pyramid,
a sort of badger-haired old merman, with a hump on his back,
takes me by the shoulders, and slews me round. 'What are
you 'bout?' says he. Slid! man, but I was frightened. Such
a phiz! But, somehow, next moment I was over the fright.
'What am I about?' says I at last. 'And what business is that
of yours, I should like to know, Mr. Humpback? Do *you* want
a kick?' By the lord, Flask, I nad no sooner said that, than
he turned round his stern to me, bent over, and dragging
up a lot of seaweed he had for a clout—what do you think,
I saw?—why thunder alive, man, his stern was stuck full
of marlinspikes, with the points out. Says I, on second

thoughts, 'I guess I won't kick you, old fellow.' 'Wise Stubb,' said he, 'wise Stubb;' and kept muttering it all the time, a sort of eating of his own gums like a chimney hag. Seeing he wasn't going to stop saying over his 'wise Stubb, wise Stubb,' I thought I might as well fall to kicking the pyramid again. But I had only just lifted my foot for it, when he roared out, 'Stop that kicking!' 'Halloa,' says I, 'what's the matter now, old fellow?' 'Look ye here,' says he; 'let's argue the insult. Captain Ahab kicked ye, didn't he?' 'Yes, he did,' says I—'right *here* it was.' 'Very good,' says he—'he used his ivory leg, didn't he?' 'Yes, he did,' says I. 'Well then,' says he, 'wise Stubb, what have you to complain of? Didn't he kick with right good will? it wasn't a common pitch pine leg he kicked with, was it? No, you were kicked by a great man, and with a beautiful ivory leg, Stubb. It's an honor; I consider it an honor. Listen, wise Stubb. In old England the greatest lords think it great glory to be slapped by a queen, and made garter-knights of; but, be *your* boast, Stubb, that ye were kicked by old Ahab, and made a wise man of. Remember what I say; *be* kicked by him; account his kicks honors; and on no account kick back; for you can't help yourself, wise Stubb. Don't you see the pyramid?' With that, he all of a sudden seemed somehow, in some queer fashion, to swim off into the air. I snored; rolled over; and there I was in my hammock! Now, what do you think of that dream, Flask?"

"I don't know; it seems a sort of foolish to me, tho'."

"May be; may be. But it's made a wise man of me, Flask. D'ye see Ahab standing there, sideways looking over the stern? Well, the best thing you can do, Flask, is to let that old man alone; never speak to him, whatever he says. Halloa! what's that he shouts? Hark!"

"Mast-head, there! Look sharp, all of ye! There are whales hereabouts! If ye see a white one, split your lungs for him!"

"What d'ye think of that now, Flask? ain't there a small drop of something queer about that, eh? A white whale—did ye mark that, man? Look ye—there's something special in the wind. Stand by for it, Flask. Ahab has that that's bloody on his mind. But, mum; he comes this way."

CETOLOGY   XXXII

ALREADY we are boldly launched upon the deep; but soon we shall be lost in its unshored, harborless immensities. Ere that come to pass; ere the Pequod's weedy hull rolls side by side with the barnacled hulls of the leviathan; at the outset it is but well to attend to a matter almost indispensable to a thorough appreciative understanding of the more special leviathanic revelations and allusions of all sorts which are to follow.

It is some systematized exhibition of the whale in his broad genera, that I would now fain put before you. Yet is it no easy task. The classification of the constituents of a chaos, nothing less is here essayed. Listen to what the best and latest authorities have laid down.

"No branch of Zoology is so much involved as that which is entitled Cetology," says Captain Scoresby, A.D. 1820.

"It is not my intention, were it in my power, to enter into the inquiry as to the true method of dividing the cetacea into groups and families. * * * Utter confusion exists among the historians of this animal" (sperm whale), says Surgeon Beale, A.D. 1839.

"Unfitness to pursue our research in the unfathomable waters." "Impenetrable veil covering our knowledge of the cetacea." "A field strewn with thorns." "All these incomplete indications but serve to torture us naturalists."

Thus speak of the whale, the great Cuvier, and John Hunter, and Lesson, those lights of zoology and anatomy. Nevertheless, though of real knowledge there be little, yet of books there are a plenty; and so in some small degree, with cetology, or the science of whales. Many are the men, small and great, old and new, landsmen and seamen, who have at large or in little, written of the whale. Run over a few:— The Authors of the Bible; Aristotle; Pliny; Aldrovandi; Sir Thomas Browne; Gesner; Ray; Linnæus; Rondeletius; Willoughby; Green; Artedi; Sibbald; Brisson; Marten; Lacépède; Bonneterre; Desmarest; Baron Cuvier; Frederick Cuvier; John Hunter; Owen; Scoresby; Beale; Bennett; J. Ross Browne; the Author of Miriam Coffin; Olmstead; and the Rev. T.

Cheever. But to what ultimate generalizing purpose all these have written, the above cited extracts will show.

Of the names in this list of whale authors, only those following Owen ever saw living whales, and but one of them was a real professional harpooneer and whaleman. I mean Captain Scoresby. On the separate subject of the Greenland or right-whale, he is the best existing authority. But Scoresby knew nothing and says nothing of the great sperm whale, compared with which the Greenland whale is almost unworthy mentioning. And here be it said, that the Greenland whale is an usurper upon the throne of the seas. He is not even by any means the largest of the whales. Yet, owing to the long priority of his claims, and the profound ignorance which, till some seventy years back, invested the then fabulous or utterly unknown sperm-whale, and which ignorance to this present day still reigns in all but some few scientific retreats and whale-ports; this usurpation has been every way complete. Reference to nearly all the leviathanic allusions in the great poets of past days, will satisfy you that the Greenland whale, without one rival, was to them the monarch of the seas. But the time has at last come for a new proclamation. This is Charing Cross; hear ye! good people all,—the Greenland whale is deposed,—the great sperm whale now reigneth!

There are only two books in being which at all pretend to put the living sperm whale before you, and at the same time, in the remotest degree succeed in the attempt. Those books are Beale's and Bennett's; both in their time surgeons to English South-Sea whale-ships, and both exact and reliable men. The original matter touching the sperm whale to be found in their volumes is necessarily small; but so far as it goes, it is of excellent quality, though mostly confined to scientific description. As yet, however, the sperm whale, scientific or poetic, lives not complete in any literature. Far above all other hunted whales, his is an unwritten life.

Now the various species of whales need some sort of popular comprehensive classification, if only an easy outline one for the present, hereafter to be filled in all its departments by subsequent laborers. As no better man advances to take this matter in hand, I hereupon offer my own poor endeavors. I promise nothing complete; because any human being supposed to be complete, must for that very reason infallibly be faulty. I shall not pretend to a minute anatomical description of the various species, or—in this place at

least—to much of any description. My object here is simply
to project the draught of a systematization of cetology. I am
the architect, not the builder.

But it is a ponderous task; no ordinary letter-sorter in the
Post-office is equal to it. To grope down into the bottom of
the sea after them; to have one's hands among the unspeakable foundations, ribs, and very pelvis of the world; this is
a fearful thing. What am I that I should essay to hook the
nose of this leviathan! The awful tauntings in Job might
well appal me. "Will he (the leviathan) make a covenant
with thee? Behold the hope of him is vain!" But I have
swam through libraries and sailed through oceans; I have had
to do with whales with these visible hands; I am in earnest;
and I will try. There are some preliminaries to settle.

First: The uncertain, unsettled condition of this science
of Cetology is in the very vestibule attested by the fact that
in some quarters it still remains a moot point whether a
whale be a fish. In his System of Nature, A.D. 1776, Linnæus declares, "I hereby separate the whales from the fish."
But of my own knowledge, I know that down to the year
1850, sharks and shad, alewives and herring, against Linnæus's express edict, were still found dividing the possession
of the same seas with the Leviathan.

The grounds upon which Linnæus would fain have banished the whales from the waters, he states as follows: "On
account of their warm bilocular heart, their lungs, their
movable eyelids, their hollow ears, penem intrantem femi-
nam mammis lactantem," and finally, "ex lege naturæ jure
meritoque." I submitted all this to my friends Simeon Macey
and Charley Coffin, of Nantucket, both messmates of mine
in a certain voyage, and they united in the opinion that the
reasons set forth were altogether insufficent. Charley profanely hinted they were humbug.

Be it known that, waiving all agrument, I take the good
old fashioned ground that the whale is a fish, and call
upon holy Jonah to back me. This fundamental thing settled, the next point is, in what internal respect does the
whale differ from other fish. Above, Linnæus has given you
those items. But in brief, they are these: lungs and warm
blood; whereas, all other fish are lungless and cold blooded.

Next: how shall we define the whale, by his obvious externals, so as conspicuously to label him for all time to
come? To be short, then, a whale is *a spouting fish with a
horizontal tail*. There you have him. However contracted,

that definition is the result of expanded meditation. A
walrus spouts much like a whale, but the walrus is not a
fish, because he is amphibious. But the last term of the definition is still more cogent, as coupled with the first. Almost
any one must have noticed that all the fish familiar to landsmen have not a flat, but a vertical, or up-and-down tail.
Whereas, among spouting fish the tail, though it may be similarly shaped, invariably assumes a horizontal position.

By the above definition of what a whale is, I do by no
means exclude from the leviathanic brotherhood any sea
creature hitherto identified with the whale by the best informed Nantucketers; nor, on the other hand, link with it
any fish hitherto authoritatively regarded as alien.* Hence,
all the smaller, spouting, and horizontal tailed fish must be
included in this ground-plan of Cetology. Now, then, come
the grand divisions of the entire whale host.

First: According to magnitude I divide the whales into
three primary BOOKS (subdivisble into CHAPTERS), and these
shall comprehend them all, both small and large.

I. The FOLIO WHALE; II. the OCTAVO WHALE; III. the
DUODECIMO WHALE.

As the type of FOLIO I present the *Sperm Whale;* of the
OCTAVO, the *Grampus;* of the DUODECIMO, the *Porpoise.*

FOLIOS. Among these I here include the following chap-
ters:—I. The *Sperm Whale;* II, the *Right Whale;* III. the
Fin Back Whale; IV. the *Hump-backed Whale;* V. the *Razor
Back Whale;* VI. the *Sulphur Bottom Whale.*

BOOK I (*Folio*), CHAPTER I. (*Sperm Whale*).—This whale,
among the English of old vaguely known as the Trumpa
whale, and the Physeter whale, and the Anvil Headed whale,
is the present Cachalot of the French, and the Pottsfich of
the Germans, and the Macrocephalus of the Long Words.
He is, without doubt, the largest inhabitant of the globe;
the most formidable of all whales to encounter; the most
majestic in aspect; and lastly, by far the most valuable in
commerce; he being the only creature from which that
valuable substance, spermaceti, is obtained. All his peculiarities will, in many other places, be enlarged upon. It is

* I am aware that down to the present time, the fish styled
Lamatins and Dugongs (Pig-fish and Sow-fish of the Coffins of
Nantucket) are included by many naturalists among the whales.
But as these pig-fish are a nosy, contemptible set, mostly lurking
in the mouths of rivers, and feeding on wet hay, and especially
as they do not spout, I deny their credentials as whales; and
have presented them with their passports to quit the Kingdom of
Cetology.

chiefly with his name that I now have to do. Philologically considered, it is absurd. Some centuries ago, when the Sperm whale was almost wholly unknown in his own proper individuality, and when his oil was only accidentally obtained from the stranded fish; in those days spermaceti, it would seem, was popularly supposed to be derived from a creature identical with the one then known in England as the Greenland or Right Whale. It was the idea also, that this same spermaceti was that quickening humor of the Greenland Whale which the first syllable of the word literally expresses. In those times, also, spermaceti was exceedingly scarce, not being used for light, but only as an ointment and medicament. It was only to be had from the druggists as you nowadays buy an ounce of rhubarb. When, as I opine, in the course of time, the true nature of spermaceti became known, its original name was still retained by the dealers; no doubt to enhance its value by a notion so strangely significant of its scarcity. And so the appellation must at last have come to be bestowed upon the whale from which this spermaceti was really derived.

BOOK I. (*Folio*), CHAPTER II. (*Right Whale*).—In one respect this is the most venerable of the leviathans, being the one first regularly hunted by man. It yields the article commonly known as whale-bone or baleen; and the oil specially known as "whale oil," an inferior article in commerce. Among the fishermen, he is indiscriminately designated by all the following titles: The Whale; the Greenland Whale; the Black Whale; the Great Whale; the True Whale; the Right Whale. There is a deal of obscurity concerning the identity of the species thus multitudinously baptized. What then is the whale, which I include in the second species of my Folios? It is the Great Mysticetus of the English naturalists; the Greenland Whale of the English whalemen; the Baliene Ordinaire of the French whalemen; the Growlands Walfish of the Swedes. It is the whale which for more than two centuries past has been hunted by the Dutch and English in the Arctic seas; it is the whale which the American fishermen have long pursued in the Indian ocean, on the Brazil Banks, on the Nor' West Coast, and various other parts of the world, designated by them Right Whale Cruising Grounds.

Some pretend to see a difference between the Greenland whale of the English and the right whale of the Americans. But they precisely agree in all their grand features; nor has there yet been presented a single determinate fact upon which to ground a radical distinction. It is by endless subdivisions based upon the most inconclusive differences, that some departments of natural history become so repellingly intricate. The right whale will be elsewhere treated of at some length, with reference to elucidating the sperm whale.

BOOK I. (*Folio*), CHAPTER III. (*Fin-Back*).—Under this head I reckon a monster which, by the various names of Fin-Back, Tall-Spout, and Long-John, has been seen almost in every sea and is commonly the whale whose distant jet is so often descried by passengers crossing the Atlantic, in the New York packet-tracks. In the length he attains, and in his baleen, the Fin-back resembles the right whale, but is of a less portly girth, and a lighter color, approaching to olive. His great lips present a cable-like aspect, formed by the intertwisting, slanting folds of large wrinkles. His grand distinguishing feature, the fin, from which he derives his name, is often a conspicuous object. This fin is some three or four feet long, growing vertically from the hinder part of the back, of an angular shape, and with a very sharp pointed end. Even if not the slightest other part of the creature be visible, this isolated fin will, at times, be seen plainly projecting from the surface. When the sea is moderately calm, and slightly marked with spherical ripples, and this gnomon-like fin stands up and casts shadows upon the wrinkled surface, it may well be supposed that the watery circle surrounding it somewhat resembles a dial, with its style and wavy hour-lines graved on it. On that Ahaz-dial the shadow often goes back. The Fin-Back is not gregarious. He seems a whale-hater, as some men are man-haters. Very shy; always going solitary; unexpectedly rising to the surface in the remotest and most sullen waters; his straight and single lofty jet rising like a tall misanthropic spear upon a barren plain; gifted with such wondrous power and velocity in swimming, as to defy all present pursuit from man; this leviathan seems the banished and unconquerable Cain of his race, bearing for his mark that style upon his back. From having the baleen in his mouth, the Fin-Back is sometimes included with the right whale, among a theoretic species denominated *Whalebone whales,* that is, whales with baleen. Of these so called Whalebone whales, there would seem to be several varieties, most of which, however, are little known. Broad-nosed whales and beaked whales; pike-headed whales; bunched whales; under-jawed whales and rostrated whales, are the fishermen's names for a few sorts.

In connexion with this appellative of "Whalebone whales,"

it is of great importance to mention, that however such a nomenclature may be convenient in facilitating allusions to some kind of whales, yet it is in vain to attempt a clear classification of the Leviathan, founded upon either his baleen, or hump, or fin, or teeth; notwithstanding that those marked parts or features very obviously seem better adapted to afford the basis for a regular system of Cetology than any other detached bodily distinctions, which the whale, in his kinds, presents. How then? The baleen, hump, back-fin, and teeth; these are things whose peculiarities are indiscriminately dispersed among all sorts of whales, without any regard to what may be the nature of their structure in other and more essential particulars. Thus, the sperm whale and the humpbacked whale, each has a hump; but there the similitude ceases. Then, this same humpbacked whale and the Greenland whale, each of these has baleen; but there again the similitude ceases. And it is just the same with the other parts above mentioned. In various sorts of whales, they form such irregular combinations; or, in the case of any one of them detached, such an irregular isolation; as utterly to defy all general methodization formed upon such a basis. On this rock every one of the whale-naturalists has split.

But it may possibly be conceived that, in the internal parts of the whale, in his anatomy—there, at least, we shall be able to hit the right classification. Nay; what thing, for example, is there in the Greenland whale's anatomy more striking than his baleen? Yet we have seen that by his baleen it is impossible correctly to classify the Greenland whale. And if you descend into the bowels of the various leviathans, why there you will not find distinctions a fiftieth part as available to the systematizer as those external ones already enumerated. What then remains? nothing but to take hold of the whales bodily, in their entire liberal volume, and boldly sort them that way. And this is the Bibliographical system here adopted; and it is the only one that can possibly succeed, for it alone is practicable. To proceed.

BOOK I. (*Folio*), CHAPTER IV. (*Hump Back*).—This whale is often seen on the northern American coast. He has been frequently captured there, and towed into harbor. He has a great pack on him like a peddler; or you might call him the Elephant and Castle whale. At any rate, the popular name for him does not sufficiently distinguish him, since the sperm whale also has a hump, though a smaller one. His oil is not very valuable. He has baleen. He is the most gamesome and light-hearted of all the whales, making more gay foam and white water generally than any other of them.

BOOK I. (*Folio*), CHAPTER V. (*Razor Back*).—Of this whale little is known but his name. I have seen him at a distance off Cape Horn. Of a retiring nature, he eludes both hunters and philosophers. Though no coward, he has never yet shown any part of him but his back, which rises in a long sharp ridge. Let him go. I know little more of him, nor does anybody else.

BOOK I. (*Folio*), CHAPTER VI. (*Sulphur Bottom*).—Another retiring gentleman, with a brimstone belly, doubtless got by scraping along the Tartarian tiles in some of his profounder divings. He is seldom seen; at least I have never seen him except in the remoter southern seas, and then always at too great a distance to study his countenance. He is never chased; he would run away with rope-walks of line. Prodigies are told of him. Adieu, Sulphur Bottom! I can say nothing more that is true of ye, nor can the oldest Nantucketer.

Thus ends BOOK I. (*Folio*), and now begins BOOK II. (*Octavo*).

OCTAVOES.* These embrace the whales of middling magnitude, among which at present may be numbered:—I., the *Grampus;* II., the *Black Fish;* III., the *Narwhale;* IV., the *Thrasher;* V., the *Killer.*

BOOK II. (*Octavo*), CHAPTER I. (*Grampus*).—Though this fish, whose loud sonorous breathing, or rather blowing, has furnished a proverb to landsmen, is so well known a denizen of the deep, yet is he not popularly classed among whales. But possessing all the grand distinctive features of the leviathan, most naturalists have recognised him for one. He is of moderate octavo size, varying from fifteen to twenty-five feet in length, and of corresponding dimensions round the waist. He swims in herds; he is never regularly hunted, though his oil is considerable in quantity, and pretty good for light. By some fishermen his approach is regarded as premonitory of the advance of the great sperm whale.

BOOK II. (*Octavo*), CHAPTER II. (*Black Fish*).—I give the

* Why this book of whales is not denominated the Quarto is very plain. Because, while the whales of this order, though smaller than those of the former order, nevertheless retain a proportionate likeness to them in figure, yet the bookbinder's Quarto volume in its diminished form does not preserve the shape of the Folio volume, but the Octavo volume does.

popular fishermen's names for all these fish, for generally they are the best. Where any name happens to be vague or inexpressive, I shall say so, and suggest another. I do so now, touching the Black Fish, so called, because blackness is the rule among almost all whales. So, call him the Hyena Whale, if you please. His voracity is well known, and from the circumstance that the inner angles of his lips are curved upwards, he carries an everlasting Mephistophelean grin on his face. This whale averages some sixteen or eighteen feet in length. He is found in almost all latitudes. He has a peculiar way of showing his dorsal hooked fin in swimming, which looks something like a Roman nose. When not more profitably employed, the sperm whale hunters sometimes capture the Hyena whale, to keep up the supply of cheap oil for domestic employment—as some frugal housekeepers, in the absence of company, and quite alone by themselves, burn unsavory tallow instead of odorous wax. Though their blubber is very thin, some of these whales will yield you upwards of thirty gallons of oil.

BOOK II. (*Octavo*), CHAPTER III. (*Narwhale*), that is, *Nostril whale*.—Another instance of a curiously named whale, so named I suppose from his peculiar horn being originally mistaken for a peaked nose. The creature is some sixteen feet in length, while its horn averages five feet, though some exceed ten, and even attain to fifteen feet. Strictly speaking, this horn is but a lengthened tusk, growing out from the jaw in a line a little depressed from the horizontal. But it is only found on the sinister side, which has an ill effect, giving its owner something analogous to the aspect of a clumsy left-handed man. What precise purpose this ivory horn or lance answers, it would be hard to say. It does not seem to be used like the blade of the sword-fish and bill-fish; though some sailors tell me that the Narwhale employs it for a rake in turning over the bottom of the sea for food. Charley Coffin said it was used for an ice-piercer; for the Narwhale, rising to the surface of the Polar Sea, and finding it sheeted with ice, thrusts his horn up, and so breaks through. But you cannot prove either of these surmises to be correct. My own opinion is, that however this one-sided horn may really be used by the Narwhale—however that may be—it would certainly be very convenient to him for a folder in reading pamphlets. The Narwhale I have heard called the Tusked whale, the Horned whale, and the Unicorn whale. He is certainly a curious example of the

Unicornism to be found in almost every kingdom of animated nature. From certain cloistered old authors I have gathered that this same sea-unicorn's horn was in ancient days regarded as the great antidote against poison, and as such, preparations of it brought immense prices. It was also distilled to a volatile salts for fainting ladies, the same way that the horns of the male deer are manufactured into hartshorn. Originally it was in itself accounted an object of great curiosity. Black Letter tells me that Sir Martin Frobisher on his return from that voyage, when Queen Bess did gallantly wave her jewelled hand to him from a window of Greenwich Palace, as his bold ship sailed down the Thames; "when Sir Martin returned from that voyage," saith Black Letter, "on bended knees he presented to her highness a prodigious long horn of the Narwhale, which for a long period after hung in the castle at Windsor." An Irish author avers that the Earl of Leicester, on bended knees, did likewise present to her highness another horn, pertaining to a land beast of the unicorn nature.

The Narwhale has a very picturesque, leopard-like look, being of a milk-white ground color, dotted with round and oblong spots of black. His oil is very superior, clear and fine; but there is little of it, and he is seldom hunted. He is mostly found in the circumpolar seas.

BOOK II. (*Octavo*), CHAPTER IV. (*Killer*).—Of this whale little is precisely known to the Nantucketer, and nothing at all to the professed naturalist. From what I have seen of him at a distance, I should say that he was about the bigness of a grampus. He is very savage—a sort of Feegee fish. He sometimes takes the great Folio whales by the lip, and hangs there like a leech, till the mighty brute is worried to death. The killer is never hunted. I never heard what sort of oil he has. Exception might be taken to the name bestowed upon this whale, on the ground of its indistinctness. For we are all killers, on land and on sea; Bonapartes and Sharks included.

BOOK II. (*Octavo*), CHAPTER V. (*Thrasher*).—This gentleman is famous for his tail, which he uses for a ferule in thrashing his foes. He mounts the Folio whale's back, and as he swims, he works his passage by flogging him; as some schoolmasters get along in the world by a similar process. Still less is known of the Thrasher than of the Killer. Both are outlaws, even in the lawless seas.

This ends BOOK II. (*Octavo*), and begins BOOK III. (*Duodecimo*).

DUODECIMOES.—These include the smaller whales. I. The Huzza Porpoise. II. The Algerine Porpoise. III. The Mealy-mouthed Porpoise.

To those who have not chanced specially to study the subject, it may possibly seem strange, that fishes not commonly exceeding four or five feet should be marshalled among WHALES—a word, which, in the popular sense, always conveys an idea of hugeness. But the creatures set down above as Duodecimoes are infallibly whales, by the terms of my definition of what a whale is—i.e. a spouting fish, with a horizontal tail.

BOOK III. (*Duodecimo*), CHAPTER I. (*Huzza Porpoise*).— This is the common porpoise found almost all over the globe. The name is of my own bestowal; for there are more than one sort of porpoises, and something must be done to distinguish them. I call him thus, because he always swims in hilarious shoals, which upon the broad sea keep tossing themselves to heaven like caps in a Fourth-of-July crowd. Their appearance is generally hailed with delight by the mariner. Full of fine spirits, they invariably come from the breezy billows to windward. They are the lads that always live before the wind. They are accounted a lucky omen. If you yourself can withstand three cheers at beholding these vivacious fish, then heaven help ye; the spirit of godly gamesomeness is not in ye. A well-fed, plump Huzza Porpoise will yield you one good gallon of good oil. But the fine and delicate fluid extracted from his jaws is exceedingly valuable. It is in request among jewellers and watchmakers. Sailors put it on their hones. Porpoise meat is good eating, you know. It may never have occurred to you that a porpoise spouts. Indeed, his spout is so small that it is not very readily discernible. But the next time you have a chance, watch him; and you will then see the great Sperm whale himself in miniature.

BOOK III. (*Duodecimo*), CHAPTER II. (*Algerine Porpoise*). —A pirate. Very savage. He is only found, I think, in the Pacific. He is somewhat larger than the Huzza Porpoise, but much of the same general make. Provoke him, and he will buckle to a shark. I have lowered for him many times, but never yet saw him captured.

BOOK III. (*Duodecimo*), CHAPTER III. (*Mealy-mouthed*

Porpoise).—The largest kind of Porpoise; and only found in the Pacific, so far as it is known. The only English name, by which he has hitherto been designated, is that of the fishers—Right-Whale Porpoise, from the circumstance that he is chiefly found in the vicinity of that Folio. In shape, he differs in some degree from the Huzza Porpoise, being of a less rotund and jolly girth; indeed, he is of quite a neat and gentleman-like figure. He has no fins on his back (most other porpoises have), he has a lovely tail, and sentimental Indian eyes of a hazel hue. But his mealy-mouth spoils all. Though his entire back down to his side fins is of a deep sable, yet a boundary line, distinct as the mark in a ship's hull, called the "bright waist," that line streaks him from stem to stern, with two separate colors, black above and white below. The white comprises part of his head, and the whole of his mouth, which makes him look as if he had just escaped from a felonious visit to a meal-bag. A most mean and mealy aspect! His oil is much like that of the common porpoise.

*   *   *   *   *

Beyond the DUODECIMO, this system does not proceed, inasmuch as the Porpoise is the smallest of the whales. Above, you have all the Leviathans of note. But there are a rabble of uncertain, fugitive, half-fabulous whales, which, as an American whaleman, I know by reputation, but not personally. I shall enumerate them by their forecastle appellations; for possibly such a list may be valuable to future investigators, who may complete what I have here but begun. If any of the following whales, shall hereafter be caught and marked, then he can readily be incorporated into this System, according to his Folio, Octavo, or Duodecimo magnitude:—The Bottle-Nose Whale; the Junk Whale; the Pudding-Headed Whale; the Cape Whale; the Leading Whale; the Cannon Whale; the Scragg Whale; the Coppered Whale; the Elephant Whale; the Iceberg Whale; the Quog Whale; the Blue Whale; &c. From Icelandic, Dutch, and old English authorities, there might be quoted other lists of uncertain whales, blessed with all manner of uncouth names. But I omit them as altogether obsolete; and can hardly help suspecting them for mere sounds, full of Leviathanism, but signifying nothing.

Finally: It was stated at the outset, that this system would not be here, and at once, perfected. You cannot but plainly see that I have kept my word. But I now leave my cetological System standing thus unfinished, even as the great Cathedral of Cologne was left, with the crane still standing upon the top of the uncompleted tower. For small erections may be finished by their first architects; grand ones, true ones, ever leave the copestone to posterity. God keep me from ever completing anything. This whole book is but a draught—nay, but the draught of a draught. Oh, Time, Strength, Cash, and Patience!

THE SPECKSYNDER   XXXIII

CONCERNING the officers of the whale-craft, this seems as good a place as any to set down a little domestic peculiarity on shipboard, arising from the existence of the harpooneer class of officers, a class unknown of course in any other marine than the whale-fleet.

The large importance attached to the harpooneer's vocation is evinced by the fact, that originally in the old Dutch Fishery, two centuries and more ago, the command of a whale ship was not wholly lodged in the person now called the captain, but was divided between him and an officer called the Specksynder. Literally this word means Fat-Cutter; usage, however, in time made it equivalent to Chief Harpooneer. In those days, the captain's authority was restricted to the navigation and general management of the vessel: while over the whale-hunting department and all its concerns, the Specksynder or Chief Harpooneer reigned supreme. In the British Greenland Fishery, under the corrupted title of Specksioneer, this old Dutch official is still retained, but his former dignity is sadly abridged. At present he ranks simply as senior Harpooneer; and as such, is but one of the captain's more inferior subalterns. Nevertheless, as upon the good conduct of the harpooneers the success of a whaling voyage largely depends, and since in the American Fishery he is not only an important officer in the boat, but under certain circumstances (night watches on a whaling ground) the command of the ship's deck is also his; therefore the grand political maxim of the sea demands, that he should nominally live apart from the men before the mast, and be in some way distinguished as their professional superior; though always, by them, familiarly regarded as their social equal.

Now, the grand distinction drawn between officer and man at sea, is this—the first lives aft, the last forward. Hence, in whaleships and merchantmen alike, the mates have their quarters with the captain; and so, too, in most of the American whalers the harpooneers are lodged in the after part of the ship. That is to say, they take their meals in the captain's cabin, and sleep in a place indirectly communicating with it.

Though the long period of a Southern whaling voyage (by far the longest of all voyages now or ever made by man), the peculiar perils of it, and the community of interest prevailing among a company, all of whom, high or low, depend for their profits, not upon fixed wages, but upon their common luck, together with their common vigilance, intrepidity, and hard work; though all these things do in some cases tend to beget a less rigorous discipline than in merchantmen generally; yet, never mind how much like an old Mesopotamian family these whalemen may, in some primitive instances, live together; for all that, the punctilious externals, at least, of the quarter-deck are seldom materially relaxed, and in no instance done away. Indeed, many are the Nantucket ships in which you will see the skipper parading his quarter-deck with an elated grandeur not surpassed in any military navy; nay, extorting almost as much outward homage as if he wore the imperial purple, and not the shabbiest of pilot-cloth.

And though of all men the moody captain of the Pequod was the least given to that sort of shallowest assumption; and though the only homage he ever exacted, was implicit, instantaneous obedience; though he required no man to remove the shoes from his feet ere stepping upon the quarter-deck; and though there were times when, owing to peculiar circumstances connected with events hereafter to be detailed, he addressed them in unusual terms, whether of condescension or *in terrorem,* or otherwise; yet even Captain Ahab was by no means unobservant of the paramount forms and usages of the sea.

Nor, perhaps, will it fail to be eventually perceived, that behind those forms and usages, as it were, he sometimes masked himself; incidentally making use of them for other and more private ends than they were legitimately intended to subserve. That certain sultanism of his brain, which had otherwise in a good degree remained unmanifested; through those forms that same sultanism became incarnate in an irresistible dictatorship. For be a man's intellectual superiority what it will, it can never assume the practical, available supremacy over other men, without the aid of some sort of external arts and entrenchments, always, in themselves, more or less paltry and base. This it is, that for ever keeps God's true princes of the Empire from the world's hustings; and leaves the highest honors that this air can give, to those men who become famous more through their infinite inferiority to the choice hidden handful of the Divine Inert, than through their undoubted superiority over the dead level of the mass. Such large virtue lurks in these small things when extreme political superstitions invest them, that in some royal instances even to idiot imbecility they have imparted potency. But when, as in the case of Nicholas the Czar, the ringed crown of geographical empire encircles an imperial brain; then, the plebeian herds crouch abased before the tremendous centralization. Nor, will the tragic dramatist who would depict mortal indomitableness in its fullest sweep and direct swing, ever forget a hint, incidentally so important in his art, as the one now alluded to.

But Ahab, my Captain, still moves before me in all his Nantucket grimness and shagginess; and in this episode touching Emperors and Kings, I must not conceal that I have only to do with a poor old whale-hunter like him; and, therefore, all outward majestical trappings and housings are denied me. Oh, Ahab! what shall be grand in thee, it must needs be plucked at from the skies, and dived for in the deep, and featured in the unbodied air!

THE CABIN-TABLE   XXXIV

IT is noon; and Dough-Boy, the steward, thrusting his pale loaf-of-bread face from the cabin-scuttle, announces dinner to his lord and master; who, sitting in the lee quarter-boat, has just been taking an observation of the sun; and is now mutely reckoning the latitude on the smooth, medallion-shaped tablet, reserved for that daily purpose on the upper part of his ivory leg. From his complete inattention to the

tidings, you would think that moody Ahab had not heard
his menial. But presently, catching hold of the mizzen
shrouds, he swings himself to the deck, and in an even,
unexhilarated voice, saying, "Dinner, Mr. Starbuck," disappears into the cabin.

When the last echo of his sultan's step has died away, and
Starbuck, the first Emir, has every reason to suppose that he
is seated, then Starbuck rouses from his quietude, takes a
few turns along the planks, and, after a grave peep into the
binnacle, says, with some touch of pleasantness, "Dinner,
Mr. Stubb," and descends the scuttle. The second Emir
lounges about the rigging awhile, and then slightly shaking
the main brace, to see whether it be all right with that important rope, he likewise takes up the old burden, and with
a rapid "Dinner, Mr. Flask," follows after his predecessors.

But the third Emir, now seeing himself all alone on the
quarterdeck, seems to feel relieved from some curious res-
traint; for, tipping all sorts of knowing winks in all sorts of
directions, and kicking off his shoes, he strikes into a sharp
but noiseless squall of a hornpipe right over the Grand
Turk's head; and then, by a dexterous sleight, pitching his
cap up into the mizen-top for a shelf, he goes down rollicking, so far at least as he remains visible from the deck,
reversing all other processions, by bringing up the rear with
music. But ere stepping into the cabin doorway below, he
pauses, ships a new face altogether, and, then, independent,
hilarious little Flask enters King Ahab's presence, in the
character of Abjectus, or the Slave.

It is not the least among the strange things bred by the
intense artificialness of sea-usages, that while in the open air
of the deck some officers will, upon provocation, bear themselves boldly and defyingly enough towards their commander; yet, ten to one, let those very officers the next moment go
down to their customary dinner in that same commander's
cabin, and straightway their inoffensive, not to say depre-
catory and humble air towards him, as he sits at the head of
the table; this is marvellous, sometimes most comical. Wherefore this difference? A problem? Perhaps not. To have been
Belshazzar, King of Babylon; and to have been Belshazzar,
not haughtily but courteously, therein certainly must have
been some touch of mundane grandeur. But he who in the
rightly regal and intelligent spirit presides over his own
private dinner-table of invited guests, that man's unchal-
lenged power and dominion of individual influence for the

time; that man's royalty of state transcends Belshazzar's, for Belshazzar was not the greatest. Who has but once dined his friends, has tasted what it is to be Caesar. It is a witchery of social czarship which there is no withstanding. Now, if to this consideration you superadd the official supremacy of a ship-master, then, by inference, you will derive the cause of that peculiarity of sea-life just mentioned.

Over his ivory-inlaid table, Ahab presided like a mute, maned sea-lion on the white coral beach, surrounded by his warlike but still deferential cubs. In his own proper turn, each officer waited to be served. They were as little children before Ahab; and yet, in Ahab, there seemed not to lurk the smallest social arrogance. With one mind, their intent eyes all fastened upon the old man's knife, as he carved the chief dish before him. I do not suppose that for the world they would have profaned that moment with the slightest observation, even upon so neutral a topic as the weather. No! And when reaching out his knife and fork, between which the slice of beef was locked, Ahab thereby motioned Starbuck's plate towards him, the mate received his meat as though receiving alms; and cut it tenderly; and a little started if, perchance, the knife grazed against the plate; and chewed it noiselessly; and swallowed it, not without circumspection. For, like the Coronation banquet at Frankfort, where the German Emperor profoundly dines with the seven Imperial Electors, so these cabin meals were somehow solemn meals, eaten in awful silence; and yet at table old Ahab forbade not conversation; only he himself was dumb. What a relief it was to choking Stubb, when a rat made a sudden racket in the hole below. And poor little Flask, he was the youngest son, and little boy of this weary family party. His were the shin-bones of the saline beef; his would have been the drumsticks. For Flask to have presumed to help himself, thus must have seemed to him tantamount to larceny in the first degree. Had he helped himself at that table, doubtless, never more would he have been able to hold his head up in this honest world; nevertheless, strange to say, Ahab never forbade him. And had Flask helped himself, the chances were Ahab had never so much as noticed it. Least of all, did Flask presume to help himself to butter. Whether he thought the owners of the ship denied it to him, on account of its clotting his clear, sunny complexion; or whether he deemed that, on so long a voyage in such marketless waters, butter was at a premium, and therefore was not for him, a subaltern; however it was, Flask, alas! was a butterless man!

Another thing. Flask was the last person down at the dinner, and Flask is the first man up. Consider! For hereby Flask's dinner was badly jammed in point of time. Starbuck and Stubb both had the start of him; and yet they also have the privilege of lounging in the rear. If Stubb even, who is but a peg higher than Flask, happens to have but a small appetite, and soon shows symptoms of concluding his repast, then Flask must bestir himself, he will not get more than three mouthfuls that day; for it is against holy usage for Stubb to precede Flask to the deck. Therefore it was that Flask once admitted in private, that ever since he had arisen to the dignity of an officer, from that moment he had never known what it was to be otherwise than hungry, more or less. For what he ate did not so much relieve his hunger, as keep it immortal in him. Peace and satisfaction, thought Flask, have for ever departed from my stomach. I am an officer; but, how I wish I could fist a bit of old-fashioned beef in the forecastle, as I used to when I was before the mast. There's the fruits of promotion now; there's the vanity of glory; there's the insanity of life! Besides, if it were so that any mere sailor of the Pequod had a grudge against Flask in Flask's official capacity, all that sailor had to do, in order to obtain ample vengeance, was to go aft at dinner-time, and get a peep at Flask through the cabin sky-light, sitting silly and dumbfoundered before awful Ahab.

Now, Ahab and his three mates formed what may be called the first table in the Pequod's cabin. After their departure, taking place in inverted order to their arrival, the canvas cloth was cleared, or rather was restored to some hurried order by the pallid steward. And then the three harpooneers were bidden to the feast, they being its residuary legatees. They made a sort of temporary servants' hall of the high and mighty cabin.

In strange contrast to the hardly tolerable constraint and nameless invisible domineerings of the captain's table, was the entire care-free license and ease, the almost frantic democracy of those inferior fellows the harpooneers. While their masters, the mates, seemed afraid of the sound of the hinges of their own jaws, the harpooneers chewed their food with such relish that there was a report to it. They dined like lords; they filled their bellies like Indian ships all day loading with spices. Such portentous appetites had Queequeg and Tashtego, that to fill out the vacancies made by the previous repast, often the pale Dough-Boy was fain to bring on a great baron of salt-junk, seemingly quarried out of the solid ox. And if he were not lively about it, if he did not go with a nimble hop-skip-and-jump, then Tashtego had an ungentlemanly way of accelerating him by darting a fork at his back, harpoonwise. And once Daggoo, seized with a sudden humor, assisted Dough-Boy's memory by snatching him up bodily, and thrusting his head into a great empty wooden trencher, while Tashtego, knife in hand, began laying out the circle preliminary to scalping him. He was naturally a very nervous, shuddering sort of little fellow, this bread-faced steward; the progeny of a bankrupt baker and a hospital nurse. And what with the standing spectacle of the black terrific Ahab, and the periodical tumultuous visitations of these three savages, Dough-Boy's whole life was one continual lip-quiver. Commonly, after seeing the harpooneers furnished with all things they demanded, he would escape from their clutches into his little pantry adjoining, and fearfully peep out at them through the blinds of its door, till all was over.

It was a sight to see Queequeg seated over against Tashtego, opposing his filed teeth to the Indian's: crosswise to them, Daggoo seated on the floor, for a bench would have brought his hearse-plumed head to the low carlines; at every motion of his colossal limbs, making the low cabin framework to shake, as when an African elephant goes passenger in a ship. But for all this, the great negro was wonderfully abstemious, not to say dainty. It seemed hardly possible that by such comparatively small mouthfuls he could keep up the vitality diffused through so broad, baronial, and superb a person. But, doubtless, this noble savage fed strong and drank deep of the abounding element of air; and through his dilated nostrils snuffed in the sublime life of the worlds. Not by beef or by bread, are giants made or nourished. But Queequeg, he had a mortal, barbaric smack of the lip in eating—an ugly sound enough—so much so, that the trembling Dough-Boy almost looked to see whether any marks of teeth lurked in his own lean arms. And when he would hear Tashtego singing out for him to produce himself, that his bones might be picked, the simple-witted Steward all but shattered the crockery hanging round him in the pantry, by his sudden fits of the palsy. Nor did the whetstone which the harpooneers carried in their pockets, for their lances and other weapons; and with which whetstones, at dinner, they would ostentatiously sharpen their knives; that grating sound did not at all tend to tranquillize poor Dough-Boy. How could he forget that in his Island days, Queequeg, for one, must certainly have been guilty of some murderous, convivial indiscretions. Alas! Dough-Boy! hard fares the white waiter who waits upon cannibals. Not a napkin should he carry on his arm, but a buckler. In good time, though, to his great delight, the three salt-sea warriors would rise and depart; to his credulous, fable-mongering ears, all their martial bones jingling in them at every step, like Moorish scimitars in scabbards.

But, though these barbarians dined in the cabin, and nominally lived there; still, being anything but sedentary in their habits, they were scarcely ever in it except at mealtimes, and just before sleeping-time, when they passed through it to their own peculiar quarters.

In this one matter, Ahab seemed no exception to most American whale captains, who, as a set, rather incline to the opinion that by rights the ship's cabin belongs to them; and that it is by courtesy alone that anybody else is, at any time, permitted there. So that, in real truth, the mates and harpooneers of the Pequod might more properly be said to have lived out of the cabin than in it. For when they did enter it, it was something as a street-door enters a house; turning inwards for a moment, only to be turned out the next; and, as a permanent thing, residing in the open air. Nor did they lose much hereby; in the cabin was no companionship; socially, Ahab was inaccessible. Though nominally included in the census of Christendom, he was still an alien to it. He lived in the world, as the last of the Grisly Bears lived in settled Missouri. And as when Spring and Summer had departed, that wild Logan of the woods, burying himself in the hollow of a tree, lived out the winter there, sucking his own paws; so, in his inclement, howling old age, Ahab's soul, shut up in the caved trunk of his body, there fed upon the sullen paws of its gloom!

THE MAST-HEAD   **XXXV**

IT was during the more pleasant weather, that in due rotation with the other seamen my first mast-head came round.

In most American whalemen the mast-heads are manned almost simultaneously with the vessel's leaving her port; even though she may have fifteen thousand miles, and more, to sail ere reaching her proper cruising ground. And if, after a three, four, or five years' voyage she is drawing nigh home with anything empty in her—say, an empty vial even—then, her mast-heads are kept manned to the last; and not till her skysail-poles sail in among the spires of the port, does she altogether relinquish the hope of capturing one whale more.

Now, as the business of standing mast-heads, ashore or afloat, is a very ancient and interesting one, let us in some measure expatiate here. I take it, that the earliest standers of mast-heads were the old Egyptians; because, in all my researches, I find none prior to them. For though their progenitors, the builders of Babel, must doubtless, by their tower, have intended to rear the loftiest mast-head in all Asia, or Africa either; yet (ere the final truck was put to it) as that great stone mast of theirs may be said to have gone by the board, in the dread gale of God's wrath; therefore, we cannot give these Babel builders priority over the Egyptians. And that the Egyptians were a nation of mast-head standers, is an assertion based upon the general belief among archæologists, that the first pyramids were founded for astronomical purposes: a theory singularly supported by the peculiar stair-like formation of all four sides of those edifices; whereby, with prodigious long upliftings of their legs, those old astronomers were wont to mount to the apex, and sing out for new stars; even as the look-outs of a modern ship sing out for a sail, or a whale just bearing in sight. In Saint Stylites, the famous Christian hermit of old times, who built him a lofty stone pillar in the desert and spent the whole latter portion of his life on its summit, hoisting his food from the ground with a tackle; in him we have a remarkable instance of a dauntless stander-of-mast-heads; who was not to be driven from his place by fogs or frosts, rain, hail, or sleet; but valiantly facing everything out to the last, literally died at his post. Of modern standers-of-mast-heads we have but a lifeless set; mere stone, iron, and bronze men; who, though well capable of facing out a stiff gale, are still entirely incompetent to the business of singing out upon discovering any strange sight. There is Napoleon; who, upon the top of the column of Vendome, stands with arms folded, some one hundred and fifty feet in the air; careless, now, who rules the decks below; whether Louis Philippe, Louis Blanc, or Louis the Devil. Great Washington, too, stands high aloft on his towering main-mast in Baltimore, and like one of Hercules' pillars, his column marks that point of human grandeur beyond which few mortals will go. Admiral Nelson, also, on a capstan of gun-metal, stands his mast-head in Trafalgar Square; and even when most obscured by that London smoke, token is yet given that a hidden hero is there; for where there is smoke, must be fire. But neither great Washington, nor Napoleon, nor Nelson, will answer a single hail from below, however madly invoked to befriend by their counsels the distracted decks upon which they gaze; however it may be surmised, that their spirits penetrate through the thick haze of the future, and descry what shoals and what rocks must be shunned.

It may seem unwarrantable to couple in any respect the mast-head standers of the land with those of the sea; but that in truth it is not so, is plainly evinced by an item for which Obed Macy, the sole historian of Nantucket, stands accountable. The worthy Obed tells us, that in the early times of the whale fishery, ere ships were regularly launched in pursuit of the game, the people of that island erected lofty spars along the sea-coast, to which the look-outs ascended by means of nailed cleats, something as fowls go upstairs in a hen-house. A few years ago this same plan was adopted by the Bay whalemen of New Zealand, who upon descrying the game, gave notice to the ready-manned boats nigh the beach. But this custom has now become obsolete; turn we then to the one proper mast-head, that of a whale-ship at sea. The three mast-heads are kept manned from sun-rise to sun-set; the seamen taking their regular turns (as at the helm), and relieving each other every two hours. In the serene weather of the tropics it is exceedingly pleasant the mast-head; nay, to a dreamy meditative man it is delightful. There you stand, a hundred feet above the silent decks, striding along the deep, as if the masts were gigantic stilts, while beneath you and between your legs, as it were, swim the hugest monsters of the sea, even as ships once sailed between the boots of the famous Colossus at old Rhodes. There you stand, lost in the infinite series of the sea, with nothing ruffled but the waves. The tranced ship indolently rolls; the drowsy trade winds blow; everything resolves you into languor. For the most part, in this tropic whaling life, a sublime uneventfulness invests you; you hear no news; read no gazettes; extras with startling accounts of commonplaces never delude you into unnecessary excitements; you hear of no domestic afflictions; bankrupt securities; fall of stocks; are never troubled with the thought of what you shall have for dinner—for all your meals for three years and more are snugly stowed in casks, and your bill of fare is immutable.

In one of those southern whalemen, on a long three or four years' voyage, as often happens, the sum of the various hours you spend at the mast-head would amount to several entire months. And it is much to be deplored that the place to which you devote so considerable a portion of the whole term of your natural life, should be so sadly destitute of anything approaching to a cosy inhabitiveness, or adapted to breed a comfortable localness of feeling, such as pertains to a bed, a hammock, a hearse, a sentry box, a pulpit, a coach, or any other of those small and snug contrivances in which men temporarily isolate themselves. Your most usual point of perch is the head of the t' gallant-mast, where you stand upon two thin sticks (almost peculiar to whalemen) called the t' gallant cross-trees. Here, tossed about by the sea, the beginner feels about as cosy as he would standing on a bull's horns. To be sure, in cold weather you may carry your house aloft with you, in the shape of a watch-coat; but properly speaking the thickest watch-coat is no more of a house than the unclad body; for as the soul is glued inside of its fleshy tabernacle, and cannot freely move about in it, nor even move out of it, without running great risk of perishing (like an ignorant pilgrim crossing the snowy Alps in winter); so a watch-coat is not so much of a house as it is a mere envelope, or additional skin encasing you. You cannot put a shelf or chest of drawers in your body, and no more can you make a convenient closet of your watch-coat.

Concerning all this, it is much to be deplored that the mast-heads of a southern whale ship are unprovided with those enviable little tents or pulpits, called *crow's-nests,* in which the lookouts of a Greenland whaler are protected from the inclement weather of the frozen seas. In the fireside narrative of Captain Sleet, entitled "A Voyage among the Icebergs, in quest of the Greenland Whale, and incidentally for the re-discovery of the Lost Icelandic Colonies of Old Greenland;" in this admirable volume, all standers of mast-heads are furnished with a charmingly circumstantial account of the then recently invented *crow's-nest* of the

Glacier, which was the name of Captain Sleet's good craft. He called it the *Sleet's crow's-nest,* in honor of himself; he being the original inventor and patentee, and free from all ridiculous false delicacy, and holding that if we call our own children after our own names (we fathers being the original inventors and patentees), so likewise should we denominate after ourselves any other apparatus we may beget. In shape, the Sleet's crow's-nest is something like a large tierce or pipe; it is open above, however, where it is furnished with a movable side-screen to keep to windward of your head in a hard gale. Being fixed on the summit of the mast, you ascend into it through a little trap-hatch in the bottom. On the after side, or side next the stern of the ship, is a comfortable seat, with a locker underneath for umbrellas, comforters, and coats. In front is a leather rack, in which to keep your speaking trumpet, pipe, telescope, and other nautical conveniences. When Captain Sleet in person stood his mast-head in this crow's nest of his, he tells us that he always had a rifle with him (also fixed in the rack), together with a powder flask and shot, for the purpose of popping off the stray narwhales, or vagrant sea unicorns infesting those waters; for you cannot successfully shoot at them from the deck owing to the resistance of the water, but to shoot down upon them is a very different thing. Now, it was plainly a labor of love for Captain Sleet to describe, as he does, all the little detailed conveniences of his crow's-nest; but though he so enlarges upon many of these, and though he treats us to a very scientific account of his experiments in this crow's-nest, with a small compass he kept there for the purpose of counteracting the errors resulting from what is called the "local attraction" of all binnacle magnets; an error ascribable to the horizontal vicinity of the iron in the ship's planks, and in the Glacier's case, perhaps, to there having been so many broken-down blacksmiths among her crew; I say, that though the Captain is very discreet and scientific here, yet, for all his learned "binnacle deviations," "azimuth compass observations," and "approximate errors," he knows very well, Captain Sleet, that he was not so much immersed in those profound magnetic meditations, as to fail being attracted occasionally towards that well replenished little case-bottle, so nicely tucked in on one side of his crow's nest, within easy reach of his hand. Though, upon the whole, I greatly admire and even love the brave, the honest, and learned Captain; yet I take it very ill of him that he should so utterly ignore that case-bottle, seeing what a faithful friend and comforter it must have been, while with mittened fingers and hooded head he was studying the mathematics aloft there in that bird's nest within three or four perches of the pole.

But if we Southern whale-fishers are not so snugly housed aloft as Captain Sleet and his Greenland-men were; yet that disadvantage is greatly counterbalanced by the widely contrasting serenity of those seductive seas in which we South fishers mostly float. For one, I used to lounge up the rigging very leisurely, resting in the top to have a chat with Queequeg, or any one else off duty whom I might find there; then ascending a little way further, and throwing a lazy leg over the top-sail yard, take a preliminary view of the watery pastures, and so at last mount to my ultimate destination.

Let me make a clean breast of it here, and frankly admit that I kept but sorry guard. With the problem of the universe revolving in me, how could I—being left completely to myself at such a thought-engendering altitude,—how could I but lightly hold my obligations to observe all whale-ships' standing orders, "Keep your weather eye open, and sing out every time."

And let me in this place movingly admonish you, ye shipowners of Nantucket! Beware of enlisting in your vigilant fisheries any lad with lean brow and hollow eye; given to unseasonable meditativeness; and who offers to ship with the Phædon instead of Bowditch in his head. Beware of such an one, I say: your whales must be seen before they can be killed; and this sunken-eyed young Platonist will tow you ten wakes round the world, and never make you one pint of sperm the richer. Nor are these monitions at all unneeded. For nowadays, the whale-fishery furnishes an asylum for many romantic, melancholy, and absent-minded young men, disgusted with the carking cares of earth, and seeking sentiment in tar and blubber. Childe Harold not unfrequently perches himself upon the mast-head of some luckless disappointed whale-ship, and in moody phrase ejaculates:—

"Roll on, thou deep and dark blue ocean, roll!
Ten thousand blubber-hunters sweep over thee in vain."

Very often do the captains of such ships take those absent-minded young philosophers to task, upbraiding them with not feeling sufficient "interest" in the voyage; half-hinting that they are so hopelessly lost to all honorable ambition, as that in their secret souls they would rather not see whales than otherwise. But all in vain; those young Platonists have a notion that their vision is imperfect; they are short-sighted; what use, then, to strain the visual nerve? They have left their opera-glasses at home.

"Why, thou monkey," said a harpooneer to one of these lads, "we've been cruising now hard upon three years, and thou hast not raised a whale yet. Whales are scarce as hen's teeth whenever thou art up here." Perhaps they were; or perhaps there might have been shoals of them in the far horizon; but lulled into such an opium-like listlessness of vacant, unconscious reverie is this absent-minded youth by the blending cadence of waves with thoughts, that at last he loses his identity; takes the mystic ocean at his feet for the visible image of that deep, blue, bottomless soul, pervading mankind and nature; and every strange, half-seen, gliding, beautiful thing that eludes him; every dimly-discovered, uprising fin of some undiscernible form, seems to him the embodiment of those elusive thoughts that only people the soul by continually flitting through it. In this enchanted mood, thy spirit ebbs away to whence it came; becomes diffused through time and space; like Cranmer's sprinkled Pantheistic ashes, forming at last a part of every shore the round globe over.

There is no life in thee, now, except that rocking life imparted by a gently rolling ship; by her, borrowed from the sea; by the sea, from the inscrutable tides of God. But while this sleep, this dream is on ye, move your foot or hand an inch; slip your hold at all; and your identity comes back in horror. Over Descartian vortices you hover. And perhaps, at mid-day, in the fairest weather, with one half-throttled shriek you drop through that transparent air into the summer sea, no more to rise for ever. Heed it well, ye Pantheists!

THE QUARTER-DECK   XXXVI

(*Enter Ahab: Then, all.*)

IT was not a great while after the affair of the pipe, that one morning shortly after breakfast, Ahab, as was his wont, ascended the cabin-gangway to the deck. There most sea-captains usually walk at that hour, as country gentlemen, after the same meal, take a few turns in the garden.

Soon his steady, ivory stride was heard, as to and fro he paced his old rounds, upon planks so familiar to his tread, that they were all over dented, like geological stones, with the peculiar mark of his walk. Did you fixedly gaze, too, upon that ribbed and dented brow; there also, you would see still stranger foot-prints—the foot-prints of his one unsleeping, ever-pacing thought.

But on the occasion in question, those dents looked deeper, even as his nervous step that morning left a deeper mark. And, so full of his thought was Ahab, that at every uniform turn that he made, now at the main-mast and now at the binnacle, you could almost see that thought turn in him as he turned, and pace in him as he paced; so completely possessing him, indeed, that it all but seemed the inward mould of every outer movement.

"D'ye mark him, Flask?" whispered Stubb; "the chick that's in him pecks the shell. 'Twill soon be out."

The hours wore on;—Ahab now shut up within his cabin; anon, pacing the deck, with the same intense bigotry of purpose in his aspect.

It drew near the close of day. Suddenly he came to a halt by the bulwarks, and inserting his bone leg into the auger-hole there, and with one hand grasping a shroud, he ordered Starbuck to send everybody aft.

"Sir!" said the mate, astonished at an order seldom or never given on ship-board except in some extraordinary case.

"Send everybody aft," repeated Ahab. "Mast-heads, there! come down!"

When the entire ship's company were assembled, and with curious and not wholly unapprehensive faces, were eyeing him, for he looked not unlike the weather horizon when a storm is coming up, Ahab, after rapidly glancing over the bulwarks, and then darting his eyes among the crew, started from his standpoint; and as though not a soul were nigh him resumed his heavy turns upon the deck. With bent head and half-slouched hat he continued to pace, unmindful of the wondering whispering among the men; till Stubb cautiously whispered to Flask, that Ahab must have summoned them there for the purpose of witnessing a pedestrian feat. But this did not last long. Vehemently pausing, he cried:—

"What do ye do when ye see a whale, men?"

"Sing out for him!" was the impulsive rejoinder from a score of clubbed voices.

"Good!" cried Ahab, with a wild approval in his tones; observing the hearty animation into which his unexpected question had so magnetically thrown them.

"And what do ye next, men?"

"Lower away, and after him!"

"And what tune is it ye pull to, men?"

"A dead whale or a stove boat!"

More and more strangely and fiercely glad and approving, grew the countenance of the old man at every shout; while the mariners began to gaze curiously at each other, as if marvelling how it was that they themselves became so excited at such seemingly purposeless questions.

But, they were all eagerness again, as Ahab, now half-revolving in his pivot-hole, with one hand reaching high up a shroud, and tightly, almost convulsively grasping it, addressed them thus:—

"All ye mast-headers have before now heard me give orders about a white whale. Look ye! d'ye see this Spanish ounce of gold?"—holding up a broad bright coin to the sun—"it is a sixteen dollar piece, men. D'ye see it? Mr. Starbuck, hand me yon top-maul."

While the mate was getting the hammer, Ahab, without speaking, was slowly rubbing the gold piece against the skirts of his jacket, as if to heighten its lustre, and without using any words was meanwhile lowly humming to himself, producing a sound so strangely muffled and inarticulate that it seemed the mechanical humming of the wheels of his vitality in him.

Receiving the top-maul from Starbuck, he advanced towards the main-mast with the hammer uplifted in one hand, exhibiting the gold with the other, and with a high raised voice exclaiming: "Whosoever of ye raises me a white-headed whale with a wrinkled brow and a crooked jaw; whosoever of ye raises me that white-headed whale, with three holes punctured in his starboard fluke—look ye, whosoever of ye raises me that same white whale, he shall have this gold ounce, my boys!"

"Huzza! huzza!" cried the seamen, as with swinging tarpaulins they hailed the act of nailing the gold to the mast.

"It's a white whale, I say," resumed Ahab, as he threw down the top-maul; "a white whale. Skin your eyes for him, men; look sharp for white water; if ye see but a bubble, sing out."

All this while Tashtego, Daggoo, and Queequeg had looked on with even more interest and surprise than the rest, and at the mention of the wrinkled brow and crooked jaw they had started as if each was separately touched by some specific recollection.

"Captain Ahab," said Tashtego, "that white whale must be the same that some call Moby Dick."

"Moby Dick?" shouted Ahab. "Do ye know the white whale then, Tash?"

"Does he fan-tail a little curious, sir, before he goes down?" said the Gay-Header deliberately.

"And has he a curious spout, too," said Daggoo, "very bushy, even for a parmacetty, and mighty quick, Captain Ahab?"

"And he have one, two, tree—oh! good many iron in him hide, too, Captain," cried Queequeg disjointedly, "all twisketee betwisk, like him—him—" faltering hard for a word, and screwing his hand round and round as though uncorking a bottle—"like him—him—"

"Corkscrew!" cried Ahab, "aye, Queequeg, the harpoons lie all twisted and wrenched in him; aye, Daggoo, his spout is a big one, like a whole shock of wheat, and white as a pile of our Nantucket wool after the great annual sheep-shearing; aye, Tashtego, and he fan-tails like a split jib in a squall. Death and devils! men, it is Moby Dick ye have seen—Moby Dick—Moby Dick!"

"Captain Ahab," said Starbuck, who, with Stubb and Flask, had thus far been eyeing his superior with increasing surprise, but at last seemed struck with a thought which somewhat explained all the wonder. "Captain Ahab, I have heard of Moby Dick—but it was not Moby Dick that took off thy leg?"

"Who told thee that?" cried Ahab; then pausing, "Aye,

Starbuck; aye, my hearties all round; it was Moby Dick that dismasted me; Moby Dick that brought me to this dead stump I stand on now. Aye, aye," he shouted with a terrific, loud, animal sob, like that of a heart-stricken moose; "Aye, aye! it was that accursed white whale that razeed me; made a poor pegging lubber of me for ever and a day!" Then tossing both arms, with measureless imprecations he shouted out: "Aye, aye! and I'll chase him round Good Hope, and round the Horn, and round the Norway Maelstrom, and round perdition's flames before I give him up. And this is what ye have shipped for, men! to chase that white whale on both sides of land, and over all sides of the earth, till he spouts black blood and rolls fin out. What say ye, men, will ye splice hands on it, now? I think ye do look brave."

"Aye, aye!" shouted the harpooneers and seamen, running closer to the excited old man: "A sharp eye for the White Whale; a sharp lance for Moby Dick!"

"God bless ye," he seemed to half sob and half shout. "God bless ye, men. Steward! go draw the great measure of grog. But what's this long face about, Mr. Starbuck; wilt thou not chase the white whale? art not game for Moby Dick?"

"I am game for his crooked jaw, and for the jaws of Death too, Captain Ahab, if it fairly comes in the way of the business we follow; but I came here to hunt whales, not my commander's vengeance. How many barrels will thy vengeance yield thee even if thou gettest it, Captain Ahab? it will not fetch thee much in our Nantucket market."

"Nantucket market! Hoot! But come closer, Starbuck; thou requirest a little lower layer. If money's to be the measurer, man, and the accountants have computed their great countinghouse the globe, by girdling it with guineas, one to every three parts of an inch; then, let me tell thee, that my vengeance will fetch a great premium *here!*"

"He smites his chest," whispered Stubb, "what's that for? methinks it rings most vast, but hollow."

"Vengeance on a dumb brute!" cried Starbuck, "that simply smote thee from blindest instinct! Madness! To be enraged with a dumb thing, Captain Ahab, seems blasphemous."

"Hark ye yet again,—the little lower layer. All visible objects, man, are but as pasteboard masks. But in each event—in the living act, the undoubted deed—there, some unknown but still reasoning thing puts forth the mouldings of its features from behind the unreasoning mask. If man will strike, strike through the mask! How can the prisoner reach outside except by thrusting through the wall? To me, the white whale is that wall, shoved near to me. Sometimes I think there's naught beyond. But 'tis enough. He tasks me; he heaps me; I see in him outrageous strength, with an inscrutable malice sinewing it. That inscrutable thing is chiefly what I hate; and be the white whale agent, or be the white whale principal, I will wreak that hate upon him. Talk not to me of blasphemy, man; I'd strike the sun if it insulted me. For could the sun do that, then could I do the other; since there is ever a sort of fair play herein, jealousy presiding over all creations. But not my master, man, is even that fair play. Who's over me? Truth hath no confines. Take off thine eye! more intolerable than fiends' glarings is a doltish stare! So, so; thou reddenest and palest; my heat has melted thee to anger-glow. But look ye, Starbuck, what is said in heat, that thing unsays itself. There are men from whom warm words are small indignity. I meant not to incense thee. Let it go. Look! see yonder Turkish cheeks of spotted tawn —living, breathing pictures painted by the sun. The Pagan leopards—the unrecking and unworshipping things, that live; and seek, and give no reasons for the torrid life they feel! The crew, man, the crew! Are they not one and all with Ahab, in this matter of the whale? See Stubb! he laughs! See yonder Chilian! he snorts to think of it. Stand up amid the general hurricane, thy one tost sapling cannot, Starbuck! And what is it? Reckon it. 'Tis but to help strike a fin; no wondrous feat for Starbuck. What is it more? From this one poor hunt, then, the best lance out of all Nantucket, surely he will not hang back, when every foremast-hand has clutched a whetstone? Ah! constrainings seize thee; I see! the billow lifts thee! Speak, but speak!—Aye, aye! thy silence, then, *that* voices thee. (*Aside*) Something shot from my dilated nostrils, he has inhaled it in his lungs. Starbuck now is mine; cannot oppose me now, without rebellion."

"God keep me!—keep us all!" murmured Starbuck, lowly.

But in his joy at the enchanted, tacit acquiescence of the mate, Ahab did not hear his foreboding invocation; nor yet the low laugh from the hold; nor yet the presaging vibrations of the winds in the cordage; nor yet the hollow flap of the sails against the masts, as for a moment their hearts sank in. For again Starbuck's downcast eyes lighted up with the stubbornness of life; the subterranean laugh died away; the winds blew on; the sails filled out; the ship heaved and rolled as before. Ah, ye admonitions and warnings! why stay ye not when ye come? But rather are ye predictions than warnings, ye shadows! Yet not so much predictions from without, as verifications of the foregoing things within. For with little external to constrain us, the innermost necessities in our being, these still drive us on.

"The measure! the measure!" cried Ahab.

Receiving the brimming pewter, and turning to the harpooneers, he ordered them to produce their weapons. Then ranging them before him near the capstan, with their harpoons in their hands, while his three mates stood at his side with their lances, and the rest of the ship's company formed a circle round the group; he stood for an instant searchingly eyeing every man of his crew. But those wild eyes met his, as the bloodshot eyes of the prairie wolves meet the eye of their leader, ere he rushes on at their head in the trail of the bison; but, alas! only to fall into the hidden snare of the Indian.

"Drink and pass!" he cried, handing the heavy charged flagon to the nearest seaman. "The crew alone now drink. Round with it, round! Short draughts—long swallows, men; 'tis hot as Satan's hoof. So, so; it goes round excellently. It spiralizes in ye; forks out at the serpent-snapping eye. Well done; almost drained. That way it went, this way it comes. Hand it me—here's a hollow! Men, ye seem the years; so brimming life is gulped and gone. Steward, refill!

"Attend now, my braves. I have mustered ye all round this capstan; and ye mates, flank me with your lances; and ye harpooneers, stand there with your irons; and ye, stout mariners, ring me in, that I may in some sort revive a noble custom of my fisherman fathers before me. O men, you will yet see that—— Ha! boy, come back? bad pennies come not sooner. Hand it me. Why, now, this pewter had run brimming again, wer't not thou St. Vitus' imp—away, thou ague!

"Advance, ye mates! Cross your lances full before me. Well done! Let me touch the axis." So saying, with extended arm, he grasped the three level, radiating lances at their crossed centre; while so doing, suddenly and nervously twitched them; meanwhile, glancing intently from Starbuck to Stubb; from Stubb to Flask. It seemed as though, by some nameless, interior volition, he would fain have shocked into them the same fiery emotion accumulated within the Leyden jar of his own magnetic life. The three mates quailed before his strong, sustained, and mystic aspect. Stubb and Flask looked sideways from him; the honest eye of Starbuck fell downright.

"In vain!" cried Ahab; "but, maybe, 'tis well. For did ye three but once take the full-forced shock, then mine own electric thing, *that* had perhaps expired from out me. Perchance, too, it would have dropped ye dead. Perchance ye need it not. Down lances! And now, ye mates, I do appoint ye three cup-bearers to my three pagan kinsmen there—yon three most honorable gentlemen and noblemen, my valiant harpooneers. Disdain the task? What, when the great Pope washes the feet of beggars, using his tiara for ewer? Oh, my sweet cardinals! your own condescension, *that* shall bend ye to it. I do not order ye; ye will it. Cut your seizings and draw the poles, ye harpooneers!"

Silently obeying the order, the three harpooneers now stood with the detached iron part of their harpoons, some three feet long, held, barbs up, before him.

"Stab me not with that keen steel! Cant them; cant them over! know ye not the goblet end? Turn up the socket! So, so; now, ye cup-bearers, advance. The irons! take them; hold them while I fill!" Forthwith, slowly going from one officer to the other, he brimmed the harpoon sockets with the fiery waters from the pewter.

"Now, three to three, ye stand. Commend the murderous chalices! Bestow them, ye who are now made parties to this indissoluble league. Ha! Starbuck! but the deed is done! Yon ratifying sun now waits to sit upon it. Drink, ye harpooneers! drink and swear, ye men that man the deathful whaleboat's bow—Death to Moby Dick! God hunt us all, if we do not hunt Moby Dick to his death!" The long, barbed steel goblets were lifted; and to cries and maledictions against the white whale, the spirits were simultaneously quaffed down with a hiss. Starbuck paled, and turned, and shivered. Once more, and finally, the replenished pewter went the rounds among the frantic crew; when, waving his free hand to them, they all dispersed; and Ahab retired within his cabin.

SUNSET   **XXXVII**

The cabin; by the stern windows; Ahab sitting alone, and gazing out.

I LEAVE a white and turbid wake; pale waters, paler cheeks, where'er I sail. The envious billows sidelong swell to whelm my track; let them; but first I pass.

Yonder, by the ever-brimming goblet's rim, the warm waves blush like wine. The gold brow plumbs the blue. The diver sun—slow dived from noon,—goes down; my soul mounts up! she wearies with her endless hill. Is, then, the crown too heavy that I wear? this Iron Crown of Lombardy. Yet is it bright with many a gem; I, the wearer, see not its far flashings; but darkly feel that I wear that, that dazzlingly confounds. 'Tis iron—that I know—not gold. 'Tis split, too—that I feel; the jagged edge galls me so, my brain seems to beat against the solid metal; aye, steel skull, mine; the sort that needs no helmet in the most brain-battering fight!

Dry heat upon my brow? Oh! time was, when as the sunrise nobly spurred me, so the sunset soothed. No more. This lovely light, it lights not me; all loveliness is anguish to me, since I can ne'er enjoy. Gifted with the high perception, I lack the low, enjoying power; damned, most subtly and most malignantly! damned in the midst of Paradise! Good night—good night! (*waving his hand, he moves from the window.*)

'Twas not so hard a task. I thought to find one stubborn, at the least; but my one cogged circle fits into all their various wheels, and they revolve. Or, if you will, like so many ant-hills of powder, they all stand before me; and I their match. Oh, hard! that to fire others, the match itself must needs be wasting! What I've dared, I've willed; and what I've willed, I'll do! They think me mad—Starbuck does; but I'm demoniac, I am madness maddened! That wild madness that's only calm to comprehend itself! The prophecy was that I should be dismembered; and—Aye! I lost this leg. I now prophesy that I will dismember my dismemberer. Now, then, be the prophet and the fulfiller one. That's more than ye, ye great gods, ever were. I laugh and hoot at ye, ye cricket-players, ye pugilists, ye deaf Burkes and blinded Bendigoes! I will not say as schoolboys do to bullies,—Take some one of your own size; don't pommel *me!* No, ye've knocked me down, and I am up again; but *ye* have run and hidden. Come forth from behind your cotton bags! I have no long gun to reach ye. Come, Ahab's compliments to ye; come and see if ye can swerve me. Swerve me? ye cannot swerve me, else ye swerve yourselves! man has ye there. Swerve me? The path to my fixed purpose is laid with iron rails, whereon my soul is grooved to run. Over unsounded gorges, through the rifled hearts of mountains, under torrents' beds, unerringly I rush! Naught's an obstacle, naught's an angle to the iron way!

DUSK   **XXXVIII**

By the Mainmast; Starbuck leaning against it.

MY soul is more than matched; she's overmanned; and by a madman! Insufferable sting, that sanity should ground arms on such a field! But he drilled deep down, and blasted all my reason out of me! I think I see his impious end; but feel that I must help him to it. Will I, nill I, the ineffable thing has tied me to him; tows me with a cable I have no knife to cut. Horrible old man! Who's over him, he cries;—aye, he would be a democrat to all above; look, how he lords it over all below! Oh! I plainly see my miserable office, —to obey, rebelling; and worse yet, to hate with touch of pity! For in his eyes I read some lurid woe shrivel me up, had I it. Yet is there hope. Time and tide flow wide. The hated whale has the round watery world to swim in, as the small gold-fish has its glassy globe. His heaven-insulting purpose, God may wedge aside. I would up heart, were it not like lead. But my whole clock's run down; my heart the all-controlling weight, I have no key to lift again.

[*A burst of revelry from the forecastle.*]
Oh, God! to sail with such a heathen crew that have small touch of human mothers in them! Whelped some-

where by the sharkish sea. The white whale is their demi-gorgon. Hark! the infernal orgies! that revelry is forward! mark the unfaltering silence aft! Methinks it pictures life. Foremost through the sparkling sea shoots on the gay, em-battled, bantering bow, but only to drag dark Ahab after it, where he broods within his sternward cabin, builded over the dead water of the wake, and further on, hunted by its wolfish gurglings. The long howl thrills me through! Peace! ye revellers, and set the watch! Oh, life! 'tis in an hour like this, with soul beat down and held to knowl-edge,—as wild, untutored things are forced to feed—Oh, life! 'tis now that I do feel the latent horror in thee! but 'tis not me! that horror's out of me! and with the soft feeling of the human in me, yet will I try to fight ye, ye grim, phantom futures! Stand by me, hold me, bind me, O ye blessed influences!

FIRST NIGHT-WATCH   XXXIX

FORE-TOP

(*Stubb solus, and mending a brace.*)

HA! ha! ha! ha! hem! clear my throat!—I've been think-ing over it ever since, and that ha, ha's the final conse-quence. Why so? Because a laugh's the wisest, easiest an-swer to all that's queer; and come what will, one comfort's always left—that unfailing comfort is, it's all predestinated. I heard not all his talk with Starbuck; but to my poor eye Starbuck then looked something as I the other evening felt. Be sure the old Mogul has fixed him, too. I twigged it, knew it; had had the gift, might readily have prophesied it—for when I clapped my eye upon his skull I saw it. Well, Stubb, *wise* Stubb—that's my title—well, Stubb, what of it, Stubb? Here's a carcase. I know not all that may be coming, but be it what it will, I'll go to it laughing. Such a waggish leering as lurks in all your horribles! I feel funny. Fa, la! lirra, skirra! What's my juicy little pear at home doing now? Cry-ing its eyes out?—Giving a party to the last arrived har-pooneers, I dare say, gay as a frigate's pennant, and so am I —fa, la! lirra, skirra! Oh—

> We'll drink to-night with hearts as light,
>   To love, as gay and fleeting
> As bubbles that swim, on the beaker's brim
>   And break on the lips while meeting.

A brave stave that—who calls? Mr. Starbuck? Aye, aye, sir— (*Aside*) he's my superior, he has his too, if I'm not mistaken.—Aye, aye, sir, just through with this job—coming.

MIDNIGHT, FORECASTLE XL

HARPOONEERS AND SAILORS

(*Foresail rises and discovers the watch standing, lounging, leaning, and lying in various attitudes, all singing in chorus.*)

> Farewell and adieu to you, Spanish ladies!
> Farewell and adieu to you, ladies of Spain!
>   Our captain's commanded.—

1ST NANTUCKET SAILOR

Oh, boys, don't be sentimental; it's bad for the digestion! Take a tonic, follow me!

(*Sings, and all follow.*)

> Our captain stood upon the deck,
>   A spy-glass in his hand,
> A viewing of those gallant whales
>   That blew at every strand.
> Oh, your tubs in your boats, my boys,
>   And by your braces stand,
> And we'll have one of those fine whales,
>   Hand, boys, over hand!
> So, be cheery, my lads! may your hearts never fail!
> While the bold harpooneer is striking the whale!

MATE'S VOICE FROM THE QUARTER-DECK

Eight bells there, forward!

2D NANTUCKET SAILOR

Avast the chorus! Eight bells there! d'ye hear, bell-boy?

Strike the bell eight, thou Pip! thou blackling! and let me call the watch. I've the sort of mouth for that—the hogshead mouth. So, so (*thrusts his head down the scuttle,*) Star—bo—l-e-e-n-s, a-h-o-y! Eight bells there below! Tumble up!

DUTCH SAILOR

Grand snoozing to-night, maty; fat night for that. I mark this in our old Mogul's wine; it's quite as deadening to some as filliping to others. We sing; they sleep—aye, lie down there, like ground-tier butts. At 'em again! There, take this copper-pump, and hail 'em through it. Tell 'em to avast dreaming of their lasses. Tell 'em it's the resurrection; they must kiss their last, and come to judgment. That's the way—*that's* it; thy throat ain't spoiled with eating Amsterdam butter.

FRENCH SAILOR

Hist, boys! let's have a jig or two before we ride to anchor in Blanket Bay. What say ye? There comes the other watch. Stand by all legs! Pip little Pip! hurrah with your tambourine!

PIP

(*Sulky and sleepy.*)
Don't know where it is.

FRENCH SAILOR

Beat thy belly, then, and wag thy ears. Jig it, men, I say; merry's the word; hurrah! Damn me, won't you dance? Form, now, Indian-file, and gallop into the double-shuffle? Throw yourselves! Legs! legs!

ICELAND SAILOR

I don't like your floor, maty; it's too springy to my taste. I'm used to ice-floors. I'm sorry to throw cold water on the subject; but excuse me.

MALTESE SAILOR

Me too; where's your girls? Who but a fool would take his left hand by his right, and say to himself, how d'ye do? Partners! I must have partners!

SICILIAN SAILOR

Aye; girls and a green!—then I'll hop with ye; yea, turn grasshopper!

LONG-ISLAND SAILOR

Well, well, ye sulkies, there's plenty more of us. Hoe corn when you may, say I. All legs go to harvest soon. Ah! here come's the music; now for it!

AZORE SAILOR

(*Ascending, and pitching the tambourine up the scuttle.*)

Here you are, Pip; and there's the windlass-bitts; up you mount! Now, boys!

(*The half of them dance to the tambourine; some go below; some sleep or lie among the coils of rigging. Oaths a-plenty.*)

AZORE SAILOR

(*Dancing.*)

Go it, Pip! Bang it, bell-boy! Rig it, dig it, stig it, quig it, bell-boy; Make fire-flies; break the jinglers!

PIP

Jinglers, you say?—there goes another, dropped off; I pound it so.

CHINA SAILOR

Rattle thy teeth, then, and pound away; make a pagoda of thyself.

FRENCH SAILOR

Merry-mad! Hold up thy hoop, Pip, till I jump through it! Split jibs! tear yourselves!

TASHTEGO

(*Quietly smoking.*)

That's à white man; he calls that fun: humph! I save my sweat.

OLD MANX SAILOR

I wonder whether those jolly lads bethink them of what they are dancing over. I'll dance over your grave, I will— that's the bitterest threat of your night-women, that beat head-winds round corners. O Christ! to think of the green navies and the green-skulled crews! Well, well; belike the whole world's a ball, as you scholars have it; and so 'tis right to make one ballroom of it. Dance on, lads, you're young; I was once.

3D NANTUCKET SAILOR

Spell oh!—whew! this is worse than pulling after whales in a calm—give us a whiff, Tash.

(*They cease dancing, and gather in clusters. Meantime the sky darkens—the wind rises.*)

LASCAR SAILOR

By Brahma! boys, it'll be douse sail soon. The sky-born, high-tide Ganges turned to wind! Thou showest thy black brow, Seeva!

MALTESE SAILOR
(*Reclining and shaking his cap.*)

It's the waves—the snow's caps turn to jig it now. They'll shake their tassels soon. Now would all the waves were women, then I'd go drown, and chassee with them ever-more! There's naught so sweet on earth—heaven may not match it!—as those swift glances of warm, wild bosoms in the dance, when the over-arboring arms hide such ripe, bursting grapes.

SICILIAN SAILOR
(*Reclining.*)

Tell me not of it! Hark ye, lad—fleet interlacings of the limbs—lithe swayings—coyings—flutterings! lip! heart! hip! all graze: unceasing touch and go! not taste, observe ye, else come satiety. Eh, Pagan? (*Nudging.*)

TAHITAN SAILOR
(*Reclining on a mat.*)

Hail, holy nakedness of our dancing girls!—the Heeva-Heeva! Ah! low veiled, high palmed Tahiti! I still rest me on thy mat, but the soft soil has slid! I saw thee woven in the wood, my mat! green the first day I brought ye thence; now worn and wilted quite. Ah me!—not thou nor I can bear the change! How then, if so be transplanted to yon sky? Hear I the roaring streams from Pirohitee's peak of spears, when they leap down the crags and drown the

villages?—The blast! the blast! Up, spine, and meet it!
(*Leaps to his feet.*)

PORTUGUESE SAILOR

How the sea rolls swashing 'gainst the side! Stand by for
reefing, hearties! the winds are just crossing swords, pell-mell
they'll go lunging presently.

DANISH SAILOR

Crack, crack, old ship! so long as thou crackest, thou
holdest! Well done! The mate there holds ye to it stiffly.
He's no more afraid than the isle fort at Cattegat, put there
to fight the Baltic with storm-lashed guns, on which the sea-
salt cakes!

4TH NANTUCKET SAILOR

He has his orders, mind ye that. I heard old Ahab tell
him he must always kill a squall, something as they burst a
waterspout with a pistol—fire your ship right into it!

ENGLISH SAILOR

Blood! but that old man's a grand old cove! We are the
lads to hunt him up his whale!

ALL

Aye! aye!

OLD MANX SAILOR

How the three pines shake! Pines are the hardest sort of
tree to live when shifted to any other soil, and here there's
none but the crew's cursed clay. Steady, helmsman! steady.
This is the sort of weather when brave hearts snap ashore,
and keeled hulls split at sea. Our captain has his birth-mark;
look yonder, boys, there's another in the sky—lurid-like, ye
see, all else pitch black.

DAGGOO

What of that? Who's afraid of black's afraid of me! I'm
quarried out of it!

SPANISH SAILOR

(*Aside.*) He wants to bully, ah!—the old grudge makes me
touchy. (*Advancing.*) Aye, harpooneer, thy race is the unde-

niable dark side of mankind—devilish dark at that. No offence.

DAGGOO (*grimly*)

None.

ST. JAGO'S SAILOR

That Spaniard's mad or drunk. But that can't be, or else in his one case our old Mogul's fire-waters are somewhat long in working.

5TH NANTUCKET SAILOR

What's that I saw—lightning? Yes.

SPANISH SAILOR

No; Daggoo showing his teeth.

DAGGOO (*springing*)

Swallow thine, mannikin! White skin, white liver!

SPANISH SAILOR (*meeting him*)

Knife thee heartily! big frame, small spirit!

ALL

A row! a row! a row!

TASHTEGO (*with a whiff*)

A row a'low, and a row aloft—Gods and men—both brawlers! Humph!

BELFAST SAILOR

A row! arrah a row! The Virgin be blessed, a row! Plunge in with ye!

ENGLISH SAILOR

Fair play! Snatch the Spaniard's knife! A ring, a ring!

OLD MANX SAILOR

Ready formed. There! the ringed horizon. In that ring Cain struck Abel. Sweet work, right work! No? Why then, God, mad'st thou the ring?

MATE'S VOICE FROM THE QUARTER DECK

Hands by the halyards! in top-gallant sails! Stand by to reef topsails!

ALL

The squall! the squall! jump, my jollies! (*They scatter.*)

PIP (*shrinking under the windlass*)

Jollies? Lord help such jollies! Crish, crash! there goes the jib-stay! Blang-whang! God! Duck lower, Pip, here comes the royal yard! It's worse than being in the whirled woods, the last day of the year! Who'd go climbing after chestnuts now? But there they go, all cursing, and here I don't. Fine prospects to 'em; they're on the road to heaven. Hold on hard! Jimmini, what a squall! But those chaps there are worse yet—they are your white squalls, they. White squalls? white whale, shirr! shirr! Here have I heard all their chat just now, and the white whale—shirr! shirr!—but spoken of once! and only this evening—it makes me jingle all over like my tambourine—that anaconda of an old man swore 'em in to hunt him! Oh, thou big white God aloft there somewhere in yon darkness, have mercy on this small black boy down here; preserve him from all men that have no bowels to feel fear!

* * * * *

MOBY DICK   XLI

I, ISHMAEL, was one of that crew; my shouts had gone up with the rest; my oath had been welded with theirs; and stronger I shouted, and more did I hammer and clinch my oath, because of the dread in my soul. A wild, mystical, sympathetical feeling was in me; Ahab's quenchless feud seemed mine. With greedy ears I learned the history of that murderous monster against whom I and all the others had taken our oaths of violence and revenge.

For some time past, though at intervals only, the unaccompanied, secluded White Whale had haunted those uncivilized seas mostly frequented by the Sperm Whale fishermen. But not all of them knew of his existence; only a few of them, comparatively, had knowingly seen him; while the number who as yet had actually and knowingly given battle to him, was small indeed. For, owing to the large number of whale-cruisers; the disorderly way they were sprinkled over the entire watery circumference, many of them adventurously pushing their quest along solitary latitudes, so as seldom or never for a whole twelvemonth or more on a stretch, to encounter a single newstelling sail of any sort; the inordinate length of each separate voyage; the irregularity of the time of sailing from home; all these, with other circumstances, direct and indirect, long obstructed the spread through the whole world-wide whaling-fleet of the special individualizing tidings concerning Moby Dick. It was hardly to be doubted, that several vessels reported to have encountered, at such or such a time, or on such or such a meridian, a Sperm Whale of uncommon magnitude and malignity, which whale, after doing great mischief to his assailants, had completely escaped them; to some minds it was not an unfair presumption, I say, that the whale in question must have been no other than Moby Dick. Yet as of late the Sperm Whale fishery had been marked by various and not infrequent instances of great ferocity, cunning, and malice in the monster attacked; therefore it was, that those who by accident ignorantly gave battle to Moby Dick; such hunters, perhaps, for the most part, were content to ascribe the peculiar terror he bred, more, as it were, to the perils of the Sperm Whale fishery at large, than to the individual cause. In that way, mostly, the disastrous encounter between Ahab and the whale had hitherto been popularly regarded.

And as for those who, previously hearing of the White Whale, by chance caught sight of him; in the beginning of the thing they had every one of them, almost, as boldly and fearlessly lowered for him, as for any other whale of that species. But at length, such calamities did ensue in these assaults—not restricted to sprained wrists and ankles, broken limbs, or devouring amputations—but fatal to the last degree of fatality; those repeated disastrous repulses, all accumulating and piling their terrors upon Moby Dick; those things had gone far to shake the fortitude of many brave hunters, to whom the story of the White Whale had eventually come.

Nor did wild rumors of all sorts fail to exaggerate, and still the more horrify the true histories of these deadly encounters. For not only do fabulous rumors naturally grow out of the very body of all surprising terrible events,—as the smitten tree gives birth to its fungi; but, in maritime life, far more than in that of terra firma, wild rumors abound, wherever there is any adequate reality for them to cling to. And as the sea surpasses the land in this matter, so the whale fishery surpasses every other sort of maritime life, in the wonderfulness and fearfulness of the rumors which sometimes circulate there. For not only are whalemen as a body unexempt from that ignorance and superstitiousness hereditary to all sailors; but of all sailors, they are by all odds the most directly brought into contact with whatever is appallingly astonishing in the sea; face to face they not only eye its greatest marvels, but, hand to jaw, give battle to them. Alone, in such remotest waters, that though you sailed a thousand miles, and passed a thousand shores, you would not come to any chiselled hearthstone, or aught hospitable beneath that part of the sun; in such latitudes and longitudes, pursuing too such a calling as he does, the whaleman is wrapped by influences all tending to make his fancy pregnant with many a mighty birth.

No wonder, then, that ever gathering volume from the mere transit over the widest watery spaces, the outblown rumors of the White Whale did in the end incorporate with themselves all manner of morbid hints, and half-formed foetal suggestions of supernatural agencies, which eventually invested Moby Dick with new terrors unborrowed from anything that visibly appears. So that in many cases such a panic did he finally strike, that few who by those rumors, at least, had heard of the White Whale, few of those hunters were willing to encounter the perils of his jaw.

But there were still other and more vital practical influences at work. Not even at the present day has the original prestige of the Sperm Whale, as fearfully distinguished from all other species of the leviathan, died out of the minds of the whalemen as a body. There are those this day among them, who, though intelligent and courageous enough in offering battle to the Greenland or Right whale, would perhaps—either from professional inexperience, or incompetency, or timidity, decline a contest with the Sperm Whale; at any rate, there are plenty of whalemen, especially among those whaling nations not sailing under the American flag, who have never hostilely encountered the Sperm Whale, but whose sole knowledge of the leviathan is restricted to the ignoble monster primitively pursued in the North; seated on their hatches, these men will hearken with a childish fireside interest and awe, to the wild, strange tales of Southern whaling. Nor is the pre-eminent tremendousness of the great Sperm Whale anywhere more feelingly comprehended, than on board of those prows which stem him.

And as if the now tested reality of his might had in former legendary times thrown its shadow before it; we find some book naturalists—Olassen and Povelson—declaring the Sperm Whale not only to be a consternation to every other creature in the sea, but also to be so incredibly ferocious as continually to be athirst for human blood. Nor even down to so late a time as Cuvier's, were these or almost similar impressions effaced. For in his Natural History, the Baron himself affirms that at sight of the Sperm Whale, all fish (sharks included) are "struck with the most lively terrors," and "often in the precipitancy of their flight dash themselves against the rocks with such violence as to cause instantaneous death." And however the general experiences in the fishery may amend such reports as these; yet in their full terribleness, even to the bloodthirsty item of Povelson, the superstitious belief in them is, in some vicissitudes of their vocation, revived in the minds of the hunters.

So that overawed by the rumors and portents concerning him, not a few of the fishermen recalled, in reference to Moby Dick, the earlier days of the Sperm Whale fishery, when it was oftentimes hard to induce long practised Right whalemen to embark in the perils of this new and daring warfare; such men protesting that although other leviathans might be hopefully pursued, yet to chase and point lance at such an apparition as the Sperm Whale was not for mortal man. That to attempt it, would be inevitably to be torn into a quick eternity. On this head, there are some remarkable documents that may be consulted.

Nevertheless, some there were, who even in the face of these things were ready to give chase to Moby Dick; and a still greater number who, chancing only to hear of him distantly and vaguely, without the specific details of any certain calamity, and without superstitious accompaniments, were sufficiently hardy not to flee from the battle if offered.

One of the wild suggestings referred to, as at last coming to be linked with the White Whale in the minds of the superstitiously inclined, was the unearthly conceit that Moby Dick was ubiquitous; that he had actually been encountered in opposite latitudes at one and the same instant of time.

Nor, credulous as such minds must have been, was this conceit altogether without some faint show of superstitious probability. For as the secrets of the currents in the seas have never yet been divulged, even to the most erudite research; so the hidden ways of the Sperm Whale when beneath the surface remain, in great part, unaccountable to his pursuers; and from time to time have originated the most curious and contradictory speculations regarding them, especially concerning the mystic modes whereby, after sounding to a great depth, he transports himself with such vast swiftness to the most widely distant points.

It is a thing well known to both American and English whaleships, and as well a thing placed upon authoritative record years ago by Scoresby, that some whales have been captured far north in the Pacific, in whose bodies have been found the barbs of harpoons darted in the Greenland seas. Nor is it to be gainsaid, that in some of these instances it has been declared that the interval of time between the two assaults could not have exceeded very many days. Hence, by inference, it has been believed by some whalemen, that the Nor' West Passage, so long a problem to man, was never a problem to the whale. So that here, in the real living experience of living men, the prodigies related in old times of the inland Strello mountain in Portugal (near whose top there was said to be a lake in which the wrecks of ships floated up to the surface); and that still more wonderful story of the Arethusa fountain near Syracuse (whose waters were believed to have come from the Holy Land by an underground passage); these fabulous narrations are almost fully equalled by the realities of the whaleman.

Forced into familiarity, then, with such prodigies as these; and knowing that after repeated, intrepid assaults, the White Whale had escaped alive; it cannot be much matter of surprise that some whalemen should go still further in their superstitions; declaring Moby Dick not only ubiquitous, but immortal (for immortality is but ubiquity in time); that though groves of spears should be planted in his flanks, he would still swim away unharmed; or if indeed he should ever be made to spout thick blood, such a sight would be but a ghastly deception; for again in unensanguined billows hundreds of leagues away, his unsullied jet would once more be seen.

But even stripped of these supernatural surmisings, there was enough in the earthly make and incontestable character of the monster to strike the imagination with unwonted power. For, it was not so much his uncommon bulk that so much distinguished him from other sperm whales, but, as was elsewhere thrown out—a peculiar snow-white wrinkled forehead, and a high, pyramidical white hump. These were his prominent features; the tokens whereby, even in the limitless, uncharted seas, he revealed his identity, at a long distance, to those who knew him.

The rest of his body was so streaked, and spotted, and marbled with the same shrouded hue, that, in the end, he had gained his distinctive appellation of the White Whale; a name, indeed, literally justified by his vivid aspect, when seen gliding at high noon through a dark blue sea, leaving a milky-way wake of creamy foam, all spangled with golden gleamings.

Nor was it unwonted magnitude, nor his remarkable hue, nor yet his deformed lower jaw, that so much invested the whale with natural terror, as that unexampled, intelligent malignity which, according to specific accounts, he had over and over again evinced in his assaults. More than all, his treacherous retreats struck more of dismay than perhaps aught else. For, when swimming before his exulting pursuers, with every apparent symptom of alarm, he had several times been known to turn round suddenly, and, bearing down upon them, either stave their boats to splinters, or drive them back in consternation to their ship.

Already several fatalities had attended his chase. But though similar disasters, however little bruited ashore, were by no means unusual in the fishery; yet, in most instances, such seemed the White Whale's infernal aforethought of ferocity, that every dismembering or death that he caused, was not wholly regarded as having been inflicted by an unintelligent agent.

Judge, then, to what pitches of inflamed, distracted fury the minds of his more desperate hunters were impelled, when amid the chips of chewed boats, and the sinking limbs of torn comrades, they swam out of the white curds of the whale's direful wrath into the serene, exasperating sunlight, that smiled on, as if at a birth or a bridal.

His three boats stove around him, and oars and men both whirling in the eddies; one captain, seizing the line-knife from his broken prow, had dashed at the whale, as an Arkansas duellist at his foe, blindly seeking with a six inch blade to reach the fathom-deep life of the whale. That captain was Ahab. And then it was, that suddenly sweeping his sickle-shaped lower jaw beneath him, Moby Dick had reaped away Ahab's leg, as a mower a blade of grass in the field. No turbaned Turk, no hired Venetian or Malay, could have smote him with more seeming malice. Small reason was there to doubt, then, that ever since that almost fatal encounter, Ahab had cherished a wild vindictiveness against the whale, all the more fell for that in his frantic morbidness he at last came to identify with him, not only all his bodily woes, but all his intellectual and spiritual exasperations. The White Whale swam before him as the monomaniac incarnation of all those malicious agencies which some deep men feel eating in them, till they are left living on with half a heart and half a lung. That intangible malignity which has been from the beginning; to whose dominion even the modern Christians ascribe one-half of the worlds; which the ancient Ophites of the east reverenced in their statue devil; —Ahab did not fall down and worship it like them; but deliriously transferring its idea to the abhorred white whale, he pitted himself, all mutilated, against it. All that most maddens and torments; all that stirs up the lees of things; all truth with malice in it; all that cracks the sinews and cakes the brain; all the subtle demonisms of life and thought; all evil, to crazy Ahab, were visibly personified, and made practically assailable in Moby Dick. He piled upon the whale's white hump the sum of all the general rage and hate felt by his whole race from Adam down; and then, as if his chest had been a mortar, he burst his hot heart's shell upon it.

It is not probable that this monomania in him took its instant rise at the precise time of his bodily dismemberment. Then, in darting at the monster, knife in hand, he had but given loose to a sudden, passionate, corporal animosity; and when he received the stroke that tore him, he probably but felt the agonizing bodily laceration, but nothing more. Yet, when by this collision forced to turn towards home, and for long months of days and weeks, Ahab and anguish lay stretched together in one hammock, rounding in mid winter that dreary, howling Patagonian Cape; then it was, that his torn body and gashed soul bled into one another; and so interfusing, made him mad. That it was only then, on the homeward voyage, after the encounter, that the final monomania seized him, seems all but certain from the fact that, at intervals during the passage, he was a raving lunatic; and, though unlimbed of a leg, yet such vital strength yet lurked in his Egyptian chest, and was moreover intensified by his delirium, that his mates were forced to lace him fast, even there, as he sailed, raving in his hammock. In a strait-jacket, he swung to the mad rockings of the gales. And, when running into more sufferable latitudes, the ship, with mild stun'sails spread, floated across the tranquil tropics, and, to all appearances, the old man's delirium seemed left behind him with the Cape Horn swells, and he came forth from his dark den into the blessed light and air; even then, when he bore that firm, collected front, however pale, and issued his calm orders once again; and his mates thanked God the direful madness was now gone; even then, Ahab, in his hidden self, raved on. Human madness is oftentimes a cunning and most feline thing. When you think it fled, it may have but become transfigured into some still subtler form. Ahab's full lunacy subsided not, but deepeningly contracted; like the unabated Hudson, when that noble Northman flows narrowly, but unfathomably through the Highland gorge. But, as in his narrow-flowing monomania, not one jot of Ahab's broad madness had been left behind; so in that broad madness, not one jot of his great natural intellect had perished. That before living agent, now became the living instrument. If such a furious trope may stand, his special lunacy stormed his general sanity, and carried it, and turned all its concentrated cannon upon its own mad mark; so that far from having lost his strength, Ahab, to that one end, did now possess a thousand fold more potency than ever he had sanely brought to bear upon any one reasonable object.

This is much; yet Ahab's larger, darker, deeper part remains unhinted. But vain to popularize profundities, and all truth is profound. Winding far down from within the very heart of this spiked Hotel de Cluny where we here stand—however grand and wonderful, now quit it;—and take your way, ye nobler, sadder souls, to those vast Roman halls of Thermes; where far beneath the fantastic towers of man's upper earth, his root of grandeur, his whole awful essence sits in bearded state; an antique buried beneath antiquities, and throned on torsoes! So with a broken throne, the great gods mock that captive king; so like a Caryatid, he patient sits, upholding on his frozen brow the piled entablatures of ages. Wind ye down there, ye prouder, sadder souls! question that proud, sad king! A family likeness! aye, he did beget ye, ye young exiled royalties; and from your grim sire only will the old State-secret come.

Now, in his heart, Ahab had some glimpse of this, namely: all my means are sane, my motive and my object mad. Yet without power to kill, or change, or shun the fact; he likewise knew that to mankind he did long dissemble; in some sort, did still. But that thing of his dissembling was only subject to his perceptibility, not to his will determinate. Nevertheless, so well did he succeed in that dissembling, that when with ivory leg he stepped ashore at last, no Nantucketer thought him otherwise than but naturally grieved, and that to the quick, with the terrible casualty which had overtaken him.

The report of his undeniable delirium at sea was likewise popularly ascribed to a kindred cause. And so too, all the added moodiness which always afterwards, to the very day of sailing in the Pequod on the present voyage, sat brooding on his brow. Nor is it so very unlikely, that far from distrusting his fitness for another whaling voyage, on account of such dark symptoms, the calculating people of that prudent isle were inclined to harbor the conceit, that for those very reasons he was all the better qualified and set on edge, for a pursuit so full of rage and wildness as the bloody hunt of whales. Gnawed within and scorched without, with the infixed, unrelenting fangs of some incurable idea; such an one, could he be found, would seem the very man to dart his iron and lift his lance against the most appalling of all brutes. Or, if for any reason thought to be corporeally incapacitated for that, yet such an one would seem superlatively competent to cheer and howl on his underlings to the attack. But be all this as it may, certain it is, that with the mad secret of his unabated rage bolted up and keyed in him, Ahab had purposely sailed upon the present voyage with the one only and all-engrossing object of hunting the White Whale. Had any one of his old acquaintances on shore but half dreamed of what was lurking in him then, how soon would their aghast and righteous souls have wrenched the ship from such a fiendish man! They were bent on profitable cruises, the profit to be counted down in dollars from the mint. He was intent on an audacious, immitigable, and supernatural revenge.

Here, then, was this grey-headed, ungodly old man, chasing with curses a Job's whale round the world, at the head of a crew, too, chiefly made up of mongrel renegades, and castaways, and cannibals—morally enfeebled also, by the incompetence of mere unaided virtue or right-mindedness in Starbuck, the invulnerable jollity of indifference and recklessness in Stubb, and the pervading mediocrity in Flask. Such a crew, so officered, seemed specially picked and packed by some infernal fatality to help him to his monomaniac revenge. How it was that they so aboundingly responded to the old man's ire—by what evil magic their souls were possessed, that at times his hate seemed almost theirs; the White Whale as much their insufferable foe as his; how all this came to be—what the White Whale was to them, or how to their unconscious understandings, also, in some dim, unsuspected way, he might have seemed the gliding great demon of the seas of life,—all this to explain, would be to dive deeper than Ishmael can go. The subterranean miner that works in us all, how can one tell whither leads his shaft by the ever shifting, muffled sound of his pick? Who does not feel the irresistible arm drag? What skiff in tow of a seventy-four can still? For one, I gave myself up to the abandonment of the time and the place; but while yet all a-rush to encounter the whale, could see naught in that brute but the deadliest ill.

THE WHITENESS OF THE WHALE   XLII

WHAT the white whale was to Ahab, has been hinted; what, at times, he was to me, as yet remains unsaid.

Aside from those more obvious considerations touching Moby Dick, which could not but occasionally awaken in any man's soul some alarm, there was another thought, or rather vague, nameless horror concerning him, which at times by its intensity completely overpowered all the rest; and yet so mystical and well nigh ineffable was it, that I almost despair of putting it in a comprehensible form. It was the whiteness of the whale that above all things appalled me. But how can I hope to explain myself here; and yet, in some dim, random way, explain myself I must, else all these chapters might be naught.

Though in many natural objects, whiteness refiningly enhances beauty, as if imparting some special virtue of its own, as in marbles, japonicas, and pearls; and though various nations have in some way recognised a certain royal preeminence in this hue; even the barbaric, grand old kings of Pegu placing the title "Lord of the White Elephants" above all their other magniloquent ascriptions of dominion; and the modern kings of Siam unfurling the same snowy-white quadruped in the royal standard; and the Hanoverian flag bearing the one figure of a snow-white charger; and the great Austrian Empire, Cæsarian, heir to overlording Rome, having for the imperial color the same imperial hue; and though this pre-eminence in it applies to the human race itself, giving the white man ideal mastership over every dusky tribe; and though, besides all this, whiteness has been even made significant of gladness, for among the Romans a white stone marked a joyful day; and though in other mortal sympathies and symbolizings, this same hue is made the emblem of many touching, noble things—the innocence of brides, the benignity of age; though among the Red Men of America the giving of the white belt of wampum was the deepest pledge of honor; though in many climes, whiteness typifies the majesty of Justice in the ermine of the Judge, and contributes to the daily state of kings and queens drawn by milk-white steeds; though even in the higher mysteries of the most august religions it has been made the symbol of the divine spotlessness and power; by the Persian fire worshippers, the white forked flame being held the holiest on the altar; and in the Greek mythologies, Great Jove himself being made incarnate in a snow-white bull; and though to the noble Iroquois, the midwinter sacrifice of the sacred White Dog was by far the holiest festival of their theology, that spotless, faithful creature being held the purest envoy they could send to the Great Spirit with the annual tidings of their own fidelity; and though directly from the Latin word for white, all Christian priests derive the name of one part of their sacred vesture, the alb or tunic, worn beneath the cassock; and though among the holy pomps of the Romish faith, white is specially employed in the celebration of the Passion of our Lord; though in the Vision of St. John, white robes are given to the redeemed, and the four-and-twenty elders stand clothed in white before the great white throne, and the Holy One that sitteth there white like wool; yet for all these accumulated associations, with whatever is sweet, and honorable, and sublime, there yet lurks an elusive something in the innermost idea of this hue, which strikes more of panic to the soul than that redness which affrights in blood.

This elusive quality it is, which causes the thought of whiteness, when divorced from more kindly associations, and coupled with any object terrible in itself, to heighten that terror to the furthest bounds. Witness the white bear of the poles, and the white shark of the tropics; what but their smooth, flaky whiteness makes them the transcendent horrors they are? That ghastly whiteness it is which imparts such an abhorrent mildness, even more loathsome than terrific, to the dumb gloating of their aspect. So that not the fierce-fanged tiger in his heraldic coat can so stagger courage as the white-shrouded bear or shark.*

Bethink thee of the albatross, whence come those clouds of spiritual wonderment and pale dread, in which that white phantom sails in all imaginations? Not Coleridge first threw that spell; but God's great, unflattering laureate, Nature.**

* With reference to the Polar bear, it may possibly be urged by him who would fain go still deeper into this matter, that it is not the whiteness, separately regarded, which heightens the intolerable hideousness of that brute; for, analysed, that heightened hideousness, it might be said, only arises from the circumstance, that the irresponsible ferociousness of the creature stands invested in the fleece of celestial innocence and love; and hence, by bringing together two such opposite emotions in our minds, the Polar bear frightens us with so unnatural a contrast. But even assuming all this to be true; yet, were it not for the whiteness, you would not have that intensified terror.

As for the white shark, the white gliding ghostliness of repose in that creature, when beheld in his ordinary moods, strangely tallies with the same quality in the Polar quadruped. This peculiarity is most vividly hit by the French in the name they bestow upon that fish. The Romish mass for the dead begins with "Requiem eternam" (eternal rest), whence *Requiem* denominating the mass itself, and any other funereal music. Now, in allusion to the white, silent stillness of death in this shark, and the mild deadliness of his habits, the French call him *Requin*.

** I remember the first albatross I ever saw. It was during a prolonged gale, in waters hard upon the Antarctic seas. From my forenoon watch below, I ascended to the overclouded deck; and there, dashed upon the main hatches, I saw a regal, feathery thing of unspotted whiteness, and with a hooked, Roman bill sublime. At intervals, it arched forth its vast archangel wings, as if to embrace some holy ark. Wondrous flutterings and throbbings shook it. Though bodily unharmed, it uttered cries, as some king's ghost in supernatural distress. Through its inexpressible, strange eyes, methought I peeped to secrets which took hold of God. As Abraham before the angels, I bowed myself; the white thing was so white, its wings so wide, and in those for ever exiled waters, I had lost the miserable warping memories of traditions and of towns. Long I gazed at that prodigy of plumage. I cannot tell, can only hint, the things that darted through me then. But at last I awoke; and turning, asked a sailor what bird was this. A goney, he replied. Goney! I never had heard that name before; is it conceivable that this glorious thing is utterly unknown to men ashore! never! But some time after, I learned that goney was some seaman's name for albatross. So that by no possibility could Coleridge's wild Rhyme have had aught to

Most famous in our Western annals and Indian traditions is that of the White Steed of the Prairies; a magnificent milk-white charger, large-eyed, small-headed, bluff-chested, and with the dignity of a thousand monarchs in his lofty, over-scorning carriage. He was the elected Xerxes of vast herds of wild horses, whose pastures in those days were only fenced by the Rocky Mountains and the Alleghanies. At their flaming head he westward trooped it like that chosen star which every evening leads on the hosts of light. The flashing cascade of his mane, the curving comet of his tail, invested him with housings more resplendent than gold and silver-beaters could have furnished him. A most imperial and archangelical apparition of that unfallen, western world, which to the eyes of the old trappers and hunters revived the glories of those primeval times when Adam walked majestic as a god, bluff-bowed and fearless as this mighty steed. Whether marching amid his aides and marshals in the van of countless cohorts that endlessly streamed it over the plains, like an Ohio; or whether with his circumambient subjects browsing all around at the horizon, the White Steed gallopingly reviewed them with warm nostrils reddening through his cool milkiness in whatever aspect he presented himself, always to the bravest Indians he was the object of trembling reverence and awe. Nor can it be questioned from what stands on legendary record of this noble horse, that it was his spiritual whiteness chiefly, which so clothed him with divineness; and that this divineness had that in it which, though commanding worship, at the same time enforced a certain nameless terror.

---

do with those mystical impressions which were mine, when I saw that bird upon our deck. For neither had I then read the Rhyme, nor knew the bird to be an albatross. Yet, in saying this, I do but indirectly burnish a little brighter the noble merit of the poem and the poet.

I assert, then, that in the wondrous bodily whiteness of the bird chiefly lurks the secret of the spell; a truth the more evinced in this, that by a solecism of terms there are birds called grey albatrosses; and these I have frequently seen, but never with such emotions as when I beheld the Antarctic fowl.

But how had the mystic thing been caught? Whisper it not, and I will tell; with a treacherous hook and line, as the fowl floated on the sea. At last the Captain made a postman of it; tying a lettered, leathern tally round its neck, with the ship's time and place; and then letting it escape. But I doubt not, that leathern tally, meant for man, was taken off in Heaven, when the white fowl flew to join the wing-folding, the invoking, and adoring cherubim!

But there are other instances where this whiteness loses all that accessory and strange glory which invests it in the White Steed and Albatross.

What is it that in the Albino man so peculiarly repels and often shocks the eye, as that sometimes he is loathed by his own kith and kin! It is that whiteness which invests him, a thing expressed by the name he bears. The Albino is as well made as other men—has no substantive deformity—and yet this mere aspect of all-pervading whiteness makes him more strangely hideous than the ugliest abortion. Why should this be so?

Nor, in quite other aspects, does Nature in her least palpable but not the less malicious agencies, fail to enlist among her forces this crowning attribute of the terrible. From its snowy aspect, the gauntleted ghost of the Southern Seas has been denominated the White Squall. Nor, in some historic instances, has the art of human malice omitted so potent an auxiliary. How wildly it heightens the effect on that passage in Froissart, when, masked in the snowy symbol of their faction, the desperate White Hoods of Ghent murder their bailiff in the market-place!

Nor, in some things, does the common, hereditary experience of all mankind fail to bear witness to the supernaturalism of this hue. It cannot well be doubted, that the one visible quality in the aspect of the dead which most appals the gazer, is the marble pallor lingering there; as if indeed that pallor were as much like the badge of consternation in the other world, as of mortal trepidation here. And from that pallor of the dead, we borrow the expressive hue of the shroud in which we wrap them. Nor even in our superstitions do we fail to throw the same snowy mantle round our phantoms; all ghosts rising in a milk-white fog—Yea, while these terrors seize us, let us add, that even the king of terrors, when personified by the evangelist, rides on his pallid horse.

Therefore, in his other moods, symbolize whatever grand or gracious thing he will by whiteness, no man can deny that in its profoundest idealized significance it calls up a peculiar apparition to the soul.

But though without dissent this point be fixed, how is mortal man to account for it? To analyse it, would seem impossible. Can we, then, by the citation of some of those instances wherein this thing of whiteness—though for the time either wholly or in great part stripped of all direct associations calculated to impart to it aught fearful, but, nevertheless, is found to exert over us the same sorcery, however modified;—can we thus hope to light upon some chance clue to conduct us to the hidden cause we seek?

Let us try. But in a matter like this, subtlety appeals to subtlety, and without imagination no man can follow another into these halls. And though, doubtless, some at least of the imaginative impressions about to be presented may have been shared by most men, yet few perhaps were entirely conscious of them at the time, and therefore may not be able to recall them now.

Why to the man of untutored ideality, who happens to be but loosely acquainted with the peculiar character of the day, does the bare mention of Whitsuntide marshal in the fancy such long, dreary, speechless processions of slow-pacing pilgrims, downcast and hooded with new-fallen snow? Or, to the unread, unsophisticated Protestant of the Middle American States, why does the passing mention of a White Friar or a White Nun, evoke such an eyeless statue in the soul?

Or what is there apart from the traditions of dungeoned warriors and kings (which will not wholly account for it) that makes the White Tower of London tell so much more strongly on the imagination of an untravelled American, than those other storied structures, its neighbors—the Byward Tower, or even the Bloody? And those sublimer towers, the White Mountains of New Hampshire, whence, in peculiar moods, comes that gigantic ghostliness over the soul at the bare mention of that name, while the thought of Virginia's Blue Ridge is full of a soft, dewy, distant dreaminess? Or why, irrespective of all latitudes and longitudes, does the name of the White Sea exert such a spectralness over the fancy, while that of the Yellow Sea lulls us with mortal thoughts of long lacquered mild afternoons on the waves, followed by the gaudiest and yet sleepiest of sunsets? Or, to choose a wholly unsubstantial instance, purely addressed to the fancy, why, in reading the old fairy tales of Central Europe, does "the tall pale man" of the Hartz forests, whose changeless pallor unrustingly glides through the green of the groves—why is this phantom more terrible than all the whooping imps of the Blocksburg?

Nor is it, altogether, the remembrance of her cathedral-toppling earthquakes; nor the stampedoes of her frantic seas; nor the tearlessness of arid skies that never rain; nor the sight of her wide field of learning spires, wrenched copestones, and crosses all adroop (like canted yards of anchored fleets); and her suburban avenues of housewalls lying over upon each other, as a tossed pack of cards;—it is not these things alone which make tearless Lima, the strangest, saddest city thou can'st see. For Lima has taken the white veil; and there is a higher horror in this whiteness of her woe. Old as Pizarro, this whiteness keeps her ruins for ever new; admits not the cheerful greenness of complete decay; spreads over her broken ramparts the rigid pallor of an apoplexy that fixes its own distortions.

I know that, to the common apprehension, this phenomenon of whiteness is not confessed to be the prime agent in exaggerating the terror of objects otherwise terrible; nor to the unimaginative mind is there aught of terror in those appearances whose awfulness to another mind almost solely consists in this one phenomenon, especially when exhibited under any form at all approaching to muteness or universality. What I mean by these two statements may perhaps be respectively elucidated by the following examples.

First: The mariner, when drawing nigh the coasts of foreign lands, if by night he hear the roar of breakers, starts to vigilance, and feels just enough of trepidation to sharpen all his faculties; but under precisely similar circumstances, let him be called from his hammock to view his ship sailing through a midnight sea of milky whiteness—as if from encircling headlands shoals of combed white bears were swimming round him, then he feels a silent, superstitious dread; the shrouded phantom of the whitened waters is horrible to him as a real ghost; in vain the lead assures him he is still off soundings; heart and helm they both go down; he never rests till blue water is under him again. Yet where is the mariner who will tell thee, "Sir, it was not so much the fear of striking hidden rocks, as the fear of that hideous whiteness that so stirred me?"

Second: To the native Indian of Peru, the continual sight of the snow-howdahed Andes conveys naught of dread, except, perhaps in the mere fancying of the eternal frosted desolateness reigning at such vast altitudes, and the natural conceit of what a fearfulness it would be to lose oneself in such inhuman solitudes. Much the same is it with the backwoodsman of the West, who with comparative indifference views an unbounded prairie sheeted with driven snow, no shadow of tree or twig to break the fixed trance of whiteness. Not so the sailor, beholding the scenery of the Antarctic seas; where at times, by some infernal trick of legerdemain in the powers of frost and air, he, shivering and half shipwrecked, instead of rainbows speaking hope and solace to his misery, views what seems a boundless church-yard grinning upon him with its lean ice monuments and splintered crosses.

But thou sayest, methinks this white-lead chapter about whiteness is but a white flag hung out from a craven soul; thou surrenderest to a hypo, Ishmael.

Tell me, why this strong young colt, foaled in some peaceful valley of Vermont, far removed from all beasts of prey—why is it that upon the sunniest day, if you but shake a fresh buffalo robe behind him, so that he cannot even see it, but only smells its wild animal muskiness—why will he start, snort, and with bursting eyes paw the ground in phrensies of affright? There is no remembrance in him of any gorings of wild creatures in his green northern home, so that the strange muskiness he smells cannot recall to him anything associated with the experience of former perils; for what knows he, this New England colt, of the black bisons of distant Oregon?

No: but here thou beholdest even in a dumb brute, the instinct of the knowledge of the demonism in the world. Though thousands of miles from Oregon, still when he smells that savage musk, the rending, goring bison herds are as present as to the deserted wild foal of the prairies, which this instant they may be trampling into dust.

Thus, then, the muffled rollings of a milky sea; the bleak rustlings of the festooned frosts of mountains; the desolate shiftings of the windrowed snows of prairies; all these, to Ishmael, are as the shaking of that buffalo robe to the frightened colt!

Though neither knows where lie the nameless things of which the mystic sign gives forth such hints; yet with me, as with the colt, somewhere those things must exist. Though in many of its aspects this visible world seems formed in love, the invisible spheres were formed in fright.

But not yet have we solved the incantation of this whiteness, and learned why it appeals with such power to the soul; and more strange and far more portentous—why, as we have seen, it is at once the most meaning symbol of spiritual things, nay, the very veil of the Christian's Deity; and yet should be as it is, the intensifying agent in things the most appalling to mankind.

Is it that by its indefiniteness it shadows forth the heartless voids and immensities of the universe, and thus stabs us from behind with the thought of annihilation, when beholding the white depths of the milky way? Or is it, that as in essence whiteness is not so much a color as the visible absence of color, and at the same time the concrete of all colors; is it for these reasons that there is such a dumb blankness, full of meaning, in a wide landscape of snows— a colorless, all-color of atheism from which we shrink? And when we consider that other theory of the natural philosophers, that all other earthly hues—every stately or lovely emblazoning—the sweet tinges of sunset skies and woods; yea, and the gilded velvets of butterflies, and the butterfly cheeks of young girls; all these are but subtile deceits, not actually inherent in substances, but only laid on from without; so that all deified Nature absolutely paints like the harlot, whose allurements cover nothing but the charnel-house within; and when we proceed further, and consider that the mystical cosmetic which produces every one of her hues, the great principle of light, for ever remains white or colorless in itself, and if operating without medium upon matter, would touch all objects, even tulips and roses, with its own blank tinge—pondering all this, the palsied universe lies before us a leper; and like wilful travellers in Lapland, who refuse to wear colored and coloring glasses upon their eyes, so the wretched infidel gazes himself blind at the monumental white shroud that wraps all the prospect around him. And of all these things the Albino whale was the symbol. Wonder ye then at the fiery hunt?

HARK!   XLIII

"HIST! Did you hear that noise, Cabaco?"

It was the middle-watch: a fair moonlight; the seamen were standing in a cordon, extending from one of the fresh-water butts in the waist, to the scuttle-butt near the taffrail. In this manner, they passed the buckets to fill the scuttle-butt. Standing, for the most part, on the hallowed precincts of the quarterdeck, they were careful not to speak or rustle their feet. From hand to hand, the buckets went in the deepest silence, only broken by the occasional flap of a sail, and the steady hum of the unceasingly advancing keel.

It was in the midst of this repose, that Archy, one of the

cordon, whose post was near the after-hatches, whispered to
his neighbor, a Cholo, the words above.

"Hist! did you hear that noise, Cabaco?"

"Take the bucket, will ye, Archy? what noise d'ye mean?"

"There it is again—under the hatches—don't you hear it
—a cough—it sounded like a cough."

"Cough be damned! Pass along that return bucket."

"There again—there it is!—it sounds like two or three
sleepers turning over, now!"

"Caramba! have done, shipmate, will ye? It's the three
soaked biscuits ye eat for supper turning over inside of ye
—nothing else. Look to the bucket!"

"Say what ye will, shipmate; I've sharp ears."

"Aye, you are the chap, ain't ye, that heard the hum of
the old Quakeress's knitting-needles fifty miles at sea from
Nantucket; you're the chap."

"Grin away; we'll see what turns up. Hark ye, Cabaco,
there is somebody down in the after-hold that has not yet
been seen on deck; and I suspect our old Mogul knows
something of it too. I heard Stubb tell Flask, one morning
watch, that there was something of that sort in the wind."

"Tish! the bucket!"

THE CHART   XLIV

HAD you followed Captain Ahab down into his cabin
after the squall that took place on the night succeeding that
wild ratification of his purpose with his crew, you would
have seen him go to a locker in the transom, and bringing
out a large wrinkled roll of yellowish sea charts, spread
them before him on his screwed-down table. Then seating
himself before it, you would have seen him intently study the
various lines and shadings which there met his eye; and with
slow but steady pencil trace additional courses over spaces
that before were blank. At intervals, he would refer to piles
of old log-books beside him, wherein were set down the
seasons and places in which, on various former voyages of
various ships, sperm whales had been captured or seen.

While thus employed, the heavy pewter lamp suspended in
chains over his head, continually rocked with the
motion of the ship, and for ever threw shifting gleams and

shadows of lines upon his wrinkled brow, till it almost seemed that while he himself was marking out lines and courses on the wrinkled charts, some invisible pencil was also tracing lines and courses upon the deeply marked chart of his forehead.

But it was not this night in particular that, in the solitude of his cabin, Ahab thus pondered over his charts. Almost every night they were brought out; almost every night some pencil marks were effaced, and others were substituted. For with the charts of all four oceans before him, Ahab was threading a maze of currents and eddies, with a view to the more certain accomplishment of that monomaniac thought of his soul.

Now, to any one not fully acquainted with the ways of the leviathans, it might seem an absurdly hopeless task thus to seek out one solitary creature in the unhooped oceans of this planet. But not so did it seem to Ahab, who knew the sets of all tides and currents; and thereby calculating the driftings of the sperm whale's food; and, also, calling to mind the regular, ascertained seasons for hunting him in particular latitudes; could arrive at reasonable surmises, almost approaching to certainties, concerning the timeliest day to be upon this or that ground in search of his prey.

So assured, indeed, is the fact concerning the periodicalness of the sperm whale's resorting to given waters, that many hunters believe that, could he be closely observed and studied throughout the world; were the logs for one voyage of the entire whale fleet carefully collated, then the migrations of the sperm whale would be found to correspond in invariability to those of the herring-shoals or the flights of swallows. On this hint, attempts have been made to construct elaborate migratory charts of the sperm whale.*

Besides, when making a passage from one feeding-ground

* Since the above was written, the statement is happily borne out by an official circular, issued by Lieutenant Maury, of the National Observatory, Washington, April 16th, 1851. By that circular, it appears that precisely such a chart is in course of completion; and portions of it are presented in the circular. "This chart divides the ocean into districts of five degrees of latitude by five degrees of longitude; perpendicularly through each of which districts are twelve columns for the twelve months; and horizontally through each of which districts are three lines; one to show the number of days that have been spent in each month in every district; and the two others to show the number of days in which whales, sperm or right, have been seen."

to another, the sperm whales, guided by some infallible instinct—say, rather, secret intelligence from the Deity—mostly swim in *veins,* as they are called; continuing their way along a given ocean-line with such undeviating exactitude, that no ship ever sailed her course, by any chart, with one tithe of such marvellous precision. Though, in these cases, the direction taken by any one whale be straight as a surveyor's parallel, and though the line of advance be strictly confined to its own unavoidable, straight wake, yet the arbitrary *vein* in which at these times he is said to swim, generally embraces some few miles in width (more or less, as the vein is presumed to expand or contract); but never exceeds the visual sweep from the whale-ship's mast-heads, when circumspectly gliding along this magic zone. The sum is, that at particular seasons within that breadth and along that path, migrating whales may with great confidence be looked for.

And hence not only at substantiated times, upon well known separate feeding-grounds, could Ahab hope to encounter his prey; but in crossing the widest expanses of water between those grounds he could, by his art, so place and time himself on his way, as even then not to be wholly without prospect of a meeting.

There was a circumstance which at first sight seemed to entangle his delirious but still methodical scheme. But not so in the reality, perhaps. Though the gregarious sperm whales have their regular seasons for particular grounds, yet in general you cannot conclude that the herds which haunted such and such a latitude or longitude this year, say, will turn out to be identically the same with those that were found there the preceding season; though there are peculiar and unquestionable instances where the contrary of this has proved true. In general, the same remark, only within a less wide limit, applies to the solitaries and hermits among the matured, aged sperm whales. So that though Moby Dick had in a former year been seen, for example, on what is called the Seychelle ground in the Indian ocean, or Volcano Bay on the Japanese Coast; yet it did not follow, that were the Pequod to visit either of those spots at any subsequent corresponding season, she would infallibly encounter him there. So, too, with some other feeding grounds, where he had at times revealed himself. But all these seemed only his casual stopping-places and ocean-inns, so to speak, not his places of prolonged abode. And where Ahab's chances of accomplishing his object have hitherto been spoken of, allusion has only been made to whatever way-side, antecedent, extra prospects were his, ere a particular set time or place were attained, when all possibilities would become probabilities, and, as Ahab fondly thought, every possibility the next thing to a certainty. That particular set time and place were conjoined in the one technical phrase—the Season-on-the-Line. For there and then, for several consecutive years, Moby Dick had been periodically descried, lingering in those waters for awhile, as the sun, in its annual round, loiters for a predicted interval in any one sign of the Zodiac. There it was, too, that most of the deadly encounters with the white whale had taken place; there the waves were storied with his deeds; there also was that tragic spot where the monomaniac old man had found the awful motive to his vengeance. But in the cautious comprehensiveness and unloitering vigilance with which Ahab threw his brooding soul into this unfaltering hunt, he would not permit himself to rest all his hopes upon the one crowning fact above mentioned, however flattering it might be to those hopes; nor in the sleeplessness of his vow could he so tranquillize his unquiet heart as to postpone all intervening quest.

Now, the Pequod had sailed from Nantucket at the very beginning of the Season-on-the-Line. No possible endeavor then could enable her commander to make the great passage southwards, double Cape Horn, and then running down sixty degrees of latitude arrive in the equatorial Pacific in time to cruise there. Therefore, he must wait for the next ensuing season. Yet the premature hour of the Pequod's sailing had, perhaps, been correctly selected by Ahab, with a view to this very complexion of things. Because, an interval of three hundred and sixty-five days and nights was before him; an interval which, instead of impatiently enduring ashore, he would spend in a miscellaneous hunt; if by chance the White Whale, spending his vacation in seas far remote from his periodical feeding-grounds, should turn up his wrinkled brow off the Persian Gulf, or in the Bengal Bay, or China Seas, or in any other waters haunted by his race. So that Monsoons, Pampas, Nor-Westers, Harmattans, Trades; any wind but the Levanter and Simoom, might blow Moby Dick into the devious zig-zag world-circle of the Pequod's circumnavigating wake.

But granting all this; yet, regarded discreetly and coolly, seems it not but a mad idea, this; that in the broad boundless ocean, one solitary whale, even if encountered, should be thought capable of individual recognition from his hunter, even as a white-bearded Mufti in the thronged thoroughfares of Constantinople? Yes. For the peculiar snow-white brow of Moby Dick, and his snow-white hump, could not but be unmistakable. And have I not tallied the whale, Ahab would mutter to himself, as after poring over his charts till long after midnight he would throw himself back in reveries— tallied him, and shall he escape? His broad fins are bored, and scalloped out like a lost sheep's ear! And here, his mad mind would run on in a breathless race; till a weariness and faintness of pondering came over him; and in the open air of the deck he would seek to recover his strength. Ah, God! what trances of torments does that man endure who is consumed with one unachieved revengeful desire. He sleeps with clenched hands; and wakes with his own bloody nails in his palms.

Often, when forced from his hammock by exhausting and intolerably vivid dreams of the night, which, resuming his own intense thoughts through the day, carried them on amid a clashing of phrensies, and whirled them round and round in his blazing brain, till the very throbbing of his life-spot became insufferable anguish; and when, as was sometimes the case, these spiritual throes in him heaved his being up from its base, and a chasm seemed opening in him, from which forked flames and lightnings shot up, and accursed fiends beckoned him to leap down among them; when this hell in himself yawned beneath him, a wild cry would be heard through the ship; and with glaring eyes Ahab would burst from his state room, as though escaping from a bed that was on fire. Yet these, perhaps, instead of being the unsuppressable symptoms of some latent weakness, or fright at his own resolve, were but the plainest tokens of its intensity. For, at such times, crazy Ahab, the scheming, unappeasedly steadfast hunter of the white whale; this Ahab that had gone to his hammock, was not the agent that so caused him to burst from it in horror again. The latter was the eternal, living principle or soul in him; and in sleep, being for the time dissociated from the characterizing mind, which at other times employed it for its outer vehicle or agent, it spontaneously sought escape from the scorching contiguity of the frantic thing, of which, for the time, it was no longer an integral. But as the mind does not exist unless leagued with the soul, therefore it must have been that, in Ahab's case, yielding up all his thoughts and fancies to his one supreme purpose; that purpose, by its own sheer inveteracy of will, forced itself against gods and devils into a kind of self-assumed, independent being of its own. Nay, could grimly live and burn, while the common vitality to which it was conjoined, fled horror-stricken from the unbidden and unfathered birth. Therefore, the tormented spirit that glared out of bodily eyes, when what seemed Ahab rushed from his room, was for the time but a vacated thing, a formless somnambulistic being, a ray of living light, to be sure, but without an object to color, and therefore a blankness in itself. God help thee, old man, thy thoughts have created a creature in thee; and he whose intense thinking thus makes him a Prometheus; a vulture feeds upon that heart for ever; that vulture the very creature he creates.

THE AFFIDAVIT   XLV

so far as what there may be of a narrative in this book; and, indeed, as indirectly touching one or two very interesting and curious particulars in the habits of sperm whales, the foregoing chapter, in its earlier part, is as important a one as will be found in this volume; but the leading matter of it requires to be still further and more familiarly enlarged upon, in order to be adequately understood, and moreover to take away any incredulity which a profound ignorance of the entire subject may induce in some minds, as to the natural verity of the main points of this affair.

I care not to perform this part of my task methodically; but shall be content to produce the desired impression by separate citations of items, practically or reliably known to me as a whaleman; and from these citations, I take it—the conclusion aimed at will naturally follow of itself.

First: I have personally known three instances where a whale, after receiving a harpoon, has effected a complete escape; and, after an interval (in one instance of three years), has been again struck by the same hand, and slain; when the two irons, both marked by the same private cypher, have been taken from the body. In the instance where three years intervened between the flinging of the two harpoons; and I

think it may have been something more than that; the man
who darted them happening, in the interval, to go in a
trading ship on a voyage to Africa, went ashore there, joined
a discovery party, and penetrated far into the interior, where
he travelled for a period of nearly two years, often endangered by serpents, savages, tigers, poisonous miasmas,
with all the other common perils incident to wandering in
the heart of unknown regions. Meanwhile, the whale he had
struck must also have been on its travels; no doubt it had
thrice circumnavigated the globe, brushing with its flanks
all the coasts of Africa; but to no purpose. This man and
this whale again came together, and the one vanquished the
other. I say I, myself, have known three instances similar to
this; that is in two of them I saw the whales struck; and,
upon the second attack, saw the two irons with the respective
marks cut in them, afterwards taken from the dead fish. In
the three-year instance, it so fell out that I was in the boat
both times, first and last, and the last time distinctly recognised a peculiar sort of huge mole under the whale's eye,
which I had observed there three years previous. I say three
years, but I am pretty sure it was more than that. Here are
three instances, then, which I personally know the truth of;
but I have heard of many other instances from persons
whose veracity in the matter there is no good ground to im-
peach.

Secondly: It is well known in the Sperm Whale Fishery,
however ignorant the world ashore may be of it, that there
have been several memorable historical instances where a particular whale in the ocean has been at distant times and places
popularly cognisable. Why such a whale became thus
marked was not altogether and originally owing to his bodily
peculiarities as distinguished from other whales; for however
peculiar in that respect any chance whale may be, they soon
put an end to his peculiarities by killing him, and boiling
him down into a peculiarly valuable oil. No: the reason was
this: that from the fatal experiences of the fishery there hung
a terrible prestige of perilousness about such a whale as there
did about Rinaldlo Rinaldini, insomuch that most fishermen
were content to recognise him by merely touching their tarpaulins when he would be discovered lounging by them on
the sea, without seeking to cultivate a more intimate acquaintance. Like some poor devils ashore that happen to
know an irascible great man, they make distant unobtrusive

salutations to him in the street, lest if they pursued the acquaintance further, they might receive a summary thump for their presumption.

But not only did each of these famous whales enjoy great individual celebrity—nay, you may call it an ocean-wide renown; not only was he famous in life and now is immortal in forecastle stories after death, but he was admitted into all the rights, privileges, and distinctions of a name; had as much a name indeed as Cambyses or Cæsar. Was it not so, O Timor Tom! thou famed leviathan, scarred like an iceberg, who so long did'st lurk in the Oriental straits of that name, whose spout was oft seen from the palmy beach of Ombay? Was it not so, O New Zealand Jack! thou terror of all cruisers that crossed their wakes in the vicinity of the Tattoo Land? Was it not so, O Morquan! King of Japan, whose lofty jet they say at times assumed the semblance of a snow-white cross against the sky? Was it not so, O Don Miguel! thou Chilian whale, marked like an old tortoise with mystic hieroglyphics upon the back! In plain prose, here are four whales as well known to the students of Cetacean History as Marius or Sylla to the classic scholar.

But this is not all. New Zealand Tom and Don Miguel, after at various times creating great havoc among the boats of different vessels, were finally gone in quest of, systematically hunted out, chased and killed by valiant whaling captains, who heaved up their anchors with that express object as much in view, as in setting out through the Narragansett Woods, Captain Butler of old had it in his mind to capture that notorious murderous savage Annawon, the headmost warrior of the Indian King Philip.

I do not know where I can find a better place than just here, to make mention of one or two other things, which to me seem important, as in printed form establishing in all respects the reasonableness of the whole story of the White Whale, more especially the catastrophe. For this is one of those disheartening instances where truth requires full as much bolstering as error. So ignorant are most landsmen of some of the plainest and most palpable wonders of the world, that without some hints touching the plain facts, historical and otherwise, of the fishery, they might scout at Moby Dick as a monstrous fable, or still worse and more detestable, a hideous and intolerable allegory.

First: Though most men have some vague flitting ideas of the general perils of the grand fishery, yet they have nothing like a fixed, vivid conception of those perils, and the frequency with which they recur. One reason perhaps is, that not one in fifty of the actual disasters and deaths by casualties in the fishery, ever finds a public record at home, however transient and immediately forgotten that record. Do you suppose that that poor fellow there, who this moment perhaps caught by the whaleline off the coast of New Guinea, is being carried down to the bottom of the sea by the sounding leviathan—do you suppose that that poor fellow's name will appear in the newspaper obituary you will read to-morrow at your breakfast? No: because the mails are very irregular between here and New Guinea. In fact, did you ever hear what might be called regular news direct or indirect from New Guinea? Yet I tell you that upon one particular voyage which I made to the Pacific, among many others we spoke thirty different ships, every one of which had had a death by a whale, some of them more than one, and three that had each lost a boat's crew. For God's sake, be economical with your lamps and candles! not a gallon you burn, but at least one drop of man's blood was spilled for it.

Secondly: People ashore have indeed some indefinite idea that a whale is an enormous creature of enormous power; but I have ever found that when narrating to them some specific example of this two-fold enormousness, they have significantly complimented me upon my facetiousness; when, I declare upon my soul, I had no more idea of being facetious than Moses, when he wrote the history of the plagues of Egypt.

But fortunately the special point I here seek can be established upon testimony entirely independent of my own. That point is this: The Sperm Whale is in some cases sufficiently powerful, knowing, and judiciously malicious, as with direct aforethought to stave in, utterly destroy, and sink a large ship; and what is more, the Sperm Whale *has* done it.

First: In the year 1820 the ship Essex, Captain Pollard, of Nantucket, was cruising in the Pacific Ocean. One day she saw spouts, lowered her boats, and gave chase to a shoal of sperm whales. Ere long, several of the whales were wounded; when, suddenly, a very large whale escaping from the boats, issued from the shoal, and bore directly down upon the ship. Dashing his forehead against her hull, he so stove her in, that in less than "ten minutes" she settled down and fell over. Not a surviving plank of her has been seen since. After the severest exposure, part of the crew reached the land in their boats. Being returned home at last, Captain Pollard once more sailed for the Pacific in command of another ship, but the gods shipwrecked .iim again upon unknown rocks and breakers; for the second time his ship was utterly lost, and forthwith forswearing the sea, he has never tempted it since. At this day Captain Pollard is a resident of Nantucket. I have seen Owen Chace, who was chief mate of the Essex at the time of the tragedy; I have read his plain and faithful narrative; I have conversed with his son; and all this within a few miles of the scene of the catastrophe.*

Secondly: The ship Union, also of Nantucket, was in the year 1807 totally lost off the Azores by a similar onset, but the authentic particulars of this catastrophe I have never chanced to encounter, though from the whale hunters I have now and then heard casual allusions to it.

Thirdly: Some eighteen or twenty years ago Commodore J—— then commanding an American sloop-of-war of the first class, happened to be dining with a party of whaling captains, on board a Nantucket ship in the harbor of Oahu, Sandwich Islands. Conversation turning upon whales, the

* The following are extracts from Chace's narrative: "'Every fact seemed to warrant me in concluding that it was anything but chance which directed his operations; he made two several attacks upon the ship, at a short interval between them, both of which, according to their direction, were calculated to do us the most injury, by being made ahead, and thereby combining the speed of the two objects for the shock; to effect which, the exact manœuvres which he made were necessary. His aspect was most horrible, and such as indicated resentment and fury. He came directly from the shoal which we had just before entered, and in which we had struck three of his companions, as if fired with revenge for their sufferings." Again: "At all events, the whole circumstances taken together, all happening before my own eyes, and producing, at the time, impressions in my mind of decided, calculating mischief, on the part of the whale (many of which impressions I cannot now recall), induce me to be satisfied that I am correct in my opinion."

Here are his reflections some time after quitting the ship, during a black night in an open boat, when almost despairing of reaching any hospitable shore. "The dark ocean and swelling waters were nothing; the fears of being swallowed up by some dreadful tempest, or dashed upon hidden rocks, with all the other ordinary subjects of fearful contemplation, seemed scarcely entitled to a moment's thought; the dismal looking wreck, and *the horrid aspect and revenge of the whale,* wholly engrossed my reflections, until day again made its appearance."

In another place—p. 45,—he speaks of *"the mysterious and mortal attack of the animal."*

Commodore was pleased to be sceptical touching the amazing strength ascribed to them by the professional gentlemen present. He peremptorily denied for example, that any whale could so smite his stout sloop-of-war as to cause her to leak so much as a thimbleful. Very good; but there is more coming. Some weeks after, the commodore set sail in this impregnable craft for Valparaiso. But he was stopped on the way by a portly sperm whale, that begged a few moments' confidential business with him. That business consisted in fetching the Commodore's craft such a thwack, that with all his pumps going he made straight for the nearest port to heave down and repair. I am not superstitious, but I consider the Commodore's interview with that whale as providential. Was not Saul of Tarsus converted from unbelief by a similar fright? I tell you, the sperm whale will stand no nonsense.

I will now refer you to Langsdorff's Voyages for a little circumstance in point, peculiarly interesting to the writer hereof. Langsdorff, you must know by the way, was attached to the Russian Admiral Krusenstern's famous Discovery Expedition in the beginning of the present century. Captain Langsdorff thus begins his seventeenth chapter.

"By the thirteenth of May our ship was ready to sail, and the next day we were out in the open sea, on our way to Ochotsh. The weather was very clear and fine, but so intolerably cold that we were obliged to keep on our fur clothing. For some days we had very little wind; it was not till the nineteenth that a brisk gale from the northwest sprang up. An uncommon large whale, the body of which was larger than the ship itself, lay almost at the surface of the water, but was not perceived by any one on board till the moment when the ship, which was in full sail, was almost upon him, so that it was impossible to prevent its striking against him. We were thus placed in the most imminent danger, as this gigantic creature, setting up its back, raised the ship three feet at least out of the water. The masts reeled, and the sails fell altogether, while we who were below all sprang instantly upon the deck, concluding that we had struck upon some rock; instead of this we saw the monster sailing off with the utmost gravity and solemnity. Captain D'Wolf applied immediately to the pumps to examine whether or not the vessel had received any damage from the shock, but we found that very happily it had escaped entirely uninjured."

Now, the Captain D'Wolf here alluded to as commanding

the ship in question, is a New Englander, who, after a long life of unusual adventures as a sea-captain, this day resides in the village of Dorchester near Boston. I have the honor of being a nephew of his. I have particularly questioned him concerning this passage in Langsdorff. He substantiates every word. The ship, however, was by no means a large one: a Russian craft built on the Siberian coast, and purchased by my uncle after bartering away the vessel in which he sailed from home.

In that up and down manly book of old-fashioned adventure, so full, too, of honest wonders—the voyage of Lionel Wafer, one of ancient Dampier's old chums—I found a little matter set down so like that just quoted from Langsdorff, that I cannot forbear inserting it here for a corroborative example, if such be needed.

Lionel, it seems, was on his way to "John Ferdinando," as he calls the modern Juan Fernandes. "In our way thither," he says, "about four o'clock in the morning, when we were about one hundred and fifty leagues from the Main of America, our ship felt a terrible shock, which put our men in such consternation that they could hardly tell where they were or what to think; but every one began to prepare for death. And, indeed, the shock was so sudden and violent, that we took it for granted the ship had struck against a rock; but when the amazement was a little over, we cast the lead, and sounded, but found no ground. The suddenness of the shock made the guns leap in their carriages, and several of the men were shaken out of their hammocks. Captain Davis, who lay with his head on a gun, was thrown out of his cabin!" Lionel then goes on to impute the shock to an earthquake, and seems to substantiate the imputation by stating that a great earthquake, somewhere about that time, did actually do great mischief along the Spanish land. But I should not much wonder if, in the darkness of that early hour of the morning, the shock was after all caused by an unseen whale vertically bumping the hull from beneath.

I might proceed with several more examples, one way or another known to me, of the great power and malice at times of the sperm whale. In more than one instance, he has been known, not only to chase the assailing boats back to their ships, but to pursue the ship itself, and long withstand all the lances hurled at him from its decks. The English ship Pusie Hall can tell a story on that head; and, as for his strength, let me say, that there have been examples where the lines attached to a running sperm whale have, in a calm, been transferred to the ship, and secured there; the whale towing her great hull through the water, as a horse walks off with a cart. Again, it is very often observed that, if the sperm whale, once struck, is allowed time to rally, he then acts, not so often with blind rage, as with wilful, deliberate designs of destruction to his pursuers; nor is it without conveying some eloquent indication of his character, that upon being attacked he will frequently open his mouth, and retain it in that dread expansion for several consecutive minutes. But I must be content with only one more and a concluding illustration; a remarkable and most significant one, by which you will not fail to see that not only is the most marvellous event in this book corroborated by plain facts of the present day, but that these marvels (like all marvels) are mere repetitions of the ages; so that for the millionth time we say amen with Solomon—Verily there is nothing new under the sun.

In the sixth Christian century lived Procopius, a Christian magistrate of Constantinople, in the days when Justinian was Emperor and Belisarius general. As many know, he wrote the history of his own times, a work every way of uncommon value. By the best authorities, he has always been considered a most trustworthy and unexaggerating historian, except in some one or two particulars, not at all affecting the matter presently to be mentioned.

Now, in this history of his, Procopius mentions that, during the term of his prefecture at Constantinople, a great sea-monster was captured in the neighboring Propontis, or Sea of Marmora, after having destroyed vessels at intervals in those waters for a period of more than fifty years. A fact thus set down in substantial history cannot easily be gainsaid. Nor is there any reason it should be. Of what precise species this sea-monster was, is not mentioned. But as he destroyed ships, as well as for other reasons, he must have been a whale; and I am strongly inclined to think a sperm whale. And I will tell you why. For a long time I fancied that the sperm whale had been always unknown in the Mediterranean and the deep waters connecting with it. Even now I am certain that those seas are not, and perhaps never can be, in the present constitution of things, a place for his habitual gregarious resort. But further investigations have recently proved to me, that in modern times there have been isolated instances of the presence of the sperm whale in the

Mediterranean. I am told, on good authority, that on the
Barbary coast, a Commodore Davis of the British navy found
the skeleton of a sperm whale. Now, as a vessel of war
readily passes through the Dardanelles, hence a sperm whale
could, by the same route, pass out of the Mediterranean into
the Propontis.

In the Propontis, as far as I can learn, none of that peculiar substance called *brit* is to be found, the aliment of the
right whale. But I have every reason to believe that the food
of the sperm whale—squid or cuttle-fish—lurks at the bottom
of that sea, because large creatures, but by no means the
largest of that sort, have been found at its surface. If, then,
you properly put these statements together, and reason upon
them a bit, you will clearly perceive that, according to all
human reasoning, Procopius's sea-monster, that for half a
century stove the ships of a Roman Emperor, must in all
probability have been a sperm whale.

SURMISES   XLVI

THOUGH consumed with the hot fire of his purpose,
Ahab in all his thoughts and actions ever had in view the
ultimate capture of Moby Dick; though he seemed ready to
sacrifice all mortal interests to that one passion; nevertheless it may have been that he was by nature and long habit-
uation far too wedded to a fiery whaleman's ways, altogether to abandon the collateral prosecution of the voyage.
Or at least if this were otherwise, there were not wanting
other motives much more influential with him. It would be
refining too much, perhaps, even considering his monomania,
to hint that his vindictiveness towards the White Whale might
have possibly extended itself in some degree to all sperm
whales, and that the more monsters he slew by so much the
more he multiplied the chances that each subsequently encountered whale would prove to be the hated one he hunted.
But if such an hypothesis be indeed exceptionable, there were
still additional considerations which, though not so strictly
according with the wildness of his ruling passion, yet were
by no means incapable of swaying him.

To accomplish his object Ahab must use tools; and of all
tools used in the shadow of the moon, men are most apt to

get out of order. He knew, for example, that however magnetic his ascendency in some respects was over Starbuck, yet that ascendency did not cover the complete spiritual man any more than mere corporeal superiority involves intellectual mastership; for to the purely spiritual, the intellectual but stand in a sort of corporeal relation. Starbuck's body and Starbuck's coerced will were Ahab's, so long as Ahab kept his magnet at Starbuck's brain; still he knew that for all this the chief mate, in his soul, abhorred his captain's quest, and could he, would joyfully disintegrate himself from it, or even frustrate it. It might be that a long interval would elapse ere the White Whale was seen. During that long interval Starbuck would ever be apt to fall into open relapses of rebellion against his captain's leadership, unless some ordinary, prudential, circumstantial influences were brought to bear upon him. Not only that, but the subtle insanity of Ahab respecting Moby Dick was noways more significantly manifested than in his superlative sense and shrewdness in foreseeing that, for the present, the hunt should in some way be stripped of that strange imaginative impiousness which naturally invested it; that the full terror of the voyage must be kept withdrawn into the obscure background (for few men's courage is proof against protracted meditation unrelieved by action); that when they stood their long night watches, his officers and men must have some nearer things to think of than Moby Dick. For however eagerly and impetuously the savage crew had hailed the announcement of his quest; yet all sailors of all sorts are more or less capricious and unreliable—they live in the varying outer weather, and they inhale its fickleness—and when retained for any object remote and blank in the pursuit, however promissory of life and passion in the end, it is above all things requisite that temporary interests and employments should intervene and hold them healthily suspended for the final dash.

Nor was Ahab unmindful of another thing. In times of strong emotion mankind disdain all base considerations; but such times are evanescent. The permanent constitutional condition of the manufactured man, thought Ahab, is sordidness. Granting that the White Whale fully incites the hearts of this my savage crew, and playing round their savageness even breeds a certain generous knight-errantism in them, still, while for the love of it they give chase to Moby Dick, they must also have food for their more common, daily appetites. For even the high lifted and chivalric

Crusaders of old times were not content to traverse two thousand miles of land to fight for their holy sepulchre, without committing burglaries, picking pockets, and gaining other pious perquisites by the way. Had they been strictly held to their one final and romantic object—that final and romantic object, too many would have turned from in disgust. I will not strip these men, thought Ahab, of all hopes of cash—aye, cash. They may scorn cash now; but let some months go by, and no perspective promise of it to them, and then this same quiescent cash all at once mutinying in them, this same cash would soon cashier Ahab.

Nor was there wanting still another precautionary motive more related to Ahab personally. Having impulsively, it is probable, and perhaps somewhat prematurely revealed the prime but private purpose of the Pequod's voyage, Ahab was now entirely conscious that, in so doing, he had indirectly laid himself open to the unanswerable charge of usurpation; and with perfect impunity, both moral and legal, his crew if so disposed, and to that end competent, could refuse all further obedience to him, and even violently wrest from him the command. From even the barely hinted imputation of usurpation, and the possible consequences of such a suppressed impression gaining ground, Ahab must of course have been most anxious to protect himself. That protection could only consist in his own predominating brain and heart and hand, backed by a heedful, closely calculating attention to every minute atmospheric influence which it was possible for his crew to be subjected to.

For all these reasons then, and others perhaps too analytic to be verbally developed here, Ahab plainly saw that he must still in a good degree continue true to the natural, nominal purpose of the Pequod's voyage; observe all customary usages; and not only that, but force himself to evince all his well known passionate interest in the general pursuit of his profession.

Be all this as it may, his voice was now often heard hailing the three mast-heads and admonishing them to keep a bright look-out, and not omit reporting even a porpoise. This vigilance was not long without reward.

THE MAT-MAKER   XLVII

IT was a cloudy, sultry afternoon; the seamen were lazily lounging about the decks, or vacantly gazing over into the lead-colored waters. Queequeg and I were mildly employed weaving what is called a sword-mat, for an additional lashing to our boat. So still and subdued and yet somehow preluding was all the scene, and such an incantation of revery lurked in the air, that each silent sailor seemed resolved into his own invisible self.

I was the attendant or page of Queequeg, while busy at the mat. As I kept passing and repassing the filling or woof of marline between the long yarns of the warp, using my own hand for the shuttle, and as Queequeg, standing sideways, ever and anon slid his heavy oaken sword between the threads, and idly looking off upon the water, carelessly and unthinkingly drove home every yarn; I say so strange a dreaminess did there then reign all over the ship and all over the sea, only broken by the intermitting dull sound of the sword, that it seemed as if this were the Loom of Time, and I myself were a shuttle mechanically weaving and weaving away at the Fates. There lay the fixed threads of the warp subject to but one single, ever returning, unchanging vibration, and that vibration merely enough to admit of the crosswise interblending of other threads with its own. This warp seemed necessity; and here, thought I, with my own hand I ply my own shuttle and weave my own destiny into these unalterable threads. Meantime, Queequeg's impulsive, indifferent sword, sometimes hitting the woof slantingly, or crookedly, or strongly, or weakly, as the case might be; and by this difference in the concluding blow producing a corresponding contrast in the final aspect of the completed fabric; this savage's sword, thought I, which thus finally shapes and fashions both warp and woof; this easy, indifferent sword must be chance—aye, chance, free will, and necessity—no wise incompatible—all interweavingly working together. The straight warp of necessity, not to be swerved from its ultimate course—its every alternating vibration, indeed, only tending to that; free will still free to ply her shuttle between given threads; and chance, though restrained in its play within the right lines of necessity, and sideways in its motions directed by free will, though thus prescribed to by both, chance by turns rules either, and has the last featuring blow at events.

* * * * *

Thus we were weaving and weaving away when I started at a sound so strange, long drawn, and musically wild and unearthly, that the ball of free will dropped from my hand, and I stood gazing up at the clouds whence that voice dropped like a wing. High aloft in the cross-trees was that mad Gay-Header, Tashtego. His body was reaching eagerly forward, his hand stretched out like a wand, and at brief sudden intervals he continued his cries. To be sure the same sound was that very moment perhaps being heard all over the seas, from hundreds of whalemen's look-outs perched as high in the air; but from few of those lungs could that accustomed old cry have derived such a marvellous cadence as from Tashtego the Indian's.

As he stood hovering over you half suspended in air, so wildly and eagerly peering towards the horizon, you would have thought him some prophet or seer beholding the shadows of Fate, and by those wild cries announcing their coming.

"There she blows! there! there! there! she blows! she blows!"

"Where-away?"

"On the lee-beam, about two miles off! a school of them!"

Instantly all was commotion.

The Sperm Whale blows as a clock ticks, with the same undeviating and reliable uniformity. And thereby whalemen distinguish this fish from other tribes of his genus.

"There go flukes!" was now the cry from Tashtego; and the whales disappeared.

"Quick, steward!" cried Ahab. "Time! time!"

Dough-Boy hurried below, glanced at the watch, and reported the exact minute to Ahab.

The ship was now kept away from the wind, and she went gently rolling before it. Tashtego reporting that the whales had gone down heading to leeward, we confidently looked to see them again directly in advance of our bows. For that singular craft at times evinced by the Sperm Whale when, sounding with his head in one direction, he nevertheless, while concealed beneath the surface, mills round, and swiftly swims off in the opposite quarter—this deceitfulness of his could not now be in action; for there was no reason to suppose that the fish seen by Tashtego had been in any way alarmed, or indeed knew at all of our vicinity. One of the men selected for shipkeepers—that is, those not appointed to the boats, by this time relieved the Indian at the main-mast head. The sailors at the fore and mizzen had come down; the line tubs were fixed in their places; the cranes were thrust out; the mainyard was backed, and the three boats swung over the sea like three samphire baskets over high cliffs. Outside of the bulwarks their eager crews with one hand clung to the rail, while one foot was expectantly poised on the gunwale. So look the long line of man-of-war's men about to throw themselves on board an enemy's ship.

But at this critical instant a sudden exclamation was heard that took every eye from the whale. With a start all glared at dark Ahab, who was surrounded by five dusky phantoms that seemed fresh formed out of air.

THE FIRST LOWERING   **XLVIII**

THE phantoms, for so they then seemed, were flitting on the other side of the deck, and, with a noiseless celerity, were casting loose the tackles and bands of the boat which swung there. This boat had always been deemed one of the spare boats, though technically called the captain's, on account of its hanging from the starboard quarter. The figure that now stood by its bows was tall and swart, with one white tooth evilly protruding from its steel-like lips. A rumpled Chinese jacket of black cotton funereally invested him, with wide black trowsers of the same dark stuff. But strangely crowning this ebonness was a glistening white plaited turban, the living hair braided and coiled round and round upon his head. Less swart in aspect, the companions of this figure were of that vivid, tiger-yellow complexion peculiar to some of the aboriginal natives of the Manillas;—a race notorious for a certain diabolism of subtilty, and by some honest white mariners supposed to be the paid spies and secret confidential agents on the water of the devil, their lord, whose counting-room they suppose to be elsewhere.

While yet the wondering ship's company were gazing upon these strangers, Ahab cried out to the white-turbaned old man at their head, "All ready there, Fedallah?"

"Ready," was the half-hissed reply.

"Lower away then; d'ye hear?" shouting across the deck. "Lower away there, I say."

Such was the thunder of his voice, that spite of their amazement the men sprang over the rail; the sheaves whirled round in the blocks; with a wallow, the three boats dropped into the sea; while, with a dexterous, off-handed daring, unknown in any other vocation, the sailors, goat-like, leaped down the rolling ship's side into the tossed boats below.

Hardly had they pulled out from under the ship's lee, when a fourth keel, coming from the windward side, pulled round under the stern, and showed the five strangers rowing Ahab, who, standing erect in the stern, loudly hailed Starbuck, Stubb, and Flask, to spread themselves widely, so as to cover a large expanse of water. But with all their eyes again riveted upon the swart Fedallah and his crew, the inmates of the other boats obeyed not the command.

"Captain Ahab?—" said Starbuck.

"Spread yourselves," cried Ahab; "give way, all four boats. Thou, Flask, pull out more to leeward!"

"Aye, aye, sir," cherrily cried little King-Post, sweeping round his great steering oar. "Lay back!" addressing his crew. "There!—there!—there again! There she blows right ahead, boys!—lay back!"

"Never heed yonder yellow boys, Archy."

"Oh, I don't mind 'em, sir," said Archy; "I knew it all before now. Didn't I hear 'em in the hold? And didn't I tell Cabaco here of it? What say ye, Cabaco? They are stowaways, Mr. Flask."

"Pull, pull, my fine hearts-alive; pull, my children; pull, my little ones," drawlingly and soothingly sighed Stubb to his crew, some of whom still showed signs of uneasiness. "Why don't you break your backbones, my boys? What is it you stare at? Those chaps in yonder boat? Tut! They are only five more hands come to help us—never mind from where—the more the merrier. Pull, then, do pull; never mind the brimstone—devils are good fellows enough. So, so; there you are now; that's the stroke for a thousand pounds; that's the stroke to sweep the stakes! Hurrah for the gold cup of sperm oil, my heroes! Three cheers, men—all hearts alive! Easy, easy; don't be in a hurry—don't be in a hurry. Why don't you snap your oars, you rascals? Bite something, you dogs! So, so, so, then;—softly, softly! That's it—that's it! long and strong. Give way there, give way! The devil fetch ye, ye ragamuffin rapscallions; ye are all asleep. Stop snoring, ye sleepers, and pull. Pull, will ye? pull, can't ye? pull, won't ye? Why in the name of gudgeons and ginger-cakes don't ye pull?—pull and break something! pull, and start your eyes out! Here!" whipping out the sharp knife from his girdle; "every mother's son of ye draw his knife, and pull with the blade between his teeth. That's it—that's it. Now ye do something; that looks like it, my steel-bits. Start her—start her, my silver-spoons! Start her, marling-spikes!"

Stubb's exordium to his crew is given here at large, because he had rather a peculiar way of talking to them in general, and especially in inculcating the religion of rowing. But you must not suppose from this specimen of his sermonizings that he ever flew into downright passions with his congregation. Not at all; and therein consisted his chief peculiarity. He would say the most terrific things to his crew, in a tone so strangely compounded of fun and fury, and the fury seemed so calculated merely as a spice to the fun, that no oarsman could hear such queer invocations without pulling for dear life, and yet pulling for the mere joke of the thing. Besides he all the time looked so easy and indolent himself, so loungingly managed his steering-oar, and so broadly gaped—open-mouthed at times—that the mere sight of such a yawning commander, by sheer force of contrast, acted like a charm upon the crew. Then again, Stubb was one of those odd sort of humorists, whose jollity is sometimes so curiously ambiguous, as to put all inferiors on their guard in the matter of obeying them.

In obedience to a sign from Ahab, Starbuck was now pulling obliquely across Stubb's bow; and when for a minute or so the two boats were pretty near to each other, Stubb hailed the mate.

"Mr. Starbuck! larboard boat there, ahoy! a word with ye, sir, if you please!"

"Halloa!" returned Starbuck, turning round not a single inch as he spoke; still earnestly but whisperingly urging his crew; his face set like a flint from Stubb's.

"What think ye of those yellow boys, sir!"

"Smuggled on board, somehow, before the ship sailed. (Strong, strong, boys!") in a whisper to his crew, then speaking out loud again: "A sad business, Mr. Stubb! (seethe her, seethe her, my lads!) but never mind, Mr. Stubb, all for the best. Let all your crew pull strong, come what will. (Spring, my men, spring!) There's hogs-heads of sperm ahead, Mr.

Stubb, and that's what ye came for. (Pull, my boys!) Sperm, sperm's the play! This at least is duty; duty and profit hand in hand!"

"Aye, aye, I thought as much," soliloquized Stubb, when the boats diverged, "as soon as I clapt eye on 'em, I thought so. Aye, and that's what he went into the after hold for, so often, as Dough-Boy long suspected. They were hidden down there. The White Whale's at the bottom of it. Well, well, so be it! Can't be helped! All right! Give way, men! It ain't the White Whale to-day! Give way!"

Now the advent of these outlandish strangers at such a critical instant as the lowering of the boats from the deck, this had not unreasonably awakened a sort of superstitious amazement in some of the ship's company; but Archy's fancied discovery having some time previous got abroad among them, though indeed not credited then, this had in some small measure prepared them for the event. It took off the extreme edge of their wonder; and so what with all this and Stubb's confident way of accounting for their appearance, they were for the time freed from superstitious surmisings; though the affair still left abundant room for all manner of wild conjectures as to dark Ahab's precise agency in the matter from the beginning. For me, I silently recalled the mysterious shadows I had seen creeping on board the Pequod during the dim Nantucket dawn, as well as the enigmatical hintings of the unaccountable Elijah.

Meantime, Ahab, out of hearing of his officers, having sided the furthest to windward, was still ranging ahead of the other boats; a circumstance bespeaking how potent a crew was pulling him. Those tiger yellow creatures of his seemed all steel and whalebone; like five trip-hammers they rose and fell with regular strokes of strength, which periodically started the boat along the water like a horizontal burst boiler out of a Mississippi steamer. As for Fedallah, who was seen pulling the harpooneer oar, he had thrown aside his black jacket, and displayed his naked chest with the whole part of his body above the gunwale, clearly cut against the alternating depressions of the watery horizon; while at the other end of the boat Ahab, with one arm, like a fencer's, thrown half backward into the air, as if to counterbalance any tendency to trip; Ahab was seen steadily managing his steering oar as in a thousand boat lowerings ere the White Whale had torn him. All at once the outstretched arm gave a peculiar motion and then remained fixed, while the boat's five oars were seen simultaneously peaked. Boat and crew sat motionless on the sea. Instantly the three spread boats in the rear paused on their way. The whales had irregularly settled bodily down into the blue, thus giving no distantly discernible token of the movement, though from his closer vicinity Ahab had observed it.

"Every man look out along his oars!" cried Starbuck. "Thou, Queequeg, stand up!"

Nimbly springing up on the triangular raised box in the bow, the savage stood erect there, and with intensely eager eyes gazed off towards the spot where the chase had last been descried. Likewise upon the extreme stern of the boat where it was also triangularly platformed level with the gunwale, Starbuck himself was seen coolly and adroitly balancing himself to the jerking tossings of his chip of a craft, and silently eyeing the vast blue eye of the sea.

Not very far distant Flask's boat was also lying breathlessly still; its commander recklessly standing upon the top of the loggerhead, a stout sort of post rooted in the keel, and rising some two feet above the level of the stern platform. It is used for catching turns with the whale line. Its top is not more spacious than the palm of a man's hand, and standing upon such a base as that, Flask seemed perched at the mast-head of some ship which had sunk to all but her trucks. But little King-Post was small and short, and at the same time little King-Post was full of a large and tall ambition, so that this loggerhead stand-point of his did by no means satisfy King-Post.

"I can't see three seas off; tip us up an oar there, and let me on to that."

Upon this, Daggoo, with either hand upon the gunwale to steady his way, swiftly slid aft, and then erecting himself volunteered his lofty shoulders for a pedestal.

"Good a mast-head as any, sir. Will you mount?"

"That I will, and thank ye very much, my fine fellow; only I wish you fifty feet taller."

Whereupon planting his feet firmly against two opposite planks of the boat, the gigantic negro, stooping a little, presented his flat palm to Flask's foot, and then putting Flask's hand on his hearse-plumed head and bidding him spring as he himself should toss, with one dexterous fling landed the little man high and dry on his shoulders. And here was Flask now standing, Daggoo with one lifted arm furnishing him with a breast-band to lean against and steady himself by.

At any time it is a strange sight to the tyro to see with what wondrous habitude of unconscious skill the whaleman will maintain an erect posture in his boat, even when pitched about by the most riotously perverse and cross-running seas. Still more strange to see him giddily perched upon the loggerhead itself, under such circumstances. But the sight of little Flask mounted upon gigantic Daggoo was yet more curious; for sustaining himself with a cool, indifferent, easy, unthought of, barbaric majesty, the noble negro to every roll of the sea harmoniously rolled his fine form. On his broad back, flaxen-haired Flask seemed a snow-flake. The bearer looked nobler than the rider. Though truly vivacious, tumultuous, ostentatious little Flask would now and then stamp with impatience; but not one added heave did he thereby give to the negro's lordly chest. So have I seen Passion and Vanity stamping the living magnanimous earth, but the earth did not alter her tides and her seasons for that.

Meanwhile Stubb, the third mate, betrayed no such fargazing solicitudes. The whales might have made one of their regular soundings, not a temporary dive from mere fright; and if that were the case, Stubb, as his wont in such cases, it seems, was resolved to solace the languishing interval with his pipe. He withdrew it from his hatband, where he always wore it aslant like a feather. He loaded it, and rammed home the loading with his thumb-end; but hardly had he ignited his match across the rough sand-paper of his hand, when Tashtego, his harpooneer, whose eyes had been setting to windward like two fixed stars, suddenly dropped like light from his erect attitude to his seat, crying out in a quick phrensy of hurry, "Down, down all, and give way!— there they are!"

To a landsman, no whale, nor any sign of a herring, would have been visible at that moment; nothing but a troubled bit of greenish white water, and thin scattered puffs of vapor hovering over it, and suffusingly blowing off to leeward, like the confused scud from white rolling billows. The air around suddenly vibrated and tingled, as it were, like the air over intensely heated plates of iron. Beneath this atmospheric waving and curling, and partially beneath a thin layer of water, also, the whales were swimming. Seen in advance of all the other indications, the puffs of vapor they spouted, seemed their fore-running couriers and detached flying outriders.

All four boats were now in keen pursuit of that one spot of troubled water and air. But it bade far to outstrip them; it flew on and on, as a mass of interblending bubbles borne down a rapid stream from the hills.

"Pull, pull, my good boys," said Starbuck, in the lowest possible but intensest concentrated whisper to his men; while the sharp fixed glance from his eyes darted straight ahead of the bow, almost seemed as two visible needles in two unerring binnacle compasses. He did not say much to his crew, though, nor did his crew say anything to him. Only the silence of the boat was at intervals startlingly pierced by one of his peculiar whispers, now harsh with command, now soft with entreaty.

How different the loud little King-Post. "Sing out and say something, my hearties. Roar and pull, my thunderbolts! Beach me, beach me on their black backs, boys; only do that for me, and I'll sign over to you my Martha's Vineyard plantation, boys; including wife and children, boys. Lay me on—lay me on! O Lord, Lord! but I shall go stark, staring mad: See! see that white water!" And so shouting, he pulled his hat from his head, and stamped up and down on it; then picking it up, flirted it far off upon the sea; and finally fell to rearing and plunging in the boat's stern like a crazed colt from the prairie.

"Look at that chap now," philosophically drawled Stubb, who, with his unlighted short pipe, mechanically retained between his teeth, at a short distance, followed after—"He's got fits, that Flask has. Fits? yes, give him fits—that's the very word—pitch fits into 'em. Merrily, merrily, hearts-alive. Pudding for supper, you know;—merry's the word. Pull, babes—pull, sucklings—pull, all. But what the devil are you hurrying about? Softly, softly, and steadily, my men. Only pull, and keep pulling; nothing more. Crack all your backbones, and bite your knives in two—that's all. Take it easy—why don't ye take it easy, I say, and burst all your livers and lungs!"

But what it was that inscrutable Ahab said to that tiger-yellow crew of his—these were words best omitted here; for you live under the blessed light of the evangelical land. Only the infidel sharks in the audacious seas may give ear to such words, when, with tornado brow, and eyes of real murder, and foam-glued lips, Ahab leaped after his prey.

Meanwhile, all the boats tore on. The repeated specific allusions of Flask to "that whale," as he called the fictitious monster which he declared to be incessantly tantalizing his boat's bow with its tail—these allusions of his were at times so vivid and life-like, that they would cause some one or two of his men to snatch a fearful look over the shoulder. But this was against all rule; for the oarsmen must put out their eyes, and ram a skewer through their necks; usage pronouncing that they must have no organs but ears, and no limbs but arms, in these critical moments.

It was a sight full of quick wonder and awe! The vast swells of the omnipotent sea; the surging, hollow roar they made, as they rolled along the eight gunwales, like gigantic bowls in a boundless bowling-green; the brief suspended agony of the boat, as it would tip for an instant on the knife-like edge of the sharper waves, that almost seemed threatening to cut it in two; the sudden profound dip into the watery glens and hollows; the keen spurrings and goadings to gain the top of the opposite hill; the headlong, sled-like slide down its other side;—all these, with the cries of the herdsmen and harpooneers, and the shuddering gasps of the oarsmen, with the wondrous sight of the ivory Pequod bearing down upon her boats with outstretched sails, like a wild hen after her screaming brood;—all this was thrilling. Not the raw recruit, marching from the bosom of his wife into the fever heat of his first battle; not the dead man's ghost encountering the first unknown phantom in the other world;—neither of these can feel stranger and stronger emotions than that man does, who for the first time finds himself pulling into the charmed, churned circle of the hunted sperm whale.

The dancing white water made by the chase was now becoming more and more visible, owing to the increasing darkness of the dun cloud-shadows flung upon the sea. The jets of vapor no longer blended, but tilted everywhere to right and left; the whales seemed separating their wakes. The boats were pulled more apart; Starbuck giving chase to three whales running dead to leeward. Our sail was now set, and, with the still rising wind, we rushed along; the boat going with such madness through the water, that the lee oars could scarcely be worked rapidly enough to escape being torn from the row-locks.

Soon we were running through a suffusing wide evil of mist; neither ship nor boat to be seen.

"Give way, men," whispered Starbuck, drawing still further aft the sheet of his sail; "there is time to kill a fish yet before the squall comes. There's white water again!—close to! Spring!"

Soon after, two cries in quick succession on each side of us denoted that the other boats had got fast; but hardly were they overheard, when with a lightning-like hurtling whisper Starbuck said: "Stand up!" and Queequeg, harpoon in hand, sprang to his feet.

Though not one of the oarsmen was then facing the life and death peril so close to them ahead, yet with their eyes on the intense countenance of the mate in the stern of the boat, they knew that the imminent instant had come; they heard, too, an enormous wallowing sound as of fifty elephants stirring in their litter. Meanwhile the boat was still booming through the mist, the waves curling and hissing around us like the erected crests of enraged serpents.

"That's his hum. *There, there,* give it to him!" whispered Starbuck.

A short rushing sound leaped out of the boat; it was the darted iron of Queequeg. Then all in one welded commotion came an invisible push from astern, while forward the boat seemed striking on a ledge; the sail collapsed and exploded; a gush of scalding vapor shot up near by; something rolled and tumbled like an earthquake beneath us. The whole crew were half suffocated as they were tossed helter-skelter into the white curdling cream of the squall. Squall, whale, and harpoon had all blended together; and the whale, merely grazed by the iron, escaped.

Though completely swamped, the boat was nearly unharmed. Swimming round it we picked up the floating oars, and lashing them across the gunwhale, tumbled back to our places. There we sat up to our knees in the sea, the water covering every rib and plank, so that to our downward gazing eyes the suspended craft seemed a coral boat grown up to us from the bottom of the ocean.

The wind increased to a howl; the waves dashed their bucklers together; the whole squall roared, forked, and crackled around us like a white fire upon the prairie, in which, unconsumed, we were burning; immortal in these jaws of death! In vain we hailed the other boats; as well roar to the live coals down the chimney of a flaming furnace as hail those boats in that storm. Meanwhile the driving scud, rack, and mist, grew darker with the shadows of night; no sign of the ship could be seen. The rising sea forbade all attempts to bale out the boat. The oars were useless as propellers, performing now the office of life-preservers. So, cutting the lashing of the waterproof match keg, after many failures Starbuck contrived to ignite the lamp in the lantern; then stretching it on a waif pole, handed it to Queequeg as the standard-bearer of this forlorn hope. There, then, he sat, holding up that imbecile candle in the heart of that almighty forlornness. There, then, he sat, the sign and symbol of a man without faith, hopelessly holding up hope in the midst of despair.

Wet, drenched through, and shivering cold, despairing of ship or boat, we lifted up our eyes as the dawn came on. The mist still spread over the sea, the empty lantern lay crushed in the bottom of the boat. Suddenly Queequeg started to his feet, hollowing his hand to his ear. We all heard a faint creaking, as of ropes and yards hitherto muffled by the storm. The sound came nearer and nearer; the thick mists were dimly parted by a huge, vague form. Affrighted, we all sprang into the sea as the ship at last loomed into view, bearing right down upon us within a distance of not much more than its length.

Floating on the waves we saw the abandoned boat, as for one instant it tossed and gaped beneath the ship's bows like a chip at the base of a cataract; and then the vast hull rolled over it, and it was seen no more till it came up weltering astern. Again we swam for it, were dashed against it by the seas, and were at last taken up and safely landed on board. Ere the squall came close to, the other boats had cut loose from their fish and returned to the ship in good time. The ship had given us up, but was still cruising, if haply it might light upon some token of our perishing,— an oar or a lance pole.

THE HYENA   XLIX

THERE are certain queer times and occasions in this strange mixed affair we call life when a man takes this whole universe for a vast practical joke, though the wit thereof he but dimly discerns, and more than suspects that the joke is at nobody's expense but his own. However, nothing dispirits, and nothing seems worth while disputing. He bolts down all events, all creeds, and beliefs, and persuasions, all hard things visible and invisible, never mind how knobby; as an ostrich of potent digestion gobbles down bullets and gun flints. And as for small difficulties and worryings, prospects of sudden disaster, peril of life and limb; all these, and death itself, seem to him only sly, good-natured hits, and jolly punches in the side bestowed by the unseen and unaccountable old joker. That odd sort of wayward mood I am speaking of, comes over a man only in some time of extreme tribulation; it comes in the very midst of his earnestness, so that what just before might have seemed to him a thing most momentous, now seems but a part of the general joke. There is nothing like the perils of whaling to breed this free and easy sort of genial, desperado philosophy; and with it I now regarded this whole voyage of the Pequod, and the great White Whale its object.

"Queequeg," said I, when they had dragged me, the last man, to the deck, and I was still shaking myself in my jacket to fling off the water; "Queequeg, my fine friend, does this sort of thing often happen?" Without much emotion, though soaked through just like me, he gave me to understand that such things did often happen.

"Mr. Stubb," said I, turning to that worthy, who, buttoned up in his oil-jacket, was now calmly smoking his pipe in the rain; "Mr. Stubb, I think I have heard you say that of all whalemen you ever met, our chief mate, Mr. Starbuck, is by far the most careful and prudent. I suppose then, that going plump on a flying whale with your sail set in a foggy squall is the height of a whaleman's discretion?"

"Certain. I've lowered for whales from a leaking ship in a gale off Cape Horn."

"Mr. Flask," said I, turning to little King-Post, who was standing close by; "you are experienced in these things, and I am not. Will you tell me whether it is an unalterable law in this fishery, Mr. Flask, for an oarsman to break his own back pulling himself back-foremost into death's jaws?"

"Can't you twist that smaller?" said Flask. "Yes, that's the law. I should like to see a boat's crew backing water up to a whale face foremost. Ha, ha! the whale would give them squint for squint, mind that!"

Here then, from three impartial witnesses, I had a deliberate statement of the entire case. Considering, therefore, that squalls and capsizings in the water and consequent bivouacks

on the deep, were matters of common occurrence in this
kind of life; considering that at the superlatively critical instant of going on to the whale I must resign my life into
the hands of him who steered the boat—oftentimes a fellow who at that very moment is in his impetuousness upon
the point of scuttling the craft with his own frantic stamp-
ings; considering that the particular disaster to our own
particular boat was chiefly to be imputed to Starbuck's
driving on to his whale almost in the teeth of a squall, and
considering that Starbuck, notwithstanding, was famous for
his great heedfulness in the fishery; considering that I belonged to this uncommonly prudent Starbuck's boat; and
finally considering in what a devil's chase I was implicated,
touching the White Whale: taking all things together, I
say, I thought I might as well go below and make a rough
draft of my will. "Queequeg," said I, "come along, you
shall be my lawyer, executor, and legatee."

It may seem strange that of all men sailors should be
tinkering at their last wills and testaments, but there are
no people in the world more fond of that diversion. This
was the fourth time in my nautical life that I had done
the same thing. After the ceremony was concluded upon
the present occasion, I felt all the easier; a stone was rolled
away from my heart. Besides, all the days I should now live
would be as good as the days that Lazarus lived after his
resurrection; a supplementary clean gain of so many months
or weeks as the case might be. I survived myself; my death
and burial were locked up in my chest. I looked round me
tranquilly and contentedly, like a quiet ghost with a clean
conscience sitting inside the bars of a snug family vault.

Now then, thought I, unconsciously rolling up the sleeves
of my frock, here goes for a cool, collected dive at death
and destruction, and the devil fetch the hindmost.

AHAB'S BOAT AND CREW. FEDALLAH   L

"who would have thought it, Flask!" cried Stubb; "if
I had but one leg you would not catch me in a boat, unless
maybe to stop the plug-hole with my timber toe. Oh! he's a
wonderful old man!"

"I don't think it so strange, after all, on that account,"

said Flask. "If his leg were off at the hip, now, it would
be a different thing. That would disable him; but he has
one knee, and good part of the other left, you know."

"I don't know that, my little man; I never yet saw him
kneel."

* * * * *

Among whale-wise people it has often been argued whether,
considering the paramount importance of his life to the
success of the voyage, it is right for a whaling captain to
jeopardize that life in the active perils of the chase. So
Tamerlane's soldiers often argued with tears in their eyes,
whether that invaluable life of his ought to be carried into
the thickest of the fight.

But with Ahab the question assumed a modified aspect.
Considering that with two legs man is but a hobbling
wight in all times of danger; considering that the pursuit of
whales is always under great and extraordinary difficulties;
that every individual moment, indeed, then comprises a peril;
under these circumstances is it wise for any maimed man
to enter a whale-boat in the hunt? As a general thing, the
joint-owners of the Pequod must have plainly thought not.

Ahab well knew that although his friends at home would
think little of his entering a boat in certain comparatively
harmless vicissitudes of the chase, for the sake of being near
the scene of action and giving his orders in person, yet for
Captain Ahab to have a boat actually apportioned to him
as a regular headsman in the hunt—above all for Captain
Ahab to be supplied with five extra men, as that same
boat's crew, he well knew that such generous conceits never
entered the heads of the owners of the Pequod. Therefore
he had not solicited a boat's crew from them, nor had he in
any way hinted his desires on that head. Nevertheless he
had taken private measures of his own touching all that matter. Until Cabaco's published discovery, the sailors had little
foreseen it, though to be sure when, after being a little while
out of port, all hands had concluded the customary business
of fitting the whaleboats for service; when some time after
this Ahab was now and then found bestirring himself in the
matter of making thole-pins with his own hands for what
was thought to be one of the spare boats, and even solicit-
ously cutting the small wooden skewers, which when the
line is running out are pinned over the groove in the bow:
when all this was observed in him, and particularly his
solicitude in having an extra coat of sheathing in the bottom

of the boat, as if to make it better withstand the pointed
pressure of his ivory limb; and also the anxiety he evinced in
exactly shaping the thigh board, or clumsy cleat, as it is
sometimes called, the horizontal piece in the boat's bow
for bracing the knee against in darting or stabbing at the
whale; when it was observed how often he stood up in that
boat with his solitary knee fixed in the semi-circular depression in the cleat, and with the carpenter's chisel gouged out
a little here and straightened it a little there; all these things,
I say, had awakened much interest and curiosity at the time.
But almost everybody supposed that this particular pre-
parative heedfulness in Ahab must only be with a view to
the ultimate chase of Moby Dick; for he had already revealed his intention to hunt that mortal monster in person.
But such a supposition did by no means involve the remotest
suspicion as to any boat's crew being assigned to that boat.

Now, with the subordinate phantoms, what wonder remained soon waned away; for in a whaler wonders soon
wane. Besides, now and then such unaccountable odds and
ends of strange nations come up from the unknown nooks
and ash-holes of the earth to man these floating outlaws of
whalers; and the ships themselves often pick up such queer
castaway creatures found tossing about the open sea on
planks, bits of wreck, oars, whaleboats, canoes, blown-off
Japanese junks, and what not; that Beelzebub himself might
climb up the side and step down into the cabin to chat
with the captain, and it would not create any unsubduable
excitement in the forecastle.

But be all this as it may, certain it is that while the subordinate phantoms soon found their place among the crew,
though still as it were somehow distinct from them, yet
that hair-turbaned Fedallah remained a muffled mystery to
the last. Whence he came in a mannerly world like this, by
what sort of unaccountable tie he soon evinced himself to
be linked with Ahab's peculiar fortunes; nay, so far as to
have some sort of a half-hinted influence; Heaven knows,
but it might have been even authority over him; all this
none knew. But one cannot sustain an indifferent air concerning Fedallah. He was such a creature as civilized, domestic people in the temperate zone only see in their dreams,
and that but dimly; but the like of whom now and then
glide among the unchanging Asiatic communities, especially
the Oriental isles to the east of the continent—those insulated, immemorial, unalterable countries, which even in these

modern days still preserve much of the ghostly aboriginalness of earth's primal generations, when the memory of the first man was a distinct recollection, and all men his descendants, unknowing whence he came, eyed each other as real phantoms, and asked of the sun and the moon why they were created and to what end; when though, according to Genesis, the angels indeed consorted with the daughters of men, the devils also, add the uncanonical Rabbins, indulged in mundane amours.

THE SPIRIT-SPOUT   LI

DAYS, weeks passed, and under easy sail, the ivory Pequod had slowly swept across four several cruisinggrounds; that off the Azores; off the Cape de Verdes; on the Plate (so called), being off the mouth of the Rio de la Plata; and the Carrol Ground, an unstaked, watery locality, southerly from St. Helena.

It was while gliding through these latter waters that one serene and moonlight night, when all the waves rolled by like scrolls of silver; and, by their soft, suffusing seethings, made what seemed a silvery silence, not a solitude: on such a silent night a silvery jet was seen far in advance of the white bubbles at the bow. Lit up by the moon, it looked celestial; seemed some plumed and glittering god uprising from the sea. Fedallah first descried this jet. For of these moonlight nights, it was his wont to mount to the mainmast head, and stand a look-out there, with the same precision as if it had been day. And yet, though herds of whales were seen by night, not one whaleman in a hundred would venture a lowering for them. You may think with what emotions, then, the seamen beheld this old Oriental perched aloft at such unusual hours; his turban and the moon, companions in one sky. But when, after spending his uniform interval there for several successive nights without uttering a single sound; when, after all this silence, his unearthly voice was heard announcing that silvery, moon-lit jet, every reclining mariner started to his feet as if some winged spirit had lighted in the rigging, and hailed the mortal crew. "There she blows!" Had the trump of judgment blown, they could not have quivered more; yet still they felt no terror;

rather pleasure. For though it was a most unwonted hour, yet so impressive was the cry, and so deliriously exciting, that almost every soul on board instinctively desired a lowering.

Walking the deck with quick, side-lunging strides, Ahab commanded the t'gallant sails and royals to be set, and every stunsail spread. The best man in the ship must take the helm. Then, with every mast-head manned, the piled-up craft rolled down before the wind. The strange, upheaving, lifting tendency of the taffrail breeze filling the hollows of so many sails, made the buoyant, hovering deck to feel like air beneath the feet; while still she rushed along, as if two antagonistic influences were struggling in her—one to mount direct to heaven, the other to drive yawingly to some horizontal goal. And had you watched Ahab's face that night, you would have thought that in him also two different things were warring. While his one live leg made lively echoes along the deck, every stroke of his dead limb sounded like a coffin-tap. On life and death this old man walked. But though the ship so swiftly sped, and though from every eye, like arrows, the eager glances shot, yet the silvery jet was no more seen that night. Every sailor swore he saw it once, but not a second time.

This midnight-spout had almost grown a forgotten thing, when, some days after, lo! at the same silent hour, it was again announced: again it was descried by all; but upon making sail to overtake it, once more it disappeared as if it had never been. And so it served us night after night, till no one heeded it but to wonder at it. Mysteriously jetted into the clear moonlight, or starlight, as the case might be; disappearing again for one whole day, or two days, or three; and somehow seeming at every distinct repetition to be advancing still further and further in our van, this solitary jet seemed for ever alluring us on.

Nor with the immemorial superstition of their race, and in accordance with the preternaturalness, as it seemed, which in many things invested the Pequod, were there wanting some of the seamen who swore that whenever and wherever described; at however remote times, or in however far apart latitudes and longitudes, that unnearable spout was cast by one self-same whale; and that whale, Moby Dick. For a time, there reigned, too, a sense of peculiar dread at this flitting apparition, as if it were treacherously beckoning us on and on, in order that the monster might turn round upon us, and rend us at last in the remotest and most savage seas.

These temporary apprehensions, so vague but so awful, derived a wondrous potency from the contrasting serenity of the weather, in which, beneath all its blue blandness, some thought there lurked a devilish charm, as for days and days we voyaged along, through seas so wearily, lonesomely mild, that all space, in repugnance to our vengeful errand, seemed vacating itself of life before our urn-like prow.

But, at last, when turning to the eastward, the Cape winds began howling around us, and we rose and fell upon the long, troubled seas that are there; when the ivory-tusked Pequod sharply bowed to the blast, and gored the dark waves in her madness, till, like showers of silver chips, the foam-flakes flew over her bulwarks; then all this desolate vacuity of life went away, but gave place to sights more dismal than before.

Close to our bows, strange forms in the water darted hither and thither before us; while thick in our rear flew the inscrutable sea-ravens. And every morning, perched on our stays, rows of these birds were seen; and spite of our hootings, for a long time obstinately clung to the hemp, as though they deemed our ship some drifting, uninhabited craft; a thing appointed to desolation, and therefore fit roosting-place for their homeless selves. And heaved and heaved, still unrestingly heaved the black sea, as if its vast tides were a conscience; and the great mundane soul were in anguish and remorse for the long sin and suffering it had bred.

Cape of Good Hope, do they call ye? Rather Cape Tormentoto, as called of yore; for long allured by the perfidious silences that before had attended us, we found ourselves launched into this tormented sea, where guilty things transformed in those fowls and these fish, seemed condemned to swim on everlastingly without any haven in store, or beat that black air without any horizon. But calm, snow-white, and unvarying; still directing its fountain of feathers to the sky; still beckoning us from before, the solitary jet would at times be descried.

During all this blackness of the elements, Ahab, though assuming for the time the almost continual command of the drenched and dangerous deck, manifested the gloomiest reserve; and more seldom than ever addressed his mates. In tempestuous times like these, after everything above and

aloft has been secured, nothing more can be done but pas-
sively to await the issue of the gale. Then Captain and crew
become practical fatalists. So, with his ivory leg inserted into
its accustomed hole, and with one hand firmly grasping a
shroud, Ahab for hours and hours would stand gazing dead
to windward, while an occasional squall of sleet or snow
would all but congeal his very eyelashes together. Meantime, the crew driven from the forward part of the ship by
the perilous seas that burstingly broke over its brows, stood
in a line along the bulwarks in the waist; and the better to
guard against the leaping waves, each man had slipped himself into a sort of bowline secured to the rail, in which he
swung as in a loosened belt. Few or no words were spoken;
and the silent ship, as if manned by painted sailors in wax,
day after day tore on through all the swift madness and
gladness of the demoniac waves. By night the same muteness
of humanity before the shrieks of the ocean prevailed; still
in silence the men swung in the bowlines; still wordless Ahab
stood up to the blast. Even when wearied nature seemed
demanding repose he would not seek that repose in his
hammock. Never could Starbuck forget the old man's aspect, when one night going down into the cabin to mark how
the barometer stood, he saw him with closed eyes sitting
straight in his floor-screwed chair; the rain and half-
melted sleet of the storm from which he had some time before emerged, still slowly dripping from the unremoved hat
and coat. On the table beside him lay unrolled one of those
charts of tides and currents which have previously been spoken of. His lantern swung from his tightly clenched hand.
Though the body was erect, the head was thrown back so
that the closed eyes were pointed towards the needle of
the tell-tale that swung from a beam in the ceiling.*

Terrible old man! thought Starbuck with a shudder, sleeping in this gale, still thou steadfastly eyes thy purpose.

---

* The cabin-compass is called the tell-tale, because without
going to the compass at the helm, the Captain, while below, can
inform himself of the course of the ship.

THE ALBATROSS LII

SOUTH-EASTWARD from the Cape, off the distant Crozetts, a good cruising ground for Right Whalemen, a sail loomed ahead, the Goney (Albatross) by name. As she slowly drew nigh, from my lofty perch at the fore-mast-head, I had a good view of that sight so remarkable to a tyro in the far ocean fisheries—a whaler at sea, and long absent from home.

As if the waves had been fullers, this craft was bleached like the skeleton of a stranded walrus. All down her sides, this spectral appearance was traced with long channels of reddened rust, while all her spars and her rigging were like the thick branches of trees furred over with hoar-frost. Only her lower sails were set. A wild sight it was to see her long-bearded look-outs at those three mast-heads. They seemed clad in the skins of beasts, so torn and bepatched the raiment that had survived nearly four years of cruising. Standing in iron hoops nailed to the mast, they swayed and swung over a fathomless sea; and though, when the ship slowly glided close under our stern, we six men in the air came so nigh to each other that we might almost have leaped from the mast-heads of one ship to those of the other; yet, those forlorn-looking fishermen, mildly eyeing us as they passed, said not one word to our own look-outs, while the quarter-deck hail was being heard from below.

"Ship ahoy! Have ye seen the White Whale?"

But as the strange captain, leaning over the pallid bulwarks, was in the act of putting his trumpet to his mouth, it somehow fell from his hand into the sea; and the wind now rising amain, he in vain strove to make himself heard without it. Meantime his ship was still increasing the distance between. While in various silent ways the seamen of the Pequod were evincing their observance of this ominous incident at the first mere mention of the White Whale's name to another ship, Ahab for a moment paused; it almost seemed as though he would have lowered a boat to board the stranger, had not the threatening wind forbade. But taking advantage of his windward position, he again seized his trumpet, and knowing by her aspect that the stranger vessel

was a Nantucketer and shortly bound home, he loudly hailed
—"Ahoy there! This is the Pequod, bound round the world!
Tell them to address all future letters to the Pacific ocean!
and this time three years, if I am not at home, tell them to
address them to ————"

At that moment the two wakes were fairly crossed, and
instantly, then, in accordance with their singular ways,
shoals of small harmless fish, that for some days before had
been placidly swimming by our side, darted away with what
seemed shuddering fins, and ranged themselves fore and aft
with the stranger's flanks. Though in the course of his continual voyagings Ahab must often before have noticed a similar sight, yet, to any monomaniac man, the veriest trifles ca-
priciously carry meanings.

"Swim away from me, do ye?" murmured Ahab, gazing
over into the water. There seemed but little in the words, but
the tone conveyed more of deep helpless sadness than the
insane old man had ever before evinced. But turning to the
steersman, who thus far had been holding the ship in the
wind to diminish her headway, he cried out in his old lion
voice,—"Up helm! Keep her off round the world!"

Round the world! There is much in that sound to inspire
proud feelings; but whereto does all that circumnavigation
conduct? Only through numberless perils to the very point
whence we started, where those that we left behind secure,
were all the time before us.

Were this world an endless plain, and by sailing eastward we could forever reach new distances, and discover
sights more sweet and strange than any Cyclades or Islands
of King Solomon, then there were promise in the voyage.
But in pursuit of those far mysteries we dream of, or in
tormented chase of that demon phantom that, some time or
other, swims before all human hearts; while chasing such
over this round globe, they either lead us on in barren mazes
or midway leave us whelmed.

THE GAM   LIII

THE ostensible reason why Ahab did not go on board
of the whaler we had spoken was this: the wind and sea
betokened storms. But even had this not been the case, he
would not after all, perhaps have boarded her—judging by

his subsequent conduct on similar occasions—if so it had been that, by the process of hailing, he had obtained a negative answer to the question he put. For, as it eventually turned out, he cared not to consort, even for five minutes, with any stranger captain, except he could contribute some of that information he so absorbingly sought. But all this might remain inadequately estimated, were not something said here of the peculiar usages of whaling-vessels when meeting each other in foreign seas, and especially on a common cruising-ground.

If two strangers crossing the Pine Barrens in New York State, or the equally desolate Salisbury Plain in England; if casually encountering each other in such inhospitable wilds, these twain, for the life of them, cannot well avoid a mutual salutation; and stopping for a moment to interchange the news; and, perhaps, sitting down for a while and resting in concert: then, how much more natural that upon the illimitable Pine Barrens and Salisbury Plains of the sea, two whaling vessels descrying each other at the ends of the earth—off lone Fanning's Island, or the far away King's Mills; how much more natural, I say, that under such circumstances these ships should not only interchange hails, but come into still closer, more friendly and sociable contact. And especially would this seem to be a matter of course, in the case of vessels owned in one seaport, and whose captains, officers, and not a few of the men are personally known to each other; and consequently, have all sorts of dear domestic things to talk about.

For the long absent ship, the outward-bounder, perhaps, has letters on board; at any rate, she will be sure to let her have some papers of a date a year or two later than the last one on her blurred and thumb-worn files. And in return for that courtesy, the outward-bound ship would receive the latest whaling intelligence from the cruising-ground to which she may be destined, a thing of the utmost importance to her. And in degree, all this will hold true concerning whaling vessels crossing each other's track on the cruising-ground itself, even though they are equally long absent from home. For one of them may have received a transfer of letters from some third, and now far remote vessel; and some of those letters may be for the people of the ship she now meets. Besides, they would exchange the whaling news, and have an agreeable chat. For not only would they meet with all the sympathies of sailors, but likewise with all the peculiar congenialities arising from a common pursuit and mutually shared privations and perils.

Nor would difference of country make any very essential difference; that is, so long as both parties speak one language, as is the case with Americans and English. Though, to be sure, from the small number of English whalers, such meetings do not very often occur, and when they do occur there is too apt to be a sort of shyness between them; for your Englishman is rather reserved, and your Yankee, he does not fancy that sort of thing in anybody but himself. Besides, the English whalers sometimes affect a kind of metropolitan superiority over the American whalers; regarding the long, lean Nantucketer, with his nondescript provincialisms, as a sort of sea-peasant. But where this superiority in the English whalemen does really consist, it would be hard to say, seeing that the Yankees in one day, collectively, kill more whales than all the English, collectively, in ten years. But this is a harmless little foible in the English whale-hunters, which the Nantucketer does not take much to heart; probably, because he knows that he has a few foibles himself.

So, then, we see that of all ships separately sailing the sea, the whalers have most reason to be sociable—and they are so. Whereas, some merchant ships crossing each other's wake in the mid-Atlantic, will oftentimes pass on without so much as a single word of recognition, mutually cutting each other on the high seas, like a brace of dandies in Broadway; and all the time indulging, perhaps, in finical criticism upon each other's rig. As for Men-of-War, when they chance to meet at sea, they first go through such a string of silly bowings and scrapings, such a ducking of ensigns, that there does not seem to be much right-down hearty good-will and brotherly love about it at all. As touching Slave-ships meeting, why, they are in such a prodigious hurry, they run away from each other as soon as possible. And as for Pirates, when they chance to cross each other's cross-bones, the first hail is—"How many skulls?"—the same way that whalers hail—"How many barrels?" And that question once answered, pirates straightway steer apart, for they are infernal villains on both sides, and don't like to see overmuch of each other's villainous likenesses.

But look at the godly, honest, unostentatious, hospitable, sociable, free-and-easy whaler! What does the whaler do when she meets another whaler in any sort of decent weather? She has a *"Gam,"* a thing so utterly unknown to all other ships that they never heard of the name even; and if by chance they should hear of it, they only grin at it, and repeat gamesome stuff about "spouters" and "blubber-boilers," and such like pretty exclamations. Why it is that all Merchant-seamen, and also all Pirates and Man-of-War's men, and Slave-ship sailors, cherish such a scornful feeling towards Whale-ships; this is a question it would be hard to answer. Because, in the case of pirates, say, I should like to know whether that profession of theirs has any peculiar glory about it. It sometimes ends in uncommon elevation, indeed; but only at the gallows. And besides, when a man is elevated in that odd fashion, he has no proper foundation for his superior altitude. Hence, I conclude, that in boasting himself to be high lifted above a whaleman, in that assertion the pirate has no solid basis to stand on.

But what is a *Gam?* You might wear out your index-finger running up and down the columns of dictionaries, and never find the word. Dr. Johnson never attained to that erudition; Noah Webster's ark does not hold it. Nevertheless, this same expressive word has now for many years been in constant use among some fifteen thousand true born Yankees. Certainly, it needs a definition, and should be incorporated into the Lexicon. With that view, let me learnedly define it.

GAM. NOUN—*A social meeting of two (or more) Whaleships, generally on a cruising-ground; when, after exchanging hails, they exchange visits by boats' crews: the two captains remaining, for the time, on board of one ship, and the two chief mates on the other.*

There is another little item about Gamming which must not be forgotten here. All professions have their own little peculiarities of detail; so has the whale fishery. In a pirate, man-of-war, or slave ship, when the captain is rowed anywhere in his boat, he always sits in the stern sheets on a comfortable, sometimes cushioned seat there, and often steers himself with a pretty little milliner's tiller decorated with gay cords and ribbons. But the whale-boat has no seat astern, no sofa of that sort whatever, and no tiller at all. High times indeed, if whaling captains were wheeled about the water on castors like gouty old aldermen in patent chairs. And as for a tiller, the whale-boat never admits of any such effeminacy; and therefore as in gamming a complete boat's crew must leave the ship, and hence as the boat steerer or harpooner

is of the number, that subordinate is the steersman upon
the occasion, and the captain, having no place to sit in, is
pulled off to his visit all standing like a pine tree. And often
you will notice that being conscious of the eyes of the
whole visible world resting on him from the sides of the
two ships, this standing captain is all alive to the importance
of sustaining his dignity by maintaining his legs. Nor is this
any very easy matter; for in his rear is the immense projecting steering oar hitting him now and then in the small
of his back, the after-oar reciprocating by rapping his
knees in front. He is thus completely wedged before and
behind, and can only expand himself sideways by settling
down on his stretched legs; but a sudden, violent pitch of the
boat will often go far to topple him, because length of
foundation is nothing without corresponding breadth. Merely
make a spread angle of two poles, and you cannot stand
them up. Then, again, it would never do in plain sight of the
world's riveted eyes, it would never do, I say, for this strad-
dling captain to be seen steadying himself the slightest
particle by catching hold of anything with his hands; indeed,
as token of his entire, buoyant self-command, he generally
carries his hands in his trowsers' pockets; but perhaps being
generally very large, heavy hands, he carries them there for
ballast. Nevertheless there have occurred instances, well authenticated ones too, where the captain has been known for
an uncommonly critical moment or two, in a sudden squall
say—to seize hold of the nearest oarsman's hair, and hold
on there like grim death.

THE TOWN-HO'S STORY   LIV

(As told at the Golden Inn.)

THE Cape of Good Hope, and all the watery region round
about there, is much like some noted four corners of a great
highway, where you meet more travellers than in any other
part.

It was not very long after speaking the Goney that another
homeward-bound whaleman, the Town-Ho,* was encoun-

---

* The ancient whale-cry upon first sighting a whale from the
mast-head, still used by whalemen in hunting the famous Gallipagos terrapin.

tered. She was manned almost wholly by Polynesians. In the short gam that ensued she gave us strong news of Moby Dick. To some the general interest in the White Whale was now wildly heightened by a circumstance of the Town-Ho's story, which seemed obscurely to involve with the whale a certain wondrous, inverted visitation of one of those so called judgments of God which at times are said to overtake some men. This latter circumstance, with its own particular accompaniments, forming what may be called the secret part of the tragedy about to be narrated, never reached the ears of Captain Ahab or his mates. For that secret part of the story was unknown to the captain of the Town-Ho himself. It was the private property of three confederate white seamen of that ship, one of whom, it seems, communicated it to Tashtego with Romish injunctions of secrecy, but the following night Tashtego rambled in his sleep, and revealed so much of it in that way, that when he was wakened he could not well withhold the rest. Nevertheless, so potent an influence did this thing have on those seamen in the Pequod who came to the full knowledge of it, and by such a strange delicacy, to call it so, were they governed in this matter, that they kept the secret among themselves so that it never transpired abaft the Pequod's main-mast. Interweaving in its proper place this darker thread with the story as publicly narrated on the ship, the whole of this strange affair I now proceed to put on lasting record.

For my humor's sake, I shall preserve the style in which I once narrated it at Lima, to a lounging circle of my Spanish friends, one saint's eve, smoking upon the thick-gilt tiled piazza of the Golden Inn. Of those fine cavaliers, the young Dons, Pedro and Sebastian, were on the closer terms with me; and hence the interluding questions they occasionally put, and which are duly answered at the time.

"Some two years prior to my first learning the events which I am about rehearsing to you, gentlemen, the Town-Ho, Sperm Whaler of Nantucket, was cruising in your Pacific here, not very many days' sail westward from the eaves of this good Golden Inn. She was somewhere to the northward of the Line. One morning upon handling the pumps, according to daily usage, it was observed that she made more water in her hold than common. They supposed a swordfish had stabbed her, gentlemen. But the captain, having some unusual reason for believing that rare good luck awaited him in those latitudes; and therefore being very averse to quit them, and the leak not being then considered at all dangerous, though, indeed, they could not find it after searching the hold as low down as was possible in rather heavy weather, the ship still continued her cruisings, the mariners working at the pumps at wide and easy intervals; but no good luck came; more days went by, and not only was the leak yet undiscovered, but it sensibly increased. So much so, that now taking some alarm, the captain, making all sail, stood away for the nearest harbor among the islands, there to have his hull hove out and repaired.

"Though no small passage was before her, yet, if the commonest chance favored, he did not at all fear that his ship would founder by the way, because his pumps were of the best, and being periodically relieved at them, those six-and-thirty men of his could easily keep the ship free; never mind if the leak should double on her. In truth, well nigh the whole of this passage being attended by very prosperous breezes, the Town-Ho had all but certainly arrived in perfect safety at her port without the occurrence of the least fatality, had it not been for the brutal overbearing of Radney, the mate, a Vineyarder, and the bitterly provoked vengeance of Steelkilt, a Lakeman and desperado from Buffalo."

" 'Lakeman!—Buffalo! Pray, what is a Lakeman, and where is Buffalo?' said Don Sebastian, rising in his swinging mat of grass.

"On the eastern shore of our Lake Erie, Don; but—I crave your courtesy—may be, you shall soon hear further of all that. Now, gentlemen, in square-sail brigs and three-masted ships, well nigh as large and stout as any that ever sailed out of your old Callao to far Manilla; this Lakeman, in the land-locked heart of our America, had yet been nurtured by all those agrarian freebooting impressions popularly connected with the open ocean. For in their interflowing aggregate, those grand freshwater seas of ours,—Erie, and Ontario, and Huron, and Superior, and Michigan,—possess an ocean-like expansiveness, with many of the ocean's noblest traits; with many of its rimmed varieties of races and of climes. They contain round archipelagoes of romantic isles, even as the Polynesian waters do; in large part, are shored by two great contrasting nations, as the Atlantic is; they furnish long maritime approaches to our numerous territorial colonies from the East, dotted all round their banks; here and there are frowned upon by batteries, and by the goat-like craggy guns of lofty Mackinaw; they have heard the fleet thunderings of naval victories; at intervals, they yield their beaches to wild barbarians, whose red painted faces flash from out their peltry wigwams; for leagues and leagues are flanked by ancient and unentered forests, where the gaunt pines stand like serried lines of kings in Gothic genealogies; those same woods harboring wild Afric beasts of prey, and silken creatures whose exported furs give robes to Tartar Emperors; they mirror the paved capitals of Buffalo and Cleveland, as well as Winnebago villages; they float alike the full-rigged merchant ship, the armed cruiser of the State, the steamer, and the beech canoe; they are swept by Borean and dismasting blasts as direful as any that lash the salted wave; they know what shipwrecks are, for out of sight of land, however inland, they have drowned full many a midnight ship with all its shrieking crew. Thus, gentlemen, though an inlander, Steelkilt was wild-ocean born, and wild-ocean nurtured; as much of an audacious mariner as any. And for Radney, though in his infancy he may have laid him down on the lone Nantucket beach, to nurse at his maternal sea; though in after life he had long followed our austere Atlantic and your contemplative Pacific; yet was he quite as vengeful and full of social quarrel as the backwoods seaman, fresh from the latitudes of buck-horn handled Bowie-knives. Yet was this Nantucketer a man with some good-hearted traits; and this Lakeman, a mariner, who though a sort of devil indeed, might yet by inflexible firmness, only tempered by that common decency of human recognition which is the meanest slave's right; thus treated, this Steelkilt had long been retained harmless and docile. At all events, he had proved so thus far; but Radney was doomed and made mad, and Steelkilt—but, gentlemen, you shall hear.

"It was not more than a day or two at the furthest after pointing her prow for her island haven, that the Town-Ho's leak seemed again increasing, but only so as to require an hour or more at the pumps every day. You must know that in a settled and civilized ocean like our Atlantic, for example, some skippers think little of pumping their whole way across it; though of a still, sleepy night, should the officer of the deck happen to forget his duty in that respect, the probability would be that he and his shipmates would never again remember it, on account of all hands gently subsiding to the bottom. Nor in the solitary and savage seas far from you to the westward, gentlemen, is it altogether unusual for ships to keep clanging at their pump-handles in full chorus even for a voyage of considerable length; that is, if it lie along a tolerably accessible coast, or if any other reasonable retreat is afforded them. It is only when a leaky vessel is in some very out of the way part of those waters, some really landless latitude, that her captain begins to feel a little anxious.

"Much this way had it been with the Town-Ho; so when her leak was found gaining once more, there was in truth some small concern manifested by several of her company; especially by Radney the mate. He commanded the upper sails to be well hoisted, sheeted home anew, and every way expanded to the breeze. Now this Radney, I suppose, was as little of a coward, and as little inclined to any sort of nervous apprehensiveness touching his own person as any fearless, unthinking creature on land or on sea that you can conveniently imagine, gentlemen. Therefore when he betrayed this solicitude about the safety of the ship, some of the seamen declared that it was only on account of his being a part owner in her. So when they were working that evening at the pumps, there was on this head no small gamesomeness slily going on among them, as they stood with their feet continually overflowed by the rippling clear water; clear as any mountain spring, gentlemen—that bubbling from the pumps ran across the deck, and poured itself out in steady spouts at the lee scupper-holes.

"Now, as you well know, it is not seldom the case in this conventional world of ours—watery or otherwise; that when a person placed in command over his fellow-men finds one of them to be very significantly his superior in general pride of manhood, straightway against that man he conceives an unconquerable dislike and bitterness; and if he have a chance he will pull down and pulverize that subaltern's tower, and make a little heap of dust of it. Be this conceit of mine as it may, gentlemen, at all events Steelkilt was a tall and noble animal with a head like a Roman, and a flowing golden beard like the tasseled housings of your last viceroy's snorting charger; and a brain, and a heart, and a soul in him, gentlemen, which had made Steelkilt Charlemagne, had he been born son to Charlemagne's father. But Radney, the mate, was ugly as a mule; yet as hardy, as stubborn, as malicious. He did not love Steelkilt, and Steelkilt knew it.

"Espying the mate drawing near as he was toiling at the pump with the rest, the Lakeman affected not to notice him, but unawed, went on with his gay banterings.

" 'Aye, aye, my merry lads, it's a lively leak this; hold a cannikin, one of ye, and let's have a taste. By the Lord, it's worth bottling! I tell ye what, men, old Rad's investment must go for it! he had best cut away his part of the hull and tow it home. The fact is, boys, that sword-fish only began the job; he's come back again with a gang of ship-carpenters, saw-fish, and file-fish, and what not; and the whole posse of 'em are now hard at work cutting and slash-ing at the bottom; making improvements, I suppose. If old Rad were here now, I'd tell him to jump overboard and scatter 'em. They're playing the devil with his estate, I can tell him. But he's a simple old soul,—Rad, and a beauty too. Boys, they say the rest of his property is invested in looking-glasses. I wonder if he'd give a poor devil like me the model of his nose.'

" 'Damn your eyes! what's that pump stopping for?' roared Radney, pretending not to have heard the sailors' talk. 'Thun-der away at it!'

" 'Aye, aye, sir,' said Steelkilt, merry as a cricket. 'Lively boys, lively, now!' And with that the pump clanged like fifty fire-engines; the men tossed their hats off to it, and ere long that peculiar gasping of the lungs was heard which denotes the fullest tension of life's utmost energies.

"Quitting the pump at last, with the rest of his band, the Lakeman went forward all panting, and sat himself down on the windlass, his face fiery red, his eyes bloodshot, and wiping the profuse sweat from his brow. Now what cozening fiend it was, gentlemen, that possessed Radney to meddle with such a man in that corporally exasperated state, I know not; but so it happened. Intolerably striding along the deck, the mate commanded him to get a broom and sweep down the planks, and also a shovel, and remove some offensive mat-ters consequent upon allowing a pig to run at large.

"Now, gentlemen, sweeping a ship's deck at sea is a piece of household work which in all times but raging gales is regularly attended to every evening; it has been known to be done in the case of ships actually foundering at the time. Such, gentlemen, is the inflexibility of sea-usages and the in-stinctive love of neatness in seamen; some of whom would not willingly drown without first washing their faces. But in all vessels this broom business is the prescriptive province of the boys, if boys there be aboard. Besides, it was the stronger men in the Town-Ho that had been divided into gangs, taking turns at the pumps; and being the most athletic seaman of them all, Steelkilt had been regularly assigned captain of one of the gangs; consequently he should have been freed from any trivial business not connected with truly nautical duties, such being the case with his comrades. I mention all these particulars so that you may understand exactly how this affair stood between the two men.

"But there was more than this: the order about the shovel was almost as plainly meant to sting and insult Steelkilt, as though Radney had spat in his face. Any man who has gone sailor in a whaleship will understand this; and all this and doubtless much more, the Lakeman fully comprehended when the mate uttered his command. But as he sat still for a moment, and as he steadfastly looked into the mate's malignant eye and perceived the stacks of powder-casks heaped up in him and the slow-match silently burning along towards them; as he instinctively saw all this, that strange forbearance and unwillingness to stir up the deeper passionateness in any already ireful being—a repugnance most felt, when felt at all, by really valiant men even when aggrieved—this nameless phantom feeling, gentlemen, stole over Steelkilt.

"Therefore, in his ordinary tone, only a little broken by the bodily exhaustion he was temporarily in, he answered him saying that sweeping the deck was not his business, and he would not do it. And then, without at all alluding to the shovel, he pointed to three lads as the customary sweepers; who, not being billeted at the pumps, had done little or nothing all day. To this, Radney replied with an oath, in a most domineering and outrageous manner unconditionally reiterating his command; meanwhile advancing upon the still seated Lakeman, with an uplifted cooper's club hammer which he had snatched from a cask near by.

"Heated and irritated as he was by his spasmodic toil at the pumps, for all his first nameless feeling of forbearance the sweating Steelkilt could but ill brook this bearing in the mate; but somehow still smothering the conflagration within him, without speaking he remained doggedly rooted to his seat, till at last the incensed Radney shook the hammer within a few inches of his face, furiously commanding him to do his bidding.

"Steelkilt rose, and slowly retreating round the windlass, steadily followed by the mate with his menacing hammer, deliberately repeated his intention not to obey. Seeing, however, that his forbearance had not the slightest effect, by an awful and unspeakable intimation with his twisted hand he warned off the foolish and infatuated man; but it was to no purpose. And in this way the two went once slowly round the windlass; when, resolved at last no longer to retreat, bethinking him that he had now forborne as much as comported with his humor, the Lakeman paused on the hatches and thus spoke to the officer:

" 'Mr. Radney, I will not obey you. Take that hammer away, or look to yourself.' But the predestinated mate coming still closer to him, where the Lakeman stood fixed, now shook the heavy hammer within an inch of his teeth; meanwhile repeating a string of insufferable maledictions. Retreating not the thousandth part of an inch; stabbing him in the eye with the unflinching poniard of his glance, Steelkilt, clenching his right hand behind him and creepingly drawing it back, told his persecutor that if the hammer but grazed his cheek he (Steelkilt) would murder him. But, gentlemen, the fool had been branded for the slaughter by the gods. Immediately the hammer touched the cheek; the next instant the lower jaw of the mate was stove in his head; he fell on the hatch spouting blood like a whale.

"Ere the cry could go aft Steelkilt was shaking one of the backstays leading far aloft to where two of his comrades were standing their mast-heads. They were both Canallers.

" 'Canallers!' cried Don Pedro. " 'We have seen many whale-ships in our harbors, but never heard of your Canallers. Pardon: who and what are they?'

" 'Canallers, Don, are the boatmen belonging to our grand Erie Canal. You must have heard of it.'

" 'Nay, Senor; hereabouts in this dull, warm, most lazy, and hereditary land, we know but little of your vigorous North.'

" 'Aye? Well then, Don, refill my cup. Your chicha's very fine; and ere proceeding further I will tell ye what our Canallers are; for such information may throw side-light upon my story.'

"For three hundred and sixty miles, gentlemen, through the entire breadth of the state of New York; through numerous populous cities and most thriving villages; through long, dismal, uninhabited swamps, and affluent, cultivated fields, unrivalled for fertility; by billiard-room and barroom; through the holy-of-holies of great forests; on Roman arches over Indian rivers; through sun and shade; by happy hearts or broken; through all the wide contrasting scenery of those noble Mohawk counties; and especially, by rows of snow-white chapels, whose spires stand almost like milestones, flows one continual stream of Venetianly corrupt and often lawless life. There's your true Ashantee, gentlemen; there howl your pagans; where you ever find them, next door to you; under the long-flung shadow, and the snug patronizing lee of churches. For by some curious fatality, as it is often noted of your metropolitan freebooters that they ever encamp around the halls of justice, so sinners, gentlemen, most abound in holiest vicinities.

" 'Is that a friar passing?' said Don Pedro, looking downwards into the crowded plazza, with humorous concern.

" 'Well for our northern friend, Dame Isabella's Inquisition wanes in Lima,' laughed Don Sebastian. 'Proceed, Senor.'

" 'A moment! Pardon!' cried another of the company. " 'In the name of all us Limeese, I but desire to express to you, sir sailor, that we have by no means overlooked your delicacy in not substituting present Lima for distant Venice in your corrupt comparison. Oh! do not bow and look surprised; you know the proverb all along this coast—"Corrupt as Lima." It but bears out your saying, too; churches more plentiful than billiard-tables, and for ever open—and "Corrupt as Lima." So, too, Venice; I have been there; the holy city of the blessed evangelist, St. Mark!—St. Dominic, purge it! Your cup! Thanks: here I refill; now, you pour out again.'

"Freely depicted in his own vocation, gentlemen, the Canaller would make a fine dramatic hero, so abundantly and picturesquely wicked is he. Like Mark Antony, for days and days along his green-turfed, flowery Nile, he indolently floats, openly toying with his red-cheeked Cleopatra, ripening his apricot thigh upon the sunny deck. But ashore, all this effeminacy is dashed. The brigandish guise which the Canaller so proudly sports; his slouched and gaily-ribboned hat betoken his grand features. A terror to the smiling innocence of the villages through which he floats; his swart visage and bold swagger are not unshunned in cities. Once a vagabond on his own canal, I have received good turns from one of these Canallers; I thank him heartily; would fain be not ungrateful; but it is often one of the prime redeeming qualities of your man of violence, that at times he has as stiff an arm to back a poor stranger in a strait, as to plunder a wealthy one. In sum, gentlemen, what the wildness of this canal life is, is emphatically evinced by this; that our wild whale-fishery contains so many of its most finished graduates, and that scarce any race of mankind, except Sydney men, are so much distrusted by our whaling captains. Nor does it at all diminish the curiousness of this matter, that to many thousands of our rural boys and young men born along its line, the probationary life of the Grand Canal furnishes the sole transition between quietly reaping in a Christian corn-field, and recklessly ploughing the waters of the most barbaric seas."

" 'I see! I see!' impetuously exclaimed Don Pedro, spilling his chicha upon his silvery ruffles. 'No need to travel! The world's one Lima. I had thought, now, that at your temperate North the generations were cold and holy as the hills.—But the story.'

"I left off, gentlemen, where the Lakeman shook the backstay. Hardly had he done so, when he was surrounded by the three junior mates and the four harpooneers, who all crowded him to the deck. But sliding down the ropes like baleful comets, the two Canallers rushed into the uproar, and sought to drag their man out of it towards the forecastle. Others of the sailors joined with them in this attempt, and a twisted turmoil ensued; while standing out of harm's way, the valiant captain danced up and down with a whalepike, calling upon his officers to manhandle that atrocious scoundrel, and smoke him along to the quarter-deck. At intervals, he ran close up to the revolving border of the confusion, and prying into the heart of it with his pike, sought to prick out the object of his resentment. But Steelkilt and his desperadoes were too much for them all; they succeeded in gaining the forecastle deck, where, hastily slewing about three or four large casks in a line with the windlass, these sea-Parisians entrenched themselves behind the barricade."

" 'Come out of that, ye pirates!' roared the captain, now menacing them with a pistol in each hand, just brought to him by the steward. 'Come out of that, ye cut-throats!'

"Steelkilt leaped on the barricade, and striding up and down there, defied the worst the pistols could do; but gave the captain to understand distinctly, that his (Steelkilt's) death would be the signal for a murderous mutiny on the part of all hands. Fearing in his heart lest this might prove but too true, the captain a little desisted, but still commanded the insurgents instantly to return to their duty.

" 'Will you promise not to touch us, if we do?' demanded their ringleader.

" 'Turn to! turn to!—I make no promise;—to your duty! Do you want to sink the ship, by knocking off at a time like this? Turn to!' and he once more raised a pistol.

" 'Sink the ship?' cried Steelkilt. 'Aye, let her sink. Not a man of us turns to, unless you swear not to raise a rope-yarn against us. What say ye, men?' turning to his comrades. A fierce cheer was their response.

"The Lakeman now patrolled the barricade, all the while keeping his eye on the Captain, and jerking out such sentences as these:—'It's not our fault; we didn't want it; I told him to take his hammer away; it was boy's business; he might have known me before this; I told him not to prick the buffalo; I believe I have broken a finger here against his cursed jaw; ain't those mincing knives down in the forecastle there, men? look to those handspikes, my hearties. Captain, by God, look to yourself; say the word; don't be a fool; forget it all; we are ready to turn to; treat us decently, and we're your men; but we won't be flogged.'

" 'Turn to! I make no promises, turn to, I say!'

" 'Look ye, now,' cried the Lakeman, flinging out his arm towards him, 'there are a few of us here (and I am one of them) who have shipped for the cruise, d'ye see; now as you well know, sir, we can claim our discharge as soon as the anchor is down; so we don't want a row; it's not our interest; we want to be peaceable; we are ready to work, but we won't be flogged.'

" 'Turn to!' roared the Captain.

"Steelkilt glanced round him for a moment, and then said:—'I tell you what it is now, Captain, rather than kill ye, and be hung for such a shabby rascal, we won't lift a hand against ye unless ye attack us; but till you say the word about not flogging us, we don't do a hand's turn.'

" 'Down into the forecastle then, down with ye, I'll keep ye there till ye're sick of it. Down ye go.'

" 'Shall we?' cried the ringleader to his men. Most of them were against it; but at length, in obedience to Steelkilt, they preceded him down into their dark den, growlingly disappearing, like bears into a cave.

"As the Lakeman's bare head was just level with the planks, the Captain and his posse leaped the barricade, and rapidly drawing over the slide of the scuttle, planted their group of hands upon it, and loudly called for the steward to bring the heavy brass padlock belonging to the companion-way. Then opening the slide a little, the Captain whispered something down the crack, closed it, and turned the key upon them—ten in number—leaving on deck some twenty or more, who thus far had remained neutral.

"All night a wide-awake watch was kept by all the officers, forward and aft, especially about the forecastle scuttle and fore hatchway; at which last place it was feared the insurgents might emerge, after breaking through the bulkhead below. But the hours of darkness passed in peace; the men who still remained at their duty toiling hard at the pumps, whose clinking and clanking at intervals through the dreary night dismally resounded through the ship.

"At sunrise the Captain went forward, and knocking on the deck, summoned the prisoners to work; but with a yell they refused. Water was then lowered down to them, and a couple of handfuls of biscuit were tossed after it; when again turning the key upon them and pocketing it, the Captain returned to the quarter-deck. Twice every day for three days this was repeated; but on the fourth morning a confused wrangling, and then a scuffling was heard, as the customary summons was delivered; and suddenly four men burst up from the forecastle, saying they were ready to turn to. The fetid closeness of the air, and a famishing diet, united perhaps to some fears of ultimate retribution, had constrained them to surrender at discretion. Emboldened by this, the Captain reiterated his demand to the rest, but Steelkilt shouted up to him a terrific hint to stop his babbling and betake himself where he belonged. On the fifth morning three others of the mutineers bolted up into the air from the desperate arms below that sought to restrain them. Only three were left.

" 'Better turn to, now?' said the Captain with a heartless jeer.

" 'Shut us up again, will ye!' cried Steelkilt.

" 'Oh! certainly,' said the Captain, and the key clicked.

"It was at this point, gentlemen, that enraged by the defection of seven of his former associates, and stung by the mocking voice that had last hailed him, and maddened by his long entombment in a place as black as the bowels of despair; it was then that Steelkilt proposed to the two Canallers, thus far apparently of one mind with him, to burst out of their hole at the next summoning of the garrison; and armed with their keen mincing knives (long, crescentic, heavy implements with a handle at each end) run a muck from the bowsprit to the taffrail; and if by any devilishness of desperation possible, seize the ship. For himself, he would do this, he said, whether they joined him or not. That was the last night he should spend in that den. But the scheme met with no opposition on the part of the other two; they swore they were ready for that, or for any other mad thing, for anything in short but a surrender. And what was more, they each insisted upon being the first man on deck, when the time to make the rush should come. But to this their leader as fiercely objected, reserving that priority for himself; particularly as his two comrades would not yield, the one to the other, in the matter; and both of them could not be first, for the ladder would but admit one man at a time. And here, gentlemen, the foul play of these miscreants must come out.

"Upon hearing the frantic project of their leader, each in his own separate soul had suddenly lighted, it would seem, upon the same piece of treachery, namely: to be foremost in breaking out, in order to be the first of the three, though the last of the ten, to surrender; and thereby secure whatever small chance of pardon such conduct might merit. But when Steelkilt made known his determination still to lead them to the last, they in some way, by some subtle chemistry of villany, mixed their before secret treacheries together; and when their leader fell into a doze, verbally opened their souls to each other in three sentences; and bound the sleeper with cords, and gagged him with cords; and shrieked out for the Captain at midnight.

"Thinking murder at hand, and smelling in the dark for the blood, he and all his armed mates and harpooneers rushed for the forecastle. In a few minutes the scuttle was opened, and, bound hand and foot, the still struggling ringleader was shoved up into the air by his perfidious allies, who at once claimed the honor of securing a man who had been fully ripe for murder. But all these were collared, and dragged along the deck like dead cattle; and, side by side, were seized up into the mizen rigging, like three quarters of meat, and there they hung till morning. 'Damn ye,' cried the Captain, pacing to and fro before them, 'the vultures would not touch ye, ye villains!'

"At sunrise he summoned all hands; and separating those who had rebelled from those who had taken no part in the mutiny, he told the former that he had a good mind to flog them all round—thought, upon the whole, he would do so—he ought to—justice demanded it; but for the present, considering their timely surrender, he would let them go with a reprimand, which he accordingly administered in the vernacular.

" 'But as for you, ye carrion rogues,' turning to the three men in the rigging—'for you, I mean to mince ye up for the trypots;' and, seizing a rope, he applied it with all his might to the backs of the two traitors, till they yelled no more, but lifelessly hung their heads sideways, as the two cruci-fied thieves are drawn.

" 'My wrist is sprained with ye!' he cried, at last; 'but there is still rope enough left for you, my fine bantam, that wouldn't give up. Take that gag from his mouth, and let us hear what he can say for himself.'

"For a moment the exhausted mutineer made a tremulous motion of his cramped jaws, and then painfully twisting round his head, said in a sort of hiss, 'What I say is this—and mind it well—if you flog me, I murder you!'

" 'Say ye so? then see how ye frighten me'—and the Cap-tain drew off with the rope to strike.

" 'Best not,' hissed the Lakeman.

" 'But I must,'—and the rope was once more drawn back for the stroke.

"Steelkilt here hissed out something, inaudible to all but the Captain; who, to the amazement of all hands, started back, paced the deck rapidly two or three times, and then suddenly throwing down his rope, said, 'I won't do it—let him go—cut him down: d'ye hear?'

"But as the junior mates were hurrying to execute the order, a pale man, with a bandaged head, arrested them—Radney the chief mate. Ever since the blow, he had lain in his berth; but that morning, hearing the tumult on the deck, he had crept out, and thus far had watched the whole scene. Such was the state of his mouth, that he could hardly speak; but mumbling something about *his* being willing and able to do what the captain dared not attempt, he snatched the rope and advanced to his pinioned foe.

" 'You are a coward!' hissed the Lakeman.

" 'So I am, but take that.' The mate was in the very act of striking, when another hiss stayed his uplifted arm. He paused: and then pausing no more, made good his word, spite of Steelkilt's threat, whatever that might have been. The three men were then cut down, all hands were turned to, and, sullenly worked by the moody seamen, the iron pumps clanged as before.

"Just after dark that day, when one watch had retired below, a clamor was heard in the forecastle; and the two trembling traitors running up, besieged the cabin door, saying they durst not consort with the crew. Entreaties, cuffs, and kicks could not drive them back, so at their own instance they were put down in the ship's run for salvation. Still, no sign of mutiny reappeared among the rest. On the contrary, it seemed, that mainly at Steelkilt's instigation, they had resolved to maintain the strictest peacefulness, obey all orders to the last, and, when the ship reached port, desert her in a body. But in order to insure the speediest end to the voyage, they all agreed to another thing—namely, not to sing out for whales, in case any should be discovered. For, spite of her leak, and spite of all her other perils, the Town-Ho still maintained her mast-heads, and her captain was just as willing to lower for a fish that moment, as on the day his craft first struck the cruising ground; and Radney the mate was quite as ready to change his berth for a boat, and with his bandaged mouth seek to gag in death the vital jaw of the whale.

"But though the Lakeman had induced the seamen to adopt this sort of passiveness in their conduct, he kept his own counsel (at least till all was over) concerning his own proper and private revenge upon the man who had stung him in the ventricles of his heart. He was in Radney the chief mate's watch; and as if the infatuated man sought to run more than half way to meet his doom, after the scene at the rigging, he insisted, against the express counsel of the captain, upon resuming the head of his watch at night. Upon this, and one or two other circumstances, Steelkilt systematically built the plan of his revenge.

"During the night, Radney had an unseamanlike way of sitting on the bulwarks of the quarter-deck, and leaning his arm upon the gunwale of the boat which was hoisted up there, a little above the ship's side. In this attitude, it was well known, he sometimes dozed. There was a considerable vacancy between the boat and the ship, and down between this was the sea. Steelkilt calculated his time, and found that his next trick at the helm would come round at two o'clock, in the morning of the third day from that in which he had been betrayed. At his leisure, he employed the interval in braiding something very carefully in his watches below.

" 'What are you making there?' said a shipmate.

" 'What do you think? what does it look like?'

" 'Like a lanyard for your bag; but it's an odd one, seems to me.'

" 'Yes, rather oddish,' said the Lakeman, holding it at

arm's length before him; 'but I think it will answer. Shipmate, I haven't enough twine,—have you any?'

"But there was none in the forecastle.

" 'Then I must get some from old Rad;' and he rose to go aft.

" 'You don't mean to go a begging to *him!*' said a sailor.

" 'Why not? Do you think he won't do me a turn, when it's to help himself in the end, shipmate?' and going to the mate, he looked at him quietly, and asked him for some twine to mend his hammock. It was given him—neither twine nor lanyard were seen again; but the next night an iron ball, closely netted, partly rolled from the pocket of the Lakeman's monkey jacket, as he was tucking the coat into his hammock for a pillow. Twenty-four hours after, his trick at the silent helm—nigh to the man who was apt to doze over the grave always ready dug to the seaman's hand—that fatal hour was then to come; and in the fore-ordaining soul of Steelkilt, the mate was already stark and stretched as a corpse, with his forehead crushed in.

"But, gentlemen, a fool saved the would-be murderer from the bloody deed he had planned. Yet complete revenge he had, and without being the avenger. For by a mysterious fatality, Heaven itself seemed to step in to take out of his hands into its own the damning thing he would have done.

"It was just between daybreak and sunrise of the morning of the second day, when they were washing down the decks, that a stupid Teneriffe man, drawing water in the main-chains, all at once shouted out, 'There she rolls! there she rolls!' Jesu, what a whale! It was Moby Dick.

" 'Moby Dick!' cried Don Sebastian; 'St. Dominic! Sir sailor, but do whales have christenings? Whom call you Moby Dick?'

" 'A very white, and famous, and most deadly immortal monster, Don;—but that would be too long a story.'

" 'How? how?' cried all the young Spaniards, crowding.

" 'Nay, Dons, Dons—nay, nay! I cannot rehearse that now. Let me get more into the air, Sirs.'

" 'The chicha! the chicha!' cried Don Pedro; 'our vigorous friend looks faint;—fill up his empty glass!'

"No need, gentlemen; one moment, and I proceed.—Now, gentlemen, so suddenly perceiving the snowy whale within fifty yards of the ship—forgetful of the compact among the crew—in the excitement of the moment, the Teneriffe man had instinctively and involuntarily lifted his voice for the monster, though for some little time past it had been plainly beheld from the three sullen mast-heads. All was now a phrensy. 'The White Whale—the White Whale!' was the cry from the captain, mates, and harpooneers, who, undeterred by fearful rumors, were all anxious to capture so famous and precious a fish; while the dogged crew eyed askance, and with curses, the appalling beauty of the vast milky mass, that lit up by a horizontal spangling sun, shifted and glistened like a living opal in the blue morning sea. Gentlemen, a strange fatality pervades the whole career of these events, as if verily mapped out before the world itself was charted. The mutineer was the bowsman of the mate, and when fast to a fish, it was his duty to sit next him, while Radney stood up with his lance in the prow, and haul in or slacken the line, at the word of command. Moreover, when the four boats were lowered, the mate's got the start; and none howled more fiercely with delight than did Steelkilt, as he strained at his oar. After a stiff pull, their harpooneer got fast, and, spear in hand, Radney sprang to the bow. He was always a furious man, it seems, in a boat. And now his bandaged cry was, to beach him on the whale's topmost back. Nothing loath, his bowsman hauled him up and up, through a blinding foam that blent two whitenesses together; till of a sudden the boat struck as against a sunken ledge, and keeling over, spilled out the standing mate. That instant, as he fell on the whale's slippery back, the boat righted, and was dashed aside by the swell, while Radney was tossed over into the sea, on the other flank of the whale. He struck out through the spray, and, for an instant, was dimly seen through that veil, wildly seeking to remove himself from the eye of Moby Dick. But the whale rushed round in a sudden maelstrom; seized the swimmer between his jaws; and rearing high up with him, plunged headlong again, and went down.

"Meantime, at the first tap of the boat's bottom, the Lakeman had slackened the line, so as to drop astern from the whirlpool; calmly looking on, he thought his own thoughts. But a sudden, terrific, downward jerking of the boat, quickly brought his knife to the line. He cut it; and the whale was free. But, at some distance, Moby Dick rose again, with some tatters of Radney's red woollen shirt, caught in the teeth that had destroyed him. All four boats gave chase again; but the whale eluded them, and finally wholly disappeared.

"In good time, the Town-Ho reached her port—a savage,

solitary place—where no civilized creature resided. There, headed by the Lakeman, all but five or six of the foremastmen deliberately deserted among the palms; eventually, as it turned out, seizing a large double war-canoe of the savages, and setting sail from some other harbor.

"The ship's company being reduced to but a handful, the captain called upon the Islanders to assist him in the laborious business of heaving down the ship to stop the leak. But to such unresting vigilance over their dangerous allies was this small band of whites necessitated, both by night and by day, and so extreme was the hard work they underwent, that upon the vessel being ready again for sea, they were in such a weakened condition that the captain durst not put off with them in so heavy a vessel. After taking counsel with his officers, he anchored the ship as far off shore as possible; loaded and ran out his two cannon from the bows; stacked his muskets on the poop; and warning the Islanders not to approach the ship at their peril, took one man with him, and setting the sail of his best whaleboat, steered straight before the wind for Tahiti, five hundred miles distant, to procure a reinforcement to his crew.

"On the fourth day of the sail, a large canoe was descried, which seemed to have touched at a low isle of corals. He steered away from it; but the savage craft bore down on him; and soon the voice of Steelkilt hailed him to heave to, or he would run him under water. The captain presented a pistol. With one foot on each prow of the yoked war-canoes, the Lakeman laughed him to scorn; assuring him that if the pistol so much as clicked in the lock, he would bury him in bubbles and foam.

" 'What do you want of me?' cried the captain.

" 'Where are you bound? and for what are you bound?' demanded Steelkilt; 'no lies.'

" 'I am bound to Tahiti for more men.'

" 'Very good. Let me board you a moment—I come in peace.' With that he leaped from the canoe, swam to the boat; and climbing the gunwale, stood face to face with the captain.

" 'Cross your arms, sir; throw back your head. Now, repeat after me. As soon as Steelkilt leaves me, I swear to beach this boat on yonder island, and remain there six days. If I do not, may lightnings strike me!'

" 'A pretty scholar,' laughed the Lakeman. 'Adios, Senor!' and leaping into the sea, he swam back to his comrades.

"Watching the boat till it was fairly beached, and drawn up to the roots of the cocoa-nut trees, Steelkilt made sail again, and in due time arrived at Tahiti, his own place of destination. There, luck befriended him; two ships were about to sail for France, and were providentially in want of precisely that number of men which the sailor headed. They embarked; and so for ever got the start of their former captain, had he been at all minded to work them legal retribution.

"Some ten days after the French ships sailed, the whale-boat arrived, and the captain was forced to enlist some of the more civilized Tahitians, who had been somewhat used to the sea. Chartering a small native schooner, he returned with them to his vessel; and finding all right there, again resumed his cruisings.

"Where Steelkilt now is, gentlemen, none know; but upon the island of Nantucket, the widow of Radney still turns to the sea which refuses to give up its dead; still in dreams sees the awful white whale that destroyed him. * * *

" 'Are you through?' said Don Sebastian, quietly.

" 'I am, Don.'

" 'Then I entreat you, tell me if to the best of your own conviction, this your story is in substance really true? It is so passing wonderful! Did you get it from an unquestionable source? Bear with me if I seem to press.'

" 'Also bear with all of us, sir sailor; for we all join in Don Sebastian's suit,' cried the company, with exceeding interest.

" 'Is there a copy of the Holy Evangelists in the Golden Inn, gentlemen?'

" 'Nay,' said Don Sebastian; 'but I know a worthy priest near by, who will quickly procure one for me. I go for it; but are you well advised? this may grow too serious.'

" 'You will be so good as to bring the priest also, Don?'

" 'Though there are no Auto-da-Fés in Lima now,' said one of the company to another; 'I fear our sailor friend runs risk of the archiepiscopacy. Let us withdraw more out of the moonlight. I see no need of this.'

" 'Excuse me for running after you, Don Sebastian; but may I also beg that you will be particular in procuring the largest sized Evangelists you can.'

* * * * *

" 'This is the priest, he brings you the Evangelists,' said

Don Sebastian, gravely, returning with a tall and solemn figure.

" 'Let me remove my hat. Now, venerable priest, further into the light, and hold the Holy Book before me that I may touch it.'

" 'So help me Heaven, and on my honor the story I have told ye, gentlemen, is in substance and its great items, true. I know it to be true; it happened on this ball; I trod the ship; I knew the crew; I have seen and talked with Steelkilt since the death of Radney."

OF THE MONSTROUS PICTURES OF WHALES

LV

I SHALL ere long paint to you as well as one can without canvas, something like the true form of the whale as he actually appears to the eye of the whaleman when in his own absolute body the whale is moored alongside the whaleship so that he can be fairly stepped upon there. It may be worth while, therefore, previously to advert to those curious imaginary portraits of him which even down to the present day confidently challenge the faith of the landsman. It is time to set the world right in this matter, by proving such pictures of the whale all wrong.

It may be that the primal source of all those pictorial delusions will be found among the oldest Hindoo, Egyptian, and Grecian sculptures. For ever since those inventive but unscrupulous times when on the marble panellings of temples, the pedestals of statues, and on shields, medallions, cups, and coins, the dolphin was drawn in scales of chain-armor like Saladin's, and a helmeted head like St. George's; ever since then has something of the same sort of license prevailed, not only in most popular pictures of the whale, but in many scientific presentations of him.

Now, by all odds, the most ancient extant portrait anyways purporting to be the whale's, is to be found in the famous cavern-pagoda of Elephanta, in India. The Brahmins maintain that in the almost endless sculptures of that immemorial pagoda, all the trades and pursuits, every conceivable avocation of man, were prefigured ages before any of them actually came into being. No wonder then, that in some sort our noble profession of whaling should have been there shadowed forth. The Hindoo whale referred to, occurs in a separate department of the wall, depicting the incarnation of Vishnu in the form of leviathan, learnedly known as the Matse Avatar. But though this sculpture is half man and half whale, so as only to give the tail of the latter, yet that small section of him is all wrong. It looks more like the tapering tail of an anaconda, than the broad palms of the true whale's majestic flukes.

But go to the old Galleries, and look now at a great Christian painter's portrait of this fish; for he succeeds no better than the antediluvian Hindoo. It is Guido's picture of Perseus rescuing Andromeda from the sea-monster or whale. Where did Guido get the model of such a strange creature as that? Nor does Hogarth, in painting the same scene in his own "Perseus Descending," make out one whit better. The huge corpulence of that Hogarthian monster undulates on the surface, scarcely drawing one inch of water. It has a sort of howdah on its back, and its distended tusked mouth into which the billows are rolling, might be taken for the Traitors' Gate leading from the Thames by water into the Tower. Then, there are the Prodromus whales of old Scotch Sibbald, and Jonah's whale, as depicted in the prints of old Bibles and the cuts of old primers. What shall be said of these? As for the book-binder's whale winding like a vine-stalk round the stock of a descending anchor— as stamped and gilded on the backs and title-pages of many books both old and new—that is a very picturesque but purely fabulous creature, imitated, I take it, from the like figures on antique vases. Though universally denominated a dolphin, I nevertheless call this book-binder's fish an attempt at a whale; because it was so intended when the device was first introduced. It was introduced by an old Italian publisher somewhere about the 15th century, during the Revival of Learning; and in those days, and even down to a comparatively late period, dolphins were popularly supposed to be a species of the Leviathan.

In the vignettes and other embellishments of some ancient books you will at times meet with very curious touches at the whale, where all manner of spouts, jets d'eau, hot springs and cold, Saratoga and Baden-Baden, come bubbling up from his unexhausted brain. In the title-page of the original edition of the "Advancement of Learning" you will find some curious whales.

But quitting all these unprofessional attempts, let us glance at those pictures of leviathan purporting to be sober, scientific delineations, by those who know. In old Harris's collection of voyages there are some plates of whales extracted from a Dutch book of voyages, A.D. 1671, entitled "A Whaling Voyage to Spitzbergen in the ship Jonas in the Whale, Peter Peterson of Friesland, master." In one of those plates the whales, like great rafts of logs, are represented lying among ice-isles, with white bears running over their living backs. In another plate, the prodigious blunder is made of representing the whale with perpendicular flukes.

Then again, there is an imposing quarto, written by one Captain Colnett, a Post Captain in the English navy, entitled "A Voyage round Cape Horn into the South Seas, for the purpose of extending the Spermaceti Whale Fisheries." In this book is an outline purporting to be a "Picture of a Physeter or Spermaceti whale, drawn by scale from one killed on the coast of Mexico, August, 1793, and hoisted on deck." I doubt not the captain had this veracious picture taken for the benefit of his marines. To mention but one thing about it, let me say that it has an eye which applied, according to the accompanying scale, to a full grown sperm whale, would make the eye of that whale a bow-window some five feet long. Ah, my gallant captain, why did ye not give us Jonah looking out of that eye!

Nor are the most conscientious compilations of Natural History for the benefit of the young and tender, free from the same heinousness of mistake. Look at that popular work "Goldsmith's Animated Nature." In the abridged London edition of 1807, there are plates of an alleged "whale" and a "narwhale." I do not wish to seem inelegant, but this unsightly whale looks much like an amputated sow; and, as for the narwhale, one glimpse at it is enough to amaze one, that in this nineteenth century such a hippogriff could be palmed for genuine upon any intelligent public of schoolboys.

Then, again, in 1825, Bernard Germain, Count de Lacépède, a great naturalist, published a scientific systemized whale book, wherein are several pictures of the different species of the Leviathan. All these are not only incorrect, but the picture of the Mysticetus or Greenland whale (that is to say, the Right whale), even Scoresby, a long experienced man as touching that species, declares not to have its counterpart in nature.

But the placing of the cap-sheaf to all this blundering business was reserved for the scientific Frederick Cuvier, brother to the famous Baron. In 1836, he published a Natural History of Whales, in which he gives what he calls a picture of the Sperm Whale. Before showing that picture to any Nantucketer, you had best provide for your summary retreat from Nantucket. In a word, Frederick Cuvier's Sperm Whale is not a Sperm Whale, but a squash. Of course, he never had the benefit of a whaling voyage (such men seldom have), but whence he derived that picture, who can tell? Perhaps he got it as his scientific predecessor in the same field, Desmarest, got one of his authentic abortions; that is, from a Chinese drawing. And what sort of lively lads with the pencil those Chinese are, many queer cups and saucers inform us.

As for the sign-painters' whales seen in the streets hanging over the shops of oil-dealers, what shall be said of them? They are generally Richard III. whales, with dromedary humps, and very savage; breakfasting on three or four sailor tarts, that is whaleboats full of mariners: their deformities floundering in seas of blood and blue paint.

But these manifold mistakes in depicting the whale are not so very surprising after all. Consider! Most of the scientific drawings have been taken from the stranded fish; and these are about as correct as a drawing of a wrecked ship, with broken back, would correctly represent the noble animal itself in all its undashed pride of hull and spars. Though elephants have stood for their full-lengths, the living Leviathan has never yet fairly floated himself for his portrait. The living whale, in his full majesty and significance, is only to be seen at sea in unfathomable waters; and afloat the vast bulk of him is out of sight, like a launched line-of-battle ship; and out of that element it is a thing eternally impossible for mortal man to hoist him bodily into the air, so as to preserve all his mighty swells and undulations. And, not to speak of the highly presumable difference of contour between a young sucking whale and a full-grown Platonian Leviathan; yet, even in the case of one of those young sucking whales hoisted to a ship's deck, such is then the outlandish, eel-like, limbered, varying shape of him, that his precise expression the devil himself could not catch.

But it may be fancied, that from the naked skeleton of

the stranded whale, accurate hints may be derived touching his true form. Not at all. For it is one of the more curious things about this Leviathan, that his skeleton gives very little idea of his general shape. Though Jeremy Bentham's skeleton, which hangs for candlelabra in the library of one of his executors, correctly conveys the idea of a burly-browed utilitarian old gentleman, with all Jeremy's other leading-personal characteristics; yet nothing of this kind could be inferred from any leviathan's articulated bones. In fact, as the great Hunter says, the mere skeleton of the whale bears the same relation to the fully invested and padded animal as the insect does to the chrysalis that so roundingly envelopes it. This peculiarity is strikingly evinced in the head, as in some part of this book will be incidentally shown. It is also very curiously displayed in the side fin, the bones of which almost exactly answer to the bones of the human hand, minus only the thumb. This fin has four regular bone-fingers, the index, middle, ring, and little finger. But all these are permanently lodged in their fleshy covering, as the human fingers in an artificial covering. "However recklessly the whale may sometimes serve us," said humorous Stubb one day, "he can never be truly said to handle us without mittens."

For all these reasons, then, any way you may look at it, you must needs conclude that the great Leviathan is that one creature in the world which must remain unpainted to the last. True, one portrait may hit the mark nearer than another, but none can hit it with any very considerable degree of exactness. So there is no earthly way of finding out precisely what the whale really looks like. And the only mode in which you can derive even a tolerable idea of his living contour, is by going a whaling yourself; but by so doing, you run no small risk of being eternally stove and sunk by him. Wherefore, it seems to me you had best not be too fastidious in your curiosity touching this Leviathan.

OF THE LESS ERRONEOUS
PICTURES OF WHALES,
AND THE TRUE PICTURES
OF WHALING SCENES   LVI

IN connexion with the monstrous pictures of whales, I am strongly tempted here to enter upon those still more monstrous stories of them which are to be found in certain books, both ancient and modern, especially in Pliny, Purchas, Hackluyt, Harris, Cuvier, &c. But I pass that matter by.

I know of only four published outlines of the great Sperm Whale; Colnett's, Huggins's, Frederick Cuvier's, and Beale's. In the previous chapter Colnett and Cuvier have been referred to. Huggins's is far better than theirs; but, by great odds, Beale's is the best. All Beale's drawings of this whale are good, excepting the middle figure in the picture of three whales in various attitudes, capping his second chapter. His frontispiece, boats attacking Sperm Whales, though no doubt calculated to excite the civil scepticism of some parlor men, is admirably correct and life-like in its general effect. Some of the Sperm Whale drawings in J. Ross Browne are pretty correct in contour; but they are wretchedly engraved. That is not his fault though.

Of the Right Whale, the best outline pictures are in Scoresby; but they are drawn on too small a scale to convey a desirable impression. He has but one picture of whaling scenes, and this is a sad deficiency, because it is by such pictures only, when at all well done, that you can derive anything like a truthful idea of the living whale as seen by his living hunters.

But, taken for all in all, by far the finest, though in some details not the most correct, presentations of whales and whaling scenes to be anywhere found, are two large French engravings, well executed, and taken from paintings by one Garnery. Respectively, they represent attacks on the Sperm and Right Whale. In the first engraving a noble Sperm Whale is depicted in full majesty of might, just risen beneath the boat from the profundities of the ocean, and bearing high in the air upon his back the terrific wreck of the stoven planks. The prow of the boat is partially unbroken, and is drawn just balancing upon the monster's spine; and standing in that prow, for that one single incomputable flash of time, you behold an oarsman, half shrouded by the incensed boiling spout of the whale, and in the act of leaping, as if from a precipice. The action of the whole thing is wonderfully good and true. The half-emptied line-tub floats on the whitened sea; the wooden poles of the spilled harpoons obliquely bob in it; the heads of the swimming crew are scattered about the whale in contrasting expressions of affright; while in the black stormy distance the ship is bearing down upon the scene. Serious fault might be found with the anatomical details of this whale, but let that pass; since, for the life of me, I could not draw so good a one.

In the second engraving, the boat is in the act of drawing alongside the barnacled flank of a large running Right Whale, that rolls his black weedy bulk in the sea like some mossy rockslide from the Patagonian cliffs. His jets are erect, full, and black like soot; so that from so abounding a smoke in the chimney, you would think there must be a brave supper cooking in the great bowels below. Sea fowls are pecking at the small crabs, shell-fish, and other sea candies and maccaroni, which the Right Whale sometimes carries on his pestilent back. And all the while the thick-lipped leviathan is rushing through the deep, leaving tons of tumultuous white curds in his wake, and causing the slight boat to rock in the swells like a skiff caught nigh the paddle-wheels of an ocean steamer. Thus, the foregoing is all raging commotion; but behind, in admirable artistic contrast, is the glassy level of a sea becalmed, the drooping unstarched sails of the powerless ship, and the inert mass of a dead whale, a conquered fortress, with the flag of capture lazily hanging from the whale-pole inserted into his spout-hole.

Who Garnery the painter is, or was, I know not. But my life for it he was either practically conversant with his subject, or else marvellously tutored by some experienced whaleman. The French are the lads for painting action. Go and gaze upon all the paintings of Europe, and where will you find such a gallery of living and breathing commotion on canvas, as in that triumphal hall at Versailles; where the beholder fights his way, pell-mell, through the consecutive great battles of France; where every sword seems a flash of the Northern Lights, and the successive armed kings and Emper-

ors dash by, like a charge of crowned centaurs? Not wholly
unworthy of a place in that gallery, are these sea battle-pieces
of Garnery.

The natural aptitude of the French for seizing the picturesqueness of things seems to be peculiarly evinced in
what paintings and engravings they have of their whaling
scenes. With not one tenth of England's experience in the
fishery, and not the thousandth part of that of the Americans, they have nevertheless furnished both nations with
the only finished sketches at all capable of conveying the real
spirit of the whale hunt. For the most part, the English and
American whale draughtsmen seem entirely content with presenting the mechanical outline of things, such as the vacant
profile of the whale; which, so far as picturesqueness of effect
is concerned, is about tantamount to sketching the profile of
a pyramid. Even Scoresby, the justly renowned Right whaleman, after giving us a stiff full length of the Greenland whale,
and three or four delicate miniatures of narwhales and porpoises, treats us to a series of classical engravings of boat
hooks, chopping knives, and grapnels; and with the microscopic diligence of a Leuwenhoeck submits to the inspection
of a shivering world ninety-six fac-similes of magnified Arctic
snow crystals. I mean no disparagement to the excellent voyager (I honor him for a veteran), but in so important a matter it was certainly an oversight not to have procured
for every crystal a sworn affidavit taken before a Greenland Justice of the Peace.

In addition to those fine engravings from Garnery, there
are two other French engravings worthy of note, by some one
who subscribes himself "H. Durand." One of them, though
not precisely adapted to our present purpose, nevertheless
deserves mention on other accounts. It is a quiet noon-scene
among the isles of the Pacific; a French whaler anchored, in-
shore, in a calm, and lazily taking water on board; the
loosened sails of the ship, and the long leaves of the palms
in the background, both drooping together in the breezeless
air. The effect is very fine, when considered with reference
to its presenting the hardy fishermen under one of their few
aspects of oriental repose. The other engraving is quite a
different affair: the ship hove-to upon the open sea, and in the
very heart of the Leviathanic life, with a Right Whale alongside; the vessel (in the act of cutting-in) hove over to the
monster as if to a quay; and a boat, hurriedly pushing off
from this scene of activity, is about giving chase to whales

in the distance. The harpoons and lances lie levelled for use; three oarsmen are just setting the mast in its hole; while from a sudden roll of the sea, the little craft stands half-erect out of the water, like a rearing horse. From the ship, the smoke of the torments of the boiling whale is going up like the smoke over a village of smithies; and to windward, a black cloud, rising up with earnest of squalls and rains, seems to quicken the activity of the excited seamen.

OF WHALES IN PAINT; IN TEETH; IN WOOD; IN SHEET-IRON; IN STONE; IN MOUNTAINS; IN STARS   LVII

ON Tower-hill, as you go down to the London docks, you may have seen a crippled beggar (or *kedger,* as the sailors say) holding a painted board before him, representing the tragic scene in which he lost his leg. There are three whales and three boats; and one of the boats (presumed to contain the missing leg in all its original integrity) is being crunched by the jaws of the foremost whale. Any time these ten years, they tell me, has that man held up that picture, and exhibited that stump to an incredulous world. But the time of his justification has now come. His three whales are as good whales as were ever published in Wapping, at any rate; and his stump as unquestionable a stump as any you will find in the western clearings. But, though for ever mounted on that stump, never a stump-speech does the poor whaleman make; but, with downcast eyes, stands ruefully contemplating his own amputation.

Throughout the Pacific, and also in Nantucket, and New Bedford, and Sag Harbor, you will come across lively sketches of whales and whaling-scenes, graven by the fishermen themselves on Sperm Whale-teeth, or ladies' busks wrought out of the Right Whale-bone, and other like skrimshander articles, as the whalemen call the numerous little ingenious contrivances they elaborately carve out of the rough material, in their hours of ocean leisure. Some of them have little boxes of dentistical-looking implements, specially intended for the skrimshandering business. But, in general, they toil with their jack-knives alone; and, with that almost

omnipotent tool of the sailor, they will turn you out anything you please, in the way of a mariner's fancy.

Long exile from Christendom and civilization inevitably
restores a man to that condition in which God placed him,
i.e. what is called savagery. Your true whale-hunter is as
much a savage as an Iroquois. I myself am a savage, owning
no allegiance but to the King of the Cannibals; and ready
at any moment to rebel against him.

Now, one of the peculiar characteristics of the savage in
his domestic hours, is his wonderful patience of industry. An
ancient Hawaiian war-club or spear-paddle, in its full multiplicity and elaboration of carving, is as great a trophy of
human perseverance as a Latin lexicon. For, with but a bit of
broken sea-shell or a shark's tooth, that miraculous intricacy
of wooden net-work has been achieved; and it has cost steady
years of steady application.

As with the Hawaiian savage, so with the white sailor-
savage. With the same marvellous patience, and with the same
single shark's tooth, of his one poor jack-knife, he will carve
you a bit of bone sculpture, not quite as workmanlike, but as
close packed in its maziness of design, as the Greek savage,
Achilles's shield; and full of barbaric spirit and suggestive-
ness, as the prints of that fine old Dutch savage, Albert
Durer.

Wooden whales, or whales cut in profile out of the small
dark slabs of the noble South Sea war-wood, are frequently
met with in the forecastles of American whalers. Some of
them are done with much accuracy.

At some old gable-roofed country houses you will see brass
whales hung by the tail for knockers to the road-side door.
When the porter is sleepy, the anvil-headed whale would be
best. But these knocking whales are seldom remarkable as
faithful essays. On the spires of some old-fashioned churches
you will see sheet-iron whales placed there for weather-cocks;
but they are so elevated, and besides that are to all intents
and purposes so labelled with *"Hands off!"* you cannot examine them closely enough to decide upon their merit.

In bony, ribby regions of the earth, where at the base of
high broken cliffs masses of rock lie strewn in fantastic
groupings upon the plain, you will often discover images as
of the petrified forms of the Leviathan partly merged in grass,
which of a windy day breaks against them in a surf of green
surges.

Then, again, in mountainous countries where the traveller

is continually girdled by amphitheatrical heights; here and there from some lucky point of view you will catch passing glimpses of the profiles of whales defined along the undulating ridges. But you must be a thorough whaleman, to see these sights; and not only that, but if you wish to return to such a sight again, you must be sure and take the exact intersecting latitude and longitude of your first stand-point, else so chance-like are such observations of the hills, that your precise, previous standpoint would require a laborious rediscovery; like the Solomon islands, which still remain incognita, though once high-ruffed Mendanna trod them and old Figuera chronicled them.

Nor when expandingly lifted by your subject, can you fail to trace out great whales in the starry heavens, and boats in pursuit of them; as when long filled with thoughts of war the Eastern nations saw armies locked in battle among the clouds. Thus at the North have I chased Leviathan round and round the Pole with the revolutions of the bright points that first defined him to me. And beneath the effulgent Antarctic skies I have boarded the Argo-Navis, and joined the chase against the starry Cetus far beyond the utmost stretch of Hydrus and the Flying Fish.

With a frigate's anchors for my bridle-bitts and fasces of harpoons for spurs, would I could mount that whale and leap the topmost skies, to see whether the fabled heavens with all their countless tents really lie encamped beyond my mortal sight!

BRIT **LVIII**

STEERING north-eastward from the Crozetts, we fell in with vast meadows of brit, the minute, yellow substance, upon which the Right Whale largely feeds. For leagues and leagues it undulated round us, so that we seemed to be sailing through boundless fields of ripe and golden wheat.

On the second day, numbers of Right Whales were seen, who, secure from the attack of a Sperm Whaler like the Pequod, with open jaws sluggishly swam through the brit, which, adhering to the fringing fibres of that wondrous Venetian blind in their mouths, was in that manner separated from the water that escaped at the lip.

As morning mowers, who side by side slowly and seething-
ly advance their scythes through the long wet grass of
marshy meads; even so these monsters swam, making a
strange, grassy, cutting sound; and leaving behind them endless swaths of blue upon the yellow sea.*

But it was only the sound they made as they parted the
brit which at all reminded one of mowers. Seen from the
mastheads, especially when they paused and were stationary
for a while, their vast black forms looked more like lifeless
masses of rock than anything else. And as in the great hunting countries of India, the stranger at a distance will sometimes pass on the plains recumbent elephants without knowing them to be such, taking them for bare, blackened ele-
vations of the soil; even so, often, with him, who for the
first time beholds this species of the leviathans of the sea.
And even when recognised at last, their immense magnitude
renders it very hard really to believe that such bulky masses
of overgrowth can possibly be instinct, in all parts, with the
same sort of life that lives in a dog or a horse.

Indeed, in other respects, you can hardly regard any
creatures of the deep with the same feelings that you do
those of the shore. For though some old naturalists have
maintained that all creatures of the land are of their kind
in the sea; and though taking a broad general view of the
thing, this may very well be; yet coming to specialities,
where, for example, does the ocean furnish any fish that in
disposition answers to the sagacious kindness of the dog?
The accursed shark alone can in any generic respect be
said to bear comparative analogy to him.

But though, to landsmen in general, the native inhabitants
of the seas have ever been regarded with emotions unspeakably unsocial and repelling; though we know the sea
to be an everlasting terra incognita, so that Columbus sailed
over numberless unknown worlds to discover his one superficial western one; though, by vast odds, the most terrific
of all mortal disasters have immemorially and indiscriminately befallen tens and hundreds of thousands of those
who have gone upon the waters; though but a moment's

---

* That part of the sea known among whalemen as the "Brazil
Banks" does not bear that name as the Banks of Newfoundland
do, because of there being shallows and soundings there, but
because of this remarkable meadow-like appearance, caused by
the vast drifts of brit continually floating in those latitudes,
where the Right Whale is often chased.

consideration will teach, that however baby man may brag
of his science and skill, and however much, in a flattering future, that science and skill may augment; yet for
ever and for ever, to the crack of doom, the sea will insult
and murder him, and pulverize the stateliest frigate he can
make; nevertheless, by the continual repetition of these very
impressions, man has lost that sense of the full awfulness
of the sea which aboriginally belongs to it.

The first boat we read of, floated on an ocean, that with
Portuguese vengeance had whelmed a whole world without
leaving so much as a widow. That same ocean rolls now;
that same ocean destroyed the wrecked ships of last year.
Yea, foolish mortals, Noah's flood is not yet subsided;
two thirds of the fair world it yet covers.

Wherein differ the sea and the land, that a miracle upon
one is not a miracle upon the other? Preternatural terrors
rested upon the Hebrews, when under the feet of Korah
and his company the live ground opened and swallowed
them up for ever; yet not a modern sun ever sets, but in
precisely the same manner the live sea swallows up ships
and crews.

But not only is the sea such a foe to man who is an alien
to it, but it is also a fiend to its own offspring; worse than
the Persian host who murdered his own guests; sparing not
the creatures which itself hath spawned. Like a savage tigress
that tossing in the jungle overlays her own cubs, so the sea
dashes even the mightiest whales against the rocks, and
leaves them there side by side with the split wrecks of ships.
No mercy, no power but its own controls it. Panting and
snorting like a mad battle steed that has lost its rider, the
masterless ocean overruns the globe.

Consider the subtleness of the sea; how its most dreaded
creatures glide under water, unapparent for the most part,
and treacherously hidden beneath the loveliest tints of azure.
Consider also the devilish brilliance and beauty of many
of its most remorseless tribes, as the dainty embellished
shape of many species of sharks. Consider, once more, the
universal cannibalism of the sea; all whose creatures prey
upon each other, carrying on eternal war since the world
began.

Consider all this; and then turn to this green, gentle, and
most docile earth; consider them both, the sea and the
land; and do you not find a strange analogy to something in
yourself? For as this appalling ocean surrounds the verdant

land, so in the soul of man there lies one insular Tahiti, full of peace and joy, but encompassed by all the horrors of the half known life. God keep thee! Push not off from that isle, thou canst never return!

SQUID   **LIX**

SLOWLY wading through the meadows of brit, the Pequod still held on her way north-eastward towards the island of Java; a gentle air impelling her keel, so that in the surrounding serenity her three tall tapering masts mildly waved to that languid breeze, as three mild palms on a plain. And still, at wide intervals in the silvery night, the lonely, alluring jet would be seen.

But one transparent blue morning, when a stillness almost preternatural spread over the sea, however unattended with any stagnant calm; when the long burnished sun-glade on the waters seemed a golden finger laid across them, enjoining some secrecy; when the slippered waves whispered together as they softly ran on; in this profound hush of the visible sphere a strange spectre was seen by Daggoo from the main-mast head.

In the distance, a great white mass lazily rose, and rising higher and higher, and disentangling itself from the azure, at last gleamed before our prow like a snow-slide, new slid from the hills. Thus glistening for a moment, as slowly it subsided, and sank. Then once more arose, and silently gleamed. It seemed not a whale; and yet is this Moby Dick? thought Daggoo. Again the phantom went down, but on reappearing once more, with a stiletto-like cry that startled every man from his nod, the negro yelled out—"There! there again! there she breaches! right ahead! The White Whale, the White Whale!"

Upon this, the seamen rushed to the yard-arms, as in swarming-time the bees rush to the boughs. Bare-headed in the sultry sun, Ahab stood on the bowsprit, and with one hand pushed far behind in readiness to wave his orders to the helmsman, cast his eager glance in the direction indicated aloft by the outstretched motionless arm of Daggoo.

Whether the flitting attendance of the one still and solitary jet had gradually worked upon Ahab, so that he was now prepared to connect the ideas of mildness and repose with the first sight of the particular whale he pursued; however this was, or whether his eagerness betrayed him; whichever way it might have been, no sooner did he distinctly perceive the white mass, than with a quick intensity he instantly gave orders for lowering.

The four boats were soon on the water; Ahab's in advance, and all swiftly pulling towards their prey. Soon it went down, and while, with oars suspended, we were awaiting its reappearance, lo! in the same spot where it sank, once more it slowly rose. Almost forgetting for the moment all thoughts of Moby Dick, we now gazed at the wondrous phenomenon which the secret seas have hitherto revealed to mankind. A vast pulpy mass, furlongs in length and breadth, of a glancing cream-color, lay floating on the water, innumerable long arms radiating from its centre, and curling and twisting like a nest of anacondas, as if blindly to clutch at any hapless object within reach. No perceptible face or front did it have; no conceivable token of either sensation or instinct; but undulated there on the billows, an unearthly, formless, chance-like apparition of life.

As with a low sucking sound it slowly disappeared again, Starbuck still gazing at the agitated waters where it had sunk, with a wild voice exclaimed—"Almost rather had I seen Moby Dick and fought him, than to have seen thee, thou white ghost!"

"What was it, Sir?" said Flask.

"The great live squid, which, they say, few whale-ships ever beheld, and returned to their ports to tell of it."

But Ahab said nothing; turning his boat, he sailed back to the vessel; the rest as silently following.

Whatever superstitions the sperm whalemen in general have connected with the sight of this object, certain it is, that a glimpse of it being so very unusual, that circumstance has gone far to invest it with portentousness. So rarely is it beheld, that though one and all of them declare it to be the largest animated thing in the ocean, yet very few of them have any but the most vague ideas concerning its true nature and form; notwithstanding, they believe it to furnish to the sperm whale his only food. For though other species of whales find their food above water, and may be seen by man in the act of feeding, the spermaceti whale obtains his whole food in unknown zones below the surface; and only by inference is it that any one can tell of what, precisely,

that food consists. At times, when closely pursued, he will
disgorge what are supposed to be the detached arms of the
squid; some of them thus exhibited exceeding twenty and
thirty feet in length. They fancy that the monster to which
these arms belonged ordinarily clings by them to the bed of
the ocean; and that the sperm whale, unlike other species,
is supplied with teeth in order to attack and tear it.

There seems some ground to imagine that the great Kraken
of Bishop Pontoppodan may ultimately resolve itself into
Squid. The manner in which the Bishop describes it, as
alternately rising and sinking, with some other particulars he
narrates, in all this the two correspond. But much abate-
ment is necessary with respect to the incredible bulk he
assigns it.

By some naturalists who have vaguely heard rumors of
the mysterious creature, here spoken of, it is included among
the class of cuttlefish, to which, indeed, in certain external
respects it would seem to belong, but only as the Anak of
the tribe.

THE LINE   **LX**

    WITH reference to the whaling scene snortly to be de-
scribed, as well as for the better understanding of all similar
scenes elsewhere presented, I have here to speak of the
magical, sometimes horrible whale-line.

The line originally used in the fishery was of the best
hemp, slightly vapored with tar, not impregnated with it, as
in the case of ordinary ropes; for while tar, as ordinarily
used, makes the hemp more pliable to the rope-maker, and
also renders the rope itself more convenient to the sailor
for common ship use; yet, not only would the ordinary
quantity too much stiffen the whale-line for the close coiling
to which it must be subjected; but as most seamen are beginning to learn, tar in general by no means adds to the
rope's durability or strength, however much it may give it
compactness and gloss.

Of late years the Manilla rope has in the American fishery
almost entirely superseded hemp as a material for whale-
lines; for, though not so durable as hemp, it is stronger, and
far more soft and elastic; and I will add (since there is an

æsthetics in all things), is much more handsome and becoming to the boat, than hemp. Hemp is a dusky, dark
fellow, a sort of Indian; but Manilla is as a golden-haired
Circassian to behold.

The whale line is only two thirds of an inch in thickness.
At first sight, you would not think it so strong as it really
is. By experiment its one and fifty yarns will each suspend
a weight of one hundred and twenty pounds; so that the
whole rope will bear a strain nearly equal to three tons. In
length, the common sperm whale-line measures something
over two hundred fathoms. Towards the stern of the boat
it is spirally coiled away in the tub, not like the worm-pipe
of a still though, but so as to form one round, cheese-
shaped mass of densely bedded "sheaves," or layers of concentric spiralizations, without any hollow but the "heart,"
or minute vertical tube formed at the axis of the cheese. As
the least tangle or kink in the coiling would, in running out,
infallibly take somebody's arm, leg, or entire body off, the
utmost precaution is used in stowing the line in its tub.
Some harpooneers will consume almost an entire morning
in this business, carrying the line high aloft and then reeving
it downwards through a block towards the tub, so as in the
act of coiling to free it from all possible wrinkles and twists.

In the English boats two tubs are used instead of one;
the same line being continuously coiled in both tubs. There
is some advantage in this; because these twin-tubs being so
small they fit more readily into the boat, and do not strain
it so much; whereas, the American tub, nearly three feet in
diameter and of proportionate depth, makes a rather bulky
freight for a craft whose planks are but one half-inch in
thickness; for the bottom of the whale-boat is like critical
ice, which will bear up a considerable distributed weight,
but not very much of a concentrated one. When the painted
canvas cover is clapped on the American line-tub, the boat
looks as if it were pulling off with a prodigious great wedding-
cake to present to the whales.

Both ends of the line are exposed; the lower end terminating in an eye-splice or loop coming up from the bottom against the side of the tub, and hanging over its edge
completely disengaged from everything. This arrangement of
the lower end is necessary on two accounts. First: In order
to facilitate the fastening to it of an additional line from
a neighboring boat, in case the stricken whale should sound
so deep as to threaten to carry off the entire line originally

attached to the harpoon. In these instances, the whale of course is shifted like a mug of ale, as it were, from one boat to the other; though the first boat always hovers at hand to assist its consort. Second: This arrangement is indispensable for common safety's sake; for were the lower end of the line in any way attached to the boat, and were the whale then to run the line out to the end almost in a single, smoking minute as he sometimes does, he would not stop there, for the doomed boat would infallibly be dragged down after him into the profundity of the sea; and in that case no town-crier would ever find her again.

Before lowering the boat for the chase, the upper end of the line is taken aft from the tub, and passing round the logger-head there, is again carried forward the entire length of the boat, resting crosswise upon the loom or handle of every man's oar, so that it joggs against his wrist in rowing; and also passing between the men, as they alternately sit at the opposite gunwales, to the leaded chocks or grooves in the extreme pointed prow of the boat, where a wooden pin or skewer the size of a common quill, prevents it from slipping out. From the chocks it hangs in a slight festoon over the bows, and is then passed inside the boat again; and some ten or twenty fathoms (called box-line) being coiled upon the box in the bows, it continues its way to the gunwale still a little further aft, and is then attached to the short-warp—the rope which is immediately connected with the harpoon; but previous to that connexion, the short-warp goes through sundry mystifications too tedious to detail.

Thus the whale-line folds the whole boat in its complicated coils, twisting and writhing around it in almost every direction. All the oarsmen are involved in its perilous contortions; so that to the timid eye of the landsman, they seem as Indian jugglers, with the deadliest snakes sportively festooning their limbs. Nor can any son of mortal woman, for the first time, seat himself amid those hempen intricacies, and while straining his utmost at the oar, bethink him that at any unknown instant the harpoon may be darted, and all these horrible contortions be put in play like ringed lightnings; he cannot be thus circumstanced without a shudder that makes the very marrow in his bones to quiver in him like a shaken jelly. Yet habit—strange thing! what cannot habit accomplish?—Gayer sallies, more merry mirth, better jokes, and brighter repartees, you never heard over your mahogany, than you will hear over the half-inch white cedar of the whaleboat, when thus hung in hangman's nooses; and, like the six burghers of Calais before King Edward, the six men composing the crew pull into the jaws of death, with a halter around every neck, as you may say.

Perhaps a very little thought will now enable you to account for those repeated whaling disasters—some few of which are casually chronicled—of this man or that man being taken out of the boat by the line, and lost. For, when the line is darting out, to be seated then in the boat, is like being seated in the midst of the manifold whizzings of a steam-engine in full play, when every flying beam, and shaft, and wheel, is grazing you. It is worse; for you cannot sit motionless in the heart of these perils, because the boat is rocking like a cradle, and you are pitched one way and the other, without the slightest warning; and only by a certain self-adjusting buoyancy and simultaneousness of volition and action, can you escape being made a Mazeppa of, and run away with where the all-seeing sun himself could never pierce you out.

Again: as the profound calm which only apparently precedes and prophesies of the storm, is perhaps more awful than the storm itself; for, indeed, the calm is but the wrapper and envelope of the storm; and contains it in itself, as the seemingly harmless rifle holds the fatal powder, and the ball, and the explosion; so the graceful repose of the line, as it silently serpentines about the oarsmen before being brought into actual play—this is a thing which carries more of true terror than any other aspect of this dangerous affair. But why say more? All men live enveloped in whale-lines. All are born with halters round their necks; but it is only when caught in the swift, sudden turn of death, that mortals realize the silent, subtle, ever-present perils of life. And if you be a philosopher, though seated in the whale-boat, you would not at heart feel one whit more of terror, than though seated before your evening fire with a poker, and not a harpoon, by your side.

STUBB KILLS A WHALE   LXI

IF to Starbuck the apparition of the Squid was a thing of portents, to Queequeg it was quite a different object.

"When you see him 'quid," said the savage, honing his
harpoon in the bow of his hoisted boat, "then you quick
see him 'parm whale."

The next day was exceedingly still and sultry, and with
nothing special to engage them, the Pequod's crew could
hardly resist the spell of sleep induced by such a vacant sea.
For this part of the Indian Ocean through which we then
were voyaging is not what whalemen call a lively ground;
that is, it affords fewer glimpses of porpoises, dolphins,
flying-fish, and other vivacious denizens of more stirring
waters, than those off the Rio de la Plata, or the in-shore
ground off Peru.

It was my turn to stand at the foremast-head; and with
my shoulders leaning against the slackened royal shrouds,
to and fro I idly swayed in what seemed an enchanted air.
No resolution could withstand it; in that dreamy mood losing all consciousness, at last my soul went out of my body;
though my body still continued to sway as a pendulum will,
long after the power which first moved it is withdrawn.

Ere forgetfulness altogether came over me, I had noticed
that the seamen at the main and mizzen mast-heads were already drowsy. So that at last all three of us lifelessly swung
from the spars, and for every swing that we made there was
a nod from below from the slumbering helmsman. The waves,
too, nodded their indolent crests; and across the wide trance
of the sea, east nodded to west, and the sun over all.

Suddenly bubbles seemed bursting beneath my closed eyes;
like vices my hands grasped the shrouds; some invisible,
gracious agency preserved me; with a shock I came back to
life. And lo! close under our lee, not forty fathoms off, a
gigantic Sperm Whale lay rolling in the water like the capsized hull of a frigate, his broad, glossy back, of an Ethiopian
hue, glistening in the sun's rays like a mirror. But lazily
undulating in the trough of the sea, and ever and anon tranquilly spouting his vapory jet, the whale looked like a portly
burgher smoking his pipe of a warm afternoon. But that
pipe, poor whale, was thy last. As if struck by some en-
chanter's wand, the sleepy ship and every sleeper in it all at
once started into wakefulness; and more than a score of
voices from all parts of the vessel, simultaneously with the
three notes from aloft, shouted forth the accustomed cry, as
the great fish slowly and regularly spouted the sparkling brine
into the air.

"Clear away the boats! Luff!" cried Ahab. And obeying

his own order, he dashed the helm down before the helmsman could handle the spokes.

The sudden exclamations of the crew must have alarmed the whale; and ere the boats were down, majestically turning, he swam away to the leeward, but with such a steady tranquillity, and making so few ripples as he swam, that thinking after all he might not as yet be alarmed, Ahab gave orders that not an oar should be used, and no man must speak but in whispers. So seated like Ontario Indians on the gunwales of the boats, we swiftly but silently paddled along; the calm not admitting of the noiseless sails being set. Presently, as we thus glided in chase, the monster perpendicularly flitted his tail forty feet into the air, and then sank out of sight like a tower swallowed up.

"There go flukes!" was the cry, an announcement immediately followed by Stubb's producing his match and igniting his pipe, for now a respite was granted. After the full interval of his sounding had elapsed, the whale rose again, and being now in advance of the smoker's boat, and much nearer to it than to any of the others, Stubb counted upon the honor of the capture. It was obvious, now, that the whale had at length become aware of his pursuers. All silence of cautiousness was therefore no longer of use. Paddles were dropped, and oars came loudly into play. And still puffing at his pipe, Stubb cheered on his crew to the assault.

Yes, a mighty change had come over the fish. All alive to his jeopardy, he was going "head out;" that part obliquely projecting from the mad yeast which he brewed.*

"Start her, start her, my men! Don't hurry yourselves; take plenty of time—but start her; start her like thunderclaps, that's all," cried Stubb, spluttering out the smoke as he spoke. "Start her, now; give 'em the long and strong stroke, Tashtego. Start her, Tash, my boy—start her, all; but keep cool, keep cool—cucumbers is the word—easy,

---

* It will be seen in some other place of what a very light substance the entire interior of the sperm whale's enormous head consists. Though apparently the most massive, it is by far the most buoyant part about him. So that with ease he elevates it in the air, and invariably does so when going at his utmost speed. Besides, such is the breadth of the upper part of the front of his head, and such the tapering cut-water formation of the lower part, that by obliquely elevating his head, he thereby may be said to transform himself from a bluff-bowed sluggish galliot into a sharp-pointed New York pilot-boat.

easy—only start her like grim death and grinning devils,
and raise the buried dead perpendicular out of their graves,
boys—that's all. Start her!"

"Woo-hoo! Wa-hee!" screamed the Gay-Header in reply,
raising some old war-whoop to the skies; as every oarsman
in the strained boat involuntarily bounced forward with the
one tremendous leading stroke which the eager Indian gave.

But his wild screams were answered by others quite as
wild. "Kee-hee! Kee-hee!" yelled Daggoo, straining forwards
and backwards on his seat, like a pacing tiger in his cage.

"Ka-la! Koo-loo!" howled Queequeg, as if smacking his
lips over a mouthful of Grenadier's steak. And thus with
oars and yells the keels cut the sea. Meanwhile, Stubb re-
taining his place in the van, still encouraged his men to the
onset, all the while puffing the smoke from his mouth. Like
desperadoes they tugged and they strained, till the welcome
cry was heard—"Stand up, Tashtego!—give it to him!" The
harpoon was hurled. "Stern all!" The oarsmen backed water;
the same moment something went hot and hissing along
every one of their wrists. It was the magical line. An instant
before, Stubb had swiftly caught two additional turns with it
round the loggerhead, whence, by reason of its increased
rapid circlings, a hempen blue smoke now jetted up and
mingled with the steady fumes from his pipe. As the line
passed round and round the loggerhead; so also, just before reaching that point, it blisteringly passed through and
through both of Stubb's hands, from which the hand-cloths,
or squares of quilted canvas sometimes worn at these times,
had accidentally dropped. It was like holding an enemy's
sharp two-edged sword by the blade, and that enemy all the
time striving to wrest it out of your clutch.

"Wet the line! wet the line!" cried Stubb to the tub oarsman (him seated by the tub) who, snatching off his hat,
dashed the sea-water into it.* More turns were taken, so
that the line began holding its place. The boat now flew
through the boiling water like a shark all fins. Stubb and
Tashtego here changed places—stem for stern—a staggering
business truly in that rocking commotion.

From the vibrating line extending the entire length of the

---

* Partly to show the indispensableness of this act, it may
here be stated, that, in the old Dutch fishery, a mop was used
to dash the running line with water; in many other ships, a
wooden piggin, or bailer, is set apart for that purpose. Your
hat, however, is the most convenient.

upper part of the boat, and from its now being more tight than a harpstring, you would have thought the craft had two keels—one cleaving the water, the other the air—as the boat churned on through both opposing elements at once. A continual cascade played at the bows; a ceaseless whirling eddy in her wake; and, at the slightest motion from within, even but of a little finger, the vibrating, cracking craft canted over her spasmodic gunwale into the sea. Thus they rushed; each man with might and main clinging to his seat, to prevent being tossed to the foam; and the tall form of Tashtego at the steering oar crouching almost double, in order to bring down his centre of gravity. Whole Atlantics and Pacifics seemed passed as they shot on their way, till at length the whale somewhat slackened his flight.

"Haul in—haul in!" cried Stubb to the bowsman! and, facing round towards the whale, all hands began pulling the boat up to him, while yet the boat was being towed on. Soon ranging up by his flank, Stubb, firmly planting his knee in the clumsy cleat, darted dart after dart into the flying fish; at the word of command, the boat alternately sterning out of the way of the whale's horrible wallow, and then ranging up for another fling.

The red tide now poured from all sides of the monster like brooks down a hill. His tormented body rolled not in brine but in blood, which bubbled and seethed for furlongs behind in their wake. The slanting sun playing upon this crimson pond in the sea, sent back its reflection into every face, so that they all glowed to each other like red men. And all the while, jet after jet of white smoke was agonizingly shot from the spiracle of the whale, and vehement puff after puff from the mouth of the excited headsman; as at every dart, hauling in upon his crooked lance (by the line attached to it), Stubb straightened it again and again, by a few rapid blows against the gunwale, then again and again sent it into the whale.

"Pull up—pull up!" he now cried to the bowsman, as the waning whale relaxed in his wrath. "Pull up!—close to!" and the boat ranged along the fish's flank. When reaching far over the bow, Stubb slowly churned his long sharp lance into the fish, and kept it there, carefully churning and churning, as if cautiously seeking to feel after some gold watch that the whale might have swallowed, and which he was fearful of breaking ere he could hook it out. But that gold watch he sought was the innermost life of the fish. And now it is struck; for, starting from his trance into that unspeakable thing called his "flurry," the monster horribly wallowed in his blood, over-wrapped himself in impenetrable, mad, boiling spray, so that the imperilled craft, instantly dropping astern, had much ado blindly to struggle out from that phrensied twilight into the clear air of the day.

And now abating in his flurry, the whale once more rolled out into view; surging from side to side; spasmodically dilating and contracting his spout-hole, with sharp, cracking, agonized respirations. At last, gush after gush of clotted red gore, as if it had been the purple lees of red wine, shot into the frighted air; and falling back again, ran dripping down his motionless flanks into the sea. His heart had burst!

"He's dead, Mr. Stubb," said Daggoo.

"Yes; both pipes smoked out!" and withdrawing his own from his mouth, Stubb scattered the dead ashes over the water; and, for a moment, stood thoughtfully eyeing the vast corpse he had made.

THE DART   LXII

A WORD concerning an incident in the last chapter.

According to the invariable usage of the fishery, the whale-boat pushes off from the ship, with the headsman or whale-killer as temporary steersman, and the harpooneer or whale-fastener pulling the foremost oar, the one known as the harpooneer-oar. Now it needs a strong, nervous arm to strike the first iron into the fish; for often, in what is called a long dart, the heavy implement has to be flung to the distance of twenty or thirty feet. But however prolonged and exhausting the chase, the harpooneer is expected to pull his oar meanwhile to the uttermost; indeed, he is expected to set an example of superhuman activity to the rest, not only by incredible rowing, but by repeated loud and intrepid exclamations; and what it is to keep shouting at the top of one's compass, while all the other muscles are strained and half started—what that is none know but those who have tried it. For one, I cannot bawl very heartily and work very recklessly at one and the same time. In this straining, bawling state, then, with his back to the fish, all at once the exhausted harpooneer hears the exciting cry—"Stand by, and

give it to him!" He now has to drop and secure his oar,
turn round on his centre half way, seize his harpoon from
the crotch, and with what little strength may remain, he
assays to pitch it somehow into the whale. No wonder, taking
the whole fleet of whalemen in a body, that out of fifty
fair chances for a dart, not five are successful; no wonder
that so many hapless harpooneers are madly cursed and dis-
rated; no wonder that some of them actually burst their
blood-vessels in the boat; no wonder that some sperm whalemen are absent four years with four barrels; no wonder
that to many ship owners, whaling is but a losing concern;
for it is the harpooneer that makes the voyage, and if you
take the breath out of his body how can you expect to find
it there when most wanted!

Again, if the dart be successful, then at the second critical
instant, that is, when the whale starts to run, the boat-header
and harpooneer likewise start to running fore and aft, to the
imminent jeopardy of themselves and every one else. It is
then they change places; and the headsman, the chief officer
of the little craft, takes his proper station in the bows of the
boat.

Now, I care not who maintains the contrary, but all this is
both foolish and unnecessary. The headsman should stay in
the bows from first to last; he should both dart the harpoon
and the lance, and no rowing whatever should be expected
of him, except under circumstances obvious to any fisherman.
I know that this would sometimes involve a slight loss of
speed in the chase; but long experience in various whalemen
of more than one nation has convinced me that in the vast
majority of failures in the fishery, it has not by any means
been so much the speed of the whale as the before described
exhaustion of the harpooneer that has caused them.

To insure the greatest efficiency in the dart, the harpooneers of this world must start to their feet from out of
idleness, and not from out of toil.

THE CROTCH   LXIII

OUT of the trunk, the branches grow; out of them, the
twigs. So, in productive subjects, grow the chapters.
The crotch alluded to on a previous page deserves inde-

pendent mention. It is a notched stick of peculiar form, some
two feet in length, which is perpendicularly inserted into the
starboard gunwale near the bow, for the purpose of furnishing a rest for the wooden extremity of the harpoon, whose
other naked, barbed end slopingly projects from the prow.
Thereby the weapon is instantly at hand to its hurler, who
snatches it up as readily from its rest as a backwoodsman
swings his rifle from the wall. It is customary to have two
harpoons reposing in the crotch, respectively called the first
and second irons.

But these two harpoons, each by its own cord, are both
connected with the line; the object being this: to dart them
both, if possible, one instantly after the other into the same
whale; so that if, in the coming drag, one should draw out,
the other may still retain a hold. It is a doubling of the
chances. But it very often happens that owing to the instantaneous, violent, convulsive running of the whale upon
receiving the first iron, it becomes impossible for the harpooneer, however lightning-like in his movements, to pitch
the second iron into him. Nevertheless, as the second iron
is already connected with the line, and the line is running,
hence that weapon must, at all events, be anticipatingly tossed
out of the boat, somehow and somewhere; else the most terrible jeopardy would involve all hands. Tumbled into the
water, it accordingly is in such cases; the spare coils of box
line (mentioned in a preceding chapter) making this feat, in
most instances, prudently practicable. But this critical act is
not always unattended with the saddest and most fatal
casualties.

Furthermore: you must know that when the second iron
is thrown overboard, it thenceforth becomes a dangling,
sharp-edged terror, skittishly curvetting about both boat and
whale, entangling the lines, or cutting them, and making a
prodigious sensation in all directions. Nor, in general, is it
possible to secure it again until the whale is fairly captured
and a corpse.

Consider, now, how it must be in the case of four boats all
engaging one unusually strong, active, and knowing whale;
when owing to these qualities in him, as well as to the thousand concurring accidents of such an audacious enterprise,
eight or ten loose second irons may be simultaneously dangling about him. For, of course, each boat is supplied with
several harpoons to bend on to the line should the first one
be ineffectually darted without recovery. All these particulars

are faithfully narrated here, as they will not fail to elucidate several most important, however intricate passages, in scenes hereafter to be painted.

STUBB'S SUPPER   LXIV

STUBB'S whale had been killed some distance from the ship. It was a calm; so, forming a tandem of three boats, we commenced the slow business of towing the trophy to the Pequod. And now, as we eighteen men with our thirty-six arms, and one hundred and eighty thumbs and fingers, slowly toiled hour after hour upon that inert, sluggish corpse in the sea; and it seemed hardly to budge at all, except at long intervals; good evidence was hereby furnished of the enormousness of the mass we moved. For, upon the great canal of Hang-Ho, or whatever they call it, in China, four or five laborers on the foot-path will draw a bulky freighted junk at the rate of a mile an hour; but this grand argosy we towed heavily forged along, as if laden with pig-lead in bulk.

Darkness came on; but three lights up and down in the Pequod's main-rigging dimly guided our way; till drawing nearer we saw Ahab dropping one of several more lanterns over the bulwarks. Vacantly eyeing the heaving whale for a moment, he issued the usual orders for securing it for the night; and then handing his lantern to a seaman, went his way into the cabin, and did not come forward again until morning.

Though, in overseeing the pursuit of this whale, Captain Ahab had evinced his customary activity, to call it so; yet now that the creature was dead, some vague dissatisfaction, or impatience, or despair, seemed working in him; as if the sight of that dead body reminded him that Moby Dick was yet to be slain; and though a thousand other whales were brought to his ship, all that would not one jot advance his grand, monomaniac object. Very soon you would have thought from the sound on the Pequod's decks, that all hands were preparing to cast anchor in the deep; for heavy chains are being dragged along the deck, and thrust rattling out of the port-holes. But by those clanking links, the vast corpse itself, not the ship, is to be moored. Tied by the head to the stern, and by the tail to the bows, the whale now lies with its black hull close to the vessel's, and seen through the darkness of the night, which obscured the spars and rigging aloft, the two—ship and whale, seemed yoked together like colossal bullocks, whereof one reclines while the other remains standing.*

If moody Ahab was now all quiescence, at least so far as could be known on deck, Stubb, his second mate, flushed with conquest, betrayed an unusual but still good-natured excitement. Such an unwonted bustle was he in that the staid Starbuck, his official superior, quietly resigned to him for the time the sole management of affairs. One small, helping cause of all this liveliness in Stubb, was soon made strangely manifest. Stubb was a high liver; he was somewhat intemperately fond of the whale as a flavorish thing to his palate.

"A steak, a steak, ere I sleep! You, Daggoo! overboard you go, and cut me one from his small!"

Here be it known, that though these wild fishermen do not as a general thing, and according to the great military maxim, make the enemy defray the current expenses of the war (at least before realizing the proceeds of the voyage), yet now and then you find some of these Nantucketers who have a genuine relish for that particular part of the Sperm Whale designated by Stubb; comprising the tapering extremity of the body.

About midnight that steak was cut and cooked; and lighted by two lanterns of sperm oil, Stubb stoutly stood up to his spermaceti supper at the capstan-head, as if that capstan were a sideboard. Nor was Stubb the only banqueter on whale's flesh that night. Mingling their mumblings with his own mastications, thousands on thousands of sharks,

---

* A little item may as well be related here. The strongest and most reliable hold which the ship has upon the whale when moored alongside, is by the flukes or tail; and as from its greater density that part is relatively heavier than any other (excepting the side-fins), its flexibility even in death, causes it to sink below the surface; so that with the hand you cannot get at it from the boat, in order to put the chain around it. But this difficulty is ingeniously overcome: a small, strong line is prepared with a wooden float at its outer end, and a weight in its middle, while the other end is secured to the ship. By adroit management the wooden float is made to rise on the other side of the mass, so that now having girdled the whale, the chain is readily made to follow suit; and being slipped along the body, is at last locked fast round the smallest part of the tail, at the point of junction with its broad flukes or lobes.

swarming round the dead leviathan, smackingly feasted on its fatness. The few sleepers below in their bunks were often startled by the sharp slapping of their tails against the hull, within a few inches of the sleepers' hearts. Peering over the side you could just see them (as before you heard them) wallowing in the sullen, black waters, and turning over on their backs as they scooped out huge globular pieces of the whale of the bigness of a human head. This particular feat of the shark seems all but miraculous. How, at such an apparently unassailable surface, they contrive to gouge out such symmetrical mouthfuls, remains a part of the universal problem of all things. The mark they thus leave on the whale, may best be likened to the hollow made by a carpenter in countersinking for a screw.

Though amid all the smoking horror and diabolism of a seafight, sharks will be seen longingly gazing up to the ship's decks, like hungry dogs round a table where red meat is being carved, ready to bolt down every killed man that is tossed to them; and though, while the valiant butchers over the deck-table are thus cannibally carving each other's live meat with carving-knives all gilded and tasselled, the sharks, also, with their jewel-hilted mouths, are quarrelsomely carving away under the table at the dead meat; and though, were you to turn the whole affair upside down, it would still be pretty much the same thing, that is to say, a shocking sharkish business enough for all parties; and though sharks also are the invariable outriders of all slave ships crossing the Atlantic, systematically trotting alongside, to be handy in case a parcel is to be carried anywhere, or a dead slave to be decently buried; and though one or two other like instances might be set down, touching the set terms, places, and occasions, when sharks do most socially congregate, and most hilariously feast; yet is there no conceivable time or occasion when you will find them in such countless numbers, and in gayer or more jovial spirits, than around a dead sperm whale, moored by night to a whale-ship at sea. If you have never seen that sight, then suspend your decision about the propriety of devil-worship, and the expediency of conciliating the devil.

But, as yet, Stubb heeded not the mumblings of the banquet that was going on so nigh him, no more than the sharks heeded the smacking of his own epicurean lips.

"Cook, cook!—where's that old Fleece?" he cried at length, widening his legs still further, as if to form a more secure base for his supper; and, at the same time darting his fork into the dish, as if stabbing with his lance; "cook, you cook! —sail this way, cook!"

The old black, not in any very high glee at having been previously roused from his warm hammock at a most unseasonable hour, came shambling along from his galley, for, like many old blacks, there was something the matter with his knee-pans, which he did not keep well scoured like his other pans; this old Fleece, as they called him, came shuffling and limping along, assisting his step with his tongs, which, after a clumsy fashion, were made of straightened iron hoops; this old Ebony floundered along, and in obedience to the word of command, came to a dead stop on the opposite side of Stubb's sideboard; when, with both hands folded before him, and resting on his two-legged cane, he bowed his arched back still further over, at the same time sideways inclining his head, so as to bring his best ear into play.

"Cook," said Stubb, rapidly lifting a rather reddish morsel to his mouth, "don't you think this steak is rather overdone? You've been beating this steak too much, cook; it's too tender. Don't I always say that to be good, a whale-steak must be tough? There are those sharks now over the side, don't you see they prefer it tough and rare? What a shindy they are kicking up! Cook, go and talk to 'em; tell 'em they are welcome to help themselves civilly, and in moderation, but they must keep quiet. Blast me, if I can hear my own voice. Away, cook, and deliver my message. Here, take this lantern," snatching one from his sideboard; "now then, go and preach to 'em!"

Sullenly taking the offered lantern, old Fleece limped across the deck to the bulwarks; and then, with one hand dropping his light low over the sea, so as to get a good view of his congregation, with the other hand he solemnly flourished his tongs, and leaning far over the side in a mumbling voice began addressing the sharks, while Stubb, softly crawling behind, overheard all that was said.

"Fellow-critters: I'se ordered here to say dat you must stop dat dam noise dare. You hear? Stop dat dam smackin' ob de lip! Massa Stubb say dat you can fill your dam bellies up to de hatchings, but by Gor! you must stop dat dam racket!"

"Cook," here interposed Stubb, accompanying the word with a sudden slap on the shoulder,—"Cook! why, damn your eyes, you mustn't swear that way when you're preaching. That's no way to convert sinners, Cook!"

"Who dat? Den preach to him yourself," sullenly turning to go.

"No, Cook; go on, go on."

"Well, den, Belubed fellow-critters:"—

"Right!" exclaimed Stubb, approvingly, "coax 'em to it; try that," and Fleece continued.

"Do you is all sharks, and by natur wery woracious, yet I zay to you, fellow-critters, dat dat woraciousness—'top dat dam slappin' ob de tail! How you tink to hear, 'spose you keep up such a dam slappin' and bitin' dare?"

"Look," cried Stubb, collaring him, "I won't have that swearing. Talk to 'em gentlemanly."

Once more the sermon proceeded.

"Your woraciousness, fellow-critters, I don't blame ye so much for; dat is natur, and can't be helped; but to gobern dat wicked natur, dat is de pint. You is sharks, sartin; but if you gobern de shark in you, why den you be angel; for all angel is not'ing more dan de shark well goberned. Now, look here, bred'ren, just try wonst to be cibil, a helping yoursebls from dat whale. Don't be tearin' de blubber out your neighbour's mout, I say. Is not one shark dood right as toder to dat whale? And, by Gor, none of you has de right to dat whale; dat whale belong to some one else. I know some o you has berry brig mout, brigger dan oders; but den de brig mouts sometimes has de small bellies; so dat de brigness ob de mout is not to swaller wid, but to bite off de blubber for de small fry ob sharks, dat can't get into de scrouge to help demselves."

"Well done, old Fleece!" cried Stubb, "that's Christianity; go on."

"No use goin' on; de dam willains will keep a scrougin' and slappin' each oder, Massa Stubb; dey don't hear one word; no use a-preachin' to such dam g'uttons as you call 'em, till dare bellies is full, and dare bellies is bottomless; and when dey do get 'em full, dey won't hear you den; for den dey sink in de sea, go fast to sleep on de coral, and can't hear not'ing at all, no more, for eber and eber."

"Upon my soul, I am about of the same opinion; so give the benediction, Fleece, and I'll away to my supper."

Upon this, Fleece, holding both hands over the fishy mob, raised his shrill voice, and cried—

"Cussed fellow-critters! Kick up de damndest row as ever

you can; fill your dam' bellies 'till dey bust—and den die."

"Now, cook," said Stubb, resuming his supper at the capstan; "Stand just where you stood before, there, over against me, and pay particular attention."

"All dention," said Fleece, again stooping over upon his tongs in the desired position.

"Well," said Stubb, helping himself freely meanwhile; "I shall now go back to the subject of this steak. In the first place, how old are you, cook?"

"What dat do wid de 'teak," said the old black, testily.

"Silence! How old are you, cook?"

" 'Bout ninety, dey say," he gloomily muttered.

"And have you lived in this world hard upon one hundred years, cook, and don't know yet how to cook a whale-steak?" rapidly bolting another mouthful at the last word, so that that morsel seemed a continuation of the question. "Where were you born, cook?"

" 'Hind de hatchway, in ferry-boat, goin' ober de Roanoke."

"Born in a ferry-boat! That's queer, too. But I want to know what country you were born in, cook?"

"Didn't I say de Roanoke country?" he cried, sharply.

"No, you didn't, cook; but I'll tell you what I'm coming to, cook. You must go home and be born over again; you don't know how to cook a whale-steak yet."

"Bress my soul, if I cook noder one," he growled, angrily, turning round to depart.

"Come back, cook;—here, hand me those tongs;—now take that bit of steak there, and tell me if you think that steak cooked as it should be? Take it, I say"—holding the tongs towards him—"take it, and taste it."

Faintly smacking his withered lips over it for a moment, the old negro muttered, "Best cooked 'teak I eber taste; joosy, berry joosy."

"Cook," said Stubb, squaring himself once more; "do you belong to the church?"

"Passed one once in Cape-Down," said the old man sullenly.

"And you once in your life passed a holy church in Cape-Town, where you doubtless overheard a holy parson addressing his hearers as his beloved fellow-creatures, have you, cook! And yet you come here, and tell me such a dreadful lie as you did just now, eh?" said Stubb. "Where do you expect to go to, cook?"

"Go to bed berry soon," he mumbled, half-turning as he spoke.

"Avast! heave to! I mean when you die, cook. It's an awful question. Now what's your answer?"

"When dis old brack man dies," said the negro slowly, changing his whole air and demeanor, "he hisself won't go nowhere; but some bressed angel will come and fetch him."

"Fetch him? How? In a coach and four, as they fetched Elijah? And fetch him where?"

"Up dere," said Fleece, holding his tongs straight over his head, and keeping it there very solemnly.

"So, then, you expect to go up into our main-top, do you, cook, when you are dead? But don't you know the higher you climb, the colder it gets? Main-top, eh?"

"Didn't say dat t'all," said Fleece, again in the sulks.

"You said up there, didn't you? and now look yourself, and see where your tongs are pointing. But, perhaps you expect to get into heaven by crawling through the lubber's hole, cook; but, no, no, cook, you don't get there, except you go the regular way, round by the rigging. It's a ticklish business, but must be done, or else it's no go. But none of us are in heaven yet. Drop your tongs, cook, and hear my orders. Do ye hear? Hold your hat in one hand, and clap t'other a'top of your heart, when I'm giving my orders, cook. What! that your heart, there?—that's your gizzard! Aloft! aloft!—that's it—now you have it. Hold it there now, and pay attention."

"All 'dention," said the old black, with both hands placed as desired, vainly wriggling his grizzled head, as if to get both ears in front at one and the same time.

"Well then, cook, you see this whale-steak of yours was so very bad, that I have put it out of sight as soon as possible; you see that, don't you? Well, for the future, when you cook another whale-steak for my private table here, the capstan, I'll tell you what to do so as not to spoil it by overdoing. Hold the steak in one hand, and show a live coal to it with the other; that done, dish it; d'ye hear? And now tomorrow, cook, when we are cutting in the fish, be sure you stand by to get the tips of his fins; have them put in pickle. As for the ends of the flukes, have them soused, cook. There, now ye may go."

But Fleece had hardly got three paces off, when he was recalled.

"Cook, give me cutlets for supper to-morrow night in the

midwatch. D'ye hear? away you sail, then.—Halloa! stop! make a bow before you go.—Avast heaving again! Whale-balls for breakfast—don't forget."

"Wish, by gor! whale eat him, 'stead of him eat whale. I'm bressed if he ain't more of shark dan Massa Shark hisself," muttered the old man, limping away; with which sage ejaculation he went to his hammock.

THE WHALE AS A DISH   LXV

THAT mortal man should feed upon the creature that feeds his lamp, and, like Stubb, eat him by his own light, as you may say; this seems so outlandish a thing that one must needs go a little into the history and philosophy of it.

It is upon record, that three centuries ago the tongue of the Right Whale was esteemed a great delicacy in France, and commanded large prices there. Also, that in Henry VIIIth's time, a certain cook of the court obtained a handsome reward for inventing an admirable sauce to be eaten with barbacued porpoises, which, you remember, are a species of whale. Porpoises, indeed, are to this day considered fine eating. The meat is made into balls about the size of billiard balls, and being well seasoned and spiced might be taken for turtleballs or veal balls. The old monks of Dumfermline were very fond of them. They had a great porpoise grant from the crown.

The fact is, that among his hunters at least, the whale would by all hands be considered a noble dish, were there not so much of him; but when you come to sit down before a meat-pie nearly one hundred feet long, it takes away your appetite. Only the most unprejudiced of men like Stubb, nowadays partake of cooked whales; but the Esquimaux are not so fastidious. We all know they live upon whales, and have rare old vintages of prime old train oil. Zogranda, one of their most famous doctors, recommends strips of blubber for infants, as being exceedingly juicy and nourishing. And this reminds me that certain Englishmen, who long ago were accidentally left in Greenland by a whaling vessel—that these men actually lived for several months on the mouldy scraps of whales which had been left ashore after trying out the blubber. Among the Dutch whalemen these scraps are called "fritters;" which, indeed, they greatly resemble, being brown and crisp, and smelling something like old Amsterdam housewives' dough-nuts or oly-cooks, when fresh. They have such an eatable look that the most self-denying stranger can hardly keep his hands off.

But what further depreciates the whale as a civilized dish, is his exceeding richness. He is the great prize ox of the sea, too fat to be delicately good. Look at his hump, which would be as fine eating as the buffalo's (which is esteemed a rare dish), were it not such a solid pyramid of fat. But the spermaceti itself, how bland and creamy that is; like the transparent, half-jellied, white meat of a cocoanut in the third month of its growth, yet far too rich to supply a substitute for butter. Nevertheless, many whalemen have a method of absorbing it into some other substance, and then partaking of it. In the long try watches of the night it is a common thing for the seamen to dip their ship-biscuit into the huge oil-pots and let them fry there awhile. Many a good supper have I thus made.

In the case of a small Sperm Whale the brains are accounted a fine dish. The casket of the skull is broken into with an axe, and the two plump, whitish lobes being withdrawn (precisely resembling two large puddings), they are then mixed with flour, and cooked into a most delectable mess, in flavor somewhat resembling calves' head, which is quite a dish among some epicures; and every one knows that some young bucks among the epicures, by continually dining upon calves' brains, by and by get to have a little brains of their own, so as to be able to tell a calf's head from their own heads; which, indeed, requires uncommon discrimination. And that is the reason why a young buck with an intelligent looking calf's head before him, is somehow one of the saddest sights you can see. The head looks a sort of reproachfully at him, with an "Et tu Brute!" expression.

It is not, perhaps, entirely because the whale is so excessively unctuous that landsmen seem to regard the eating of him with abhorrence; that appears to result, in some way, from the consideration before mentioned: i.e. that a man should eat a newly murdered thing of the sea, and eat it too by its own light. But no doubt the first man that ever murdered an ox was regarded as a murderer; perhaps he was hung; and if he had been put on his trial by oxen, he certainly would have been; and he certainly deserved it if any murderer does. Go to the meatmarket of a Saturday night and see the crowds of live bipeds staring up at the long rows of dead quadrupeds. Does not that sight take a tooth out of the cannibal's jaw? Cannibals? who is not a cannibal? I tell you it will be more tolerable for the Fejee that salted down a lean missionary in his cellar against a coming famine; it will be more tolerable for that provident Fejee, I say, in the day of judgment, than for thee, civilized and enlightened gourmand, who nailest geese to the ground and feastest on their bloated livers in thy paté-de-foie-gras.

But Stubb, he eats the whale by its own light, does he? and that is adding insult to injury, is it? Look at your knife-handle, there, my civilized and enlightened gourmand dining off that roast beef, what is that handle made of?—what but the bones of the brother of the very ox you are eating? And what do you pick your teeth with, after devouring that fat goose? With a feather of the same fowl. And with what quill did the Secretary of the Society for the Suppression of Cruelty to Ganders formally indite his circulars? It is only within the last month or two that that society passed a resolution to patronize nothing but steel pens.

THE SHARK MASSACRE   LXVI

WHEN in the Southern Fishery, a captured Sperm Whale, after long and weary toil, is brought alongside late at night, it is not, as a general thing at least, customary to proceed at once to the business of cutting him in. For that business is an exceedingly laborious one; is not very soon completed; and requires all hands to set about it. Therefore, the common usage is to take in all sail; lash the helm a'lee; and then send every one below to his hammock till daylight, with the reservation that, until that time, anchor-watches shall be kept; that is, two and two for an hour, each couple, the crew in rotation shall mount the deck to see that all goes well.

But sometimes, especially upon the Line in the Pacific, this plan will not answer at all; because such incalculable hosts of sharks gather round the moored carcase, that were he left so for six hours, say, on a stretch, little more than the skeleton would be visible by morning. In most other parts of the ocean, however, where these fish do not so largely abound, their wondrous voracity can be at times considerably diminished, by vigorously stirring them up with sharp whaling-spades, a procedure notwithstanding, which, in some instances, only seems to tickle them into still greater activity. But it was not thus in the present case with the Pequod's sharks; though, to be sure, any man unaccustomed to such sights, to have looked over her side that night, would have almost thought the whole round sea was one huge cheese, and those sharks the maggots in it.

Nevertheless, upon Stubb setting the anchor-watch after his supper was concluded; and when, accordingly, Queequeg and a forecastle seaman came on deck, no small excitement was created among the sharks; for immediately suspending the cutting stages over the side, and lowering three lanterns, so that they cast long gleams of light over the turbid sea, these two mariners, darting their long whaling-spades, kept up an incessant murdering of the sharks,* by striking the keen steel deep into their skulls, seemingly their only vital part. But in the foamy confusion of their mixed and strug- gling hosts, the marksmen could not always hit their mark; and this brought about new revelations of the incredible ferocity of the foe. They viciously snapped, not only at each other's disembowelments, but like flexible bows, bent round, and bit their own; till those entrails seemed swallowed over and over again by the same mouth, to be oppositely voided by the gaping wound. Nor was this all. It was unsafe to med- dle with the corpses and ghosts of these creatures. A sort of generic or Pantheistic vitality seemed to lurk in their very joints and bones, after what might be called the individual life had departed. Killed and hoisted on deck for the sake of his skin, one of these sharks almost took poor Queequeg's hand off, when he tried to shut down the dead lid of his murderous jaw.

"Queequeg no care what god made him shark," said the savage, agonizingly lifting his hand up and down; "wedder Fejee god or Nantucket god; but de god wat made shark must be one dam Ingin."

* The whaling-spade used for cutting-in is made of the very best steel; is about the bigness of a man's spread hand; and in general shape, corresponds to the garden implement after which it is named; only its sides are perfectly flat, and its upper end considerably narrower than the lower. This weapon is always kept as sharp as possible; and when being used is occasionally honed, just like a razor. In its socket, a stiff pole, from twenty to thirty feet long, is inserted for a handle.

CUTTING IN   LXVII

IT was a Saturday night, and such a Sabbath as followed! Ex officio professors of Sabbath breaking are all
whalemen. The ivory Pequod was turned into what seemed
a shamble; every sailor a butcher. You would have thought
we were offering up ten thousand red oxen to the sea gods.

In the first place, the enormous cutting tackles, among
other ponderous things comprising a cluster of blocks generally painted green, and which no single man can possibly
lift—this vast bunch of grapes was swayed up to the main-
top and firmly lashed to the lower mast-head, the strongest
point anywhere above a ship's deck. The end of the hawser-
like rope winding through these intricacies, was then conducted to the windlass, and the huge lower block of the
tackles was swung over the whale; to this block the great
blubber hook, weighing some one hundred pounds, was attached. And now suspended in stages over the side, Starbuck
and Stubb, the mates, armed with their long spades, began
cutting a hole in the body for the insertion of the hook just
above the nearest of the two side-fins. This done, a broad,
semicircular line is cut round the hole, the hook is inserted,
and the main body of the crew striking up a wild chorus,
now commence heaving in one dense crowd at the windlass.
When instantly, the entire ship careens over on her side;
every bolt in her starts like the nail-heads of an old house in
frosty weather; she trembles, quivers, and nods her frighted
mast-heads to the sky. More and more she leans over to the
whale, while every gasping heave of the windlass is answered
by a helping heave from the billows; till at last, a swift,
startling snap is heard; with a great swash the ship rolls upwards and backwards from the whale, and the triumphant
tackle rises into sight dragging after it the disengaged semi-
circular end of the first strip of blubber. Now as the blubber
envelopes the whale precisely as the rind does an orange, so
is it stripped off from the body precisely as an orange is
sometimes stripped by spiralizing it. For the strain constantly
kept up by the windlass continually keeps the whale rolling
over and over in the water, and as the blubber in one strip
uniformly peels off along the line called the "scarf," simul-

taneously cut by the spades of Starbuck and Stubb, the mates; and just as fast as it is thus peeled off, and indeed by that very act itself, it is all the time being hoisted higher and higher aloft till its upper end grazes the main-top; the men at the windlass then cease heaving, and for a moment or two the prodigious blood-dripping mass sways to and fro as if let down from the sky, and every one present must take good heed to dodge it when it swings, else it may box his ears and pitch him headlong overboard.

One of the attending harpooneers now advances with a long, keen weapon called a boarding-sword, and watching his chance he dexterously slices out a considerable hole in the lower part of the swaying mass. Into this hole, the end of the second alternating great tackle is then hooked so as to retain a hold upon the blubber, in order to prepare for what follows. Whereupon, this accomplished swordsman, warning all hands to stand off, once more makes a scientific dash at the mass, and with a few sidelong, desperate, lunging slicings, severs it completely in twain; so that while the short lower part is still fast, the long upper strip, called a blanket-piece, swings clear, and is all ready for lowering. The heavers forward now resume their song, and while the one tackle is peeling and hoisting a second strip from the whale, the other is slowly slackened away, and down goes the first strip through the main hatchway right beneath, into an unfurnished parlor called the blubber-room. Into this twilight apartment sundry nimble hands keep coiling away the long blanket-piece as if it were a great live mass of plaited serpents. And thus the work proceeds; the two tackles hoisting and lowering simultaneously; both whale and windlass heaving, the heavers singing, the blubber-room gentlemen coiling, the mates scarfing, the ship straining, and all hands swearing occasionally, by way of assuaging the general friction.

THE BLANKET   LXVIII

I HAVE given no small attention to that not unvexed subject, the skin of the whale. I have had controversies about it with experienced whalemen afloat, and learned naturalists ashore. My original opinion remains unchanged; but it is only an opinion.

The question is, what and where is the skin of the whale?
Already you know what his blubber is. That blubber is something of the consistence of firm, close-grained beef, but
tougher, more elastic and compact, and ranges from eight
or ten to twelve and fifteen inches in thickness.

Now, however preposterous it may at first seem to talk of
any creature's skin as being of that sort of consistence and
thickness, yet in point of fact these are no arguments
against such a presumption; because you cannot raise any
other dense enveloping layer from the whale's body but that
same blubber; and the outermost enveloping layer of any animal, if reasonably dense, what can that be but the skin? True,
from the unmarred dead body of the whale, you may scrape
off with your hand an infinitely thin, transparent substance,
somewhat resembling the thinnest shreds of isinglass, only it
is almost as flexible and soft as satin; that is, previous to
being dried, when it not only contracts and thickens, but becomes rather hard and brittle. I have several such dried bits,
which I use for marks in my whalebooks. It is transparent, as
I said before; and being laid upon the printed page, I have
sometimes pleased myself with fancying it exerted a magnifying influence. At any rate, it is pleasant to read about
whales through their own spectacles, as you may say. But
what I am driving at here is this. That some infinitely thin,
isinglass substance, which, I admit, invests the entire body of
the whale, is not so much to be regarded as the skin of the
creature, as the skin of the skin, so to speak; for it were
simply ridiculous to say, that the proper skin of the tremendous whale is thinner and more tender than the skin of a new-
born child. But no more of this.

Assuming the blubber to be the skin of the whale; then,
when this skin, as in the case of a very large Sperm Whale,
will yield the bulk of one hundred barrels of oil; and, when
it is considered that, in quantity, or rather weight, that oil, in
its expressed state, is only three fourths, and not the entire
substance of the coat; some idea may hence be had of the
enormousness of that animated mass, a mere part of whose
mere integument yields such a lake of liquid as that. Reckoning ten barrels to the ton, you have ten tons for the net weight
of only three quarters of the stuff of the whale's skin.

In life, the visible surface of the Sperm Whale is not the
least among the many marvels he presents. Almost invariably
it is all over obliquely crossed and re-crossed with numberless straight marks in thick array, something like those in the

finest Italian line engravings. But these marks do not seem to be impressed upon the isinglass substance above mentioned, but seem to be seen through it, as if they were engraved upon the body itself. Nor is this all. In some instances, to the quick, observant eye, those linear marks, as in a veritable engraving, but afford the ground for far other delineations. These are hieroglyphical; that is, if you call those mysterious cyphers on the walls of pyramids hieroglyphics, then that is the proper word to use in the present connexion. By my retentive memory of the hieroglyphics upon one Sperm Whale in particular, I was much struck with a plate representing the old Indian characters chiselled on the famous hieroglyphic palisades on the banks of the Upper Mississippi. Like those mystic rocks, too, the mystic-marked whale remains undecipherable. This allusion to the Indian rocks reminds me of another thing. Besides all the other phenomena which the exterior of the Sperm Whale presents, he not seldom displays the back, and more especially his flanks, effaced in great part of the regular linear appearance, by reason of numerous rude scratches, altogether of an irregular, random aspect. I should say that those New England rocks on the seacoast, which Agassiz imagines to bear the marks of violent scraping contact with vast floating icebergs—I should say, that those rocks must not a little resemble the Sperm Whale in this particular. It also seems to me that such scratches in the whale are probably made by hostile contact with other whales; for I have most remarked them in the large, full-grown bulls of the species.

A word or two more concerning this matter of the skin or blubber of the whale. It has already been said, that it is stript from him in long pieces, called blanket-pieces. Like most sea-terms, this one is very happy and significant. For the whale is indeed wrapt up in his blubber as in a real blanket or counterpane; or, still better, an Indian poncho slipt over his head, and skirting his extremity. It is by reason of this cosy blanketing of his body, that the whale is enabled to keep himself comfortable in all weathers, in all seas, times, and tides. What would become a Greenland whale, say, in those shuddering, icy seas of the North, if unsupplied with his cozy surtout? True, other fish are found exceedingly brisk in those Hyperborean waters; but these, be it observed, are your cold-blooded, lungless fish, whose very bellies are refrigerators; creatures, that warm themselves under the lee of an iceberg, as a traveller in winter would bask before an inn fire;

whereas, like man, the whale has lungs and warm blood.
Freeze his blood, and he dies. How wonderful is it then—
except after explanation—that this great monster, to whom
corporeal warmth is as indispensable as it is to man; how
wonderful that he should be found at home, immersed to
his lips for life in those Arctic waters! where, when seamen
fall overboard, they are sometimes found, months afterwards,
perpendicularly frozen into the hearts of fields of ice, as a
fly is found glued in amber. But more surprising is it to
know, as has been proved by experiment, that the blood of
a Polar whale is warmer than that of a Borneo negro in
summer.

It does seem to me, that herein we see the rare virtue of a
strong individual vitality, and the rare virtue of thick walls,
and the rare virtue of interior spaciousness. Oh, man! admire
and model thyself after the whale! Do thou, too, remain
warm among ice. Do thou, too, live in this world without
being of it. Be cool at the equator; keep thy blood fluid at the
Pole. Like the great dome of St. Peter's, and like the great
whale, retain, O man! in all seasons a temperature of thine
own.

But how easy and how hopeless to teach these fine things!
Of erections, how few are domed like St. Peter's! of creatures, how few vast as the whale!

THE FUNERAL   LXIX

"HAUL in the chains! Let the carcase go astern!"
The vast tackles have now done their duty. The peeled
white body of the beheaded whale flashes like a marble
sepulchre; though changed in hue, it has not perceptibly lost
anything in bulk. It is still colossal. Slowly it floats more and
more away, the water round it torn and splashed by the insatiate sharks, and the air above vexed with rapacious flights
of screaming fowls, whose beaks are like so many insult-
ing poniards in the whale. The vast white headless phantom
floats further and further from the ship, and every rod that
it so floats, what seem square roods of sharks and cubic roods
of fowls, augment the murderous din. For hours and hours
from the almost stationary ship that hideous sight is seen.
Beneath the unclouded and mild azure sky, upon the fair face

of the pleasant sea, wafted by the joyous breezes, that great mass of death floats on and on, till lost in infinite perspectives.

There's a most doleful and most mocking funeral! The sea-vultures all in pious mourning, the air-sharks all punctiliously in black or speckled. In life but few of them would have helped the whale, I ween, if peradventure he had needed it; but upon the banquet of his funeral they most piously do pounce. Oh, horrible vultureism of earth! from which not the mightiest whale is free.

Nor is this the end. Desecrated as the body is, a vengeful ghost survives and hovers over it to scare. Espied by some timid man-of-war or blundering discovery-vessel from afar, when the distance obscuring the swarming fowls, nevertheless still shows the white mass floating in the sun, and the white spray heaving high against it; straightway the whale's unharming corpse, with trembling fingers is set down in the log—*shoals, rocks, and breakers hereabouts: beware!* And for years afterwards, perhaps, ships shun the place; leaping over it as silly sheep leap over a vacuum, because their leader originally leaped there when a stick was held. There's your law of precedents; there's your utility of traditions; there's the story of your obstinate survival of old beliefs never bottomed on the earth, and now not even hovering in the air! There's orthodoxy!

Thus, while in life the great whale's body may have been a real terror to his foes, in his death his ghost becomes a powerless panic to a world.

Are you a believer in ghosts, my friend? There are other ghosts than the Cock-Lane one, and far deeper men than Doctor Johnson who believe in them.

THE SPHYNX   LXX

IT should not have been omitted that previous to completely stripping the body of the leviathan, he was beheaded. Now, the beheading of the Sperm Whale is a scientific anatomical feat, upon which experienced whale surgeons very much pride themselves: and not without reason.

Consider that the whale has nothing that can properly be called a neck; on the contrary, where his head and body seem to join, there, in that very place, is the thickest part of him. Remember, also, that the surgeon must operate from above, some eight or ten feet intervening between him and his subject, and that subject almost hidden in a discolored, rolling, and oftentimes tumultuous and bursting sea. Bear in mind, too, that under these untoward circumstances he has to cut many feet deep in the flesh; and in that subterraneous manner, without so much as getting one single peep into the ever-contracting gash thus made, he must skilfully steer clear of all adjacent, interdicted parts, and exactly divide the spine at a critical point hard by its insertion into the skull. Do you not marvel, then, at Stubb's boast, that he demanded but ten minutes to behead a sperm whale?

When first severed, the head is dropped astern and held there by a cable till the body is stripped. That done, if it belong to a small whale it is hoisted on deck to be deliberately disposed of. But, with a full grown leviathan this is impossible; for the sperm whale's head embraces nearly one third of his entire bulk, and completely to suspend such a burden as that, even by the immense tackles of a whaler, this were as vain a thing as to attempt weighing a Dutch barn in jewellers' scales.

The Pequod's whale being decapitated and the body stripped, the head was hoisted against the ship's side—about half way out of the sea, so that it might yet in great part be buoyed up by its native element. And there with the strained craft steeply leaning over to it, by reason of the enormous downward drag from the lower mast-head, and every yard-arm on that side projecting like a crane over the waves; there, that blood-dripping head hung to the Pequod's waist like the giant Holofernes's from the girdle of Judith.

When this last task was accomplished it was noon, and the seamen went below to their dinner. Silence reigned over the before tumultuous but now deserted deck. An intense copper calm, like a universal yellow lotus, was more and more unfolding its noiseless measureless leaves upon the sea.

A short space elapsed, and up into this noiselessness came Ahab alone from his cabin. Taking a few turns on the quarter-deck, he paused to gaze over the side, then slowly getting into the main-chains he took Stubb's long spade—still remaining there after the whale's decapitation—and striking it into the lower part of the half-suspended mass, placed its other end crutch-wise under one arm, and so stood leaning over with eyes attentively fixed on this head.

It was a black and hooded head; and hanging there in the midst of so intense a calm, it seemed the Sphynx's in the desert. "Speak, thou vast and venerable head," muttered Ahab, "which, though ungarnished with a beard, yet here and there lookest hoary with mosses; speak, mighty head, and tell us the secret thing that is in thee. Of all divers, thou hast dived the deepest. That head upon which the upper sun now gleams, has moved amid the world's foundations. Where unrecorded names and navies rust, and untold hopes and anchors rot; where in her murderous hold this frigate earth is ballasted with bones of millions of the drowned; there, in that awful water-land, there was thy most familiar home. Thou hast been where bell or diver never went; has slept by many a sailor's side, where sleepless mothers would give their lives to lay them down. Thou saw'st the locked lovers when leaping from their flaming ship; heart to heart they sank beneath the exulting wave; true to each other, when heaven seemed false to them. Thou saw'st the murdered mate when tossed by pirates from the midnight deck; for hours he fell into the deeper midnight of the insatiate maw; and his murderers still sailed on unharmed—while swift lightnings shivered the neighboring ship that would have borne a righteous husband to outstretched, longing arms. O head! thou hast seen enough to split the planets and make an infidel of Abraham, and not one syllable is thine!"

"Sail ho!" cried a triumphant voice from the main-mast-head.

"Aye? Well, now, that's cheering," cried Ahab, suddenly erecting himself, while whole thunder-clouds swept aside from his brow. "That lively cry upon this deadly calm might almost convert a better man.—Where away?"

"Three points on the starboard bow, sir, and bringing down her breeze to us!"

"Better and better, man. Would now St. Paul would come along that way, and to my breezelessness bring his breeze! O Nature, and O soul of man! how far beyond all utterance are your linked analogies! not the smallest atom stirs or lives on matter, but has its cunning duplicate in mind."

THE JEROBOAM'S STORY   LXXI

HAND in hand, ship and breeze blew on; but the breeze
came faster than the ship, and soon the Pequod began to
rock.

By and by, through the glass the strangers' boats and
manned mast-heads proved her a whale-ship. But as she was
so far to windward, and shooting by, apparently making a
passage to some other ground, the Pequod could not hope to
reach her. So the signal was set to see what response would
be made.

Here be it said, that like the vessels of military marines,
the ships of the American Whale Fleet have each a private
signal; all of which signals being collected in a book with the
names of the respective vessels attached, every captain is provided with it. Thereby, the whale commanders are enabled to
recognise each other upon the ocean, even at considerable distances, and with no small facility.

The Pequod's signal was at last responded to by the
stranger's setting her own; which proved the ship to be the
Jeroboam of Nantucket. Squaring her yards, she bore down,
ranged abeam under the Pequod's lee, and lowered a boat;
it soon drew nigh; but, as the side-ladder was being rigged
by Starbuck's order to accommodate the visiting captain, the
stranger in question waved his hand from his boat's stern in
token of that proceeding being entirely unnecessary. It turned
out that the Jeroboam had a malignant epidemic on board;
and that Mayhew, her captain, was fearful of infecting the
Pequod's company. For, though himself and boat's crew remained untainted, and though his ship was half a rifle-shot
off, and an incorruptible sea and air rolling and flowing between; yet conscientiously adhering to the timid quarantine
of the land, he peremptorily refused to come into direct contact with the Pequod.

But this did by no means prevent all communications. Preserving an interval of some few yards between itself and the
ship, the Jeroboam's boat by the occasional use of its oars
contrived to keep parallel to the Pequod, as she heavily
forged through the sea (for by this time it blew very fresh),
with her main-topsail aback; though, indeed, at times by

the sudden onset of a large rolling wave, the boat would be pushed some way ahead; but would be soon skilfully brought to her proper bearings again. Subject to this, and other the like interruptions now and then, a conversation was sustained between the two parties; but at intervals not without still another interruption of a very different sort.

Pulling an oar in the Jeroboam's boat, was a man of a singular appearance, even in that wild whaling life where individual notabilities make up all totalities. He was a small, short, youngish man, sprinkled all over his face with freckles, and wearing redundant yellow hair. A long-skirted, cabalistically-cut coat of a faded walnut tinge enveloped him; the overlapping sleeves of which were rolled up on his wrists. A deep, settled, fanatic delirium was in his eyes.

So soon as this figure had been first descried, Stubb had exclaimed—"That's he! that's he!—the long-togged scaramouch the Town-Ho's company told us of!" Stubb here alluded to a strange story of the Jeroboam, and a certain man among her crew, some time previous when the Pequod spoke the Town-Ho. According to this account and what was subsequently learned, it seemed that the scaramouch in question had gained a wonderful ascendency over almost everybody in the Jeroboam. His story was this:

He had been originally nurtured among the crazy society of Neskyeuna Shakers, where he had been a great prophet; in their cracked, secret meetings having several times descended from heaven by the way of a trap-door, announcing the speedy opening of the seventh vial, which he carried in his vest-pocket; but, which, instead of containing gunpowder, was supposed to be charged with laudanum. A strange, apostolic whim having seized him, he had left Neskyeuna for Nantucket, where, with that cunning peculiar to craziness, he assumed a steady, common sense exterior, and offered himself as a green-hand candidate for the Jeroboam's whaling voyage. They engaged him; but straightway upon the ship's getting out of sight of land, his insanity broke out in a freshet. He announced himself as the archangel Gabriel, and commanded the captain to jump overboard. He published his manifesto, whereby he set himself forth as the deliverer of the isles of the sea and vicar-general of all Oceanica. The unflinching earnestness with which he declared these things;—the dark, daring play of his sleepless, excited imagination, and all the preternatural terrors of real delirium, united to invest this Gabriel in the minds of the majority of the ignorant crew, with an atmosphere of sacredness. Moreover, they were afraid of him. As such a man, however, was not of much practical use in the ship, especially as he refused to work except when he pleased, the incredulous captain would fain have been rid of him; but apprised that that individual's intention was to land him in the first convenient port, the archangel forthwith opened all his seals and vials—devoting the ship and all hands to unconditional perdition, in case this intention was carried out. So strongly did he work upon his disciples among the crew, that at last in a body they went to the captain and told him if Gabriel was sent from the ship, not a man of them would remain. He was therefore forced to relinquish his plan. Nor would they permit Gabriel to be any way maltreated, say or do what he would; so that it came to pass that Gabriel had the complete freedom of the ship. The consequence of all this was, that the archangel cared little or nothing for the captain and mates; and since the epidemic had broken out, he carried a higher hand than ever; declaring that the plague, as he called it, was at his sole command; nor should it be stayed but according to his good pleasure. The sailors, mostly poor devils, cringed, and some of them fawned before him; in obedience to his instructions, sometimes rendering him personal homage, as to a god. Such things may seem incredible; but, however wondrous, they are true. Nor is the history of fanatics half so striking in respect to the measureless self-deception of the fanatic himself, as his measureless power of deceiving and bedeviling so many others. But it is time to return to the Pequod.

"I fear not thy epidemic, man," said Ahab from the bulwarks, to Captain Mayhew, who stood in the boat's stern; "come on board."

But now Gabriel started to his feet.

"Think, think of the fevers, yellow and bilious! Beware of the horrible plague!"

"Gabriel, Gabriel!" cried Captain Mayhew; "thou must either—" But that instant a headlong wave shot the boat far ahead, and its seethings drowned all speech.

"Hast thou seen the White Whale?" demanded Ahab, when the boat drifted back.

"Think, think of thy whale-boat, stoven and sunk! Beware of the horrible tail!"

"I tell thee again, Gabriel, that—" But again the boat tore ahead as if dragged by fiends. Nothing was said for some moments, while a succession of riotous waves rolled by, which by one of those occasional caprices of the seas were tumbling, not heaving it. Meantime, the hoisted sperm whale's head jogged about very violently, and Gabriel was seen eyeing it with rather more apprehensiveness than his archangel nature seemed to warrant.

When this interlude was over, Captain Mayhew began a dark story concerning Moby Dick; not, however, without frequent interruptions from Gabriel, whenever his name was mentioned, and the crazy sea that seemed leagued with him.

It seemed that the Jeroboam had not long left home, when upon speaking a whale-ship, her people were reliably apprised of the existence of Moby Dick, and the havoc he had made. Greedily sucking in this intelligence, Gabriel solemnly warned the captain against attacking the White Whale, in case the monster should be seen; in his gibbering insanity, pronouncing the White Whale to be no less a being than the Shaker God incarnated; the Shakers receiving the Bible. But when, some year or two afterwards, Moby Dick was fairly sighted from the mast-heads, Macey, the chief mate, burned with ardor to encounter him; and the captain himself being not unwilling to let him have the opportunity, despite all the archangel's denunciations and forewarnings. Macey succeeded in persuading five men to man his boat. With them he pushed off; and, after much weary pulling, and many perilous, unsuccessful onsets, he at last succeeded in getting one iron fast. Meantime, Gabriel, ascending to the main-royal mast-head, was tossing one arm in frantic gestures, and hurling forth prophecies of speedy doom to the sacrilegious assailants of his divinity. Now, while Macey, the mate, was standing up in his boat's bow, and with all the reckless energy of his tribe was venting his wild exclamations upon the whale, and essaying to get a fair chance for his poised lance, lo! a broad white shadow rose from the sea; by its quick, fanning motion, temporarily taking the breath out of the bodies of the oarsmen. Next instant, the luckless mate, so full of furious life, was smitten bodily into the air, and making a long arc in his descent, fell into the sea at the distance of about fifty yards. Not a chip of the boat was harmed, not a hair of any oarsman's head; but the mate for ever sank.

It is well to parenthesize here, that of the fatal accidents in the Sperm-Whale Fishery, this kind is perhaps almost as frequent as any. Sometimes, nothing is injured but the man who is thus annihilated; oftener the boat's bow is knocked off, or the thigh-board, in which the headsman stands, is torn from its place and accompanies the body. But strangest of all is the circumstance, that in more instances than one, when the body has been recovered, not a single mark of violence is discernible; the man being stark dead.

The whole calamity, with the falling form of Macey, was plainly descried from the ship. Raising a piercing shriek—"The vial! the vial!" Gabriel called off the terror-stricken crew from the further hunting of the whale. This terrible event clothed the archangel with added influence; because his credulous disciples believed that he had specifically fore-announced it, instead of only making a general prophecy, which any one might have done, and so have chanced to hit one of many marks in the wide margin allowed. He became a nameless terror to the ship.

Mayhew having concluded his narration, Ahab put such questions to him, that the stranger captain could not forbear inquiring whether he intended to hunt the White Whale, if opportunity should offer. To which Ahab answered—"Aye." Straightway, then, Gabriel once more started to his feet, glaring upon the old man, and vehemently exclaimed, with downward pointed finger—"Think, think of the blasphemer—dead, and down there!—beware of the blasphemer's end!"

Ahab stolidly turned aside; then said to Mayhew, "Captain, I have just bethought me of my letter-bag; there is a letter for one of thy officers, if I mistake not. Starbuck, look over the bag."

Every whale-ship takes out a goodly number of letters for various ships, whose delivery to the persons to whom they may be addressed, depends upon the mere chance of encountering them in the four oceans. Thus, most letters never reach their mark; and many are only received after attaining an age of three years or more.

Soon Starbuck returned with a letter in his hand. It was sorely tumbled, damp, and covered with a dull, spotted, green mould, in consequence of being kept in a dark locker of the cabin. Of such a letter, Death himself might well have been the post-boy.

"Can'st not read it?" cried Ahab. "Give it me, man. Aye, aye, it's but a dim scrawl;—what's this?" As he was studying it out, Starbuck took a long cutting-spade pole, and with his knife slightly split the end, to insert the letter there, and in that way, hand it to the boat, without its coming any closer to the ship.

Meantime, Ahab holding the letter, muttered, "Mr. Har— yes, Mr. Harry—(a woman's pinny hand,—the man's wife, I'll wager)—Aye—Mr. Harry Macey, Ship Jeroboam;—why it's Macey, and he's dead!"

"Poor fellow! poor fellow! and from his wife," sighed Mayhew; "but let me have it."

"Nay, keep it thyself," cried Gabriel to Ahab; "thou art soon going that way."

"Curses throttle thee!" yelled Ahab. "Captain Mayhew, stand by now to receive it;" and taking the fatal missive from Starbuck's hands, he caught it in the slit of the pole, and reached it over towards the boat. But as he did so, the oarsmen expectantly desisted from rowing; the boat drifted a little towards the ship's stern; so that, as if by magic, the letter suddenly ranged along with Gabriel's eager hand. He clutched it in an instant, seized the boat-knife, and impaling the letter on it, sent it thus loaded back into the ship. It fell at Ahab's feet. Then Gabriel shrieked out to his comrades to give way with their oars, and in that manner the mutinous boat rapidly shot away from the Pequod.

As, after this interlude, the seamen resumed their work upon the jacket of the whale, many strange things were hinted in reference to this wild affair.

THE MONKEY-ROPE   LXXII

IN the tumultuous business of cutting-in and attending to a whale, there is much running backwards and forwards among the crew. Now hands are wanted here, and then again hands are wanted there. There is no staying in any one place; for at one and the same time everything has to be done everywhere. It is much the same with him who endeavors the description of the scene. We must now retrace our way a little. It was mentioned that upon first breaking ground in the whale's back, the blubber-hook was inserted into the original hole there cut by the spades of the mates. But how did so clumsy and weighty a mass as that same hook get fixed in that hole? It was inserted there by my particular friend Queequeg, whose duty it was, as harpooneer, to descend upon the monster's back for the special purpose referred to. But in very many cases, circumstances require that the harpooneer

shall remain on the whale till the whole flensing or stripping
operation is concluded. The whale, be it observed, lies almost
entirely submerged, excepting the immediate parts operated
upon. So down there, some ten feet below the level of the
deck, the poor harpooneer flounders about, half on the whale
and half in the water, as the vast mass revolves like a tread-
mill beneath him. On the occasion in question, Queequeg
figured in the Highland costume—a shirt and socks—in
which to my eyes, at least, he appeared to uncommon advantage; and no one had a better chance to observe him, as
will presently be seen.

Being the savage's bowsman, that is, the person who pulled
the bow-oar in his boat (the second one from forward), it
was my cheerful duty to attend upon him while taking that
hard-scrabble scramble upon the dead whale's back. You have
seen Italian organ-boys holding a dancing-ape by a long cord.
Just so, from the ship's steep side, did I hold Queequeg down
there in the sea, by what is technically called in the fishery
a monkey-rope, attached to a strong strip of canvas belted
round his waist.

It was a humorously perilous business for both of us. For,
before we proceed further, it must be said that the monkey-
rope was fast at both ends; fast to Queequeg's broad canvas belt, and fast to my narrow leather one. So that for better or for worse, we two, for the time, were wedded;
and should poor Queequeg sink to rise no more, then both
usage and honor demanded, that instead of cutting the cord,
it should drag me down in his wake. So then, an elongated
Siamese ligature united us. Queequeg was my own inseparable
twin brother; nor could I any way get rid of the dangerous
liabilities which the hempen bond entailed.

So strongly and metaphysically did I conceive of my situation then, that while earnestly watching his motions, I seemed
distinctly to perceive that my own individuality was now
merged in a joint stock company of two: that my free will
had received a mortal wound; and that another's mistake or
misfortune might plunge innocent me into unmerited disaster and death. Therefore, I saw that here was a sort of inter-
regnum in Providence; for its even-handed equity never could
have sanctioned so gross an injustice. And yet still further
pondering—while I jerked him now and then from between
the whale and the ship, which would threaten to jam him—
still further pondering, I say, I saw that this situation of
mine was the precise situation of every mortal that breathes;

only, in most cases, he, one way or other, has this Siamese connexion with a plurality of other mortals. If your banker breaks, you snap; if your apothecary by mistake sends you poison in your pills, you die. True, you may say that, by exceeding caution, you may possibly escape these and the multitudinous other evil chances of life. But handle Queequeg's monkey-rope heedfully as I would, sometimes he jerked it so, that I came very near sliding overboard. Nor could I possibly forget that, do what I would, I only had the management of one end of it.*

I have hinted that I would often jerk poor Queequeg from between the whale and the ship—where he would occasionally fall, from the incessant rolling and swaying of both. But this was not the only jamming jeopardy he was exposed to. Unappalled by the massacre made upon them during the night, the sharks now freshly and more keenly allured by the before pent blood which began to flow from the carcase —the rabid creatures swarmed round it like bees in a beehive.

And right in among those sharks was Queequeg; who often pushed them aside with his floundering feet. A thing altogether incredible were it not that attracted by such prey as a dead whale, the otherwise miscellaneously carnivorous shark will seldom touch a man.

Nevertheless, it may well be believed that since they have such a ravenous finger in the piè, it is deemed but wise to look sharp to them. Accordingly, besides the monkey-rope, with which I now and then jerked the poor fellow from too close a vicinity to the maw of what seemed a peculiarly ferocious shark—he was provided with still another protection. Suspended over the side in one of the stages, Tashtego and Daggoo continually flourished over his head a couple of keen whale-spades, wherewith they slaughtered as many sharks as they could reach. This procedure of theirs, to be sure, was very disinterested and benevolent of them. They meant Queequeg's best happiness, I admit; but in their hasty zeal to befriend him, and from the circumstance that both he and the sharks were at times half hidden by the blood-mudded water, those indiscreet spades of theirs would come

* The monkey-rope is found in all whalers; but it was only in the Pequod that the monkey and his holder were ever tied together. This improvement upon the original usage was introduced by no less a man than Stubb, in order to afford to the imperilled harpooneer the strongest guarantee for the faithfulness and vigilance of his monkey-rope holder.

nearer amputating a leg than a tail. But poor Queequeg, I suppose, straining and gasping there with that great iron hook—poor Queequeg, I suppose, only prayed to his Yojo, and gave up his life into the hands of his gods.

Well, well, my dear comrade and twin-brother, thought I, as I drew in and then slacked off the rope to every swell of the sea—what matters it, after all? Are you not the precious image of each and all of us men in this whaling world? That unsounded ocean you gasp in, is Life; those sharks, your foes; those spades, your friends; and what between sharks and spades you are in a sad pickle and peril, poor lad.

But courage! there is good cheer in store for you, Queequeg. For now, as with blue lips and bloodshot eyes the exhausted savage at last climbs up the chains and stands all dripping and involuntarily trembling over the side; the steward advances, and with a benevolent, consolatory glance hands him—what? Some hot Cogniac? No! hands him, ye gods! hands him a cup of tepid ginger and water!

"Ginger? Do I smell ginger?" suspiciously asked Stubb, coming near. "Yes, this must be ginger," peering into the as yet untasted cup. Then standing as if incredulous for a while, he calmly walked towards the astonished steward slowly saying, "Ginger? ginger? and will you have the goodness to tell me, Mr. Dough-Boy, where lies the virtue of ginger? Ginger! is ginger the sort of fuel you use, Dough-Boy, to kindle a fire in this shivering cannibal? Ginger!—what the devil is ginger?—sea-coal?—fire-wood?—lucifer matches?—tinder?—gun-powder?—what the devil is ginger, I say, that you offer this cup to our poor Queequeg here?"

"There is some sneaking Temperance Society movement about this business," he suddenly added, now approaching Starbuck, who had just come from forward. "Will you look at that kannakin, sir: smell of it, if you please." Then watching the mate's countenance, he added: "The steward, Mr. Starbuck, had the face to offer that calomel and jalap to Queequeg, there, this instant off the whale. Is the steward an apothecary, sir? and may I ask whether this is the sort of bitters by which he blows back the life into a half-drowned man?"

"I trust not," said Starbuck, "it is poor stuff enough."

"Aye, aye, steward," cried Stubb, "we'll teach you to drug a harpooneer; none of your apothecary's medicine here; you want to poison us, do ye? You have got out insurances on our lives and want to murder us all, and pocket the proceeds, do ye?"

"It was not me," cried Dough-Boy, "it was Aunt Charity that brought the ginger on board; and bade me never give the harpooneers any spirits, but only this ginger-jub—so she called it."

"Ginger-jub! you gingerly rascal! take that! and run along with ye to the lockers, and get something better. I hope I do no wrong, Mr. Starbuck. It is the captain's orders—grog for the harpooneer on a whale."

"Enough," replied Starbuck, "only don't hit him again, but—"

"Oh, I never hurt when I hit, except when I hit a whale or something of that sort; and this fellow's a weazel. What were you about saying, sir?"

"Only this: go down with him, and get what thou wantest thyself."

When Stubb reappeared, he came with a dark flask in one hand, and a sort of tea-caddy in the other. The first contained strong spirits, and was handed to Queequeg; the second was Aunt Charity's gift, and that was freely given to the waves.

STUBB AND FLASK KILL A RIGHT WHALE; AND THEN HAVE A TALK OVER HIM   LXXIII

IT must be borne in mind that all this time we have a Sperm Whale's prodigious head hanging to the Pequod's side. But we must let it continue hanging there a while till we can get a chance to attend to it. For the present other matters press, and the best we can do now for the head, is to pray heaven the tackles may hold.

Now, during the past night and forenoon, the Pequod had gradually drifted into a sea, which, by its occasional patches of yellow brit, gave unusual tokens of the vicinity of Right Whales, a species of the Leviathan that but few supposed to be at this particular time lurking anywhere near. And though all hands commonly disdained the capture of those inferior creatures; and though the Pequod was not commissioned to cruise for them at all, and though she had passed numbers of them near the Crozetts without lowering a boat; yet now that a Sperm Whale had been brought alongside and beheaded, to the surprise of all, the announcement was made that a Right Whale should be captured that day, if opportunity offered.

Nor was this long wanting. Tall spouts were seen to leeward; and two boats, Stubb's and Flask's, were detached in pursuit. Pulling further and further away, they at last became almost invisible to the men at the mast-head. But suddenly in the distance, they saw a great heap of tumultuous white water, and soon after news came from aloft that one or both of the boats must be fast. An interval passed and the boats were in plain sight, in the act of being dragged right towards the ship by the towing whale. So close did the monster come to the hull, that at first it seemed as if he meant it malice; but suddenly going down in a maelstrom, within three rods of the planks, he wholly disappeared from view, as if diving under the keel. "Cut, cut!" was the cry from the ship to the boats, which, for one instant, seemed on the point of being brought with a deadly dash against the vessel's side. But having plenty of line yet in the tubs, and the whale not sounding very rapidly, they paid out abundance of rope, and at the same time pulled with all their might so as to get ahead of the ship. For a few minutes the struggle was intensely critical; for while they still slacked out the tightened line in one direction, and still plied their oars in another, the contending strain threatened to take them under. But it was only a few feet advance they sought to gain. And they stuck to it till they did gain it; when instantly, a swift tremor was felt running like lightning along the keel, as the strained line, scraping beneath the ship, suddenly rose to view under her bows, snapping and quivering; and so flinging off its drippings, that the drops fell like bits of broken glass on the water, while the whale beyond also rose to sight, and once more the boats were free to fly. But the fagged whale abated his speed, and blindly altering his course, went round the stern of the ship towing the two boats after him, so that they performed a complete circuit.

Meantime, they hauled more and more on their lines, till close flanking him on both sides, Stubb answered Flask with lance for lance; and thus round and round the Pequod the battle went, while the multitudes of sharks that had before swum round the Sperm Whale's body, rushed to the fresh blood that was spilled, thirstily drinking at every new gash, as the eager Israelites did at the new bursting fountains that poured from the smitten rock.

At last his spout grew thick, and with a frightful roll and vomit, he turned upon his back a corpse.

While the two headsmen were engaged in making fast cords to his flukes, and in other ways getting the mass in readiness for towing, some conversation ensued between them.

"I wonder what the old man wants with this lump of foul lard," said Stubb, not without some disgust at the thought of having to do with so ignoble a leviathan.

"Wants with it?" said Flask, coiling some spare line in the boat's bow, "did you never hear that the ship which but once has a Sperm Whale's head hoisted on her starboard side, and at the same time a Right's Whale on the larboard; did you never hear, Stubb, that that ship can never afterwards capsize?"

"Why not?"

"I don't know, but I heard that gamboge ghost of a Fedallah saying so, and he seems to know all about ships' charms. But I sometimes think he'll charm the ship to no good at last. I don't half like that chap, Stubb. Did you ever notice how that tusk of his is a sort of carved into a snake's head, Stubb?"

"Sink him! I never look at him at all; but if ever I get a chance of a dark night, and he standing hard by the bulwarks, and no one by; look down there, Flask"—pointing into the sea with a peculiar motion of both hands—"Aye, will I! Flask, I take that Fedallah to be the devil in disguise. Do you believe that cock and bull story about his having been stowed away on board ship? He's the devil, I say. The reason why you don't see his tail, is because he tucks it up out of sight; he carries it coiled away in his pocket, I guess. Blast him! now that I think of it, he's always wanting oakum to stuff into the toes of his boots."

"He sleeps in his boots, don't he? He hasn't got any hammock; but I've seen him lay of nights in a coil of rigging."

"No doubt, and it's because of his cursed tail; he coils it down, do ye see, in the eye of the rigging."

"What's the old man have so much to do with him for?"

"Striking up a swap or a bargain, I suppose."

"Bargain?—about what?"

"Why, do ye see, the old man is hard bent after that White Whale, and the devil there is trying to come round him, and get him to swap away his silver watch, or his soul, or something of that sort, and then he'll surrender Moby Dick."

"Pooh! Stubb, you are skylarking; how can Fedallah do that?"

"I don't know, Flask, but the devil is a curious chap, and a wicked one, I tell ye. Why, they say as how he went a sauntering into the old flag-ship once, switching his tail about devilish easy and gentlemanlike, and inquiring if the old governor was at home. Well, he was at home, and asked the devil what he wanted. The devil, switching his hoofs, up and says, 'I want John.' 'What for?' says the old governor. 'What business is that of yours,' says the devil, getting mad,—'I want to use him.' 'Take him,' says the governor—and by the Lord, Flask, if the devil didn't give John the Asiatic cholera before he got through with him, I'll eat this whale in one mouthful. But look sharp—ain't you all ready there? Well, then, pull ahead, and let's get the whale alongside."

"I think I remember some such story as you were telling," said Flask, when at last the two boats were slowly advancing with their burden towards the ship, "but I can't remember where."

"Three Spaniards? Adventures of those three bloody-minded soldadoes? Did ye read it there, Flask? I guess ye did?"

"No: never saw such a book; heard of it, though. But now, tell me, Stubb, do you suppose that that devil you was speaking of just now, was the same you say is now on board the Pequod?"

"Am I the same man that helped kill this whale? Doesn't the devil live for ever; who ever heard that the devil was dead? Did you ever see any parson a wearing mourning for the devil? And if the devil has a latch-key to get into the admiral's cabin, don't you suppose he can crawl into a port-hole? Tell me that, Mr. Flask?"

"How old do you suppose Fedallah is, Stubb?"

"Do you see that mainmast there?" pointing to the ship; "well, that's the figure one; now take all the hoops in the Pequod's hold, and string 'em along in a row with that mast, for oughts, do you see; well, that wouldn't begin to be Fedallah's age. Nor all the coopers in creation couldn't show hoops enough to make oughts enough."

"But see here, Stubb, I thought you a little boasted just now, that you meant to give Fedallah a sea-toss, if you got a good chance. Now, if he's so old as all those hoops of yours come to, and if he is going to live for ever, what good will it do to pitch him overboard—tell me that?"

"Give him a good ducking, anyhow."

"But he'd crawl back."

"Duck him again; and keep ducking him."

"Suppose he should take it into his head to duck you, though—yes, and drown you—what then?"

"I should like to see him try it; I'd give him such a pair of black eyes that he wouldn't dare to show his face in the admiral's cabin again for a long while, let alone down in the orlop there, where he lives, and hereabouts on the upper decks where he sneaks so much. Damn the devil, Flask; do you suppose I'm afraid of the devil? Who's afraid of him, except the old governor who daresn't catch him and put him in double-darbies, as he deserves, but let's him go about kidnapping people; aye, and signed a bond with him, that all the people the devil kidnapped, he'd roast for him? There's a governor!"

"Do you suppose Fedallah wants to kidnap Captain Ahab?"

"Do I suppose it? You'll know it before long, Flask. But I am going now to keep a sharp look-out on him; and if I see anything very suspicious going on, I'll just take him by the nape of his neck, and say—Look here, Beelzebub, you don't do it; and if he makes any fuss, by the Lord I'll make a grab into his pocket for his tail, take it to the capstan, and give him such a wrenching and heaving, that his tail will come short off at the stump—do you see; and then, I rather guess when he finds himself docked in that queer fashion, he'll sneak off without the poor satisfaction of feeling his tail between his legs."

"And what will you do with the tail, Stubb?"

"Do with it? Sell it for an ox whip when we get home;—what else?"

"Now, do you mean what you say, and have been saying all along, Stubb?"

"Mean or not mean, here we are at the ship."

The boats were here hailed, to tow the whale on the larboard side, where fluke chains and other necessaries were already prepared for securing him.

"Didn't I tell you so?" said Flask; "yes, you'll soon see this right whale's head hoisted up opposite that parmacetti's."

In good time, Flask's saying proved true. As before, the Pequod steeply leaned over towards the sperm whale's head,

now, by the counterpoise of both heads, she regained her
even keel; though sorely strained, you may well believe. So,
when on one side you hoist in Locke's head, you go over
that way; but now, on the other side, hoist in Kant's and you
come back again; but in very poor plight. Thus, some minds
for ever keep trimming boat. Oh, ye foolish! throw all these
thunder-heads overboard, and then you will float light and
right.

In disposing of the body of a right whale, when brought
alongside the ship, the same preliminary proceedings commonly take place as in the case of a sperm whale; only, in the
latter instance, the head is cut off whole, but in the former
the lips and tongue are separately removed and hoisted on
deck, with all the well known black bone attached to what is
called the crown-piece. But nothing like this, in the present
case, had been done. The carcases of both whales had dropped
astern; and the head-laden ship not a little resembled a mule
carrying a pair of overburdening panniers.

Meantime, Fedallah was calmly eyeing the right whale's
head, and ever and anon glancing from the deep wrinkles
there to the lines in his own hand. And Ahab chanced so to
stand, that the Parsee occupied his shadow; while, if the
Parsee's shadow was there at all it seemed only to blend
with, and lengthen Ahab's. As the crew toiled on, Laplandish
speculations were bandied among them, concerning all these
passing things.

THE SPERM WHALE'S HEAD—
CONTRASTED VIEW　　　　　　　　LXXIV

HERE, now, are two great whales, laying their heads together; let us join them, and lay together our own.

Of the grand order of folio leviathans, the Sperm Whale
and the Right Whale are by far the most noteworthy. They
are the only whales regularly hunted by man. To the Nantucketer, they present the two extremes of all the known
varieties of the whale. As the external difference between
them is mainly observable in their heads; and as a head of
each is this moment hanging from the Pequod's side; and as
we may freely go from one to the other, by merely stepping
across the deck:——where, I should like to know, will you
obtain a better chance to study practical cetology than here?

In the first place, you are struck by the general contrast between these heads. Both are massive enough in all conscience; but there is a certain mathematical symmetry in the Sperm Whale's which the Right Whale's sadly lacks. There is more character in the Sperm Whale's head. As you behold it, you involuntarily yield the immense superiority to him, in point of pervading dignity. In the present instance, too, this dignity is heightened by the pepper and salt color of his head at the summit, giving token of advanced age and large experience. In short, he is what the fishermen technically call a "grey-headed whale."

Let us now note what is least dissimilar in these heads—namely, the two most important organs, the eye and the ear. Far back on the side of the head, and low down, near the angle of either whale's jaw, if you narrowly search, you will at last see a lashless eye, which you would fancy to be a young colt's eye; so out of all proportion is it to the magnitude of the head.

Now, from this peculiar sideway position of the whale's eyes, it is plain that he can never see an object which is exactly ahead, no more than he can one exactly astern. In a word, the position of the whale's eyes corresponds to that of a man's ears; and you may fancy, for yourself, how it would fare with you, did you sideways survey objects through your ears. You would find that you could only command some thirty degrees of vision in advance of the straight side-line of sight; and about thirty more behind it. If your bitterest foe were walking straight towards you, with dagger uplifted in broad day, you would not be able to see him, any more than if he were stealing upon you from behind. In a word, you would have two backs, so to speak; but, at the same time, also, two fronts (side fronts): for what is it that makes the front of a man—what, indeed, but his eyes?

Moreover, while in most other animals that I can now think of, the eyes are so planted as imperceptibly to blend their visual power, so as to produce one picture and not two to the brain; the peculiar position of the whale's eyes, effectually divided as they are by many cubic feet of solid head, which towers between them like a great mountain separating two lakes in valleys; this, of course, must wholly separate the impressions which each independent organ imparts. The whale, therefore, must see one distinct picture on this side, and another distinct picture on that side; while all between must be profound darkness and nothingness to him.

Man may, in effect, be said to look out on the world from a
sentry-box with two joined sashes for his window. But with
the whale, these two sashes are separately inserted, making
two distinct windows, but sadly impairing the view. This
peculiarity of the whale's eyes is a thing always to be borne
in mind in the fishery; and to be remembered by the reader
in some subsequent scenes.

A curious and most puzzling question might be started
concerning this visual matter as touching the Leviathan. But
I must be content with a hint. So long as a man's eyes are
open in the light, the act of seeing is involuntary; that is, he
cannot then help mechanically seeing whatever objects are before him. Nevertheless, any one's experience will teach him,
that though he can take in an undiscriminating sweep of
things at one glance, it is quite impossible for him, attentively, and completely, to examine any two things—however large or however small—at one and the same instant of
time; never mind if they lie side by side and touch each
other. But if you now come to separate these two objects, and
surround each by a circle of profound darkness; then, in order
to see one of them, in such a manner as to bring your mind
to bear on it, the other will be utterly excluded from your
contemporary consciousness. How is it, then, with the whale?
True, both his eyes, in themselves, must simultaneously act;
but is his brain so much more comprehensive, combining, and
subtle than man's, that he can at the same moment of time
attentively examine two distinct prospects, one on one side
of him, and the other in an exactly opposite direction? If he
can, then is it as marvellous a thing in him, as if a man
were able simultaneously to go through the demonstrations
of two distinct problems in Euclid. Nor, strictly investigated,
is there any incongruity in this comparison.

It may be but an idle whim, but it has always seemed to
me, that the extraordinary vacillations of movement displayed
by some whales when beset by three or four boats; the
timidity and liability to queer frights, so common to such
whales; I think that all this indirectly proceeds from the
helpless perplexity of volition, in which their divided and
diametrically opposite powers of vision must involve them.

But the ear of the whale is full as curious as the eye. If
you are an entire stranger to their race, you might hunt over
these two heads for hours, and never discover that organ.
The ear has no external leaf whatever; and into the hole

itself you can hardly insert a quill, so wondrously minute is it. It is lodged a little behind the eye. With respect to their ears, this important difference is to be observed between the sperm whale and the right. While the ear of the former has an external opening, that of the latter is entirely and evenly covered over with a membrane, so as to be quite imperceptible from without.

Is it not curious, that so vast a being as the whale should see the world through so small an eye, and hear the thunder through an ear which is smaller than a hare's? But if his eyes were broad as the lens of Herschel's great telescope; and his ears capacious as the porches of cathedrals; would that make him any longer of sight, or sharper of hearing? Not at all.— Why then do you try to "enlarge" your mind? Subtilize it.

Let us now with whatever levers and steam-engines we have at hand, cant over the sperm whale's head, so that it may lie bottom up; then, ascending by a ladder to the summit, have a peep down the mouth; and were it not that the body is now completely separated from it, with a lantern we might descend into the great Kentucky Mammoth Cave of his stomach. But let us hold on here by this tooth, and look about us where we are. What a really beautiful and chaste-looking mouth! from floor to ceiling, lined, or rather papered with a glistening white membrane, glossy as bridal satins.

But come out now, and look at this portentous lower jaw, which seems like the long narrow lid of an immense snuff-box, with the hinge at one end, instead of one side. If you pry it up, so as to get it overhead, and expose its rows of teeth, it seems a terrific portcullis; and such, alas! it proves to many a poor wight in the fishery, upon whom these spikes fall with impaling force. But far more terrible is it to behold, when fathoms down in the sea, you see some sulky whale, floating there suspended, with his prodigious jaw, some fifteen feet long, hanging straight down at right-angles with his body, for all the world like a ship's jib-boom. This whale is not dead; he is only dispirited; out of sorts, perhaps; hypochondriac; and so supine, that the hinges of his jaw have relaxed, leaving him there in that ungainly sort of plight, a reproach to all his tribe, who must, no doubt, imprecate lock-jaws upon him.

In most cases this lower jaw—being easily unhinged by a practised artist—is disengaged and hoisted on deck for the purpose of extracting the ivory teeth, and furnishing a supply of that hard white whalebone with which the fishermen fashion all sorts of curious articles, including canes, umbrellastocks, and handles to riding-whips.

With a long, weary hoist the jaw is dragged on board, as if it were an anchor; and when the proper time comes—some few days after the other work—Queequeg, Daggoo, and Tashtego, being all accomplished dentists, are set to drawing teeth. With a keen cutting-spade, Queequeg lances the gums; then the jaw is lashed down to ringbolts, and a tackle being rigged from aloft, they drag out these teeth, as Michigan oxen drag stumps of old oaks out of wild wood-lands. There are generally forty-two teeth in all; in old whales, much worn down, but undecayed; nor filled after our artificial fashion. The jaw is afterwards sawn into slabs, and piled away like joists for building houses.

THE RIGHT WHALE'S HEAD— CONTRASTED VIEW   LXXV

CROSSING the deck, let us now have a good long look at the Right Whale's head.

As in general shape the noble Sperm Whale's head may be compared to a Roman war-chariot (especially in front, where it is so broadly rounded); so, at a broad view, the Right Whale's head bears a rather inelegant resemblance to a gigantic galliot-toed shoe. Two hundred years ago an old Dutch voyager likened its shape to that of a shoemaker's last. And in this same last or shoe, that old woman of the nursery tale, with the swarming brood, might very comfortably be lodged, she and all her progeny.

But as you come nearer to this great head it begins to assume different aspects, according to your point of view. If you stand on its summit and look at these two *f*-shaped spoutholes, you would take the whole head for an enormous bassviol, and these spiracles, the apertures in its sounding-board. Then, again, if you fix your eye upon this strange, crested, comb-like incrustation on the top of the mass—this green, barnacled thing, which the Greenlanders call the "crown," and the Southern fishers the "bonnet" of the Right Whale;

fixing your eyes solely on this, you would take the head for the trunk of some huge oak, with a bird's nest in its crotch. At any rate, when you watch those live crabs that nestle here on this bonnet, such an idea will be almost sure to occur to you; unless, indeed, your fancy has been fixed by the technical term "crown" also bestowed upon it; in which case you will take great interest in thinking how this mighty monster is actually a diademed king of the sea, whose green crown has been put together for him in this marvellous manner. But if this whale be a king, he is a very sulky looking fellow to grace a diadem. Look at that hanging lower lip! what a huge sulk and pout is there! a sulk and pout, by carpenter's measurement, about twenty feet long and five feet deep; a sulk and pout that will yield you some 500 gallons of oil and more.

A great pity, now, that this unfortunate whale should be hare-lipped. The fissure is about a foot across. Probably the mother during an important interval was sailing down the Peruvian coast, when earthquakes caused the beach to gape. Over this lip, as over a slippery threshold, we now slide into the mouth. Upon my word were I at Mackinaw, I should take this to be the inside of an Indian wigwam. Good Lord! is this the road that Jonah went? The roof is about twelve feet high, and runs to a pretty sharp angle, as if there were a regular ridge-pole there; while these ribbed, arched, hairy sides, present us with those wondrous, half vertical, scimetar-shaped slats of whalebone, say three hundred on a side, which depending from the upper part of the head or crown bone, form those Venetian blinds which have elsewhere been cursorily mentioned. The edges of these bones are fringed with hairy fibres, through which the Right Whale strains the water, and in whose intricacies he retains the small fish, when openmouthed he goes through the seas of brit in feeding time. In the central blinds of bone, as they stand in their natural order, there are certain curious marks, curves, hollows, and ridges, whereby some whalemen calculate the creature's age, as the age of an oak by its circular rings. Though the certainty of this criterion is far from demonstrable, yet it has the savor of analogical probability. At any rate, if we yield to it, we must grant a far greater age to the Right Whale than at first glance will seem reasonable.

In old times, there seem to have prevailed the most curious fancies concerning these blinds. One voyager in Purchas calls

them the wondrous "whiskers" inside of the whale's mouth; *
another, "hogs' bristles;" a third old gentleman in Hackluyt
uses the following elegant language: "There are about two
hundred and fifty fins growing on each side of his upper
chop, which arch over his tongue on each side of his mouth."

As every one knows, these same "hogs' bristles," "fins,"
"whiskers," "blinds," or whatever you please, furnish to the
ladies their busks and other stiffening contrivances. But in
this particular, the demand has long been on the decline. It
was in Queen Anne's time that the bone was in its glory,
the farthingale being then all the fashion. And as those ancient dames moved about gaily, though in the jaws of the
whale, as you may say; even so, in a shower, with the like
thoughtlessness, do we nowadays fly under the same jaws for
protection; the umbrella being a tent spread over the same
bone.

But now forget all about blinds and whiskers for a moment, and, standing in the Right Whale's mouth, look around
you afresh. Seeing all these colonnades of bone so methodically ranged about, would you not think you were inside of
the great Haarlem organ, and gazing upon its thousand pipes?
For a carpet to the organ we have a rug of the softest
Turkey—the tongue, which is glued, as it were, to the floor
of the mouth. It is very fat and tender, and apt to tear in
pieces in hoisting it on deck. This particular tongue now
before us; at a passing glance I should say it was a six-
barreler; that is, it will yield you about that amount of oil.

Ere this, you must have plainly seen the truth of what I
started with—that the Sperm Whale and the Right Whale
have almost entirely different heads. To sum up, then: in
the Right Whale's there is no great well of sperm; no ivory
teeth at all; no long, slender mandible of a lower jaw, like
the Sperm Whale's. Nor in the Sperm Whale are there any
of those blinds of bone; no huge lower lip; and scarcely
anything of a tongue. Again, the Right Whale has two external spout-holes, the Sperm Whale only one.

Look your last, now, on these venerable hooded heads,
while they yet lie together; for one will soon sink, unre-

* This reminds us that the Right Whale really has a sort of
whisker, or rather a moustache, consisting of a few scattered
white hairs on the upper part of the outer end of the lower
jaw. Sometimes these tufts impart a rather brigandish expression
to his otherwise solemn countenance.

corded, in the sea; the other will not be very long in following.

Can you catch the expression of the Sperm Whale's there? It is the same he died with, only some of the longer wrinkles in the forehead seem now faded away. I think his broad brow to be full of a prairie-like placidity, born of a speculative indifference as to death. But mark the other head's expression. See that amazing lower lip, pressed by accident against the vessel's side, so as firmly to embrace the jaw. Does not this whole head seem to speak of an enormous practical resolution in facing death? This Right Whale I take to have been a Stoic; the Sperm Whale, a Platonian, who might have taken up Spinoza in his latter years.

THE BATTERING-RAM   LXXVI

ERE quitting, for the nonce, the Sperm Whale's head, I would have you, as a sensible physiologist, simply—particularly remark its front aspect, in all its compacted collectedness. I would have you investigate it now with the sole view of forming to yourself some unexaggerated, intelligent estimate of whatever battering-ram power may be lodged there. Here is a vital point; for you must either satisfactorily settle this matter with yourself, or for ever remain an infidel as to one of the most appalling, but not the less true events, perhaps anywhere to be found in all recorded history.

You observe that in the ordinary swimming position of the Sperm Whale, the front of his head presents an almost wholly vertical plane to the water; you observe that the lower part of that front slopes considerably backwards, so as to furnish more of a retreat for the long socket which receives the boom-like lower jaw; you observe that the mouth is entirely under the head, much in the same way, indeed, as though your own mouth were entirely under your chin. Moreover you observe that the whale has no external nose; and that what nose he has—his spout hole—is on the top of his head; you observe that his eyes and ears are at the sides of his head, nearly one third of his entire length from the front. Wherefore, you must now have perceived that the front of the Sperm Whale's head is a dead, blind wall, without a single organ or tender prominence of any sort whatsoever. Furthermore, you are now to consider that only in the extreme, lower, backward sloping part of the front of the head, is there the slightest vestige of bone; and not till you get near twenty feet from the forehead do you come to the full cranial development. So that this whole enormous boneless mass is as one wad. Finally, though, as will soon be revealed, its contents partly comprise the most delicate oil; yet, you are now to be apprised of the nature of the substance which so impregnably invests all that apparent effeminacy. In some previous place I have described to you how the blubber wraps the body of the whale, as the rind wraps an orange. Just so with the head; but with this difference: about the head this envelope, though not so thick, is of a boneless toughness, inestimable by any man who has not handled it. The severest pointed harpoon, the sharpest lance darted by the strongest human arm, impotently rebounds from it. It is as though the forehead of the Sperm Whale were paved with horses's hoofs. I do not think that any sensation lurks in it.

Bethink yourself also of another thing. When two large, loaded Indiamen chance to crowd and crush towards each other in the docks, what do the sailors do? They do not suspend between them, at the point of coming contact, any merely hard substance, like iron or wood. No, they hold there a large, round wad of tow and cork, enveloped in the thickest and toughest of ox-hide. That bravely and uninjured takes the jam which would have snapped all their oaken handspikes and iron crowbars. By itself this sufficiently illustrates the obvious fact I drive at. But supplementary to this, it has hypothetically occurred to me, that as ordinary fish possess what is called a swimming bladder in them, capable, at will, of distention or contraction; and as the Sperm Whale, as far as I know, has no such provision in him; considering, too, the otherwise inexplicable manner in which he now depresses his head altogether beneath the surface, and anon swims with it high elevated out of the water; considering the unobstructed elasticity of its envelope; considering the unique interior of his head; it has hypothetically occurred to me, I say, that those mystical lung-celled honeycombs there may possibly have some hitherto unknown and unsuspected connexion with the outer air, so as to be susceptible to atmospheric distention and contraction. If this be so, fancy the irresistibleness of that might, to which the most impalpable and destructive of all elements contributes.

Now, mark. Unerringly impelling this dead, impregnable, uninjurable wall, and this most buoyant thing within; there swims behind it all a mass of tremendous life, only to be adequately estimated as piled wood is—by the cord; and all obedient to one volition, as the smallest insect. So that when I shall hereafter detail to you all the specialties and concentrations of potency everywhere lurking in this expansive monster; when I shall show you some of his more inconsiderable braining feats; I trust you will have renounced all ignorant incredulity, and be ready to abide by this; that though the Sperm Whale stove a passage through the Isthmus of Darien, and mixed the Atlantic with the Pacific, you would not elevate one hair of your eye-brow. For unless you own the whale, you are but a provincial and sentimentalist in Truth. But clear Truth is a thing for salamander giants only to encounter; how small the chances for the provincials then? What befel the weakling youth lifting the dread goddess's veil at Sais?

THE GREAT HEIDELBURGH TUN   LXXVII

NOW comes the Baling of the Case. But to comprehend it aright, you must know something of the curious internal structure of the thing operated upon.

Regarding the Sperm Whale's head as a solid oblong, you may, on an inclined plane, sideways divide it into two quoins,* whereof the lower is the bony structure, forming the cranium and jaws, and the upper an unctuous mass wholly free from bones; its broad forward end forming the expanded vertical apparent forehead of the whale. At the middle of the forehead horizontally subdivide this upper quoin, and then you have two almost equal parts, which before were naturally divided by an internal wall of a thick tendinous substance.

* Quoin is not a Euclidean term. It belongs to the pure nautical mathematics. I know not that it has been defined before. A quoin is a solid which differs from a wedge in having its sharp end formed by the steep inclination of one side, instead of the mutual tapering of both sides.

The lower subdivided part, called the junk, is one immense honeycomb of oil, formed by the crossing and recrossing, into ten thousand infiltrated cells, of tough elastic white fibres throughout its whole extent. The upper part known as the Case, may be regarded as the great Heidelburgh Tun of the Sperm Whale. And as that famous great tierce is mystically carved in front, so the whale's vast plaited forehead forms innumerable strange devices for the emblematical adornment of his wondrous tun. Moreover, as that of Heidelburgh was always replenished with the most excellent of the wines of the Rhenish valleys, so the tun of the whale contains by far the most precious of all his oily vintages; namely, the highly-prized spermaceti, in its absolutely pure, limpid, and odoriferous state. Nor is this precious substance found unalloyed in any other part of the creature. Though in life it remains perfectly fluid, yet, upon exposure to the air, after death, it soon begins to concrete; sending forth beautiful crystalline shoots, as when the first thin delicate ice is just forming in water. A large whale's case generally yields about five hundred gallons of sperm, though from unavoidable circumstances, considerable of it is spilled, leaks, and dribbles away, or is otherwise irrevocably lost in the ticklish business of securing what you can.

I know not with what fine and costly material the Heidelburgh was coated within, but in superlative richness that coating could not possibly have compared with the silken pearl-colored membrane, like the lining of a fine pelisse, forming the inner surface of the Sperm Whale's case.

It will have been seen that the Heidelburgh Tun of the Sperm Whale embraces the entire length of the entire top of the head; and since—as has been elsewhere set forth—the head embraces one third of the whole length of the creature, then setting that length down at eighty feet for a good sized whale, you have more than twenty-six feet for the depth of the tun, when it is lengthwise hoisted up and down against a ship's side.

As in decapitating the whale, the operator's instrument is brought close to the spot where an entrance is subsequently forced into the spermaceti magazine; he has, therefore, to be uncommonly heedful, lest a careless, untimely stroke should invade the sanctuary and wastingly let out its invaluable contents. It is this decapitated end of the head, also, which is at last elevated out of the water, and retained in that position by the enormous cutting tackles, whose hempen combinations, on one side, make quite a wilderness of ropes in that quarter.

Thus much being said, attend now, I pray you, to that marvellous and—in this particular instance—almost fatal operation whereby the Sperm Whale's great Heidelburgh Tun is tapped.

CISTERN AND BUCKETS   LXXVIII

NIMBLE as a cat, Tashtego mounts aloft; and without altering his erect posture, runs straight out upon the over-hanging main-yard-arm, to the part where it exactly projects over the hoisted Tun. He has carried with him a light tackle called a whip, consisting of only two parts, travelling through a single-sheaved block. Securing this block, so that it hangs down from the yard-arm, he swings one end of the rope, till it is caught and firmly held by a hand on deck. Then, hand-over-hand, down the other part, the Indian drops through the air, till dexterously he lands on the summit of the head. There—still high elevated above the rest of the company, to whom he vivaciously cries—he seems some Turkish Muezzin calling the good people to prayers from the top of a tower. A short-handled sharp spade being sent up to him, he diligently searches for the proper place to begin breaking into the Tun. In this business he proceeds very heedfully, like a treasure-hunter in some old house, sounding the walls to find where the gold is masoned in. By the time this cautious search is over, a stout iron-bound bucket, precisely like a well-bucket, has been attached to one end of the whip; while the other end, being stretched across the deck, is there held by two or three alert hands. These last now hoist the bucket within grasp of the Indian, to whom another person has reached up a very long pole. Inserting this pole into the bucket, Tashtego downward guides the bucket into the Tun, till it entirely disappears; then giving the word to the seamen at the whip, up comes the bucket again, all bubbling like a dairymaid's pail of new milk. Carefully lowered from its height, the full-freighted vessel is caught by an appointed hand, and quickly emptied into a large tub. Then re-mounting aloft, it again goes through the same round until the deep cistern will yield no more. Towards the end, Tashtego has to ram his long pole harder and harder, and deeper and deeper into the Tun, until some twenty feet of the pole have gone down.

Now, the people of the Pequod had been baling some time in this way; several tubs had been filled with the fragrant sperm; when all at once a queer accident happened. Whether it was that Tashtego, that wild Indian, was so heedless and reckless as to let go for a moment his one-handed hold on the great cabled tackles suspending the head; or whether the place where he stood was so treacherous and oozy; or whether the Evil One himself would have it to fall out so, without stating his particular reasons; how it was exactly, there is no telling now; but, on a sudden, as the eightieth or ninetieth bucket came suckingly up—my God! poor Tashtego—like the twin reciprocating bucket in a veritable well, dropped head-foremost down into this great Tun of Heidelburgh, and with a horrible oily gurgling, went clean out of sight!

"Man overboard!" cried Daggoo, who amid the general consternation first came to his senses. "Swing the bucket this way!" and putting one foot into it, so as the better to secure his slippery handhold on the whip itself, the hoisters ran him high up to the top of the head, almost before Tashtego could have reached its interior bottom. Meantime, there was a terrible tumult. Looking over the side, they saw the before lifeless head throbbing and heaving just below the surface of the sea, as if that moment seized with some momentous idea; whereas it was only the poor Indian unconsciously revealing by those struggles the perilous depth to which he had sunk.

At this instant, while Daggoo, on the summit of the head, was clearing the whip—which had somehow got foul of the great cutting tackles—a sharp cracking noise was heard; and to the unspeakable horror of all, one of the two enormous hooks suspending the head tore out, and with a vast vibration the enormous mass sideways swung, till the drunk ship reeled and shook as if smitten by an iceberg. The one remaining hook, upon which the entire strain now depended, seemed every instant to be in the point of giving way; an event still more likely from the violent motions of the head.

"Come down, come down!" yelled the seamen to Daggoo, but with one hand holding on to the heavy tackles, so that if the head should drop, he would still remain suspended; the negro having cleared the foul line, rammed down the bucket

into the now collapsed well, meaning that the buried harpooneer should grasp it, and so be hoisted out.

"In heaven's name, man," cried Stubb, "are you ramming
home a cartridge there?—Avast! How will that help him;
jamming that iron-bound bucket on top of his head? Avast,
will ye!"

"Stand clear of the tackle!" cried a voice like the bursting
of a rocket.

Almost in the same instant, with a thunder-boom, the
enormous mass dropped into the sea, like Niagara's Table-
Rock into the whirlpool; the suddenly relieved hull rolled
away from it, to far down her glittering copper; and all
caught their breath, as half swinging—now over the sailors'
heads, and now over the water—Daggoo, through a thick
mist of spray, was dimly beheld clinging to the pendulous
tackles, while poor, buried-alive Tashtego was sinking utterly
down to the bottom of the sea! But hardly had the blinding
vapor cleared away, when a naked figure with a boarding-
sword in its hand, was for one swift moment seen hovering
over the bulwarks. The next, a loud splash announced that
my brave Queequeg had dived to the rescue. One packed
rush was made to the side, and every eye counted every
ripple, as moment followed moment, and no sign of either
the sinker or the diver could be seen. Some hands now
jumped into a boat alongside, and pushed a little off from
the ship.

"Ha! ha!" cried Daggoo, all at once, from his now quiet,
swinging perch overhead; and looking further off from the
side, we saw an arm thrust upright from the blue waves;
a sight strange to see, as an arm thrust forth from the
grass over a grave.

"Both! both!—it is both!"—cried Daggoo again with a
joyful shout; and soon after, Queequeg was seen boldly striking out with one hand, and with the other clutching the long
hair of the Indian. Drawn into the waiting boat, they were
quickly brought to the deck; but Tashtego was long in coming to, and Queequeg did not look very brisk.

Now, how had this noble rescue been accomplished? Why,
diving after the slowly descending head, Queequeg with
his keen sword had made side lunges near its bottom, so as
to scuttle a large hole there; then dropping his sword, had
thrust his long arm far inwards and upwards, and so hauled
out our poor Tash by the head. He averred, that upon first

thrusting in for him, a leg was presented; but well knowing that that was not as it ought to be, and might occasion great trouble;—he had thrust back the leg, and by a dexterous heave and toss, had wrought a somerset upon the Indian; so that with the next trial, he came forth in the good old way—head foremost. As for the great head itself, that was doing as well as could be expected.

And thus, through the courage and great skill in obstetrics of Queequeg, the deliverance, or rather, delivery of Tashtego, was successfully accomplished, in the teeth, too, of the most untoward and apparently hopeless impediments; which is a lesson by no means to be forgotten. Midwifery should be taught in the same course with fencing and boxing, riding and rowing.

I know that this queer adventure of the Gay-Header's will be sure to seem incredible to some landsmen, though they themselves may have either seen or heard of some one's falling into a cistern ashore; an accident which not seldom happens, and with much less reason too than the Indian's, considering the exceeding slipperiness of the curb of the Sperm Whale's well.

But, peradventure, it may be sagaciously urged, how is this? We thought the tissued, infiltrated head of the Sperm Whale, was the lightest and most corky part about him; and yet thou makest it sink in an element of a far greater specific gravity than itself. We have thee there. Not at all, but I have ye; for at the time poor Tash fell in, the case had been nearly emptied of its lighter contents, leaving little but the dense tendinous wall of the well—a double welded, hammered substance, as I have before said, much heavier than the sea water; and a lump of which sinks in it like lead almost. But the tendency to rapid sinking in this substance was in the present instance materially counteracted by the other parts of the head remaining undetached from it, so that it sank very slowly and deliberately indeed, affording Queequeg a fair chance for performing his agile obstetrics on the run, as you may say. Yes, it was a running delivery, so it was.

Now, had Tashtego perished in that head, it had been a very precious perishing; smothered in the very whitest and daintiest of fragrant spermaceti; coffined, hearsed, and tombed in the secret inner chamber and sanctum sanctorum of the whale. Only one sweeter end can readily be recalled —the delicious death of an Ohio honey-hunter, who seeking

honey in the crotch of a hollow tree, found such exceeding
store of it, that leaning too far over, it sucked him in, so
that he died embalmed. How many, think ye, have likewise
fallen into Plato's honey head, and sweetly perished there?

THE PRAIRE   LXXIX

TO scan the lines of his face, or feel the bumps on the
head of this Leviathan; this is a thing which no Physiog-
nomist or Phrenologist has as yet undertaken. Such an enterprise would seem almost as hopeful as for Lavater to have
scrutinized the wrinkles on the Rock of Gibraltar, or for
Gall to have mounted a ladder and manipulated the Dome
of the Pantheon. Still, in that famous work of his, Lavater
not only treats of the various faces of men, but also attentively studies the faces of horses, birds, serpents, and fish;
and dwells in detail upon the modifications of expression
discernible therein. Nor have Gall and his disciple Spurzheim
failed to throw out some hints touching the phrenological
characteristics of other beings than man. Therefore, though
I am but ill qualified for a pioneer, in the application of
these two semi-sciences to the whale, I will do my endeavor.
I try all things; I achieve what I can.

Physiognomically regarded, the Sperm Whale is an anomalous creature. He has no proper nose. And since the nose is
the central and most conspicuous of the features; and since
it perhaps most modifies and finally controls their combined
expression; hence it would seem that its entire absence, as
an external appendage, must very largely affect the countenance of the whale. For as in landscape gardening, a spire,
cupola, monument, or tower of some sort is deemed almost
indispensable to the completion of the scene; so no face
can be physiognomically in keeping without the elevated
open-work belfry of the nose. Dash the nose from Phidias's
marble Jove, and what a sorry remainder! Nevertheless,
Leviathan is of so mighty a magnitude, all his proportions
are so stately, that the same deficiency which in the sculptured
Jove were hideous, in him is no blemish at all. Nay, it is
an added grandeur. A nose to the whale would have been
impertinent. As on your physiognomical voyage you sail
round his vast head in your jolly-boat, your noble concep-

tions of him are never insulted by the reflection that he has a nose to be pulled. A pestilent conceit, which so often will insist upon obtruding even when beholding the mightiest royal beadle on his throne.

In some particular, perhaps the most imposing physiognomical view to be had of the Sperm Whale, is that of the full front of his head. This aspect is sublime.

In thought, a fine human brow is like the East when troubled with the morning. In the repose of the pasture, the curled brow of the bull has a touch of the grand in it. Pushing heavy cannon up mountain defiles, the elephant's brow is majestic. Human or animal, the mystical brow is as that great golden seal affixed by the German emperors to their decrees. It signifies—"God: done this day by my hand." But in most creatures, nay in man himself, very often the brow is but a mere strip of alpine land lying along the snow line. Few are the foreheads which like Shakespeare's or Melancthon's rise so high, and descend so low, that the eyes themselves seem clear, eternal, tideless mountain lakes; and all above them in the forehead's wrinkles, you seem to track the antlered thoughts descending there to drink, as the Highland hunters track the snow prints of the deer. But in that great Sperm Whale, this high and mighty god-like dignity inherent in the brow is so immensely amplified, that gazing on it, in that full front view, you feel the Deity and the dread powers more forcibly than in beholding any other object in living nature. For you see no one point precisely; not one distinct feature is revealed; no nose, eyes, ears, or mouth; no face; he has none, proper; nothing but that one broad firmament of a forehead, pleated with riddles; dumbly lowering with the doom of boats, and ships, and men. Nor, in profile, does this wondrous brow diminish; though that way viewed, its grandeur does not domineer upon you so. In profile, you plainly perceive that horizontal, semi-crescentic depression in the forehead's middle, which, in man, is Lavater's mark of genius.

But how? Genius in the Sperm Whale? Has the Sperm Whale ever written a book, spoken a speech? No, his great genius is declared in his doing nothing particular to prove it. It is moreover declared in his pyramidical silence. And this reminds me that had the great Sperm Whale been known to the young Orient World, he would have been deified by their child-magian thoughts. They deified the crocodile of the Nile, because the crocodile is tongueless; and the Sperm

Whale has no tongue, or at least it is so exceedingly small, as to be incapable of protrusion. If hereafter any highly cultured, poetical nation shall lure back to their birth-right, the merry May-day gods of old; and livingly enthrone them again in the now egotistical sky; in the now unhaunted hill; then be sure, exalted to Jove's high seat, the great Sperm Whale shall lord it.

Champollion deciphered the wrinkled granite hieroglyphics. But there is no Champollion to decipher the Egypt of every man's and every being's face. Physiognomy, like every other human science, is but a passing fable. If then, Sir William Jones, who read in thirty languages, could not read the simplest peasant's face in its profounder and more subtle meanings, how may unlettered Ishmael hope to read the awful Chaldee of the Sperm Whale's brow? I but put that brow before you. Read it if you can.

THE NUT   LXXX

IF the Sperm Whale be physiognomically a Sphinx, to the phrenologist his brain seems that geometrical circle which it is impossible to square.

In the full-grown creature the skull will measure at least twenty feet in length. Unhinge the lower jaw, and the side view of this skull is as the side view of a moderately inclined plane resting throughout on a level base. But in life —as we have elsewhere seen—this inclined plane is angularly filled up, and almost squared by the enormous superincumbent mass of the junk and sperm. At the high end the skull forms a crater to bed that part of the mass; while under the long floor of this crater—in another cavity seldom exceeding ten inches in length and as many in depth—reposes the mere handful of this monster's brain. The brain is at least twenty feet from his apparent forehead in life; it is hidden away behind its vast outworks, like the innermost citadel within the amplified fortifications of Quebec. So like a choice casket is it secreted in him, that I have known some whalemen who peremptorily deny that the Sperm Whale has any other brain than that palpable semblance of one formed by the cubic-yards of his sperm magazine. Lying in strange folds, courses, and convolutions, to their apprehensions, it

seems more in keeping with the idea of his general might
to regard that mystic part of him as the seat of his intelligence.

It is plain, then, that phrenologically the head of this
Leviathan, in the creature's living intact state, is an entire
delusion. As for his true brain, you can then see no indications of it, nor feel any. The whale, like all things that
are mighty, wears a false brow to the common world.

If you unload his skull of its spermy heaps and then
take a rear view of its rear end, which is the high end, you
will be struck by its resemblance to the human skull, beheld
in the same situation, and from the same point of view.
Indeed, place this reversed skull (scaled down to the human
magnitude) among a plate of men's skulls, and you would
involuntarily confound it with them; and remarking the depressions on one part of its summit, in phrenological phrase
you would say—This man had no self-esteem, and no veneration. And by those negations, considered along with the
affirmative fact of his prodigious bulk and power, you can
best form to yourself the truest, though not the most exhilarating conception of what the most exalted potency is.

But if from the comparative dimensions of the whale's
proper brain, you deem it incapable of being adequately
charted, then I have another idea for you. If you attentively
regard almost any quadruped's spine, you will be struck with
the resemblance of its vertebrae to a strung necklace of
dwarfed skulls, all bearing rudimental resemblance to the
skull proper. It is a German conceit, that the vertebrae are
absolutely undeveloped skulls. But the curious external resemblance, I take it the Germans were not the first men to
perceive. A foreign friend once pointed it out to me, in the
skeleton of a foe he had slain, and with the vertebrae of
which he was inlaying, in a sort of basso-relievo, the beaked
prow of his canoe. Now, I consider that the phrenologists
have omitted an important thing in not pushing their investigations from the cerebellum through the spinal canal. For
I believe that much of a man's character will be found betokened in his backbone. I would rather feel your spine than
your skull, whoever you are. A thin joist of a spine never
yet upheld a full and noble soul. I rejoice in my spine, as
in the firm audacious staff of that flag which I fling half
out to the world.

Apply this spinal branch of phrenology to the Sperm

Whale. His cranial cavity is continuous with the first neck-vertebra; and in that vertebra the bottom of the spinal canal will measure ten inches across, being eight in height, and of a triangular figure with the base downwards. As it passes through the remaining vertebrae the canal tapers in size, but for a considerable distance remains of large capacity. Now, of course, this canal is filled with much the same strangely fibrous substance—the spinal cord—as the brain; and directly communicates with the brain. And what is still more, for many feet after emerging from the brain's cavity, the spinal cord remains of an undecreasing girth, almost equal to that of the brain. Under all these circumstances, would it be unreasonable to survey and map out the whale's spine phrenologically? For, viewed in this light, the wonderful comparative smallness of his brain proper is more than compensated by the wonderful comparative magnitude of his spinal cord.

But leaving this hint to operate as it may with the phrenologists, I would merely assume the spinal theory for a moment, in reference to the Sperm Whale's hump. This august hump, if I mistake not, rises over one of the larger vertebrae, and is, therefore, in some sort, the outer convex mould of it. From its relative situation then, I should call this high hump the organ of firmness or indomitableness in the Sperm Whale. And that the great monster is indomitable, you will yet have reason to know.

THE PEQUOD MEETS THE VIRGIN   LXXXI

THE predestined day arrived, and we duly met the ship Jungfrau, Derick De Deer, master, of Bremen.

At one time the greatest whaling people in the world, the Dutch and Germans are now among the least; but here and there at very wide intervals of latitude and longitude, you still occasionally meet with their flag in the Pacific.

For some reason, the Jungfrau seemed quite eager to pay her respects. While yet some distance from the Pequod, she rounded to, and dropping a boat, her captain was impelled towards us, impatiently standing in the bows instead of the stern.

"What has he in his hand there?" cried Starbuck, pointing to something wavingly held by the German. "Impossible! —a lamp-feeder!"

"Not that," said Stubb, "no, no, it's a coffee-pot, Mr. Starbuck; he's coming off to make us our coffee, is the Yarman; don't you see that big tin can there alongside of him?—that's his boiling water. Oh! he's all right, is the Yarman."

"Go along with you," cried Flask, "it's a lamp-feeder and an oil-can. He's out of oil, and has come a-begging."

However curious it may seem for an oil-ship to be borrowing oil on the whale-ground, and however much it may invertedly contradict the old proverb about carrying coals to Newcastle, yet sometimes such a thing really happens; and in the present case Captain Derick De Deer did indubitably conduct a lamp-feeder as Flask did declare.

As he mounted the deck Ahab abruptly accosted him, without at all heeding what he had in his hand; but in his broken lingo, the German soon evinced his complete ignorance of the White Whale; immediately turning the conversation to his lamp-feeder and oil can, with some remarks touching his having to turn into his hammock at night in profound darkness—his last drop of Bremen oil being gone, and not a single flying-fish yet captured to supply the deficiency; concluding by hinting that his ship was indeed what in the Fishery is technically called a *clean* one (that is, an empty one), well deserving the name of Jungfrau or the Virgin.

His necessities supplied, Derick departed; but he had not gained his ship's side, when whales were almost simultaneously raised from the mast-heads of both vessels; and so eager for the chase was Derick, that without pausing to put his oil-can and lamp-feeder aboard, he slewed round his boat and made after the leviathan lamp-feeders.

Now, the game having risen to leeward, he and the other three German boats that soon followed him, had considerably the start of the Pequod's heels. There were eight whales, an average pod. Aware of their danger, they were going all abreast with great speed straight before the wind, rubbing their flanks as closely as so many spans of horses in harness. They left a great, wide wake, as though continually unrolling a great wide parchment upon the sea.

Full in this rapid wake, and many fathoms in the rear, swam a huge, humped old bull, which by his comparatively slow progress, as well as by the unusual yellowish incrustations overgrowing him, seemed afflicted with the jaundice, or some other infirmity. Whether this whale belonged to the pod in advance, seemed questionable; for it is not customary for such venerable leviathans to be at all social. Nevertheless, he stuck to their wake, though indeed their back water must have retarded him, because the white-bone or swell at his broad muzzle was a dashed one, like the swell formed when two hostile currents meet. His spout was short, slow, and laborious; coming forth with a choking sort of gush, and spending itself in torn shreds, followed by strange subterranean commotions in him, which seemed to have egress at his other buried extremity, causing the waters behind him to upbubble.

"Who's got some paregoric?" said Stubb, "he has the stomach-ache, I'm afraid. Lord, think of having half an acre of stomach-ache! Adverse winds are holding mad Christmas in him, boys. It's the first foul wind I ever knew to blow from astern; but look, did ever whale yaw so before? it must be, he's lost his tiller."

As an overladen Indiaman bearing down the Hindostan coast with a deck load of frightened horses, careens, buries, rolls, and wallows on her way; so did this old whale heave his aged bulk, and now and then partly turning over on his cumbrous rib-ends, expose the cause of his devious wake in the unnatural stump of his starboard fin. Whether he had lost that fin in battle, or had been born without it, it were hard to say.

"Only wait a bit, old chap, and I'll give ye a sling for that wounded arm," cried cruel Flask, pointing to the whale-line near him.

"Mind he don't sling thee with it," cried Starbuck. "Give way, or the German will have him."

With one intent all the combined rival boats were pointed for this one fish, because not only was he the largest, and therefore the most valuable whale, but he was nearest to them, and the other whales were going with such great velocity, moreover, as almost to defy pursuit for the time. At this juncture, the Pequod's keels had shot by the three German boats last lowered; but from the great start he had had, Derick's boat still led the chase, though every moment neared by his foreign rivals. The only thing they feared, was, that from being already so nigh to his mark, he would be enabled to dart his iron before they could completely overtake and pass him. As for Derick, he seemed quite confident that this would be the case, and occasionally with a deriding gesture shook his lamp-feeder at the other boats.

"The ungracious and ungrateful dog!" cried Starbuck; "he mocks and dares me with the very poor-box I filled for him not five minutes ago!"—then in his old intense whisper— "give way, greyhounds! Dog to it!"

"I tell ye what it is, men"—cried Stubb to his crew—"It's against my religion to get mad; but I'd like to eat that villanous Yarman—Pull—won't ye? Are ye going to let that rascal beat ye? Do ye love brandy? A hogshead of brandy, then, to the best man. Come, why don't some of ye burst a blood-vessel? Who's that been dropping an anchor overboard —we don't budge an inch—we're becalmed. Halloo, here's grass growing in the boat's bottom—and by the Lord, the mast there's budding. This won't do, boys. Look at that Yarman! The short and long of it is, men, will ye spit fire or not?"

"Oh! see the suds he makes!" cried Flask, dancing up and down—"What a hump—Oh, *do* pile on the beef—lays like a log! Oh! my lads, *do* spring—slap-jacks and quohogs for supper, you know, my lads—baked clams and muffins—oh, *do, do,* spring—he's a hundred barreler—don't lose him now —don't, oh, *don't!*—see that Yarman—Oh! won't ye pull for your duff, my lads—such a sog! such a sogger! Don't ye love sperm? There goes three thousand dollars, men!—a bank!—a whole bank! The bank of England!—Oh, *do, do, do!*—What's that Yarman about now?"

At this moment Derick was in the act of pitching his lamp-feeder at the advancing boats, and also his oil-can; perhaps with the double view of retarding his rivals' way, and at the same time economically accelerating his own by the momentary impetus of the backward toss.

"The unmannerly Dutch dogger!" cried Stubb. "Pull now, men, like fifty thousand line-of-battle-ship loads of red-haired devils. What d'ye say, Tashtego; are you the man to snap your spine in two-and-twenty pieces for the honor of old Gay-head? What d'ye say?"

"I say, pull like god-dam,"—cried the Indian.

Fiercely, but evenly incited by the taunts of the German, the Pequod's three boats now began ranging almost abreast; and, so disposed, momentarily neared him. In that fine, loose, chivalrous attitude of the headsman when drawing near to his prey, the three mates stood up proudly, occasionally backing the after oarsman with an exhilarating cry of, "There she slides, now! Hurrah for the white-ash breeze! Down with the Yarman! Sail over him!"

But so decided an original start had Derick had, that spite of all their gallantry, he would have proved the victor in this race, had not a righteous judgment descended upon him in a crab which caught the blade of his midship oarsman. While this clumsy lubber was striving to free his white-ash, and while, in consequence, Derick's boat was nigh to capsizing, and he thundering away at his men in a mighty rage; —that was a good time for Starbuck, Stubb, and Flask. With a shout, they took a mortal start forwards, and slantingly ranged up on the German's quarter. An instant more, and all four boats were diagonally in the whale's immediate wake, while stretching from them, on both sides, was the foaming swell that he made.

It was a terrific, most pitiable, and maddening sight. The whale was now going head out, and sending his spout before him in a continual tormented jet; while his one poor fin beat his side in an agony of fright. Now to this hand, now to that, he yawed in his faltering flight, and still at every billow that he broke, he spasmodically sank in the sea, or sideways rolled towards the sky his one beating fin. So have I seen a bird with clipped wing, making affrighted broken circles in the air, vainly striving to escape the piratical hawks. But the bird has a voice, and with plaintive cries will make known her fear; but the fear of this vast dumb brute of the sea, was chained up and enchanted in him; he had no voice, save that choking respiration through his spiracle, and this made the sight of him unspeakably pitiable; while still, in his amazing bulk, portcullis jaw, and omnipotent tail, there was enough to appal the stoutest man who so pitied.

Seeing now that but a very few moments more would give the Pequod's boats the advantage, and rather than be thus foiled of his game, Derick chose to hazard what to him must have seemed a most usually long dart, ere the last chance would for ever escape.

But no sooner did this harpooneer stand up for the stroke, than all three tigers—Queequeg, Tashtego, Daggoo—instinctively sprang to their feet, and standing in a diagonal row, simultaneously pointed their barbs; and darted over the head of the German harpooneer, their three Nantucket irons entered the whale. Blinding vapors of foam and white-fire! The three boats, in the first fury of the whale's headlong rush, bumped the German's aside with such force, that both

Derick and his baffled harpooneer were spilled out, and sailed over by the three flying keels.

"Don't be afraid, my butter-boxes," cried Stubb, casting a passing glance upon them as he shot by; "ye'll be picked up presently—all right—I saw some sharks astern—St. Bernard's dogs, you know—relieve distressed travellers. Hurrah! this is the way to sail now. Every keel a sun-beam! Hurrah! —Here we go like three tin kettles at the tail of a mad cougar! This puts me in mind of fastening to an elephant in a tilbury on a plain—makes the wheel-spokes fly, boys, when you fasten to him that way; and there's danger of being pitched out too, when you strike a hill. Hurrah! this is the way a fellow feels when he's going to Davy Jones—all a rush down an endless inclined plane! Hurrah! this whale carries the everlasting mail!"

But the monster's run was a brief one. Giving a sudden gasp, he tumultuously sounded. With a grating rush, the three lines flew round the loggerheads with such a force as to gouge deep grooves in them; while so fearful were the harpooneers that this rapid sounding would soon exhaust the lines, that using all their dexterous might, they caught repeated smoking turns with the rope to hold on; till at last— owing to the perpendicular strain from the lead-lined chocks of the boats, whence the three ropes went straight down into the blue—the gunwales of the bows were almost even with the water, while the three sterns tilted high in the air. And the whale soon ceasing to sound, for some time they remained in that attitude, fearful of expending more line, though the position was a little ticklish. But though boats have been taken down and lost in this way, yet it is this "holding on," as it is called; this hooking up by the sharp barbs of his live flesh from the back; this it is that often torments the Leviathan into soon rising again to meet the sharp lance of his foes. Yet not to speak of the peril of the thing, it is to be doubted whether this course is always the best; for it is but reasonable to presume, that the longer the stricken whale stays under water, the more he is exhausted. Because, owing to the enormous surface of him—in a full grown sperm whale something less than 2000 square feet— the pressure of the water is immense. We all know what an astonishing atmospheric weight we ourselves stand up under; even here, above-ground, in the air; how vast, then, the burden of a whale, bearing on his back a column of two hundred fathoms of ocean! It must at least equal the weight of fifty atmospheres. One whaleman has estimated it at the weight of twenty line-of-battle ships, with all their guns, and stores, and men on board.

As the three boats lay there on that gently rolling sea, gazing down into its eternal blue noon; and as not a single groan or cry of any sort, nay, not so much as a ripple or a bubble came up from its depths; what landsman would have thought, that beneath all that silence and placidity, the utmost monster of the seas was writhing and wrenching in agony! Not eight inches of perpendicular rope were visible at the bows. Seems it credible that by three such thin threads the great Leviathan was suspended like the big weight to an eight day clock. Suspended? and to what? To three bits of board. Is this the creature of whom it was once so triumphantly said—"Canst thou fill his skin with barbed irons? or his head with fish-spears? The sword of him that layeth at him cannot hold, the spear, the dart, nor the habergeon; he esteemeth iron as straw; the arrow cannot make him flee; darts are counted as stubble; he laughed at the shaking of a spear!" This the creature? this he? Oh! that unfulfilments should follow the prophets. For with the strength of a thousand thighs in his tail, Leviathan had run his head under the mountains of the sea, to hide him from the Pequod's fishspears!

In that sloping afternoon sunlight, the shadows that the three boats sent down beneath the surface, must have been long enough and broad enough to shade half Xerxes' army. Who can tell how appalling to the wounded whale must have been such huge phantoms flitting over his head!

"Stand by, men; he stirs," cried Starbuck, as the three lines suddenly vibrated in the water, distinctly conducting upwards to them, as by magnetic wires, the life and death throbs of the whale, so that every oarsman felt them in his seat. The next moment, relieved in great part from the downward strain at the bows, the boats gave a sudden bounce upwards, as a small icefield will, when a dense herd of white bears are scared from it into the sea.

"Haul in! Haul in!" cried Starbuck again; "he's rising."

The lines, of which, hardly an instant before, not one hand's breadth could have been gained, were now in long quick coils flung back all dripping into the boats, and soon the whale broke water within two ship's lengths of the hunters.

His motions plainly denoted his extreme exhaustion. In

most land animals there are certain valves or flood-gates in many of their veins, whereby when wounded, the blood is in some degree at least instantly shut off in certain directions. Not so with the whale; one of whose peculiarities it is, to have an entire non-valvular structure of the blood-vessels, so that when pierced even by so small a point as a harpoon, a deadly drain is at once begun upon his whole arterial system; and when this is heightened by the extraordinary pressure of water at a great distance below the surface, his life may be said to pour from him in incessant streams. Yet so vast is the quantity of blood in him, and so distant and numerous its interior fountains, that he will keep thus bleeding and bleeding for a considerable period; even as in drought a river will flow, whose source is in the well-springs of far-off and undiscernible hills. Even now, when the boats pulled upon this whale, and perilously drew over his swaying flukes, and the lances were darted into him, they were followed by steady jets from the new made wound, which kept continually playing, while the natural spout-hole in his head was only at intervals, however rapid, sending its affrighted moisture into the air. From this last vent no blood yet came, because no vital part of him had thus far been struck. His life, as they significantly call it, was untouched.

As the boats now more closely surrounded him, the whole upper part of his form, with much of it that is ordinarily submerged, was plainly revealed. His eyes, or rather the places where his eyes had been, were beheld. As strange misgrown masses gather in the knotholes of the noblest oaks when prostrate, so from the points which the whale's eyes had once occupied, now protruded blind bulbs, horribly pitiable to see. But pity there was none. For all his old age, and his one arm, and his blind eyes, he must die the death and be murdered, in order to light the gay bridals and other merry-makings of men, and also to illuminate the solemn churches that preach unconditional inoffensiveness by all to all. Still rolling in his blood, at last he partially disclosed a strangely discolored bunch or protuberance, the size of a bushel, low down on the flank.

"A nice spot," cried Flask; "just let me prick him there once."

"Avast!" cried Starbuck, "there's no need of that!"

But humane Starbuck was too late. At the instant of the dart an ulcerous jet shot from this cruel wound, and goaded by it into more than sufferable anguish, the whale now spouting thick blood, with swift fury blindly darted at the craft, bespattering them and their glorying crews all over with showers of gore, capsizing Flask's boat and marring the bows. It was his death stroke. For, by this time, so spent was he by loss of blood, that he helplessly rolled away from the wreck he had made; lay panting on his side, impotently flapped with his stumped fin, then over and over slowly revolved like a waning world; turned up the white secrets of his belly; lay like a log, and died. It was most piteous, that last expiring spout. As when by unseen hands the water is gradually drawn off from some mighty fountain, and with half-stifled melancholy gurglings the spray-column lowers and lowers to the ground——so the last long dying spout of the whale.

Soon, while the crews were awaiting the arrival of the ship, the body showed symptoms of sinking with all its treasures unrifled. Immediately, by Starbuck's orders, lines were secured to it at different points, so that ere long every boat was a buoy; the sunken whale being suspended a few inches beneath them by the cords. By very heedful management, when the ship drew nigh, the whale was transferred to her side, and was strongly secured there by the stiffest fluke-chains, for it was plain that unless artificially upheld, the body would at once sink to the bottom.

It so chanced that almost upon first cutting into him with the spade, the entire length of a corroded harpoon was found imbedded in his flesh, on the lower part of the bunch before described. But as the stumps of harpoons are frequently found in the dead bodies of captured whales, with the flesh perfectly healed around them, and no prominence of any kind to denote their place; therefore there must needs have been some other unknown reason in the present case fully to account for the ulceration alluded to. But still more curious was the fact of a lance-head of stone being found in him, not far from the buried iron, the flesh perfectly firm about it. Who had darted that stone lance? And when? It might have been darted by some Nor' West Indian long before America was discovered.

What other marvels might have been rummaged out of this monstrous cabinet there is no telling. But a sudden stop was put to further discoveries, by the ship's being unprecedentedly dragged over sideways to the sea, owing to the body's immensely increasing tendency to sink. However, Starbuck, who had the ordering of affairs, hung on to it to the last; hung onto it so resolutely, indeed, that when at length the ship would have been capsized, if still persisting in locking arms with the body; then, when the command was given to break clear from it, such was the immovable strain upon the timber-heads to which the fluke-chains and cables were fastened, that it was impossible to cast them off. Meantime everything in the Pequod was aslant. To cross to the other side of the deck was like walking up the steep gabled roof of a house. The ship groaned and gasped. Many of the ivory inlayings of her bulwarks and cabins were started from their places, by the unnatural dislocation. In vain handspikes and crows were brought to bear upon the immovable fluke-chains, to pry them adrift from the timber-heads; and so low had the whale now settled that the submerged ends could not be at all approached, while every moment whole tons of ponderosity seemed added to the sinking bulk, and the ship seemed on the point of going over.

"Hold on, hold on, won't ye?" cried Stubb to the body, "don't be in such a devil of a hurry to sink! By thunder, men, we must do something or go for it. No use prying there; avast, I say with your handspikes, and run one of ye for a prayer book and a pen-knife, and cut the big chains."

"Knife? Aye, aye," cried Queequeg, and seizing the carpenter's heavy hatchet, he leaned out of a porthole, and steel to iron, began slashing at the largest fluke-chains. But a few strokes, full of sparks, were given, when the exceeding strain effected the rest. With a terrific snap, every fastening went adrift; the ship righted, the carcase sank.

Now, this occasional inevitable sinking of the recently killed Sperm Whale is a very curious thing; nor has any fisherman yet adequately accounted for it. Usually the dead Sperm Whale floats with great buoyancy, with its side or belly considerably elevated above the surface. If the only whales that thus sank were old, meagre, and broken-hearted creatures, their pads of lard diminished and all their bones heavy and rheumatic; then you might with some reason assert that this sinking is caused by an uncommon specific gravity in the fish so sinking, consequent upon this absence of buoyant matter in him. But it is not so. For young whales, in the highest health, and swelling with noble aspirations, prematurely cut off in the warm flush and May of life, with all their panting lard about them; even these brawny, buoyant heroes do sometimes sink.

Be it said, however, that the Sperm Whale is far less liable to this accident than any other species. Where one of that sort go down, twenty Right Whales do. This difference in the species is no doubt imputable in no small degree to the greater quantity of bone in the Right Whale; his Venetian blinds alone sometimes weighing more than a ton; from this incumbrance the Sperm Whale is wholly free. But there are instances where, after the lapse of many hours or several days, the sunken whale again rises, more buoyant than in life. But the reason of this is obvious. Gasses are generated in him; he swells to a prodigious magnitude; becomes a sort of animal balloon. A line-of-battle ship could hardly keep him under then. In the Shore Whaling, on soundings, among the Bays of New Zealand, when a Right Whale gives token of sinking, they fasten buoys to him, with plenty of rope; so that when the body has gone down, they know where to look for it when it shall have ascended again.

It was not long after the sinking of the body that a cry was heard from the Pequod's mast-heads, announcing that the Jungfrau was again lowering her boats; though the only spout in sight was that of a Fin-Back, belonging to the species of uncapturable whales, because of its incredible power of swimming. Nevertheless, the Fin-Back's spout is so similar to the Sperm Whale's, that by unskilful fishermen it is often mistaken for it. And consequently Derick and all his host were now in valiant chase of this unnearable brute. The Virgin crowding all sail, made after her four young keels, and thus they all disappeared far to leeward, still in bold, hopeful chase.

Oh! many are the Fin-Backs, and many are the Dericks, my friend.

THE HONOR AND GLORY OF WHALING

LXXXII

THERE are some enterprises in which a careful disorderliness is the true method.

The more I dive into this matter of whaling, and push my researches up to the very spring-head of it, so much the more am I impressed with its great honorableness and antiquity; and especially when I find so many great demi-gods and heroes, prophets of all sorts, who one way or other have shed distinction upon it, I am transported with the reflection that I myself belong, though but subordinately, to so emblazoned a fraternity.

The gallant Perseus, a son of Jupiter, was the first whaleman; and to the eternal honor of our calling be it said, that the first whale attacked by our brotherhood was not killed with any sordid intent. Those were the knightly days of our profession, when we only bore arms to succor the distressed, and not to fill men's lamp-feeders. Every one knows the fine story of Perseus and Andromeda; how the lovely Andromeda, the daughter of a king, was tied to a rock on the seacoast, and as Leviathan was in the very act of carrying her off, Perseus, the prince of whalemen, intrepidly advancing, harpooned the monster, and delivered and married the maid. It was an admirable artistic exploit, rarely achieved by the best harpooneers of the present day; inasmuch as this Leviathan was slain at the very first dart. And let no man doubt this Arkite story; for in the ancient Joppa, now Jaffa, on the Syrian coast, in one of the Pagan temples, there stood for many ages the vast skeleton of a whale, which the city's legends and all the inhabitants asserted to be the identical bones of the monster that Perseus slew. When the Romans took Joppa, the same skeleton was carried to Italy in triumph. What seems most singular and suggestively important in this story, is this: it was from Joppa that Jonah set sail.

Akin to the adventure of Perseus and Andromeda—indeed, by some supposed to be indirectly derived from it—is that famous story of St. George and the Dragon; which dragon I maintain to have been a whale; for in many old chronicles whales and dragons are strangely jumbled together, and often stand for each other. "Thou art as a lion of the waters, and as a dragon of the sea," said Ezekiel; hereby, plainly meaning a whale; in truth, some versions of the Bible use that word itself. Besides, it would much abstract from the glory of the exploit had St. George but encountered a crawling reptile of the land, instead of doing battle with the great monster of the deep. Any man may kill a snake, but only a Perseus, a St. George, a Coffin, have the heart in them to march boldly up to a whale.

Let not the modern paintings of this scene mislead us; for though the creature encountered by that valiant whaleman of old is vaguely represented of a griffin-like shape, and though the battle is depicted on land and the saint on horseback, yet considering the great ignorance of those times, when the true form of the whale was unknown to artists; and considering that as in Perseus' case, St. George's whale might have crawled up out of the sea on the beach; and considering that the animal ridden by St. George might have been only a large seal, or sea-horse; bearing all this in mind, it will not appear altogether incompatible with the sacred legend and the ancientest draughts of the scene, to hold this so-called dragon no other than the great Leviathan himself. In fact, placed before the strict and piercing truth, this whole story will fare like that fish, flesh, and fowl idol of the Philistines, Dagon by name; who being planted before the ark of Israel, his horse's head and both the palms of his hands fell off from him, and only the stump or fishy part of him remained. Thus, then, one of our own noble stamp, even a whaleman, is the tutelary guardian of England; and by good rights, we harpooneers of Nantucket should be enrolled in the most noble order of St. George. And therefore, let not the knights of that honorable company (none of whom, I venture to say, have ever had to do with a whale like their great patron), let them never eye a Nantucketer with disdain, since even in our woollen frocks and tarred trowsers we are much better entitled to St. George's decoration than they.

Whether to admit Hercules among us or not, concerning this I long remained dubious: for though according to the Greek mythologies, that antique Crockett and Kit Carson—that brawny doer of rejoicing good deeds, was swallowed down and thrown up by a whale; still, whether that strictly makes a whaleman of him, that might be mooted. It nowhere appears that he ever actually harpooned his fish, unless, indeed, from the inside. Nevertheless, he may be deemed a sort of involuntary whaleman; at any rate the whale caught him, if he did not the whale. I claim him for one of our clan.

But, by the best contradictory authorities, this Grecian story of Hercules and the whale is considered to be derived from the still more ancient Hebrew story of Jonah and the whale; and vice versâ; certainly they are very similar. If I claim the demi-god then, why not the prophet?

Nor do heroes, saints, demigods, and prophets alone comprise the whole roll of our order. Our grand master is still to be named; for like royal kings of old times, we find the headwaters of our fraternity in nothing short of the great gods themselves. That wondrous oriental story is now to be rehearsed from the Shaster, which gives us the dread Vishnoo, one of the three persons in the godhead of the Hindoos; gives us this divine Vishnoo himself for our Lord;—Vishnoo, who, by the first of his ten earthy incarnations, has for ever set apart and sanctified the whale. When Brahma, or the God of Gods, saith the Shaster, resolved to recreate the world after one of its periodical dissolutions, he gave birth to Vishnoo, to preside over the work; but the Vedas, or mystical books, whose perusal would seem to have been indispensable to Vishnoo before beginning the creation, and which therefore must have contained something in the shape of practical hints to young architects, these Vedas were lying at the bottom of the waters; so Vishnoo became incarnate in a whale, and sounding down in him to the uttermost depths, rescued the sacred volumes. Was not this Vishnoo a whaleman, then? even as a man who rides a horse is called a horseman?

Perseus, St. George, Hercules, Jonah, and Vishnoo! there's a member-roll for you! What club but the whaleman's can head off like that?

JONAH HISTORICALLY REGARDED   LXXXIII

REFERENCE was made to the historical study of Jonah and the whale in the preceding chapter. Now some Nantucketers rather distrust this historical story of Jonah and the whale. But then there were some sceptical Greeks and Romans, who, standing out from the orthodox pagans of their times, equally doubted the story of Hercules and the whale, and Arion and the dolphin; and yet their doubting those traditions did not make those traditions one whit the less facts, for all that.

One old Sag-Harbor whaleman's chief reason for questioning the Hebrew story was this:—He had one of those quaint old-fashioned Bibles, embellished with curious, unscientific plates; one of which represented Jonah's whale with two spouts in his head—a peculiarity only true with respect to a species of the Leviathan (the Right Whale, and the varieties of that order), concerning which the fishermen have this saying, "A penny roll would choke him;" his swallow is so very small. But, to this, Bishop Jebb's anticipative answer

is ready. It is not necessary, hints the Bishop, that we consider Jonah as tombed in the whale's belly, but as temporarily lodged in some part of his mouth. And this seems
reasonable enough in the good Bishop. For truly, the Right
Whale's mouth would accommodate a couple of whist-tables,
and comfortably seat all the players. Possibly, too, Jonah
might have ensconced himself in a hollow tooth; but, on
second thoughts, the Right Whale is toothless.

Another reason which Sag-Harbor (he went by that name)
urged for his want of faith in this matter of the prophet,
was something obscurely in reference to his incarcerated body
and the whale's gastric juices. But this objection likewise falls
to the ground, because a German exegetist supposes that
Jonah must have taken refuge in the floating body of a *dead*
whale—even as the French soldiers in the Russian campaign
turned their dead horses into tents, and crawled into them.
Besides, it has been divined by other continental commentators, that when Jonah was thrown overboard from the
Joppa ship, he straightway effected his escape to another
vessel near by, some vessel with a whale for a figure-head;
and, I would add, possibly called "The Whale," as some
craft are nowadays christened the "Shark," the "Gull," the
"Eagle." Nor have there been wanting learned exegetists who
have opined that the whale mentioned in the book of Jonah
merely meant a life-preserver—an inflated bag of wind—
which the endangered prophet swam to, and so was saved
from a watery doom. Poor Sag-Harbor, therefore, seems
worsted all round. But he had still another reason for his
want of faith. It was this, if I remember right: Jonah was
swallowed by the whale in the Mediterranean Sea, and after
three days he was vomited up somewhere within three days'
journey of Nineveh, a city on the Tigris, very much more
than three days' journey across from the nearest point of the
Mediterranean coast. How is that?

But was there no other way for the whale to land the
prophet within that short distance of Nineveh? Yes. He
might have carried him round by the way of the Cape of
Good Hope. But not to speak of the passage through the
whole length of the Mediterranean, and another passage up
the Persian Gulf and Red Sea, such a supposition would involve the complete circumnavigation of all Africa in three
days, not to speak of the Tigris waters, near the site of
Nineveh, being too shallow for any whale to swim in.
Besides, this idea of Jonah's weathering the Cape of Good

Hope at so early a day would wrest the honor of the discovery of that great headland from Bartholomew Diaz, its
reputed discoverer, and so make modern history a liar.

But all these foolish arguments of old Sag-Harbor only
evinced his foolish pride of reason—a thing still more repre-
hensible in him, seeing that he had but little learning except
what he had picked up from the sun and the sea. I say it
only shows his foolish, impious pride, and abominable,
devilish rebellion against the reverend clergy. For by a
Portuguese Catholic priest, this very idea of Jonah's going
to Nineveh viâ the Cape of Good Hope was advanced as a
signal magnification of the general miracle. And so it was.
Besides, to this day, the highly enlightened Turks devoutly
believe in the historical story of Jonah. And some three centuries ago, an English traveller in old Harris's Voyages,
speaks of a Turkish Mosque built in honor of Jonah, in
which mosque was a miraculous lamp that burnt without
any oil.

PITCHPOLING   **LXXXIV**

TO make them run easily and swiftly, the axles of carriages are anointed; and for much the same purpose, some
whalers perform an analogous operation upon their boat;
they grease the bottom. Nor is it to be doubted that as such
a procedure can do no harm, it may possibly be of no contemptible advantage; considering that oil and water are
hostile; that oil is a sliding thing, and that the object in
view is to make the boat slide bravely. Queequeg believed
strongly in anointing his boat, and one morning not long after
the German ship Jungfrau disappeared, took more than customary pains in that occupation; crawling under its bottom,
where it hung over the side, and rubbing in the unctuousness as though diligently seeking to insure a crop of hair
from the craft's bald keel. He seemed to be working in
obedience to some particular presentiment. Nor did it remain
unwarranted by the event.

Towards noon whales were raised; but so soon as the ship
sailed down to them, they turned and fled with swift precipitancy; a disordered flight, as of Cleopatra's barges from
Actium.

Nevertheless, the boats pursued, and Stubb's was foremost. By great exertion, Tashtego at last succeeded in planting one iron; but the stricken whale, without at all sounding, still continued his horizontal flight, with added fleetness. Such unintermitted strainings upon the planted iron must sooner or later inevitably extract it. It became imperative to lance the flying whale, or be content to lose him. But to haul the boat up to his flank was impossible, he swam so fast and furious. What then remained?

Of all the wondrous devices and dexterities, the sleights of hand and countless subtleties, to which the veteran whale-man is so often forced, none exceed that fine manœuvre with the lance called pitchpoling. Small sword, or broad sword, in all its exercises boasts nothing like it. It is only indispensable with an inveterate running whale; its grand fact and feature is the wonderful distance to which the long lance is accurately darted from a violently rocking, jerking boat, under extreme headway. Steel and wood included, the entire spear is some ten or twelve feet in length; the staff is much slighter than that of the harpoon, and also of a lighter material—pine. It is furnished with a small rope called a warp, of considerable length, by which it can be hauled back to the hand after darting.

But before going further, it is important to mention here, that though the harpoon may be pitchpoled in the same way with the lance, yet it is seldom done; and when done, is still less frequently successful, on account of the greater weight and inferior length of the harpoon as compared with the lance, which in effect become serious drawbacks. As a general thing, therefore, you must first get fast to a whale, before any pitchpoling comes into play.

Look now at Stubb; a man who from his humorous, delib-erate coolness and equanimity in the direst emergencies, was specially qualified to excel in pitchpoling. Look at him; he stands upright in the tossed bow of the flying boat; wrapt in fleecy foam, the towing whale is forty feet ahead. Handling the long lance lightly, glancing twice or thrice along its length to see if it be exactly straight, Stubb whistlingly gathers up the coil of the warp in one hand, so as to secure its free end in his grasp, leaving the rest unobstructed. Then holding the lance full before his waistband's middle, he levels it at the whale; when, covering him with it, he steadily depresses the butt-end in his hand, thereby elevating the point till the weapon stands fairly balanced upon his palm, fifteen feet in the air. He minds you somewhat of a juggler, balancing a long staff on his chin. Next moment with a rapid, nameless impulse, in a superb lofty arch the bright steel spans the foaming distance, and quivers in the life spot of the whale. Instead of sparkling water, he now spouts red blood.

"That drove the spigot out of him!" cries Stubb. " 'Tis July's immortal Fourth; all fountains must run wine to-day! Would now, it were old Orleans whiskey, or old Ohio, or unspeakable old Monongahela! Then, Tashtego, lad, I'd have ye hold a canakin to the jet, and we'd drink round it! Yea, verily, hearts alive, we'd brew choice punch in the spread of his spout-hole there, and from that live punch-bowl quaff the living stuff!"

Again and again to such gamesome talk, the dexterous dart is repeated, the spear returning to its master like a greyhound held in skilful leash. The agonized whale goes into his flurry; the tow-line is slackened, and the pitchpoler dropping astern, folds his hands, and mutely watches the monster die.

THE FOUNTAIN   LXXXV

THAT for six thousand years—and no one knows how many millions of ages before—the great whales should have been spouting all over the sea, and sprinkling and mistifying the gardens of the deep, as with so many sprinkling or mistifying pots; and that for some centuries back, thousands of hunters should have been close by the fountain of the whale, watching these sprinklings and spoutings—that all this should be, and yet, that down to this blessed minute (fifteen and a quarter minutes past one o'clock P.M. of this sixteenth day of December, A.D. 1851), it should still remain a problem, whether these spoutings are, after all, really water, or nothing but vapor—this is surely a noteworthy thing.

Let us, then, look at this matter, along with some interesting items contingent. Every one knows that by the peculiar cunning of their gills, the finny tribes in general breathe the air which at all times is combined with the element in which they swim; hence, a herring or a cod might live a century, and never once raise its head above the surface.

But owing to his marked internal structure which gives him regular lungs, like a human being's, the whale can only live by inhaling the disengaged air in the open atmosphere. Wherefore the necessity for his periodical visits to the upper world. But he cannot in any degree breathe through his mouth, for, in his ordinary attitude, the Sperm Whale's mouth is buried at least eight feet beneath the surface; and what is still more, his windpipe has no connexion with his mouth. No, he breathes through his spiracle alone; and this is on the top of his head.

If I say, that in any creature breathing is only a function indispensable to vitality, inasmuch as it withdraws from the air a certain element, which being subsequently brought into contact with the blood imparts to the blood its vivifying principle, I do not think I shall err; though I may possibly use some superfluous scientific words. Assume it, and it follows that if all the blood in a man could be ærated with one breath, he might then seal up his nostrils and not fetch another for a considerable time. That is to say, he would then live without breathing. Anomalous as it may seem, this is precisely the case with the whale, who systematically lives, by intervals, his full hour and more (when at the bottom) without drawing a single breath, or so much as in any way inhaling a particle of air; for, remember, he has no gills. How is this? Between his ribs and on each side of his spine he is supplied with a remarkable involved Cretan labyrinth of vermicelli-like vessels, which vessels, when he quits the surface, are completely distended with oxygenated blood. So that for an hour or more, a thousand fathoms in the sea, he carries a surplus stock of vitality in him, just as the camel crossing the waterless desert carries a surplus supply of drink for future use in its four supplementary stomachs. The anatomical fact of this labyrinth is indisputable; and that the supposition founded upon it is reasonable and true, seems the more cogent to me, when I consider the otherwise inexplicable obstinacy of that leviathan in *having his spoutings out,* as the fishermen phrase it. This is what I mean. If unmolested, upon rising to the surface, the Sperm Whale will continue there for a period of time exactly uniform with all his other unmolested risings. Say he stays eleven minutes, and jets seventy times, that is, respires seventy breaths; then whenever he rises again, he will be sure to have his seventy breaths over again, to a minute. Now, if after he fetches a few breaths you alarm him, so that he sounds, he will be always dodging up again to make good his regular allowance of air. And not till those seventy breaths are told, will he finally go down to stay out his full term below. Remark, however, that in different individuals these rates are different; but in any one they are alike. Now, why should the whale thus insist upon having his spoutings out, unless it be to replenish his reservoir of air, ere descending for good? How obvious is it too, that this necessity for the whale's rising exposes him to all the fatal hazards of the chase. For not by hook or by net could this vast leviathan be caught, when sailing a thousand fathoms beneath the sunlight. Not so much thy skill, then, O hunter, as the great necessities that strike the victory to thee!

In man, breathing is incessantly going on—one breath only serving for two or three pulsations; so that whatever other business he has to attend to, waking, or sleeping, breathe he must, or die he will. But the Sperm Whale only breathes about one seventh or Sunday of his time.

It has been said that the whale only breathes through his spout-hole; if it could truthfully be added that his spouts are mixed with water, then I opine we should be furnished with the reason why his sense of smell seems obliterated in him; for the only thing about him that at all answers to his nose is that identical spout-hole; and being so clogged with two elements, it could not be expected to have the power of smelling. But owing to the mystery of the spout—whether it be water or whether it be vapor—no absolute certainty can as yet be arrived at on this head. Sure it is, nevertheless, that the Sperm Whale has no proper olfactories. But what does he want of them? No roses, no violets, no Cologne-water in the sea.

Furthermore, as his windpipe solely opens into the tube of his spouting canal, and as that long canal—like the grand Erie Canal—is furnished with a sort of locks (that open and shut) for the downward retention of air or the upward exclusion of water, therefore the whale has no voice; unless you insult him by saying, that when he so strangely rumbles, he talks through his nose. But then again, what has the whale to say? Seldom have I known any profound being that had anything to say to this world, unless forced to stammer out something by way of getting a living. Oh! happy that the world is such an excellent listener!

Now, the spouting canal of the Sperm Whale, chiefly intended as it is for the conveyance of air, and for several feet laid along, horizontally, just beneath the upper surface of his head, and a little to one side; this curious canal is very much like a gas-pipe laid down in a city on one side of a street. But the question returns whether this gas-pipe is also a water-pipe; in other words, whether the spout of the Sperm Whale is the mere vapor of the exhaled breath, or whether that exhaled breath is mixed with water taken in at the mouth, and discharged through the spiracle. It is certain that the mouth indirectly communicates with the spouting canal; but it cannot be proved that this is for the purpose of discharging water through the spiracle. Because the greatest necessity for so doing would seem to be, when in feeding he accidentally takes in water. But the Sperm Whale's food is far beneath the surface, and there he cannot spout even if he would. Besides, if you regard him very closely, and time him with your watch, you will find that when unmolested, there is an undeviating rhyme between the periods of his jets and the ordinary periods of respiration.

But why pester one with all this reasoning on the subject? Speak out! You have seen him spout; then declare what the spout is; can you not tell water from air? My dear sir, in this world it is not so easy to settle these plain things. I have ever found your plain things the knottiest of all. And as for this whale spout, you might almost stand in it, and yet be undecided as to what it is precisely.

The central body of it is hidden in the snowy sparkling mist enveloping it; and how can you certainly tell whether any water falls from it, when, always, when you are close enough to a whale to get a close view of his spout, he is in a prodigious commotion, the water cascading all around him. And if at such times you should think that you really perceived drops of moisture in the spout, how do you know that they are not merely condensed from its vapor; or how do you know that they are not those identical drops superficially lodged in the spout-hole fissure, which is countersunk into the summit of the whale's head? For even when tranquilly swimming through the mid-day sea in a calm, with his elevated hump sun-dried as a dromedary's in the desert; even then, the whale always carries a small basin of water on his head, as under a blazing sun you will sometimes see a cavity in a rock filled up with rain.

Nor is it at all prudent for the hunter to be over curious touching the precise nature of the whale spout. It will not do for him to be peering into it, and putting his face in it.

You cannot go with your pitcher to this fountain and fill it, and bring it away. For even when coming into slight contact with the outer, vapory shreds of the jet, which will often happen, your skin will feverishly smart, from the acridness of the thing so touching it. And I know one, who coming into still closer contact with the spout, whether with some specific object in view, or otherwise, I cannot say, the skin peeled off from his cheek and arm. Wherefore, among whalemen, the spout is deemed poisonous; they try to evade it. Another thing; I have heard it said, and I do not much doubt it, that if the jet is fairly spouted into your eyes, it will blind you. The wisest thing the investigator can do then, it seems to me, is to let this deadly spout alone.

Still, we can hypothesize, even if we cannot prove and establish. My hypothesis is this: that the spout is nothing but mist. And besides other reasons, to this conclusion I am impelled, by considerations touching the great inherent dignity and sublimity of the Sperm Whale; I account him no common, shallow being, inasmuch as it is an undisputed fact that he is never found on soundings, or near shores; all other whales sometimes are. He is both ponderous and profound. And I am convinced that from the heads of all ponderous profound beings, such as Plato, Pyrrho, the Devil, Jupiter, Dante, and so on, there always goes up a certain semi-visible steam, while in the act of thinking deep thoughts. While composing a little treatise on Eternity, I had the curiosity to place a mirror before me; and ere long saw reflected there, a curious involved worming and undulation in the atmosphere over my head. The invariable moisture of my hair, while plunged in deep thought, after six cups of hot tea in my thin shingled attic, of an August noon; this seems an additional argument for the above supposition.

And how nobly it raises our conceit of the mighty, misty monster, to behold him solemnly sailing through a calm tropical sea; his vast, mild head overhung by a canopy of vapor, engendered by his incommunicable contemplations, and that vapor—as you will sometimes see it—glorified by a rainbow, as if Heaven itself had put its seal upon his thoughts. For, d'ye see, rainbows do not visit the clear air; they only irradiate vapor. And so, through all the thick mists of the dim doubts in my mind, divine intuitions now and then shoot, enkindling my fog with a heavenly ray. And for this I thank God; for all have doubts; many deny; but doubts or denials, few along with them, have intuitions. Doubts of all things earthly, and intuitions of some things heavenly; this combination makes neither believer nor infidel, but makes a man who regards them both with equal eye.

THE TAIL   LXXXVI

OTHER poets have warbled the praises of the soft eye of the antelope, and the lovely plumage of the bird that never alights; less celestial, I celebrate a tail.

Reckoning the largest sized Sperm Whale's tail to begin at that point of the trunk where it tapers to about the girth of a man, it comprises upon its upper surface alone, an area of at least fifty square feet. The compact round body of its root expands into two broad, firm, flat palms or flukes, gradually shoaling away to less than an inch in thickness. At the crotch or junction, these flukes slightly overlap, then sideways recede from each other like wings, leaving a wide vacancy between. In no living thing are the lines of beauty more exquisitely defined than in the crescentic borders of these flukes. At its utmost expansion in the full grown whale, the tail will considerably exceed twenty feet across.

The entire member seems a dense webbed bed of welded sinews; but cut into it, and you find that three distinct strata compose it:—upper, middle, and lower. The fibres in the upper and lower layers, are long and horizontal; those of the middle one, very short, and running crosswise between the outside layers. This triune structure, as much as anything else, imparts power to the tail. To the student of old Roman walls, the middle layer will furnish a curious parallel to the thin course of tiles always alternating with the stone in those wonderful relics of the antique, and which undoubtedly contribute so much to the great strength of the masonry.

But as if this vast local power in the tendinous tail were not enough, the whole bulk of the leviathan is knit over with a warp and woof of muscular fibres and filaments, which passing on either side the loins and running down into the flukes, insensibly blend with them, and largely contribute to their might; so that in the tail the confluent measureless force of the whole whale seems concentrated to a point. Could annihilation occur to matter, this were the thing to do it.

Nor does this—its amazing strength, at all tend to cripple

the graceful flexion of its motions; where infantileness of ease undulates through a Titanism of power. On the contrary, those motions derive their most appalling beauty from it. Real strength never impairs beauty or harmony, but it often bestows it; and in everything imposingly beautiful, strength has much to do with the magic. Take away the tied tendons that all over seem bursting from the marble in the caved Hercules, and its charm would be gone. As devout Eckerman lifted the linen sheet from the naked corpse of Goethe, he was overwhelmed with the massive chest of the man, that seemed as a Roman triumphal arch. When Angelo paints even God the Father in human form, mark what robustness is there. And whatever they may reveal of the divine love in the Son, the soft, curled, hermaphroditical Italian pictures, in which his idea has been most successfully embodied; these pictures, so destitute as they are of all brawniness, hint nothing of any power, but the mere negative, feminine one of submission and endurance, which on all hands it is conceded, form the peculiar practical virtues of his teachings.

Such is the subtle elasticity of the organ I treat of, that whether wielded in sport, or in earnest, or in anger, whatever be the mood it be in, its flexions are invariably marked by exceeding grace. Therein no fairy's arm can transcend it.

Five great motions are peculiar to it. First, when used as a fin for progression; Second, when used as a mace in battle; Third, in sweeping; Fourth, in lobtailing; Fifth, in peaking flukes.

First: Being horizontal in its position, the Leviathan's tail acts in a different manner from the tails of all other sea creatures. It never wriggles. In man or fish, wriggling is a sign of inferiority. To the whale, his tail is the sole means of propulsion. Scroll-wise coiled forwards beneath the body, and then rapidly sprung backwards, it is this which gives that singular darting, leaping motion to the monster when furiously swimming. His side-fins only serve to steer by.

Second: It is a little significant, that while one sperm whale only fights another sperm whale with his head and jaw, nevertheless, in his conflicts with man, he chiefly and contemptuously uses his tail. In striking at a boat, he swiftly curves away his flukes from it, and the blow is only inflicted by the recoil. If it be made in the unobstructed air, especially if it descend to its mark, the stroke is then simply irre-

sistible. No ribs of man or boat can withstand it. Your only
salvation lies in eluding it; but if it comes sideways through
the opposing water, then partly owing to the light buoyancy
of the whale-boat, and the elasticity of its materials, a
cracked rib or a dashed plank or two, a sort of stitch in the
side, is generally the most serious result. These submerged
side blows are so often received in the fishery, that they are
accounted mere child's play. Some one strips off a frock, and
the hole is stopped.

Third: I cannot demonstrate it, but it seems to me, that
in the whale the sense of touch is concentrated in the tail;
for in this respect there is a delicacy in it only equalled by
the daintiness of the elephant's trunk. This delicacy is chiefly
evinced in the action of sweeping, when in maidenly gen-
tleness the whale with a certain soft slowness moves his immense flukes from side to side upon the surface of the sea;
and if he feel but a sailor's whisker, woe to that sailor,
whiskers and all. What tenderness there is in that preliminary
touch! Had this tail any prehensile power, I should straightway bethink me of Darmonodes' elephant that so frequented
the flower-market, and with low salutations presented nose-
gays to damsels, and then caressed their zones. On more accounts than one, a pity it is that the whale does not possess
this prehensile virtue in his tail; for I have heard of yet
another elephant, that when wounded in the fight, curved
round his trunk and extracted the dart.

Fourth: Stealing unawares upon the whale in the fancied
security of the middle of solitary seas, you find him unbent
from the vast corpulence of his dignity, and kitten-like, he
plays on the ocean as if it were a hearth. But still you see his
power in his play. The broad palms of his tail are flirted high
into the air; then smiting the surface, the thunderous concussion resounds for miles. You would almost think a great
gun had been discharged; and if you noticed the light wreath
of vapor from the spiracle at his other extremity, you would
think that that was the smoke from the touch-hole.

Fifth: As in the ordinary floating posture of the leviathan
the flukes lies considerably below the level of his back, they
are then completely out of sight beneath the surface; but
when he is about to plunge into the deeps, his entire flukes
with at least thirty feet of his body are tossed erect in the
air, and so remain vibrating a moment, till they downwards
shoot out of view. Excepting the sublime *breach*—somewhere
else to be described—this peaking of the whale's flukes is

perhaps the grandest sight to be seen in all animated nature.
Out of the bottomless profundities the gigantic tail seems
spasmodically snatching at the highest heaven. So in dreams,
have I seen majestic Satan thrusting forth his tormented
colossal claw from the flame Baltic of Hell. But in gazing
at such scenes, it is all in all what mood you are in; if in the
Dantean, the devils will occur to you; if in that of Isaiah,
the archangels. Standing at the mast-head of my ship during
a sunrise that crimsoned sky and sea, I once saw a large
herd of whales in the east, all heading towards the sun, and
for a moment vibrating in concert with peaked flukes. As
it seemed to me at the time, such a grand embodiment of
adoration of the gods was never beheld, even in Persia, the
home of the fire worshippers. As Ptolemy Philopater testified of the African elephant, I then testified of the whale, pronouncing him the most devout of all beings. For according
to King Juba, the military elephants of antiquity often hailed
the morning with their trunks uplifted in the profoundest
silence.

The chance comparison in this chapter, between the whale
and the elephant, so far as some aspects of the tail of the
one and the trunk of the other are concerned, should not
tend to place those two opposite organs on an equality,
much less the creatures to which they respectively belong.
For as the mightiest elephant is but a terrier to Leviathan,
so, compared with Leviathan's tail, his trunk is but the stalk
of a lily. The most direful blow from the elephant's trunk
were as the playful tap of a fan, compared with the measureless crush and crash of the sperm whale's ponderous flukes,
which in repeated instances have one after the other hurled
entire boats with all their oars and crews into the air, very
much as an Indian juggler tosses his balls.*

The more I consider this mighty tail, the more do I de-
plore my inability to express it. At times there are gestures
in it, which, though they would well grace the hand of man,
remain wholly inexplicable. In an extensive herd, so remarkable, occasionally, are these mystic gestures, that I have

---

* Though all comparison in the way of general bulk between
the whale and the elephant is preposterous, inasmuch as in that
particular the elephant stands in much the same respect to the
whale that a dog does to the elephant; nevertheless, there are
not wanting some points of curious similitude; among these is
the spout. It is well known that the elephant will often draw
up water or dust in his trunk, and then elevating it, jet it
forth in a stream.

heard hunters who have declared them akin to Free-Mason signs and symbols; that the whale, indeed, by these methods intelligently conversed with the world. Nor are there wanting other motions of the whale in his general body, full of strangeness, and unaccountable to his most experienced assailant. Dissect him how I may, then, I but go skin deep; I know him not, and never will. But if I know not even the tail of this whale, how understand his head? much more, how comprehend his face, when face he has none? Thou shalt see my back parts, my tail, he seems to say, but my face shall not be seen. But I cannot completely make out his back parts; and hint what he will about his face, I say again he has no face.

THE GRAND ARMADA **LXXXVII**

THE long and narrow peninsula of Malacca, extending southeastward from the territories of Birmah, forms the most southerly point of all Asia. In a continuous line from that peninsula stretch the long islands of Sumatra, Java, Bally, and Timor; which, with many others, form a vast mole, or rampart, lengthwise, connecting Asia with Australia, and dividing the long unbroken Indian ocean from the thickly studded oriental archipelagoes. This rampart is pierced by several sally-ports for the convenience of ships and whales; conspicuous among which are the straits of Sunda and Malacca. By the straits of Sunda, chiefly, vessels bound to China from the west, emerge into the China seas.

Those narrow straits of Sunda divide Sumatra from Java; and standing midway in that vast rampart of islands, buttressed by that bold green promontory, known to seamen as Java Head; they not a little correspond to the central gateway opening into some vast walled empire: and considering the inexhaustible wealth of spices, and silks, and jewels, and gold, and ivory, with which the thousand islands of that oriental sea are enriched, it seems a significant provision of nature, that such treasures, by the very formation of the land, should at least bear the appearance, however ineffectual, of being guarded from the all-grasping western world. The shores of the Straits of Sunda are unsupplied with those domineering fortresses which guard the entrances to the

Mediterranean, the Baltic, and the Propontis. Unlike the Danes, these Orientals do not demand the obsequious homage of lowered top-sails from the endless procession of ships before the wind, which for centuries past, by night and by day, have passed between the islands of Sumatra and Java, freighted with the costliest cargoes of the east. But while they freely waive a ceremonial like this, they do by no means renounce their claim to more solid tribute.

Time out of mind the piratical proas of the Malays, lurking among the low shaded coves and islets of Sumatra, have sallied out upon the vessels through the straits, fiercely demanding tribute at the point of their spears. Though by the repeated bloody chastisements they have received at the hands of European cruisers, the audacity of these corsairs has of late been somewhat repressed; yet, even at the present day, we occasionally hear of English and American vessels, which, in those waters, have been remorselessly boarded and pillaged.

With a fair, fresh wind, the Pequod was now drawing nigh to these straits; Ahab purposing to pass through them into the Javan sea, and thence, cruising northwards, over waters known to be frequented here and there by the Sperm Whale, sweep inshore by the Philippine Islands, and gain the far coast of Japan, in time for the great whaling season there. By these means, the circumnavigating Pequod would sweep almost all the known Sperm Whale cruising grounds of the world, previous to descending upon the Line in the Pacific; where Ahab, though everywhere else foiled in his pursuit, firmly counted upon giving battle to Moby Dick, in the sea he was most known to frequent; and at a season when he might most reasonably be presumed to be haunting it.

But how now? in this zoned quest, does Ahab touch no land? does his crew drink air? Surely, he will stop for water. Nay. For a long time, now, the circus-running sun has raced within his fiery ring, and needs no sustenance but what's in himself. So Ahab. Mark this, too, in the whaler. While other hulls are loaded down with alien stuff, to be transferred to foreign wharves; the world-wandering whaleship carries no cargo but herself and crew, their weapons and their wants. She has a whole lake's contents bottled in her ample hold. She is ballasted with utilities; not altogether with unusable pig-lead and kentledge. She carries years' water in her. Clear old prime Nantucket water; which, when three years afloat, the Nantucketer, in the Pacific, prefers to drink before the brackish fluid, but yesterday rafted off in casks, from the Peruvian or Indian streams. Hence it is, that, while other ships may have gone to China from New York, and back again, touching at a score of ports, the whale-ship, in all that interval, may not have sighted one grain of soil; her crew having seen no man but floating seamen like themselves. So that did you carry them the news that another flood had come; they would only answer—"Well, boys, here's the ark!"

Now, as many Sperm Whales had been captured off the western coast of Java, in the near vicinity of the Straits of Sunda; indeed, as most of the ground, roundabout, was generally recognised by the fishermen as an excellent spot for cruising; therefore, as the Pequod gained more and more upon Java Head, the look-outs were repeatedly hailed, and admonished to keep wide awake. But though the green palmy cliffs of the land soon loomed on the starboard bow, and with delighted nostrils the fresh cinnamon was snuffed in the air, yet not a single jet was descried. Almost renouncing all thought of falling in with any game hereabouts, the ship had well nigh entered the straits, when the customary cheering cry was heard from aloft, and ere long a spectacle of singular magnificence saluted us.

But here be it premised, that owing to the unwearied activity with which of late they have been hunted over all four oceans, the Sperm Whales, instead of almost invariably sailing in small detached companies, as in former times, are now frequently met with in extensive herds, sometimes embracing so great a multitude, that it would almost seem as if numerous nations of them had sworn solemn league and covenant for mutual assistance and protection. To this aggregation of the Sperm Whale into such immense caravans, may be imputed the circumstance that even in the best cruising grounds, you may now sometimes sail for weeks and months together, without being greeted by a single spout; and then be suddenly saluted by what sometimes seems thousands on thousands.

Broad on both bows, at the distance of some two or three miles, and forming a great semicircle, embracing one half of the level horizon, a continuous chain of whale-jets were up-playing and sparkling in the noon-day air. Unlike the straight perpendicular twin-jets of the Right Whale, which, dividing at top, fall over in two branches, like the cleft drooping boughs of a willow, the single forward-slanting spout

of the Sperm Whale presents a thick curled bush of white
mist, continually rising and falling away to leeward.

Seen from the Pequod's deck, then, as she would rise on
a high hill of the sea, this host of vapory spouts, individually
curling up into the air, and beheld through a blending atmosphere of bluish haze, showed like the thousand cheerful
chimneys of some dense metropolis, descried of a balmy
autumnal morning, by some horseman on a height.

As marching armies approaching an unfriendly defile in
the mountains, accelerate their march, all eagerness to place
that perilous passage in their rear, and once more expand in
comparative security upon the plain; even so did this vast
fleet of whales now seem hurrying forward through the
straits; gradually contracting the wings of their semicircle,
and swimming on, in one solid, but still crescentic centre.

Crowding all sail the Pequod pressed after them; the harpooneers handling their weapons, and loudly cheering from
the heads of their yet suspended boats. If the wind only
held, little doubt had they, that chased through these Straits
of Sunda, the vast host would only deploy into the Oriental
seas to witness the capture of not a few of their numbers.
And who could tell whether, in that congregated caravan,
Moby Dick himself might not temporarily be swimming, like
the worshipped white-elephant in the coronation procession
of the Siamese! So with stun-sail piled on stun-sail, we
sailed along, driving these leviathans before us; when, of a
sudden, the voice of Tashtego was heard, loudly directing
attention to something in our wake.

Corresponding to the crescent in our van, we beheld another in our rear. It seemed formed of detached white vapors,
rising and falling something like the spouts of the whales;
only they did not so completely come and go; for they constantly hovered, without finally disappearing. Levelling his
glass at this sight, Ahab quickly revolved in his pivot-hole,
crying, "Aloft there, and rig whips and buckets to wet the
sails;—Malays, sir, and after us!"

As if too long lurking behind the headlands, till the
Pequod should fairly have entered the straits, these rascally
Asiatics were now in hot pursuit, to make up for their over-
cautious delay. But when the swift Pequod, with a fresh
leading wind, was herself in hot chase; how very kind of
these tawny philanthropists to assist in speeding her on to
her own chosen pursuit,—mere riding-whips and rowels to
her, that they were. As with glass under arm, Ahab to-and-

fro paced the deck; in his forward turn beholding the monsters he chased, and in the after one the bloodthirsty pirates chasing *him;* some such fancy as the above seemed his. And when he glanced upon the green walls of the watery defile in which the ship was then sailing, and bethought him that through that gate lay the route to his vengeance, and beheld, how that through that same gate he was now both chasing and being chased to his deadly end; and not only that, but a herd of remorseless wild pirates and inhuman atheistical devils were infernally cheering him on with their curses;—when all these conceits had passed through his brain, Ahab's brow was left gaunt and ribbed, like the black sand beach after some stormy tide has been gnawing it, without being able to drag the firm thing from its place.

But thoughts like these troubled very few of the reckless crew; and when, after steadily dropping and dropping the pirates astern, the Pequod at last shot by the vivid green Cockatoo Point on the Sumatra side, emerging at last upon the broad waters beyond; then, the harpooneers seemed more to grieve that the swift whales had been gaining upon the ship, than to rejoice that the ship had so victoriously gained upon the Malays. But still driving on in the wake of the whales, at length they seemed abating their speed; gradually the ship neared them; and the wind now dying away, word was passed to spring to the boats. But no sooner did the herd, by some presumed wonderful instinct of the Sperm Whale, become notified of the three keels that were after them,—though as yet a mile in their rear,—than they rallied again, and forming in close ranks and battalions, so that their spouts all looked like flashing lines of stacked bayonets, moved on with redoubled velocity.

Stripped to our shirts and drawers, we sprang to the white-ash; and after several hours' pulling were almost disposed to renounce the chase, when a general pausing commotion among the whales gave animating token that they were now at last under the influence of that strange perplexity of inert irresolution, which, when the fishermen perceive it in the whale, they say he is gallied. The compact martial columns in which they had been hitherto rapidly and steadily swimming, were now broken up in one measureless rout; and like King Porus' elephants in the Indian battle with Alexander, they seemed going mad with consternation. In all directions expanding in vast irregular circles, and aimlessly swimming hither and thither, by their short thick spoutings, they plainly betrayed their distraction of panic. This was still more strangely evinced by those of their number, who, completely paralysed as it were, helplessly floated like water-logged dismantled ships on the sea. Had these leviathans been but a flock of simple sheep, pursued over the pasture by three fierce wolves, they could not possibly have evinced such excessive dismay. But this occasional timidity is characteristic of almost all herding creatures. Though banding together in tens of thousands, the lion-maned buffaloes of the West have fled before a solitary horseman. Witness, too, all human beings, how when herded together in the sheepfold of a theatre's pit, they will, at the slightest alarm of fire, rush helter-skelter for the outlets, crowding, trampling, jamming, and remorselessly dashing each other to death. Best, therefore, withhold any amazement at the strangely gallied whales before us, for there is no folly of the beasts of the earth which is not infinitely outdone by the madness of men.

Though many of the whales, as has been said, were in violent motion, yet it is to be observed that as a whole the herd neither advanced nor retreated, but collectively remained in one place. As is customary in those cases, the boats at once separated, each making for some one lone whale on the outskirts of the shoal. In about three minutes' time, Queequeg's harpoon was flung; the stricken fish darted blinding spray in our faces, and then running away with us like light, steered straight for the heart of the herd. Though such a movement on the part of the whale struck under such circumstances, is in no wise unprecedented; and indeed is almost always more or less anticipated; yet does it present one of the more perilous vicissitudes of the fishery. For as the swift monster drags you deeper and deeper into the frantic shoal, you bid adieu to circumspect life and only exist in a delirious throb.

As, blind and deaf, the whale plunged forward, as if by sheer power of speed to rid himself of the iron leech that had fastened to him; as we thus tore a white gash in the sea, on all sides menaced as we flew, by the crazed creatures to and fro rushing about us; our beset boat was like a ship mobbed by ice-isles in a tempest, and striving to steer through their complicated channels and straits, knowing not at what moment it may be locked in and crushed.

But not a bit daunted, Queequeg steered us manfully; now sheering off from this monster directly across our route in advance; now edging away from that, whose colossal flukes were suspended overhead, while all the time, Starbuck stood up in the bows, lance in hand, pricking out of our way whatever whales he could reach by short darts, for there was no time to make long ones. Nor were the oarsmen quite idle, though their wonted duty was now altogether dispensed with. They chiefly attended to the shouting part of the business. "Out of the way, Commodore!" cried one, to a great dromedary that of a sudden rose bodily to the surface, and for an instant threatened to swamp us. "Hard down with your tail, there!" cried a second to another, which, close to our gunwale, seemed calmly cooling himself with his own fan-like extremity.

All whaleboats carry certain curious contrivances, originally invented by the Nantucket Indians, called druggs. Two thick squares of wood of equal size are stoutly clenched together, so that they cross each other's grain at right angles; a line of considerable length is then attached to the middle of this block, and the other end of the line being looped, it can in a moment be fastened to a harpoon. It is chiefly among gallied whales that this drugg is used. For then, more whales are close round you than you can possibly chase at one time. But sperm whales are not every day encountered; while you may, then, you must kill all you can. And if you cannot kill them all at once, you must wing them, so that they can be afterwards killed at your leisure. Hence it is, that at times like these the drugg comes into requisition. Our boat was furnished with three of them. The first and second were successfully darted, and we saw the whales staggeringly running off, fettered by the enormous sidelong resistance of the towing drugg. They were cramped like malefactors with the chain and ball. But upon flinging the third, in the act of tossing overboard the clumsy wooden block, it caught under one of the seats of the boat, and in an instant tore it out and carried it away, dropping the oarsman in the boat's bottom as the seat slid from under him. On both sides the sea came in at the wounded planks, but we stuffed two or three drawers and shirts in, and so stopped the leaks for the time.

It had been next to impossible to dart these drugged-harpoons, were it not that as we advanced into the herd, our whale's way greatly diminished; moreover, that as we went still further and further from the circumference of commotion, the direful disorders seemed waning. So that when at last the jerking harpoon drew out, and the towing whale

sideways vanished then, with the tapering force of his parting momentum, we glided between two whales into the innermost heart of the shoal, as if from some mountain torrent
we had slid into a serene valley lake. Here the storms in the
roaring glens between the outermost whales, were heard but
not felt. In this central expanse the sea presented that
smooth, satin-like surface, called a sleek, produced by the
subtle moisture thrown off by the whale in his more quiet
moods. Yes, we were now in that enchanted calm which
they say lurks at the heart of every commotion. And still in
the distracted distance we beheld the tumults of the outer
concentric circles, and saw successive pods of whales, eight
or ten in each, swiftly going round and round, like multiplied
spans of horses in a ring; and so closely shoulder to shoulder,
that a Titanic circus-rider might easily have overarched the
middle ones, and so have gone round on their backs. Owing
to the density of the crowd of reposing whales, more immediately surrounding the embayed axis of the herd, no possible chance of escape was at present afforded us. We must
watch for a breach in the living wall that hemmed us in;
the wall that had only admitted us in order to shut us up.
Keeping at the centre of the lake, we were occasionally
visited by small tame cows and calves; the women and children of this routed host.

Now, inclusive of the occasional wide intervals between
the revolving outer circles, and inclusive of the spaces between the various pods in any one of those circles, the entire
area at this juncture, embraced by the whole multitude,
must have contained at least two or three square miles.
At any rate—though indeed such a test at such a time
might be deceptive—spoutings might be discovered from our
low boat that seemed playing up almost from the rim of
the horizon. I mention this circumstance, because, as if the
cows and calves had been purposely locked up in this innermost fold; and as if the wide extent of the herd had hitherto
prevented them from learning the precise cause of its stopping; or, possibly, being so young, unsophisticated, and every
way innocent and inexperienced; however it may have been,
these smaller whales—now and then visiting our becalmed
boat from the margin of the lake—evinced a wondrous fearlessness and confidence, or else a still becharmed panic which
it was impossible not to marvel at. Like household dogs
they came snuffling round us, right up to our gunwales,

and touching them; till it almost seemed that some spell had suddenly domesticated them. Queequeg patted their foreheads; Starbuck scratched their backs with his lance; but fearful of the consequences, for the time refrained from darting it.

But far beneath this wondrous world upon the surface, another and still stranger world met our eyes as we gazed over the side. For, suspended in those watery vaults, floated the forms of the nursing mothers of the whales, and those that by their enormous girth seemed shortly to become mothers. The lake, as I have hinted, was to a considerable depth exceedingly transparent; and as human infants while suckling will calmly and fixedly gaze away from the breast, as if leading two different lives at the time; and while yet drawing mortal nourishment, be still spiritually feasting upon some unearthly reminiscence;—even so did the young of these whales seem looking up towards us, but not at us, as if we were but a bit of Gulf-weed in their new-born sight. Floating on their sides, the mothers also seemed quietly eyeing us. One of these little infants, that from certain queer tokens seemed hardly a day old, might have measured some fourteen feet in length, and some six feet in girth. He was a little frisky; though as yet his body seemed scarce yet recovered from that irksome position it had so lately occupied in the maternal reticule; where, tail to head, and all ready for the final spring, the unborn whale lies bent like a Tartar's bow. The delicate side-fins, and the palms of his flukes, still freshly retained the plaited crumpled appearance of a baby's ears newly arrived from foreign parts.

"Line! line!" cried Queequeg, looking over the gunwale; "him fast! him fast!—Who line him! Who struck?—Two whale; one big, one little!"

"What ails ye, man?" cried Starbuck.

"Look-e here," said Queequeg pointing down.

As when the stricken whale, that from the tub has reeled out hundreds of fathoms of rope; as, after deep sounding, he floats up again, and shows the slackened curling line buoyantly rising and spiralling towards the air; so now, Starbuck saw long coils of the umbilical cord of Madame Leviathan, by which the young cub seemed still tethered to its dam. Not seldom in the rapid vicissitudes of the chase, this natural line, with the maternal end loose, becomes entangled with the hempen one, so that the cub is thereby trapped. Some of the subtlest secrets of the seas seemed divulged to us in this enchanted pond. We saw young Leviathan amours in the deep.*

And thus, though surrounded by circle upon circle of consternations and affrights, did these inscrutable creatures at the centre freely and fearlessly indulge in all peaceful concernments; yea, serenely revelled in dalliance and delight. But even so, amid the tornadoed Atlantic of my being, do I myself still for ever centrally disport in mute calm; and while ponderous planets of unwaning woe revolve round me, deep down and deep inland there I still bathe me in eternal mildness of joy.

Meanwhile, as we thus lay entranced, the occasional sudden frantic spectacles in the distance evinced the activity of the other boats, still engaged in drugging the whales on the frontier of the host; or possibly carrying on the war within the first circle, where abundance of room and some convenient retreats were afforded them. But the sight of the enraged drugged whales now and then blindly darting to and fro across the circles, was nothing to what at last met our eyes. It is sometimes the custom when fast to a whale more than commonly powerful and alert, to seek to hamstring him, as it were, by sundering or maiming his gigantic tail-tendon. It is done by darting a short-handled cutting-spade, to which is attached a rope for hauling it back again. A whale wounded (as we afterwards learned) in this part, but not effectually, as it seemed, had broken away from the boat, carrying along with him half of the harpoon line; and in the extraordinary agony of the wound, he was now dashing among the revolving circles like the lone mounted desperado Arnold, at the battle of Saratoga, carrying dismay wherever he went.

But agonizing as was the wound of this whale, and an

---

* The sperm whale, as with all other species of the Leviathan, but unlike most other fish, breeds indifferently at all seasons; after a gestation which may probably be set down at nine months, producing but one at a time; though in some few known instances giving birth to an Esau and Jacob:—a contingency provided for in suckling by two teats, curiously situated, one on each side of the anus; but the breasts themselves extend upwards from that. When by chance these precious parts in a nursing whale are cut by the hunter's lance, the mother's pouring milk and blood rivallingly discolor the sea for rods. The milk is very sweet and rich; it has been tasted by man; it might do well with strawberries. When overflowing with mutual esteem, the whales salute *more hominum*.

appalling spectacle enough, any way; yet the peculiar horror with which he seemed to inspire the rest of the herd, was owing to a cause which at first the intervening distance obscured from us. But at length we perceived that by one of the unimaginable accidents of the fishery, this whale had become entangled in the harpoon-line that he towed; he had also run away with the cutting-spade in him; and while the free end of the rope attached to that weapon, had permanently caught in the coils of the harpoon-line round his tail, the cutting-spade itself had worked loose from his flesh. So that tormented to madness, he was now churning through the water, violently flailing with his flexible tail, and tossing the keen spade about him, wounding and murdering his own comrades.

This terrific object seemed to recall the whole herd from their stationary fright. First, the whales forming the margin of our lake began to crowd a little, and tumble against each other, as if lifted by half spent billows from afar; then the lake itself began faintly to heave and swell; the submarine bridal-chambers and nurseries vanished; in more and more contracting orbits the whales in the more central circles began to swim in thickening clusters. Yes, the long calm was departing. A low advancing hum was soon heard; and then like to the tumultuous masses of block-ice when the great river Hudson breaks up in Spring, the entire host of whales came tumbling upon their inner centre, as if to pile themselves up in one common mountain. Instantly Starbuck and Queequeg changed places; Starbuck taking the stern.

"Oars! Oars!" he intensely whispered, seizing the helm—"gripe your oars, and clutch your souls, now! My God, men, stand by! Shove him off, you Queequeg—the whale there!—prick him! hit him! Stand up—stand up, and stay so! Spring, men—pull, men; never mind their backs—scrape them!—scrape away!"

The boat was now all but jammed between two vast black bulks, leaving a narrow Dardanelles between their long lengths. But by desperate endeavor we at last shot into a temporary opening; then giving way rapidly, and at the same time earnestly watching for another outlet. After many similar hair-breadth escapes, we at last swiftly glided into what had just been one of the outer circles, but now crossed by random whales, all violently making for one centre. This lucky salvation was cheaply purchased by the loss of Queequeg's hat, who, while standing in the bows to prick the

fugitive whales, had his hat taken clean from his head by the
air-eddy made by the sudden tossing of a pair of broad
flukes close by.

Riotous and disordered as the universal commotion now
was, it soon resolved itself into what seemed a systematic
movement; for having clumped together at last in one dense
body, they then renewed their onward flight with augmented
fleetness. Further pursuit was useless; but the boats still
lingered in their wake to pick up what drugged whales might
be dropped astern, and likewise to secure one which Flask
had killed and waifed. The waif is a pennoned pole, two or
three of which are carried by every boat; and which, when
additional game is at hand, are inserted upright into the
floating body of a dead whale, both to mark its place on the
sea, and also as token of prior possession, should the boats
of any other ship draw near.

The result of this lowering was somewhat illustrative of
that sagacious saying in the Fishery,—the more whales the
less fish. Of all the drugged whales only one was captured.
The rest contrived to escape for the time, but only to be
taken, as will hereafter be seen, by some other craft than
the Pequod.

SCHOOLS AND SCHOOLMASTERS . LXXXVIII

THE previous chapter gave account of an immense body
or herd of Sperm Whales, and there was also then given the
probable cause inducing those vast aggregations.

Now, though such great bodies are at times encountered,
yet, as must have been seen, even at the present day, small
detached bands are occasionally observed, embracing from
twenty to fifty individuals each. Such bands are known as
schools. They generally are of two sorts; those composed almost entirely of females, and those mustering none but young
vigorous males, or bulls, as they are familiarly designated.

In cavalier attendance upon the school of females, you invariably see a male of full grown magnitude, but not old;
who, upon any alarm, evinces his gallantry by falling in the
rear and covering the flight of his ladies. In truth, this gentleman is a luxurious Ottoman, swimming about over the watery
world, surroundingly accompanied by all the solaces and en-

dearments of the harem. The contrast between this Ottoman and his concubines is striking; because, while he is always of the largest leviathanic proportions, the ladies, even at full growth, are not more than one third of the bulk of an average-sized male. They are comparatively delicate, indeed; I dare say, not to exceed half a dozen yards round the waist. Nevertheless, it cannot be denied, that upon the whole they are hereditarily entitled to *en bon point*.

It is very curious to watch this harem and its lord in their indolent ramblings. Like fashionables, they are for ever on the move in leisurely search of variety. You meet them on the Line in time for the full flower of the Equatorial feeding season, having just returned, perhaps, from spending the summer in the Northern seas, and so cheating summer of all unpleasant weariness and warmth. By the time they have lounged up and down the promenade of the Equator awhile, they start for the Oriental waters in anticipation of the cool season there, and so evade the other excessive temperature of the year.

When serenely advancing on one of these journeys, if any strange suspicious sights are seen, my lord whale keeps a wary eye on his interesting family. Should any unwarrantably pert young Leviathan coming that way, presume to draw confidentially close to one of the ladies, with what prodigious fury the Bashaw assails him, and chases him away! High times, indeed, if unprincipled young rakes like him are to be permitted to invade the sanctity of domestic bliss; though do what the Bashaw will, he cannot keep the most notorious Lothario out of his bed; for, alas! all fish bed in common. As ashore, the ladies often cause the most terrible duels among their rival admirers; just so with the whales, who sometimes come to deadly battle, and all for love. They fence with their long lower jaws, sometimes locking them together, and so striving for the supremacy like elks that warringly interweave their antlers. Not a few are captured having the deep scars of these encounters,—furrowed heads, broken teeth, scalloped fins; and in some instances, wrenched and dislocated mouths.

But supposing the invader of domestic bliss to betake himself away at the first rush of the harem's lord, then is it very diverting to watch that lord. Gently he insinuates his vast bulk among them again and revels there awhile, still in tantalizing vicinity to young Lothario, like pious Solomon devoutly worshipping among his thousand concubines. Granting other whales to be in sight, the fishermen will seldom give chase to one of these Grand Turks; for these Grand Turks are too lavish of their strength, and hence their unctuousness is small. As for the sons and the daughters they beget, why, those sons and daughters must take care of themselves; at least, with only the maternal help. For like certain other omnivorous roving lovers that might be named, my Lord Whale has no taste for the nursery, however much for the bower; and so, being a great traveller, he leaves his anonymous babies all over the world; every baby an exotic. In good time, nevertheless, as the ardor of youth declines; as years and dumps increase; as reflection lends her solemn pauses; in short, as a general lassitude overtakes the sated Turk; then a love of ease and virtue supplants the love for maidens; our Ottoman enters upon the impotent, repentant, admonitory stage of life, forswears, disbands the harem, and grown to an exemplary, sulky old soul, goes about all alone among the meridians and parallels saying his prayers, and warning each young Leviathan from his amorous errors.

Now, as the harem of whales is called by the fishermen a school, so is the lord and master of that school technically known as the schoolmaster. It is therefore not in strict character, however admirably satirical, that after going to school himself, he should then go abroad inculcating not what he learned there, but the folly of it. His title, schoolmaster, would very naturally seem derived from the name bestowed upon the harem itself, but some have surmised that the man who first thus entitled this sort of Ottoman whale, must have read the memoirs of Vidocq, and informed himself what sort of a country-schoolmaster that famous Frenchman was in his younger days, and what was the nature of those occult lessons he inculcated into some of his pupils.

The same secludedness and isolation to which the schoolmaster whale betakes himself in his advancing years, is true of all aged Sperm Whales. Almost universally, a lone whale —as a solitary Leviathan is called—proves an ancient one. Like venerable moss-bearded Daniel Boone, he will have no one near him but Nature herself; and her he takes to wife in the wilderness of waters, and the best of wives she is, though she keeps so many moody secrets.

The schools composing none but young and vigorous males, previously mentioned, offer a strong contrast to the harem schools. For while those female whales are characteristically timid, the young males, or forty-barrel-bulls, as

they call them, are by far the most pugnacious of all Leviathans, and proverbially the most dangerous to encounter; excepting those wondrous grey-headed, grizzled whales, sometimes met, and these will fight you like grim fiends exasperated by a penal gout.

The Forty-barrel-bull schools are larger than the harem
schools. Like a mob of young collegians, they are full of
fight, fun, and wickedness, tumbling round the world at such
a reckless, rollicking rate, that no prudent underwriter would
insure them any more than he would a riotous lad at Yale
or Harvard. They soon relinquish this turbulence though,
and when about three fourths grown, break up, and separately
go about in quest of settlements, that is, harems.

Another point of difference between the male and female
schools is still more characteristic of the sexes. Say you strike
a Forty-barrel-bull—poor devil! all his comrades quit him.
But strike a member of the harem school, and her companions swim around her with every token of concern, sometimes lingering so near her and so long, as themselves to fall
a prey.

FAST-FISH AND LOOSE-FISH   LXXXIX

THE allusion to the waifs and waif-poles in the last
chapter but one, necessitates some account of the laws and
regulations of the whale fishery, of which the waif may be
deemed the grand symbol and badge.

It frequently happens that when several ships are cruising
in company, a whale may be struck by one vessel, then escape, and be finally killed and captured by another vessel;
and herein are indirectly comprised many minor contingen-
cies, all partaking of this one grand feature. For example,—
after a weary and perilous chase and capture of a whale, the
body may get loose from the ship by reason of a violent
storm; and drifting far away to leeward, be retaken by a
second whaler, who, in a calm, snugly tows it alongside,
without risk of life or line. Thus the most vexatious and
violent disputes would often arise between the fishermen,
were there not some written or unwritten, universal, undisputed law applicable to all cases.

Perhaps the only formal whaling code authorized by legislative enactment, was that of Holland. It was decreed by the States-General in A.D. 1695. But though no other nation has ever had any written whaling law, yet the American fishermen have been their own legislators and lawyers in this matter. They have provided a system which for terse comprehensiveness surpasses Justinian's Pandects and the By-laws of the Chinese Society for the Suppression of Meddling with other People's Business. Yes; these laws might be engraven on a Queen Anne's farthing, or the barb of a harpoon, and worn round the neck, so small are they.

I.   A Fast-Fish belongs to the party fast to it.

II. A Loose-Fish is fair game for anybody who can soonest catch it.

But what plays the mischief with this masterly code is the admirable brevity of it, which necessitates a vast volume of commentaries to expound it.

First: What is a Fast-Fish? Alive or dead a fish is technically fast, when it is connected with an occupied ship or boat, by any medium at all controllable by the occupant or occupants,—a mast, an oar, a nine-inch cable, a telegraph wire, or a strand of cobweb, it is all the same. Likewise a fish is technically fast when it bears a waif, or any other recognised symbol of possession; so long as the party waifing it plainly evince their ability at any time to take it alongside, as well as their intention so to do.

These are scientific commentaries; but the commentaries of the whalemen themselves sometimes consist in hard words and harder knocks—the Coke-upon-Littleton of the fist. True, among the more upright and honorable whalemen allowances are always made for peculiar cases, where it would be an outrageous moral injustice for one party to claim possession of a whale previously chased or killed by another party. But others are by no means so scrupulous.

Some fifty years ago there was a curious case of whale-trover litigated in England, wherein the plaintiffs set forth that after a hard chase of a whale in the Northern seas; and when indeed they (the plaintiffs) had succeeded in harpooning the fish; they were at last, through peril of their lives, obliged to forsake not only their lines, but their boat itself. Ultimately the defendants (the crew of another ship) came up with the whale, struck, killed, seized, and finally appropriated it before the very eyes of the plaintiffs. And when those defendants were remonstrated with, their captain snapped his fingers in the plaintiff's teeth, and assured them that by way of doxology to the deed he had done, he would now retain their line, harpoons, and boat, which had remained attached to the whale at the time of the seizure. Wherefore the plaintiffs now sued for the recovery of the value of their whale, line, harpoons, and boat.

Mr. Erskine was counsel for the defendants; Lord Ellenborough was the judge. In the course of the defence, the witty Erskine went on to illustrate his position, by alluding to a recent crim. con. case, wherein a gentleman, after in vain trying to bridle his wife's viciousness, had at last abandoned her upon the seas of life; but in the course of years, repenting of that step, he instituted an action to recover possession of her. Erskine was on the other side; and he then supported it by saying, that though the gentleman had originally harpooned the lady, and had once had her fast, and only by reason of the great stress of her plunging viciousness, had at last abandoned her; yet abandon her he did, so that she became a loose-fish; and therefore when a subsequent gentleman re-harpooned her, the lady then became that subsequent gentleman's property, along with whatever harpoon might have been found sticking in her.

Now in the present case Erskine contended that the examples of the whale and the lady were reciprocally illustrative of each other.

These pleadings, and the counter pleadings, being duly heard, the very learned judge in set terms decided, to wit,— That as for the boat, he awarded it to the plaintiffs, because they had merely abandoned it to save their lives; but that with regard to the controverted whale, harpoons, and line, they belonged to the defendants; the whale, because it was a Loose-Fish at the time of the final capture; and the harpoons and line because when the fish made off with them, it (the fish) acquired a property in those articles; and hence anybody who afterwards took the fish had a right to them. Now the defendants afterwards took the fish; ergo, the aforesaid articles were theirs.

A common man looking at this decision of the very learned Judge, might possibly object to it. But ploughed up to the primary rock of the matter, the two great principles laid down in the twin whaling laws previously quoted, and applied and elucidated by Lord Ellenborough in the above cited case; these two laws touching Fast-Fish and Loose-Fish, I say, will, on reflection, be found the fundamentals of all human jurisprudence; for notwithstanding its complicated tracery of sculpture, the Temple of the Law, like the Temple of the Philistines, has but two props to stand on.

Is it not a saying in every one's mouth, Possession is half of the law: that is, regardless of how the thing came into possession? But often possession is the whole of the law. What are the sinews and souls of Russian serfs and Republican slaves but Fast-Fish, whereof possession is the whole of the law? What to the rapacious landlord is the widow's last mite but a Fast-Fish? What is yonder undetected villain's marble mansion with a door-plate for a waif; what is that but a Fast-Fish? What is the ruinous discount which Mordecai, the broker, gets from poor Woebegone, the bankrupt, on a loan to keep Woebegone's family from starvation; what is that ruinous discount but a Fast-Fish? What is the Archbishop of Savesoul's income of £100,000 seized from the scant bread and cheese of hundreds of thousands of broken-backed laborers (all sure of heaven without any of Savesoul's help) what is that globular 100,000 but a Fast-Fish? What are the Duke of Dunder's hereditary towns and hamlets but Fast-Fish? What to that redoubted harpooneer, John Bull, is poor Ireland, but a Fast-Fish? What to that apostolic lancer, Brother Jonathan, is Texas but a Fast-Fish? And concerning all these, is not Possession the whole of the law?

But if the doctrine of Fast-Fish be pretty generally applicable, the kindred doctrine of Loose-Fish is still more widely so. That is internationally and universally applicable.

What was America in 1492 but a Loose-Fish, in which Columbus struck the Spanish standard by way of waifing it for his royal master and mistress? What was Poland to the Czar? What Greece to the Turk? What India to England? What at last will Mexico be to the United States? All Loose-Fish.

What are the Rights of Man and the Liberties of the World but Loose-Fish? What all men's minds and opinions but Loose-Fish? What is the principle of religious belief in them but a Loose-Fish? What to the ostentatious smuggling verbalists are the thoughts of thinkers but Loose-Fish? What is the great globe itself but a Loose-Fish? And what are you, reader, but a Loose-Fish and a Fast-Fish, too?

HEADS OR TAILS   XC

"De balena vero sufficit, si rex habeat caput, et regina
caudam."   *Bracton, l. 3, c. 3.*

LATIN from the books of the Laws of England, which
taken along with the context, means, that of all whales captured by anybody on the coast of that land, the King, as
Honorary Grand Harpooneer, must have the head, and the
Queen be respectfully presented with the tail. A division
which, in the whale, is much like halving an apple; there
is no intermediate remainder. Now as this law, under a modified form, is to this day in force in England; and as it
offers in various respects a strange anomaly touching the
general law of Fast and Loose-Fish, it is here treated of in a
separate chapter, on the same courteous principle that
prompts the English railways to be at the expense of a separate car, specially reserved for the accommodation of royalty.
In the first place, in curious proof of the fact that the above-
mentioned law is still in force, I proceed to lay before you a
circumstance that happened within the last two years.

It seems that some honest mariners of Dover, or Sandwich,
or some one of the Cinque Ports, had after a hard chase
succeeded in killing and beaching a fine whale which they
had originally descried afar off from the shore. Now the
Cinque Ports are partially or somehow under the jurisdic-
tion of a sort of policeman or beadle, called a Lord Warden.
Holding the office directly from the crown, I believe, all
the royal emoluments incident to the Cinque Port territories
become by assignment his. By some writers this office is
called a sinecure. But not so. Because the Lord Warden is
busily employed at times in fobbing his perquisites; which
are his chiefly by virtue of that same fobbing of them.

Now when these poor sun-burnt mariners, bare-footed,
and with their trowsers rolled high up on their eely legs, had
wearily hauled their fat fish high and dry, promising themselves a good £150 from the precious oil and bone; and in
fantasy sipping rare tea with their wives, and good ale with
their cronies, upon the strength of their respective shares; up
steps a very learned and most Christian and charitable gen-

tleman, with a copy of Blackstone under his arm; and laying it upon the whale's head, he says—"Hands off! this fish, my masters, is a Fast-Fish. I seize it as the Lord Warden's." Upon this the poor mariners in their respectful consternation—so truly English—knowing not what to say, fall to vigorously scratching their heads all round; meanwhile ruefully glancing from the whale to the stranger. But that did in nowise mend the matter, or at all soften the hard heart of the learned gentleman with the copy of Blackstone. At length one of them, after long scratching about for his ideas, made bold to speak.

"Please, sir, who is the Lord Warden?"

"The Duke."

"But the duke had nothing to do with taking this fish?"

"It is his."

"We have been at great trouble, and peril, and some expense, and is all that to go to the Duke's benefit; we getting nothing at all for our pains but our blisters?"

"It is his."

"Is the Duke so very poor as to be forced to this desperate mode of getting a livelihood?"

"It is his."

"I thought to relieve my old bed-ridden mother by part of my share of this whale."

"It is his."

"Won't the Duke be content with a quarter or a half?"

"It is his."

In a word, the whale was seized and sold, and his Grace the Duke of Wellington received the money. Thinking that viewed in some particular lights, the case might by a bare possibility in some small degree be deemed, under the circumstances, a rather hard one, an honest clergyman of the town respectfully addressed a note to his Grace, begging him to take the case of those unfortunate mariners into full consideration. To which my Lord Duke in substance replied (both letters were published) that he had already done so, and received the money, and would be obliged to the reverend gentleman if for the future he (the reverend gentleman) would decline meddling with other people's business. Is this the still militant old man, standing at the corners of the three kingdoms, on all hands coercing alms of beggars?

It will readily be seen that in this case the alleged right of the Duke to the whale was a delegated one from the Sovereign. We must needs inquire then on what principle the Sovereign is originally invested with that right. The law itself has already been set forth. But Plowdon gives us the reason for it. Says Plowdon, the whale so caught belongs to the King and Queen, "because of its superior excellence." And by the soundest commentators this has ever been held a cogent argument in such matters.

But why should the King have the head, and the Queen the tail? A reason for that, ye lawyers!

In his treatise on "Queen-Gold," or Queen-pinmoney, an old King's Bench author, one William Prynne, thus discourseth: "Ye tail is ye Queen's, that ye Queen's wardrobe may be supplied with ye whalebone." Now this was written at a time when the black limber bone of the Greenland or Right whale was largely used in ladies' bodices. But this same bone is not in the tail; it is in the head, which is a sad mistake for a sagacious lawyer like Prynne. But is the Queen a mermaid, to be presented with a tail? An allegorical meaning may lurk here.

There are two royal fish so styled by the English law writers—the whale and the sturgeon; both royal property under certain limitations, and nominally supplying the tenth branch of the crown's ordinary revenue. I know not that any other author has hinted of the matter; but by inference it seems to me that the sturgeon must be divided in the same way as the whale, the King receiving the highly dense and elastic head peculiar to that fish, which, symbolically regarded, may possibly be humorously grounded upon some presumed congeniality. And thus there seems a reason in all things, even in law.

THE PEQUOD MEETS THE ROSE-BUD   XCI

"In vain it was to rake for Ambergriese in the paunch of this Leviathan, insufferable fetor denying not inquiry."
Sir T. Browne, V. E.

IT was a week or two after the last whaling scene recounted, and when we were slowly sailing over a sleepy, vapory, mid-day sea, that the many noses on the Pequod's deck proved more vigilant discoverers than the three pairs of eyes aloft. A peculiar and not very pleasant smell was smelt in the sea.

"I will bet something now," said Stubb, "that somewhere hereabouts are some of those drugged whales we tickled the other day. I thought they would keel up before long."

Presently, the vapors in advance slid aside; and there in the distance lay a ship, whose furled sails betokened that some sort of whale must be alongside. As we glided nearer, the stranger showed French colors from his peak; and by the eddying cloud of vulture sea-fowl that circled, and hovered, and swooped around him, it was plain that the whale alongside must be what the fishermen call a blasted whale, that is, a whale that has died unmolested on the sea, and so floated an unappropriated corpse. It may well be conceived, what an unsavory odor such a mass must exhale; worse than an Assyrian city in the plague, when the living are incompetent to bury the departed. So intolerable indeed is it regarded by some, that no cupidity could persuade them to moor alongside of it. Yet are there those who will still do it; notwithstanding the fact that the oil obtained from such subjects is of a very inferior quality, and by no means of the nature of attar-of-rose.

Coming still nearer with the expiring breeze, we saw that the Frenchman had a second whale alongside; and this second whale seemed even more of a nosegay than the first. In truth, it turned out to be one of those problematical whales that seem to dry up and die with a sort of prodigious dyspepsia, or indigestion; leaving their defunct bodies almost entirely bankrupt of anything like oil. Nevertheless, in the proper place we shall see that no knowing fisherman will ever turn up his nose at such a whale as this, however much he may shun blasted whales in general.

The Pequod had now swept so nigh to the stranger, that Stubb vowed he recognized his cutting spade-pole entangled in the lines that were knotted round the tail of one of these whales.

"There's a pretty fellow, now," he banteringly laughed, standing in the ship's bows, "there's a jackal for ye! I well know that these Crappoes of Frenchmen are but poor devils in the fishery; sometimes lowering their boats for breakers, mistaking them for Sperm Whale spouts; yes, and sometimes sailing from their port with their hold full of boxes of tallow candles, and cases of snuffers, foreseeing that all the oil they will get won't be enough to dip the Captain's wick into; aye, we all know these things; but look ye, here's a Crappo that is content with our leavings, the drugged whale there, I mean; aye, and is content too with scraping the dry bones of that other precious fish he has there. Poor devil! I say, pass round a hat, some one, and let's make him a present of a little oil for dear charity's sake. For what oil he'll get from that drugged whale there, wouldn't be fit to burn in a jail; no, not in a condemned cell. And as for the other whale, why, I'll agree to get more oil by chopping up and trying out these three masts of ours, than he'll get from that bundle of bones; though, now that I think of it, it may contain something worth a good deal more than oil; yes, ambergris. I wonder now if our old man has thought of that. It's worth trying. Yes, I'm in for it;" and so saying he started for the quarter-deck.

By this time the faint air had become a complete calm; so that whether or no, the Pequod was now fairly entrapped in the smell, with no hope of escaping except by its breezing up again. Issuing from the cabin, Stubb now called his boat's crew, and pulled off for the stranger. Drawing across her bow, he perceived that in accordance with the fanciful French taste, the upper part of her stem-piece was carved in the likeness of a huge drooping stalk, was painted green, and for thorns had copper spikes projecting from it here and there; the whole terminating in a symmetrical folded bulb of a bright red color. Upon her head boards, in large gilt letters, he read "Bouton de Rose,"—Rose button, or Rose-bud; and this was the romantic name of this aromatic ship.

Though Stubb did not understand the *Bouton* part of the inscription, yet the word *rose,* and the bulbous figure-head put together, sufficiently explained the whole to him.

"A wooden rose-bud, eh?" he cried with his hand to his nose, "that will do very well; but how like all creation it smells!"

Now in order to hold direct communication with the people on deck, he had to pull round the bows to the starboard side, and thus come close to the blasted whale; and so talk over it.

Arrived then at this spot, with one hand still to his nose, he bawled—"Bouton-de-Rose, ahoy! are there any of you Bouton-de-Roses that speak English?"

"Yes," rejoined a Guernsey-man from the bulwarks, who turned out to be the chief-mate.

"Well, then, my Bouton-de-Rose-bud, have you seen the White Whale?"

"*What* whale?"

"The *White* Whale—a Sperm Whale—Moby Dick, have ye seen him?"

"Never heard of such a whale. Cachalot Blanche! White Whale—no."

"Very good, then; good bye now, and I'll call again in a minute."

Then rapidly pulling back towards the Pequod, and seeing Ahab leaning over the quarter-deck rail awaiting his report, he moulded his two hands into a trumpet and shouted—"No, Sir! No!" Upon which Ahab retired, and Stubb returned to the Frenchman.

He now perceived that the Guernsey-man, who had just got into the chains, and was using a cutting-spade, had slung his nose in a sort of bag.

"What's the matter with your nose, there?" said Stubb. "Broke it?"

"I wish it was broken, or that I didn't have any nose at all!" answered the Guernsey-man, who did not seem to relish the job he was at very much. "But what are you holding *yours* for?"

"Oh, nothing! It's a wax nose; I have to hold it on. Fine day, ain't it? Air rather gardenny, I should say; throw us a bunch of posies, will ye, Bouton-de-Rose?"

"What in the devil's name do you want here?" roared the Guernsey-man, flying into a sudden passion.

"Oh! keep cool—cool? yes, that's the word; why don't you pack those whales in ice while you're working at 'em? But joking aside, though; do you know, Rose-bud, that it's all nonsense trying to get any oil out of such whales? As for that dried up one, there, he hasn't a gill in his whole carcase."

"I know that well enough; but, d'ye see, the Captain here won't believe it; this is his first voyage; he was a Cologne manufacturer before. But come aboard, and mayhap he'll believe you, if he won't me; and so I'll get out of this dirty scrape."

"Anything to oblige ye, my sweet and pleasant fellow," rejoined Stubb, and with that he soon mounted to the deck. There a queer scene presented itself. The sailors, in tasselled caps of red worsted, were getting the heavy tackles in readiness for the whales. But they worked rather slow and talked very fast, and seemed in anything but a good humor. All their

noses upwardly projected from their faces like so many jib-
booms. Now and then pairs of them would drop their work,
and run up to the mast-head to get some fresh air. Some
thinking they would catch the plague, dipped oakum in coal-
tar, and at intervals held it to their nostrils. Others having
broken the stems of their pipes almost short off at the bowl,
were vigorously puffing tobacco-smoke, so that it constantly
filled their olfactories.

Stubb was struck by a shower of outcries and anathemas
proceeding from the Captain's round-house abaft; and looking
in that direction saw a fiery face ,thrust from behind the door,
which was held ajar from within. This was the tormented surgeon, who, after in vain remonstrating against the proceedings of the day, had betaken himself to the Captain's round-
house (*cabinet* he called it) to avoid the pest; but still, could
not help yelling out his entreaties and indignations at times.

Marking all this, Stubb argued well for his scheme, and
turning to the Guernsey-man had a little chat with him, during which the stranger mate expressed his detestation of his
Captain as a conceited ignoramus, who had brought them all
into so unsavory and unprofitable a pickle. Sounding him
carefully, Stubb further perceived that the Guernsey-man
had not the slightest suspicion concerning the ambergris.
He therefore held his peace on that head, but otherwise was
quite frank and confidential with him, so that the two quickly
concocted a little plan for both circumventing and satirizing
the Captain, without his at all dreaming of distrusting their
sincerity. According to this little plan of theirs, the Guernsey-
man, under cover of an interpreter's office, was to tell the
Captain what he pleased, but as coming from Stubb; and as
for Stubb, he was to utter any nonsense that should come
uppermost in him during the interview.

By this time their destined victim appeared from his cabin.
He was a small and dark, but rather delicate looking man for
a sea-captain, with large whiskers and moustache, however;
and wore a red cotton velvet vest with watch-seals at his side.
To this gentleman, Stubb was now politely introduced by the
Guernsey-man, who at once ostentatiously put on the aspect
of interpreting between them.

"What shall I say to him first?" said he.

"Why," said Stubb, eyeing the velvet vest and the watch
and seals, "you may as well begin by telling him that he
looks a sort of babyish to me, though I don't pretend to be a
judge."

"He says, Monsieur," said the Guernsey-man, in French, turning to his captain, "that only yesterday his ship spoke a vessel, whose captain and chief-mate, with six sailors, had all died of a fever caught from a blasted whale they had brought alongside."

Upon this the captain started, and eagerly desired to know more.

"What now?" said the Guernsey-man to Stubb.

"Why, since he takes it so easy, tell him that now I have eyed him carefully, I'm quite certain that he's no more fit to command a whale-ship than a St. Jago monkey. In fact, tell him from me he's a baboon."

"He vows and declares, Monsieur, that the other whale, the dried one, is far more deadly than the blasted one; in fine, Monsieur, he conjures us, as we value our lives, to cut loose from these fish."

Instantly the captain ran forward, and in a loud voice commanded his crew to desist from hoisting the cutting-tackles, and at once cast loose the cables and chains confining the whales to the ship.

"What now?" said the Guernsey-man, when the captain had returned to them.

"Why, let me see; yes, you may as well tell him now that—that—in fact, tell him I've diddled him, and (aside to himself) perhaps somebody else."

"He says, Monsieur, that he's very happy to have been of any service to us."

Hearing this, the captain vowed that they were the grateful parties (meaning himself and mate) and concluded by inviting Stubb down into his cabin to drink a bottle of Bordeaux.

"He wants you to take a glass of wine with him," said the interpreter.

"Thank him heartily; but tell him it's against my principles to drink with the man I've diddled. In fact, tell him I must go."

"He says, Monsieur, that his principles won't admit of his drinking; but that if Monsieur wants to live another day to drink, then Monsieur had best drop all four boats, and pull the ship away from these whales, for it's so calm they won't drift."

By this time Stubb was over the side, and getting into his boat, hailed the Guernsey-man to this effect,—that having a long tow-line in his boat, he would do what he could to help them, by pulling out the lighter whale of the two from the ship's side. While the Frenchman's boats, then, were engaged in towing the ship one way, Stubb benevolently towed away at his whale the other way, ostentatiously slacking out a most unusually long tow-line.

Presently a breeze sprang up; Stubb feigned to cast off from the whale; hoisting his boats, the Frenchman soon increased his distance, while the Pequod slid in between him and Stubb's whale. Whereupon Stubb quickly pulled to the floating body, and hailing the Pequod to give notice of his intentions, at once proceeded to reap the fruit of his unrighteous cunning. Seizing his sharp boatspade, he commenced an excavation in the body, a little behind the side fin. You would almost have thought he was digging a cellar there in the sea; and when at length his spade struck against the gaunt ribs, it was like turning up old Roman tiles and pottery buried in fat English loam. His boat's crew were all in high excitement, eagerly helping their chief, and looking as anxious as gold-hunters.

And all the time numberless fowls were diving, and ducking, and screaming, and yelling, and fighting around them. Stubb was beginning to look disappointed, especially as the horrible nosegay increased, when suddenly from out the very heart of this plague, there stole a faint stream of perfume, which flowed through the tide of bad smells without being absorbed by it, as one river will flow into and then along with another, without at all blending with it for a time.

"I have it, I have it," cried Stubb, with delight, striking something in the subterranean regions, "a purse! a purse!"

Dropping his spade, he thrust both hands in, and drew out handfuls of something that looked like ripe Windsor soap, or rich mottled old cheese; very unctuous and savory withal. You might easily dent it with your thumb; it is of a hue between yellow and ash color. And this, good friends, is ambergris, worth a gold guinea an ounce to any druggist. Some six handfuls were obtained; but more was unavoidably lost in the sea, and still more, perhaps, might have been secured were it not for impatient Ahab's loud command to Stubb to desist, and come on board, else the ship would bid them good bye.

AMBERGRIS   XCII

NOW this ambergris is a very curious substance, and so
important as an article of commerce, that in 1791 a certain
Nantucket-born Captain Coffin was examined at the bar of
the English House of Commons on that subject. For at that
time, and indeed until a comparatively late day, the precise
origin of ambergris remained, like amber itself, a problem to
the learned. Though the word ambergris is but the French
compound for grey amber, yet the two substances are quite
distinct. For amber, though at times found on the sea-coast,
is also dug up in some far inland soils, whereas ambergris
is never found except upon the sea. Besides, amber is a hard,
transparent, brittle, odorless substance, used for mouth-pieces
to pipes, for beads and ornaments; but ambergris is soft,
waxy, and so highly fragrant and spicy, that it is largely used
in perfumery, in pastiles, precious candles, hair-powders, and
pomatum. The Turks use it in cooking, and also carry it to
Mecca, for the same purpose that frankincense is carried to
St. Peter's in Rome. Some wine merchants drop a few grains
into claret, to flavor it.

Who would think, then, that such fine ladies and gentlemen should regale themselves with an essence found in the
inglorious bowels of a sick whale! Yet so it is. By some,
ambergris is supposed to be the cause, and by others the
effect, of the dyspepsia in the whale. How to cure such a
dyspepsia it were hard to say, unless by administering three
or four boat loads of Brandreth's pills, and then running out
of harm's way, as laborers do in blasting rocks.

I have forgotten to say that there were found in this
ambergris, certain hard, round, bony plates, which at first
Stubb thought might be sailors' trousers buttons; but it afterwards turned out that they were nothing more than pieces of
small squid bones embalmed in that manner.

Now that the incorruption of this most fragrant ambergris
should be found in the heart of such decay; is this nothing?
Bethink thee of that saying of St. Paul in Corinthians, about
corruption and incorruption; how that we are sown in dishonor, but raised in glory. And likewise call to mind that
saying of Paracelsus about what it is that maketh the best

musk. Also forget not the strange fact that of all things of ill-savor, Cologne-water, in its rudimental manufacturing stages, is the worst.

I should like to conclude the chapter with the above appeal, but cannot, owing to my anxiety to repel a charge often made against whalemen, and which, in the estimation of some already biased minds, might be considered as indirectly substantiated by what has been said of the Frenchman's two whales. Elsewhere in this volume the slanderous aspersion has been disproved, that the vocation of whaling is throughout a slatternly, untidy business. But there is another thing to rebut. They hint that all whales always smell bad. Now how did this odious stigma originate?

I opine, that it is plainly traceable to the first arrival of the Greenland whaling ships in London, more than two centuries ago. Because those whalemen did not then, and do not now, try out their oil at sea as the Southern ships have always done; but cutting up the fresh blubber in small bits, thrust it through the bung holes of large casks, and carry it home in that manner; the shortness of the season in those Icy Seas, and the sudden and violent storms to which they are exposed, forbidding any other course. The consequence is, that upon breaking into the hold, and unloading one of these whale cemeteries, in the Greenland dock, a savor is given forth somewhat similar to that arising from excavating an old city grave-yard, for the foundation of a Lying-in Hospital.

I partly surmise also, that this wicked charge against whalers may be likewise imputed to the existence on the coast of Greenland, in former times, of a Dutch village called Schmerenburgh or Smeerenberg, which latter name is the one used by the learned Fogo Von Slack, in his great work on Smells, a textbook on that subject. As its name imports (smeer, fat; berg, to put up), this village was founded in order to afford a place for the blubber of the Dutch whale fleet to be tried out, without being taken home to Holland for that purpose. It was a collection of furnaces, fat-kettles, and oil sheds; and when the works were in full operation certainly gave forth no very pleasant savor. But all this is quite different with a South Sea Sperm Whaler; which in a voyage of four years perhaps, after completely filling her hold with oil, does not, perhaps, consume fifty days in the business of boiling out; and in the state that it is casked, the oil is nearly scentless. The truth is, that living or dead, if but decently treated, whales as a species are by no means crea-

tures of ill odor; nor can whalemen be recognised, as the
people of the middle ages affected to detect a Jew in the
company, by the nose. Nor indeed can the whale possibly be
otherwise than fragrant, when, as a general thing, he enjoys
such high health; taking abundance of exercise; always out of
doors; though, it is true, seldom in the open air. I say, that
the motion of a Sperm Whale's flukes above water dispenses
a perfume, as when a musk-scented lady rustles her dress in a
warm parlor. What then shall I liken the Sperm Whale to
for fragrance, considering his magnitude? Must it not be to
that famous elephant, with jewelled tusks, and redolent
with myrrh, which was led out of an Indian town to do
honor to Alexander the Great?

THE CASTAWAY   XCIII

IT was but some few days after encountering the Frenchman, that a most significant event befell the most insignificant of the Pequod's crew; an event most lamentable; and
which ended in providing the sometimes madly merry and
predestinated craft with a living and ever accompanying
prophecy of whatever shattered sequel might prove her own.

Now, in the whale ship, it is not every one that goes in the
boats. Some few hands are reserved called ship-keepers, whose
province it is to work the vessel while the boats are pursuing
the whale. As a general thing, these ship-keepers are as hardy
fellows as the men comprising the boats' crew. But if there
happen to be an unduly slender, clumsy, or timorous wight
in the ship, that wight is certain to be made a ship-keeper.
It was so in the Pequod with the little negro Pippin by nick-
name, Pip by abbreviation. Poor Pip! ye have heard of him
before; ye must remember his tambourine on that dramatic
midnight, so gloomy-jolly.

In outer aspect, Pip and Dough-Boy made a match, like a
black pony and a white one, of equal developments, though
of dissimilar color, driven in one eccentric span. But while
hapless Dough-Boy was by nature dull and torpid in his in-
tellects, Pip, though over tender-hearted, was at bottom very
bright, with that pleasant, genial, jolly brightness peculiar to
his tribe; a tribe, which ever enjoy all holidays and festivities
with finer, freer relish than any other race. For blacks, the

year's calendar should show naught but three hundred and sixty-five Fourth of Julys and New Year's Days. Nor smile so, while I write that this little black was brilliant, for even blackness has its brilliancy; behold yon lustrous ebony, panelled in king's cabinets. But Pip loved life, and all life's peaceable securities; so that the panic-striking business in which he had somehow unaccountably become entrapped, had most sadly blurred his brightness; though, as ere long will be seen, what was thus temporarily subdued in him, in the end was destined to be luridly illumined by strange wild fires, that fictitiously showed him off to ten times the natural lustre with which in his native Tolland County in Connecticut, he had once enlivened many a fiddler's frolic on the green; and at medodious even-tide, with his gay ha-ha! had turned the round horizon into one star-belled tambourine. So, though in the clear air of day, suspended against a blue-veined neck, the pure-watered diamond drop will healthful glow; yet, when the cunning jeweler would show you the diamond in its most impressive lustre, he lays it against a gloomy ground, and then lights it up, not by the sun, but by some unnatural gases. Then come out those fiery effulgences, infernally superb; then the evil-blazing diamond, once the divinest symbol of the crystal skies, looks like some crown-jewel stolen from the King of Hell. But let us to the story.

It came to pass, that in the ambergris affair Stubb's after-oarsman chanced so to sprain his hand, as for a time to become quite maimed; and, temporarily, Pip was put into his place.

The first time Stubb lowered with him, Pip evinced much nervousness; but happily, for that time, escaped close contact with the whale; and therefore came off not altogether discreditably; though Stubb observing him, took care, afterwards, to exhort him to cherish his courageousness to the utmost, for he might often find it needful.

Now upon the second lowering, the boat paddled upon the whale; and as the fish received the darted iron, it gave its customary rap, which happened, in this instance, to be right under poor Pip's seat. The involuntary consternation of the moment caused him to leap, paddle in hand, out of the boat; and in such a way, that part of the slack whale line coming against his chest, he breasted it overboard with him, so as to become entangled in it, when at last plumping into the water. That instant the stricken whale started on a fierce run, the line swiftly straightened; and presto! poor Pip came all foaming up to the chocks of the boat, remorsely dragged there by the line, which had taken several turns around his chest and neck.

Tashtego stood in the bows. He was full of the fire of the hunt. He hated Pip for a poltroon. Snatching the boat-knife from its sheath, he suspended its sharp edge over the line, and turning towards Stubb, exclaimed interrogatively, "Cut?" Meantime Pip's blue, choked face plainly looked, Do, for God's sake! All passed in a flash. In less than half a minute, this entire thing happened.

"Damn him, cut!" roared Stubb; and so the whale was lost and Pip was saved.

So soon as he recovered himself, the poor little negro was assailed by yells and execrations from the crew. Tranquilly permitting these irregular cursings to evaporate, Stubb then in a plain, business-like, but still half humorous manner, cursed Pip officially; and that done, unofficially gave him much wholesome advice. The substance was, Never jump from a boat, Pip, except—but all the rest was indefinite, as the soundest advice ever is. Now, in general, *Stick to the boat,* is your true motto in whaling; but cases will sometimes happen when *Leap from the boat,* is still better. Moreover, as if perceiving at last that if he should give undiluted conscientious advice to Pip, he would be leaving him too wide a margin to jump in for the future; Stubb suddenly dropped all advice, and concluded with a peremptory command, "Stick to the boat, Pip, or by the Lord, I won't pick you up if you jump; mind that. We can't afford to lose whales by the likes of you; a whale would sell for thirty times what you would, Pip, in Alabama. Bear that in mind, and don't jump any more." Hereby perhaps Stubb indirectly hinted, that though man loved his fellow, yet man is a money-making animal, which propensity too often interferes with his benevolence.

But we are all in the hands of the Gods; and Pip jumped again. It was under very similar circumstances to the first performance; but this time he did not breast out the line; and hence, when the whale started to run, Pip was left behind on the sea, like a hurried traveller's trunk. Alas! Stubb was but too true to his word. It was a beautiful, bounteous, blue day; the spangled sea calm and cool, and flatly stretching away, all round, to the horizon, like gold-beater's skin hammered out to the extremest. Bobbing up and down in the sea,

Pip's ebon head showed like a head of cloves. No boat-knife was lifted when he fell so rapidly astern. Stubb's inexorable back was turned upon him; and the whale was winged. In three minutes, a whole mile of shoreless ocean was between Pip and Stubb. Out from the centre of the sea, poor Pip turned his crisp, curling, black head to the sun, another lonely castaway, though the loftiest and the brightest.

Now, in calm weather, to swim in the open ocean is as easy to the practised swimmer as to ride in a spring-carriage ashore. But the awful lonesomeness is intolerable. The intense concentration of self in the middle of such a heartless immensity, my God! who can tell it? Mark, how when sailors in a dead calm bathe in the open sea—mark how closely they hug their ship and only coast along her sides.

But had Stubb really abandoned the poor little negro to his fate? No; he did not mean to, at least. Because there were two boats in his wake, and he supposed, no doubt, that they would of course come up to Pip very quickly, and pick him up; though, indeed, such considerations towards oarsmen jeopardized through their own timidity, is not always manifested by the hunters in all similar instances; and such instances not unfrequently occur; almost invariably in the fishery, a coward, so called, is marked with the same ruthless detestation peculiar to military navies and armies.

But it so happened, that those boats, without seeing Pip, suddenly spying whales close to them on one side, turned, and gave chase; and Stubb's boat was now so far away, and he and all his crew so intent upon his fish, that Pip's ringed horizon began to expand around him miserably. By the merest chance the ship itself at last rescued him; but from that hour the little negro went about the deck an idiot; such, at least, they said he was. The sea had jeeringly kept his finite body up, but drowned the infinite of his soul. Not drowned entirely, though. Rather carried down alive to wondrous depths, where strange shapes of the unwarped primal world glided to and fro before his passive eyes; and the miser-merman, Wisdom, revealed his hoarded heaps; and among the joyous, heartless, ever-juvenile eternities, Pip saw the multitudinous, God-omnipresent, coral insects, that out of the firmament of waters heaved the colossal orbs. He saw God's foot upon the treadle of the loom, and spoke it; and therefore his shipmates called him mad. So man's insanity is heaven's sense; and wandering from all mortal reason, man comes at last to that celestial thought, which, to reason, is absurd and frantic; and weal or woe, feels then uncompromised, indifferent as his God.

For the rest, blame not Stubb too hardly. The thing is common in that fishery; and in the sequel of the narrative, it will then be seen what like abandonment befell myself.

A SQUEEZE OF THE HAND   XCIV

THAT whale of Stubb's so dearly purchased, was duly brought to the Pequod's side, where all those cutting and hoisting operations previously detailed, were regularly gone through, even to the baling of the Heidelburgh Tun, or Case.

While some were occupied with this latter duty, others were employed in dragging away the larger tubs, so soon as filled with the sperm; and when the proper time arrived, this same sperm was carefully manipulated ere going to the try-works, of which anon.

It had cooled and crystallized to such a degree, that when, with several others, I sat down before a large Constantine's bath of it, I found it strangely concreted into lumps, here and there rolling about in the liquid part. It was our business to squeeze these lumps back into fluid. A sweet and unctuous duty! No wonder that in old times this sperm was such a favorite cosmetic. Such a clearer! such a sweetener! such a softener! such a delicious mollifier! After having my hands in it for only a few minutes, my fingers felt like eels, and began, as it were, to serpentine and spiralize.

As I sat there at my ease, cross-legged on the deck; after the bitter exertion at the windlass; under a blue tranquil sky; the ship under indolent sail, and gliding so serenely along; as I bathed my hands among those soft, gentle globules of infiltrated tissues, woven almost within the hour; as they richly broke to my fingers, and discharged all their opulence, like fully ripe grapes their wine; as I snuffed up that uncontaminated aroma,—literally and truly, like the smell of spring violets; I declare to you, that for the time I lived as in a musky meadow; I forgot all about our horrible oath; in that inexpressible sperm, I washed my hands and my heart of it; I almost began to credit the old Paracelsan superstition that sperm is of rare virtue in allaying the heat of anger: while bathing in that bath, I felt divinely free from all ill-will, or petulance, or malice, of any sort whatsoever.

Squeeze! squeeze! squeeze! all the morning long; I squeezed that sperm till I myself almost melted into it; I squeezed that sperm till a strange sort of insanity came over me; and I found myself unwittingly squeezing my co-laborers' hands in it, mistaking their hands for the gentle globules. Such an abounding, affectionate, friendly, loving feeling did this avocation beget; that at last I was continually squeezing their hands, and looking up into their eyes sentimentally; as much as to say,—Oh! my dear fellow beings, why should we longer cherish any social acerbities, or know the slightest ill-humor or envy! Come; let us squeeze hands all round; nay, let us all squeeze ourselves into each other; let us squeeze ourselves universally into the very milk and sperm of kindness.

Would that I could keep squeezing that sperm for ever! For now, since by many prolonged, repeated experiences, I have perceived that in all cases man must eventually lower, or at least shift, his conceit of attainable felicity; not placing it anywhere in the intellect or the fancy; but in the wife, the heart, the bed, the table, the saddle, the fire-side, the country; now that I have perceived all this, I am ready to squeeze case eternally. In thoughts of the visions of the night, I saw long rows of angels in paradise, each with his hands in a jar of spermaceti.

* * * * *

Now, while discoursing of sperm, it behooves to speak of other things akin to it, in the business of preparing the sperm whale for the try-works.

First comes white-horse, so called, which is obtained from the tapering part of the fish, and also from the thicker portions of his flukes. It is tough with congealed tendons—a wad of muscle—but still contains some oil. After being severed from the whale, the white-horse is first cut into portable oblongs ere going to the mincer. They look much like blocks of Berkshire marble.

Plum-pudding is the term bestowed upon certain fragmentary parts of the whale's flesh, here and there adhering to the blanket of blubber, and often participating to a considerable degree in its unctuousness. It is a most refreshing, convivial, beautiful object to behold. As its name imports, it is of an exceedingly rich, mottled tint, with a bestreaked snowy and golden ground, dotted with spots of the deepest crimson and purple. It is plums of rubies, in pictures of citron. Spite of reason, it is hard to keep yourself from eating it. I confess, that once I stole behind the foremast to try it. It tasted something as I should conceive a royal cutlet from the thigh of Louis le Gros might have tasted, supposing him to have been killed the first day after the venison season, and that particular venison season contemporary with an unusually fine vintage of the vineyards of Champagne.

There is another substance, and a very singular one, which turns up in the course of this business, but which I feel it to be very puzzling adequately to describe. It is called slobgollion; an appellation original with the whalemen, and even so is the nature of the substance. It is an ineffably, oozy, stringy affair, most frequently found in the tubs of sperm, after a prolonged squeezing, and subsequent decanting. I hold it to be the wondrously thin, ruptured membranes of the case, coalescing.

Gurry, so called, is a term properly belonging to right whalemen, but sometimes incidentally used by the sperm fishermen. It designates the dark, glutinous substance which is scraped off the back of the Greenland or right whale, and much of which covers the decks of those inferior souls who hunt that ignoble Leviathan.

Nippers. Strictly this word is not indigenous to the whale's vocabulary. But as applied by whalemen, it becomes so. A whaleman's nipper is a short firm strip of tendinous stuff cut from the tapering part of Leviathan's tail: it averages an inch in thickness, and for the rest, is about the size of the iron part of a hoe. Edgewise moved along the oily deck, it operates like a leathern squilgee; and by nameless blandishments, as of magic, allures along with it all impurities.

But to learn all about these recondite matters, your best way is at once to descend into the blubber-room, and have a long talk with its inmates. This place has previously been mentioned as the receptacle for the blanket-pieces, when stript and hoisted from the whale. When the proper time arrives for cutting up its contents, this apartment is a scene of terror to all tyros, especially by night. On each side, lit by a dull lantern, a space has been left clear for the workmen. They generally go in pairs,—a pike-and-gaff-man and a spademan. The whaling-pike is similar to a frigate's boarding-weapon of the same name. The gaff is something like a boathook. With his gaff, the gaffman hooks on to a sheet of blubber, and strives to hold it from slipping, as the ship pitches and lurches about. Meanwhile, the spade-man stands on the sheet itself, perpendicularly chopping it into the portable horse-pieces. This spade is sharp as hone can make it; the spade-man's feet are shoeless; the thing he stands on will sometimes irresistibly slide away from him, like a sledge. If he cuts off one of his own toes, or one of his assistants', would you be very much astonished? Toes are scarce among veteran blubber-room men.

THE CASSOCK   XCV

HAD you stepped on board the Pequod at a certain juncture of this post-mortemizing of the whale; and had you strolled forward nigh the windlass, pretty sure am I that you would have scanned with no small curiosity a very strange, enigmatical object, which you would have seen there, lying along lengthwise in the lee scuppers. Not the wondrous cistern in the whale's huge head; not the prodigy of his unhinged lower jaw; not the miracle of his symmetrical tail; none of these would so surprise you, as half a glimpse of that unaccountable cone,—longer than a Kentuckian is tall, nigh a foot in diameter at the base, and jet-black as Yojo, the ebony idol of Queequeg. And an idol, indeed, it is; or, rather, in old times, its likeness was. Such an idol as that found in the secret groves of Queen Maachah in Judea; and for worshipping which, king Asa, her son, did depose her, and destroyed the idol, and burnt it for an abomination at the brook Kedron, as darkly set forth in the 15th chapter of the first book of Kings.

Look at the sailor, called the mincer, who now comes along, and assisted by two allies, heavily backs the grandissimus, as the mariners call it, and with bowed shoulders, staggers off with it, as if he were a grenadier carrying a dead comrade from the field. Extending it upon the forecastle deck, he now proceeds cylindrically to remove its dark pelt, as an African hunter the pelt of a boa. This done he turns the pelt inside out, like a pantaloon leg; gives it a good stretching, so as almost to double its diameter; and at last hangs it, well spread, in the rigging, to dry. Ere long, it is taken down; when removing some three feet of it, towards

the pointed extremity, and then cutting two slits for arm-
holes at the other end, he lengthwise slips himself bodily into
it. The mincer now stands before you invested in the full
canonicals of his calling. Immemorial to all his order, this investiture alone will adequately protect him, while employed
in the peculiar functions of his office.

That office consists in mincing the horse-pieces of blubber
for the pots; an operation which is conducted at a curious
wooden horse, planted endwise against the bulwarks, and
with a capacious tub beneath it, into which the minced pieces
drop, fast as the sheets from a rapt orator's desk. Arrayed in
decent black; occupying a conspicuous pulpit; intent on
bible leaves; what a candidate for an archbishoprick, what a
lad for a Pope were this mincer!*

THE TRY-WORKS   XCVI

BESIDES her hoisted boats, an American whaler is out-
wardly distinguished by her try-works. She presents the curious anomaly of the most solid masonry joining with oak
and hemp in constituting the completed ship. It is as if from
the open field a brick-kiln were transported to her planks.

The try-works are planted between the foremast and main-
mast, the most roomy part of the deck. The timbers beneath
are of a peculiar strength, fitted to sustain the weight of an
almost solid mass of brick and mortar, some ten feet by eight
square, and five in height. The foundation does not penetrate
the deck, but the masonry is firmly secured to the surface
by ponderous knees of iron bracing it on all sides, and screwing it down to the timbers. On the flanks it is cased with
wood, and at top completely covered by a large, sloping, bat-
tened hatchway. Removing this hatch we expose the great
try-pots, two in number, and each of several barrels' capacity.
When not in use, they are kept remarkably clean. Sometimes
they are polished with soapstone and sand, till they shine
within like silver punchbowls. During the night-watches some

---

* Bible leaves! Bible leaves! This is the invariable cry from
the mates to the mincer. It enjoins him to be careful, and cut his
work into as thin slices as possible, inasmuch as by so doing
the business of boiling out the oil is much accelerated, and its
quantity considerably increased, besides perhaps improving it in
quality.

cynical old sailors will crawl into them and coil themselves
away there for a nap. While employed in polishing them—
one man in each pot, side by side—many confidential communications are carried on, over the iron lips. It is a place
also for profound mathematical meditation. It was in the
left hand try-pot of the Pequod, with the soapstone diligently circling round me, that I was first indirectly struck by
the remarkable fact, that in geometry all bodies gliding along
the cycloid, my soapstone for example, will descend from
any point in precisely the same time.

Removing the fire-board from the front of the try-works,
the bare masonry of that side is exposed, penetrated by the
two iron mouths of the furnaces, directly underneath the
pots. These mouths are fitted with heavy doors of iron. The
intense heat of the fire is prevented from communicating itself to the deck, by means of a shallow reservoir extending
under the entire inclosed surface of the works. By a tunnel
inserted at the rear, this reservoir is kept replenished with
water as fast as it evaporates. There are no external chimneys; they open direct from the rear wall. And here let us go
back for a moment.

It was about nine o'clock at night that the Pequod's try-
works were first started on this present voyage. It belonged to
Stubb to oversee the business.

"All ready there? Off hatch, then, and start her. You cook,
fire the works." This was an easy thing, for the carpenter had
been thrusting his shavings into the furnace throughout the
passage. Here be it said that in a whaling voyage the first
fire in the try-works has to be fed for a time with wood.
After that no wood is used, except as a means of quick igni-
tion to the staple fuel. In a word, after being tried out, the
crisp, shrivelled blubber, now called scraps or fritters, still
contains considerable of its unctuous properties. These fritters feed the flames. Like a plethoric burning martyr, or a
self-consuming misanthrope, once ignited, the whale supplies
his own fuel and burns by his own body. Would that he consumed his own smoke! for his smoke is horrible to inhale,
and inhale it you must, and not only that, but you must live
in it for the time. It has an unspeakable, wild, Hindoo odor
about it, such as may lurk in the vicinity of funereal pyres.
It smells like the left wing of the day of judgment; it is an
argument for the pit.

By midnight the works were in full operation. We were
clear from the carcase; sail had been made; the wind was

freshening; the wild ocean darkness was intense. But that darkness was licked up by the fierce flames, which at intervals forked forth from the sooty flues, and illuminated every lofty rope in the rigging, as with the famed Greek fire. The burning ship drove on, as if remorselessly commissioned to some vengeful deed. So the pitch and sulphur-freighted brigs of the bold Hydriote, Canaris, issuing from their midnight harbors, with broad sheets of flame for sails, bore down upon the Turkish frigates, and folded them in conflagrations.

The hatch, removed from the top of the works, now afforded a wide hearth in front of them. Standing on this were the Tartarean shapes of the pagan harpooneers, always the whaleship's stokers. With huge pronged poles they pitched hissing masses of blubber into the scalding pots, or stirred up the fires beneath, till the snaky flames darted, curling, out of the doors to catch them by the feet. The smoke rolled away in sullen heaps. To every pitch of the ship there was a pitch of the boiling oil, which seemed all eagerness to leap into their faces. Opposite the mouth of the works, on the further side of the wide wooden hearth, was the windlass. This served for a sea-sofa. Here lounged the watch, when not otherwise employed, looking into the red heat of the fire, till their eyes felt scorched in their heads. Their tawny features, now all begrimed with smoke and sweat, their matted beards, and the contrasting barbaric brilliancy of their teeth, all these were strangely revealed in the capricious emblazonings of the works. As they narrated to each other their unholy adventures, their tales of terror told in words of mirth; as their uncivilized laughter forked upwards out of them, like the flames from the furnace; as to and fro, in their front, the harpooneers wildly gesticulated with their huge pronged forks and dippers; as the wind howled on, and the sea leaped, and the ship groaned and dived, and yet steadfastly shot her red hell further and further into the blackness of the sea and the night, and scornfully champed the white bone in her mouth, and viciously spat round her on all sides; then the rushing Pequod, freighted with savages, and laden with fire, and burning a corpse, and plunging into that blackness of darkness, seemed the material counterpart of her monomaniac commander's soul.

So seemed it to me, as I stood at her helm, and for long hours silently guided the way of this fire-ship on the sea. Wrapped, for that interval, in darkness myself, I but the better saw the redness, the madness, the ghastliness of others.

The continual sight of the fiend shapes before me, capering half in smoke and half in fire, these at last begat kindred visions in my soul, so soon as I began to yield to that unaccountable drowsiness which ever would come over me at a midnight helm.

But that night, in particular, a strange (and ever since inexplicable) thing occurred to me. Starting from a brief standing sleep, I was horribly conscious of something fatally wrong. The jaw-bone tiller smote my side, which leaned against it; in my ears was the low hum of sails, just beginning to shake in the wind; I thought my eyes were open; I was half conscious of putting my fingers to the lids and mechanically stretching them still further apart. But, spite of all this, I could see no compass before me to steer by; though it seemed but a minute since I had been watching the card, by the steady binnacle lamp illuminating it. Nothing seemed before me but a jet gloom, now and then made ghastly by flashes of redness. Uppermost was the impression, that whatever swift, rushing thing I stood on was not so much bound to any haven ahead as rushing from all havens astern. A stark, bewildered feeling, as of death, came over me. Convulsively my hand grasped the tiller, but with the crazy conceit that the tiller was, somehow, in some enchanted way, inverted. My God! what is the matter with me? thought I. Lo! in my brief sleep I had turned myself about, and was fronting the ship's stern, with my back to her prow and the compass. In an instant I faced back, just in time to prevent the vessel from flying up into the wind, and very probably capsizing her. How glad and how grateful the relief from this unnatural hallucination of the night, and the fatal contingency of being brought by the lee!

Look not too long in the face of the fire, O man! Never dream with thy hand on the helm! Turn not thy back to the compass; accept the first hint of the hitching tiller; believe not the artificial fire, when its redness makes all things look ghastly. To-morrow, in the natural sun, the skies will be bright; those who glared like devils in the forking flames, the morn will show in far other, at least gentler, relief; the glorious, golden, glad sun, the only true lamp—all others but liars!

Nevertheless the sun hides not Virginia's Dismal Swamp, nor Rome's accursed Campagna, nor wide Sahara, nor all the millions of miles of deserts and of griefs beneath the moon. The sun hides not the ocean, which is the dark side of this earth, and which is two thirds of this earth. So, therefore, that mortal man who hath more of joy than sorrow in him, that mortal man cannot be true—not true, or undeveloped. With books the same. The truest of all men was the Man of Sorrows, and the truest of all books is Solomon's, and Ecclesiastes is the fine hammered steel of woe. "All is vanity." ALL. This wilful world hath not got hold of unchristian Solomon's wisdom yet. But he who dodges hospitals and jails, and walks fast crossing graveyards, and would rather talk of operas than hell; calls Cowper, Young, Pascal, Rousseau, poor devils all of sick men; and throughout a care-free lifetime swears by Rabelais as passing wise, and therefore jolly;—not that man is fitted to sit down on tomb-stones, and break the green damp mould with unfathomably wondrous Solomon.

But even Solomon, he says, "the man that wandereth out of the way of understanding shall remain" (*i.e.* even while living) "in the congregation of the dead." Give not thyself up, then, to fire, lest it invert thee, deaden thee; as for the time it did me. There is a wisdom that is woe; but there is a woe that is madness. And there is a Catskill eagle in some souls that can alike dive down into the blackest gorges, and soar out of them again and become invisible in the sunny spaces. And even if he for ever flies within the gorge, that gorge is in the mountains; so that even in his lowest swoop the mountain eagle is still higher than other birds upon the plain, even though they soar.

THE LAMP   XCVII

HAD you descended from the Pequod's try-works to the Pequod's forecastle, where the off duty watch were sleeping, for one single moment you would have almost thought you were standing in some illuminated shrine of canonized kings and counsellors. There they lay in their triangular oaken vaults, each mariner a chiselled muteness; a score of lamps flashing upon his hooded eyes.

In merchantmen, oil for the sailor is more scarce than the milk of queens. To dress in the dark, and eat in the dark, and stumble in darkness to his pallet, this is his usual lot. But the whaleman, as he seeks the food of light, so he lives in light. He makes his berth an Aladdin's lamp, and lays him down in it; so that in the pitchiest night the ship's black hull still houses an illumination.

See with what entire freedom the whaleman takes his handful of lamps—often but old bottles and vials, though—to the copper cooler at the try-works, and replenishes them there, as mugs of ale at a vat. He burns, too, the purest of oil, in its unmanufactured, and, therefore, unvitiated state; a fluid unknown to solar, lunar, or astral contrivances ashore. It is sweet as early grass butter in April. He goes and hunts for his oil, so as to be sure of its freshness and genuineness, even as the traveller on the prairie hunts up his own supper of game.

STOWING DOWN AND CLEARING UP   XCVIII

ALREADY has it been related how the great leviathan is afar off descried from the mast-head; how he is chased over the watery moors, and slaughtered in the valleys of the deep; how he is then towed alongside and beheaded; and how (on the principle which entitled the headsman of old to the garments in which the beheaded was killed) his great padded surtout becomes the property of his executioner; how, in due time, he is condemned to the pots, and, like Shadrach, Meshach, and Abednego, his spermaceti, oil, and bone pass unscathed through the fire;—but now it remains to conclude the last chapter of this part of the description by rehearsing—singing, if I may—the romantic proceeding of decanting off his oil into the casks and striking them down into the hold, where once again leviathan returns to his native profundities, sliding along beneath the surface as before; but, alas! never more to rise and blow.

While still warm, the oil, like hot punch, is received into the six-barrel casks; and while, perhaps, the ship is pitching and rolling this way and that in the midnight sea, the enormous casks are slewed round and headed over, end for end, and sometimes perilously scoot across the slippery deck, like so many land slides, till at last man-handled and stayed in their course; and all round the hoops, rap, rap, go as many hammers as can play upon them, for now, *ex officio*, every sailor is a cooper.

At length, when the last pint is casked, and all is cool, then the great hatchways are unsealed, the bowels of the ship are thrown open, and down go the casks to their final rest in the sea. This done, the hatches are replaced, and hermetically closed, like a closet walled up.

In the sperm fishery, this is perhaps one of the most remarkable incidents in all the business of whaling. One day the planks stream with freshets of blood and oil; on the sacred quarter-deck enormous masses of the whale's head are profanely piled; great rusty casks lie about, as in a brewery yard; the smoke from the try-works has besooted all the bulwarks; the mariners go about suffused with unctuousness; the entire ship seems great leviathan himself; while on all hands the din is deafening.

But a day or two after, you look about you, and prick your ears in this self-same ship; and were it not for the tell-tale boats and try-works, you would all but swear you trod some silent merchant vessel, with a most scrupulously neat commander. The unmanufactured sperm oil possesses a singularly cleansing virtue. This is the reason why the decks never look so white as just after what they call an affair of oil. Besides, from the ashes of the burned scraps of the whale, a potent ley is readily made; and whenever any adhesiveness from the back of the whale remains clinging to the side, that ley quickly exterminates it. Hands go diligently along the bulwarks, and with buckets of water and rags restore them to their full tidiness. The soot is brushed from the lower rigging. All the numerous implements which have been in use are likewise faithfully cleansed and put away. The great hatch is scrubbed and placed upon the try-works, completely hiding the pots; every cask is out of sight; all tackles are coiled in unseen nooks; and when by the combined and simultaneous industry of almost the entire ship's company, the whole of this conscientious duty is at last concluded, then the crew themselves proceed to their own ablutions; shift themselves from top to toe; and finally issue to the immaculate deck, fresh and all aglow, as bridegrooms new-leaped from out the daintiest Holland.

Now, with elated step, they pace the planks in twos and threes, and humorously discourse of parlors, sofas, carpets, and fine cambrics; propose to mat the deck; think of having hangings to the top; object not to taking tea by moonlight on the piazza of the forecastle. To hint to such musked mariners of oil, and bone, and blubber, were little short of audacity. They know not the thing you distantly allude to. Away, and bring us napkins!

But mark; aloft there, at the three mast-heads, stand three men intent on spying out more whales, which, if caught, infallibly will again soil the old oaken furniture, and drop at least one small grease-spot somewhere. Yes; and many is the time, when, after the severest uninterrupted labors, which know no night; continuing straight through for ninety-six hours; when from the boat, where they have swelled their wrists with all day rowing on the Line,—they only step to the deck to carry vast chains, and heave the heavy windlass, and cut the slash, yea, and in their very sweatings to be smoked and burned anew by the combined fires of the equatorial sun and the equatorial try-works; when, on the heel of all this, they have finally bestirred themselves to cleanse the ship, and make a spotless dairy room of it; many is the time the poor fellows, just buttoning the necks of their clean frocks, are startled by the cry of "There she blows!" and away they fly to fight another whale, and go through the whole weary thing again. Oh! my friends, but this is man-killing! Yet this is life. For hardly have we mortals by long toilings extracted from this world's vast bulk its small but valuable sperm; and then, with weary patience, cleansed ourselves from its defilements, and learned to live here in clean tabernacles of the soul; hardly is this done, when—*There she blows!*—the ghost is spouted up, and away we sail to fight some other world, and go through young life's old routine again.

Oh! the metempsychosis! Oh! Pythagoras, that in bright Greece, two thousand years ago, did die, so good, so wise, so mild; I sailed with thee along the Peruvian coast last voyage—and, foolish as I am, taught thee, a green simple boy, how to splice a rope!

THE DOUBLOON   XCIX

ERE now it has been related how Ahab was wont to pace his quarter-deck, taking regular turns at either limit, the binnacle and mainmast; but in the multiplicity of other things requiring narration it has not been added how that sometimes in these walks, when most plunged in his mood, he was wont to pause in turn at each spot, and stand there strangely eyeing the particular object before him. When he halted before the binnacle, with his glance fastened on the pointed needle in the compass, that glance shot like a javelin with the pointed intensity of his purpose; and when resuming his walk he again paused before the mainmast, then, as the same riveted glance fastened upon the riveted gold coin there, he still wore the same aspect of nailed firmness, only dashed with a certain wild longing, if not hopefulness.

But one morning, turning to pass the doubloon, he seemed to be newly attracted by the strange figures and inscriptions stamped on it, as though now for the first time beginning to interpret for himself in some monomaniac way whatever significance might lurk in them. And some certain significance lurks in all things, else all things are little worth, and the round world itself but an empty cipher, except to sell by the cartload, as they do hills about Boston, to fill up some morass in the Milky Way.

Now this doubloon was of purest, virgin gold, raked somewhere out of the heart of gorgeous hills, whence, east and west, over golden sands, the head-waters of many a Pactolus flows. And though now nailed amidst all the rustiness of iron bolts and the verdigris of copper spikes, yet, untouchable and immaculate to any foulness, it still preserved its Quito glow. Nor, though placed amongst a ruthless crew and every hour passed by ruthless hands, and through the live-long nights shrouded with thick darkness which might cover any pilfering approach, nevertheless every sunrise found the doubloon where the sunset left it last. For it was set apart and sanctified to one awe-striking end; and however wanton in their sailor ways, one and all, the mariners revered it as the white whale's talisman. Sometimes they talked it over in the weary watch by night, wondering whose it was to be at last, and whether he would ever live to spend it.

Now those noble golden coins of South America are as medals of the sun and tropic token-pieces. Here palms, alpacas, and volcanoes; sun's disks and stars; ecliptics, horns-of-plenty, and rich banners waving, are in luxuriant profusion stamped; so that the precious gold seems almost to derive an added preciousness and enhancing glories, by passing through those fancy mints, so Spanishly poetic.

It so chanced that the doubloon of the Pequod was a most wealthy example of these things. On its round border it bore the letters, REPUBLICA DEL ECUADOR: QUITO. So this bright coin came from a country planted in the middle of the world, and beneath the great equator, and named after it; and it had been cast midway up the Andes, in the unwaning clime that knows no autumn. Zoned by those letters you saw the likeness of three Andes' summits; from one a flame; a tower on another; on the third a crowing cock; while arching over all was a segment of the partitioned zodiac, the signs all marked with their usual cabalistics, and the keystone sun entering the equinoctial point at Libra.

Before this equatorial coin, Ahab, not unobserved by others, was now pausing.

"There's something ever egotistical in mountain-tops and towers, and all other grand and lofty things; look here,— three peaks as proud as Lucifer. The firm tower, that is Ahab; the volcano, that is Ahab; the courageous, the undaunted, and victorious fowl, that, too, is Ahab; all are Ahab; and this round gold is but the image of the rounder globe, which, like a magician's glass, to each and every man in turn but mirrors back his own mysterious self. Great pains, small gains for those who ask the world to solve them; it cannot solve itself. Methinks now this coined sun wears a ruddy face; but see! aye, he enters the sign of storms, the equinox! and but six months before he wheeled out of a former equinox at Aries! From storm to storm! So be it, then. Born in throes, 't is fit that man should live in pains and die in pangs! So be it, then! Here's stout stuff for woe to work on. So be it, then."

"No fairy fingers can have pressed the gold, but devil's claws must have left their mouldings there since yesterday," murmured Starbuck to himself, leaning against the bulwarks. "The old man seems to read Belshazzar's awful writing. I have never marked the coin inspectingly. He goes below; let me read. A dark valley between three mighty, heaven-abiding peaks, that almost seem the Trinity, in some faint earthly symbol. So in this vale of Death, God girds us round; and over all our gloom, the sun of Righteousness still shines a beacon and a hope. If we bend down our eyes, the dark vale shows her mouldy soil; but if we lift them, the bright sun meets our glance half way, to cheer. Yet, oh, the great sun is no fixture; and if, at midnight, we would fain snatch some sweet solace from him, we gaze for him in vain! This coin speaks wisely, mildly, truly, but still sadly to me. I will quit it, lest Truth shake me falsely."

"There now's the old Mogul," soliloquized Stubb by the try-works, "he's been twigging it; and there goes Starbuck from the same, and both with faces which I should say might be somewhere within nine fathoms long. And all from looking at a piece of gold, which did I have it now on Negro Hill or in Corlaer's Hook, I'd not look at it very long ere spending it. Humph! in my poor, insignificant opinion, I regard this as queer. I have seen doubloons before in my voyagings; your doubloons of old Spain, your doubloons of Peru, your doubloons of Chili, your doubloons of Bolivia, your doubloons of Popayan; with plenty of gold moidores and pistoles, and joes, and half joes, and quarter joes. What then should there be in this doubloon of the Equator that is so killing wonderful? By Golconda! let me read it once. Halloa! here's signs and wonders truly! That, now, is what old Bowditch in his Epitome calls the zodiac, and what my almanack below calls ditto. I'll get the almanack and as I have heard devils can be raised with Daboll's arithmetic, I'll try my hand at raising a meaning out of these queer curvicues here with the Massachusetts calendar. Here's the book. Let's see now. Signs and wonders; and the sun, he's always among 'em. Hem, hem, hem; here they are—here they go—all alive:— Aries, or the Ram; Taurus, or the Bull and Jimimi! here's Gemini himself, or the Twins. Well; the sun he wheels among 'em. Aye, here on the coin he's just crossing the threshold between two of twelve sitting-rooms all in a ring. Book! you lie there; the fact is, you books must know your places. You'll do to give us the bare words and facts, but we come in to supply the thoughts. That's my small experience, so far as the Massachusetts calendar, and Bowditch's navigator, and Daboll's arithmetic go. Signs and wonders, eh? Pity if there is nothing wonderful in signs, and significant in wonders! There's a clue somewhere; wait a bit; hist—hark! By Jove, I have it! Look you, Doubloon, your zodiac here is the life of man in one round chapter; and now I'll read it off, straight out of the book. Come, Almanack! To begin: there's Aries, or the Ram—lecherous dog, he begets us; then, Taurus, or the Bull—he bumps us the first thing; then Gemini, or the Twins—that is, Virtue and

Vice: we try to reach Virtue, when lo! comes Cancer the Crab, and drags us back; and here, going from Virtue, Leo, a roaring Lion, lies in the path—he gives a few fierce bites and surly dabs with his paw; we escape, and hail Virgo, the Virgin! that's our first love; we marry and think to be happy for aye, when pop comes Libra, or the Scales—happiness weighed and found wanting; and while we are very sad about that, Lord! how we suddenly jump, as Scorpio, or the Scorpion, stings us in rear; we are curing the wound, when whang come the arrows all round; Sagittarius, or the Archer, is amusing himself. As we pluck out the shafts, stand aside! here's the battering-ram, Capricornus, or the Goat; full tilt, he comes rushing, and headlong we are tossed; when Aquarius, or the Water-bearer, pours out his whole deluge and drowns us; and to wind up with Pisces, or the Fishes, we sleep. There's a sermon now, writ in high heaven, and the sun goes through it every year, and yet comes out of it all alive and hearty. Jollily he, aloft there, wheels through toil and trouble; and so, alow here, does jolly Stubb. Oh, jolly's the word for aye! Adieu, Doubloon! But stop; here comes little King-Post; dodge round the try-works, now, and let's hear what he'll have to say. There; he's before it; he'll out with something presently. So, so; he's beginning."

"I see nothing here, but a round thing made of gold, and whoever raises a certain whale, this round thing belongs to him. So, what's all this staring been about? It's worth sixteen dollars, that's true; and at two cents the cigar, that's nine hundred and sixty cigars. I won't smoke dirty pipes like Stubb, but I like cigars, and here's nine hundred and sixty of them, so here goes Flask aloft to spy them out."

"Shall I call that wise or foolish, now; if it be really wise it has a foolish look to it; yet, if it be really foolish, then has it a sort of wiseish look to it. But, avast; here comes our old Manxman—the old hearse-driver, he must have been, that is, before he took to the sea. He luffs up before the doubloon; halloa, and goes round on the other side of the mast; why, there's a horse-shoe nailed on that side; and now he's back again; what does that mean? Hark! he's muttering—voice like an old wornout coffee-mill. Prick ears and listen!"

"If the White Whale be raised, it must be in a month and a day, when the sun stands in some one of these signs. I've studied signs, and know their marks; they were taught me two score years ago, by the old witch in Copenhagen. Now, in what sign will the sun then be? The horse-shoe sign; for there it is, right opposite the gold. And what's the horse-shoe sign? The lion is the horse-shoe sign—the roaring and devouring lion. Ship, old ship! my old head shakes to think of thee."

"There's another rendering now; but still one text. All sorts of men in one kind of world, you see. Dodge again! here comes Queequeg—all tattooing—looks like the signs of the Zodiac himself. What says the Cannibal? As I live he's com-paring notes; looking at his thigh bone; thinks the sun is in the thigh, or in the calf, or in the bowels, I suppose, as the old women talk Surgeon's Astronomy in the back coun-try. And by Jove, he's found something there in the vicinity of his thigh—I guess it's Sagittarius, or the Archer. No: he don't know what to make of the doubloon; he takes it for an old button off some king's trowsers. But, aside again! here comes that ghost-devil, Fedallah; tail coiled out of sight as usual, oakum in the toes of his pumps as usual. What does he say, with that look of his? Ah, only makes a sign to the sign and bows himself; there is a sun on the coin—fire wor-shipper, depend upon it. Ho! more and more. This way comes Pip—poor boy! would he had died, or I; he's half hor-rible to me. He too has been watching all of these inter-preters—myself included—and look now, he comes to read, with that unearthly idiotic face. Stand away again and hear him. Hark!"

"I look, you look, he looks; we look, ye look, they look."

"Upon my soul, he's been studying Murray's Grammar! Improving his mind, poor fellow! But what's that he says now—hist!"

"I look, you look, he looks; we look, ye look, they look."

"Why, he's getting it by heart—hist! again."

"I look, you look, he looks; we look, ye look, they look."

"Well, that's funny."

"And I, you, and he; and we, ye, and they, are all bats; and I'm a crow, especially when I stand a'top of this pine tree here. Caw! caw! caw! caw! caw! caw! Ain't I a crow? And where's the scarecrow? There he stands; two bones stuck into a pair of old trowsers, and two more poked into the sleeves of an old jacket."

"Wonder if he means me?—complimentary!—poor lad!—I could go hang myself. Any way, for the present, I'll quit Pip's vicinity. I can stand the rest, for they have plain wits; but he's too crazy-witty for my sanity. So, so, I leave him muttering."

"Here's the ship's navel, this doubloon here, and they

are all on fire to unscrew it. But, unscrew your navel, and what's the consequence? Then again, if it stays here, that is ugly, too, for when aught's nailed to the mast it's a sign that things grow desperate. Ha, ha! old Ahab! the White Whale; he'll nail ye! This is a pine tree. My father, in old Tolland county, cut down a pine tree once, and found a silver ring grown over in it; some old darkey's wedding ring. How did it get there? And so they'll say in the resurrection, when they come to fish up this old mast, and find a doubloon lodged in it, with bedded oysters for the shaggy bark. Oh, the gold! the precious, precious gold!—the green miser'll hoard ye soon! Hish! hish! God goes 'mong the worlds blackberrying. Cook! ho, cook! and cook us! Jenny! hey, hey, hey, hey, hey, Jenny, Jenny! and get your hoe-cake done!"

LEG AND ARM
THE PEQUOD, OF NANTUCKET, MEETS
THE SAMUEL ENDERBY, OF LONDON
C

"ship, ahoy! Hast seen the White Whale?"

So cried Ahab, once more hailing a ship showing English colors, bearing down under the stern. Trumpet to mouth, the old man was standing in his hoisted quarter-boat, his ivory leg plainly revealed to the stranger captain, who was carelessly reclining in his own boat's bow. He was a darkly-tanned, burly, good-natured, fine-looking man, of sixty or thereabout, dressed in a spacious roundabout, that hung round him in festoons of blue pilot-cloth; and one empty arm of this jacket streamed behind him like the broidered arm of a huzzar's surcoat.

"Hast seen the White Whale?"

"See you this?" and withdrawing it from the folds that had hidden it, he held up a white arm of sperm whale bone, terminating in a wooden head like a mallet.

"Man my boat!" cried Ahab, impetuously, and tossing about the oars near him—"Stand by to lower!"

In less than a minute, without quitting his little craft, he and his crew were dropped to the water, and were soon alongside of the stranger. But here a curious difficulty presented itself. In the excitement of the moment, Ahab had forgotten that since the loss of his leg he had never once stepped on board of any vessel at sea but his own, and then it was always by an ingenious and very handy mechanical contrivance peculiar to the Pequod, and a thing not to be rigged and shipped in any other vessel at a moment's warning. Now, it is no very easy matter for anybody—except those who are almost hourly used to it, like whalemen— to clamber up a ship's side from a boat on the open sea; for the great swells now lift the boat high up towards the bulwarks, and then instantaneously drop it half way down to the kelson. So, deprived of one leg, and the strange ship of course being altogether unsupplied with the kindly invention, Ahab now found himself abjectly reduced to a clumsy landsman again; hopelessly eyeing the uncertain changeful height he could hardly hope to attain.

It has before been hinted, perhaps, that every little untoward circumstance that befel him, and which indirectly sprang from his luckless mishap, almost invariably irritated or exasperated Ahab. And in the present instance, all this was heightened by the sight of the two officers of the strange ship, leaning over the side, by the perpendicular ladder of nailed cleets there, and swinging towards him a pair of tastefully-ornamented man-ropes; for at first they did not seem to bethink them that a one-legged man must be too much of a cripple to use their sea bannisters. But this awkwardness only lasted a minute, because the strange captain, observing at a glance how affairs stood, cried out, "I see, I see!—avast heaving there! Jump, boys, and swing over the cutting tackle."

As good luck would have it, they had had a whale alongside a day or two previous, and the great tackles were still aloft, and the massive curved blubber-hook, now clean and dry, was still attached to the end. This was quickly lowered to Ahab, who at once comprehending it all, slid his solitary thigh into the curve of the hook (it was like sitting in the fluke of an anchor, or the crotch of an apple tree), and then giving the word, held himself fast, and at the same time also helped to hoist his own weight, by pulling hand-over-hand upon one of the running parts of the tackle. Soon he was carefully swung inside the high bulwarks, and gently landed upon the capstan head. With his ivory arm frankly thrust forth in welcome, the other captain advanced, and Ahab, putting out his ivory leg, and crossing the ivory arm (like two sword-fish blades) cried out in his walrus way, "Aye, aye, hearty! let us shake bones together!—an arm and a leg!—an arm that never can shrink, d'ye see; and a leg

that never can run. Where did'st thou see the White Whale?——
—how long ago?"

"The White Whale," said the Englishman, pointing his
ivory arm towards the East, and taking a rueful sight along it,
as if it had been a telescope; "There I saw him, on the
Line, last season."

"And he took that arm off, did he?" asked Ahab, now sliding down from the capstan, and resting on the Englishman's shoulder, as he did so.

"Aye, he was the cause of it, at least; and that leg, too?"

"Spin me the yarn," said Ahab; "how was it?"

"It was the first time in my life that I ever cruised on the
Line," began the Englishman. "I was ignorant of the White
Whale at that time. Well, one day we lowered for a pod of
four or five whales, and my boat fastened to one of them; a
regular circus horse he was, too, that went milling and milling round so, that my boat's crew could only trim dish, by
sitting all their sterns on the outer gunwale. Presently up
breaches from the bottom of the sea a bouncing great whale,
with a milky-white head and hump, all crows' feet and
wrinkles."

"It was he, it was he!" cried Ahab, suddenly letting out his
suspended breath.

"And harpoons sticking in near his starboard fin."

"Aye, aye—they were mine—*my* irons," cried Ahab,
exultingly—"but on!"

"Give me a chance, then," said the Englishman, good-
humoredly. "Well, this old great-grandfather, with the white
head and hump, runs all afoam into the pod, and goes to
snapping furiously at my fast-line."

"Aye, I see!—wanted to part it; free the fast-fish—an old
trick—I know him."

"How it was exactly," continued the one-armed commander, "I do not know; but in biting the line, it got foul of his
teeth, caught there somehow; but we didn't know it then;
so that when we afterwards pulled on the line, bounce we
came plump on to his hump! instead of the other whale's that
went off to windward, all fluking. Seeing how matters stood,
and what a noble great whale it was—the noblest and biggest
I ever saw, sir, in my life—I resolved to capture him, spite
of the boiling rage he seemed to be in. And thinking the
haphazard line would get loose, or the tooth it was tangled
to might draw (for I have a devil of a boat's crew for a pull
on a whale-line); seeing all this, I say, I jumped into my

first mate's boat—Mr. Mounttop's here (by the way, Captain—Mounttop; Mounttop—the captain);—as I was saying, I jumped into Mounttop's boat, which, d'ye see, was gunwale and gunwale with mine, then; and snatching the first harpoon, let this old great-grandfather have it. But, Lord, look you, sir—hearts and souls alive, man—the next instant, in a jiff, I was blind as a bat—both eyes out—all befogged and bedeadened with black foam—the whale's tail looming straight up out of it, perpendicular in the air, like a marble steeple. No use sterning all, then; but as I was groping at midday, with a blinding sun, all crown-jewels; as I was groping, I say, after second iron, to toss it overboard—down comes the tail like a Lima tower, cutting my boat in two, leaving each half in splinters; and, flukes first, the white hump backed through the wreck, as though it was all chips. We all struck out. To escape his terrible flailings, I seized hold of my harpoon-pole sticking in him, and for a moment clung to that like a sucking fish. But a combing sea dashed me off, and at the same instant, the fish, taking one good dart forwards, went down like a flash; and the barb of that cursed second iron towing along near me caught me here" (clapping his hand just below his shoulder); "yes, caught me here, I say, and bore me down to Hell's flames, I was thinking; when, when, all of a sudden, thank the good God, the barb ript its way along the flesh—clear along the whole length of my arm—come out nigh my wrist, and up I floated;—and that gentleman there will tell you the rest (by the way, captain—Dr. Bunger, ship's surgeon: Bunger, my lad,—the captain). Now, Bunger boy, spin your part of the yarn."

The professional gentleman thus familiarly pointed out, had been all the time standing near them, with nothing specific visible, to denote his gentlemanly rank on board. His face was an exceedingly round but sober one; he was dressed in a faded blue woolen frock or shirt, and patched trowsers; and had thus far been dividing his attention between a marlingspike he held in one hand, and a pill-box held in the other, occasionally casting a critical glance at the ivory limbs of the two crippled captains. But, at his superior's introduction of him to Ahab, he politely bowed, and straightway went on to do his captain's bidding.

"It was a shocking bad wound," began the whale-surgeon; "and, taking my advice, Captain Boomer here, stood our old Sammy—"

"Samuel Enderby is the name of my ship," interrupted

the one-armed captain, addressing Ahab; "go on, boy."

"Stood our old Sammy off to the northward, to get out of the blazing hot weather there on the Line. But it was no use—I did all I could; sat up with him nights; was very severe with him in the matter of diet—"

"Oh, very severe!" chimed in the patient himself; then suddenly altering his voice, "Drinking hot rum toddies with me every night, till he couldn't see to put on the bandages; and sending me to bed, half seas over, about three o'clock in the morning. Oh, ye stars! he sat up with me indeed, and was very severe in my diet. Oh! a great watcher, and very dietetically severe, is Dr. Bunger. (Bunger, you dog, laugh out! why don't ye? You know you're a precious jolly rascal.) But, heave ahead, boy, I'd rather be killed by you than kept alive by any other man."

"My captain, you must have ere this perceived, respected sir"—said the imperturbably godly-looking Bunger, slightly bowing to Ahab—"is apt to be facetious at times; he spins us many clever things of that sort. But I may as well say—en passant, as the French remark—that I myself—that is to say, Jack Bunger, late of the reverend clergy—am a strict total abstinence man; I never drink—"

"Water!" cried the captain; "he never drinks it; it's a sort of fits to him; fresh water throws him into the hydrophobia; but go on—go on with the arm story."

"Yes, I may as well," said the surgeon, coolly. "I was about observing, sir, before Captain Boomer's facetious interruption, that spite of my best and severest endeavors, the wound kept getting worse and worse; the truth was, sir, it was as ugly gaping wound as surgeon ever saw; more than two feet and several inches long. I measured it with the lead line. In short, it grew black; I knew what was threatened, and off it came. But I had no hand in shipping that ivory arm there; that thing is against all rule"—pointing at it with the marlingspike—"that is the captain's work, not mine; he ordered the carpenter to make it; he had that club-hammer there put to the end, to knock some one's brains out with, I suppose, as he tried mine once. He flies into diabolical passions sometimes. Do ye see this dent, sir"—removing his hat, and brushing aside his hair, and exposing a bowl-like cavity in his skull, but which bore not the slightest scarry trace, or any token of ever having been a wound—"Well, the captain there will tell you how that came here; he knows."

"No, I don't," said the captain, "but his mother did; he

was born with it. Oh, you solemn rogue, you—you Bunger! was there ever such another Bunger in the watery world? Bunger, when you die, you ought to die in pickle, you dog; you should be preserved to future ages, you rascal."

"What became of the White Whale?" now cried Ahab, who thus far had been impatiently listening to this bye-play between the two Englishmen.

"Oh!" cried the one-armed captain, "Oh, yes! Well; after he sounded, we didn't see him again for some time; in fact, as I before hinted, I didn't then know what whale it was that had served me such a trick, till some time afterwards, when coming back to the Line, we heard about Moby Dick— as some call him—and then I knew it was he."

"Did'st thou cross his wake again?"

"Twice."

"But could not fasten?"

"Didn't want to try to: ain't one limb enough? What should I do without this other arm? And I'm thinking Moby Dick doesn't bite so much as he swallows."

"Well, then," interrupted Bunger, "give him your left arm for bait to get the right. Do you know, gentlemen"—very gravely and mathematically bowing to each Captain in succession—"Do you know, gentlemen, that the digestive organs of the whale are so inscrutably constructed by Divine Providence, that it is quite impossible for him to completely digest even a man's arm? And he knows it too. So that what you take for the White Whale's malice is only his awkwardness. For he never means to swallow a single limb; he only thinks to terrify by feints. But sometimes he is like the old juggling fellow, formerly a patient of mine in Ceylon, that making believe swallow jack-knives, once upon a time let one drop into him in good earnest, and there it stayed for a twelvemonth or more; when I gave him an emetic, and he heaved it up in small tacks, d'ye see. No possible way for him to digest that jack-knife, and fully incorporate it into his general bodily system. Yes, Captain Boomer, if you are quick enough about it, and have a mind to pawn one arm for the sake of the privilege of giving decent burial to the other, why in that case the arm is yours; only let the whale have another chance at you shortly, that's all."

"No, thank ye, Bunger," said the English Captain, "he's welcome to the arm he has, since I can't help it, and didn't know him then; but not to another one. No more White Whales for me; I've lowered for him once, and that has satisfied me. There would be great glory in killing him, I know that; and there is a ship-load of precious sperm in him, but, hark ye, he's best let alone; don't you think so, Captain?"—glancing at the ivory leg.

"He is. But he will still be hunted, for all that. What is best let alone, that accursed thing is not always what least allures. He's all a magnet! How long since thou saw'st him last? Which way heading?"

"Bless my soul, and curse the foul fiend's," cried Bunger, stoopingly walking round Ahab, and like a dog, strangely snuffing; "this man's blood—bring the thermometer;—it's at the boiling point!—his pulse makes these planks beat!—sir!"—taking a lancet from his pocket, and drawing near to Ahab's arm.

"Avast!" roared Ahab, dashing him against the bulwarks—"Man the boat! Which way heading?"

"Good God!" cried the English Captain, to whom the question was put. "What's the matter? He is heading east, I think.—Is your Captain crazy?" whispering Fedallah.

But Fedallah, putting a finger on his lip, slid over the bulwarks to take the boat's steering oar, and Ahab, swinging the cutting-tackle towards him, commanded the ship's sailors to stand by to lower.

In a moment he was standing on the boat's stern, and the Manilla men were springing to their oars. In vain the English Captain hailed him. With back to the stranger ship, and face set like a flint to his own, Ahab stood upright till alongside of the Pequod.

THE DECANTER   CI

ERE the English ship fades from sight, be it set down here, that she hailed from London, and was named after the late Samuel Enderby, merchant of that city, the original of the famous whaling house of Enderby & Sons; a house which in my poor whaleman's opinion, comes not far behind the united royal houses of the Tudors and Bourbons, in point of real historical interest. How long, prior to the year of our Lord, 1775, this great whaling house was in existence, my numerous fish-documents do not make plain; but in that year (1775) it fitted out the first English ships

that ever regularly hunted the Sperm Whale; though for
some score of years previous (ever since 1726) our valiant
Coffins and Maceys of Nantucket and the Vineyard had in
large fleets pursued that Leviathan, but only in the North
and South Atlantic: not elsewhere. Be it distinctly recorded
here, that the Nantucketers were the first among mankind
to harpoon with civilized steel the great Sperm Whale; and
that for half a century they were the only people of the
whole globe who so harpooned him.

In 1778, a fine ship, the Amelia, fitted out for the express
purpose, and at the sole charge of the vigorous Enderbys,
boldly rounded Cape Horn, and was the first among the
nations to lower a whale-boat of any sort in the great South
Sea. The voyage was a skilful and lucky one; and returning to her berth with her hold full of the precious sperm,
the Amelia's example was soon followed by other ships,
English and American, and thus the vast Sperm Whale
grounds of the Pacific were thrown open. But not content
with this good deed, the indefatigable house again bestirred
itself: Samuel and all his Sons—how many, their mother only
knows—and under their immediate auspices, and partly, I
think, at their expense, the British government was induced
to send the sloop-of-war Rattler on a whaling voyage of discovery into the South Sea. Commanded by a naval Post-
Captain, the Rattler made a rattling voyage of it, and did
some service; how much does not appear. But this is not all.
In 1819, the same house fitted out a discovery whale ship
of their own, to go on a tasting cruise to the remote waters
of Japan. That ship—well called the "Syren"—made a noble
experimental cruise; and it was thus that the great Japanese
Whaling Ground first became generally known. The Syren
in this famous voyage was commanded by a Captain Coffin,
a Nantucketer.

All honor to the Enderbies, therefore, whose house, I
think, exists to the present day; though doubtless the original Samuel must long ago have slipped his cable for the
great South Sea of the other world.

The ship named after him was worthy of the honor, being a very fast sailer and a noble craft every way. I boarded
her once at mid-night somewhere off the Patagonian coast,
and drank good flip down in the forecastle. It was a fine gam
we had, and they were all trumps—every soul on board. A
short life to them, and a jolly death. And that fine gam I
had—long, very long after old Ahab touched her planks

with his ivory heel—it minds me of the noble, solid, Saxon hospitality of that ship; and may my parson forget me, and the devil remember me, if I ever lose sight of it. Flip? Did I say we had flip? Yes, and we flipped it at the rate of ten gallons the hour; and when the squall came (for it's squally off there by Patagonia), and all hands—visitors and all—were called to reep topsails, we were so top-heavy that we had to swing each other aloft in bowlines; and we ignorantly furled the skirts of our jackets into the sails, so that we hung there, reefed fast in the howling gale, a warning example to all drunken tars. However, the masts did not go overboard; and by and bye we scrambled down, so sober, that we had to pass the flip again, though the savage salt spray bursting down the forecastle scuttle, rather too much diluted and pickled it to my taste.

The beef was fine—tough, but with body in it. They said it was bull-beef; others, that it was dromedary beef; but I do not know, for certain, how that was. They had dumplings too; small, but substantial, symmetrically globular, and indestructible dumplings. I fancied that you could feel them, and roll them about in you after they were swallowed. If you stooped over too far forward, you risked their pitching out of you like billiard balls. The bread—but that couldn't be helped; besides, it was an anti-scorbutic; in short, the bread contained the only fresh fare they had. But the forecastle was not very light, and it was very easy to step over into a dark corner when you ate it. But all in all, taking her from truck to helm, considering the dimensions of the cook's boilers, including his own live parchment boilers; fore and aft, I say, the Samuel Enderby was a jolly ship; of good fare and plenty; fine flip and strong, crack fellows all, and capital from boot heels to hat-band.

But why was it, think ye, that the Samuel Enderby, and some other English whalers I know of—not all though—were such famous, hospitable ships; that passed round the beef, and the bread, and the can, and the joke; and were not soon weary of eating, and drinking, and laughing? I will tell you. The abounding good cheer of these English whalers is matter for historical research. Nor have I been at all sparing of historical whale research, when it has seemed needed.

The English were preceded in the whale fishery by the Hollanders, Zealanders, and Danes; from whom they derived many terms still extant in the fishery; and what is yet more, their fat old fashions, touching plenty to eat and drink. For, as a general thing, the English merchant-ship scrimps her crew; but not so the English whaler. Hence, in the English, this thing of whaling good cheer is not normal and natural, but incidental and particular; and, therefore, must have some special origin, which is here pointed out, and will be still further elucidated.

During my researches in the Leviathanic histories, I stumbled upon an ancient Dutch volume, which, by the musty whaling smell of it, I knew must be about whalers. The title was, "Dan Coopman," wherefore I concluded that this must be the invaluable memoirs of some Amsterdam cooper in the fishery, as every whale ship must carry its cooper. I was reinforced in this opinion by seeing that it was the production of one "Fitz Swackhammer." But my friend Dr. Snodhead, a very learned man, professor of Low Dutch and High German in the college of Santa Claus and St. Pott's, to whom I handed the work for translation, giving him a box of sperm candles for his trouble—this same Dr. Snodhead, so soon as he spied the book, assured me that "Dan Coopman" did not mean "The Cooper," but "The Merchant." In short, this ancient and learned Low Dutch book treated of the commerce of Holland; and, among other subjects, contained a very interesting account of its whale fishery. And in this chapter it was, headed "Smeer," or "Fat," that I found a long detailed list of the outfits for the larders and cellars of 180 sail of Dutch whalemen; from which list, as translated by Dr. Snodhead, I transcribe the following:

```
400,000  lbs. of beef.
 60,000  lbs. Friesland pork.
150,000  lbs. of stock fish.
550,000  lbs. of biscuit.
 72,000  lbs. of soft bread.
  2,800  firkins of butter.
 20,000  lbs. Texel & Leyden cheese.
144,000  lbs. cheese (probably an inferior article).
    550  ankers of Geneva.
 10,800  barrels of beer.
```

Most statistical tables are parchingly dry in the reading; not so in the present case, however, where the reader is flooded with whole pipes, barrels, quarts, and gills of good gin and good cheer.

At the time, I devoted three days to the studious digesting of all this beer, beef, and bread, during which many profound thoughts were incidentally suggested to me, capable of a transcendental and Platonic application; and, furthermore, I compiled supplementary tables of my own, touching the probable quantity of stock-fish, &c., consumed by every Low Dutch harpooneer in that ancient Greenland and Spitbergen whale fishery. In the first place, the amount of butter, and Texel and Leyden cheese consumed, seems amazing, I impute it, though, to their naturally unctuous natures, being rendered still more unctuous by the nature of their vocation, and especially by their pursuing their game in those frigid Polar Seas, on the very coasts of that Esquimaux country where the convivial natives pledge each other in bumpers of train oil.

The quantity of beer, too, is very large, 10,800 barrels. Now, as those polar fisheries could only be prosecuted in the short summer of that climate, so that the whole cruise of one of these Dutch whalemen, including the short voyage to and from the Spitzbergen sea, did not much exceed three months, say, and reckoning 30 men to each of their fleet of 180 sail, we have 5,400 Low Dutch seamen in all; therefore, I say, we have precisely two barrels of beer per man, for a twelve weeks' allowance, exclusive of his fair proportion of that 550 ankers of gin. Now, whether these gin and beer harpooners, so fuddled as one might fancy them to have been, were the right sort of men to stand up in a boat's head, and take good aim at flying whales; this would seem somewhat improbable. Yet they did aim at them, and hit them too. But this was very far North, be it remembered, where beer agrees well with the constitution; upon the Equator, in our southern fishery, beer would be apt to make the harpooneer sleepy at the mast-head and boozy in his boat; and grievous loss might ensue to Nantucket and New Bedford.

But no more; enough has been said to show that the old Dutch whalers of two or three centuries ago were high livers; and that the English whalers have not neglected so excellent an example. For, say they, when cruising in an empty ship, if you can get nothing better out of the world, get a good dinner out of it, at least. And this empties the decanter.

A BOWER IN THE ARSACIDES   CII

HITHERTO, in descriptively treating of the Sperm Whale,
I have chiefly dwelt upon the marvels of his outer aspect;
or separately and in detail upon some few interior struc-
tural features. But to a large and thorough sweeping comprehension of him, it behooves me now to unbutton him
still further, and untagging the points of his hose, unbuckling
his garters, and casting loose the hooks and the eyes of the
joints of his innermost bones, set him before you in his
ultimatum; that is to say, in his unconditional skeleton.

But how now, Ishmael? How is it, that you, a mere oarsman in the fishery, pretend to know aught about the subterranean parts of the whale? Did erudite Stubb, mounted
upon your capstan, deliver lectures on the anatomy of the
Cetacea; and by help of the windlass, hold up a specimen
rib for exhibition? Explain thyself, Ishmael. Can you land
a full-grown whale on your deck for examination, as a cook
dishes a roast-pig? Surely not. A veritable witness have you
hitherto been, Ishmael; but have a care how you seize the
privilege of Jonah alone; the privilege of discoursing upon
the joists and beams; the rafters, ridge-pole, sleepers, and
under-pinnings, making up the framework of leviathan; and
belike of the tallow-vats, dairy-rooms, butteries, and cheeseries
in his bowels.

I confess, that since Jonah, few whalemen have penetrated very far beneath the skin of the adult whale; nevertheless, I have been blessed with an opportunity to dissect
him in miniature. In a ship I belonged to, a small cub
Sperm Whale was once bodily hoisted to the deck for his
poke or bag, to make sheaths for the barbs of the harpoons, and for the heads of the lances. Think you I let
that chance go, without using my boat-hatchet and jack-
knife, and breaking the seal and reading all the contents of
that young cub?

And as for my exact knowledge of the bones of the
leviathan in their gigantic, full grown development, for that
rare knowledge I am indebted to my late royal friend Tranquo, king of Tranque, one of the Arsacides. For being at
Tranque, years ago, when attached to the trading-ship Dey

of Algiers, I was invited to spend part of the Arsacidean holidays with the lord of Tranque, at his retired palm villa at Pupella; a sea-side glen not very far distant from what our sailors called Bamboo-Town, his capital.

Among many other fine qualities, my royal friend Tranquo, being gifted with a devout love for all matters of barbaric vertù, had brought together in Pupella whatever rare things the more ingenious of his people could invent; chiefly carved woods of wonderful devices, chiselled shells, inlaid spears, costly paddles, aromatic canoes; and all these distributed among whatever natural wonders, the wonder-freighted, tribute-rendering waves had cast upon his shores.

Chief among these latter was a great Sperm Whale, which, after an unusually long raging gale, had been found dead and stranded, with his head against a cocoa-nut tree, whose plumage-like, tufted droopings seemed his verdant jet. When the vast body had at last been stripped of its fathom-deep enfoldings, and the bones become dust dry in the sun, then the skeleton was carefully transported up the Pupella glen, where a grand temple of lordly palms now sheltered it.

The ribs were hung with trophies; the vertebrae were carved with Arsacidean annals, in strange hieroglyphics; in the skull, the priests kept up an unextinguishable aromatic flame, so that the mystic head again sent forth its vapory spout; while, suspended from a bough, the terrific lower jaw vibrated over all the devotees, like the hair-hung sword that so affrighted Damocles.

It was a wondrous sight. The wood was green as mosses of the Icy Glen; the trees stood high and haughty, feeling their living sap; the industrious earth beneath was as a weaver's loom, with a gorgeous carpet on it, whereof the ground-vine tendrils formed the warp and woof, and the living flowers the figures. All the trees, with all their laden branches; all the shrubs, and ferns, and grasses; the message-carrying air; all these unceasingly were active. Through the lacings of the leaves, the great sun seemed a flying shuttle weaving the unwearied verdure. Oh, busy weaver! unseen weaver!—pause!—one word!—whither flows the fabric? what palace may it deck? wherefore all these ceaseless toilings? Speak, weaver!—stay thy hand!—but one single word with thee! Nay—the shuttle flies—the figures float from forth the loom; the freshet-rushing carpet for ever slides away. The weaver-god, he weaves; and by that weaving he is deafened, that he hears no mortal voice; and by that humming, we, too, who look on the loom are deafened; and only when we escape it shall we hear the thousand voices that speak through it. For even so it is in all material factories. The spoken words that are inaudible among the flying spindles; those same words are plainly heard without the walls, bursting from the opened casements. Thereby have villanies been detected. Ah, mortal! then, be heedful; for so, in all this din of the great world's loom, thy subtlest thinkings may be overheard afar.

Now, amid the green, life-restless loom of that Arsacidean wood, the great, white, worshipped skeleton lay lounging—a gigantic idler! Yet, as the ever-woven verdant warp and woof intermixed and hummed around him, the mighty idler seemed the cunning weaver; himself all woven over with the vines; every month assuming greener, fresher verdure; but himself a skeleton. Life folded Death; Death trellised Life; the grim god wived with youthful Life, and begat him curly-headed glories.

Now, when with royal Tranquo I visited this wondrous whale, and saw the skull an altar, and the artificial smoke ascending from where the real jet had issued, I marvelled that the king should regard a chapel as an object of vertù. He laughed. But more I marvelled that the priests should swear that smoky jet of his was genuine. To and fro I paced before this skeleton—brushed the vines aside—broke through the ribs—and with a ball of Arsacidean twine, wandered, eddied long amid its many winding, shaded collonades and arbors. But soon my line was out; and following it back, I emerged from the opening where I entered. I saw no living thing within; naught was there but bones.

Cutting me a green measuring-rod, I once more dived within the skeleton. From their arrow-slit in the skull, the priests perceived me taking the altitude of the final rib. "How now!" they shouted; "Dar'st thou measure this our god! That's for us." "Aye, priests—well, how long do ye make him, then?" But hereupon a fierce contest rose among them, concerning feet and inches; they cracked each other's sconces with their yard-sticks—the great skull echoed—and seizing that lucky chance, I quickly concluded my own admeasurements.

These admeasurements I now propose to set before you. But first, be it recorded, that, in this matter, I am not free to utter any fancied measurement I please. Because there are skeleton authorities you can refer to, to test my accuracy. There is a Leviathanic Museum, they tell me, in Hull, England, one of the whaling ports of that country, where they have some fine specimens of fin-backs and other whales. Likewise, I have heard that in the museum of Manchester, in New Hampshire, they have what the proprietors call "the only perfect specimen of a Greenland or River Whale in the United States." Moreover, at a place in Yorkshire, England, Burton Constable by name, a certain Sir Clifford Constable has in his possession the skeleton of a Sperm Whale, but of moderate size, by no means of the full-grown magnitude of my friend King Tranquo's.

In both cases, the stranded whales to which these two skeletons belonged, were originally claimed by their proprietors upon similar grounds. King Tranquo seizing his because he wanted it; and Sir Clifford, because he was lord of the seignories of those parts. Sir Clifford's whale has been articulated throughout; so that, like a great chest of drawers, you can open and shut him, in all his bony cavities—spread out his ribs like a gigantic fan—and swing all day upon his lower jaw. Locks are to be put upon some of his trap-doors and shutters; and a footman will show round future visitors with a bunch of keys at his side. Sir Clifford thinks of charging twopence for a peep at the whispering gallery in the spinal column; threepence to hear the echo in the hollow of his cerebellum; and sixpence for the unrivalled view from his forehead.

The skeleton dimension I shall now proceed to set down are copied verbatim from my right arm, where I had been tattooed; as in my wild wanderings at that period, there was no other secure way of preserving such valuable statistics. But as I was crowded for space, and wished the other parts of my body to remain a blank page for a poem I was then composing—at least, what untattooed parts might remain—I did not trouble myself with the odd inches; nor, indeed, should inches at all enter into a congenial admeasurement of the whale.

MEASUREMENT
OF THE WHALE'S SKELETON   CIII

IN the first place, I wish to lay before you a particular, plain statement, touching the living bulk of this leviathan, whose skeleton we are briefly to exhibit. Such a statement may prove useful here.

According to a careful calculation I have made, and which I partly base upon Captain Scoresby's estimate, of seventy tons for the largest sized Greenland whale of sixty feet in length; according to my careful calculation, I say, a Sperm Whale of the largest magnitude, between eighty-five and ninety feet in length, and something less than forty feet in its fullest circumference, such a whale will weigh at least ninety tons; so that, reckoning thirteen men to a ton, he would considerably outweigh the combined population of a whole village of one thousand one hundred inhabitants.

Think you not then that brains, like yoked cattle, should be put to this leviathan, to make him at all budge to any landsman's imagination?

Having already in various ways put before you his skull, spout-hole, jaw, teeth, tail, forehead, fins, and divers other parts I shall now simply point out what is most interesting in the general bulk of his unobstructed bones. But as the colossal skull embraces so very large a proportion of the entire extent of the skeleton; as it is by far the most complicated part; and as nothing is to be repeated concerning it in this chapter, you must not fail to carry it in your mind, or under your arm, as we proceed, otherwise you will not gain a complete notion of the general structure we are about to view.

In length, the Sperm Whale's skeleton at Tranque measured seventy-two feet; so that when fully invested and extended in life, he must have been ninety feet long; for in the whale, the skeleton loses about one-fifth in length compared with the living body. Of this seventy-two feet, his skull and jaw comprised some twenty feet, leaving some fifty feet of plain back-bone. Attached to this back-bone, for something less than a third of its length, was the mighty circular basket of ribs which once enclosed his vitals.

To me this vast ivory-ribbed chest, with the long, unrelieved spine, extending far away from it in a straight line, not a little resembled the hull of a great ship new-laid upon the stocks, when only some of her naked bow-ribs are inserted, and the keel is otherwise, for the time, but a long, disconnected timber.

The ribs were ten on a side. The first, to begin from the neck, was nearly six feet long; the second, third, and fourth were each successively longer, till you came to the climax of the fifth, or one of the middle ribs, which measured eight feet and some inches. From that part, the remaining ribs diminished, till the tenth and last only spanned five feet and some inches. In general thickness, they all bore a seemly correspondence to their length. The middle ribs were the most arched. In some of the Arsacides they are used for beams whereon to lay footpath bridges over small streams.

In considering these ribs, I could not but be struck anew with the circumstance, so variously repeated in this book, that the skeleton of the whale is by no means the mould of his invested form. The largest of the Tranque ribs, one of the middle ones, occupied that part of the fish which, in life, is greatest in depth. Now, the greatest depth of the invested body of this particular whale must have been at least sixteen feet; whereas, the corresponding rib measured but little more than eight feet. So that this rib only conveyed half of the true notion of the living magnitude of that part. Besides, for some way, where I now saw but a naked spine, all that had been once wrapped round with tons of added bulk in flesh, muscle, blood, and bowels. Still more, for the ample fins, I here saw but a few disordered joints; and in place of the weighty and majestic, but boneless flukes, an utter blank!

How vain and foolish, then, thought I, for timid untravelled man to try to comprehend aright this wondrous whale, by merely poring over his dead attenuated skeleton, stretched in this peaceful wood. No. Only in the heart of quickest perils; only when within the eddyings of his angry flukes; only on the profound unbounded sea, can the fully invested whale be truly and livingly found out.

But the spine. For that, the best way we can consider it is, with a crane, to pile its bones high up on end. No speedy enterprise. But now it's done, it looks much like Pompey's Pillar.

There are forty and odd vertebræ in all, which in the skeleton are not locked together. They mostly lie like the great knobbed blocks on a Gothic spire, forming solid courses of heavy masonry. The largest, a middle one, is in width something less than three feet, and in depth more than four. The smallest, where the spine tapers away into the tail, is only two inches in width, and looks something like a white billiard-ball. I was told that there were still smaller ones, but they had been lost by some little cannibal urchins, the priest's children, who had stolen them to play marbles with. Thus we see how that the spine of even the hugest of living things tapers off at last into simple child's play.

THE FOSSIL WHALE   CIV

FROM his mighty bulk the whale affords a most congenial theme whereon to enlarge, amplify, and generally expatiate. Would you, you could not compress him. By good rights he should only be treated of in imperial folio. Not to tell over again his furlongs from spiracle to tail, and the yards he measures about the waist; only think of the gigantic involutions of his intestines, where they lie in him like great cables and hausers coiled away in the subterranean orlop-deck of a line-of-battleship.

Since I have undertaken to manhandle this Leviathan, it behooves me to approve myself omnisciently exhaustive in the enterprise; not overlooking the minutest seminal germs of his blood, and spinning him out to the uttermost coil of his bowels. Having already described him in most of his present habitatory and anatomical peculiarities, it now remains to magnify him in an archæological, fossiliferous, and antediluvian point of view. Applied to any other creature than the Leviathan—to an ant or a flea—such portly terms might justly be deemed unwarrantably grandiloquent. But when Leviathan is the text, the case is altered. Fain am I to stagger to this emprise under the weightiest words of the dictionary. And here be it said, that whenever it has been convenient to consult one in the course of these dissertations, I have invariably used a huge quarto edition of Johnson, expressly purchased for that purpose; because that famous lexicographer's uncommon personal bulk more fitted him to compile a lexicon to be used by a whale author like me.

One often hears of writers that rise and swell with their subject, though it may seem but an ordinary one. How, then, with me, writing of this Leviathan? Unconsciously my chirography expands into placard capitals. Give me a condor's quill! Give me Vesuvius' crater for an inkstand! Friends, hold my arms! For in the mere act of penning my thoughts of this Leviathan, they weary me, and make me faint with their out-reaching comprehensiveness of sweep, as if to include the whole circle of the sciences, and all the generations of whales, and men, and mastodons, past, present, and to come, with all the revolving panoramas of empire on earth, and throughout the whole universe, not excluding its suburbs. Such, and so magnifying, is the virtue of a large and liberal theme! We expand to its bulk. To produce a mighty book, you must choose a mighty theme. No great and enduring volume can ever be written on the flea, though many there be who have tried it.

Ere entering upon the subject of Fossil Whales, I present my credentials as a geologist, by stating that in my miscellaneous time I have been a stone-mason, and also a great digger of ditches, canals and wells, wine-vaults, cellars, and cisterns of all sorts. Likewise, by way of preliminary, I desire to remind the reader, that while in the earlier geological strata there are found the fossils of monsters now almost completely extinct; the subsequent relics discovered in what are called the Tertiary formations seem the connecting, or at any rate intercepted links, between the antichronical creatures, and those whose remote posterity are said to have entered the Ark; all the Fossil Whales hitherto discovered belong to the Tertiary period, which is the last preceding the superficial formations. And though none of them precisely answer to any known species of the present time, they are yet sufficiently akin to them in general respects, to justify their taking rank as Cetacean fossils.

Detached broken fossils of pre-adamite whales, fragments of their bones and skeletons, have within thirty years past, at various intervals, been found at the base of the Alps, in Lombardy, in France, in England, in Scotland, and in the States of Louisiana, Mississippi, and Alabama. Among the more curious of such remains is part of a skull, which in the year 1779 was disinterred in the Rue Dauphiné in Paris, a short street opening almost directly upon the palace of

the Tuileries; and bones disinterred in excavating the great
docks of Antwerp, in Napoleon's time. Cuvier pronounced
these fragments to have belonged to some utterly unknown
Leviathanic species.

But by far the most wonderful of all cetacean relics was
the almost complete vast skeleton of an extinct monster,
found in the year 1842, on the plantation of Judge Creagh,
in Alabama. The awe-stricken credulous slaves in the vicinity took it for the bones of one of the fallen angels. The
Alabama doctors declared it a huge reptile, and bestowed
upon it the name of Basilosaurus. But some specimen bones
of it being taken across the sea to Owen, the English Anat-
omist, it turned out that this alleged reptile was a whale,
though of a departed species. A significant illustration of the
fact, again and again repeated in this book, that the skeleton
of the whale furnishes but little clue to the shape of his
fully invested body. So Owen rechristened the monster
Zeuglodon; and in his paper read before the London Geological Society, pronounced it, in substance, one of the most
extraordinary creatures which the mutations of the globe
have blotted out of existence.

When I stand among these mighty Leviathan skeletons,
skulls, tusks, jaws, ribs, and vertebræ, all characterized by
partial resemblances to the existing breeds of sea-monsters;
but at the same time bearing on the other hand similar af-
finities to the annihilated antichronical Leviathans, their incalculable seniors; I am, by a flood, borne back to that
wondrous period, ere time itself can be said to have begun;
for time began with man. Here Saturn's grey chaos rolls
over me, and I obtain dim, shuddering glimpses into those
Polar eternities; when wedged bastions of ice pressed hard
upon what are now the Tropics; and in all the 25,000 miles
of this world's circumference, not an inhabitable hand's
breadth of land was visible. Then the whole world was the
whale's; and, king of creation, he left his wake along the
present lines of the Andes and the Himmalehs. Who can
show a pedigree like Leviathan? Ahab's harpoon had shed
older blood than the Pharaoh's. Methuselah seems a school-
boy. I look round to shake hands with Shem. I am horror-
struck at this antemosaic, unsourced existence of the unspeakable terrors of the whale, which, having been before
all time, must needs exist after all humane ages are over.

But not alone has this Leviathan left his pre-adamite traces
in the stereotype plates of nature, and in limestone and

marl bequeathed his ancient bust; but upon Egyptian tablets, whose antiquity seems to claim for them an almost fossiliferous character, we find the unmistakable print of his fin. In an apartment of the great temple of Denderah, some fifty years ago, there was discovered upon the granite ceiling a sculptured and painted planisphere, abounding in centaurs, griffins, and dolphins, similar to the grotesque figures on the celestial globe of the moderns. Gliding among them, old Leviathan swam as of yore; was there swimming in that plainisphere, centuries before Solomon was cradled.

Nor must there be omitted another strange attestation of the antiquity of the whale, in his own osseous post-diluvian reality, as set down by the venerable John Leo, the old Barbary traveller.

"Not far from the Sea-side, they have a Temple, the Rafters and Beams of which are made of Whale-Bones; for Whales of a monstrous size are oftentimes cast up dead upon that shore. The Common People imagine, that by a secret Power bestowed by God upon the Temple, no Whale can pass it without immediate death. But the truth of the Matter is, that on either side of the Temple, there are Rocks that shoot two Miles into the Sea, and wound the Whales when they light upon 'em. They keep a Whale's Rib of an incredible length for a Miracle, which lying upon the Ground with its convex part uppermost, makes an Arch, the Head of which cannot be reached by a Man upon a Camel's Back. This Rib (says John Leo) is said to have layn there a hundred Years before I saw it. Their Historians affirm, that a Prophet who prophesy'd of Mahomet, came from this Temple, and some do not stand to assert, that the Prophet Jonas was cast forth by the Whale at the Base of the Temple."

In this Afric Temple of the Whale I leave you, reader, and if you be a Nantucketer, and a whaleman, you will silently worship there.

DOES THE WHALE'S MAGNITUDE DIMINISH? WILL HE PERISH? CV

INASMUCH, then, as this Leviathan comes floundering down upon us from the head-waters of the Eternities, it may be fitly inquired, whether, in the long course of his generations, he has not degenerated from the original bulk of his sires.

But upon investigation we find, that not only are the whales of the present day superior in magnitude to those whose fossil remains are found in the Tertiary system (embracing a distinct geological period prior to man), but of the whales found in that Tertiary system, those belonging to its latter formations exceed in size those of its earlier ones.

Of all the pre-adamite whales yet exhumed, by far the largest is the Alabama one mentioned in the last chapter, and that was less then seventy feet in length in the skeleton. Whereas, we have already seen, that the tape-measure gives seventy-two feet for the skeleton of a large sized modern whale. And I have heard, on whalemen's authority, that Sperm Whales have been captured near a hundred feet long at the time of capture.

But may it not be, that while the whales of the present hour are an advance in magnitude upon those of all previous geological periods; may it not be, that since Adam's time they have degenerated?

Assuredly, we must conclude so, if we are to credit the accounts of such gentlemen as Pliny, and the ancient naturalists generally. For Pliny tells us of whales that embraced acres of living bulk, and Aldrovandus of others which measured eight hundred feet in length—Rope Walks and Thames Tunnels of Whales! And even in the days of Banks and Solander, Cooke's naturalists, we find a Danish member of the Academy of Sciences setting down certain Iceland Whales (reydan-siskur, or Wrinkled Bellies) at one hundred and twenty yards; that is, three hundred and sixty feet. And Lacépède, the French naturalist, in his elaborate history of whales, in the very beginning of his work (page 3), sets down the Right Whale at one hundred metres, three hundred and twenty-eight feet. And this work was published so late as A.D. 1825.

But will any whaleman believe these stories? No. The whale of to-day is as big as his ancestors in Pliny's time. And if ever I go where Pliny is, I, a whaleman (more than he was), will make bold to tell him so. Because I cannot understand how it is, that while the Egyptian mummies that were buried thousands of years before even Pliny was born, do not measure so much in their coffins as a modern

Kentuckian in his socks; and while the cattle and other animals sculptured on the oldest Egyptian and Nineveh tablets, by the relative proportions in which they are drawn, just as plainly prove that the high-bred, stall-fed, prize cattle of Smithfield, not only equal, but far exceed in magnitude the fattest of Pharaoh's fat kine; in the face of all this, I will admit that of all animals the whale alone should have degenerated.

But still another inquiry remains; one often agitated by the more recondite Nantucketers. Whether owing to the almost omniscient look-outs at the mast-heads of the whale-ships, now penetrating even through Behring's straits, and into the remotest secret drawers and lockers of the world; and the thousand harpoons and lances darted along all continental coasts; the moot point is, whether Leviathan can long endure so wide a chase, and so remorseless a havoc; whether he must not at last be exterminated from the waters, and the last whale, like the last man, smoke his last pipe, and then himself evaporate in the final puff.

Comparing the humped herds of whales with the humped herds of buffalo, which, not forty years ago, overspread by tens of thousands the prairies of Illinois and Missouri, and shook their iron manes and scowled with their thunder-clotted brows upon the sites of populous river-capitals, where now the polite broker sells you land at a dollar an inch; in such a comparison an irresistible argument would seem furnished, to show that the hunted whale cannot now escape speedy extinction.

But you must look at this matter in every light. Though so short a period ago—not a good life-time—the census of the buffalo in Illinois exceeded the census of men now in London, and though at the present day not one horn or hoof of them remains in all that region; and though the cause of this wondrous extermination was the spear of man; yet the far different nature of the whale-hunt peremptorily forbids so inglorious an end to the Leviathan. Forty men in one ship hunting the Sperm Whale for forty-eight months think they have done extremely well, and thank God, if at last they carry home the oil of forty fish. Whereas, in the days of the old Canadian and Indian hunters and trappers of the West, when the far west (in whose sunset suns still rise) was a wilderness and a virgin, the same number of moccasined men, for the same number of months, mounted on horse instead of sailing in ships, would have slain not forty, but forty thousand and more buffaloes; a fact that, if need were, could be statistically stated.

Nor, considered aright, does it seem any argument in favor of the gradual extinction of the Sperm Whale, for example, that in former years (the latter part of the last century, say) these Leviathans, in small pods, were encountered much oftener than at present, and, in consequence, the voyages were not so prolonged, and were also much more remunerative. Because, as has been elsewhere noticed, those whales, influenced by some views to safety, now swim the seas in immense caravans, so that to a large degree the scattered solitaries, yokes, and pods, and schools of other days are now aggregated into vast but widely separated, unfrequent armies. That is all. And equally fallacious seems the conceit, that because the so-called whalebone whales no longer haunt many grounds in former years abounding with them, hence that species also is declining. For they are only being driven from promontory to cape; and if one coast is no longer enlivened with their jets, then, be sure, some other and remoter strand has been very recently startled by the unfamiliar spectacle.

Furthermore: concerning these last mentioned Leviathans, they have two firm fortresses, which, in all human probability, will for ever remain impregnable. And as upon the invasion of their valleys, the frosty Swiss have retreated to their mountains; so, hunted from the savannas and glades of the middle seas, the whale-bone whales can at last resort to their Polar citadels, and diving under the ultimate glassy barriers and walls there, come up among icy fields and floes; and in a charmed circle of everlasting December, bid defiance to all pursuit from man.

But as perhaps fifty of these whale-bone whales are harpooned for one cachalot, some philosophers of the forecastle have concluded that this positive havoc has already very seriously diminished their battalions. But though for some time past a number of these whales, not less than 13,000, have been annually slain on the nor' west coast by the Americans alone; yet there are considerations which render even this circumstance of little or no account as an opposing argument in this matter.

Natural as it is to be somewhat incredulous concerning the populousness of the more enormous creatures of the globe, yet what shall we say to Harto, the historian of Goa, when he tells us that at one hunting the King of Siam took 4000 elephants; that in those regions elephants are numerous as droves of cattle in the temperate climes. And there seems no reason to doubt that if these elephants, which have now been hunted for thousands of years, by Semiramis, by Porus, by Hannibal, and by all the successive monarchs of the East—if they still survive there in great numbers, much more may the great whale outlast all hunting, since he has a pasture to expatiate in, which is precisely twice as large as all Asia, both Americas, Europe and Africa, New Holland, and all the Isles of the sea combined.

Moreover: we are to consider, that from the presumed great longevity of whales, their probably attaining the age of a century and more, therefore at any one period of time, several distinct adult generations must be contemporary. And what that is, we may soon gain some idea of, by imagining all the grave-yards, cemeteries, and family vaults of creation yielding up the live bodies of all the men, women, and children who were alive seventy-five years ago; and adding this countless host to the present human population of the globe.

Wherefore, for all these things, we account the whale immortal in his species, however perishable in his individuality. He swam the seas before the continents broke water; he once swam over the site of the Tuileries, and Windsor Castle, and the Kremlin. In Noah's flood he despised Noah's Ark; and if ever the world is to be again flooded, like the Netherlands, to kill off its rats, then the eternal whale will still survive, and rearing upon the topmost crest of the equatorial flood, spout his frothed defiance to the skies.

AHAB'S LEG   CVI

THE precipitating manner in which Captain Ahab had quitted the Samuel Enderby of London, had not been unattended with some small violence to his own person. He had lighted with such energy upon a thwart of his boat that his ivory leg had received a half-splintering shock. And when after gaining his own deck, and his own pivot-hole there, he so vehemently wheeled round with an urgent command to the steersman (it was, as ever, something about his not steering inflexibly enough); then, the already shaken ivory received such an additional twist and wrench, that though it still remained entire, and to all appearances lusty, yet Ahab did not deem it entirely trustworthy.

And, indeed, it seemed small matter for wonder, that for all his pervading, mad recklessness, Ahab did at times give careful heed to the condition of that dead bone upon which he partly stood. For it had not been very long prior to the Pequod's sailing from Nantucket, that he had been found one night lying prone upon the ground, and insensible; by some unknown, and seemingly inexplicable, unimaginable casualty, his ivory limb having been so violently displaced, that it had stake-wise smitten, and all but pierced his groin; nor was it without extreme difficulty that the agonizing wound was entirely cured.

Nor, at the time, had it failed to enter his monomaniac mind, that all the anguish of that then present suffering was but the direct issue of a former woe; and he too plainly seemed to see, that as the most poisonous reptile of the marsh perpetuates his kind as inevitably as the sweetest songster of the grove; so, equally with every felicity, all miserable events do naturally beget their like. Yea, more than equally, thought Ahab; since both the ancestry and posterity of Grief go further than the ancestry and posterity of Joy. For, not to hint of this: that it is an inference from certain canonic teachings, that while some natural enjoyments here shall have no children born to them for the other world, but, on the contrary, shall be followed by the joy-childlessness of all hell's despair; whereas, some guilty mortal miseries shall still fertilely beget to themselves an eternally progressive progeny of griefs beyond the grave; not at all to hint of this, there still seems an inequality in the deeper analysis of the thing. For, thought Ahab, while even the highest earthly felicities ever have a certain unsignifying pettiness lurking in them, but, at bottom, all heart-woes, a mystic significance, and, in some men, an archangelic grandeur; so do their diligent tracings-out not belie the obvious deduction. To trail the genealogies of these high mortal miseries, carries us at last among the sourceless primogenitures of the gods; so that, in the face of all the glad, hay-making suns, and soft-cymballing, round harvest-moons, we must needs give in to this: that the gods themselves are not for ever glad. The ineffaceable, sad birthmark in the brow of man, is but the stamp of sorrow in the signers.

Unwittingly here a secret has been divulged, which perhaps might more properly, in set way, have been disclosed before. With many other particulars concerning Ahab, always had it remained a mystery to some, why it was, that for a certain period, both before and after the sailing of the Pequod, he had hidden himself away with such Grand-Lama-like exclusiveness; and, for that one interval, sought speechless refuge, as it were, among the marble senate of the dead. Captain Peleg's bruited reason for this thing appeared by no means adequate; though, indeed, as touching all Ahab's deeper part, every revelation partook more of significant darkness than of explanatory light. But, in the end, it all came out; this one matter did, at least. That direful mishap was at the bottom of his temporary recluseness. And not only this, but to that ever-contracting, dropping circle ashore, who, for any reason, possessed the privilege of a less banned approach to him; to that timid circle the above hinted casualty—remaining, as it did, moodily unaccounted for by Ahab—invested itself with terrors, not entirely underived from the land of spirits and of wails. So that, through their zeal for him, they had all conspired, so far as in them lay, to muffle up the knowledge of this thing from others; and hence it was, that not till a considerable interval had elapsed, did it transpire upon the Pequod's decks.

But be all this as it may; let the unseen, ambiguous synod in the air, or the vindictive princes and potentates of fire, have to do or not with earthly Ahab, yet in this present matter of his leg, he took plain practical procedures;—he called the carpenter.

And when that functionary appeared before him, he bade him without delay set about making a new leg, and directed the mates to see him supplied with all the studs and joists of jaw-ivory (Sperm Whale) which had thus far been accumulated on the voyage, in order that a careful selection of the stoutest, clearest-grained stuff might be secured. This done, the carpenter received orders to have the leg completed that night; and to provide all the fittings for it, independent of those pertaining to the distrusted one in use. Moreover, the ship's forge was ordered to be hoisted out of its temporary idleness in the hold; and, to accelerate the affair, the blacksmith was commanded to proceed at once to the forging of whatever iron contrivances might be needed.

THE CARPENTER   CVII

SEAT thyself sultanically among the moons of Saturn, and take high abstracted man alone; and he seems a wonder, a grandeur, and a woe. But from the same point, take mankind in mass, and for the most part, they seem a mob of unnecessary duplicates, both contemporary and hereditary. But most humble though he was, and far from furnishing an example of the high, humane abstraction; the Pequod's carpenter was no duplicate; hence, he now comes in person on this stage.

Like all sea-going ship carpenters, and more especially those belonging to whaling vessels, he was, to a certain offhanded, practical extent, alike experienced in numerous trades and callings collateral to his own; the carpenter's pursuit being the ancient and outbranching trunk of all those numerous handicrafts which more or less have to do with wood as an auxiliary material. But, besides the application to him of the generic remark above, this carpenter of the Pequod was singularly efficient in those thousand nameless mechanical emergencies continually recurring in a large ship, upon a three or four years' voyage, in uncivilized and far-distant seas. For not to speak of his readiness in ordinary duties:— repairing stove boats, sprung spars, reforming the shape of clumsy-bladed oars, inserting bull's eyes in the deck, or new tree-nails in the side planks, and other miscellaneous matters more directly pertaining to his special business; he was moreover unhesitatingly expert in all manner of conflicting aptitudes, both useful and capricious.

The one grand stage where he enacted all his various parts so manifold, was his vice-bench; a long rude ponderous table furnished with several vices, of different sizes, and both of iron and of wood. At all times except when whales were alongside, this bench was securely lashed athwartships against the rear of the try-works.

A belaying pin is found too large to be easily inserted into its hole: the carpenter claps it into one of his every-ready vices, and straightway files it smaller. A lost land-bird of strange plumage strays on board, and is made a captive: out of clean shaved rods of right-whale bone, and cross-beams of sperm whale ivory, the carpenter makes a pagoda-looking cage for it. An oarsman sprains his wrist: the carpenter concocts a soothing lotion. Stubb longed for vermillion stars to be painted upon the blade of his every oar; screwing each oar in his big vice of wood, the carpenter symmetrically supplies the constellation. A sailor takes a fancy to wear shark-bone ear-rings: the carpenter drills his ears. Another has the toothache: the carpenter out pincers, and clapping one hand upon his bench bids him be seated there; but the poor fellow unmanageably winces under the unconcluded operation; whirling round the handle of his wooden vice, the carpenter signs him to clap his jaw in that, if he would have him draw the tooth.

Thus, this carpenter was prepared at all points, and alike indifferent and without respect in all. Teeth he accounted bits of ivory; heads he deemed but top-blocks; men themselves he lightly held for capstans. But while now upon so wide a field thus variously accomplished, and with such liveliness of expertness in him, too; all this would seem to argue some uncommon vivacity of intelligence. But not precisely so. For nothing was this man more remarkable, than for a certain impersonal stolidity as it were; impersonal, I say; for it so shaded off into the surrounding infinite of things, that it seemed one with the general stolidity discernible in the whole visible world; which while pauselessly active in uncounted modes, still eternally holds its peace, and ignores you, though you dig foundations for cathedrals. Yet was this half-horrible stolidity in him, involving, too, as it appeared, an all-ramifying heartlessness;—yet was it oddly dashed at times, with an old, crutch-like, antediluvian, wheezing humorousness, not unstreaked now and then with a certain grizzled wittiness; such as might have served to pass the time during the midnight watch on the bearded forecastle of Noah's ark. Was it that this old carpenter had been a life-long wanderer, whose much rolling, to and fro, not only had gathered no moss; but what is more, had rubbed off whatever small outward clingings might have originally pertained to him? He was a stript abstract; an unfractioned integral; uncompromised as a new-born babe; living without premeditated reference to this world or the next. You might almost say, that this strange uncompromisedness in him involved a sort of unintelligence; for in his numerous trades, he did not seem to work so much by reason or by instinct, or simply because he had been tutored to it, or by any intermixture of all these, even or uneven; but merely by a kind of deaf and dumb, spontaneous literal process. He was a pure manipulator; his brain, if he had ever had one, must have early oozed along into the muscles of his fingers. He was like one of those unreasoning but still highly useful, *multum in parvo*, Sheffield contrivances, assuming the exterior—though a little swelled—of a common pocket knife; but containing, not only blades of various sizes, but also screw-drivers, cork-screws, tweezers, awls, pens, rulers, nail-filers, counter-sinkers. So, if his superiors wanted to use the carpenter for a screw-driver, all they had to do was to open that part of him, and the screw was fast: or if for tweezers, take him up by the legs, and there they were.

Yet, as previously hinted, this omnitooled, open-and-shut carpenter, was, after all, no mere machine of an automaton. If he did not have a common soul in him, he had a subtle something that somehow anomalously did its duty. What that was, whether essence of quicksilver, or a few drops of hartshorn, there is no telling. But there it was; and there it had abided for now some sixty years or more. And this it was, this same unaccountable, cunning life-principle in him; this it was, that kept him a great part of the time soliloquizing; but only like an unreasoning wheel, which also hummingly soliloquizes; or rather, his body was a sentry-box and this soliloquizer on guard there, and talking all the time to keep himself awake.

AHAB AND THE CARPENTER
THE DECK—FIRST NIGHT WATCH   CVIII

(*Carpenter standing before his vice-bench, and by the light of two lanterns busily filing the ivory joist for the leg, which joist is firmly fixed in the vice. Slabs of ivory, leather straps, pads, screws, and various tools of all sorts lying about the bench. Forward the red flame of the forge is seen, where the blacksmith is at work.*)

DRAT the file, and drat the bone! That is hard which should be soft, and that is soft which should be hard. So we go, who file old jaws and shinbones. Let's try another. Aye, now, this works better (*sneezes*). Halloa, this bone dust is (*sneezes*)—why it's (*sneezes*)—yes it's (*sneezes*)—bless my soul, it won't let me speak! This is what an old fellow gets now for working in dead lumber. Saw a live tree, and you don't get this dust; amputate a live bone, and you don't get it (*sneezes*). Come, come, you old Smut, there, bear a hand, and let's have that ferule and buckle-screw; I'll be ready for them presently. Lucky now (*sneezes*) there's no knee-joint to make; that might puzzle a little; but a mere shinbone—why it's easy as making hop-poles; only I should like to put a good finish on. Time, time; if I but only had the time, I could turn him out as neat a leg now as ever (*sneezes*) scraped to a lady in a parlor. Those buckskin legs and calves of legs I've seen in shop windows wouldn't compare at all. They soak water, they do; and of course get rheumatic, and have to be doctored (*sneezes*) with washes and lotions, just like live legs. There; before I saw it off, now, I must call his old Mogulship, and see whether the length will be all right; too short, if anything, I guess. Ha! that's the heel; we are in luck; here he comes, or it's somebody else, that's certain.

AHAB (*advancing*).
(*During the ensuing scene, the carpenter continues sneezing at times.*)

Well, manmaker!
Just in time, sir. If the captain pleases, I will now mark the length. Let me measure, sir.
Measured for a leg! good. Well, it's not the first time. About it! There; keep thy finger on it. This is a cogent vice thou hast here, carpenter; let me feel its grip once. So, so; it does pinch some.
Oh, sir, it will break bones—beware, beware!
No fear; I like a good grip; I like to feel something in this slippery world that can hold, man. What's Prometheus about there?—the blacksmith, I mean—what's he about?
He must be forging the buckle-screw, sir, now.
Right. It's a partnership; he supplies the muscle part. He makes a fierce red flame there!
Aye, sir; he must have the white heat for this kind of fine work.
Um-m. So he must. I do deem it now a most meaning thing, that that old Greek, Prometheus, who made men, they say, should have been a blacksmith, and animated

them with fire; for what's made in fire must properly belong to fire; and so hell's probable. How the soot flies! This must be the remainder the Greek made the Africans of. Carpenter, when he's through with that buckle, tell him to forge a pair of steel shoulder-blades; there's a pedlar aboard with a crushing pack.

Sir?

Hold; while Prometheus is about it, I'll order a complete man after a desirable pattern. Imprimis, fifty feet high in his socks; then, chest modelled after the Thames Tunnel; then, legs with roots to 'em, to stay in one place; then, arms three feet through the wrist; no heart at all, brass forehead, and about a quarter of an acre of fine brains; and let me see—shall I order eyes to see outwards? No, but put a sky-light on top of his head to illuminate inwards. There, take the order, and away.

Now, what's he speaking about, and who's he speaking to, I should like to know? Shall I keep standing here? (aside.)

'Tis but indifferent architecture to make a blind dome; here's one. No, no, no; I must have a lantern.

Ho, ho! That's it, hey? Here are two, sir; one will serve my turn.

What art thou thrusting that thief-catcher into my face for, man? Thrusted light is worse than presented pistols.

I thought, sir, that you spoke to carpenter.

Carpenter? why that's—but no;—a very tidy, and, I may say, an extremely gentlemanlike sort of business thou art in here, carpenter;—or would'st thou rather work in clay?

Sir?—Clay? clay, sir? That's mud; we leave clay to ditchers, sir.

The fellow's impious! What art thou sneezing about?

Bone is rather dusty, sir.

Take the hint, then; and when thou art dead, never bury thyself under living people's noses.

Sir?—oh! ah!—I guess so;—yes—oh, dear!

Look ye, carpenter, I dare say thou callest thyself a right good workmanlike workman, eh? Well, then, will it speak thoroughly well for thy work, if, when I come to mount this leg thou makest, I shall nevertheless feel another leg in the same identical place with it; that is, carpenter, my old lost leg; the flesh and blood one, I mean. Canst thou not drive that old Adam away?

Truly, sir, I begin to understand somewhat now. Yes, I have heard something curious on that score, sir; how that a dismasted man never entirely loses the feeling of his old spar, but it will be still pricking him at times. May I humbly ask if it be really so, sir?

It is, man. Look, put thy live leg here in the place where mine once was; so, now, here is only one distinct leg to the eye, yet two to the soul. Where thou feelest tingling life; there, exactly there, there to a hair, do I. Is't a riddle?

I should humbly call it a poser, sir.

Hist, then. How dost thou know that some entire, living, thinking thing may not be invisibly and uninterpenetratingly standing precisely where thou now standest; aye, and standing there in thy spite? In thy most solitary hours, then, dost thou not fear eavesdroppers? Hold, don't speak! And if I still feel the smart of my crushed leg, though it be now so long dissolved; then, why mayst not thou, carpenter, feel the fiery pains of hell for ever, and without a body? Hah!

Good Lord! Truly, sir, if it comes to that, I must calculate over again; I think I didn't carry a small figure, sir.

Look ye, pudding-heads should never grant premises.— How long before the leg is done?

Perhaps an hour, sir.

Bungle away at it then, and bring it to me (*turns to go*). Oh, Life! Here I am, proud as Greek god, and yet standing debtor to this blockhead for a bone to stand on! Cursed be that mortal inter-indebtedness which will not do away with ledgers. I would be free as air; and I'm down in the whole world's books. I am so rich, I could have given bid for bid with the wealthiest Prætorians at the auction of the Roman empire (which was the world's); and yet I owe for the flesh in the tongue I brag with. By heavens! I'll get a crucible, and into it, and dissolve myself down to one small, compendious vertebra. So.

CARPENTER (*resuming his work*).

Well, well, well! Stubb knows him best of all, and Stubb always says he's queer; says nothing but that one sufficient little word queer; he's queer, says Stubb; he's queer—queer, queer; and keeps dinning it into Mr. Starbuck all the time— queer, sir—queer, queer, very queer. And here's his leg! Yes, now that I think of it, here's his bedfellow! has a stick of whale's jaw-bone for a wife! And this is his leg; he'll stand on this. What was that now about one leg standing in three places, and all three places standing in one hell— how was that? Oh! I don't wonder he looked so scornful at

me! I'm a sort of strange-thoughted sometimes, they say; but
that's only haphazard-like. Then, a short, little old body
like me, should never undertake to wade out into deep
waters with tall, heron-built captains; the water chucks
you under the chin pretty quick, and there's a great cry
for life-boats. And here's the heron's leg! long and slim,
sure enough! Now, for most folks one pair of legs lasts a
lifetime, and that must be because they use them mercifully, as a tender-hearted old lady uses her roly-poly old
coach-horses. But Ahab; oh he's a hard driver. Look, driven
one leg to death, and spavined the other for life, and now
wears out bone legs by the cord. Halloa, there, you Smut!
bear a hand there with those screws, and let's finish it before the resurrection fellow comes a-calling with his horn
for all legs, true or false, as brewery-men go round collecting
old beer barrels, to fill 'em up again. What a leg this is! It
looks like a real live leg, filed down to nothing but the core;
he'll be standing on this to-morrow; he'll be taking altitudes
on it. Halloa! I almost forgot the little oval slate, smoothed
ivory, where he figures up the latitude. So, so; chisel, file, and
sand-paper now!

AHAB AND STARBUCK IN THE CABIN   CIX

ACCORDING to usage they were pumping the ship next
morning; and lo! no inconsiderable oil came up with the
water; the casks below must have sprung a bad leak. Much
concern was shown; and Starbuck went down into the cabin
to report this unfavorable affair.*

Now, from the South and West the Pequod was drawing
nigh to Formosa and the Bashee Isles, between which lies
one of the tropical outlets from the China waters into the
Pacific. And so Starbuck found Ahab with a general chart
of the oriental archipelagoes spread before him; and an-

---

* In Sperm-whalemen with any considerable quantity of oil
on board, it is a regular semi-weekly duty to conduct a hose
into the hold, and drench the casks with sea-water; which afterwards, at varying intervals, is removed by the ship's pumps.
Hereby the casks are sought to be kept damply tight; while by
the changed character of the withdrawn water, the mariners
readily detect any serious leakage in the precious cargo.

other separate one representing the long eastern coasts of the Japanese islands—Niphon, Matsmai, and Sikoke. With his snow-white new ivory leg braced against the screwed leg of his table, and with a long pruning-hook of a jack-knife in his hand, the wondrous old man, with his back to the gangway door, was wrinkling his brow, and tracing his old courses again.

"Who's there?" hearing the footstep at the door, but not turning round to it. "On deck! Begone!"

"Captain Ahab mistakes; it is I. The oil in the hold is leaking, sir. We must up Burtons and break out."

"Up Burtons and break out? Now that we are nearing Japan; heave-to here for a week to tinker a parcel of old hoops?"

"Either do that, sir, or waste in one day more oil than we may make good in a year. What we come twenty thousand miles to get is worth saving, sir."

"So it is, so it is; if we get it."

"I was speaking of the oil in the hold, sir."

"And I was not speaking or thinking of that at all. Begone! Let it leak! I'm all aleak myself. Aye! leaks in leaks! not only full of leaky casks, but those leaky casks are in a leaky ship; and that's a far worse plight than the Pequod's, man. Yet I don't stop to plug my leak; for who can find it in the deep-loaded hull; or how hope to plug it, even if found, in this life's howling gale? Starbuck! I'll not have the Burtons hoisted."

"What will the owners say, sir?"

"Let the owners stand on Nantucket beach and outyell the Typhoons. What cares Ahab? Owners, owners? Thou art always prating to me, Starbuck, about those miserly owners, as if the owners were my conscience. But look ye, the only real owner of anything is its commander; and hark ye, my conscience is in this ship's keel.—On deck!"

"Captain Ahab," said the reddening mate, moving further into the cabin, with a daring so strangely respectful and cautious that it almost seemed not only every way seeking to avoid the slightest outward manifestation of itself, but within also seemed more than half distrustful of itself; "A better man than I might well pass over in thee what he would quickly enough resent in a younger man; aye, and in a happier, Captain Ahab."

"Devils! Dost thou then so much as dare to critically think of me?—On deck!"

"Nay, sir, not yet; I do entreat. And I do dare, sir—to be forbearing! Shall we not understand each other better than hitherto, Captain Ahab?"

Ahab seized a loaded musket from the rack (forming part of most South-Sea-men's cabin furniture), and pointing it towards Starbuck, exclaimed: "There is one God that is Lord over the earth, and one Captain that is lord over the Pequod.—On deck!"

For an instant in the flashing eyes of the mate, and his fiery cheeks, you would have almost thought that he had really received the blaze of the levelled tube. But, mastering his emotion, he half calmly rose, and as he quitted the cabin, paused for an instant and said: "Thou hast outraged, not insulted me, sir; but for that I ask thee not to beware of Starbuck; thou wouldst but laugh; but let Ahab beware of Ahab; beware of thyself, old man."

"He waxes brave, but nevertheless obeys; most careful bravery that!" murmured Ahab, as Starbuck disappeared. "What's that he said—Ahab beware of Ahab—there's something there!" Then unconsciously using the musket for a staff, with an iron brow he paced to and fro in the little cabin; but presently the thick plaits of his forehead relaxed, and returning the gun to the rack, he went to the deck.

"Thou art but too good a fellow, Starbuck," he said lowly to the mate; then raising his voice to the crew: "Furl the t'gallant-sails and close-reef the top-sails, fore and aft; back the main-yard; up Burtons, and break out in the main-hold."

It were perhaps vain to surmise exactly why it was, that as respecting Starbuck, Ahab thus acted. It may have been a flash of honesty in him; or mere prudential policy which, under the circumstance, imperiously forbade the slightest symptom of open disaffection, however transient, in the important chief officer of his ship. However it was, his orders were executed; and the Burtons were hoisted.

QUEEQUEG IN HIS COFFIN   CX

UPON searching, it was found that the casks last struck into the hold were perfectly sound, and that the leak must be further off. So, it being calm weather, they broke out

deeper and deeper, disturbing the slumbers of the huge
ground-tier butts; and from that black midnight sending
those gigantic moles into the daylight above. So deep did
they go; and so ancient, and corroded, and weedy the aspect
of the lowermost puncheons, that you almost looked next
for some mouldy corner-stone cask containing coins of
Captain Noah, with copies of the posted placards, vainly
warning the infatuated old world from the flood. Tierce after
tierce, too, of water, and bread, and beef, and shooks of
staves, and iron bundles of hoops, were hoisted out, till at
last the piled decks were hard to get about; and the hollow
hull echoed under foot, as if you were treading over empty
catacombs, and reeled and rolled in the sea like an air-
freighted demijohn. Top-heavy was the ship as a dinnerless
student with all Aristotle in his head. Well was it that the
Typhoons did not visit them then.

Now, at this time it was that my poor pagan companion,
and fast bosom-friend, Queequeg, was seized with a fever,
which brought him nigh to his endless end.

Be it said, that in this vocation of whaling, sinecures are
unknown; dignity and danger go hand in hand; till you get
to be Captain, the higher you rise the harder you toil. So
with poor Queequeg, who, as harpooneer, must not only
face all the rage of the living whale, but—as we have elsewhere seen—mount his dead back in a rolling sea; and finally
descend into the gloom of the hold, and bitterly sweating
all day in that subterraneous confinement, resolutely manhandle the clumsiest casks and see to their stowage. To be
short, among whalemen, the harpooneers are the holders,
so called.

Poor Queequeg! when the ship was about half disembow-
elled, you should have stooped over the hatchway, and
peered down upon him there; where, stripped to his woollen
drawers, the tattooed savage was crawling about amid that
dampness and slime, like a green spotted lizard at the bottom
of a well. And a well, or an ice-house, it somehow proved to
him, poor pagan; where, strange to say, for all the heat of
his sweatings, he caught a terrible chill which lapsed into a
fever; and at last, after some days' suffering, laid him in
his hammock, close to the very sill of the door of death.
How he wasted and wasted away in those few long-lingering
days, till there seemed but little left of him but his frame
and tattooing. But as all else in him thinned, and his cheek-
bones grew sharper, his eyes, nevertheless, seemed growing

fuller and fuller; they became of a strange softness of
lustre; and mildly but deeply looked out at you there from
his sickness, a wondrous testimony to that immortal health
in him which could not die, or be weakened. And like circles on the water, which, as they grow fainter, expand; so
his eyes seemed rounding and rounding, like the rings of
Eternity. An awe that cannot be named would steal over
you as you sat by the side of this waning savage, and saw
as strange things in his face, as any beheld who were by-
standers when Zoroaster died. For whatever is truly wondrous and fearful in man, never yet was put into words or
books. And the drawing near of Death, which alike levels
all, alike impresses all with a last revelation, which only
an author from the dead could adequately tell. So that—let
us say it again—no dying Chaldee or Greek had higher and
holier thoughts than those, whose mysterious shades you
saw creeping over the face of poor Queequeg, as he quietly
lay in his swaying hammock, and the rolling sea seemed
gently rocking him to his final rest, and the ocean's invisible
flood-tide lifted him higher and higher towards his destined heaven.

Not a man of the crew but gave him up; and, as for
Queequeg himself, what he thought of his case was forcibly
shown by a curious favor he asked. He called one to him in
the grey morning watch, when the day was just breaking,
and taking his hand, said that while in Nantucket he had
chanced to see certain little canoes of dark wood, like the
rich war-wood of his native isle; and upon inquiry, he had
learned that all whalemen who died in Nantucket, were laid
in those same dark canoes, and that the fancy of being so
laid had much pleased him; for it was not unlike the custom of his own race, who, after embalming a dead warrior,
stretched him out in his canoe, and so left him to be floated
away to the starry archipelagoes; for not only do they believe that the stars are isles, but that far beyond all visible
horizons, their own mild, uncontinented seas, interflow with
the blue heavens; and so form the white breakers of the
milky way. He added, that he shuddered at the thought of
being buried in his hammock, according to the usual sea-
custom, tossed like something vile to the death-devouring
sharks. No: he desired a canoe like those of Nantucket, all
the more congenial to him, being a whaleman, that like a
whale-boat these coffin-canoes were without a keel; though

that involved but uncertain steering, and much lee-way adown the dim ages.

Now, when this strange circumstance was made known aft, the carpenter was at once commanded to do Queequeg's bidding, whatever it might include. There was some heathenish, coffin-colored old lumber aboard, which, upon a long previous voyage, had been cut from the aboriginal groves of the Lackaday islands, and from these dark planks the coffin was recommended to be made. No sooner was the carpenter apprised of the order, than taking his rule, he forthwith with all the indifferent promptitude of his character, proceeded into the forecastle and took Queequeg's measure with great accuracy, regularly chalking Queequeg's person as he shifted the rule.

"Ah! poor fellow! he'll have to die now," ejaculated the Long Island sailor.

Going to his vice-bench, the carpenter for convenience sake and general reference, now transferringly measured on it the exact length the coffin was to be, and then made the transfer permanent by cutting two notches at its extremities. This done, he marshalled the planks and his tools, and to work.

When the last nail was driven, and the lid duly planed and fitted, he lightly shouldered the coffin and went forward with it, inquiring whether they were ready for it yet in that direction.

Overhearing the indignant but half-humorous cries with which the people on deck began to drive the coffin away, Queequeg, to every one's consternation, commanded that the thing should be instantly brought to him, nor was there any denying him; seeing that, of all mortals, some dying men are the most tyrannical; and certainly, since they will shortly trouble us so little for evermore, the poor fellows ought to be indulged.

Leaning over in his hammock, Queequeg long regarded the coffin with an attentive eye. He then called for his harpoon, had the wooden stock drawn from it, and then had the iron part placed in the coffin along with one of the paddles of his boat. All by his own request, also, biscuits were then ranged round the sides within: a flask of fresh water was placed at the head, and a small bag of woody earth scraped up in the hold at the foot; and a piece of sail-cloth being rolled up for a pillow, Queequeg now entreated to be lifted into his final bed, that he might make trial of its comforts, if any it had. He lay without moving a few minutes, then told one to go to his bag and bring out his little god, Yojo. Then crossing his arms on his breast with Yojo between, he called for the coffin lid (hatch he called it) to be placed over him. The head part turned over with a leather hinge, and there lay Queequeg in his coffin with little but his composed countenance in view. "Rarmai" (it will do; it is easy), he murmured at last, and signed to be replaced in his hammock.

But ere this was done, Pip, who had been slily hovering near by all this while, drew nigh to him where he lay, and with soft sobbings, took him by the hand; in the other, holding his tambourine.

"Poor rover! will ye never have done with all this weary roving? where go ye now? But if the currents carry ye to those sweet Antilles where the beaches are only beat with water-lilies, will ye do one little errand for me? Seek out one Pip, who's now been missing long: I think he's in those far Antilles. If ye find him, then comfort him; for he must be very sad; for look! he's left his tambourine behind;—I found it. Rig-a-dig, dig, dig! Now, Queequeg, die; and I'll beat ye your dying march."

"I have heard," murmured Starbuck, gazing down the scuttle, "that in violent fevers, men, all ignorance, have talked in ancient tongues; and that when the mystery is probed, it turns out always that in their wholly forgotten childhood those ancient tongues had been really spoken in their hearing by some lofty scholars. So, to my fond faith, poor Pip, in this strange sweetness of his lunacy, brings heavenly vouchers of all our heavenly homes. Where learned he that, but there?—Hark! he speaks again: but more wildly now."

"Form two and two! Let's make a General of him! Ho, where's his harpoon? Lay it across here.—Rig-a-dig, dig dig! huzza! Oh for a game cock now to sit upon his head and crow! Queequeg dies game!—mind ye that; Queequeg dies game!—take ye good heed of that; Queequeg dies game! I say; game, game, game! but base little Pip, he died a coward; died all a'shiver;—out upon Pip! Hark ye; if ye find Pip, tell all the Antilles he's a runaway; a coward, a coward, a coward! Tell them he jumped from a whale-boat! I'd never beat my tambourine over base Pip, and hail him General, if he were once more dying here. No, no! shame upon all cowards—shame upon them! Let 'em go drown like Pip, that jumped from a whale-boat. Shame! shame!"

During all this, Queequeg lay with closed eyes, as if in a dream. Pip was led away, and the sick man was replaced in his hammock.

But now that he had apparently made every preparation for death; now that his coffin was proved a good fit, Queequeg suddenly rallied; soon there seemed no need of the carpenter's box: and thereupon, when some expressed their delighted surprise, he, in substance, said, that the cause of his sudden convalescence was this;—at a critical moment, he had just recalled a little duty ashore, which he was leaving undone; and therefore had changed his mind about dying: he could not die yet, he averred. They asked him, then, whether to live or die was a matter of his own sovereign will and pleasure. He answered, certainly. In a word, it was Queequeg's conceit, that if a man made up his mind to live, mere sickness could not kill him: nothing but a whale, or a gale, or some violent, ungovernable, unintelligent destroyer of that sort.

Now, there is this noteworthy difference between savage and civilized; that while a sick, civilized man may be six months convalescing, generally speaking, a sick savage is almost half-well again in a day. So, in good time my Queequeg gained strength; and at length after sitting on the windlass for a few indolent days (but eating with a vigorous appetite) he suddenly leaped to his feet, threw out arms and legs, gave himself a good stretching, yawned a little bit, and then springing into the head of his hoisted boat, and poising a harpoon, pronounced himself fit for a fight.

With a wild whimsiness, he now used his coffin for a sea-chest; and emptying into it his canvas bag of clothes, set them in order there. Many spare hours he spent, in carving the lid with all manner of grotesque figures and drawings; and it seemed that hereby he was striving, in his rude way, to copy parts of the twisted tattooing on his body. And this tattooing, had been the work of a departed prophet and seer of his island, who, by those hieroglyphic marks, had written out on his body a complete theory of the heavens and the earth, and a mystical treatise on the art of attaining truth; so that Queequeg in his own proper person was a riddle to unfold; a wondrous work in one volume; but whose mysteries not even himself could read, though his own live heart beat against them; and these mysteries were there-

fore destined in the end to moulder away with the living
parchment whereon they were inscribed, and so be unsolved
to the last. And this thought it must have been which suggested to Ahab that wild exclamation of his, when one morning turning away from surveying poor Queequeg—"Oh, devilish tantalization of the gods!"

THE PACIFIC   **CXI**

WHEN gliding by the Bashee isles we emerged at last
upon the great South Sea; were it not for other things, I
could have greeted my dear Pacific with uncounted thanks,
for now the long supplication of my youth was answered;
that serene ocean rolled eastwards from me a thousand
leagues of blue.

There is, one knows not what sweet mystery about this
sea, whose gently awful stirrings seem to speak of some hidden soul beneath; like those fabled undulations of the Ephe-
sian sod over the buried Evangelist St. John. And meet it is,
that over these sea-pastures, wide-rolling watery prairies and
Potters' Fields of all four continents, the waves should rise
and fall, and ebb and flow unceasingly; for here, millions
of mixed shades and shadows, drowned dreams, somnambu-
lisms, reveries; all that we call lives and souls, lie dreaming,
dreaming, still; tossing like slumberers in their beds; the
ever-rolling waves but made so by their restlessness.

To any meditative Magian rover, this serene Pacific, once
beheld, must ever after be the sea of his adoption. It rolls
the midmost waters of the world, the Indian ocean and Atlantic being but its arms. The same waves wash the moles
of the new-built California towns, but yesterday planted by
the recentest race of men, and lave the faded but still gorgeous skirts of Asiatic lands, older than Abraham; while
all between float milky-ways of coral isles, and low-lying,
endless, unknown Archipelagoes, and impenetrable Japans.
Thus this mysterious, divine Pacific zones the world's whole
bulk about; makes all coasts one bay to it; seems the tide-
beating heart of earth. Lifted by those eternal swells, you
needs must own the seductive god, bowing your head to Pan.

But few thoughts of Pan stirred Ahab's brain, as standing
like an iron statue at his accustomed place beside the mizen

rigging, with one nostril he unthinkingly snuffed the sugary musk from the Bashee isles (in whose sweet woods mild lovers must be walking), and with the other consciously inhaled the salt breath of the new found sea; that sea in which the hated White Whale must even then be swimming. Launched at length upon these almost final waters, and gliding towards the Japanese cruising-ground, the old man's purpose intensified itself. His firm lips met like the lips of a vice; the Delta of his forehead's veins swelled like overladen brooks; in his very sleep, his ringing cry ran through the vaulted hull, "Stern all! the White Whale spouts thick blood!"

THE BLACKSMITH   CXII

AVAILING himself of the mild, summer-cool weather that now reigned in these latitudes, and in preparation for the peculiarly active pursuits shortly to be anticipated, Perth, the begrimed, blistered old blacksmith, had not removed his portable forge to the hold again, after concluding his contributory work for Ahab's leg, but still retained it on deck, fast lashed to ringbolts by the foremast; being now almost incessantly invoked by the headsmen, and harpooneers, and bowsmen to do some little job for them; altering, or repairing, or new shaping their various weapons and boat furniture. Often he would be surrounded by an eager circle, all waiting to be served; holding boat-spades, pike-heads, harpoons, and lances, and jealously watching his every sooty movement, as he toiled. Nevertheless, this old man's was a patient hammer wielded by a patient arm. No murmur, no impatience, no petulance did come from him. Silent, slow, and solemn; bowing over still further his chronically broken back, he toiled away, as if toil were life itself, and the heavy beating of his hammer the heavy beating of his heart. And so it was. —Most miserable!

A peculiar walk in this old man, a certain slight but painful appearing yawing in his gait, had at an early period of the voyage excited the curiosity of the mariners. And to the importunity of their persisted questionings he had finally given in; and so it came to pass that every one now knew the shameful story of his wretched life.

Belated, and not innocently, one bitter winter's midnight,

on the road running between two country towns, the black-smith half-stupidly felt the deadly numbness stealing over him, and sought refuge in a leaning, dilapidated barn. The issue was, the loss of the extremities of both feet. Out of this revelation, part by part, at last came out the four acts of the gladness, and the one long, and as yet uncatastrophied fifth act of the grief of his life's drama.

He was an old man, who, at the age of nearly sixty, had postponedly encountered that thing in sorrow's technicals called ruin. He had been an artisan of famed excellence, and with plenty to do; owned a house and garden; embraced a youthful, daughter-like, loving wife, and three blithe, ruddy children; every Sunday went to a cheerful-looking church, planted in a grove. But one night, under cover of darkness, and further concealed in a most cunning disguisement, a desperate burglar slid into his happy home, and robbed them all of everything. And darker yet to tell, the blacksmith himself did ignorantly conduct this burglar into his family's heart. It was the Bottle Conjuror! Upon the opening of that fatal cork, forth flew the fiend, and shrivelled up his home. Now, for prudent, most wise, and economic reasons, the blacksmith's shop was in the basement of his dwelling, but with a separate entrance to it; so that always had the young and loving healthy wife listened with no unhappy nerv-ousness, but with vigorous pleasure, to the stout ringing of her young-armed old husband's hammer; whose reverberations, muffled by passing through the floors and walls, came up to her, not unsweetly, in her nursery; and so, to stout Labor's iron lullaby, the blacksmith's infants were rocked to slumber.

Oh, woe on woe! Oh, Death, why canst thou not sometimes be timely? Hadst thou taken this old blacksmith to thyself ere his full ruin came upon him, then had the young widow had a delicious grief, and her orphans a truly venerable, leg-endary sire to dream of in their after years; and all of them a care-killing competency. But Death plucked down some vir-tuous elder brother, on whose whistling daily toil solely hung the responsibilities of some other family, and left the worse than useless old man standing, till the hideous rot of life should make him easier to harvest.

Why tell the whole? The blows of the basement hammer every day grew more and more between; and each blow every day grew fainter than the last; the wife sat frozen at the win-dow, with tearless eyes, glitteringly gazing into the weeping faces of her children; the bellows fell; the forge choked up with cinders; the house was sold; the mother dived down into the long church-yard grass; her children twice followed her thither; and the houseless, familyless old man staggered off a vagabond in crape; his every woe unreverenced; his grey head a scorn to flaxen curls!

Death seems the only desirable sequel for a career like this; but Death is only a launching into the region of the strange Untried; it is but the first salutation to the possibilities of the immense Remote, the Wild, the Watery, the Unshored; therefore, to the death-longing eyes of such men, who still have left in them some interior compunctions against suicide, does the all-contributed and all-receptive ocean alluringly spread forth his whole plain of unimaginable, taking terrors, and wonderful, new-life adventures; and from the hearts of infinite Pacific, the thousand mermaids sing to them—"Come hither, brokenhearted; here is another life without the guilt of intermediate death; here are wonders supernatural, without dying for them. Come hither! bury thyself in a life which, to your now equally abhorred and abhorring, landed world, is more oblivious than death. Come hither! put up *thy* gravestone, too, within the churchyard, and come hither, till we marry thee!"

Hearkening to these voices, East and West, by early sunrise, and by fall of eve, the blacksmith's soul responded, Aye, I come! And so Perth went a-whaling.

THE FORGE   CXIII

WITH matted beard, and swathed in a bristling shark-skin apron, about mid-day, Perth was standing between his forge and anvil, the latter placed upon an iron-wood log, with one hand holding a pike-head in the coals, and with the other at his forge's lungs, when Captain Ahab came along, carrying in his hand a small rusty-looking leathern bag. While yet a little distance from the forge, moody Ahab paused; till at last, Perth, withdrawing his iron from the fire, began hammering it upon the anvil—the red mass sending off the sparks in thick hovering flights, some of which flew close to Ahab.

"Are these thy Mother Carey's chickens, Perth? they are

always flying in thy wake; birds of good omen, too, but not to all;—look here, they burn; but thou—thou liv'st among them without a scorch."

"Because I am scorched all over, Captain Ahab," answered Perth, resting for a moment on his hammer; "I am past scorching; not easily can'st thou scorch a scar."

"Well, well; no more. Thy shrunk voice sounds too calmly, sanely woful to me. In no Paradise myself, I am impatient of all misery in others that is not mad. Thou should'st go mad, blacksmith; say, why dost thou not go mad? How can'st thou endure without being mad? Do the heavens yet hate thee, that thou can'st not go mad?—What wert thou making there?"

"Welding an old pike-head, sir; there were seams and dents in it."

"And can'st thou make it all smooth again, blacksmith, after such hard usage as it had?"

"I think so, sir."

"And I suppose thou can'st smoothe almost any seams and dents; never mind how hard the metal, blacksmith?"

"Aye, sir, I think I can; all seams and dents but one."

"Look ye here, then," cried Ahab, passionately advancing, and leaning with both hands on Perth's shoulder; "look ye here—*here*—can ye smoothe out a seam like this, blacksmith," sweeping one hand across his ribbed brow; "if thou could'st, blacksmith, glad enough would I lay my head upon thy anvil, and feel thy heaviest hammer between my eyes. Answer! Can'st thou smoothe this seam?"

"Oh! that is the one, sir! Said I not all seams and dents but one?"

"Aye, blacksmith, it is the one; aye, man, it is unsmoothable; for though thou only see'st it here in my flesh, it has worked down into the bone of my skull—*that* is all wrinkles! But, away with child's play; no more gaffs and pikes to-day. Look ye here!" jingling the leathern bag, as if it were full of gold coins. "I, too, want a harpoon made; one that a thousand yoke of fiends could not part, Perth; something that will stick in a whale like his own fin-bone. There's the stuff," flinging the pouch upon the anvil. "Look ye, blacksmith, these are the gathered nailstubbs of the steel shoes of racing horses."

"Horse-shoe stubbs, sir? Why, Captain Ahab, thou hast here, then, the best and stubbornest stuff we blacksmiths ever work."

"I know it, old man; these stubbs will weld together like, glue from the melted bones of murderers. Quick! forge me the harpoon. And forge me first, twelve rods for its shank; then wind, and twist, and hammer these twelve together like the yarns and strands of a tow-line. Quick! I'll blow the fire."

When at last the twelve rods were made, Ahab tried them, one by one, by spiralling them, with his own hand, round a long, heavy iron bolt. "A flaw!" rejecting the last one. "Work that over again, Perth."

This done, Perth was about to begin welding the twelve into one, when Ahab stayed his hand, and said he would weld his own iron. As, then, with regular, gasping hems, he hammered on the anvil, Perth passing to him the glowing rods, one after the other, and the hard pressed forge shooting up its intense straight flame, the Parsee passed silently, and bowing over his head towards the fire, seemed invoking some curse or some blessing on the toil. But, as Ahab looked up, he slid aside.

"What's that bunch of lucifers dodging about there for?" muttered Stubb, looking on from the forecastle. "That Parsee smells fire like a fusee; and smells of it himself, like a hot musket's powder-pan."

At last the shank, in one complete rod, received its final heat; and as Perth, to temper it, plunged it all hissing into the cask of water near by, the scalding steam shot up into Ahab's bent face.

"Would'st thou brand me, Perth?" wincing for a moment with the pain; "have I been but forging my own branding-iron, then?"

"Pray God, not that; yet I fear something, Captain Ahab. Is not this harpoon for the White Whale?"

"For the white fiend! But now for the barbs; thou must make them thyself, man. Here are my razors—the best of steel; here, and make the barbs sharp as the needle-sleet of the Icy Sea."

For a moment, the old blacksmith eyed the razors as though he would fain not use them.

"Take them, man, I have no need for them; for I now neither shave, sup, nor pray till—but here—to work!"

Fashioned at last into an arrowy shape, and welded by Perth to the shank, the steel soon pointed the end of the iron; and as the blacksmith was about giving the barbs their final heat, prior to tempering them, he cried to Ahab to place the watercask near.

"No, no—no water for that; I want it of the true death-temper. Ahoy, there! Tashtego, Queequeg, Daggoo! What say ye, pagans! Will ye give me as much blood as will cover this barb?" holding it high up. A cluster of dark nods replied, Yes. Three punctures were made in the heathen flesh, and the White Whale's barbs were then tempered.

"Ego non baptizo te in nomine patris, sed in nomine diaboli!" deliriously howled Ahab, as the malignant iron scorchingly devoured the baptismal blood.

Now, mustering the spare poles from below, and selecting one of hickory, with the bark still investing it, Ahab fitted the end to the socket of the iron. A coil of new tow-line was then unwound, and some fathoms of it taken to the windlass, and stretched to a great tension. Pressing his foot upon it, till the rope hummed like a harpstring, then eagerly bending over it, and seeing no strandings, Ahab exclaimed, "Good! and now for the seizings."

At one extremity the rope was unstranded, and the separate spread yarns were all braided and woven round the socket of the harpoon; the pole was then driven hard up into the socket; from the lower end the rope was traced half way along the pole's length, and firmly secured so, with inter-twistings of twine. This done, pole, iron, and rope—like the Three Fates—remained inseparable, and Ahab moodily stalked away with the weapon; the sound of his ivory leg, and the sound of the hickory pole, both hollowly ringing along every plank. But ere he entered his cabin, a light, unnatural, half-bantering, yet most piteous sound was heard. Oh, Pip! thy wretched laugh, thy idle but unresting eye; all thy strange mummeries not unmeaningly blended with the black tragedy of the melancholy ship, and mocked it!

THE GILDER   CXIV

PENETRATING further and further into the heart of the Japanese cruising ground, the Pequod was soon all astir in the fishery. Often, in mild, pleasant weather, for twelve, fifteen, eighteen, and twenty hours on the stretch, they were engaged in the boats, steadily pulling, or sailing, or paddling after the whales, or for an interlude of sixty or seventy minutes calmly awaiting their uprising; though with but small success for their pains.

At such times, under an abated sun; afloat all day upon smooth, slow heaving swells; seated in his boat, light as a birch canoe; and so sociably mixing with the soft waves themselves, that like hearth-stone cats they purr against the gunwale; these are the times of dreamy quietude, when beholding the tranquil beauty and brilliancy of the ocean's skin, one forgets the tiger heart that pants beneath it; and would not willingly remember, that this velvet paw but conceals a remorseless fang.

These are the times, when in his whale-boat the rover softly feels a certain filial, confident, land-like feeling towards the sea; that he regards it as so much flowery earth; and the distant ship revealing only the tops of her masts, seems struggling forward, not through high rolling waves, but through the tall grass of a rolling prairie: as when the western emigrants' horses only show their erected ears, while their hidden bodies widely wade through the amazing verdure.

The long-drawn virgin vales; the mild blue hill-sides; as over these there steals the hush, the hum; you almost swear that play-wearied children lie sleeping in these solitudes, in some glad May-time, when the flowers of the woods are plucked. And all this mixes with your most mystic mood; so that fact and fancy, half-way meeting, interpenetrate, and form one seamless whole.

Nor did such soothing scenes, however temporary, fail of at least as temporary an effect on Ahab. But if these secret golden keys did seem to open in him his own secret golden treasuries, yet did his breath upon them prove but tarnishing.

Oh, grassy glades! oh, ever vernal endless landscapes in the soul; in ye,—though long parched by the dead drought of the earthly life—in ye, men yet may roll, like young horses in new morning clover; and for some few fleeting moments, feel the cool dew of the life immortal on them. Would to God these blessed calms would last. But the mingled, mingling threads of life are woven by warp and woof: calms crossed by storms, a storm for every calm. There is no steady unretracing progress in this life; we do not advance through fixed gradations, and at the last one pause:—through infancy's unconscious spell, boyhood's thoughtless faith, adolescence' doubt (the common doom), then scepticism, then disbelief, resting at last in manhood's pondering repose of If. But once gone through, we trace the round again; and are infants, boys, and men, and Ifs eternally. Where lies the final harbor, whence we unmoor no more? In what rapt ether sails the world, of which the weariest will never weary? Where is the foundling's father hidden? Our souls are like those orphans whose unwedded mothers die in bearing them: the secret of our paternity lies in their grave, and we must there to learn it.

And that same day, too, gazing far down from his boat's side into that same golden sea, Starbuck lowly murmured:—

"Loveliness unfathomable, as ever lover saw in his young bride's eye!—Tell me not of thy teeth-tiered sharks, and thy kidnapping cannibal ways. Let faith oust fact; let fancy oust memory; I look deep down and do believe."

And Stubb, fish-like, with sparkling scales, leaped up in that same golden light:—

"I am Stubb, and Stubb has his history; but here Stubb takes oaths that he has always been jolly!"

THE PEQUOD MEETS THE BACHELOR   CXV

AND jolly enough were the sights and the sounds that came bearing down before the wind, some few weeks after Ahab's harpoon had been welded.

It was a Nantucket ship, the Bachelor, which had just wedged in her last cask of oil, and bolted down her bursting hatches; and now, in glad holiday apparel, was joyously, though somewhat vain-gloriously, sailing round among the widely-separated ships on the ground, previous to pointing her prow for home.

The three men at her mast-head wore long streamers of narrow red bunting at their hats; from the stern, a whaleboat was suspended, bottom down; and hanging captive from the bowsprit was seen the long lower jaw of the last whale they had slain. Signals, ensigns, and jacks of all colors were flying from her rigging, on every side. Sideways lashed in each of her three basketed tops were two barrels of sperm; above which, in her top-mast cross-trees, you saw slender breakers of the same precious fluid; and nailed to her main truck was a brazen lamp.

As was afterwards learned, the Bachelor had met with the

most surprising success; all the more wonderful, for that while cruising in the same seas numerous other vessels had gone entire months without securing a single fish. Not only had barrels of beef and bread been given away to make room for the far more valuable sperm, but additional supplemental casks had been bartered for, from the ships she had met; and these were stowed along the deck, and in the captain's and officer's staterooms. Even the cabin table itself had been knocked into kindling-wood; and the cabin mess dined off the broad head of an oil-butt, lashed down to the floor for a centerpiece. In the forecastle, the sailors had actually caulked and pitched their chests, and filled them; it was humorously added, that the cook had clapped a head on his largest boiler, and filled it; that the steward had plugged his spare coffee-pot and filled it; that the harpooneers had headed the sockets of their irons and filled them; that indeed everything was filled with sperm, except the captain's pantaloons pockets, and those he reserved to thrust his hands into, in self-complacent testimony of his entire satisfaction.

As this glad ship of good luck bore down upon the moody Pequod, the barbarian sound of enormous drums came from her forecastle; and drawing still nearer, a crowd of her men were seen standing round her huge try-pots, which, covered with the parchment-like *poke* or stomach skin of the black fish, gave forth a loud roar to every stroke of the clenched hands of the crew. On the quarter-deck, the mates and harpooneers were dancing with the olive-hued girls who had eloped with them from the Polynesian Isles; while suspended in an ornamented boat, firmly secured aloft between the foremast and mainmast, three Long Island negroes, with glittering fiddle-bows of whale ivory, were presiding over the hilarious jig. Meanwhile, others of the ship's company were tumultuously busy at the masonry of the try-works, from which the huge pots had been removed. You would have almost thought they were pulling down the cursed Bastile, such wild cries they raised, as the now useless brick and mortar were being hurled into the sea.

Lord and master over all this scene, the captain stood erect on the ship's elevated quarter-deck, so that the whole rejoicing drama was full before him, and seemed merely contrived for his own individual diversion.

And Ahab, he too was standing on his quarter-deck, shaggy and black, with a stubborn gloom; and as the two ships crossed each other's wakes—one all jubilations for things passed, the other all forebodings as to things to come—their two captains in themselves impersonated the whole striking contrast of the scene.

"Come aboard, come aboard!" cried the gay Bachelor's commander, lifting a glass and a bottle in the air.

"Hast seen the White Whale?" gritted Ahab in reply.

"No; only heard of him; but don't believe in him at all," said the other good-humoredly. "Come aboard!"

"Thou art too damned jolly. Sail on. Hast lost any men?"

"Not enough to speak of—two islanders, that's all;—but come aboard, old hearty, come along. I'll soon take that black from your brow. Come along, will ye (merry's the play); a full ship and homeward-bound."

"How wondrous familiar is a fool!" muttered Ahab; then aloud, "Thou art a full ship and homeward bound, thou sayst; well, then, call me an empty ship, and outward-bound. So go thy ways, and I will mine. Forward there! Set all sail, and keep her to the wind!"

And thus, while the one ship went cheerily before the breeze, the other stubbornly fought against it; and so the two vessels parted; the crew of the Pequod looking with grave, lingering glances towards the receding Bachelor; but the Bachelor's men never heeding their gaze for the lively revelry they were in. And as Ahab, leaning over the taffrail, eyed the homeward-bound craft, he took from his pocket a small vial of sand, and then looking from the ship to the vial, seemed thereby bringing two remote associations together, for that vial was filled with Nantucket soundings.

THE DYING WHALE   CXVI

NOT seldom in this life, when, on the right side, fortune's favorites sail close by us, we, though all adroop before, catch somewhat of the rushing breeze, and joyfully feel our bagging sails fill out. So seemed it with the Pequod. For next day after encountering the gay Bachelor, whales were seen and four were slain; and one of them by Ahab.

It was far down the afternoon; and when all the spearings of the crimson fight were done: and floating in the lovely sunset sea and sky, sun and whale both stilly died together; then, such a sweetness and such plaintiveness, such inwreathing orisons curled up in that rosy air, that it almost seemed as if far over from the deep green convent valleys of the Manilla isles, the Spanish land-breeze, wantonly turned sailor, had gone to sea, freighted with these vesper hymns.

Soothed again, but only soothed to deeper gloom, Ahab, who had sterned off from the whale, sat intently watching his final wanings from the now tranquil boat. For that strange spectacle observable in all sperm whales dying—the turning sunwards of the head, and so expiring—that strange spectacle, beheld of such a placid evening, somehow to Ahab conveyed a wondrousness unknown before.

"He turns and turns him to it,—how slowly, but how steadfastly, his homage-rendering and invoking brow, with his last dying motions. He too worships fire; most faithful, broad, baronial vassal of the sun!—Oh that these too-favoring eyes should see these too-favoring sights. Look! here, far waterlocked; beyond all hum of human weal or woe; in these most candid and impartial seas; where to traditions no rocks furnish tablets; where for long Chinese ages, the billows have still rolled on speechless and unspoken to, as stars that shine upon the Niger's unknown source; here, too, life dies sunwards full of faith; but see! no sooner dead, than death whirls round the corpse, and it heads some other way.—

"Oh, thou dark Hindoo half of nature, who of drowned bones hast builded thy separate throne somewhere in the heart of these unverdured seas; thou art an infidel, thou queen, and too truly speakest to me in the wide-slaughtering Typhoon, and the hushed burial of its after calm. Nor has this thy whale sunwards turned his dying head, and then gone round again, without a lesson to me.

"Oh, trebly hooped and welded hip of power! Oh, high aspiring, rainbowed jet!—that one strivest, this one jettest all in vain! In vain, oh whale, dost thou seek intercedings with yon all-quickening sun, that only calls forth life, but gives it not again. Yet dost thou, darker half, rock me with a prouder, if a darker faith. All thy unnamable imminglings float beneath me here; I am buoyed by breaths of once living things, exhaled as air, but water now.

"Then hail, for ever hail, O sea, in whose eternal tossings the wild fowl finds his only rest. Born of earth, yet suckled by the sea; though hill and valley mothered me, ye billows are my foster-brothers!"

THE WHALE WATCH   CXVII

THE four whales slain that evening had died wide apart;
one, far to windward; one, less distant, to leeward; one
ahead; one astern. These last three were brought alongside
ere nightfall; but the windward one could not be reached till
morning; and the boat that had killed it lay by its side all
night; and that boat was Ahab's.

The waif-pole was thrust upright into the dead whale's
spout-hole; and the lantern hanging from its top, cast a
troubled flickering glare upon the black, glossy back, and far
out upon the midnight waves, which gently chafed the
whale's broad flank, like soft surf upon a beach.

Ahab and all his boat's crew seemed asleep but the Parsee;
who crouching in the bow, sat watching the sharks, that spec-
trally played round the whale, and tapped the light cedar
planks with their tails. A sound like the moaning in squadrons
over Asphaltites of unforgiven ghosts of Gomorrah, ran
shuddering through the air.

Started from his slumbers, Ahab, face to face, saw the Parsee; and hooped round by the gloom of the night they seemed
the last men in a flooded world. "I have dreamed it again,"
said he.

"Of the hearses? Have I not said, old man, that neither
hearse nor coffin can be thine?"

"And who are hearsed that die on the sea?"

"But I said, old man, that ere thou couldst die on this
voyage, two hearses must verily be seen by thee on the sea;
the first not made by mortal hands; and the visible wood of
the last one must be grown in America."

"Aye, aye! a strange sight that, Parsee:—a hearse and its
plumes floating over the ocean with the waves for the pall-
bearers. Ha! Such a sight we shall not soon see."

"Believe it or not, thou canst not die till it be seen, old
man."

"And what was that saying about thyself?"

"Though it come to the last, I shall still go before thee
thy pilot."

"And when thou art so gone before—if that ever befall—
then ere I can follow, thou must still appear to me, to pilot

me still?—Was it not so? Well, then, did I believe all ye say, oh my pilot! I have here two pledges that I shall yet slay Moby Dick and survive it."

"Take another pledge, old man," said the Parsee, as his eyes lighted up like fire-flies in the gloom—"Hemp only can kill thee."

"The gallows, ye mean.—I am immortal then, on land and on sea," cried Ahab, with a laugh of derision;—"Immortal on land and on sea!"

Both were silent again, as one man. The grey dawn came on, and the slumbering crew arose from the boat's bottom, and ere noon the dead whale was brought to the ship.

THE QUADRANT   CXVIII

THE season for the Line at length drew near; and every day when Ahab, coming from his cabin, cast his eyes aloft, the vigilant helmsman would ostentatiously handle his spokes, and the eager mariners quickly run to the braces, and would stand there with all their eyes centrally fixed on the nailed doubloon; impatient for the order to point the ship's prow for the equator. In good time the order came. It was hard upon high noon; and Ahab, seated in the bows of his high-hoisted boat, was about taking his wonted daily observation of the sun to determine his latitude.

Now, in that Japanese sea, the days in summer are as freshets of effulgences. That unblinkingly vivid Japanese sun seems the blazing focus of the glassy ocean's immeasurable burning-glass. The sky looks lacquered; clouds there are none; the horizon floats; and this nakedness of unrelieved radiance is as the insufferable splendors of God's throne. Well that Ahab's quadrant was furnished with colored glasses, through which to take sight of that solar fire. So, swinging his seated form to the roll of the ship, and with his astrological-looking instrument placed to his eye, he remained in that posture for some moments to catch the precise instant when the sun should gain its precise meridian. Meantime while his whole attention was absorbed, the Parsee was kneeling beneath him on the ship's deck, and with face thrown up like Ahab's, was eyeing the same sun with him; only the lids of his eyes half hooded their orbs, and his

wild face was subdued to an earthly passionlessness. At
length the desired observation was taken; and with his pencil
upon his ivory leg, Ahab soon calculated what his latitude
must be at that precise instant. Then falling into a moment's
revery, he again looked up towards the sun and murmured
to himself: "Thou sea-mark! thou high and mighty Pilot!
thou tellest me truly where I *am*—but canst thou cast the
least hint where I *shall* be? Or canst thou tell where some
other thing beside me is this moment living? Where is Moby
Dick? This instant thou must be eyeing him. These eyes of
mine look into the very eye that is even now beholding him;
aye, and into the eye that is even now equally beholding the
objects on the unknown, thither side of thee, thou sun!"

Then gazing at his quadrant, and handling, one after the
other, its numerous cabalistical contrivances, he pondered
again, and muttered: "Foolish toy! babies' plaything of
haughty Admirals, and Commodores, and Captains; the
world brags of thee, of thy cunning and might; but what
after all canst thou do, but tell the poor, pitiful point, where
thou thyself happenest to be on this wide planet, and the
hand that holds thee: no! not one jot more! Thou canst not
tell where one drop of water or one grain of sand will be to-
morrow noon; and yet with thy impotence thou insultest the
sun! Science! Curse thee, thou vain toy; and cursed be all
things that cast man's eyes aloft to that heaven, whose live
vividness but scorches him, as these old eyes are even now
scorched with thy light, O sun! Level by nature to this earth's
horizon are the glances of man's eyes; not shot from the
crown of his head, as if God had meant him to gaze on his
firmament. Curse thee, thou quadrant!" dashing it to the
deck, "no longer will I guide my earthly way by thee; the
level ship's compass, and the level dead-reckoning, by log
and by line; *these* shall conduct me, and show me my
place on the sea. Aye," lighting from the boat to the deck,
"thus I trample on thee, thou paltry thing that feebly pointest
on high! thus I split and destroy thee!"

As the frantic old man thus spoke and thus trampled with
his live and dead feet, a sneering triumph that seemed meant
for Ahab, and a fatalistic despair that seemed meant for himself—these passed over the mute, motionless Parsee's face.
Unobserved he rose and glided away; while, awestruck by the
aspect of their commander, the seamen clustered together on
the forecastle, till Ahab, troubledly pacing the deck, shouted
out—"To the braces! Up helm!—square in!"

In an instant the yards swung round; and as the ship half-wheeled upon her heel, her three firm-seated graceful masts erectly poised upon her long, ribbed hull, seemed as the three Horatii pirouetting on one sufficient steed.

Standing between the knight-heads, Starbuck watched the Pequod's tumultuous way, and Ahab's also, as he went lurching along the deck.

"I have sat before the dense coal fire and watched it all aglow, full of its tormented flaming life; and I have seen it wane at last, down, down, to dumbest dust. Old man of oceans! of all this fiery life of thine, what will at length remain but one little heap of ashes!"

"Aye," cried Stubb, "but sea-coal ashes—mind ye that, Mr. Starbuck—sea-coal, not your common charcoal. Well, well; I heard Ahab mutter, 'Here some one thrusts these cards into these old hands of mine; swears that I must play them, and no others.' And damn me, Ahab, but thou actest right; live in the game, and die it!"

THE CANDLES   CXIX

WARMEST climes but nurse the cruellest fangs: the tiger of Bengal crouches in spiced groves of ceaseless verdure. Skies the most effulgent but basket the deadliest thunders: gorgeous Cuba knows tornadoes that never swept tame northern lands. So, too, it is, that in these resplendent Japanese seas the mariner encounters the direst of all storms, the Typhoon. It will sometimes burst from out that cloudless sky, like an exploding bomb upon a dazed and sleepy town.

Towards evening of that day, the Pequod was torn of her canvas, and bare-poled was left to fight a Typhoon which had struck her directly ahead. When darkness came on, sky and sea roared and split with the thunder, and blazed with the lightning, that showed the disabled masts fluttering here and there with the rags which the first fury of the tempest had left for its after sport.

Holding by a shroud, Starbuck was standing on the quarter-deck; at every flash of the lightning glancing aloft, to see what additional disaster might have befallen the intricate hamper there; while Stubb and Flask were directing the men in the higher hoisting and firmer lashing of the boats. But

all their pains seemed naught. Though lifted to the very top
of the cranes, the windward quarter boat (Ahab's) did not
escape. A great rolling sea, dashing high up against the reeling ship's high tetering side, stove in the boat's bottom at
the stern, and left it again, all dripping through like a sieve.

"Bad work, bad work! Mr. Starbuck," said Stubb, regarding
the wreck, "but the sea will have its way. Stubb, for one,
can't fight it. You see, Mr. Starbuck, a wave has such a
great long start before it leaps, all round the world it runs,
and then comes the spring! But as for me, all the start
I have to meet it, is just across the deck here. But never
mind; it's all in fun: so the old song says;"—(*sings.*)

> Oh! jolly is the gale,
> And a joker is the whale,
> A' flourishin' his tail,—

Such a funny, sporty, gamy, jesty, joky, hoky-poky lad, is the
Ocean, oh!

> The scud all a flyin',
> That's his flip only foamin';
> When he stirs in the spicin',—

Such a funny, sporty, gamy, jesty, joky, hoky-poky lad, is the
Ocean, oh!

> Thunder splits the ships,
> But he only smacks his lips,
> A tastin' of this flip,—

Such a funny, sporty, gamy, jesty, joky, hoky-poky lad, is the
Ocean, oh!

"Avast Stubb," cried Starbuck, "let the Typhoon sing, and
strike his harp here in our rigging; but if thou art a brave
man thou wilt hold thy peace."

"But I am not a brave man; never said I was a brave man;
I am a coward; and I sing to keep up my spirits. And I tell
you what it is, Mr. Starbuck, there's no way to stop my singing in this world but to cut my throat. And when that's done,
ten to one I sing ye the doxology for a wind-up."

"Madman! look through my eyes if thou hast none of thine
own."

"What! how can you see better of a dark night than anybody else, never mind how foolish?"

"Here!" cried Starbuck, seizing Stubb by the shoulder, and
pointing his hand towards the weather bow, "markest thou
not that the gale comes from the eastward, the very course
Ahab is to run for Moby Dick? the very course he swung to
this day noon? now mark his boat there; where is that

stove? In the stern-sheets, man; where he is wont to stand—his stand-point is stove, man! Now jump overboard, and sing away, if thou must!"

"I don't half understand ye; what's in the wind?"

"Yes, yes, round the Cape of Good Hope is the shortest way to Nantucket," soliloquized Starbuck, suddenly, heedless of Stubb's question. "The gale that now hammers at us to stave us, we can turn it into a fair wind that will drive us towards home. Yonder, to windward, all is blackness of doom; but to leeward, homeward—I see it lightens up there; but not with the lightning."

At that moment in one of the intervals of profound darkness, following the flashes, a voice was heard at his side; and almost at the same instant a volley of thunder peals rolled overhead.

"Who's there?"

"Old Thunder!" said Ahab, groping his way along the bulwarks to his pivot-hole; but suddenly finding his path made plain to him by elbowed lances of fire.

Now, as the lightning rod to a spire on shore is intended to carry off the perilous fluid into the soil; so the kindred rod which at sea some ships carry to each mast, is intended to conduct it into the water. But as this conductor must descend to considerable depth, that its end may avoid all contact with the hull; and as moreover, if kept constantly towing there, it would be liable to many mishaps, besides interfering not a little with some of the rigging, and more or less impeding the vessel's way in the water; because of all this, the lower parts of a ship's lightning-rods are not always overboard; but are generally made in long slender links, so as to be the more readily hauled up into the chains outside, or thrown down into the sea, as occasion may require.

"The rods! the rods!" cried Starbuck to the crew, suddenly admonished to vigilance by the vivid lightning that had just been darting flambeaux, to light Ahab to his post. "Are they overboard? drop them over, fore and aft. Quick!"

"Avast!" cried Ahab; "let's have fair play here, though we be the weaker side. Yet I'll contribute to raise rods on the Himmalehs and Andes, that all the world may be secured; but out on privileges! Let them be, sir."

"Look aloft!" cried Starbuck. "The corpusants! the corpusants!"

All the yard-arms were tipped with a pallid fire; and touched at each tri-pointed lightning-rod-end with three ta-

pering white flames, each of the three tall masts was silently
burning in that sulphurous air, like three gigantic wax tapers
before an altar.

"Blast the boat! let it go!" cried Stubb at this instant, as a
swashing sea heaved up under his own little craft, so that its
gunwale violently jammed his hand, as he was passing a
lashing. "Blast it!"—but slipping backward on the deck, his
uplifted eyes caught the flames; and immediately shifting his
tone, he cried—"The corpusants have mercy on us all!"

To sailors, oaths are household words; they will swear in
the trance of the calm, and in the teeth of the tempest; they
will imprecate curses from the topsail-yard-arms, when most
they teter over to a seething sea; but in all my voyagings, seldom have I heard a common oath when God's burning finger has been laid on the ship; when His "Mene, Mene, Tekel
Upharsin" has been woven into the shrouds and the cordage.

While this pallidness was burning aloft, few words were
heard from the enchanted crew; who in one thick cluster
stood on the forecastle, all their eyes gleaming in that pale
phosphorescence, like a far away constellation of stars. Relieved against the ghostly light, the gigantic jet negro, Daggoo, loomed up to thrice his real stature, and seemed the
black cloud from which the thunder had come. The parted
mouth of Tashtego revealed his shark-white teeth, which
strangely gleamed as if they too had been tipped by corpusants; while lit up by the preternatural light, Queequeg's tattooing burned like Satanic blue flames on his body.

The tableau all waned at last with the pallidness aloft; and
once more the Pequod and every soul on her decks were
wrapped in a pall. A moment or two passed, when Starbuck, going forward, pushed against some one. It was Stubb.
"What thinkest thou now, man; I heard thy cry; it was not
the same in the song."

"No, no, it wasn't; I said the corpusants have mercy on
us all; and I hope they will, still. But do they only have
mercy on long faces?—have they no bowels for a laugh? And
look ye, Mr. Starbuck—but it's too dark to look. Hear me,
then: I take that mast-head flame we saw for a sign of good
luck; for those masts are rooted in a hold that is going to be
chock a' block with sperm-oil, d'ye see; and so, all that sperm
will work up into the masts, like sap in a tree. Yes, our
three masts will yet be as three spermaceti candles—that's
the good promise we saw."

At that moment Starbuck caught sight of Stubb's face

slowly beginning to glimmer into sight. Glancing upwards, he cried: "See! see!" and once more the high tapering flames were beheld with what seemed redoubled supernaturalness in their pallor.

"The corpusants have mercy on us all," cried Stubb, again.

At the base of the mainmast, full beneath the doubloon and the flame, the Parsee was kneeling in Ahab's front, but with his head bowed away from him; while near by, from the arched and overhanging rigging, where they had just been engaged securing a spar, a number of the seamen, arrested by the glare, now cohered together, and hung pendulous, like a knot of numbed wasps from a drooping, orchard twig. In various enchanted attitudes, like the standing, or stepping, or running skeletons in Herculaneum, others remained rooted to the deck; but all their eyes upcast.

"Aye, aye, men!" cried Ahab. "Look up at it; mark it well; the white flame but lights the way to the White Whale! Hand me those main-mast links there; I would fain feel this pulse, and let mine beat against it; blood against fire! So."

Then turning—the last link held fast in his left hand, he put his foot upon the Parsee; and with fixed upward eye, and high-flung right arm, he stood erect before the lofty tri-pointed trinity of flames.

"Oh! thou clear spirit of clear fire, whom on these seas I as Persian once did worship, till in the sacramental act so burned by thee, that to this hour I bear the scar; I now know thee, thou clear spirit, and I now know that thy right worship is defiance. To neither love nor reverence wilt thou be kind; and e'en for hate thou canst but kill; and all are killed. No fearless fool now fronts thee. I own thy speechless, placeless power; but to the last gasp of my earthquake life will dispute its unconditional, unintegral mastery in me. In the midst of the personified impersonal, a personality stands here. Though but a point at best; whencesoe'er I came; wheresoe'er I go; yet while I earthly live, the queenly personality lives in me, and feels her royal rights. But war is pain, and hate is woe. Come in thy lowest form of love, and I will kneel and kiss thee; but at thy highest, come as mere supernal power; and though thou launchest navies of full-freighted worlds, there's that in here that still remains indifferent. Oh, thou clear spirit, of thy fire thou madest me, and like a true child of fire, I breathe it back to thee."

[Sudden, repeated flashes of lightning; the nine flames leap lengthwise to thrice their previous height; Ahab, with the *rest, closes his eyes, his right hand pressed hard upon them.*]

"I own thy speechless, placeless power; said I not so? Nor was it wrung from me; nor do I now drop these links. Thou canst blind; but I can then grope. Thou canst consume; but I can then be ashes. Take the homage of these poor eyes, and shutter-hands. I would not take it. The lightning flashes through my skull; mine eye-balls ache and ache; my whole beaten brain seems as beheaded, and rolling on some stunning ground. Oh, oh! Yet blindfold, yet will I talk to thee. Light though thou be, thou leapest out of darkness; but I am darkness leaping out of light, leaping out of thee! The javelins cease; open eyes; see, or not? There burn the flames! Oh! thou magnanimous! now I do glory in my genealogy. But thou art but my fiery father; my sweet mother, I know not. Oh, cruel! what hast thou done with her? There lies my puzzle; but thine is greater. Thou knowest not how came ye, hence callest thyself unbegotten; certainly knowest not thy beginning, hence callest thyself unbegun. I know that of me, which thou knowest not of thyself, oh, thou omnipotent. There is some unsuffusing thing beyond thee, thou clear spirit, to whom all thy eternity is but time, all thy creativeness mechanical. Through thee, thy flaming self, my scorched eyes do dimly see it. Oh, thou foundling fire, thou hermit immemorial, thou too hast thy incommunicable riddle, thy unparticipated grief. Here again with haughty agony, I read my sire. Leap! leap up, and lick the sky! I leap with thee; I burn with thee; would fain be welded with thee; defyingly I worship thee!"

"The boat! the boat!" cried Starbuck, "look at thy boat, old man!"

Ahab's harpoon, the one forged at Perth's fire, remained firmly lashed in conspicuous crotch, so that it projected beyond his whale-boat's bow; but the sea that had stove its bottom had caused the loose leather sheath to drop off; and from the keen steel barb there now came a levelled flame of pale, forked fire. As the silent harpoon burned there like a serpent's tongue, Starbuck grasped Ahab by the arm— "God, God is against thee, old man; forbear! t'is an ill voyage! ill begun, ill continued; let me square the yards, while we may, old man, and make a fair wind of it homewards, to go on a better voyage than this."

Overhearing Starbuck, the panic-stricken crew instantly ran to the braces—though not a sail was left aloft. For the moment all the aghast mate's thoughts seemed theirs; they raised a half mutinous cry. But dashing the rattling lightning links to the deck, and snatching the burning harpoon, Ahab waved it like a torch among them; swearing to transfix with it the first sailor that but cast loose a rope's end. Petrified by his aspect, and still more shrinking from the fiery dart that he held, the men fell back in dismay, and Ahab again spoke:—

"All your oaths to hunt the White Whale are as binding as mine; and heart, soul, and body, lungs and life, old Ahab is bound. And that ye may know to what tune this heart beats; look ye here; thus I blow out the last fear!" And with one blast of his breath he extinguished the flame.

As in the hurricane that sweeps the plain, men fly the neighborhood of some lone, gigantic elm, whose very height and strength but render it so much the more unsafe, because so much the more a mark for thunderbolts; so at those last words of Ahab's many of the mariners did run from him in a terror of dismay.

THE DECK TOWARDS THE END OF THE FIRST NIGHT WATCH CXX

Ahab standing by the helm. Starbuck approaching him.

"WE must send down the main-top-sail yard, sir. The band is working loose, and the lee lift is half-stranded. Shall I strike it, sir?"

"Strike nothing; lash it. If I had sky-sail poles, I'd sway them up now."

"Sir?—in God's name!—sir?"

"Well."

"The anchors are working, sir. Shall I get them inboard?"

"Strike nothing, and stir nothing, but lash everything. The wind rises, but it has not got up to my table-lands yet. Quick, and see to it.—By masts and keels! he takes me for the hunch-backed skipper of some coasting smack. Send down my main-top-sail yard! Ho, gluepots! Loftiest trucks were made for wildest winds, and this brain-truck of mine now sails amid the cloud-scud. Shall I strike that? Oh, none but cowards send down their brain-trucks in tempest time. What

a hooroosh aloft there! I would e'en take it for sublime, did
I not know that the colic is a noisy malady. Oh, take medicine, take medicine!"

MIDNIGHT—
THE FORECASTLE BULWARKS   CXXI

*Stubb and Flask mounted on them, and passing additional
lashings over the anchors there hanging.*

"NO, Stubb; you may pound that knot there as much
as you please, but you will never pound into me what you
were just now saying. And how long ago is it since you said
the very contrary? Didn't you once say that whatever ship
Ahab sails in, that ship should pay something extra on its
insurance policy, just as though it were loaded with powder
barrels aft and boxes of lucifers forward? Stop now; didn't
you say so?"

"Well, suppose I did? What then? I've part changed my
flesh since that time, why not my mind? Besides, supposing
we *are* loaded with powder barrels aft and lucifers forward;
how the devil could the lucifers get afire in this drenching
spray here? Why, my little man, you have pretty red hair,
but you couldn't get afire now. Shake yourself; you're Aquarius, or the water-bearer, Flask; might fill pitchers at
your coat collar. Don't you see, then, that for these extra risks
the Marine Insurance companies have extra guarantees? Here
are hydrants, Flask. But hark, again, and I'll answer ye the
other thing. First take your leg off from the crown of the
anchor here, though, so I can pass the rope; now listen.
What the mighty difference between holding a mast's lightning-rod in the storm, and standing close by a mast that
hasn't got any lightning-rod at all in a storm? Don't you see,
you timber-head, that no harm can come to the holder of
the rod, unless the mast is first struck? What are you
talking about, then? Not one ship in a hundred carries rods,
and Ahab—aye, man, and all of us,—were in no more danger
then, in my poor opinion, than all the crews in ten thousand
ships now sailing the seas. Why, you King-Post, you, I suppose you would have every man in the world go about with
a small lightning-rod running up the corner of his hat, like

a militia officer's skewered feather, and trailing behind like
his sash. Why don't ye be sensible, Flask? it's easy to be sensible; why don't ye, then? any man with half an eye can
be sensible."

"I don't know that, Stubb. You sometimes find it rather
hard."

"Yes, when a fellow's soaked through, it's hard to be
sensible, that's a fact. And I am about drenched with this
spray. Never mind; catch the turn there, and pass it. Seems
to me we are lashing down these anchors now as if they
were never going to be used again. Tying these two anchors
here, Flask, seems like tying a man's hands behind him.
And what big generous hands they are, to be sure. These are
your iron fists, hey? What a hold they have, too! I wonder,
Flask, whether the world is anchored anywhere; if she is, she
swings with an uncommon long cable, though. There, hammer that knot down, and we've done. So; next to touching
land, lighting on deck is the most satisfactory. I say, just
wring out my jacket skirts, will ye? Thank ye. They laugh
at long-togs so, Flask; but seems to me, a long tailed coat
ought always to be worn in all storms afloat. The tails tapering down that way, serve to carry off the water, d'ye
see. Same with cocked hats; the cocks form gable-end eave-
troughs, Flask. No more monkey-jackets and tarpaulins for
me; I must mount a swallowtail, and drive down a beaver;
so. Halloa! whew! there goes my tarpaulin overboard; Lord,
Lord, that the winds that come from heaven should be so
unmannerly! This is a nasty night, lad."

MIDNIGHT ALOFT— THUNDER AND LIGHTNING CXXII

*The Main-top-sail yard.—Tashtego passing new
lashings around it.*

"UM, um, um. Stop that thunder! Plenty too much
thunder up here. What's the use of thunder? Um, um, um. We
don't want thunder; we want rum; give us a glass of rum. Um,
um, um!"

THE MUSKET CXXIII

DURING the most violent shocks of the Typhoon, the man at the Pequod's jaw-bone tiller had several times been reelingly hurled to the deck by its spasmodic motions, even though preventer tackles had been attached to it—for they were slack—because some play to the tiller was indispensable.

In a severe gale like this, while the ship is but a tossed shuttlecock to the blast, it is by no means uncommon to see the needles in the compasses, at intervals, go round and round. It was thus with the Pequod's; at almost every shock the helmsman had not failed to notice the whirling velocity with which they revolved upon the cards; it is a sight that hardly any one can behold without some sort of unwonted emotion.

Some hours after midnight, the Typhoon abated so much, that through the strenuous exertions of Starbuck and Stubb —one engaged forward and the other aft—the shivered remnants of the jib and fore and main-top-sails were cut adrift from the spars, and went eddying away to leeward, like the feathers of an albatross, which sometimes are cast to the winds when that storm-tossed bird is on the wing.

The three corresponding new sails were now bent and reefed, and a storm-trysail was set further aft; so that the ship soon went through the water with some precision again; and the course—for the present, East-south-east—which he was to steer, if practicable, was once more given to the helmsman. For during the violence of the gale, he had only steered according to its vicissitudes. But as he was now bringing the ship as near her course as possible, watching the compass meanwhile, lo! a good sign! the wind seemed coming round astern; aye, the foul breeze became fair!

Instantly the yards were squared, to the lively song of "Ho! the fair wind! oh-he-yo, cheerly, men!" the crew singing for joy, that so promising an event should so soon have falsified the evil portents preceding it.

In commonplace with the standing order of his commander—to report immediately, and at any one of the twenty-four hours, any decided change in the affairs of the deck,—

Starbuck had no sooner trimmed the yards to the breeze—however reluctantly and gloomily,—than he mechanically went below to apprise Captain Ahab of the circumstance.

Ere knocking at his state-room, he involuntarily paused before it a moment. The cabin lamp—taking long swings this way and that—was burning fitfully, and casting fitful shadows upon the old man's bolted door,—a thin one, with fixed blinds inserted, in place of upper panels. The isolated subterraneousness of the cabin made a certain humming silence to reign there, though it was hooped round by all the roar of the elements. The loaded muskets in the rack were shiningly revealed, as they stood upright against the forward bulkhead. Starbuck was an honest, upright man; but out of Starbuck's heart, at that instant when he saw the muskets, there strangely evolved an evil thought; but so blent with its neutral or good accompaniments that for the instant he hardly knew it for itself.

"He would have shot me once," he murmured, "yes, there's the very musket that he pointed at me;—that one with the studded stock; let me touch it—lift it. Strange, that I, who have handled so many deadly lances, strange, that I should shake so now. Loaded? I must see. Aye, aye; and powder in the pan;—that's not good. Best spill it?—wait. I'll cure myself of this. I'll hold the musket boldly while I think.—I come to report a fair wind to him. But how fair? Fair for death and doom,—*that's* fair for Moby Dick. It's a fair wind that's only fair for that accursed fish. —The very tube he pointed at me!—the very one; *this* one —I hold it here; he would have killed me with the very thing I handle now.—Aye and he would fain kill all his crew. Does he not say he will not strike his spars to any gale? Has he not dashed his heavenly quadrant? and in these same perilous seas, gropes he not his way by mere dead reckoning of the error-abounding log? and in this very Typhoon, did he not swear that he would have no lightning-rods? But shall this crazed old man be tamely suffered to drag a whole ship's company down to doom with him?—Yes, it would make him the wilful murderer of thirty men and more, if this ship come to any deadly harm; and come to deadly harm, my soul swears this ship will, if Ahab have his way. If, then, he were this instant—put aside, that crime would not be his. Ha! is he muttering in his sleep? Yes, just there,—in there, he's sleeping. Sleeping? aye, but still alive, and soon awake again. I can't withstand thee,

then, old man. Not reasoning; not remonstrance; not entreaty wilt thou hearken to; all this thou scornest. Flat
obedience to thy own flat commands, this is all thou breath-
est. Aye, and say'st the men have vow'd thy vow; say'st
all of us are Ahabs. Great God forbid!—But is there
no other way? no lawful way?—Make him a prisoner to
be taken home? What! hope to wrest this old man's living
power from his own living hands? Only a fool would try it.
Say he were pinioned even; knotted all over with ropes and
hawsers; chained down to ring-bolts on this cabin floor;
he would be more hideous than a caged tiger, then. I could
not endure the sight; could not possibly fly his howlings; all
comfort, sleep itself, inestimable reason would leave me on
the long intolerable voyage. What, then, remains? The
land is hundreds of leagues away, and locked Japan the
nearest. I stand alone here upon an open sea, with two
oceans and a whole continent between me and law.—Aye,
aye, 'tis so.—Is heaven a murderer when its lightning strikes
a would-be murderer in his bed, tindering sheets and skin
together?—And would I be a murderer, then, if"——and
slowly, stealthily, and half sideways looking, he placed the
loaded musket's end against the door.

"On this level, Ahab's hammock swings within; his head
this way. A touch, and Starbuck may survive to hug his
wife and child again.—Oh Mary! Mary!—boy! boy! boy!—
But if I wake thee not to death, old man, who can tell to what
unsounded deeps Starbuck's body this day week may sink,
with all the crew! Great God, where art thou? Shall I?
shall I?——The wind has gone down and shifted, sir; the
fore and main topsails are reefed and set; she heads her
course."

"Stern all! Oh Moby Dick, I clutch thy heart at last!"

Such were the sounds that now came hurtling from out the
old man's tormented sleep, as if Starbuck's voice had caused
the long dumb dream to speak.

The yet levelled musket shook like a drunkard's arm
against the panel; Starbuck seemed wrestling with an angel;
but turning from the door, he placed the death-tube in its
rack, and left the place.

"He's too sound asleep, Mr. Stubb; go thou down, and
wake him, and tell him. I must see to the deck here. Thou
know'st what to say."

THE NEEDLE   CXXIV

NEXT morning the not-yet-subsided sea rolled in long slow billows of mighty bulk, and striving in the Pequod's gurgling track, pushed her on like giants' palms outspread. The strong, unstaggering breeze abounded so, that sky and air seemed vast outbellying sails; the whole world boomed before the wind. Muffled in the full morning light, the invisible sun was only known by the spread intensity of his place; where his bayonet rays moved on in stacks. Emblazonings, as of crowned Babylonian kings and queens, reigned over everything. The sea was as a crucible of molten gold, that bubblingly leaps with light and heat.

Long maintaining an enchanted silence, Ahab stood apart; and every time the tetering ship loweringly pitched down her bowsprit, he turned to eye the bright sun's rays produced ahead; and when she profoundly settled by the stern, he turned behind, and saw the sun's rearward place, and how the same yellow rays were blending with his undeviating wake.

"Ha, ha, my ship! thou mightest well be taken now for the sea-chariot of the sun. Ho, ho! all ye nations before my prow, I bring the sun to ye! Yoke on the further billows; hallo! a tandem, I drive the sea!"

But suddenly reined back by some counter thought, he hurried towards the helm, huskily demanding how the ship was heading.

"East-sou-east, sir," said the frightened steersman.

"Thou liest!" smiting him with his clenched fist. "Heading East at this hour in the morning, and the sun astern?"

Upon this every soul was confounded; for the phenomenon just then observed by Ahab had unaccountably escaped every one else; but its very blinding palpableness must have been the cause.

Thrusting his head half way into the binnacle, Ahab caught one glimpse of the compasses; his uplifted arm slowly fell; for a moment he almost seemed to stagger. Standing behind him Starbuck looked, and lo! the two compasses pointed East, and the Pequod was as infallibly going West.

But ere the first wild alarm could get out abroad among

the crew, the old man with a rigid laugh exclaimed, "I have it! It has happened before. Mr. Starbuck, last night's thunder turned our compasses—that's all. Thou hast before now heard of such a thing, I take it."

"Aye; but never before has it happened to me, sir," said the pale mate, gloomily.

Here, it must needs be said, that accidents like this have in more than one case occurred to ships in violent storms. The magnetic energy, as developed in the mariner's needle, is, as all know, essentially one with the electricity beheld in heaven; hence it is not to be much marvelled at, that such things should be. In instances where the lightning has actually struck the vessel, so as to smite down some of the spars and rigging, the effect upon the needle has at times been still more fatal; all its loadstone virtue being annihilated, so that the before magnetic steel was of no more use than an old wife's knitting needle. But in either case, the needle never again, of itself, recovers the original virtue thus marred or lost; and if the binnacle compasses be affected, the same fate reaches all the others that may be in the ship; even were the lowermost one inserted into the kelson.

Deliberately standing before the binnacle, and eyeing the transpointed compasses, the old man, with the sharp of his extended hand, now took the precise bearing of the sun, and satisfied that the needles were exactly inverted, shouted out his orders for the ship's course to be changed accordingly. The yards were hard up; and once more the Pequod thrust her undaunted bows into the opposing wind, for the supposed fair one had only been juggling her.

Meanwhile, whatever were his own secret thoughts, Starbuck said nothing, but quietly he issued all requisite orders; while Stubb and Flask—who in some small degree seemed then to be sharing his feelings—likewise unmurmuringly acquiesced. As for the men, though some of them lowly rumbled, their fear of Ahab was greater than their fear of Fate. But as ever before, the pagan harpooneers remained almost wholly unimpressed; or if impressed, it was only with a certain magnetism shot into their congenial hearts from inflexible Ahab's.

For a space the old man walked the deck in rolling reveries. But chancing to slip with his ivory heel, he saw the crushed copper sight-tubes of the quadrant he had the day before dashed to the deck.

"Thou poor, proud heaven-gazer and sun's pilot! yesterday I wrecked thee, and to-day the compasses would feign have wrecked me. So, so. But Ahab is lord over the level loadstone yet. Mr. Starbuck—a lance without the pole; a topmaul, and the smallest of the sail-maker's needles. Quick!"

Accessory, perhaps, to the impulse dictating the thing he was now about to do, were certain prudential motives, whose object might have been to revive the spirits of his crew by a stroke of his subtile skill, in a matter so wondrous as that of the inverted compasses. Besides, the old man well knew that to steer by transpointed needles, though clumsily practicable, was not a thing to be passed over by superstitious sailors, without some shudderings and evil portents.

"Men," said he, steadily turning upon the crew, as the mate handed him the things he had demanded, "my men, the thunder turned old Ahab's needles; but out of this bit of steel Ahab can make one of his own, that will point as true as any."

Abashed glances of servile wonder were exchanged by the sailors, as this was said; and with fascinated eyes they awaited whatever magic might follow. But Starbuck looked away.

With a blow from the top-maul Ahab knocked off the steel head of the lance, and then handing to the mate the long iron rod remaining, bade him hold it upright, without its touching the deck. Then, with the maul, after repeatedly smiting the upper end of this iron rod, he placed the blunted needle endwise on the top of it, and less strongly hammered that, several times, the mate still holding the rod as before. Then going through some small strange motions with it—whether indispensable to the magnetizing of the steel, or merely intended to augment the awe of the crew, is uncertain—he called for linen thread; and moving to the binnacle, slipped out the two reversed needles there, and horizontally suspended the sail-needle by its middle, over one of the compass-cards. At first, the steel went round and round, quivering and vibrating at either end; but at last it settled to its place, when Ahab, who had been intently watching for this result, stepped frankly back from the binnacle, and pointing his stretched arm towards it, exclaimed,—"Look ye, for yourselves, if Ahab be not lord of the level loadstone! The sun is East, and that compass swears it!"

One after another they peered in, for nothing but their

own eyes could persuade such ignorance as theirs, and one after another they slunk away.

In his fiery eyes of scorn and triumph, you then saw Ahab in all his fatal pride.

THE LOG AND LINE   CXXV

WHILE now the fated Pequod had been so long afloat this voyage, the log and line had but very seldom been in use. Owing to a confident reliance upon other means of determining the vessel's place, some merchantmen, and many whalemen, especially when cruising, wholly neglect to heave the log; though at the same time, and frequently more for form's sake than anything else, regularly putting down upon the customary slate the course steered by the ship, as well as the presumed average rate of progression every hour. It had been thus with the Pequod. The wooden reel and angular log attached hung, long untouched, just beneath the railing of the after bulwarks. Rains and spray had damped it; sun and wind had warped it; all the elements had combined to rot a thing that hung so idly. But heedless of all this, his mood seized Ahab, as he happened to glance upon the reel, not many hours after the magnet scene, and he remembered how his quadrant was no more, and recalled his frantic oath about the level log and line. The ship was sailing plungingly; astern the billows rolled in riots.

"Forward, there! Heave the log!"

Two seamen came. The golden-hued Tahitian and the grizzly Manxman. "Take the reel, one of ye, I'll heave."

They went towards the extreme stern, on the ship's lee side, where the deck, with the oblique energy of the wind, was now almost dipping into the creamy, sidelong-rushing sea.

The Manxman took the reel, and holding it high up, by the projecting handle-ends of the spindle, round which the spool of line revolved, so stood with the angular log hanging downwards, till Ahab advanced to him.

Ahab stood before him, and was lightly unwinding some thirty or forty turns to form a preliminary hand-coil to

toss overboard, when the old Manxman, who was intently
eyeing both him and the line, made bold to speak.

"Sir, I mistrust it; this line looks far gone, long heat and
wet have spoiled it."

" 'Twill hold, old gentleman. Long heat and wet, have
they spoiled thee? Thou seem'st to hold. Or, truer perhaps,
life holds thee; not thou it."

"I hold the spool, sir. But just as my captain says. With
these grey hairs of mine 'tis not worth while disputing,
'specially with a superior, who'll ne'er confess."

"What's that? There now's a patched professor in Queen
Nature's granite-founded College; but methinks he's too sub-
servient. Where wert thou born?"

"In the little rocky Isle of Man, sir."

"Excellent! Thou'st hit the world by that."

"I know not, sir, but I was born there."

"In the Isle of Man, hey? Well, the other way, it's good.
Here's a man from Man; a man born in once independent
Man, and now unmanned of Man; which is sucked in—by
what? Up with the reel! The dead, blind wall butts all inquiring heads at last. Up with it! So."

The log was heaved. The loose coils rapidly straightened
out in a long dragging line astern, and then, instantly, the
reel began to whirl. In turn, jerkingly raised and lowered
by the rolling billows, the towing resistance of the log
caused the old reelman to stagger strangely.

"Hold hard!"

Snap! the overstrained line sagged down in one long
festoon; the tugging log was gone.

"I crush the quadrant, the thunder turns the needles, and
now the mad sea parts the log-line. But Ahab can mend all.
Haul in here, Tahitian; reel up, Manxman. And look ye, let
the carpenter make another log, and mend thou the line.
See to it."

"There he goes now; to him nothing's happened; but to
me, the skewer seems loosening out of the middle of the
world. Haul in, haul in, Tahitian! These lines run whole, and
whirling out: come in broken, and dragging slow. Ha, Pip?
come to help; eh, Pip?"

"Pip? whom call ye Pip? Pip jumped from the whale-boat.
Pip's missing. Let's see now if ye haven't fished him up here,
fisherman. It drags hard; I guess he's holding on. Jerk him,
Tahiti! Jerk him off; we haul in no cowards here. Ho!

there's his arm just breaking water. A hatchet! a hatchet! cut if off—we haul in no cowards here. Captain Ahab! sir, sir! here's Pip, trying to get on board again."

"Peace, thou crazy loon," cried the Manxman, seizing him by the arm. "Away from the quarter-deck!"

"The greater idiot ever scolds the lesser," muttered Ahab, advancing. "Hands off from that holiness! Where sayest thou Pip was, boy?"

"Astern there, sir, astern! Lo, lo!"

"And who art thou, boy? I see not my reflection in the vacant pupils of thy eyes. Oh God! that man should be a thing for immortal souls to sieve through! Who art thou, boy?"

"Bell-boy, sir; ship's-crier; ding, dong, ding! Pip! Pip! Pip! One hundred pounds of clay reward for Pip; five feet high—looks cowardly—quickest known by that! Ding, dong, ding! Who's seen Pip the coward?"

"There can be no hearts above the snow-line. Oh, ye frozen heavens! look down here. Ye did beget this luckless child, and have abandoned him, ye creative libertines. Here, boy; Ahab's cabin shall be Pip's home henceforth, while Ahab lives. Thou touchest my inmost centre, boy; thou art tied to me by cords woven of my heart-strings. Come, let's down."

"What's this? here's velvet shark-skin," intently gazing at Ahab's hand, and feeling it. "Ah, now, had poor Pip but felt so kind a thing as this, perhaps he had ne'er been lost! This seems to me, sir, as a man-rope; something that weak souls may hold by. Oh, sir, let old Perth now come and rivet these two hands together; the black one with the white, for I will not let this go."

"Oh, boy, nor will I thee, unless I should thereby drag thee to worse horrors than are here. Come, then, to my cabin. Lo! ye believers in gods all goodness, and in man all ill, lo you! see the omniscient gods oblivious of suffering man; and man, though idiotic, and knowing not what he does, yet full of the sweet things of love and gratitude. Come! I feel prouder leading thee by thy black hand, than though I grasped an Emperor's!"

"There go two daft ones now," muttered the old Manxman. "One daft with strength, the other daft with weakness. But here's the end of the rotten line—all dripping, too. Mend it, eh? I think we had best have a new line altogether. I'll see Mr. Stubb about it."

THE LIFE-BUOY   CXXVI

STEERING now south-eastward by Ahab's levelled steel, and her progress solely determined by Ahab's level log and line; the Pequod held on her path towards the Equator. Making so long a passage through such unfrequented waters, descrying no ships, and ere long, sideways impelled by unvarying trade winds, over waves monotonously mild; all these seemed the strange calm things preluding some riotous and desperate scene.

At last, when the ship drew near to the outskirts, as it were, of the Equatorial fishing-ground, and in the deep darkness that goes before the dawn, was sailing by a cluster of rocky islets; the watch—then headed by Flask—was startled by a cry so plaintively wild and unearthly—like half-articulated wailings of the ghosts of all Herod's murdered Innocents—that one and all, they started from their reveries, and for the space of some moments stood, or sat, or leaned all transfixedly listening, like the carved Roman slave, while that wild cry remained within hearing. The Christian or civilized part of the crew said it was mermaids, and shuddered; but the pagan harpooneers remained unappalled. Yet the grey Manxman—the oldest mariner of all—declared that the wild thrilling sounds that were heard, were the voices of newly drowned men in the sea.

Below in his hammock, Ahab did not hear of this till grey dawn, when he came to the deck; it was then recounted to him by Flask, not unaccompanied with hinted dark meanings. He hollowly laughed, and thus explained the wonder.

Those rocky islands the ship had passed were the resort of great numbers of seals, and some young seals that had lost their dams, or some dams that had lost their cubs, must have risen nigh the ship and kept company with her, crying and sobbing with their human sort of wail. But this only the more affected some of them, because most mariners cherish a very supersititious feeling about seals, arising not only from their peculiar tones when in distress, but also from the human look of their round heads and semi-intelligent faces, seen uprising from the water alongside. In the sea, under certain circumstances, seals have more than once been mistaken for men.

But the bodings of the crew were destined to receive a most plausible confirmation in the fate of one of their number that morning. At sun-rise this man went from his hammock to his mast-head at the fore; and whether it was that he was not yet half waked from his sleep (for sailors sometimes go aloft in a transition state), whether it was thus with the man, there is now no telling; but, be that as it may, he had not been long at his perch, when a cry was heard—a cry and a rushing—and looking up, they saw a falling phantom in the air; and looking down, a little tossed heap of white bubbles in the blue of the sea.

The life-buoy—a long slender cask—was dropped from the stern, where it always hung obedient to a cunning spring; but no hand rose to seize it, and the sun having long beat upon this cask it had shrunken, so that it slowly filled, and the parched wood also filled at its every pore; and the studded iron-bound cask followed the sailor to the bottom, as if to yield him his pillow, though in sooth but a hard one.

And thus the first man of the Pequod that mounted the mast to look out for the White Whale, on the White Whale's own peculiar ground; that man was swallowed up in the deep. But few, perhaps, thought of that at the time. Indeed, in some sort, they were not grieved at this event, at least as a portent; for they regarded it, not as a foreshadowing of evil in the future, but as the fulfilment of an evil already presaged. They declared that now they knew the reason of those wild shrieks they had heard the night before. But again the old Manxman said nay.

The lost life-buoy was now to be replaced; Starbuck was directed to see to it; but as no cask of sufficient lightness could be found, and as in the feverish eagerness of what seemed the approaching crisis of the voyage, all hands were impatient of any toil but what was directly connected with its final end, whatever that might prove to be; therefore, they were going to leave the ship's stern unprovided with a buoy, when by certain strange signs and inuendoes Queequeg hinted a hint concerning his coffin.

"A life-buoy of a coffin!" cried Starbuck, starting.

"Rather queer, that, I should say," said Stubb.

"It will make a good enough one," said Flask, "the carpenter here can arrange it easily."

"Bring it up; there's nothing else for it," said Starbuck, after a melancholy pause. "Rig it, carpenter; do not look at me so—the coffin, I mean. Dost thou hear me? Rig it."

"And shall I nail down the lid, sir?" moving his hand as with a hammer.

"Aye."

"And shall I caulk the seams, sir?" moving his hand as with a caulking-iron.

"Aye."

"And shall I then pay over the same with pitch, sir?" moving his hand as with a pitch-pot.

"Away! what possesses thee to this? Make a life-buoy of the coffin, and no more.—Mr. Stubb, Mr. Flask, come forward with me."

"He goes off in a huff. The whole he can endure; at the parts he baulks. Now I don't like this. I make a leg for Captain Ahab, and he wears it like a gentleman; but I make a bandbox for Queequeg, and he won't put his head into it. Are all my pains to go for nothing with that coffin? And now I'm ordered to make a life-buoy of it. It's like turning an old coat; going to bring the flesh on the other side now. I don't like this cobbling sort of business—I don't like it at all; it's undignified; it's not my place. Let tinkers' brats do tinkerings; we are their betters. I like to take in hand none but clean, virgin, fair-and-square mathematical jobs, something that regularly begins at the beginning, and is at the middle when midway, and comes to an end at the conclusion; not a cobbler's job, that's at an end in the middle, and at the beginning at the end. It's the old woman's tricks to be giving cobbling jobs. Lord! what an affection all old women have for tinkers. I know an old woman of sixty-five who ran away with a bald-headed young tinker once. And that's the reason I never would work for lonely widow old women ashore, when I kept my job-shop in the Vineyard; they might have taken it into their lonely old heads to run off with me. But heigh-ho! there are no caps at sea but snow-caps. Let me see. Nail down the lid; caulk the seams; pay over the same with pitch; batten them down tight, and hang it with the snap-spring over the ship's stern. Were ever such things done before with a coffin? Some superstitious old carpenters, now, would be tied up in the rigging, ere they would do the job. But I'm made of knotty Aroostook hemlock; I don't budge. Cruppered with a coffin! Sailing about with a grave-yard tray! But never mind. We workers

in woods make bridal-bedsteads and card-tables, as well as
coffins and hearses. We work by the month, or by the job,
or by the profit; not for us to ask the why and wherefore
of our work, unless it be too confounded cobbling, and
then we stash it if we can. Hem! I'll do the job, now,
tenderly. I'll have me—let's see—how many in the ship's
company, all told? But I've forgotten. Any way, I'll have me
thirty separate, Turk's-headed life-lines, each three feet long
hanging all round to the coffin. Then, if the hull go down,
there'll be thirty lively fellows all fighting for one coffin, a
sight not seen very often beneath the sun! Come hammer,
caulking-iron, pitch-pot, and marling-spike! Let's to it."

THE DECK   CXXVII

*The coffin laid upon two line-tubs, between the vice-bench
and the open hatchway; the Carpenter caulking its seams;
the string of twisted oakum slowly unwinding from a
large roll of it placed in the bosom of his frock.—Ahab
comes slowly from the cabin-gangway, and hears Pip
following him.*

"BACK, lad; I will be with ye again presently. He goes!
Not this hand complies with my humor more genially than
that boy.—Middle aisle of a church! What's here?"

"Life-buoy, sir. Mr. Starbuck's orders. Oh, look, sir! Beware the hatchway!"

"Thank ye, man. Thy coffin lies handy to the vault."

"Sir? The hatchway? oh! So it does, sir, so it does."

"Art not thou the leg-maker? Look, did not this stump
come from thy shop?"

"I believe it did, sir; does the ferrule stand, sir?"

"Well enough. But art thou not also the undertaker?"

"Aye, sir; I patched up this thing here as a coffin for
Queequeg; but they've set me now to turning it into something else."

"Then tell me; art thou not an arrant, all-grasping, inter-
meddling, monopolizing, heathenish old scamp, to be one
day making legs, and the next day coffins to clap them in,
and yet again life-buoys out of those same coffins? Thou

art as unprincipled as the gods, and as much of a jack-of-all-trades."

"But I do not mean anything, sir. I do as I do."

"The gods again. Hark ye, dost thou not ever sing working about a coffin? The Titans, they say, hummed snatches when chipping out the craters for volcanoes; and the grave-digger in the play sings, spade in hand. Dost thou never?"

"Sing, sir? Do I sing? Oh, I'm indifferent enough, sir, for that; but the reason why the grave-digger made music must have been because there was none in his spade, sir. But the caulking mallet is full of it. Hark to it."

"Aye, and that's because the lid there's a sounding-board; and what in all things makes the sounding-board is this —there's naught beneath. And yet, a coffin with a body in it rings pretty much the same, Carpenter. Hast thou ever helped carry a bier, and heard the coffin knock against the churchyard gate, going in?"

"Faith, sir, I've——"

"Faith? What's that?"

"Why, faith, sir, it's only a sort of exclamation-like—that's all, sir."

"Um, um; go on."

"I was about to say, sir, that——"

"Art thou a silk-worm? Dost thou spin thy own shroud out of thyself? Look at thy bosom! Despatch! and get these traps out of sight."

"He goes aft. That was sudden, now; but squalls come sudden in hot latitudes. I've heard that the Isle of Albermarle, one of the Gallipagos, is cut by the Equator right in the middle. Seems to me some sort of Equator cuts yon old man, too, right in his middle. He's always under the Line—fiery hot, I tell ye! He's looking this way—come, oakum; quick. Here we go again. This wooden mallet is the cork, and I'm the professor of musical glasses—tap, tap!"

(Ahab to himself)

"There's a sight! There's a sound! The greyheaded woodpecker tapping the hollow tree! Blind and dumb might well be envied now. See! that thing rests on two line-tubs, full of two-lines. A most malicious wag, that fellow. Rat-tat! So man's seconds tick! Oh! how immaterial are all materials! What things real are there, but imponderable thoughts? Here now's the very dreaded symbol of grim death, by a mere

hap, made the expressive sign of the help and hope of most
endangered life. A life-buoy of a coffin! Does it go further?
Can it be that in some spiritual sense the coffin is, after all,
but an immortality-preserver! I'll think of that. But no. So
far gone am I in the dark side of earth, that its other side,
the theoretic bright one, seems but uncertain twilight to me.
Will ye never have done, Carpenter, with that accursed
sound? I go below; let me not see that thing here when I
return again. Now, then, Pip, we'll talk this over; I do suck
most wondrous philosophies from thee! Some unknown con-
duits from the unknown worlds must empty into thee!"

THE PEQUOD MEETS THE RACHEL   CXXVIII

NEXT day, a large ship, the Rachel, was descried, bearing directly down upon the Pequod, all her spars thickly
clustering with men. At the time the Pequod was making
good speed through the water; but as the broad-winged
windward stranger shot nigh to her, the boastful sails all
fell together as blank bladders that are burst, and all life
fled from the smitten hull.

"Bad news; she brings bad news," muttered the old Manxman. But ere her commander, who, with trumpet to mouth,
stood up in his boat; ere he could hopefully hail, Ahab's
voice was heard.

"Hast seen the White Whale?"

"Aye, yesterday. Have ye seen a whale-boat adrift?"

Throttling his joy, Ahab negatively answered this unexpected question; and would then have fain boarded the
stranger, when the stranger captain himself, having stopped
his vessel's way, was seen descending her side. A few keen
pulls, and his boat-hook soon clinched the Pequod's main-
chains, and he sprang to the deck. Immediately he was
recognized by Ahab for a Nantucketer he knew. But no
formal salutation was exchanged.

"Where was he?—not killed!—not killed!" cried Ahab,
closely advancing. "How was it?"

It seemed that somewhat late on the afternoon of the day
previous, while three of the stranger's boats were engaged
with a shoal of whales, which had led them some four or
five miles from the ship; and while they were yet in swift

chase to windward, the white hump and head of Moby
Dick had suddenly loomed up out of the blue water, not
very far to leeward; whereupon, the fourth rigged boat—a reserved one—had been instantly lowered in chase. After a
keen sail before the wind, this fourth boat—the swiftest
keeled of all—seemed to have succeeded in fastening—at
least, as well as the man at the masthead could tell anything
about it. In the distance he saw the diminished dotted boat;
and then a swift-gleam of bubbling white water; and after
that nothing more; whence it was concluded that the stricken
whale must have indefinitely run away with his pursuers, as
often happens. There was some apprehension, but no positive
alarm, as yet. The recall signals were placed in the rigging;
darkness came on; and forced to pick up her three far to
windward boats—ere going in quest of the fourth one in
the precisely opposite direction—the ship had not only been
necessitated to leave that boat to its fate till near midnight,
but, for the time, to increase her distance from it. But the
rest of her crew being at last safe aboard, she crowded all
sail—stunsail on stunsail—after the missing boat; kindling a
fire in her try-pots for a beacon; and every other man aloft
on the look-out. But though when she had thus sailed a
sufficient distance to gain the presumed place of the absent
ones when last seen; though she then paused to lower her
spare boats to pull all around her; and not finding anything, had again dashed on; again paused, and lowered her
boats; and though she had thus continued doing till day
light; yet not the least glimpse of the missing keel had been
seen.

The story told, the stranger Captain immediately went on
to reveal his object in boarding the Pequod. He desired that
ship to unite with his own in the search; by sailing over the
sea some four or five miles apart, on parallel lines, and so
sweeping a double horizon, as it were.

"I will wager something now," whispered Stubb to Flask,
"that some one in that missing boat wore off that Captain's
best coat; mayhap, his watch—he's so cursed anxious to get
it back. Who ever heard of two pious whale-ships cruising
after one missing whale-boat in the height of the whaling
season? See, Flask, only see how pale he looks—pale in the
very buttons of his eyes—look—it wasn't the coat—it must
have been the ——"

"My boy, my own boy is among them. For God's sake
—I beg, I conjure"—here exclaimed the stranger Captain

to Ahab, who thus far had icily received his petition. "For eight-and-forty hours let me charter your ship—I will gladly pay for it, and roundly pay for it—if there be no other way—for eight-and-forty hours ónly—only that—you must, oh, you must, and you *shall* do this thing."

"His son!" cried Stubb, "oh, it's his son he's lost! I take back the coat and watch—what says Ahab? We must save that boy."

"He's drowned with the rest on 'em, last night," said the old Manx sailor standing behind them; "I heard; all of ye heard their spirits."

Now, as it shortly turned out, what made this incident of the Rachel's the more melancholy, was the circumstance, that not only was one of the Captain's sons among the number of the missing boat's crew; but among the number of the other boat's crews, at the same time, but on the other hand, separated from the ship during the dark vicissitudes of the chase, there had been still another son; as that for a time, the wretched father was plunged to the bottom of the cruellest perplexity; which was only solved for him by his chief mate's instinctively adopting the ordinary procedure of a whale-ship in such emergencies, that is, when placed between jeopardized but divided boats, always to pick up the majority first. But the captain, for some unknown constitutional reason, had refrained from mentioning all this, and not till forced to it by Ahab's iciness did he allude to his one yet missing boy; a little lad, but twelve years old, whose father with the earnest but unmisgiving hardihood of a Nantucketer's paternal love, had thus early sought to initiate him in the perils and wonders of a vocation almost immemorially the destiny of all his race. Nor does it unfrequently occur, that Nantucket captains will send a son of such tender age away from them, for a protracted three or four years' voyage in some other ship than their own; so that their first knowledge of a whaleman's career shall be unenervated by any chance display of a father's natural but untimely partiality, or undue apprehensiveness and concern.

Meantime, now the stranger was still beseeching his poor boon of Ahab; and Ahab still stood like an anvil, receiving every shock, but without the least quivering of his own.

"I will not go," said the stranger, "till you say *aye* to me. Do to me as you would have me do to you in the like case. For *you* too have a boy, Captain Ahab—though but a child, and nestling safely at home now—a child of your old age too—Yes, yes, you relent; I see it—run, run, men, now, and stand by to square in the yards."

"Avast," cried Ahab—"touch not a rope-yard;" then in a voice that prolongingly moulded every word—"Captain Gardiner, I will not do it. Even now I lose time. Good bye, good bye. God bless ye, man, and may I forgive myself, but I must go. Mr. Starbuck, look at the binnacle watch, and in three minutes from this present instant warn off all strangers: then brace forward again, and let the ship sail as before."

Hurriedly turning, with averted face, he descended into his cabin, leaving the strange captain transfixed at this unconditional and utter rejection of his so earnest suit. But starting from his enchantment, Gardiner silently hurried to the side; more fell than stepped into his boat, and returned to his ship.

Soon the two ships diverged their wakes; and long as the strange vessel was in view, she was seen to yaw hither and thither at every dark spot, however small, on the sea. This way and that her yards were swung round; starboard and larboard, she continued to tack; now she beat against a head sea; and again it pushed her before it; while all the while, her masts and yards were thickly clustered with men, as three tall cherry trees, when the boys are cherrying among the boughs.

But by her still halting course and winding, woful way, you plainly saw that this ship that so wept with spray, still remained without comfort. She was Rachel, weeping for her children, because they were not.

THE CABIN   **CXXIX**

(*Ahab moving to go on deck; Pip catches him by the hand to follow.*)

"LAD, lad, I tell thee thou must not follow Ahab now. The hour is coming when Ahab would not scare thee from him, yet would not have thee by him. There is that in thee, poor lad, which I feel too curing to my malady. Like cures like; and for this hunt, my malady becomes my most desired health. Do thou abide below here, where they shall

serve thee, as if thou wert the captain. Aye, lad, thou shalt
sit here in my own screwed chair; another screw to it, thou
must be."

"No, no, no! ye have not a whole body, sir; do ye but
use poor me for your one lost leg; only tread upon me, sir;
I ask no more, so I remain a part of ye."

"Oh! spite of million villains, this makes me a bigot in
the fadeless fidelity of man!—and a black! and crazy!—
but methinks like-cures-like applies to him too; he grows
so sane again."

"They tell me, sir, that Stubb did once desert poor little
Pip, whose drowned bones now show white, for all the black-
ness of his living skin. But I will never desert ye, sir, as
Stubb did him. Sir, I must go with ye."

"If thou speakest thus to me much more, Ahab's purpose
keels up in him. I tell thee no; it cannot be."

"Oh good master, master, master!"

"Weep so, and I will murder thee! have a care, for Ahab
too is mad. Listen, and thou wilt often hear my ivory foot
upon the deck, and still know that I am there. And now I
quit thee. Thy hand!—Met! True art thou, lad, as the circumference to its centre. So: God for ever bless thee; and
if it come to that,—God for ever save thee, let what will
befall."

(Ahab goes; Pip steps one step forward.)

"Here he this instant stood; I stand in his air,—but I'm
alone. Now were even poor Pip here I could endure it, but
he's missing. Pip! Pip! Ding, dong, ding! Who's seen Pip?
He must be up here; let's try the door. What? neither lock,
nor bolt, nor bar; and yet there's no opening it. It must be
the spell; he told me to stay here: Aye, and told me
this screwed chair was mine. Here, then, I'll seat me, against
the transom, in the ship's full middle, all her keel and her
three masts before me. Here, our old sailors say, in their
black seventy-fours great admirals sometimes sit at table,
and lord it over rows of captains and lieutenants. Ha! what's
this? epaulets! epaulets! the epaulets all come crowding!
Pass round the decanters; glad to see ye; fill up, monsieurs!
What an odd feeling, now, when a black boy's host to white
men with gold lace upon their coats!—Monsieurs, have ye
seen one Pip?—a little negro lad, five feet high, hang-dog
look, and cowardly! Jumped from a whale-boat once;—seen

him? No! Well then, fill up again, captains, and let's drink
shame upon all cowards! I name no names. Shame upon
them! Put one foot upon the table. Shame upon all cowards.
—Hist! above there, I hear ivory—Oh, master! master! I am
indeed downhearted when you walk over me. But here I'll
stay, though this stern strikes rocks; and they bulge through;
and oysters come to join me."

THE HAT   **CXXX**

AND now that at the proper time and place, after so
long and wide a preliminary cruise, Ahab,—all other whaling waters swept—seemed to have chased his foe into an
ocean-fold, to slay him the more securely there; now, that
he found himself hard by the very latitude and longitude
where his tormenting wound had been inflicted; now that a
vessel had been spoken which on the very day preceding
had actually encountered Moby Dick;—and now that all his
successive meetings with various ships constrastingly con-
curred to show the demoniac indifference with which the
white whale tore his hunters, whether sinning or sinned
against; now it was that there lurked a something in the old
man's eyes, which it was hardly sufferable for feeble souls to
see. As the unsetting polar star, which through the live-
long, arctic, six months' night sustains its piercing, steady,
central gaze; so, Ahab's purpose now fixedly gleamed down
upon the constant midnight of the gloomy crew. It domi-
neered above them so, that all their bodings, doubts, misgivings, fears, were fain to hide beneath their souls, and
not sprout forth a single spear or leaf.

In this foreshadowing interval too, all humor, forced or
natural, vanished. Stubb no more strove to raise a smile;
Starbuck no more strove to check one. Alike, joy and sorrow, hope and fear, seemed ground to finest dust, and
powdered, for the time, in the clamped mortar of Ahab's
iron soul. Like machines, they dumbly moved about the
deck, ever conscious that the old man's despot eye was on
them.

But did you deeply scan him in his more secret confidential hours; when he thought no glance but one was on
him; then you would have seen that even as Ahab's eyes

so awed the crew's, the inscrutable Parsee's glance awed his;
or somehow, at least, in some wild way, at times affected it.
Such an added, gliding strangeness began to invest the thin
Fedallah now; such ceaseless shudderings shook him; that
the men looked dubious at him; half uncertain, as it seemed,
whether indeed he were a mortal substance, or else a tremulous shadow cast upon the deck by some unseen being's
body. And that shadow was always hovering there. For not
by night, even, had Fedallah ever certainly been known to
slumber, or go below. He would stand still for hours: but
never sat or leaned; his wan but wondrous eyes did plainly
say—We two watchmen never rest.

Nor, at any time, by night or day could the mariners
now step up the deck, unless Ahab was before them; either
standing in his pivot-hole, or exactly pacing the planks between two undeviating limits,—the main-mast and the mizen;
or else they saw him standing in the cabin-scuttle,—his living foot advanced upon the deck, as if to step; his hat
slouched heavily over his eyes; so that however motionless
he stood, however the days and nights were added on, that
he had not swung in his hammock; yet hidden beneath that
slouching hat, they could never tell unerringly whether, for
all this, his eyes were really closed at times: or whether he
was still intently scanning them; no matter, though he stood
so in the scuttle for a whole hour on the stretch, and the unheeded night-damp gathered in beads of dew upon that
stone-carved coat and hat. The clothes that the night had
wet, the next day's sunshine dried upon him; and so, day
after day, and night after night; he went no more beneath
the planks; whatever he wanted from the cabin that thing
he sent for.

He ate in the same open air; that is, his two only meals,—
breakfast and dinner: supper he never touched; nor reaped
his beard; which darkly grew all gnarled, as unearthed roots
of trees blown over, which still grow idly on at naked
base, though perished in the upper verdure. But though his
whole life was now become one watch on deck; and though
the Parsee's mystic watch was without intermission as his
own; yet these two never seemed to speak—one man to the
other—unless at long intervals some passing unmomentous
matter made it necessary. Though such a potent spell
seemed secretly to join the twain; openly, and to the awestruck crew, they seemed pole-like asunder. If by day they
chanced to speak one word; by night, dumb men were both,

so far as concerned the slightest verbal interchange. At times, for longest hours, without a single hail, they stood far parted in the starlight; Ahab in his scuttle, the Parsee by the main-mast; but still fixedly gazing upon each other; as if in the Parsee Ahab saw his forethrown shadow, in Ahab the Parsee his abandoned substance.

And yet, somehow, did Ahab—in his own proper self, as daily, hourly, and every instant, commandingly revealed to his subordinates,—Ahab seemed an independent lord; the Parsee but his slave. Still again both seemed yoked together, and an unseen tyrant driving them; the lean shade siding the solid rib. For be this Parsee what he may, all rib and keel was solid Ahab.

At the first faintest glimmering of the dawn, his iron voice was heard from aft—"Man the mast-heads!"—and all through the day, till after sunset and after twilight, the same voice every hour, at the striking of the helmsman's bell, was heard—"What d'ye see?—sharp! sharp!"

But when three or four days had slided by, after meeting the children-seeking Rachel; and no spout had yet been seen; the monomaniac old man seemed distrustful of his crew's fidelity; at least, of nearly all except the Pagan harpooneers; he seemed to doubt, even, whether Stubb and Flask might not willingly overlook the sight he sought. But if these suspicions were really his, he sagaciously refrained from verbally expressing them, however his actions might seem to hint them.

"I will have the first sight of the whale myself,"—he said. "Aye! Ahab must have the doubloon!" and with his own hands he rigged a nest of basketed bowlines; and sending a hand aloft, with a single sheaved block, to secure to the main-mast head, he received the two ends of the downward-reeved rope; and attaching one to his basket prepared a pin for the other end, in order to fasten it at the rail. This done, with that end yet in his hand and standing beside the pin, he looked round upon his crew, sweeping from one to the other; pausing his glance long upon Daggoo, Queequeg, Tashtego; but shunning Fedallah; and then settling his firm relying eye upon the chief mate, said,—"Take the rope, sir—I give it into thy hands, Starbuck." Then arranging his person in the basket, he gave the word for them to hoist him to his perch, Starbuck being the one who secured the rope at last; and afterwards stood near it. And thus, with one hand clinging round the royal mast, Ahab gazed abroad upon the sea for miles and miles,—ahead, astern, this side,

and that,—within the wide expanded circle commanded at
so great a height.

When in working with his hands at some lofty almost
isolated place in the rigging, which chances to afford no foot-
hold, the sailor at sea is hoisted up to that spot, and sustained there by the rope; under these circumstances, its fastened end on deck is always given in strict charge to some
one man who has the special watch of it. Because in such
a wilderness of running rigging, whose various different relations aloft cannot always be infallibly discerned by what
is seen of them at the deck; and when the deck-ends of
these ropes are being every few minutes cast down from the
fastenings, it would be but a natural fatality, if, unprovided
with a constant watchman, the hoisted sailor should by some
carelessness of the crew be cast adrift and fall all swooping
to the sea. So Ahab's proceedings in this matter were not
unusual; the only strange thing about them seemed to be,
that Starbuck, almost the one only man who had ever ventured to oppose him with anything in the slightest degree
approaching to decision—one of those too, whose faithfulness on the look-out he had seemed to doubt somewhat;—
it was strange, that this was the very man he should select
for his watchman; freely giving his whole life into such an
otherwise distrusted person's hands.

Now, the first time Ahab was perched aloft; ere he had
been there ten minutes; one of those red-billed savage sea-
hawks which so often fly incommodiously close round the
manned mast-heads of whalemen in these latitudes; one of
these birds came wheeling and screaming round his head in a
maze of untrackably swift circlings. Then it darted a thousand feet straight up into the air; then spiralized downwards,
and went eddying again round his head.

But with his gaze fixed upon the dim and distant horizon,
Ahab seemed not to mark this wild bird; nor, indeed, would
any one else have marked it much, it being no uncommon
circumstance; only now almost the least heedful eye seemed
to see some sort of cunning meaning in almost every sight.

"Your hat, your hat, sir!" suddenly cried the Sicilian seaman, who being posted at the mizen-mast-head, stood directly behind Ahab, though somewhat lower than his level,
and with a deep gulf of air dividing them.

But already the sable wing was before the old man's eyes;
the long hooked bill at his head; with a scream, the black
hawk darted away with his prize.

An eagle flew thrice round Tarquin's head, removing his cap to replace it, and thereupon Tanaquil, his wife, declared that Tarquin would be king of Rome. But only by the replacing of the cap was that omen accounted good. Ahab's hat was never restored; the wild hawk flew on and on with it; far in advance of the prow: and at last disappeared; while from the point of that disappearance, a minute black spot was dimly discerned, falling from that vast height into the sea.

THE PEQUOD MEETS THE DELIGHT   CXXXI

THE intense Pequod sailed on; the rolling waves and days went by; the life-buoy-coffin still lightly swung; and another ship, most miserably misnamed the Delight, was descried. As she drew nigh, all eyes were fixed upon her broad beams, called shears, which, in some whaling-ships, cross the quarter-deck at the height of eight or nine feet; serving to carry the spare, unrigged, or disabled boats.

Upon the stranger's shears were beheld the shattered, white ribs, and some few splintered planks, of what had once been a whale-boat; but you now saw through this wreck, as plainly as you see through the peeled, half-unhinged, and bleaching skeleton of a horse.

"Hast seen the White Whale?"

"Look!" replied the hollow-cheeked captain from his taffrail; and with his trumpet he pointed to the wreck.

"Hast killed him?"

"The harpoon is not yet forged that will ever do that," answered the other, sadly glancing upon a rounded hammock on the deck, whose gathered sides some noiseless sailors were busy in sewing together.

"Not forged!" and snatching Perth's levelled iron from the crotch, Ahab held it out, exclaiming—"Look ye, Nantucketer; here in this hand I hold his death! Tempered in blood, and tempered by lightning are these barbs; and I swear to temper them triply in that hot place behind the fin, where the White Whale most feels his accursed life!"

"Then God keep thee, old man—see'st thou that"—pointing to the hammock—"I bury but one of five stout men, who were alive only yesterday; but were dead ere night. Only *that* one I bury; the rest were buried before they died; you sail upon their tomb." Then turning to his crew—"Are ye ready there? place the plank then on the rail, and lift the body; so, then—Oh! God"—advancing towards the hammock with uplifted hands—"may the resurrection and the life—"

"Brace forward! Up helm!" cried Ahab like lightning to his men.

But the suddenly started Pequod was not quick enough to escape the sound of the splash that the corpse soon made as it struck the sea; not so quick, indeed, but that some of the flying bubbles might have sprinkled her hull with their ghostly baptism.

As Ahab now glided from the dejected Delight, the strange life-buoy hanging at the Pequod's stern came into conspicuous relief.

"Ha! yonder! look yonder, men!" cried a foreboding voice in her wake. "In vain, oh, ye strangers, ye fly our sad burial; ye but turn us your taffrail to show us your coffin!"

THE SYMPHONY   **CXXXII**

IT was a clear steel-blue day. The firmaments of air and sea were hardly separable in that all-pervading azure; only, the pensive air was transparently pure and soft, with a woman's look, and the robust and man-like sea heaved with long, strong, lingering swells, as Samson's chest in his sleep.

Hither, and thither, on high, glided the snow-white wings of small, unspeckled birds; these were the gentle thoughts of the feminine air; but to and fro in the deeps, far down in the bottomless blue, rushed mightly leviathans, sword-fish, and sharks; and these were the strong, troubled, murderous thinkings of the masculine sea.

But though thus contrasting within, the contrast was only in shades and shadows without; those two seemed one; it was only the sex, as it were, that distinguished them.

Aloft, like a royal czar and king, the sun seemed giving this gentle air to this bold and rolling sea; even as bride to groom. And at the girdling line of the horizon—denoted the fond, throbbing trust, the loving alarms, with which the poor bride gave her bosom away.

Tied up and twisted; gnarled and knotted with wrinkles; haggardly firm and unyielding; his eyes glowing like coals, that still glow in the ashes of ruin; untottering Ahab stood forth in the clearness of the morn; lifting his splintered helmet of a brow to the fair girl's forehead of heaven.

Oh, immortal infancy, and innocency of the azure! Invisible winged creatures that frolic all round us! Sweet childhood of air and sky! how oblivious were ye of old Ahab's close-coiled woe! But so have I seen little Miriam and Martha, laughing-eyed elves, heedlessly gambol around their old sire; sporting with the circle of singed locks which grew on the marge of that burnt-out crater of his brain.

Slowly crossing the deck from the scuttle, Ahab leaned over the side, and watched how his shadow in the water sank and sank to his gaze, the more and the more that he strove to pierce the profundity. But the lovely aromas in that enchanted air did at last seem to dispel, for a moment, the cankerous thing in his soul. That glad, happy air, that winsome sky, did at last stroke and caress him; the stepmother world, so long cruel—forbidding—now threw affectionate arms round his stubborn neck, and did seem to joyously sob over him, as if over one, that however wilful and erring, she could yet find it in her heart to save and to bless. From beneath his slouched hat Ahab dropped a tear into the sea; nor did all the Pacific contain such wealth as that one wee drop.

Starbuck saw the old man; saw him, how he heavily leaned over the side; and he seemed to hear in his own true heart the measureless sobbing that stole out of the centre of the serenity around. Careful not to touch him, or be noticed by him, he yet drew near to him, and stood there.

Ahab turned.

"Starbuck!"

'Sir."

"Oh, Starbuck! it is a mild, mild wind, and a mild looking sky. On such a day—very much such a sweetness as this—I struck my first whale—a boy-harpooneer of eighteen! Forty—forty—forty years ago!—ago! Forty years of continual whaling! forty years of privation, and peril, and storm-time! forty years on the pitiless sea! for forty years has Ahab forsaken the peaceful land, for forty years to make war on the horrors of the deep! Aye and yes, Starbuck, out of those forty years I have not spent three ashore. When I think of this life I have led; the desolation of solitude it has been; the masoned, walled-town of a Captain's exclusiveness, which admits but small entrance to any sympathy from the green country without—oh, weariness! heaviness! Guinea-cost slavery of solitary command!—when I think of all this; only half-suspected, not so keenly known to me before—and how for forty years I have fed upon dry salted fare—fit emblem of the dry nourishment of my soul!—when the poorest landsman has had fresh fruit to his daily hand, and broken the world's fresh bread to my mouldy crusts—away, whole oceans away, from that young girl-wife I wedded past fifty, and sailed for Cape Horn the next day, leaving but one dent in my marriage pillow—wife? wife?—rather a widow with her husband alive! Aye, I widowed that poor girl when I married her, Starbuck; and then, the madness, the frenzy, the boiling blood and the smoking brow, with which, for a thousand lowerings old Ahab has furiously, foamingly chased his prey—more a demon than a man!—aye, aye! what a forty years' fool—fool—old fool, has old Ahab been! Why this strife of the chase? why weary, and palsy the arm at the oar, and the iron, and the lance? how the richer or better is Ahab now? Behold. Oh, Starbuck! is it not hard, that with this weary load I bear, one poor leg should have been snatched from under me? Here, brush this old hair aside; it blinds me, that I seem to weep. Locks so grey did never grow but from out some ashes! But do I look very old, so very, very old, Starbuck? I feel deadly faint, bowed, and humped, as though I were Adam, staggering beneath the piled centuries since Paradise. God! God! God!—crack my heart!—stave my brain!—mockery! mockery! bitter, biting mockery of grey hairs, have I lived enough joy to wear ye; and seem and feel thus intolerably old? Close! stand close to me, Starbuck; let me look into a human eye; it is better than to gaze into sea or sky; better than to gaze upon God. By the green land; by the bright hearth-stone! this is the magic glass, man; I see my wife and my child in thine eye. No, no; stay on board, on board!—lower not when I do; when branded Ahab gives chase to Moby Dick. That hazard shall not be thine. No, no! not with the far away home I see in that eye!"

"Oh, my Captain! my Captain! noble soul! grand old heart, after all! why should any one give chase to that hated fish! Away with me! let us fly these deadly waters! let us home! Wife and child, too, are Starbuck's—wife and child of his brotherly, sisterly, play-fellow youth; even as thine, sir, are the wife and child of thy loving, longing, paternal old age! Away! let us away!—this instant let me alter the course! How cheerily, how hilariously, O my Captain, would we bowl on our way to see old Nantucket again! I think, sir, they have some such mild blue days, even as this, in Nantucket."

"They have, they have. I have seen them—some summer days in the morning. About this time—yes, it is his noon nap now—the boy vivaciously wakes; sits up in bed; and his mother tells him of me, of cannibal old me; how I am abroad upon the deep, but will yet come back to dance him again."

" 'Tis my Mary, my Mary herself! She promised that my boy, every morning, should be carried to the hill to catch the first glimpse of his father's sail! Yes, yes! no more! it is done! we head for Nantucket! Come, my Captain, study out the course, and let us away! See, see! the boy's face from the window! the boy's hand on the hill!"

But Ahab's glance was averted; like a blighted fruit tree he shook, and cast his last, cindered apple to the soil.

"What is it, what nameless inscrutable, unearthly thing is it; what cozzening, hidden lord and master, and cruel, remorseless emperor commands me; that against all natural lovings and longings, I so keep pushing, and crowding, and jamming myself on all the time; recklessly making me ready to do what in my own proper, natural heart, I durst not so much as dare? Is Ahab, Ahab? Is it I, God, or who, that lifts this arm? But if the great sun move not of himself; but is as an errand-boy in heaven; nor one single star can revolve, but by some invisible power; how then can this one small heart beat; this one small brain think thoughts; unless God does that beating, does that thinking, does that living, and not I. By heaven, man, we are turned round and round in this world, like yonder windlass, and Fate is the handspike. And all the time, lo! that smiling sky, and this unsounded sea! Look! see yon Albicore! who put it into him to chase and fang that flying-fish? Where do murderers go, man! Who's to doom, when the judge himself is dragged to the bar? But it is a mild, mild wind, and a mild looking sky; and the air smells now, as if it blew from a faraway meadow; they have been making hay somewhere under the slopes of the Andes, Starbuck, and the mowers are sleeping among the new-mown hay. Sleeping? Aye, toil we how we may, we all sleep at last on the field. Sleep? Aye, and rust amid greenness; as last year's scythes flung down, and left in the half-cut swaths—Starbuck!"

But blanched to a corpse's hue with despair, the Mate had stolen away.

Ahab crossed the deck to gaze over on the other side; but started at two reflected, fixed eyes in the water there. Fedallah was motionlessly leaning over the same rail.

THE CHASE—FIRST DAY   CXXXIII

THAT night, in the mid-watch, when the old man—as his wont at intervals—stepped forth from the scuttle in which he leaned, and went to his pivot-hole, he suddenly thrust out his face fiercely, snuffing up the sea air as a sagacious ship's dog will, in drawing nigh to some barbarous isle. He declared that a whale must be near. Soon that peculiar odor, sometimes to a great distance given forth by the living sperm whale, was palpable to all the watch; nor was any mariner surprised when, after inspecting the compass, and then the dog-vane, and then ascertaining the precise bearing of the odor as nearly as possible, Ahab rapidly ordered the ship's course to be slightly altered, and the sail to be shortened.

The acute policy dictating these movements was sufficiently vindicated at daybreak, by the sight of a long sleek on the sea directly and lengthwise ahead, smooth as oil, and resembling in the pleated watery wrinkles bordering it, the polished metallic-like marks of some swift tide-rip, at the mouth of a deep, rapid stream.

"Man the mast-heads! Call all hands!"

Thundering with the butts of three clubbed handspikes on the forecastle deck, Daggoo roused the sleepers with such judgment claps that they seemed to exhale from the scuttle, so instantaneously did they appear with their clothes in their hands.

"What d'ye see?" cried Ahab, flattening his face to the sky.

"Nothing, nothing, sir!" was the sound hailing down in reply.

"T'gallant sails!—stunsails! alow and aloft, and on both sides!"

All sail being set, he now cast loose the life-line, reserved for swaying him to the main royal-mast head; and in a few moments they were hoisting him thither, when, while but two thirds of the way aloft, and while peering ahead through the horizontal vacancy between the main-top-sail and top-gallant-sail, he raised a gull-like cry in the air, "There she blows!—there she blows! A hump like a snow-hill! It is Moby Dick!"

Fired by the cry which seemed simultaneously taken up by the three look-outs, the men on deck rushed to the rigging to behold the famous whale they had so long been pursuing. Ahab had now gained his final perch, some feet above the other look-outs, Tashtego standing just beneath him on the cap of the top-gallant-mast, so that the Indian's head was almost on a level with Ahab's heel. From this height the whale was now seen some mile or so ahead, at every roll of the sea revealing his high sparkling hump, and regularly jetting his silent spout into the air. To the credulous mariners it seemed the same silent spout they had so long ago beheld in the moonlit Atlantic and Indian Oceans.

"And did none of ye see it before?" cried Ahab, hailing the perched men all around him.

"I saw him almost that same instant, sir, that Captain Ahab did, and I cried out," said Tashtego.

"Not the same instant; not the same—no, the doubloon is mine, Fate reserved the doubloon for me. I only; none of ye could have raised the White Whale first. There she blows! there she blows!—there she blows! There again!—there again!" he cried, in long-drawn, lingering, methodic tones, attuned to the gradual prolongings of the whale's visible jets. "He's going to sound! In stunsails! Down top-gallant-sails! Stand by three boats. Mr. Starbuck, remember, stay on board, and keep the ship. Helm there! Luff, luff a point! So; steady, man, steady! There go flukes! No, no, only black water! All ready the boats there? Stand by, stand by! Lower me, Mr. Starbuck; lower, lower,—quick, quicker!" and he slid through the air to the deck.

"He is heading straight to leeward, sir," cried Stubb, "right away from us; cannot have seen the ship yet."

"Be dumb, man! Stand by the braces! Hard down the helm!—brace up! Shiver her!—shiver her! So; well that! Boats, boats!"

Soon all the boats but Starbuck's were dropped; all the boatsails set—all the paddles plying; with rippling swiftness, shooting to leeward; and Ahab heading the onset. A pale, death-glimmer lit up Fedallah's sunken eyes; a hideous motion gnawed his mouth.

Like noiseless nautilus shells, their light prows sped through the sea; but only slowly they neared the foe. As they neared him, the ocean grew still more smooth; seemed drawing a carpet over its waves; seemed a noon-meadow, so serenely it spread. At length the breathless hunter came so nigh his seemingly unsuspecting prey, that his entire dazzling hump was distinctly visible, sliding along the sea as if an isolated thing, and continually set in a revolving ring of finest, fleecy, greenish foam. He saw the vast, involved wrinkles of the slightly projecting head beyond. Before it, far out on the soft Turkish-rugged waters, went the glistening white shadow from his broad, milky forehead, a musical rippling playfully accompanying the shade; and behind, the blue waters interchangeably flowed over into the moving valley of his steady wake; and on either hand bright bubbles arose and danced by his side. But these were broken again by the light toes of hundreds of gay fowl softly feathering the sea, alternate with their fitful flight; and like to some flagstaff rising from the painted hull of an argosy, the tall but shattered pole of a recent lance projected from the white whale's back; and at intervals one of the cloud of soft-toed fowls hovering, and to and fro skimming like a canopy over the fish, silently perched and rocked on this pole, the long tail feathers streaming like pennons.

A gentle joyousness—a mighty mildness of repose in swiftness, invested the gliding whale. Not the white bull Jupiter swimming away with ravished Europa clinging to his graceful horns; his lovely, leering eyes sideways intent upon the maid; with smooth bewitching fleetness, rippling straight for the nuptial bower in Crete; not Jove, not that great majesty Supreme! did surpass the glorified White Whale as he so divinely swam.

On each soft side—coincident with the parted swell, that but once leaving him, then flowed so wide away—on each bright side, the whale shed off enticings. No wonder there had been some among the hunters who namelessly transported and allured by all this serenity, had ventured to assail it; but had fatally found that quietude but the vesture of tornadoes. Yet calm, enticing calm, oh, whale! thou glidest on, to all who for the first time eye thee, no matter how many in that same way thou may'st have bejuggled and destroyed before.

And thus, through the serene tranquillities of the tropical sea, among waves whose hand-clappings were suspended by exceeding rapture, Moby Dick moved on, still withholding from sight the full terrors of his submerged trunk, entirely hiding the wrenched hideousness of his jaw. But soon the fore part of him slowly rose from the water; for an instant his whole marbleized body formed a high arch, like Virginia's Natural Bridge, and warningly waving his bannered flukes in the air, the grand god revealed himself, sounded, and went out of sight. Hoveringly halting, and dipping on the wing, the white sea-fowls longingly lingered over the agitated pool that he left.

With oars apeak, and paddles down, the sheets of their sails adrift, the three boats now stilly floated, awaiting Moby Dick's reappearance.

"An hour," said Ahab, standing rooted in his boat's stern; and he gazed beyond the whale's place, towards the dim blue spaces and wide wooing vacancies to leeward. It was only an instant; for again his eyes seemed whirling round in his head as he swept the watery circle. The breeze now freshened; the sea began to swell.

"The birds!—the birds!" cried Tashtego.

In long Indian file, as when herons take wing, the white birds were now all flying towards Ahab's boat; and when within a few yards began fluttering over the water there, wheeling round and round, with joyous, expectant cries. Their vision was keener than man's; Ahab could discover no sign in the sea. But suddenly as he peered down and down into its depths, he profoundly saw a white living spot no bigger than a white weasel, with wonderful celerity uprising, and magnifying as it rose, till it turned, and then there were plainly revealed two long crooked rows of white, glistening teeth, floating up from the undiscoverable bottom. It was Moby Dick's open mouth and scrolled jaw; his vast, shadowed bulk still blending with the blue of the sea. The glittering mouth yawned beneath the boat like an open-doored marble tomb; and giving one sidelong sweep with his steering oar, Ahab whirled the craft aside from this tremendous apparition. Then, calling upon Fedallah to change places with him, went forward to the bows, and seizing Perth's harpoon, commanded his crew to grasp their oars and stand by to stern.

Now, by reason of this timely spinning round the boat upon its axis, its bow, by anticipation, was made to face the whale's head while yet under water. But as if perceiving this stratagem, Moby Dick, with that malicious intelligence ascribed to him, sidelingly transplanted himself, as it were, in an instant, shooting his pleated head lengthwise beneath the boat.

Through and through; through every plank and each rib, it thrilled for an instant, the whale obliquely lying on his back, in the manner of a biting shark, slowly and feelingly taking its bows full within his mouth, so that the long, narrow, scrolled lower jaw curled high up into the open air, and one of the teeth caught in a row-lock. The bluish pearl-white of the inside of the jaw was within six inches of Ahab's head, and reached higher than that. In this attitude the White Whale now shook the slight cedar as a mildly cruel cat her mouse. With unastonished eyes Fedallah gazed, and crossed his arms; but the tiger-yellow crew were tumbling over each other's heads to gain the uttermost stern.

And now, while both elastic gunwales were springing in and out, as the whale dallied with the doomed craft in this devilish way; and from his body being submerged beneath the boat, he could not be darted at from the bows, for the bows were almost inside of him, as it were; and while the other boats involuntarily paused, as before a quick crisis impossible to withstand, then it was that monomaniac Ahab, furious with this tantalizing vicinity of his foe, which placed him all alive and helpless in the very jaws he hated; frenzied with all this, he seized the long bone with his naked hands, and wildly strove to wrench it from its gripe. As now he thus vainly strove, the jaw slipped from him; the frail gunwales bent in, collapsed, and snapped, as both jaws, like an enormous shears, sliding further aft, bit the craft completely in twain, and locked themselves fast again in the sea, midway between the two floating wrecks. These floated aside, the broken ends drooping, the crew at the stern-wreck clinging to the gunwales, and striving to hold fast to the oars to lash them across.

At that preluding moment, ere the boat was yet snapped, Ahab, the first to perceive the whale's intent, by that crafty upraising of his head, a movement that loosed his hold for the time; at that moment his hand made one final effort to push the boat out of the bite. But only slipping further into the whale's mouth, and tilting over sideways as it slipped, the boat had shaken off his hold on the jaw; spilled him out of it, as he leaned to the push; and so he fell flat-faced upon the sea.

Ripplingly withdrawing from his prey, Moby Dick now lay at a little distance, vertically thrusting his oblong white head up and down in the billows; and at the same time slowly revolving his whole spindled body; so that when his vast wrinkled forehead rose—some twenty or more feet out of the water—the now rising swells, with all their confluent waves, dazzlingly broke against it; vindictively tossing their shivered spray still higher into the air.* So, in a gale, the but half baffled Channel billows only recoil from the base of the Eddystone, triumphantly to overlap its summit with their scud.

But soon resuming his horizontal attitude, Moby Dick swam swiftly round and round the wrecked crew; sideways churning the water in his vengeful wake, as if lashing himself up to still another and more deadly assault. The sight of the splintered boat seemed to madden him, as the blood of grapes and mulberries cast before Antiochus's elephants in the book of Maccabees. Meanwhile Ahab half smothered in the foam of the whale's insolent tail, and too much of a cripple to swim,—though he could still keep afloat, even in the heart of such a whirlpool as that; helpless Ahab's head was seen, like a tossed bubble which the least chance shock might burst. From the boat's fragmentary stern, Fedallah incuriously and mildly eyed him; the clinging crew, at the other drifting end, could not succor him; more than enough was it for them to look to themselves. For so revolvingly appalling was the White Whale's aspect, and so planetarily swift the ever-contracting circles he made, that he seemed horizontally swooping upon them. And though the other boats, unharmed, still hovered hard by; still they dared not pull into the eddy to strike, lest that should be the signal for the instant destruction of the jeopardized castaways, Ahab and all; nor in that case could they themselves hope to escape. With straining eyes, then, they remained on the outer edge of the direful zone, whose centre had now become the old man's head.

Meantime, from the beginning all this had been des-

---

* This motion is peculiar to the sperm whale. It receives its designation (pitchpoling) from its being likened to that preliminary up-and-down poise of the whale-lance, in the exercise called pitchpoling, previously described. By this motion the whale must best and most comprehensively view whatever objects may be encircling him.

cried from the ship's mast heads; and squaring her yards, she had borne down upon the scene; and was now so nigh, that Ahab in the water hailed her;—"Sail on the"—but that moment a breaking sea dashed on him from Moby Dick, and whelmed him for the time. But struggling out of it again, and chancing to rise on a towering crest, he shouted, —"Sail on the whale!—Drive him off!"

The Pequod's prows were pointed; and breaking up the charmed circle, she effectually parted the white whale from his victim. As he sullenly swam off, the boats flew to the rescue.

Dragged into Stubb's boat with blood-shot, blinded eyes, the white brine caking in his wrinkles, the long tension of Ahab's bodily strength did crack, and helplessly he yielded to his body's doom: for a time, lying all crushed in the bottom of Stubb's boat, like one trodden under foot of herds of elephants. Far inland, nameless wails came from him, as desolate sounds from out ravines.

But this intensity of his physical prostration did but so much the more abbreviate it. In an instant's compass, great hearts sometimes condense to one deep pang, the sum total of those shallow pains kindly diffused through feebler men's whole lives. And so, such hearts, though summary in each one suffering; still, if the gods decree it, in their lifetime aggregate a whole age of woe, wholly made up of instantaneous intensities; for even in their pointless centres, those noble natures contain the entire circumferences of inferior souls.

"The harpoon," said Ahab, half way rising, and draggingly leaning on one bended arm—"is it safe?"

"Aye, sir, for it was not darted; this is it," said Stubb, showing it.

"Lay it before me;—any missing men?"

"One, two, three, four, five;—there were five oars, and here are five men."

"That's good.—Help me, man; I wish to stand. So, so, I see him! there! there! going to leeward still; what a leaping spout!—Hands off from me! The eternal sap runs up in Ahab's bones again! Set the sail; out oars; the helm!"

It is often the case that when a boat is stove, its crew, being picked up by another boat, help to work that second boat; and the chase is thus continued with what is called double-banked oars. It was thus now. But the added power of the boat did not equal the added power of the whale, for he seemed to have treble-banked his every fin; swimming with a velocity which plainly showed, that if now, under these circumstances, pushed on, the chase would prove an indefinitely prolonged, if not a hopeless one; nor could any crew endure for so long a period, such an unintermitted, intense straining at the oar; a thing barely tolerable only in some one brief vicissitude. The ship itself, then, as it sometimes happens, offered the most promising intermediate means of overtaking the chase. Accordingly, the boats now made for her, and were soon swayed up to their cranes—the two parts of the wrecked boat having been previously secured by her—and then hoisting everything to her side, and stacking her canvas high up, and sideways outstretching it with stun-sails, like the double-jointed wings of an albatross; the Pequod bore down in the leeward wake of Moby Dick. At the well known, methodic intervals, the whale's glittering spout was regularly announced from the manned mast-heads; and when he would be reported as just gone down, Ahab would take the time, and then pacing the deck, binnacle-watch in hand, so soon as the last second of the allotted hour expired, his voice was heard.—"Whose is the doubloon now? D'ye see him?" and if the reply was, No, sir! straightway he commanded them to lift him to his perch. In this way the day wore on; Ahab, now aloft and motionless; anon, unrestingly pacing the planks.

As he was thus walking, uttering no sound, except to hail the men aloft, or to bid them hoist a sail still higher, or to spread one to a still greater breadth—thus to and fro pacing, beneath his slouched hat, at every turn he passed his own wrecked boat, which had been dropped upon the quarter-deck, and lay there reversed; broken bow to shattered stern. At last he paused before it; and as in an already over-clouded sky fresh troops of clouds will sometimes sail across, so over the old man's face there now stole some such added gloom as this.

Stubb saw him pause; and perhaps intending, not vainly, though, to evince his own unabated fortitude, and thus keep up a valiant place in his Captain's mind, he advanced, and eyeing the wreck exclaimed—"The thistle the ass refused; it pricked his mouth too keenly, sir; ha! ha!"

"What soulless thing is this that laughs before a wreck? Man, man! did I now know thee brave as fearless fire (and as mechanical) I could swear thou wert a poltroon. Groan nor laugh should be heard before a wreck."

"Aye, sir," said Starbuck drawing near, " 'tis a solemn sight; an omen, and an ill one."

"Omen? omen?—the dictionary! If the gods think to speak outright to man, they will honorably speak outright; not shake their heads, and give an old wives' darkling hint.— Begone! Ye two are the opposite poles of one thing; Starbuck is Stubb reversed, and Stubb is Starbuck; and ye two are all mankind; and Ahab stands alone among the millions of the peopled earth, nor gods nor men his neighbors! Cold, cold—I shiver!—How now? Aloft there! D'ye see him? Sing out for every spout, though he spouts ten times a second!"

The day was nearly done; only the hem of his golden robe was rustling. Soon, it was almost dark; but the look-out men still remained unset.

"Can't see the spout now, sir;—too dark"—cried a voice from the air.

"How heading when last seen?"

"As before, sir,—straight to leeward."

"Good! he will travel slower now 'tis night. Down royals and top-gallant stun-sails, Mr. Starbuck. We must not run over him before morning; he's making a passage now, and may heave-to a while. Helm there! keep her full before the wind!—Aloft! come down!—Mr. Stubb, send a fresh hand to the fore-mast head, and see it manned till morning."—Then advancing towards the doubloon in the main-mast—"Men, this gold is mine, for I earned it; but I shall let it abide here till the White Whale is dead; and then, whosoever of ye first raises him, upon the day he shall be killed, this gold is that man's; and if on that day I shall again raise him, then, ten times its sum shall be divided among all of ye! Away now!—the deck is thine, sir."

And so saying, he placed himself half way within the scuttle, and slouching his hat, stood there till dawn, except when at intervals rousing himself to see how the night wore on.

THE CHASE—SECOND DAY   CXXXIV

AT day-break, the three mast-heads were punctually manned afresh.

"D'ye see him?" cried Ahab, after allowing a little space for the light to spread.

"See nothing, sir."

"Turn up all hands and make sail! he travels faster than

I thought for;—the top-gallant sails!—aye, they should have been kept on her all night. But no matter—'tis but resting for the rush."

Here be it said, that this pertinacious pursuit of one particular whale, continued through day and night, and through night into day, is a thing by no means unprecedented in the South sea fishery. For such is the wonderful skill, prescience of experience, and invincible confidence acquired by some great natural geniuses among the Nantucket commanders; that from the simple observation of a whale when last descried, they will, under certain circumstances, pretty accurately foretell both the direction in which he will continue to swim for a time, while out of sight, as well as his probable rate of progression during that period. And, in these cases, somewhat as a pilot, when about losing sight of a coast, whose general trending he well knows, and which he desires shortly to return to again, but at some further point; like as this pilot stands by his compass, and takes the precise bearing of the cape at present visible, in order the more certainly to hit aright the remote, unseen headland, eventually to be visited: so does the fisherman, at his compass, with the whale; for after being chased, and diligently marked, through several hours of daylight, then, when night obscures the fish, the creature's future wake through the darkness is almost as established to the sagacious mind of the hunter, as the pilot's coast is to him. So that to this hunter's wondrous skill, the proverbial evanescence of a thing writ in water, a wake, is to all desired purposes well nigh as reliable as the steadfast land. And as the mighty iron Leviathan of the modern railway is so familiarly known in its every pace, that, with watches in their hands, men time his rate as doctors that of a baby's pulse; and lightly say of it, the up train or the down train will reach such or such a spot, at such or such an hour; even so, almost, there are occasions when these Nantucketers time that other Leviathan of the deep, according to the observed humor of his speed; and say to themselves, so many hours hence this whale will have gone two hundred miles, will have about reached this or that degree of latitude or longitude. But to render this acuteness at all successful in the end, the wind and the sea must be the whaleman's allies; for of what present avail to the becalmed or windbound mariner is the skill that assures him he is exactly ninety-three leagues and a quarter from his port? Inferable from these statements, are many collateral subtile matters touching the chase of whales.

The ship tore on; leaving such a furrow in the sea as when a cannon-ball, missent, becomes a plough-share and turns up the level field.

"By salt and hemp!" cried Stubb, "but this swift motion of the deck creeps up one's legs and tingles at the heart. This ship and I are two brave fellows!—Ha! ha! Some one take me up, and launch me, spine-wise, on the sea,—for by live-oaks! my spine's a keel. Ha! ha! we go the gait that leaves no dust behind!"

"There she blows—she blows!—she blows!—right ahead!" was now the mast-head cry.

"Aye, aye" cried Stubb, "I knew it—ye can't escape—blow on and split your spout, O whale! the mad fiend himself is after ye! blow your trump—blister your lungs!—Ahab will dam off your blood, as a miller shuts his water-gate upon the stream!"

And Stubb did but speak out for well nigh all that crew. The frenzies of the chase had by this time worked them bubblingly up, like old wine worked anew. Whatever pale fears and forebodings some of them might have felt before; these were not only now kept out of sight through the growing awe of Ahab, but they were broken up, and on all sides routed, as timid prairie hares that scatter before the bounding bison. The hand of Fate had snatched all their souls; and by the stirring perils of the previous day; the rack of the past night's suspense; the fixed, unfearing, blind, reckless way in which their wild craft went plunging towards its flying mark; by all these things, their hearts were bowled along. The wind that made great bellies of their sails, and rushed the vessel on by arms invisible as irresistible; this seemed the symbol of that unseen agency which so enslaved them to the race.

They were one man, not thirty. For as the one ship that held them all; though it was put together of all contrasting things—oak, and maple, and pine wood; iron, and pitch, and hemp—yet all these ran into each other in the one concrete hull, which shot on its way, both balanced and directed by the long central keel; even so, all the individualities of the crew, this man's valor, that man's fear; guilt and guiltiness, all varieties were welded into oneness, and were all directed to that fatal goal which Ahab their one lord and keel did point to.

The rigging lived. The mast-heads, like the tops of tall palms, were outspreadingly tufted with arms and legs.

Clinging to a spar with one hand, some reached forth the other with impatient wavings; others, shading their eyes from the vivid sunlight, sat far out on the rocking yards; all the spars in full bearing of mortals, ready and ripe for their fate. Ah! how they still strove through that infinite blueness to seek out the thing that might destroy them!

"Why sing ye not out for him, if ye see him?" cried Ahab, when, after the lapse of some minutes since the first cry, no more had been heard. "Sway me up, men; ye have been deceived; not Moby Dick casts one odd jet that way, and then disappears."

It was even so; in their headlong eagerness, the men had mistaken some other thing for the whale-spout, as the event itself soon proved; for hardly had Ahab reached his perch; hardly was the rope belayed to its pin on deck, when he struck the key-note to an orchestra, that made the air vibrate as with the combined discharge of rifles. The triumphant halloo of thirty buckskin lungs was heard, as— much nearer to the ship than the place of the imaginary jet, less than a mile ahead—Moby Dick bodily burst into view! For not by any calm and indolent spoutings; not by the peaceable gush of that mystic fountain in his head, did the White Whale now reveal his vicinity; but by the far more wondrous phenomenon of breaching. Rising with his utmost velocity from the furthest depths, the Sperm Whale thus booms his entire bulk into the pure element of air, and piling up a mountain of dazzling foam, shows his place to the distance of seven miles and more. In those moments, the torn, enraged waves he shakes off, seem his mane; in some cases, this breaching is his act of defiance.

"There she breaches! there she breaches!" was the cry, as in his immeasurable bravadoes the White Whale tossed himself salmon-like to Heaven. So suddenly seen in the blue plain of the sea, and relieved against the still bluer margin of the sky, the spray that he raised, for the moment, intolerably glittered and glared like a glacier; and stood there gradually fading and fading away from its first sparkling intensity, to the dim mistiness of an advancing shower in a vale.

"Aye, breach your last to the sun, Moby Dick!" cried Ahab, "thy hour and thy harpoon are at hand!—Down! down all of ye, but one man at the fore. The boats!—stand by!"

Unmindful of the tedious rope-ladders of the shrouds,

the men, like shooting stars, slid to the deck, by the isolated
backstays and halyards; while Ahab, less dartingly, but still
rapidly was dropped from his perch.

"Lower away," he cried, so soon as he had reached his
boat—a spare one, rigged the afternoon previous. "Mr. Starbuck, the ship is thine—keep away from the boats, but
keep near them. Lower, all!"

As if to strike a quick terror into them, by this time being the first assailant himself, Moby Dick had turned, and
was now coming for the three crews. Ahab's boat was central; and cheering his men, he told them he would take
the whale head-and-head,—that is, pull straight up to his
forehead,—a not uncommon thing; for when within a certain limit, such a course excludes the coming onset from the
whale's sidelong vision. But ere that close limit was gained,
and while yet all three boats were plain as the ship's three
masts to his eye; the White Whale churning himself into
furious speed, almost in an instant as it were, rushing among
the boats with open jaws, and a lashing tail, offered appalling
battle on every side; and heedless of the irons darted at him
from every boat, seemed only intent on annihilating each
separate plank of which those boats were made. But skilfully manœuvred, incessantly wheeling like trained charg-
ers in the field; the boats for a while eluded him; though, at
times, but by a plank's breadth; while all the time, Ahab's unearthly slogan tore every other cry but his to shreds.

But at last in his untraceable evolutions, the White Whale
so crossed and recrossed, and in a thousand ways entangled
the slack of the three lines now fast to him, that they fore-
shortened, and, of themselves, warped the devoted boats
towards the planted irons in him; though now for a moment
the whale drew aside a little, as if to rally for a more
tremendous charge. Seizing that opportunity, Ahab first paid
out more line: and then was rapidly hauling and jerking in
upon it again—hoping that way to disencumber it of some
snarls—when lo!—a sight more savage than the embattled
teeth of sharks!

Caught and twisted—corkscrewed in the mazes of the line,
loose harpoons and lances, with all their bristling barbs and
points, came flashing and dripping up to the chocks in the
bows of Ahab's boat. Only one thing could be done. Seizing
the boat-knife, he critically reached within—through—and
then, without—the rays of steel; dragged in the line beyond,
passed it, inboard, to the bowsman, and then, twice sundering the rope near the chocks—dropped the intercepted fagot

of steel into the sea; and was all fast again. That instant,
the White Whale made a sudden rush among the remaining tangles of the other lines; by so doing, irresistibly dragged
the more involved boats of Stubb and Flask towards his
flukes; dashed them together like two rolling husks on a surf-
beaten beach, and then, diving down into the sea, disappeared in a boiling maelstrom, in which, for a space, the
odorous cedar chips of the wrecks danced round and round,
like the grated nutmeg in a swiftly stirred bowl of punch.

While the two crews were yet circling in the waters,
reaching out after the revolving line-tubs, oars, and other
floating furniture, while aslope little Flask bobbed up and
down like an empty vial, twitching his legs upwards to escape the dreaded jaws of sharks; and Stubb was lustily singing out for some one to ladle him up; and while the old
man's line—now parting—admitted of his pulling into the
creamy pool to rescue whom he could;—in that wild simultaneousness of a thousand concreted perils,—Ahab's yet un-
stricken boat seemed drawn up towards Heaven by invisible
wires,—as, arrow-like, shooting perpendicularly from the sea,
the White Whale dashed his broad forehead against its bottom, and sent it, turning over and over, into the air; till it
fell again—gunwale downwards—and Ahab and his men
struggled out from under it, like seals from a seaside cave.

The first uprising momentum of the whale—modifying
its direction as he struck the surface—involuntarily launched
him along it, to a little distance from the centre of the
destruction he had made; and with his back to it, he now
lay for a moment slowly feeling with his flukes from side
to side; and whenever a stray oar, bit of plank, the least
chip or crumb of the boats touched his skin, his tail swiftly
drew back, and came sideways smiting the sea. But soon,
as if satisfied that his work for that time was done, he
pushed his pleated forehead through the ocean, and trailing after him the intertangled lines, continued his leeward
way at a traveller's methodic pace.

As before, the attentive ship having descried the whole
fight, again came bearing down to the rescue, and dropping
a boat, picked up the floating mariners, tubs, oars, and whatever else could be caught at, and safely landed them on her
decks. Some sprained shoulders, wrists, and ankles; livid
contusions; wrenched harpoons and lances; inextricable intricacies of rope; shattered oars and planks; all these were
there; but no fatal or even serious ill seemed to have befallen any one. As with Fedallah the day before, so Ahab

was now found grimly clinging to his boat's broken half, which afforded a comparatively easy float; nor did it so exhaust him as the previous day's mishap.

But when he was helped to the deck, all eyes were fastened upon him; as instead of standing by himself he still half-hung upon the shoulder of Starbuck, who had thus far been the foremost to assist him. His ivory leg had been snapped off, leaving but one short sharp splinter.

"Aye aye, Starbuck, 'tis sweet to lean sometimes, be the leaner who he will; and would old Ahab had leaned oftener than he has."

"The ferrule has not stood, sir," said the carpenter, now coming up; "I put good work into that leg."

"But no bones broken, sir, I hope," said Stubb with true concern.

"Aye! and all splintered to pieces, Stubb! d'ye see it.— But even with a broken bone, old Ahab is untouched; and I account no living bone of mine one jot more me, than this dead one that's lost. Nor white whale, nor man, nor fiend, can so much as graze old Ahab in his own proper and inaccessible being. Can any lead touch yonder floor, any mast scrape yonder roof?—Aloft there! which way?"

"Dead to leeward, sir."

"Up helm, then; pile on the sail again, ship keepers! down the rest of the spare boats and rig them—Mr. Starbuck away, and muster the boat's crews."

"Let me first help thee towards the bulwarks, sir."

"Oh, oh, oh! how this splinter gores me now! Accursed fate! that the unconquerable captain in the soul should have such a craven mate!"

"Sir?"

"My body, man, not thee. Give me something for a cane— there, that shivered lance will do. Muster the men. Surely I have not seen him yet. By heaven it cannot be!—missing? —quick! call them all."

The old man's hinted thought was true. Upon mustering the company, the Parsee was not there.

"The Parsee!" cried Stubb—"he must have been caught in——"

"The black vomit wrench thee!—run all of ye above, alow, cabin, forecastle—find him—not gone—not gone!"

But quickly they returned to him with the tidings that the Parsee was nowhere to be found.

"Aye, sir," said Stubb—"caught among the tangles of your line—I thought I saw him dragging under."

"*My* line! *my* line? Gone?—gone? What means that little word?—What death-knell rings in it, that old Ahab shakes as if he were the belfry. The harpoon, too!—toss over the litter there,—d'ye see it?—the forged iron, men, the white whale's—no, no, no,—blistered fool! this hand did dart it!—'tis in the fish!—Aloft there! Keep him nailed—Quick!—all hands to the rigging of the boats—collect the oars—harpooneers! the irons, the irons!—hoist the royals higher—a pull on all the sheets!—helm there! steady, steady for your life! I'll ten times girdle the unmeasured globe; yea and dive straight through it, but I'll slay him yet!"

"Great God! but for one single instant show thyself," cried Starbuck; "never, never wilt thou capture him, old man—In Jesus' name no more of this, that's worse than devil's madness. Two days chased; twice stove to splinters; thy very leg once more snatched from under thee; thy evil shadow gone—all good angels mobbing thee with warnings:—what more wouldst thou have?—Shall we keep chasing this murderous fish till he swamps the last man? Shall we be dragged by him to the bottom of the sea? Shall we be towed by him to the infernal world? Oh, oh,—Impiety and blasphemy to hunt him more!"

"Starbuck, of late I've felt strangely moved to thee; ever since that hour we both saw—thou know'st what, in one another's eyes. But in this matter of the whale, be the front of thy face to me as the palm of this hand—a lipless, unfeatured blank. Ahab is for ever Ahab, man. This whole act's immutably decreed. 'Twas rehearsed by thee and me a billion years before this ocean rolled. Fool! I am the Fates' lieutenant; I act under orders. Look thou, underling! that thou obeyest mine.—Stand round me, men. Ye see an old man cut down to the stump; leaning on a shivered lance; propped up on a lonely foot. 'Tis Ahab—his body's part; but Ahab's soul's a centipede, that moves upon a hundred legs. I feel strained, half stranded, as ropes that tow dismasted frigates in a gale; and I may look so. But ere I break, ye'll hear me crack; and till ye hear *that,* know that Ahab's hawser tows his purpose yet. Believe ye, men, in the things called omens? Then laugh aloud, and cry encore! For ere they drown, drowning things will twice rise to the surface; then rise again, to sink for evermore. So with Moby Dick—two days he's floated—to-morrow will be the third. Aye, men, he'll rise once more,—but only to spout his last! D'ye feel brave men, brave?"

"As fearless fire," cried Stubb.

"And as mechanical," muttered Ahab. Then as the men went forward, he muttered on:—"The things called omens! And yesterday I talked the same to Starbuck there, concerning my broken boat. Oh! how valiantly I seek to drive out of others' hearts what's clinched so fast in mine!—The Parsee —the Parsee!—gone, gone? and he was to go before:—but still was to be seen again ere I could perish—How's that?— There's a riddle now might baffle all the lawyers backed by the ghosts of the whole line of judges:—like a hawk's beak it pecks my brain. *I'll, I'll* solve it, though!"

When dusk descended, the whale was still in sight to leeward.

So once more the sail was shortened, and everything passed nearly as on the previous night; only, the sound of hammers, and the hum of the grindstone was heard till nearly daylight, as the men toiled by lanterns in the complete and careful rigging of the spare boats and sharpening their fresh weapons for the morrow. Meantime, of the broken keel of Ahab's wrecked craft the carpenter made him another leg; while still as on the night before, slouched Ahab stood fixed within his scuttle; his hid, heliotrope glance anticipatingly gone backward on its dial; sat due eastward for the earliest sun.

THE CHASE—THIRD DAY   CXXXV

THE morning of the third day dawned fair and fresh, and once more the solitary man at the fore-mast-head was relieved by crowds of the daylight look-outs, who dotted every mast and almost every spar.

"D'ye see him?" cried Ahab; but the whale was not yet in sight.

"In his infallible wake, though; but follow that wake, that's all. Helm there; steady, as thou goest, and hast been going. What a lovely day again! were it a new-made world, and made for a summerhouse to the angels, and this morning the first of its throwing open to them, a fairer day could not dawn upon that world. Here's food for thought, had Ahab time to think; but Ahab never thinks; he only feels, feels, feels; *that's* tingling enough for mortal man! to think's audacity. God only has that right and privilege. Thinking is, or ought to be, a coolness and a calmness; and our poor hearts throb, and our poor brains beat too much for that. And yet, I've sometimes thought my brain was very calm—frozen calm, this old skull cracks so, like a glass in which the contents turned to ice, and shiver it. And still this hair is growing now; this moment growing, and heat must breed it; but no, it's like that sort of common grass that will grow anywhere, between the earthy clefts of Greenland ice or in Vesuvius lava. How the wild winds blow it; they whip it about me as the torn shreds of split sails lash the tossed ship they cling to. A vile wind that has no doubt blown ere this through prison corridors and cells, and wards of hospitals, and ventilated them, and now comes blowing hither as innocent as fleeces. Out upon it!—it's tainted. Were I the wind, I'd blow no more on such a wicked, miserable world. I'd crawl somewhere to a cave, and slink there. And yet, 'tis a noble and heroic thing, the wind! who ever conquered it? In every fight it has the last and bitterest blow. Run tilting at it, and you but run through it. Ha! a coward wind that strikes stark naked men, but will not stand to receive a single blow. Even Ahab is a braver thing—a nobler thing than *that*. Would now the wind but had a body; but all the things that most exasperate and outrage mortal man, all these things are bodiless, but only bodiless as objects, not as agents. There's a most special, a most cunning, oh, a most malicious difference! And yet, I say again, and swear it now, that there's something all glorious and gracious in the wind. These warm Trade Winds, at least, that in the clear heavens blow straight on, in strong and steadfast, vigorous mildness; and veer not from their mark, however the baser currents of the sea may turn and tack, and mightiest Mississippies of the land swift and swerve about, uncertain where to go at last. And by the eternal Poles! these same Trades that so directly blow my good ship on; these Trades, or something like them—something so unchangeable, and full as strong, blow my keeled soul along! To it! Aloft there! What d'ye see?"

"Nothing, sir."

"Nothing! and noon at hand! The doubloon goes a-begging! See the sun! Aye, aye, it must be so. I've oversailed him. How, got the start? Aye, he's chasing *me* now; not I *him*—that's bad; I might have known it, too. Fool! the lines—the harpoons he's towing. Aye, aye, I have run him by last night. About! about! Come down, all of ye, but the regular look outs! Man the braces!"

Steering as she had done, the wind had been somewhat

on the Pequod's quarter, so that now being pointed in the reverse direction, the braced ship sailed hard upon the breeze as she rechurned the cream in her own white wake.

"Against the wind he now steers for the open jaw," murmured Starbuck to himself, as he coiled the new-hauled main-brace upon the rail. "God keep us, but already my bones feel damp within me, and from the inside wet my flesh. I misdoubt me that I obey my God in obeying him!"

"Stand by to sway me up!" cried Ahab, advancing to the hempen basket. "We should meet him soon."

"Aye, aye, sir," and straightway Starbuck did Ahab's bidding, and once more Ahab swung on high.

A whole hour now passed; gold-beaten out to ages. Time itself now held long breaths with keen suspense. But at last, some three points off the weather bow, Ahab descried the spout again, and instantly from the three mast-heads three shrieks went up as if the tongues of fire had voiced it.

"Forehead to forehead I meet thee, this third time, Moby Dick! On deck there!—brace sharper up; crowd her into the wind's eye. He's too far off to lower yet, Mr. Starbuck. The sails shake! Stand over that helmsman with a top-maul! So, so; he travels fast, and I must down. But let me have one more good round look aloft here at the sea; there's time for that. An old, old sight, and yet somehow so young; aye, and not changed a wink since I first saw it, a boy, from the sand-hills of Nantucket! The same!—the same!—the same to Noah as to me. There's a soft shower to leeward. Such lovely leewardings! They must lead somewhere—to something else than common land, more plamy than the palms. Leeward! the white whale goes that way; look to windward, then; the better if the bitterer quarter. But good bye, good bye, old mast-head! What's this?—green? aye, tiny mosses in these warped cracks. No such green weather stains on Ahab's head! There's the difference now between man's old age and matter's. But aye, old mast, we both grow old together; sound in our hulls, though, are we not, my ship? Aye, minus a leg, that's all. By heaven this dead wood has the better of my live flesh every way. I can't compare with it; and I've known some ships made of dead trees outlast the lives of men made of the most vital stuff of vital fathers. What's that he said? he should still go before me, my pilot; and yet to be seen again? But where? Will I have eyes at the bottom of the sea, supposing I descend those endless stairs? and all night I've been sailing from him, wherever he did sink to. Aye, aye, like many more thou told'st direful truth as touching thyself, O Parsee; but, Ahab, there thy shot fell short. Good bye, mast-head—keep a good eye upon the whale, the while I'm gone. We'll talk to-morrow, nay, to-night, when the white whale lies down there, tied by head and tail."

He gave the word; and still gazing round him, was steadily lowered through the cloven blue air to the deck.

In due time the boats were lowered; but as standing in his shallop's stern, Ahab just hovered upon the point of the descent, he waved to the mate,—who held one of the tackle-ropes on deck—and bade him pause.

"Starbuck!"

"Sir?"

"For the third time my soul's ship starts upon this voyage, Starbuck."

"Aye, sir, thou wilt have it so."

"Some ships sail from their ports, and ever afterwards are missing, Starbuck!"

"Truth, sir: saddest truth."

"Some men die at ebb tide; some at low water; some at the full of the flood;—and I feel now like a billow that's all one crested comb, Starbuck. I am old;—shake hands with me, man."

Their hands met; their eyes fastened; Starbuck's tears the glue.

"Oh, my captain, my captain!—noble heart—go not—go not!—see, it's a brave man that weeps; how great the agony of the persuasion then!"

"Lower away!"—cried Ahab, tossing the mate's arm from him. "Stand by the crew!"

In an instant the boat was pulling round close under the stern. "The sharks! the sharks!" cried a voice from the low cabin-window there; "O master, my master, come back!"

But Ahab heard nothing; for his own voice was high-lifted then; and the boat leaped on.

Yet the voice spake true; for scarce had he pushed from the ship, when numbers of sharks, seemingly rising from out the dark waters beneath the hull, maliciously snapped at the blades of the oars, every time they dipped in the water; and in this way accompanied the boat with their bites. It is a thing not uncommonly happening to the whale-boats in those swarming seas; the sharks at times apparently following them in the same prescient way that vultures hover over the banners of marching regiments in the east. But these were the first sharks that had been observed by

the Pequod since the White Whale had been first descried;
and whether it was that Ahab's crew were all such tiger-
yellow barbarians, and therefore their flesh more musky
to the senses of the sharks—a matter sometimes well known
to affect them,—however it was, they seemed to follow that
one boat without molesting the others.

"Heart of wrought steel!" murmured Starbuck gazing over
the side, and following with his eyes the receding boat—
"canst thou yet ring boldly to that sight?—lowering thy keel
among ravening sharks, and followed by them, open-mouthed
to the chase; and this the critical third day?—For when
three days flow together in one continuous pursuit; be sure
the first is the morning, the second the noon, and the third
the evening and the end of that thing—be that end what it
may. Oh! my God! what is this that shoots through me,
and leaves me so deadly calm, yet expectant,—fixed at the top
of a shudder! Future things swim before me, as in empty
outlines and skeletons; all the past is somehow grown dim.
Mary, girl! thou fadest in pale glories behind me; boy! I
seem to see but thy eyes grown wondrous blue. Strangest
problems of life seem clearing; but clouds sweep between—
Is my journey's end coming? My legs feel faint; like his
who has footed it all day. Feel thy heart,—beats it yet?—
Stir thyself, Starbuck!—stave it off—move, move! speak
aloud!—Mast-head there! See ye my boy's hand on the
hill?—Crazed;—aloft there!—keep thy keenest eye upon the
boats:—mark well the whale!—Ho! again!—drive off that
hawk! see! he pecks—he tears the vane"—pointing to the
red flag flying at the main-truck—"Ha! he soars away with
it!—Where's the old man now? sees't thou that sight, oh
Ahab!—shudder, shudder!"

The boats had not gone very far, when by a signal from
the mast-heads—a downward pointed arm, Ahab knew that
the whale had sounded; but intending to be near him at the
next rising, he held on his way a little sideways from the
vessel; the becharmed crew maintaining the profoundest silence, as the head-beat waves hammered and hammered
against the opposing bow.

"Drive, drive in your nails, oh ye waves! to their uttermost heads drive them in! ye but strike a thing without a
lid; and no coffin and no hearse can be mine:—and hemp
only can kill me! Ha! ha!"

Suddenly the waters around them slowly swelled in broad
circles; then quickly upheaved, as if sideways sliding from
a submerged berg of ice, swiftly rising to the surface. A low

rumbling sound was heard; a subterranean hum; and then all held their breaths; as bedraggled with trailing ropes, and harpoons, and lances, a vast form shot lengthwise, but obliquely from the sea. Shrouded in a thin drooping veil of mist, it hovered for a moment in the rainbowed air; and then fell swamping back into the deep. Crushed thirty feet upwards, the waters flashed for an instant like heaps of fountains, then brokenly sank in a shower of flakes, leaving the circling surface creamed like new milk round the marble trunk of the whale.

"Give way!" cried Ahab to the oarsmen, and the boats darted forward to the attack; but maddened by yesterday's fresh irons that corroded in him, Moby Dick seemed combinedly possessed by all the angels that fell from heaven. The wide tiers of welded tendons overspreading his broad white forehead, beneath the transparent skin, looked knitted together; as head on, he came churning his tail among the boats; and once more flailed them apart; spilling out the irons and lances from the two mates' boats, and dashing in one side of the upper part of their bows, but leaving Ahab's almost without a scar.

While Daggoo and Queequeg were stopping the strained planks; and as the whale swimming out from them, turned, and showed one entire flank as he shot by them again; at that moment a quick cry went up. Lashed round and round to the fish's back; pinioned in the turns upon turns in which, during the past night, the whale had reeled the involutions of the lines around him, the half torn body of the Parsee was seen; his sable raiment frayed to shreds; his distended eyes turned full upon old Ahab.

The harpoon dropped from his hand.

"Befooled, befooled!"—drawing in a long lean breath— "Aye, Parsee! I see thee again.—Aye, and thou goest before; and this, *this* then is the hearse that thou didst promise. But I hold thee to the last letter of thy word. Where is the second hearse? Away, mates, to the ship! those boats are useless now; repair them if ye can in time, and return to me; if not, Ahab is enough to die—Down, men! the first thing that but offers to jump from this boat I stand in, that thing I harpoon. Ye are not other men, but my arms and my legs; and so obey me.—Where's the whale? gone down again?"

But he looked too nigh the boat; for as if bent upon escaping with the corpse he bore, and as if the particular place of the last encounter had been but a stage in his leeward voyage, Moby Dick was now again steadily swimming forward; and had almost passed the ship,—which thus far had been sailing in the contrary direction to him, though for the present her headway had been stopped. He seemed swimming with his utmost velocity, and now only intent upon pursuing his own straight path in the sea.

"Oh! Ahab," cried Starbuck, "not too late is it, even now, the third day, to desist. See! Moby Dick seeks thee not. It is thou, thou, that madly seekest him!"

Setting sail to the rising wind, the lonely boat was swiftly impelled to leeward, by both oars and canvas. And at last when Ahab was sliding by the vessel, so near as plainly to distinguish Starbuck's face as he leaned over the rail, he hailed him to turn the vessel about, and follow him, not too swiftly, at a judicious interval. Glancing upwards, he saw Tashtego, Queequeg, and Daggoo, eagerly mounting to the three mast-heads; while the oarsmen were rocking in the two staved boats which had just been hoisted to the side, and were busily at work in repairing them. One after the other, through the portholes, as he sped, he also caught flying glimpses of Stubb and Flask, busying themselves on deck among bundles of new irons and lances. As he saw all this; as he heard the hammers in the broken boats; far other hammers seemed driving a nail into his heart. But he rallied. And now marking that the vane or flag was gone from the main-mast-head, he shouted to Tashtego, who had just gained that perch, to descend again for another flag, and a hammer and nails, and so nail it to the mast.

Whether fagged by the three days' running chase, and the resistance to his swimming in the knotted hamper he bore; or whether it was some latent deceitfulness and malice in him: whichever was true, the White Whale's way now began to abate, as it seemed, from the boat so rapidly nearing him once more; though indeed the whale's last start had not been so long a one as before. And still as Ahab glided over the waves the unpitying sharks accompanied him; and so pertinaciously stuck to the boat; and so continually bit at the plying oars, that the blades became jagged and crunched, and left small splinters in the sea, at almost every dip.

"Heed them not! those teeth but give new rowlocks to your oars. Pull on! 'tis the better rest, the shark's jaw than the yielding water."

"But at every bite, sir, the thin blades grow smaller and smaller!"

"They will last long enough! pull on!—But who can tell"
—he muttered—"whether these sharks swim to feast on
the whale or on Ahab?—But pull on! Aye, all alive, now—
we near him. The helm! take the helm; let me pass,"—
and so saying, two of the oarsmen helped him forward to the
bows of the still flying boat.

At length as the craft was cast to one side, and ran ranging along with the White Whale's flank, he seemed strangely
oblivious of its advance—as the whale sometimes will—and
Ahab was fairly within the smoky mountain mist, which,
thrown off from the whale's spout, curled round his great,
Monadnock hump; he was even thus close to him; when,
with body arched back, and both arms lengthwise high-
lifted to the poise, he darted his fierce iron, and his far
fiercer curse into the hated whale. As both steel and curse
sank to the socket, as if sucked into a morass, Moby Dick
sideways writhed; spasmodically rolled his nigh flank against
the bow, and, without staving a hole in it, so suddenly
canted the boat over, that had it not been for the elevated
part of the gunwale to which he then clung, Ahab would
once more have been tossed into the sea. As it was, three
of the oarsmen—who foreknew not the precise instant of the
dart, and were therefore unprepared for its effects—these
were flung out; but so fell, that, in an instant two of them
clutched the gunwale again, and rising to its level on a
combing wave, hurled themselves bodily inboard again; the
third man helplessly dropping astern, but still afloat and
swimming.

Almost simultaneously, with a mighty volition of ungrad-
uated, instantaneous swiftness, the White Whale darted
through the weltering sea. But when Ahab cried out to the
steersman to take new turns with the line, and hold it so;
and commanded the crew to turn round on their seats, and
tow the boat up to the mark; the moment the treacherous
line felt that double strain and tug, it snapped in the empty
air!

"What breaks in me? Some sinew cracks!—'tis whole again;
oars! oars! Burst in upon him!"

Hearing the tremendous rush of the sea-crashing boat,
the whale wheeled round to present his blank forehead at
bay; but in that evolution, catching sight of the nearing
black hull of the ship; seemingly seeing in it the source of
all his persecutions; bethinking it—it may be—a larger and
nobler foe; of a sudden, he bore down upon its advancing
prow, smiting his jaws amid fiery showers of foam.

Ahab staggered; his hand smote his forehead. "I grow blind; hands! stretch out before me that I may yet grope my way. Is't night?"

"The whale! The ship!" cried the cringing oarsmen.

"Oars! oars! Slope downwards to thy depths, O sea, that ere it be for ever too late, Ahab may slide this last, last time upon his mark! I see: the ship! the ship! Dash on, my men! Will ye not save my ship?"

But as the oarsmen violently forced their boat through the sledge-hammering seas, the before whale-smitten bow-ends of two planks burst through, and in an instant almost, the temporarily disabled boat lay nearly level with the waves; its half-wading, splashing crew, trying hard to stop the gap and bale out the pouring water.

Meantime, for that one beholding instant, Tashtego's mast-head hammer remained suspended in his hand; and the red flag, half-wrapping him as with a plaid, then streamed itself straight out from him, as his own forward-flowing heart; while Starbuck and Stubb, standing upon the bowsprit beneath, caught sight of the downcoming monster just as soon as he.

"The whale, the whale! Up helm, up helm! Oh, all ye sweet powers of air, now hug me close! Let not Starbuck die, if die he must, in a woman's fainting fit. Up helm, I say—ye fools, the jaw! the jaw! Is this the end of all my bursting prayers? all my life-long fidelities? Oh, Ahab, Ahab, lo, thy work. Steady! helmsman, steady. Nay, nay! Up helm again! He turns to meet us! Oh, his unappeasable brow drives on towards one, whose duty tells him he cannot depart. My God, stand by me now!"

"Stand not by me, but stand under me, whoever you are that will now help Stubb; for Stubb, too, sticks here. I grin at thee, thou grinning whale! Who ever helped Stubb, or kept Stubb awake, but Stubb's own unwinking eye? And now poor Stubb goes to bed upon a mattress that is all too soft; would it were stuffed with brushwood! I grin at thee, thou grinning whale! Look ye, sun, moon, and stars! I call ye assassins of as good a fellow as ever spouted up his ghost. For all that, I would yet ring glasses with ye, would ye but hand the cup! Oh, oh! oh, oh! thou grinning whale, but there'll be plenty of gulping soon! Why fly ye not, O Ahab! For me, off shoes and jacket to it; let Stubb die in his drawers! A most mouldy and over salted death, though; —cherries! cherries! cherries! Oh, Flask, for one red cherry ere we die!"

"Cherries? I only wish that we were where they grow. Oh, Stubb, I hope my poor mother's drawn my part-pay ere this; if not, few coppers will now come to her, for the voyage is up."

From the ship's bows, nearly all the seamen now hung inactive; hammers, bits of plank, lances, and harpoons, mechanically retained in their hands, just as they had darted from their various employments; all their enchanted eyes intent upon the whale, which from side to side strangely vibrating his predestinating head, sent a broad band of overspreading semicircular foam before him as he rushed. Retribution, swift vengeance, eternal malice were in his whole aspect, and spite of all that mortal man could do, the solid white buttress of his forehead smote the ship's starboard bow, till men and timbers reeled. Some fell flat upon their faces. Like dislodged trucks, the heads of the harpooneers aloft shook on their bull-like necks. Through the breach, they heard the waters pour, as mountain torrents down a flume.

"The ship! The hearse!—the second hearse!" cried Ahab from the boat; "its wood could only be American!"

Diving beneath the settling ship, the whale ran quivering along its keel; but turning under water, swiftly shot to the surface again, far off the other bow, but within a few yards of Ahab's boat, where, for a time, he lay quiescent.

"I turn my body from the sun. What ho, Tashtego! let me hear thy hammer. Oh! ye three unsurrendered spires of mine; thou uncracked keel; and only god-bullied hull; thou firm deck, and haughty helm, and Pole-pointed prow,—death-glorious ship! must ye then perish, and without me? Am I cut off from the last fond pride of meanest shipwrecked captains? Oh, lonely death on lonely life! Oh, now I feel my topmost greatness lies in my topmost grief. Ho, ho! from all your furthest bounds, pour ye now in, ye bold billows of my whole foregone life, and top this one piled comber of my death! Towards thee I roll, thou all-destroying but unconquering whale; to the last I grapple with thee; from hell's heart I stab at thee; for hate's sake I spit my last breath at thee. Sink all coffins and all hearses to one common pool! and since neither can be mine, let me then tow to pieces, while still chasing thee, though tied to thee, thou damned whale! *Thus*, I give up the spear!"

The harpoon was darted; the stricken whale flew forward; with igniting velocity the line ran through the groove;— ran foul. Ahab stooped to clear it; he did clear it; but the flying turn caught him round the neck, and voicelessly as Turkish mutes bowstring their victim, he was shot out of the boat, ere the crew knew he was gone. Next instant, the heavy eye-splice in the rope's final end flew out of the dark-empty tub, knocked down an oarsman, and smiting the sea, disappeared in its depths.

For an instant, the tranced boat's crew stood still; then turned. "The ship? Great God, where is the ship?" Soon they through dim, bewildering mediums saw her sidelong fading phantom, as in the gaseous Fata Morgana; only the uppermost masts out of water; while fixed by infatuation, or fidelity, or fate, to their once lofty perches, the pagan harpooneers still maintained their sinking lookouts on the sea. And now, concentric circles seized the lone boat itself, and all its crew, and each floating oar, and every lance-pole, and spinning, animate and inanimate, all round and round in one vortex, carried the smallest chip of the Pequod out of sight.

But as the last whelmings intermixingly poured themselves over the sunken head of the Indian at the mainmast, leaving a few inches of the erect spar yet visible, together with long streaming yards of the flag, which calmly undulated, with ironical coincidings, over the destroying billows they almost touched;—at that instant, a red arm and a hammer hovered backwardly uplifted in the open air, in the act of nailing the flag faster and yet faster to the subsiding spar. A sky-hawk that tauntingly had followed the main-truck downwards from its natural home among the stars, pecking at the flag, and incommoding Tashtego there; this bird now chanced to intercept its broad fluttering wing between the hammer and the wood; and simultaneously feeling that ethereal thrill, the submerged savage beneath, in his death-gasp, kept his hammer frozen there; and so the bird of heaven, with archangelic shrieks, and his imperial beak thrust upwards, and his whole captive form folded in the flag of Ahab, went down with his ship, which, like Satan, would not sink to hell till she had dragged a living part of heaven along with her, and helmeted herself with it.

Now small fowls flew screaming over the yet yawning gulf; a sullen white surf beat against its steep sides; then all collapsed, and the great shroud of the sea rolled on as it rolled five thousand years ago.

EPILOGUE

"AND I ONLY AM ESCAPED ALONE TO TELL THEE."
                                                    Job.

The drama's done. Why then here does any one step forth?—Because one did survive the wreck.

It so chanced, that after the Parsee's disappearance, I was he whom the Fates ordained to take the place of Ahab's bowsman, when that bowsman assumed the vacant post; the same, who, when on the last day the three men were tossed from out the rocking boat, was dropped astern. So, floating on the margin of the ensuing scene, and in full sight of it, when the half-spent suction of the sunk ship reached me, I was then, but slowly, drawn towards the closing vortex. When I reached it, it had subsided to a creamy pool. Round and round, then, and ever contracting towards the button-like black bubble at the axis of that slowly wheeling circle, like another Ixion I did revolve. Till, gaining that vital centre, the black bubble upward burst; and now, liberated by reason of its cunning spring, and, owing to its great buoyancy, rising with great force, the coffin life-buoy shot lengthwise from the sea, fell over, and floated by my side. Buoyed up by that coffin, for almost one whole day and night, I floated on a soft and dirge-like main. The unharming sharks, they glided by as if with padlocks on their mouths; the savage sea-hawks sailed with sheathed beaks. On the second day, a sail drew near, nearer, and picked me up at last. It was the devious-cruising Rachel, that in her retracing search after her missing children, only found another orphan.

FINIS.

CRITICISM AND CONTEXT

HERMAN MELVILLE: A Biographical Note

A life of more variety and intensity than Herman Melville's is not easy to imagine. Born in 1819 in New York City, third child of Allan Melvill (the final *e* was added to the name in 1832), Herman was the scion of two notable aristocratic American families. His mother, Maria Gansevoort, of Dutch ancestry, was the only daughter of the distinguished General Peter Gansevoort, a hero of the American Revolution and reputed to be "the richest man in Albany." His grandfather, Major Thomas Melvill, had been one of the "Indians" who participated in the Boston Tea Party and also served with honor in the Revolution. His father was an importer of elegant clothes and fabrics, and the family home in New York was marked by a cultivated formality that verged on the pretentious. From about 1826 the business took a downward turn, because of a general depression, and by 1830 Allan Melvill returned to Albany in an attempt to recoup his fortune. There he died in 1832, his mind unbalanced by his financial troubles. The notion of madness stayed with Herman through his life; there are some indications in his letters that he wondered how long he would be able to stand up under the strains of writing, poverty, and struggling with new ideas.

Until his father's death, Herman was a student at the Albany Academy and thereafter, from the age of twelve, he worked in a bank, a farm, and a store, while his older brother, Gansevoort, prospered in a fur business and restored the family to relative opulence. At fifteen Herman joined his brother in the fur business, which flourished for two years, while Herman enrolled in the Albany Classical School and developed a taste for debating. But in 1837 the business failed, and Herman, now nearly eighteen, took a position as a country schoolmaster near Pittsfield—a position he kept for only a few months. After searching fruitlessly for employment in New York, he found a berth on the three-masted ship *St. Lawrence* and sailed for Liverpool in June, 1839. The brutal sort of experience a young man of twenty did not foresee, it seems to have disenchanted his dream of the sea to the extent that when he next decided to try his fortunes it was in the West. The story of this first voyage later served as the basis for *Redburn* (1849), and the unprofitable trip to the West appeared in *The Confidence Man* (1857), but richer adventures were to come before there was any writing.

In spite of the hardship of his first voyage, by the end of 1840 Melville had made a momentous decision, and on January 3, 1841, he sailed on the whaler *Acushnet* on her maiden voyage to the South Seas. This most important voyage in American literature was to have carried him four years. It started well, but it soon deteriorated under bad fortune in the fishery and the bad temper of its captain. After about eighteen months, Melville deserted in Nuku Hiva in the Marquesas on June 23, 1842, with Richard Tobias Greene, a fellow crewman who shared his discontent. They made their way into the valley of the Taipis (Typees), who were reputed to be cannibals but turned out to be friendly, or so it seemed, for the two young Americans could not be sure that they were not being fattened up for a feast. Melville had injured his leg and suffered from an infection. "Toby" persuaded the savages to let him go in search of medicine or a doctor; he was impressed aboard another whaler, and that was the last that Melville saw of him on that island. Torn, perhaps, between his romance with the beautiful Fayaway, who is described in *Typee,* and his fear of the cannibals, Melville escaped after two weeks and shipped aboard another whaler, the *Lucy Ann,* which proved more unpleasant than the *Acushnet:* the mate was drunk, the captain sick and incompetent, some of the crew had deserted, and some were in the brig of a warship waiting to be tried for mutiny. Melville and some other sailors were also put ashore to be tried for mutiny; but he escaped with a friend, explored Tahiti, and later made his way to the island of Eimeo, where for some time he worked on a potato farm. These adventures were to be described in *Omoo* (1847). In November, 1842, he shipped on a third whaler, the *Charles and Henry.* And the following April, after a pleasant voyage, he was honorably discharged, with a tiny profit, in the Hawaiian Islands. In Honolulu he worked for a time as a clerk, observing the degradation of the natives by civilized white men who came to convert and enlighten them. These observations, subsequently expressed in *Omoo,* elicited resentment instead of promoting reform.

After less than four months in Honolulu, Melville shipped as a common sailor aboard the frigate *United States.* He was shocked by the brutality of naval discipline, particularly the punishment of flogging for minor offenses; and he heard of the warship *Somers* on which three sailors were hanged for mutiny after a court-martial under his own cousin, Lieutenant Guert Gansevoort. These events provided materials for *White Jacket* (1850) and *Billy Budd,* a short novel published after the author's death. After nearly a year's cruise, he was honorably discharged in Boston, in October, 1844, at the age of twenty-five. This date explains the particular significance of the passage, several years later in a letter to Hawthorne, in which Melville declared that "Until I was twenty-five, I had no development at all. From my twenty-fifth year I date my life." He found his family prospering now, and they were enthralled by the tales of his adventures. At their urging he began to write. *Typee* was published in May, 1846, and as a result the boy whom his father had regarded as intellectually the least promising of his three sons enjoyed a sudden and extraordinary fame in England and America.

The acceptance of *Typee* and the writing of a sequel, *Omoo,* were confused by a public demand to know that the events described in *Typee* were true. Melville was asked to provide an affidavit that he had indeed been to the South Seas and lived with cannibals. When his long-lost companion, Toby, wrote from Buffalo that the story was completely true to his recollections, Melville was so relieved and gratified that he made a trip to see Toby and wrote a long addendum on Toby's adventures after he left Melville with the Typees. Melville was also in trouble for the raciness of his tales and for his attacks on the missionaries, which became stronger in *Omoo.* The first publisher to consider the manuscript made such severe criticisms that Melville decided on the deletion of three chapters and revision of eight others.

When *Omoo* was revised and sold, Melville made some new moves that tell us something about his family. Instead of starting another book, he applied for a job as clerk in the Treasury Department at Washington. He persuaded his influential uncle, Peter Gansevoort, to write a supporting letter to Senator John Dix, and he traveled to Washington for an interview. In spite of family connections and "strong letters from various prominent persons," he did not get the job. The abortive flurry of job hunting coincided with his intention to marry Elizabeth Shaw, daughter of the distinguished Chief Justice of Massachusetts, Judge Lemuel Shaw. Melville had decided to buy a large house in New York with his brother Allen, who was also planning to marry soon, where they would set up housekeeping with their brides, their mother, and their four sisters. The family ties were very strong; it was through one of his sisters that he had met Elizabeth, and the courting was carried on while she was visiting this sister.

Melville married Elizabeth in early August, 1847, and after a rainy honeymoon in Canada returned to New York to settle in the new house late in September. The young couple found themselves in a household completely dominated by the senior Mrs. Melville. Herman had six peaceful hours a day for writing, but Elizabeth had no duties except to tidy the two rooms that constituted her little domain. She disliked the fashionable Melville atmosphere, dictated by her mother-in-law, and the round of formal calls through which that lady maintained her hold on the aristocratic world in which she had thriven when her husband was alive and to which she did not wish to become unaccustomed, cost what it might. The young couple enjoyed a walk together after dinner, and a couple of hours in their rooms later, while Herman read what he had written that day. Elizabeth was often busy copying material for the printer, but she was to write worried letters about the obscurity of *Mardi*, which appeared in 1849, and she longed for the simpler life of her family in Boston.

Mardi purported to be a sea voyage, but it was also a complicated allegory, touching on religion, politics, human nature, and cosmic absolutes. The new Melville, reading, thinking, and developing every day, was beginning to show, and the public did not welcome the change from the spirit of *Typee*. To restore his finances and his place in the public eye, Melville rapidly completed two sea books, which he considered pot-boilers: *Redburn,* published in 1849, and *White Jacket* in 1850. Returning to New York in February, 1850 after a trip to England and the Continent, he found himself once more successful and acclaimed. Four books were selling well, Elizabeth had given him a son, and his head was throbbing with plots for future books.

He set to work immediately on *Moby-Dick* and wrote until midsummer, when he moved his family to a farm he had just bought near Pittsfield, Massachusetts. There he met various literary notables —most important of all, Nathaniel Hawthorne—and underwent some sort of spiritual revolution that led him to rewriting his novel. It was not finished until the fall of 1851, and when published brought a confusing mixture of praise, blame, and misapprehension, as one may judge from the reviews printed in the present volume. Melville's style of living—the fine house named Arrowhead, full of family and guests, the 160 acres of land—was beyond his means. He had overdrawn his account at Harper's, his publisher; *Moby-Dick* after a good start was not selling well; and he had to plunge into another novel. He seems to have intended *Pierre* to be a romantic pot-boiler, guaranteed to appeal to the reading ladies of his day, but as his plot carried him into gothic mysteries reminiscent of those of the late eighteenth-century English novel, he found himself probing deeper and deeper, once again, into the cosmic and human enigmas that had sustained *Moby-Dick*. This time the result was so gloomy, so tormented, and so shocking that it brought a storm of censure down upon him. One moral critic was sure he had gone mad.

The same suspicion may have occurred to his family, who now worried about his health and used every means to persuade him to give up his literary career and turn to something more substantial. There is an incongruity in the picture of a gentleman farmer with money in the bank and numerous rich and illustrious relatives who nevertheless was gnawed by debt and somewhat shattered by the agonies of creating. He turned to shorter works, doing stories for *Putnam's Magazine* and planning a book on tortoise hunting, which probably led to the sketch, "The Encantadas or Enchanted Islands," about the Galapagos Islands, printed in 1854; his novel *Israel Potter* was serialized in *Putnam's Magazine* in 1854 and published as a book in 1855; and he finished a remarkable long story, "Benito Cereno," in 1855. Eyestrain, rheumatism, and general ill-health brought on such depressions that his family renewed their efforts to persuade him away from the farm and back to New York, where he might get a steady job. His writing, even in the short pieces, continued (he published *The Piazza Tales* in 1856) to be too philosophical, even "allegorical," to suit the public or his publishers, but nevertheless he stuck to his craft. When his health took a turn for the better, Melville began the last novel to be published during his lifetime, *The Confidence Man,* which appeared in 1857 and turned out to be the most bitter, ambiguous, and troubling of all his works, with the possible exception of *Pierre.* His wife and relatives now got together and raised money to send him on a cruise to the Mediterranean, hoping to restore his health and perhaps by new perspectives to lead him into a new way of life. Melville saw Hawthorne in Liverpool, in November, 1856, where the old friendship was quickly renewed; and Hawthorne, now United States Consul, agreed to handle the British publication of *The Confidence Man.* Melville visited Greece, Egypt, Constantinople, and got to the Holy Land in January, 1857. Under the Mediterranean sun he was feeling much better, but the desolate Holy Land depressed and discouraged him. In Rome he fell ill again, and when he landed in New York in June he had not recovered his spirits.

His family had moved to New York, where they renewed unsuccessful efforts that had extended over many years to get him a position in the New York Customs. Failing that, Melville now put his farm up for sale and set forth as a lecturer. He spoke on Rome, travel, and the South Seas, generating considerable interest as "the man who had lived among cannibals," and for three seasons made a very small income. Meanwhile he was writing poetry, an occupation that filled his wife with anxiety and his pocket not at all, for he could not find a publisher. When he stopped lecturing, his family encouraged him to go off on another voyage. In May, 1860 he went on the clipper ship *Meteor,* of which his brother Thomas was the captain, bound for the Pacific. In order to straighten out his tangled finances, he deeded all his property to his father-in-law, Judge Shaw, who cancelled his notes and forthwith signed all the deeds and property over to Elizabeth, Melville's wife. His voyage came to an end in San Francisco, where the prospect of a long delay oppressed him so that he embarked on another ship and returned to New York. His poems had not sold, his publisher had gone bankrupt three years earlier, and now finally he agreed to seek a government post. In 1861, when he was considering an appointment as consul to Glasgow, his father-in-law, Judge Shaw, died. The Melvilles came into an inheritance and he arranged at last to get rid of his farm and move permanently to New York. While moving furniture from the farm, he was badly injured in a fall from a wagon. His recovery was slow, and his depressions and moodiness increased. By the time the Civil War swept over the nation, he was forgotten as a writer, although he still enjoyed the love of his relatives and the acclaim of associates and friends.

By 1863 the family was re-established in New York, where apparently they were living well enough. Melville repaid his long-overdue debt to Harper's, lived sociably among his family and friends, and wrote poetry. A small flurry of literary success came with publication of several of his Civil War poems in *Harper's Magazine,* followed by a volume, *Battle Pieces and Aspects of the War* (1866), perhaps his first piece of writing that did not offend the standard middle-class sentimental people who constituted the market for books, especially fiction. After having been always in some sense subversive of the proprieties, Melville had become respectable—and the change was signalized by his appointment as deputy inspector of customs for the Port of New York. Then his older son, Malcolm, committed suicide with a pistol, apparently because his father had locked him in his room for returning home too late the night before. (The authorities later called it an accident.) With such a blow, plus various maladies, Melville retreated further into obscurity. He finished a long poem, *Clarel: A Poem and Pilgrimage in the Holy Land,* which was published in two volumes in 1876 at his uncle Peter Gansevoort's expense. It represented a return to the old spirit of *Mardi* and *Pierre* and had no success, although recently critics have praised it.

The years that followed were marked by worry and illness, combined with depressions that frightened his wife. Financial security—even prosperity—finally came as bequests from wealthy relatives accumulated; and in 1885, after nineteen years of service, Melville retired from the customs, aged sixty-five, to rest from the long struggle with disappointment, ill-health, and financial worries. In 1886 his son Stanwix died in San Francisco. Resisting this new blow, Melville gathered a collection of miscellaneous poetry and prose as *John Marr and Other Sailors,* which he published in an edition of twenty-five copies in 1888. Thereafter, he worked slowly on the manuscript of his last novel, which was published after his death as *Billy Budd, Sailor,* and another volume of poems, *Timoleon,* which was privately printed in May, 1891. Melville died in September of the same year, unknown to the general public, and vanished into an obscurity that lasted until 1920, when the great revival of his name and work began.

After the phenomenal creative activity of his first years—he wrote seven novels and many shorter pieces between 1845 and 1852—Melville seems to have fulfilled the hint in his 1851 letter to Hawthorne: "I feel that I am now come to the inmost leaf of the bulb, and that shortly the flower must fall to the mould." The impious probes and daring speculations, which so offended many critics and so bored sentimental readers, also generated imperfect sympathies in his host of aristocratic relatives. They came to regard him as a dark horse (if not a black sheep), slightly discreditable, possibly dangerous, and perhaps even unbalanced. They recommended change of occupation and underwrote sea voyages. But these were unavailing. Melville retreated into depression and inactivity, the long twilight of his years witnessing a steady drying up of his inspiration and energies and it was left to the twentieth century to give him recognition as having written the greatest of all American novels.

LETTERS

As a member of an aristocratic family, who had made a reputation with two romantic travel books, Typee *and* Omoo, *Melville found himself increasingly isolated as he voyaged deeper and deeper into uncharted seas of speculation. The letters he wrote during the composition of* Moby-Dick, *and just after its publication, to Nathaniel Hawthorne and his wife, are particularly illuminating.*

Passages from Some Letters by Herman Melville*

To Evert A. Duyckinck
13 December 1850
Pittsfield

My Dear Duyckinck, If you overhaul your old diaries you will see that a long period ago you were acquainted with one Herman Melvill(e); that he then resided in New York; but removing after a time into a remote region called Berkshire, and failing to answer what letters you sent him, you but reasonably supposed him dead; at any rate did not hear anything of him again, & so by degrees you thought no more about him.

I now write to inform you that this man has turned up—in short, My Dear Fellow in spite of my incivility I am alive & well, & would fain be remembered. . . .

I have a sort of sea-feeling here in the country, now that the ground is all covered with snow. I look out of my window in the morning when I rise as I would out of a port-hole of a ship in the Atlantic. My room seems a ship's cabin; & at nights when I wake up & hear the wind shrieking, I almost fancy there is too much sail on the house, & I had better go on the roof & rig in the chimney.

* Merrell R. Davis and William H. Gilman (eds.), *The Letters of Herman Melville.* New Haven: Yale University Press (1960). Used with the permission of the editors and the Yale University Press.

Do you want to know how I pass my time?—I rise at eight—
thereabouts—& go to my barn—say good-morning to the horse,
& give him his breakfast. (It goes to my heart to give him a cold
one, but it can't be helped) Then, pay a visit to my cow—cut up
a pumpkin or two for her, & stand by to see her eat it—for it's
a pleasant sight to see a cow move her jaws—she does it so mildly
& with such a sanctity.—My own breakfast over, I go to my work-
room & light my fire—then spread my M.S.S. on the table—take
one business squint at it, & fall to with a will. At 2½ P.M. I hear
a preconcerted knock at my door, which (by request) continues till
I rise & go to the door, which serves to wean me effectively from
my writing, however interested I may be. My friends the horse &
cow now demand their dinner—& I go & give it them. My own
dinner over, I rig my sleigh & with my mother or sisters start off
for the village—& if it be a Literary World day, great is the satisfaction thereof.—My evenings I spend in a sort of mesmeric state
in my room—not being able to read—only now & then skimming
over some large-printed book.—Can you send me about fifty fast-
writing youths, with an easy style & not averse to polishing their
labors? If you can, I wish you would, because since I have been
here I have planned about that number of future works & cant
find enough time to think about them separately.—But I dont
know but a book in a man's brain is better off than a book bound
in calf—at any rate it is safer from criticism. And taking a book
off the brain, is akin to the ticklish & dangerous business of taking
an old painting off a panel—you have to scrape off the whole
brain in order to get at it with due safety—& even then, the painting may not be worth the trouble. . . .

To Nathaniel Hawthorne
April [?] 1851
Pittsfield

. . . There is a certain tragic phase of humanity which, in our
opinion, was never more powerfully embodied than by Hawthorne.
We mean the tragicalness of human thought in its own unbiassed,
native, and profounder workings. We think that into no recorded
mind has the intense feeling of the visable truth ever entered more
deeply than into this man's. By visable truth, we mean the apprehension of the absolute condition of present things as they strike the
eye of the man who fears them not, though they do their worst to
him,—the man who, like Russia or the British Empire, declares

himself a sovereign nature (in himself) amid the powers of heaven, hell, and earth. He may perish; but so long as he exists he insists upon treating with all Powers upon an equal basis. If any of those other Powers choose to withhold certain secrets, let them; that does not impair my sovereignty in myself; that does not make me tributary. And perhaps, after all, there is *no* secret. We incline to think that the Problem of the Universe is like the Freemason's mighty secret, so terrible to all children. It turns out, at last, to consist in a triangle, a mallet, and an apron,—nothing more! We incline to think that God cannot explain His own secrets, and that He would like a little information upon certain points Himself. We mortals astonish Him as much as He us. But it is this *Being* of the matter; there lies the knot with which we choke ourselves. As soon as you say *Me,* a *God,* a *Nature,* so soon you jump off from your stool and hang from the beam. Yes, that word is the hangman. Take God out of the dictionary, and you would have Him in the street.

There is the grand truth about Nathaniel Hawthorne. He says NO! in thunder; but the Devil himself cannot make him say *yes.* For all men who say *yes,* lie; and all men who say *no,*—why, they are in the happy condition of judicious, unincumbered travellers in Europe; they cross the frontiers into Eternity with nothing but a carpet-bag,—that is to say, the Ego. Whereas those *yes*-gentry, they travel with heaps of baggage, and, damn them! they will never get through the Custom House. What's the reason, Mr. Hawthorne, that in the last stages of metaphysics a fellow always falls to *swearing* so? I could rip an hour. You see, I began with a little criticism extracted for your benefit from the "Pittsfield Secret Review," and here I have landed in Africa.

Walk down one of these mornings and see me. No nonsense; come. Remember me to Mrs. Hawthorne and the children.

H. Melville.

P.S. The marriage of Phoebe with the daguerreotypist is a fine stroke, because of his turning out to be a *Maule.* If you pass Hepzibah's cent-shop, buy me a Jim Crow (fresh) and send it to me by Ned Higgins.

To Nathaniel Hawthorne
1? June 1851
Pittsfield

My Dear Hawthorne,—I should have been rumbling down to you in my pine-board chariot a long time ago, were it not that for

some weeks past I have been more busy than you can well imagine,
—out of doors,—building and patching and tinkering away in all
directions. Besides, I had my crops to get in,—corn and potatoes
(I hope to show you some famous ones by and by),—and many
other things to attend to, all accumulating upon this one particular
season. I work myself; and at night my bodily sensations are akin
to those I have so often felt before, when a hired man, doing
my day's work from sun to sun. But I mean to continue visiting
you until you tell me that my visits are both supererogatory and
superfluous. With no son of man do I stand upon any etiquette or
ceremony, except the Christian ones of charity and honesty. I am
told, my fellow-man, that there is an aristocracy of the brain. Some
men have boldly advocated and asserted it. Schiller seems to have
done so, though I don't know much about him. At any rate, it is
true that there have been those who, while earnest in behalf of
political equality, still accept the intellectual estates. And I can
well perceive, I think, how a man of superior mind can, by its intense cultivation, bring himself, as it were, into a certain spontaneous aristocracy of feeling,—exceedingly nice and fastidious,—
similar to that which, in an English Howard, conveys a torpedo-
fish thrill at the slightest contact with a social plebeian. So, when
you see or hear of my ruthless democracy on all sides, you may possibly feel a touch of a shrink, or something of that sort. It is but
nature to be shy of a mortal who boldly declares that a thief in
jail is as honorable a personage as Gen. George Washington. This is
ludicrous. But Truth is the silliest thing under the sun. Try to get
a living by the Truth—and go to the Soup Societies. Heavens!
Let any clergyman try to preach the Truth from its very stronghold, the pulpit, and they would ride him out of his church on
his own pulpit bannister. It can hardly be doubted that all Reformers are bottomed upon the truth, more or less; and to the
world at large are not reformers almost universally laughing-
stocks? Why so? Truth is ridiculous to men. Thus easily in my
room here do I, conceited and garrulous, reverse the test of my Lord
Shaftesbury.

It seems an inconsistency to assert unconditional democracy
in all things, and yet confess a dislike to all mankind—in the
mass. But not so.—But it's an endless sermon,—no more of it. I
began by saying that the reason I have not been to Lenox is this,—
in the evening I feel completely done up, as the phrase is, and incapable of the long jolting to get to your house and back. In a
week or so, I go to New York, to bury myself in a third-story
room, and work and slave on my "Whale" while it is driving
through the press. *That* is the only way I can finish it now,—I am
so pulled hither and thither by circumstances. The calm, the
coolness, the silent grass-growing mood in which a man *ought*
always to compose,—that, I fear, can seldom be mine. Dollars
damn me; and the malicious Devil is forever grinning in upon me,
holding the door ajar. My dear Sir, a presentiment is on me,—

I shall at last be worn out and perish, like an old nutmeg-grater, grated to pieces by the constant attrition of the wood, that is, the nutmeg. What I feel most moved to write, that is banned,—it will not pay. Yet, altogether, write the *other* way I cannot. So the product is a final hash, and all my books are botches. I'm rather sore, perhaps, in this letter; but see my hand!—four blisters on this palm, made by hoes and hammers within the last few days. It is a rainy morning; so I am indoors, and all work suspended. I feel cheerfully disposed, and therefore I write a little bluely. Would the Gin were here! If ever, my dear Hawthorne, in the eternal times that are to come, you and I shall sit down in Paradise, in some little shady corner by ourselves; and if we shall by any means be able to smuggle a basket of champagne there (I won't believe in a Temperance Heaven), and if we shall then cross our celestial legs in the celestial grass that is forever tropical, and strike our glasses and our heads together, till both musically ring in concert, —then, O my dear fellow-mortal, how shall we pleasantly discourse of all the things manifold which now so distress us,—when all the earth shall be but a reminiscence, yea, its final dissolution an antiquity. Then shall songs be composed as when wars are over; humorous, comic songs,—"Oh, when I lived in that queer little hole called the world," or, "Oh, when I toiled and sweated below," or, "Oh, when I knocked and was knocked in the fight!"—yes, let us look forward to such things. Let us swear that, though now we sweat, yet it is because of the dry heat which is indispensable to the nourishment of the vine which is to bear the grapes that are to give us the champagne hereafter.

But I was talking about the "Whale." As the fishermen say, "he's in his flurry" when I left him some three weeks ago. I'm going to take him by his jaw, however, before long, and finish him up in some fashion or other. What's the use of elaborating what, in its very essence, is so short-lived as a modern book? Though I wrote the Gospels in this century, I should die in the gutter. —I talk all about myself, and this is selfishness and egotism. Granted. But how help it? I am writing to you; I know little about you, but something about myself. So I write about myself,— at least, to you. Don't trouble yourself, though, about writing; and don't trouble yourself about visiting; and when you *do* visit, don't trouble yourself about talking. I will do all the writing and visiting and talking myself.—By the way, in the last "Dollar Magazine" I read "The Unpardonable Sin." He was a sad fellow, that Ethan Brand. I have no doubt you are by this time responsible for many a shake and tremor of the tribe of "general readers." It is a frightful poetical creed that the cultivation of the brain eats out the heart. But it's my *prose* opinion that in most cases, in those men who have fine brains and work them well, the heart extends down to hams. And though you smoke them with the fire of tribulation, yet, like veritable hams, the head only gives the richer and the better flavor. I stand for the heart. To the dogs with the head! I had rather be a fool with a heart, than Jupiter Olympus with his head. The reason the mass of men fear God, and *at bottom dislike* Him, is because they rather distrust His heart, and fancy Him all brain like a watch. (You perceive I employ a capital initial in the pronoun referring to the Deity; don't you think there is a slight dash of flunkeyism in that usage?) Another thing, I was in New York for four-and-twenty hours the other day, and saw a portrait of N.H. And I have seen and heard many flattering (in a publisher's point of view) allusions to the "Seven Gables." And I have seen "Tales," and "A New Volume" announced, by N.H. So upon the whole, I say to myself, this N.H. is in the ascendant. My dear Sir, they begin to patronize. All Fame is patronage. Let me be infamous: there is no patronage in *that*. What "reputation" H.M. has is horrible. Think of it! To go down to posterity is bad enough, any way; but to go down as a "man who lived among the cannibals"! When I speak of posterity, in reference to myself, I only mean the babies who will probably be born in the moment immediately ensuing upon my giving up the ghost. I shall go down to some of them, in all likelihood. "Typee" will be given to them, perhaps, with their gingerbread. I have come to regard this matter of Fame as the most transparent of all vanities. I read Solomon more and more, and every time see deeper and deeper and unspeakable meanings in him. I did not think of Fame, a year ago, as I do now. My development has been all within a few years past. I am like one of those seeds taken out of the Egyptian Pyramids, which, after being three thousand years a seed and nothing but a seed, being planted in English soil, it developed itself, grew to greenness, and then fell to mould. So I. Until I was twenty-five, I had no development at all. From my twenty-fifth year I date my life. Three weeks have scarcely passed, at any time between then and now, that I have not unfolded within myself. But I feel that I am now come to the inmost leaf of the bulb, and that shortly the flower must fall to the mould. It seems to me now that Solomon was the truest man who ever spoke, and yet that he a little *managed* the truth with a view to popular conservatism; or else there have been many corruptions and interpolations of the text.—In reading some of Goethe's sayings, so worshipped by his votaries, I came across this, *"Live in the all."* That is to say, your separate identity is but a wretched one, —good; but get out of yourself, spread and expand yourself, and bring to yourself the tinglings of life that are felt in the flowers and the woods, that are felt in the planets Saturn and Venus, and the Fixed Stars. What nonsense! Here is a fellow with a raging toothache. "My dear boy," Goethe says to him, "you are sorely afflicted with that tooth; but you must *live in the all*, and then you will be happy!" As with all great genius, there is an immense deal of flummery in Goethe, and in proportion to my own contact with him, a monstrous deal of it in me.

                                                                    H. Melville.

P.S. "Amen!" saith Hawthorne.

N.B. This "all" feeling, though, there is some truth in. You must often have felt it, lying on the grass on a warm summer's day. Your legs seem to send out shoots into the earth. Your hair feels like leaves upon your head. This is the *all* feeling. But what plays the mischief with the truth is that men will insist upon the universal application of a temporary feeling or opinion.

P.S. You must not fail to admire my discretion in paying the postage on this letter.

To Nathaniel Hawthorne
November 1851
Pittsfield, Monday afternoon

My Dear Hawthorne,—People think that if a man has undergone any hardship, he should have a reward; but for my part, if I have done the hardest possible day's work, and then come to sit down in a corner and eat my supper comfortably—why, then I don't think I deserve any reward for my hard day's work—for am I not now at peace? Is not my supper good? My peace and my supper are my reward, my dear Hawthorne. So your joy-giving and exultation-breeding letter is not my reward for my ditcher's work with that book, but is the good goddess's bonus over and above what was stipulated for—for not one man in five cycles, who is wise, will expect appreciative recognition from his fellows, or any one of them. Appreciation! Recognition! Is love appreciated? Why, ever since Adam, who has got to the meaning of this great allegory —the world? Then we pygmies must be content to have our paper allegories but ill comprehended. I say your appreciation is my glorious gratuity. In my proud, humble way,—a shepherd-king,— I was lord of a little vale in the solitary Crimea; but you have now given me the crown of India. But on trying it on my head, I found it fell down on my ears, notwithstanding their asinine length—for it's only such ears that sustain such crowns.

Your letter was handed me last night on the road going to Mr. Morewood's, and I read it there. Had I been at home, I would have sat down at once and answered it. In me divine magnanimities are spontaneous and instantaneous—catch them while you can. The world goes round, and the other side comes up. So now I can't write what I felt. But I felt pantheistic then—your heart beat in my ribs and mine in yours, and both in God's. A sense of unspeakable security is in me this moment, on account of your hav-

ing understood the book. I have written a wicked book, and feel
spotless as the lamb. Ineffable socialities are in me. I would sit
down and dine with you and all the gods in old Rome's Pantheon.
It is a strange feeling—no hopefulness is in it, no despair. Content—that is it; and irresponsibility; but without licentious inclination. I speak now of my profoundest sense of being, not of
an incidental feeling.

Whence come you, Hawthorne? By what right do you drink
from my flagon of life? And when I put it to my lips—lo, they
are yours and not mine. I feel that the Godhead is broken up like
the bread at the Supper, and that we are the pieces. Hence this
infinite fraternity of feeling. Now, sympathizing with the paper,
my angel turns over another page. You did not care a penny for
the book. But, now and then as you read, you understood the
pervading thought that impelled the book—and that you praised.
Was it not so? You were archangel enough to despise the imperfect
body, and embrace the soul. Once you hugged the ugly Socrates
because you saw the flame in the mouth, and heard the rushing
of the demon,—the familiar,—and recognized the sound; for you
have heard it in your own solitudes.

My dear Hawthorne, the atmospheric skepticisms steal into me
now, and make me doubtful of my sanity in writing you thus.
But, believe me, I am not mad, most noble Festus! But truth is
ever incoherent, and when the big hearts strike together, the
concussion is a little stunning. Farewell. Don't write a word about
the book. That would be robbing me of my miserly delight. I am
heartily sorry I ever wrote anything about it—it was paltry.
Lord, when shall we be done growing? As long as we have anything more to do, we have done nothing. So, now, let us add Moby
Dick to our blessing, and step from that. Leviathan is not the
biggest fish;—I have heard of Krakens.

This is a long letter, but you are not at all bound to answer it.
Possibly, if you do answer it, and direct it to Herman Melville,
you will missend it—for the very fingers that now guide this pen
are not precisely the same that just took it up and put it on this
paper. Lord, when shall we be done changing? Ah! it's a long stage,
and no inn in sight, and night coming, and the body cold. But
with you for a passenger, I am content and can be happy. I shall
leave the world, I feel, with more satisfaction for having come to
know you. Knowing you persuades me more than the Bible of our
immortality.

What a pity, that, for your plain, bluff letter, you should get
such gibberish! Mention me to Mrs. Hawthorne and to the children, and so, good-by to you, with my blessing.

                                                      Herman.

P.S. I can't stop yet. If the world was entirely made up of
Magians, I'll tell you what I should do. I should have a paper-mill
established at one end of the house, and so have an endless riband
of foolscap rolling in upon my desk; and upon that endless riband

I should write a thousand—a million—billion thoughts, all under the form of a letter to you. The divine magnet is on you, and my magnet responds. Which is the biggest? A foolish question—they are *One*.

H.

P.P.S. Don't think that by writing me a letter you shall always be bored with an immediate reply to it—and so keep both of us delving over a writing-desk eternally. No such thing! I sh'n't always answer your letters, and you may do just as you please.

To Sophia Hawthorne
8 January 1852
New York

My Dear Mrs. Hawthorne, I have hunted up the finest Bath I could find, gilt-edged and stamped, whereon to inscribe my humble acknowledgment of your highly flattering letter of the 29th Dec: —it really amazed me that you should find any satisfaction in that book. It is true that some *men* have said they were pleased with it, but you are the only *woman*—for as a general thing, women have small taste for the sea. But, then, since you, with your spiritualizing nature, see more things than other people, and by the same process, refine all you see, so that they are not the same things that other people see, but things which while you think you but humbly discover them, you do in fact create them for yourself—Therefore, upon the whole, I do not so much marvel at your expressions concerning Moby Dick. At any rate, your allusion for example to the "Spirit Spout" first showed to me that there was a subtle significance in that thing—but I did not, in that case, *mean* it. I had some vague idea while writing it, that the whole book was susceptible of an allegoric construction, & also that *parts* of it were—but the speciality of many of the particular subordinate allegories, were first revealed to me, after reading Mr. Hawthorne's letter, which, without citing any particular examples, yet intimated the part-&-parcel allegoricalness of the whole.—But, My Dear Lady, I shall not again send you a bowl of salt water. The next chalice I shall commend, will be a rural bowl of milk. . . .

MOBY-DICK AND ITS CONTEMPORARY REVIEWS

Book reviews in Melville's time were apt to be at once elaborate and facetious. It is an interesting mark of the nineteenth century that the language then available tended to be richer than the people who used it. They had enormous vocabularies and a command of elaborate sentence patterns more often perhaps than they had something considerable to say; they waved the big stick therefore somewhat aimlessly.

The reviews that follow reveal some of these qualities; they are judicial without being judicious, severe without being informed, and sympathetic without understanding.

From **The Literary World**
NEW YORK, NOVEMBER 15-22, 1851, *by* Evert Duyckinck

MELVILLE'S MOBY DICK; OR, THE WHALE.

Every reader throughout the United States has probably perused in the newspapers the account of a recent incident in the whale fishery which would stagger the mind by its extent of the marvellous, were it not paralleled by a well known case—that of the *Essex* of Nantucket, still authenticated by living witnesses. It appears from a narrative published in the *Panama Herald* (an American newspaper in that region, itself one of the wonders of the age!), taken down from the lips of the captain of the vessel, John S. Deblois, that the ship Ann Alexander, of New Bedford, having left that port in June of last year with the usual vicissitudes of Cape Horn service, losing a New Hampshire man overboard in a storm at that point, had entered upon her Pacific hunting-grounds, and in the recent month of August was coursing within a few degrees of the Equator—a well known haunt of the whale. On the 20th of that month, nine in the morning, fish were discovered; two boats were lowered in pursuit, and by mid-day a particular sperm whale was struck and fast to the line. The first mate commanded the boat, thus far successful, and the Captain himself the other. After running some time, in the words of the narrative, the whale turned upon the boat to which he was attached, and rushing at it with tremendous violence, lifted open its enormous jaws, and taking the boat in, actually crushed it to fragments as small as a common-sized chair. Captain Deblois struck for the spot, and rescued the nine members of the boat's crew—a feat, we presume, which could only be accomplished among men hardy, resolute, and full of vitality as whalemen, strung at the moment by excitement to almost super-human energy and superiority to the elements. The Captain, with his double boat's crew, proceeded to the ship, some six miles off. There the waist-boat was fitted out, the men divided, and both parties went again in pursuit of the whale, the mate again taking the lead. The whale perceived the coming renewal of the attack, made for the boat, crushed it with his jaw, the men again throwing themselves into the deep. The Captain once more rescuing them, was himself pursued by the whale, which passed the boat with distended jaw; but they reached the ship in safety. A boat was sent for the oars of the broken vessels floating on the water, which were secured. Sail was set on the ship, and it was determined to proceed after the whale. He was overtaken, and a lance thrown into his head! The ship passed on, when it was immediately discovered that the whale was in pursuit. The ship manœuvred out of his way. *After he had fairly passed they kept off to overtake and attack him again.* The whale settled down deep below the surface. It was then near sundown. Capt. Deblois, continues the account, was at this time standing on the knight-heads on the larboard bow, with shaft in hand, ready to strike the monster a deadly blow should he appear, the ship moving about five knots, when looking over the side of the ship he discerned the whale rushing towards her at the rate of fifteen knots. In an instant the monster struck the ship with tremendous violence, shaking her from stem to stern. She quivered under the violence of the shock as if she had struck upon a rock. Captain Deblois descending to the forecastle, discovered that *the whale had struck the ship about two feet from the keel, abreast the foremast, knocking a great hole entirely through her bottom.* The ship was sinking rapidly. All hands were ordered into the boats, the captain leaving the deck last, throwing himself into the sea, and swimming to his comrades. That night was passed in the boats, with but twelve quarts of water saved, and no provisions for twenty-two men. In the morning the ship still lay on her beam-ends. Not a man would board her to cut away the masts, right the vessel, and procure provisions—fearing her sinking instantly—except the captain, who undertook the work with a single hatchet, and succeeded in getting the ship nearly on her keel. Nothing could be procured by cutting through the decks but some vinegar and a small quantity of wet bread, with which they abandoned the dangerous vessel. At the close of the next day they hailed the ship Nantucket of Nantucket, and were welcomed by its Captain, Gibbs, with the utmost hospitality. They were landed at Paita, where an authenticated protest of this extraordinary series of occurrences was made before the United States Consul.

By a singular coincidence this extreme adventure is, even to very many of the details, the catastrophe of Mr. Melville's new book, which is a natural-historical, philosophical, romantic account of the person, habits, manners, ideas of the great sperm whale; of his haunts and of his belongings; of his associations with the world of the deep, and of the not less remarkable individuals and combinations of individuals who hunt him on the oceans. Nothing like it has ever before been written of the whale; for no man who has at once seen so much of the actual conflict, and weighed so carefully all that has been recorded on the subject, with equal powers of perception and reflection, has attempted to write at all on it—the labors of Scoresby covering a different and inferior branch of the history. To the popular mind this book of Herman Melville, touching the Leviathan of the deep, is as much of a discovery in Natural History as was the revelation of America by Christopher Columbus in geography. Let any one read this book with the attention which it deserves, and then converse with the best informed of his friends and acquaintances who have not seen it, and he will notice the extent and variety of treatment; while scientific men must admit the original observation and speculation.

Such an infuriated, resolute sperm whale as pursued and destroyed the Ann Alexander is the hero, Moby Dick, of Mr. Melville's book. The vengeance with which he is hunted, which with Capt. Deblois was the incident of a single, though most memorable day, is the leading passion and idea of Captain Ahab of the Pequod for years, and throughout the seas of the world. Incidentally with this melo-dramatic action and spiritual development of the character of Ahab, is included a full, minute, thorough investigation, and description of the whale and its fishery. Such is a short-hand account of this bulky and multifarious volume.

It opens, after a dedication to Nathaniel Hawthorne, with a preliminary flourish in the style of Carlyle and the "Doctor" of etymology, followed by a hundred or so of extracts of "Old Burton," passages of a quaint and pithy character from Job and King Alfred to Miriam Coffin; in lieu of the old style of Scott, Cooper, and others, of distributing such flourishes about the heads of chapters. Here they are all in a lump, like the grace over the Franklin barrel of pork, and may be taken as a kind of bitters, a whet and fillip to the imagination, exciting it to the curious, ludicrous, sublime traits and contemplations which are to follow.

It is some time after opening with Chapter I. before we get fairly afloat, but the time is very satisfactorily occupied with some very strange, romantic, and, withal, highly humorous adventures at New Bedford and Nantucket. A scene at the Spouter Inn, of the former town, a night in bed with a Pacific Islander, and a mid-ocean adventure subsequently with a Frenchman over some dead whales in the Pacific, treat the reader to a laugh worthy of Smollet. We might perhaps as well introduce this at once. The Pequod, the ship in which the reader embarks from Nantucket, one day meets a French whaler under peculiar circumstances, in a calm, with two carcasses of whales secured to her, which the unadventurous crew had picked up, dead waifs of previous conflicts on the ocean. The Mate, Stubb, had boarded this vessel seeking information for Capt. Ahab, of Moby Dick, and returns to circumvent the ambergris, a product found in the diseased animal. . . .

A difficulty in the estimate of this, in common with one or two other of Mr. Melville's books, occurs from the double character under which they present themselves. In one light they are romantic fictions, in another statements of absolute fact. When to this is added that the romance is made a vehicle of opinion and satire through a more or less opaque allegorical veil, as particularly in the latter half of Mardi, and to some extent in this present volume, the critical difficulty is considerably thickened. It becomes quite impossible to submit such books to a distinct classification as fact, fiction, or essay. Something of a parallel may be found in Jean Paul's German tales, with an admixture of Southey's Doctor. Under these combined influences of personal observation, actual fidelity to local truthfulness in description, a taste for reading and sentiment, a fondness for fanciful analogies, near and remote, a rash daring in speculation, reckless at times of taste and propriety, again refined and eloquent, this volume of Moby Dick may be pronounced a most remarkable sea-dish—an intellectual chowder of romance, philosophy, natural history, fine writing, good feeling, bad sayings—but over which, in spite of all uncertainties, and in spite of the author himself, predominates his keen perceptive faculties, exhibited in vivid narration.

There are evidently two if not three books in Moby Dick rolled into one. Book No. I. we could describe as a thorough exhaustive account admirably given of the great Sperm Whale. The information is minute, brilliantly illustrated, as it should be—the whale himself so generously illuminating the midnight page on which his memoirs are written—has its level passages, its humorous touches, its quaint suggestion, its incident usually picturesque and occasionally sublime. All this is given in the most delightful manner in "The Whale." Book No. 2 is the romance of Captain Ahab, Queequeg, Tashtego, Pip & Co., who are more or less spiritual personages talking and acting differently from the general business run of the conversation on the decks of whalers. They are for the most part very serious people, and seem to be concerned a great deal about the problem of the universe. They are striking characters withal, of the romantic spiritual cast of the German drama; realities of some kinds at bottom, but veiled in all sorts of poetical incidents and expressions.

As a bit of German melodrama, with Captain Ahab for the Faust of the quarter-deck, and Queequeg with the crew, for Walpurgis night revellers in the forecastle, it has its strong points, though here the limits as to space and treatment of the stage would improve it. Moby Dick in this view becomes a sort of fishy moralist, a leviathan metaphysician, a folio Ductor Dubitantium, in fact, in the fresh water illustration of Mrs. Malaprop, "an allegory on the banks of the Nile." After pursuing him in this melancholic company over a few hundred squares of latitude and longitude, we begin to have some faint idea of the association of whaling and lamentation, and why blubber is popularly synonymous with tears.

The intense Captain Ahab is too long drawn out; something more of *him* might, we think, be left to the reader's imagination. The value of this kind of writing can only be through the personal consciousness of the reader, what he brings to the book; and all this is sufficiently evoked by a dramatic trait or suggestion. If we had as much of Hamlet or Macbeth as Mr. Melville gives us of Ahab, we should be tired even of their sublime company. Yet Captain Ahab is a striking conception, firmly planted on the wild deck of the Pequod—a dark disturbed soul arraying itself with every ingenuity of material resources for a conflict at once natural and supernatural in his eye, with the most dangerous extant physical monster of the earth, embodying, in strongly drawn lines of mental association, the vaster moral evil of the world. The pursuit of the White Whale thus interweaves with the literal perils of the fishery —a problem of fate and destiny—to the tragic solution of which Ahab hurries on, amidst the wild stage scenery of the ocean. To this end the motley crew, the air, the sky, the sea, its inhabitants are idealized throughout. It is a noble and praiseworthy conception; and though our sympathies may not always accord with the train of thought, we would caution the reader against a light or hasty condemnation of this part of the work.

Book III., appropriating perhaps a fourth of the volume, is a vein of moralizing, half essay, half rhapsody, in which much refinement and subtlety, and no little poetical feeling, are mingled with quaint conceit and extravagant daring speculation. This is to be taken as in some sense dramatic; the narrator throughout among the personages of the Pequod being one Ishmael, whose wit may be allowed to be against everything on land, as his hand is against everything at sea. This piratical running down of creeds and opinions, the conceited indifferentism of Emerson, or the run-a-muck style of Carlyle is, we will not say dangerous in such cases, for there are various forces at work to meet more powerful onslaught, but it is out of place and uncomfortable. We do not like to see what, under any view, must be to the world the most sacred associations of life violated and defaced.

We call for fair play in this matter. Here is Ishmael, telling the story of this volume, going down on his knees with a cannibal to a piece of wood, in the second story fireplace of a New-Bedford tavern, in the spirit of amiable and transcendent charity, which may be all very well in its way; but why dislodge from heaven, with contumely, "long-pampered Gabriel, Michael and Raphael." Surely Ishmael, who is a scholar, might have spoken respectfully of the Archangel Gabriel, out of consideration, if not for the Bible (which might be asking too much of the school), at least for one John Milton, who wrote Paradise Lost.

Nor is it fair to inveigh against the terrors of priestcraft, which, skilful though it may be in making up its woes, at least seeks to provide a remedy for the evils of the world, and attribute the existence of conscience to "hereditary dyspepsias, nurtured by Ramadans"—and at the same time go about petrifying us with imaginary horrors, and all sorts of gloomy suggestions, all the world through. It is a curious fact that there are no more bilious people in the world, more completely filled with megrims and head shakings, than some of these very people who are constantly inveighing against the religious melancholy of priestcraft.

So much for the consistency of Ishmael—who, if it is the author's object to exhibit the painful contradictions of this self-dependent, self-torturing agency of a mind driven hither and thither as a flame in a whirlwind, is, in a degree, a successful embodiment of opinions, without securing from us, however, much admiration for the result.

With this we make an end of what we have been reluctantly compelled to object to this volume. With far greater pleasure, we acknowledge the acuteness of observation, the freshness of perception, with which the author brings home to us from the deep, "things unattempted yet in prose or rhyme," the weird influences of his ocean scenes, the salient imagination which connects them with the past and distant, the world of books and the life of experience—certain prevalent traits of manly sentiment. These are strong powers with which Mr. Melville wrestles in this book. It would be a great glory to subdue them to the highest uses of fiction. It is still a great honor, among the crowd of successful mediocrities which throng our publishers' counters, and know nothing of divine impulses, to be in the company of these nobler spirits on any terms.

From **Harper's New Monthly Magazine**
NEW YORK, DECEMBER, 1851

A new work by HERMAN MELVILLE, entitled *Moby Dick; or, The Whale,* has just been issued by Harper and Brothers, which, in point of richness and variety of incident, originality of conception, and splendor of description, surpasses any of the former productions of this highly successful author. *Moby Dick* is the name of an old White Whale; half fish and half devil; the terror of the Nantucket cruisers; the scourge of distant oceans; leading an invulnerable, charmed life; the subject of many grim and ghostly traditions. This huge sea monster has a conflict with one Captain Ahab; the veteran Nantucket salt comes off second best; not only loses a leg in the affray, but receives a twist in the brain; becomes the victim of a deep, cunning monomania; believes himself predestined to take a bloody revenge on his fearful enemy; pursues him with fierce demoniac energy of purpose; and at last perishes in the dreadful fight, just as he deems that he has reached the goal of his frantic passion. On this slight framework, the author has constructed a romance, a tragedy, and a natural history, not without numerous gratuitous suggestions on psychology, ethics, and theology. Beneath the whole story, the subtle, imaginative reader may perhaps find a pregnant allegory, intended to illustrate the mystery of human life. Certain it is that the rapid, pointed hints which are often thrown out, with the keenness and velocity of a harpoon, penetrate deep into the heart of things, showing that the genius of the author for moral analysis is scarcely surpassed by his wizard power of description.

In the course of the narrative the habits of the whale are fully and ably described. Frequent graphic and instructive sketches of the fishery, of sea-life in a whaling vessel, and of the manners and customs of strange nations are interspersed with excellent artistic effect among the thrilling scenes of the story. The various processes of procuring oil are explained with the minute, painstaking fidelity of a statistical record, contrasting strangely with the weird, phantom-like character of the plot, and of some of the leading personages, who present a no less unearthly appearance than the witches in Macbeth. These sudden and decided transitions form a striking feature of the volume. Difficult of management, in the highest degree, they are wrought with consummate skill. To a less gifted author, they would inevitably have proved fatal. He has not only deftly avoided their dangers, but made them an element of great power. They constantly pique the attention of the reader, keeping curiosity alive, and presenting the combined charm of surprise and alternation.

The introductory chapters of the volume, containing sketches of life in the great marts of Whalingdom, New Bedford and Nantucket, are pervaded with a fine vein of comic humor, and reveal a succession of portraitures, in which the lineaments of nature shine forth, through a good deal of perverse, intentional exaggeration. To many readers, these will prove the most interesting portions of the work. Nothing can be better than the description of the owners of the vessel, Captain Peleg and Captain Bildad, whose acquaintance we make before the commencement of the voyage. The character of Captain Ahab also opens upon us with wonderful power. He exercises a wild, bewildering fascination by his dark and mysterious nature, which is not at all diminished when we obtain a clearer insight into his strange history. Indeed, all the members of the ship's company, the three mates, Starbuck, Stubbs, and Flash, the wild, savage Gayheader, the case-hardened old blacksmith, to say nothing of the pearl of a New Zealand harpooner, the bosom friend of the narrator—all stand before us in the strongest individual relief, presenting a unique picture gallery, which every artist must despair of rivaling.

From **The Athenaeum**
LONDON, OCTOBER 25, 1851

THIS is an ill-compounded mixture of romance and matter-of-fact. The idea of a connected and collected story has obviously visited and abandoned its writer again and again in the course of composition. The style of his tale is in places disfigured by mad (rather than bad) English; and its catastrophe is hastily, weakly, and obscurely managed. The second title—'Moby Dick'—is the name given to a particular sperm whale, or white sea monster, more malignant and diabolical even than the sperm whale in general is known to be. This ocean fiend is invested with especial horrors for our ship's crew;—because, once upon a time, a conflict with him cost their Captain a limb. Captain Ahab had an ivory leg made,—took an oath of retribution,—grew crazy,—lashed himself up into a purpose of cruising in quest of his adversary,—and bound all who sailed with him to stand by him in his wrath. With this cheerful Captain, on such a wise and Christian voyage of discovery, went to sea Ishmael, the imaginary writer of this narrative.

Frantic though such an invention seems to be, it might possibly have been accepted as the motive and purpose of an *extravaganza* had its author been consistent with himself. Nay, in such a terrible cause—when Krakens and Typhoons and the wonders of Mid-Ocean, &c. &c. were the topics and toys to be arranged and manœuvred—we might have stretched a point in admission of electrical verbs and adjectives as hoarse as the hurricane. There is a time for everything in imaginative literature;—and, according to its order, a place—for rant as well as for reserve; but the rant must be good, honest, shameless rant, without flaw or misgiving. The voice of "the storm wind Euroclydon" must not be interrupted by the facts of Scoresby and the figures of Cocker. Ravings and scraps of useful knowledge flung together salad-wise make a dish in which there

may be much surprise, but in which there is little savour. The real
secret of this patchiness in the present case is disclosed in Mr.
Melville's appendix; which contains such an assortment of curious
quotations as Southey might have wrought up into a whale-chapter
for 'The Doctor,'—suggesting the idea that a substantial work
on the subject may have been originally contemplated. Either Mr.
Melville's purpose must have changed, or his power must have
fallen short. The result is, at all events, a most provoking book,—
neither so utterly extravagant as to be entirely comfortable, nor
so instructively complete as to take place among documents on
the subject of the Great Fish, his capabilities, his home and his
capture. Our author must be henceforth numbered in the company
of the incorrigibles who occasionally tantalize us with indications
of genius, while they constantly summon us to endure monstrosities,
carelessnesses, and other such harassing manifestations of bad taste
as daring or disordered ingenuity can devise. . . .

The dark-complexioned harpooner turned out to be a cannibal,
one Queequeg,—as sweet-tempered a savage as if he had been a
prize vegetarian. It seemed odd enough to find Miss Martineau
in her 'Eastern Travel' professing that "she had never rested till
she had mastered the religious idea involved in cannibalism,"—
but Mr. Melville's impersonation of the virtues and humanities
which are to light up and relieve his terrible story is yet odder
as a selection. The Battas, who, as Sir Stamford Raffles assures
us, eat their progenitors when the latter are sixty years old, are
henceforth not beyond the reach of *réhabilitation:*—nay, those
most dismal of Gnomes, the aborigines who devour clay, may now
expect their laureate and their apologist. To such lengths will a
craving for effect carry a sane man!

We have little more to say in reprobation or in recommendation
of this absurd book,—having detailed its leading incident. Mr.
Melville has been on former occasions characterized by us as one
who thoroughly understands the tone of sea superstition. There
is a wild humorous poetry in some of his terrors which distinguishes
him from the vulgar herd of fustian-weavers. For instance, his
interchapter on 'The Whiteness of the Whale' is full of ghostly
suggestions for which a Maturin or a Monk Lewis would have
been thankful. Mr. Melville has to thank himself only if his horrors
and his heroics are flung aside by the general reader, as so much
trash belonging to the worst school of Bedlam literature,—since
he seems not so much unable to learn as disdainful of learning the
craft of an artist.

From **The Spectator**
LONDON, OCTOBER 25, 1851
HERMAN MELVILLE'S WHALE.

THIS sea novel is a singular medley of naval observation, magazine article writing, satiric reflection upon the conventionalism of civilized life, and rhapsody run mad. So far as the nautical parts are appropriate and unmixed, the portraiture is truthful and interesting. Some of the satire, especially in the early parts, is biting and reckless. The chapter-spinning is various in character; now powerful from the vigorous and fertile fancy of the author, now little more than empty though sounding phrases. The rhapsody belongs to wordmongering where ideas are the staple; where it takes the shape of narrative or dramatic fiction, it is phantasmal—an attempted description of what is impossible in nature and without probability in art; it repels the reader instead of attracting him.

The elements of the story are a South Sea whaling voyage, narrated by Ishmael, one of the crew of the ship Pequod, from Nantucket. Its "probable" portions consist of the usual sea matter in that branch of the industrial marine; embracing the preparations for departure, the voyage, the chase and capture of whale, with the economy of cutting up, &c., and the peculiar discipline of the service. This matter is expanded by a variety of digressions on the nature and characteristics of the sperm whale, the history of the fishery, and similar things, in which a little knowledge is made the excuse for a vast many words. The voyage is introduced by several chapters in which life in American seaports is rather broadly depicted.

The "marvellous" injures the book by disjointing the narrative, as well as by its inherent want of interest, at least as managed by Mr. Melville. In the superstition of some whalers, (grounded upon the malicious foresight which occasionally characterizes the attacks of the sperm fish upon the boats sent to capture it,) there is a *white* whale which possesses supernatural power. To capture or even to hurt it is beyond the art of man; the skill of the whaler is useless; the harpoon does not wound it; it exhibits a contemptuous strategy in its attacks upon the boats of its pursuers; and happy is the vessel where only loss of limb, or of a single life, attends its chase. Ahab, the master of the Pequod—a mariner of long experience, stern resolve, and indomitable courage, the high hero of romance, in short, transferred to a whale-ship—has lost his leg in a contest with the white whale. Instead of daunting Ahab, the loss exasperates him; and by long brooding over it his reason becomes shaken. In this condition he undertakes the voyage; making the chase of his fishy antagonist the sole object of his thoughts, and, so far as he can without exciting overt insubordination among his officers, the object of his proceedings.

Such a groundwork is hardly natural enough for a regular-built novel, though it might form a tale, if properly managed. But Mr.

Melville's mysteries provoke wonder at the author rather than terror at the creation; the soliloquies and dialogues of Ahab, in which the author attempts delineating the wild imaginings of monomania, and exhibiting some profoundly speculative views of things in general, induce weariness or skipping; while the whole scheme mars, as we have said, the nautical continuity of story— greatly assisted by various chapters of a bookmaking kind.

Perhaps the earliest chapters are the best, although they contain little adventure. Their topics are fresher to English readers than the whale-chase, and they have more direct satire. One of the leading personages in the voyage is Queequeg, a South Sea Islander, that Ishmael falls in with at New Bedford, and with whom he forms a bosom friendship. . . .

The strongest point of the book is its "characters." Ahab, indeed, is a melodramatic exaggeration, and Ishmael is little more than a mouthpiece; but the harpooners, the mates, and several of the seamen, are truthful portraitures of the sailor as modified by the whaling service. The persons ashore are equally good, though they are soon lost sight of. The two Quaker owners are the author's means for a hit at the religious hypocrisies. Captain Bildad, an old sea-dog, has got rid of everything pertaining to the meeting-house save an occasional "thou" and "thee." Captain Peleg, in American phrase "professes religion." . . .

It is a canon with some critics that nothing should be introduced into a novel which it is physically impossible for the writer to have known: thus, he must not describe the conversation of miners in a pit if they *all* perish. Mr. Melville hardly steers clear of this rule, and he continually violates another, by beginning in the autobiographical form and changing ad libitum into the narrative. His catastrophe overrides all rule: not only is Ahab, with his boat's-crew, destroyed in his last desperate attack upon the white whale, but the Pequod herself sinks with all on board into the depths of the illimitable ocean. Such is the go-ahead method.

MOBY-DICK AND ITS MODERN CRITICS

The great Melville revival began in 1921 with the publication of Raymond Weaver's Herman Melville: Mariner and Mystic, *and since then there has been a prodigious amount of excellent scholarship and criticism. Melville has become a sort of myth himself—in the sense of an archetype of the American problem—for almost every important critic has tested his doctrinal weapons on the writer's shield, or hide. The selections that follow are only the smallest sample, but give some idea of the* kinds *of critical approaches that have been made to* Moby-Dick.

From Herman Melville*
by Newton Arvin

When we read *Moby-Dick* in this manner [as a "dreamlike projection of Melville's unconscious wishes and obscure inward contests"] we are conscious of being presented at the very outset with one dominating oneiric image, the image of self-destruction; and then, as the action unrolls itself, and Ahab advances slowly to the forescene, we are given its counterpart and equivalent, the image of murderous destructiveness directed outward against the Other. From one point of view, what is dreamlike in the book may be said to move back and forth between these two poles, the suicidal wish, the longing for self-extinction, and its necessary antithesis, so deeply dependent upon it emotionally, the desire to inflict death upon what is, or what one imagines to be, the source of one's suffering. To undergo a kind of suicide is the motive that, along with the idea of the Whale (so closely bound up with it), impels Ishmael in the first place to go off to sea. Whenever, he says, he finds himself involuntarily pausing before coffin warehouses, and bringing up the rear of every funeral he meets, then he accounts it high time to get to sea as soon as he can: "With a philosophical flourish

* Newton Arvin, *Herman Melville*. New York: William Sloane Associates (1950), pp. 170–190.

549

Cato throws himself upon his sword; I quietly take to the ship."
There follows a series of hypnotic meditations on the allurements
of the sea, of water generally, in which that element figures, though
in a complex and iridescent way, as a symbol of death; of a return
to the primal liquidity, oblivion, nonbeing. The sailing of the *Pequod*
is to be for Ishmael a temporary passage out of existence. . . .

From this point on we are only intermittently and in flashes
aware of him. It is Ahab in whom the most intense emotions of
the dream are now concentrated. He is what our wildest, most
egoistic, most purely destructive malevolence could wish to be,
this old Quaker skipper from Nantucket; obsessed to the point of
monomania with the will to destroy the hated thing, yet free from
all mere smallnesses, "a grand, ungodly, godlike man." He is our
hatred ennobled, as we would wish to have it, up to heroism. Moreover, he has in fact been terribly and vitally injured by Moby Dick.
The Whale, in what looks like conscious malice, has reaped Ahab's
leg away with his frightful, sickle-shaped jaw, and Ahab must
now rely on a dead, artificial leg made of a Sperm Whale's jaw-
bone. A kind of castration, in short, has been not only imagined
and dreaded but inflicted, and the phallic source of vital potency
has been replaced by an image of impotence and lifelessness, constructed from the skeleton of the injurer himself. Not only so, but
in a kind of redoubled, repetitive, dreamlike manner, we hear that
this apparently impotent limb has itself turned upon Ahab, and
that before the sailing of the *Pequod* he had been found one night
fallen in the streets of Nantucket with his artificial leg so twisted
about that it had smitten his groin like a stake and almost pierced it.

A profound sexual injury is transparently symbolized here, and
Ahab's "ivory" leg is an equivocal symbol both of his own impotence and of the independent male principle directed cripplingly
against him. It had been fashioned from the polished bone of a
Sperm Whale's jaw, though not of course from Moby Dick's own:
what, then, does Moby Dick himself, on this deep instinctive plane,
shadow forth? It would be easiest to say simply the father, the
father who imposes constraint upon the most powerful instincts,
both egoistic and sexual; the father also who threatens even to
destroy the latter by castration and may indeed, in all but the
literal sense, carry out the threat. On the deepest level, this is the
oneiric truth about Moby Dick, but it is Melville with whom we
have to reckon throughout, and for whom we have to remember
how soon, and how overbearingly, the paternal role was played
by Maria Melville. On every ground we are forced to confront a
profound ambiguity in Moby Dick and to end by confessing that
he embodies neither the father merely nor the mother but, by a
process of condensation, the *parental* principle inclusively. Of his
basic maleness there can be no question, not only because we are
everywhere reminded of his preternatural power and masculine
strength but because, in detail, we are required to contemplate the
"battering-ram" of his head, the highly prized spermaceti with which

it is so richly stored, his phallus ("The Cassock"), and his tail (with its "Titanism of power"); there is even a suggested association with the phallic serpent-god of the Ophites. Yet along with all this we cannot ignore a certain bisexuality in the image, if not literally of Moby Dick, then of the Sperm Whale generally; a bisexuality that is conveyed to us partly by the glimpses we have into his "beautiful" mouth and "the great Kentucky Mammoth Cave of his stomach"—that stomach in which, as Father Mapple's sermon reminds us, Jonah was swallowed up as in a womb—but also, and chiefly, by the obstetric imagery of the chapter (LXXVIII) in which Tashtego falls into the liquid depths of a Sperm Whale's severed head and is rescued or "delivered," like a baby, by Queequeg.

Moby Dick is thus the archetypal Parent; the father, yes, but the mother also, so far as she becomes a substitute for the father. And the emotions Moby Dick evokes in us are the violently contradictory emotions that prevail between parent and child. Too little, curiously, has been made of this; what dominates most accounts of the White Whale is the simple vindictive emotion that Ahab is alleged to feel toward him, and of course there can be no question of his Oedipal bitterness toward Moby Dick: his conviction that the Whale is the embodiment of "all the subtle demonisms of life and thought"; in short, "all evil." Yet hatred of this obsessive and even paranoid sort is but the deformation of a still more deepseated love, and Ahab is as tightly bound to Moby Dick as an unhappy child to a parent too passionately loved. The emotion, however, that the Sperm Whale inspires is not restricted to Ahab's monomaniac vengefulness: from the very outset we are conscious also of Ishmael's feelings, and though at one pole these are identified with Ahab's, at the other they are by no means the same. They are, at any rate, more openly and obviously contradictory: the "grand hooded phantom," as it swims before Ishmael's fancy, may inspire a kind of fear but it inspires also an intensity of mystical longing that is something like love. It is a sort of love that lies behind that passionate preoccupation with every detail, however trifling, that characterizes the regarded object, and it is a sort of love, though an imperfectly fulfilled one, that brings Moby Dick before our imaginations as a creature of "majestic bulk," "pervading dignity," and "appalling beauty." . . .

Meanwhile the unconscious and instinctive sources of the fable have expressed themselves in still other oneiric symbols. The very setting of the whole narrative, on board a ship from which of necessity everything female has been excluded, is itself dreamlike and wishful. Of all the countersailing vessels the *Pequod* meets, only one is an image of prosperity and jolliness, and this vessel is revealingly named the *Bachelor*—that "glad ship of good luck" which is heading back to Nantucket laden to its very bulwarks and mastheads with abounding spermaceti. The weapons with which the Sperm Whale is attacked and slaughtered are appropriately phallic symbols—harpoons, lances, cutting-spades, and the like—and if there were any uncertainty about the nature of Ahab's injury, on this instinctive plane, it would not survive a careful scrutiny of the doubloon he nails to the mainmast as a promised reward for the man who first sights Moby Dick. This golden coin from Ecuador bears on its exposed side three unmistakable symbols in the form of three Andean mountain-peaks, one of them flaming like a volcano, one bearing a tower on its top, and the third a crowing cock. Queequeg, gazing at it, as Stubb watches him from a little distance, glances from the coin to his thighbone, "comparing notes," and seems, as Stubb fancies, to find something in that vicinity: "I guess it's Sagittarius, or the Archer." The coin that is to reward the sailor who first glimpses the White Whale, and who proves to be Ahab himself, is one that symbolizes, among other things, the virility that Moby Dick has destroyed.

The moral meanings of *Moby Dick,* though of course they tran-scend its oneiric meanings and exist in a sense on another plane, are by no means independent of them: on the contrary, the unity of the book is so masterly that only by artifice can we disentangle its various strands of significance. From the oneiric point of view Ahab is the suffering and neurotic self, lamed by early experience so vitally that it can devote itself only to destructive ends and find rest only in self-annihilation. No reader of the book, to be sure, could fail to feel how imperfectly this clinical description fits the grandiose captain of the *Pequod:* he embodies a form of sickness, certainly, but in doing so he embodies also, and on a higher imag-inative plane, a form of tragedy. The two, however, originate and eventuate together.

Ahab is not only the sick self; he is, for his time and place, the noblest and most complete embodiment of the tragic hero. He is modern man, and particularly American man, in his role as "free" and "independent" Individual, as self-sustaining and self-assertive Ego, of forcible will and unbending purpose all compact, inflexible, unpitying, and fell, but enlarged by both his vices and his strength to dimensions of legendary grandeur. About Ahab's moral largeness there can be no uncertainty: the cleansing effect of *Moby-Dick* depends vitally upon that. He is described as not only "grand" but even "godlike," and godlike—in a sense that is at once Greek and Yankee, at once classical and contemporary—everyone feels him to be. He has such Areté, says Melville in effect, as a grim and shaggy old whale-hunter from Nantucket can have, and that is much; his very appearance suggests a demigod: "His whole high, broad form seemed made of solid bronze, and shaped in an unalter-able mould, like Cellini's cast Perseus." He calls himself "proud as a Greek god," and indeed his pride is noble enough to endure the comparison. In its highest expression it is the heroic self-trust and self-regard of the modern Western man asserted in the teeth of all that would overbear and diminish him, whether natural or beyond nature. This is what Ahab affirms in the Aeschylean scene in which he defies the flaming corposants: "I own thy speechless, placeless power; but to the last gasp of my earthquake life will dispute its unconditional, unintegral mastery in me. In the midst of the personified impersonal, a personality stands here."

This is the very rapture of ideal individualism: neither Carlyle nor Emerson nor Nietzsche ever uttered it more loftily. Yet even as he pronounces his great tirade Ahab is dimly and bitterly aware that what he says is not true: what stands there is not, in the high sense, a personality, but only a proud and defiant will. Ahab has long since ceased to be a personality, if that word is to be understood as signifying a human being in all his wholeness and roundness. He has ceased to be anything but an Ego; a noble Ego, to be sure; a heroic one; but *that* rather than a Self. He is no longer a free mind: his thought has become the slave of his insane purpose. He is no longer emotionally free: his heart has become the slave of his consuming hate. Nor is he any longer morally free: his conscience too has allowed itself to be deadened and stupefied by the compulsive quest for Moby Dick. Just how empty, in this sense, is his claim to be a "queenly personality," he himself betrays when he exhibits what his monomania has done to his very conception of humanity, of "a complete man after a desirable pattern." In the scene with the old carpenter, who is making a new leg for him, Ahab, half soliloquizing, half addressing the carpenter, imagines such a man as, first, physically gigantic, and then as having "no heart at all, brass forehead, and about a quarter of an acre of fine brains." . . .

It is partly his momentary gleams of insight, nevertheless, that preserve Ahab's tragic stature even in his perdition. He has penetrated to one of the fatal truths about himself when he uses the phrase, "against all natural lovings and longings." His ideal man would have "no heart at all," and he himself has striven with terrible success to destroy his own great native capacity for love. To have yielded to it—to have yielded to what is clearly his ardor of affection for his wife and child, to his love for little Pip, to his spontaneous movement of compassion for the bereaved Captain Gardiner—this would have been to open a breach in the massive wall of his self-sufficiency; and so rigid is his egoistic fixity that he cannot afford or admit the slightest concession to a self-forgetful thought. The idea of pure independence has become an insanity with him: the thought of dependence in any form is a torment. It enrages him that he must be a debtor to "this blockhead" of a carpenter for a bone to stand on: "Cursed be that mortal interindebtedness which will not do away with ledgers. I would be free as air; and I'm down in the whole world's books." Again, with his wonderful, intermittent self-knowledge, Ahab is right: he is not genuinely independent, but on the contrary peculiarly dependent, and on the whole world. It is a sterile dependence, however, not a creative one, because it is imposed from without by circumstance, not accepted from within by the ethical imagination; and Ahab has his reward. He gets not independence but isolation; and, since he is after all human, it is unendurable. He has lived, as he himself says, "in a desolation of solitude," and it destroys him. He has refused to accept the interdependence that is the condition of genuinely human existence, and we can at least imagine that, like Jonah in Father Mapple's sermon, "he feels that his dreadful punishment is just." Objectively it is so. . . .

The tragic error for which Ahab suffers is an archetypal one; it has both its general and its particular aspects, both its placeless and its local application. The raging egoism Ahab embodies has something in common with the Hubris of Greek tragedy, as it has also something, and still more, in common with the Christian sin of pride; but it is neither quite the one nor quite the other. There is something of Prometheus, of Agamemnon, of Oedipus in Ahab: he is guilty of an inflated arrogance similar to theirs, a similar conviction of his superiority to the mass of ordinary men. The true antithesis of Hubris, however, is moderation, and moderation is no cardinal virtue in Melville's calendar; Starbuck embodies that, and Starbuck hovers between a golden *mediocritas* and plain mediocrity. So with the sin of pride: we are far closer to Ahab's error here, as with Melville's deep spiritual derivation from Calvinist Christianity we are bound to be. Father Mapple's sermon is intended to make us understand that Ahab, like Jonah, has in a certain sense sinned through his proud refusal to obey God's will, or its equivalent; pride and disobedience, in at any rate some dimly Christian senses, are at the root of Ahab's wickedness. The true antithesis of spiritual pride, however, is Christian humility; and this is only somewhat closer to Melville's positive thought than moderation is. . . .

In the fullest conscious sense, however, he believed in neither. What he felt as a menace in himself, and what he saw at work in the scene about him, was very like what Hawthorne felt and saw: a complex moral reality of which one pole was a pure and strong affirmation of the grandeur of the individual, and the other pole a wild egoism, anarchic, irresponsible, and destructive, that masqueraded in the kingly weeds of self-reliance. It is no accident that Ahab, as a whale-hunter, represents one of the great exploitative, wasteful, predatory industries of the nineteenth century; from this point of view the Whale embodies nothing so much as the normally innocent and indifferent forces of wild nature—the forests, the soil, the animal life of land and sea—that nineteenth-century man was bent on raping to his own egoistic ends. On the last day of the chase, in spite of what he has suffered at their hands, Moby Dick seems intent only on swimming as swiftly and as straight as possible away from the *Pequod*. "See!" cries the good Starbuck to Ahab. "Moby Dick seeks thee not! It is thou, thou, that madly seekest him!"

The alternative to Ahab's egoism is not, then, the ideal of "Nothing too much," nor is it a broken and a contrite heart. On one level it is an intuition that carries us beyond morality, in the usual sense, into the realm of cosmic piety; on the usual ethical level, however, it is a strong intuition of human solidarity as a priceless good. . . .

Deep as are the psychological meanings, and serious as are the moral meanings, of *Moby Dick,* they by no means exhaust between them the richness of its interest or the scope of its significance. In the end, as one reflects on the book, one is aware that one must reckon with the most comprehensive of all its qualities, the quality that can only be called mythic. Few words even in our time have been used more glibly than the word "myth"; it has ended by taking on some of the hollow sanctity of the mystic syllable Ôm in the mouths of the unenlightened. When one uses it, however, in association with *Moby Dick,* it means something precise and indispensable; and it is used here in the sense of an imagined narrative in which the leading roles are played by divine or god-like personages, engaged in symbolic actions amid symbolic objects; which embodies some form of the conflict between human wishes and nonhuman forces, and which has its roots in a philosophically serious desire to comprehend the meaning of nature and the destiny of man. The literary expression toward which myth in this sense typically moves is the epic or some closely comparable form.

If *Moby Dick* has a strongly mythic character, it is partly because the human setting out of which it emerged, as we have repeatedly seen, reproduced many of the conditions of a myth-making phase of culture. There was much in Melville's own experience too—his life among the Taipis and Tahitians, as well as much else—that, along with the bias of his own creative faculty, led straight in the mythic direction. There was a mingling in his nature, as in that of every greatly endowed poet, of the primitive and the highly civilized; of the naive and the literate, even the bookish; of the primitive capacity to "think" in symbols and the cultivated capacity to deal in abstractions. He was unique, moreover, among American writers of his time in the particular quality of his intellectual and moral seriousness; unique in his troubled preoccupation with problems that Emerson and Thoreau simply passed by, and that Hawthorne was intellectually too incurious to consider deeply. Like a truly myth-making poet's, Melville's imagination was obsessed by the spectacle of a natural and human scene in which the instinctive need for order and meaning seems mainly to be confronted by meaninglessness and disorder; in which the human will seems sometimes to be sustained but oftener to be thwarted by the forces of physical nature, and even by agencies that lie behind it; in which goodness and evil, beneficence and destructiveness, light and darkness, seem bafflingly intermixed. In none of the great formulations that were available to him, neither in Calvinist Christianity nor in romantic optimism, could Melville discover a myth that for him was adequate to the lighting up of these obscurities.

Moby Dick is his endeavor to construct his own myth. The personages of the fable, ordinary as they begin by seeming, very soon take on the large outlines and the poetic typicality of figures in legend or edda. They are engaged, moreover, in an action that is profoundly archetypal—that is, in a voyage by sea that is also a hunt or a quest, and that reaches its culmination in an all but complete catastrophe. As they do so they move among primordial forces in which their destinies seem involved almost as if they were Greek or Norse or Polynesian demigods or heroes—forces such as the sea that is both the source of life and the extinction of it, the solid land that is both safety and peril, the spires of flame that must be defied but also worshipped, the wind that is sometimes "glorious and gracious" and sometimes tainted and cowardly, the sun "like a royal czar and king," and the moonlight or starlight that serves to irradiate the mystic Spirit Spout. So intense is the animation, so nearly personal is the vitality, of these elemental forces that hardly a step would be needed to transform them into actual deities. Melville himself indeed remarks that the Greeks gave the sea a deity of its own; he calls the northeast wind by its Greek name, Euroclydon, and Ahab defies the fire of the corposants in language that leaves no doubt of its mythic deification. Nowhere, however, is Melville's myth-making power at work in a more truly primordial sense than in the creation of the White Whale himself.

Here chiefly, in the aggrandizement of a huge and fearsome animal to deiform proportions, does Melville surpass all other poets of his century in the rejuvenation of myth. On this ground he is quite incomparable; no other writer of the century can be set beside him. He himself could not wholly have realized how deep a descent he was making into the quarry of the past by penetrating so far as he did into the region of animal existence. He had some sense of this, but it was a flickering one: unavailable to him in his generation was the knowledge of primitive thought and belief that enables us now to see Moby Dick for the deeply primordial symbol he is. Only a man who had himself been a hunter of wild beasts—only a man who had been in at the kill of a tormented Sperm Whale—could have re-entered so far into the intense and complex feelings with which the primitive hunter regards the animals about him and especially his chief prey; into that lost, archaic mingling of fear and gratitude, of resentment and veneration, in which all the savage's emotions toward the animal are steeped, and which leads him again and again to endow it with an awful divinity. Of all this Melville had little or no "knowledge" but a penetrating intuition. The three pagan harpooneers on the Pequod, Queequeg, Tashtego, and Daggoo, have all seen Moby Dick before; when Ahab speaks for the first time of the White Whale to his crew, they and they alone are at once aware what creature it is that he means.

"Your true whale-hunter is as much a savage as an Iroquois," Melville himself says, and he adds: "I myself am a savage." Certainly in his half-fearful, half-worshipful attitude toward the Sperm Whale he was closer to the primitive than to the civilized mind;

and he gives us his own clues to this when he identifies the Whale with the dragons of Perseus and St. George, or recalls that the Hindu god Vishnu was incarnate in a whale. Yet he probably did not know, literally, that for many primitive peoples—for peoples as remote from one another as the Annamese, the Tongans, and the Unalit Eskimos—the whale is, or once was, the object of a solemn cult, a sacred animal as truly as the cow or the bear was elsewhere. He probably had not heard that some of these peoples prepared themselves for a whale-hunt by fasting for days beforehand, by bathing themselves repeatedly, and by other rites; that some of them, after a whale's life had been taken, propitiated his ghost by holding a communal festival; and that others, when a dead whale was washed ashore, accorded it solemn burial and preserved its bones in a small pagoda near the sea.

Melville knew that whiteness in animals had often been a mark of special sanctity; he alludes to the sacred White Dog of the Iroquois and the White Elephant of Pegu; did he know, however, that the White Whale itself was so superstitiously regarded by the Eskimos of Bering Strait that a hunter who had helped to kill one was forbidden to do any work for four days thereafter, and that the shore where a dead White Whale had been beached was thenceforth tabu? It is of no real importance whether he knew of these things or not; in the contemplation of the great white monster and its mystic ways, he could rely upon a deeper and more primeval knowledge than any he could have acquired from Tylor or Frazer. His imagination ran before the anthropologists; he forefelt, as other poets have done, what the savants would later confirm.

He could rely, in all this, upon the aboriginal myth-making fancy, still strong in his own nature, for which birds and beasts were not simply "lower animals" but creatures somehow identifiable with the beneficent or the malignant potencies of all nature; the fancy that again and again transformed these creatures into gods—eagle-gods, bear-gods, fish-gods, and the like. Even among nineteenth-century whalers generally there may have survived, obscurely and dumbly, much more of this fearful and worshipful emotion than has ever been supposed, and Melville may be pointing to this when he makes Starbuck say of the heathen crew of the Pequod that the White Whale is their "demigorgon"—Demogorgon, as he should have said if he meant the mysterious infernal deity to whom Milton and Shelley allude, but he may well have been confusing Demogorgon with the creative Demiurgos of Platonic or Gnostic thought. In any case, there can be no doubt about Moby Dick's deific attributes. There is something godlike in the mere crude fact of his physical magnitude, his "majestic bulk." Physically he is the greatest of all animals that have ever existed, and in proportion to his vast magnitude is his potency, the potency that exhibits itself in his terrific speed, in the dreadful strength of his great jaw, and in the "Titanism of power" with which he wields his massive tail. He is not only physically huge and appallingly powerful, but—as one realizes when one reflects on the problem of his spout—there is in his whole being a "great inherent dignity and sublimity." Moby Dick is godlike in his beauty too, and when, after so many months of search, we at last sight him, gliding swiftly and mildly through the sea, he seems more beautiful even than Zeus himself swimming in the shape of a white bull, with Europa, toward his nuptial bower in Crete: "not Jove, not that great majesty Supreme! did surpass the glorified White Whale as he so divinely swam."

Beautiful he may be, yet to the whalemen who have encountered him, or even to those who have only heard of such encounters, there is something so terrible, so mysterious, in the ferocity and the apparently intelligent malignity with which Moby Dick has rounded upon his attackers, that they have ended by refusing to believe that such a creature is fit prey for mortal man. Some of them have persuaded themselves that he is actually ubiquitous; that he has been sighted in opposite latitudes at the same instant of time; and not only so, but that he is immortal, and that no lance forged of earthly iron can ever destroy him. . . .

This is a nature myth such as only a nineteenth-century imagination, obsessed with the spectacle of impersonal force and ceaseless physical change, could have created, though Melville had unconsciously drawn, in creating it, on a whole complex of thoughts that had come to him from reading, or reading about, Job, the Stoics, the Gnostics and Manicheans, Spinoza, and the men of science. It is a myth such as other minds of the nineteenth century were groping toward, and one can see dim analogies to Moby Dick in Schopenhauer's blind irrational Will, in Herbert Spencer's Unknowable, and still more truly in Hardy's Immanent Will or Urging Immanence. In the traditional Christian God, the omniscient and loving Father, Melville had now lost all confident belief; *that* God survived in his mind, when he wrote *Moby Dick,* only as a symbol of human fraternity and the quasi-religious sense of equality: "The great God absolute! The centre and circumference of all democracy! His omnipresence, our divine equality!" The language here seems traditional enough, but it is unsupported by anything else in the action or the imagery of the book, and the truth is that the God of Melville's fathers has yielded place, at every other point, to the godlike and portentous White Whale.

Seven Moby-Dicks*
by John Parke

"Hark ye yet again,—the little lower layer."—AHAB

Moby-Dick has been justly and sufficiently acclaimed as a peerless saga of physical adventure, appealing to young and old just like any other good yarn. Its external action takes place in a world of athletic heroism, the kind of man's world that many girls at one time or another and all boys fervently wish to enter. It is filled with boasting talk, odd characters, rough deeds, alarums, accidents, mysteries, and narrow escapes. The exciting paradox of the fragility of men's bodies and the sturdiness of their ingenuries is vividly present; and the technical descriptions—of the process of killing a whale, for instance—with their robustly metaphoric picturization and their hallmark of cleanly observant intimacy with materials and elements, arouse the most imaginative sort of manipulative interest. Merely as marine exposition the book is expert; merely as action narrative the story is a good one, as the frequent appearance of "The Chase" in anthologies and school readers attests.

But let us descend one layer. Mere good narrative or exposition is exhaustible. Even those readers least disposed or equipped to interpret *Moby-Dick* metaphorically often feel its power as something strange and haunting. This phenomenon did not escape critical notice even prior to the Melville renaissance of the 1920's; Melville's version of the old struggle with the sea and monsters simply seems to excel as a producer of what might be called the spiritual sensation of marine adventure. For here the sea and the universe are perhaps most unconquerable (and does man not tire of "conquests" over nature at last?). Here civilized insulation from the cosmos is least purchasable; the very fierceness with which it is scorned should challenge the creeping spirit of the most troglodytic reader. "The Lee Shore," an early heroic chapter, sets this spiritual tone (if Chapter I has not already), vigorously lifting the adventure story to a supraphysical level; and though from here on the central narrative and theme go in a morally oblique direction (or does Bulkington? and would *he* have bent to Ahab's will?), this "six-inch chapter" is as it were a harmonic which vibrates again and again throughout the book, particularly in relation to the landlessness of Ahab, and the crew's gradual involvement in it, on the one hand, and the far-voyaging speculations of the narrator-adventurer on the other. And when the majesty of the antagonist whale, or the alluring terror of the putative drop from masthead to water, is dramatized against such a background of material observation, we surely have adventure writing of the highest order, even as we do in the fight with Grendel's mother or the escape from Circe.

But leaving behind that self-limiting view which is pleased to

* John Parke, "Seven *Moby-Dicks*." New Brunswick, Maine: *New England Quarterly* (XXVIII, 1955), pp. 319–338.

regard *Moby-Dick* as a mere physical adventure story with a certain exotic spiritual tonality, we can proceed to discover next a sort of emblem-story of man and nature, in which are revealed certain accumulated meanings of an age-long struggle. Several generations of readers have seen in these emblems, the more obvious ones at least, what man does to nature and nature to man—the imprint left on each by the other. At times, as in the descriptions of Flask's pugnacity concerning whales or of Moby Dick's accumulated tangle of barbs and line, they are presented in fairly literal terms—so literal, in fact, that the reader predisposed to literalness will contend, again, that they are nothing more than what they seem. At other times, as with the albatross, the mat-weaving, or the final vignette of the flag, the hammer, and the bird, they are in more figurative, and hence more suggestive and extendible, terms. (We except here the more dramatic metaphors or symbolic constructions which relate directly to dynamic aspects of the theme, such as Ishmael's hallucination at the helm when he gazes into the nocturnal try-works, or Ahab's magnetizing of the needle.) These symbolic vignettes, often explicitly—even heavily—interpreted by the author, were Melville's delight; indeed, he had a connoisseur's penchant for them. This is held against him by readers unreceptive to the central symbolism of *Moby-Dick;* and if the subject-matter exclusive of strict narration consisted largely of a heavy sprinkling of unrelated emblematic tableaux, they would have solid grounds for objection. But such is not the case. The various symbols, static and otherwise, do indeed "add up"; they are, ultimately, part of the tissue of drama and inner theme. These latter elements must now be dealt with on their own proper level.

For Ahab's wound and mania, the preternatural Fedallah, Starbuck's tense and ambivalent relation to his captain, the prophetic soliloquies, Pip, and the "Whiteness of the Whale"—these are entities of another sort. When we examine the complicated moral drama, with the much disputed theme—that "hideous and intolerable allegory" which Melville more than half facetiously disavowed —we are indeed working on a much "lower layer," or series of layers. In the story of Ahab and his crew, and the one articulate antagonist, Starbuck, we discover a grimly joined inner battle, a searing and terrible symbolic representation of a profound conflict in the soul of man. There is no mistaking Melville's intent so to generalize. There is only the necessary search for applicability.

As with *Hamlet,* where three hundred years have not sufficed for the emergence of a definitive thematic interpretation, we have here a host of contenders for authoritative explication. This can mean one of two things: that the text, due to confusion in concept or execution, is at fault; or that, as a sort of master metaphor, it embodies an archetypal situation capable of a considerable variation of perfectly relevant responses or "meanings." Of course, this state of affairs always produces at some time a school of critics whose compulsion is to debunk all symbolic interpretations and to deny all levels of meaning in the work except the "factual" or phenomenal. It is our privilege to ignore these dogmatic skeptics and to assume, pending close examination, that the second alternative above fairly describes the novel. It is our further privilege to work for as specific an interpretation as possible according to our own lights, in the hope that all thoughtful contributions to an understanding of the work may enrich the experience of its readers, whether or not final agreement is yet—or ever—possible.

The primary and indisputable fact of the inner drama is that Captain Ahab has been led to attribute deliberation ("inscrutable malignity") on the part of the universe against himself. Thereafter, instead of minding his whaling business prudently, as Starbuck or any good Quaker would, he conjured up a soul's antagonist in The Whale. With this phantasm he then had to do unceasing battle, magnifying it to the proportions of a life-usurping fetish, until its power over his soul destroyed him, just as the actual whale sank his ship and left him to drown. This inner human destruction is the core of the drama, as two utterances by Ahab at the denouement show: "For the third time my soul's ship starts upon this voyage, Starbuck"; and finally:

> Oh, now I feel my topmost greatness lies in my topmost grief.
> Ho, ho! from all your furthest bounds, pour ye now in, ye
> bold billows of my whole foregone life, and top this one piled
> comber of my death! Towards thee I roll, thou all-destroying
> but unconquering whale; to the last I grapple with thee; from
> hell's heart I stab at thee; for hate's sake I spit my last breath
> at thee. Sink all coffins and all hearses to one common pool!
> and since neither can be mine, let me then tow to pieces, while
> still chasing thee, though tied to thee, thou damned whale!
> Thus, I give up the spear!

Now, what brought about this titanic nemesis? What is at issue in the conflict within the particular man Ahab, and between him and Starbuck? What is Melville's "mighty theme" for which the drama serves as vehicle? What is the archetypal situation?

The title points to The Whale as chief protagonist, not to Ahab; The Whale was there before Ahab, and outlived him, so we had best find out about it. Moby Dick, with his ambivalent whiteness, his solitariness, his mildness and transient fury, his ubiquitousness and his scars, is, as more than one critic has suggested, the noumenon of nature itself—a comprehensive dynamic symbol for the whole immense, riddling, uncaring cosmos in which man finds himself nurtured, stunned, challenged, and (if he choose and can) at home. The *uncaringness* is the point. A significant part of the thematic framework of the book is the strong auctorial suggestion that the universe is neutral and unpurposeful in terms of human values and purposes. From this it follows that man's adaptation to the universe, to the limitations, opportunities, and destiny (favorable or otherwise) with which it presents him, shapes his whole concept of it.

For, if external nature simply does not concern itself with man's destiny, the malevolence or benevolence he attributes to it is obviously a mere projection of his own hate or love, fear or faith. But if he believes it malevolent—i.e., cannot accept whatever is accorded him of fate—and attacks it, it will prove malevolent, or prove to seem so, and expertly accommodate him in his own undoing—either physically, or inwardly through upheaval in his own nature, or both. Melville drives home this neutrality of nature in the chapter on The Whale's mysterious whiteness, where the ambivalence (to man) is marvelously exhibited through countless and ageless instances: the evil white and the beneficent white in man's vision, but always the irresistible white, the dazzling summit of all colors, the emblem of his most intense spiritual energy. The energy, in man and outside him, is impersonal and neutral: it is man personally or collectively who, by free choice or inward compulsion, turns it to destructive or creative ends in himself and so sees it in malevolent or benevolent aspects outside him.

It is further evident that man in this universe is equipped to observe, marvel, deduce; that he can minutely and partially manipulate, deflect, exploit; but that he cannot influence the power of created life at its source; and, strangely, that he cannot even attempt this with impunity. The mighty Whale is content to let Ahab and other men live, so long as they do not seek power over the principle of nature itself, the "phantom of life"; so long as they attack only whales and not The Great Whale of the Universe.

"Oh! Ahab," cried Starbuck, "not too late is it, even now, the third day, to desist. See! Moby Dick seeks thee not. It is thou, thou, that madly seekest him!"

Consider normal man (Starbuck), rational and sane, submitting his heart and his behavior not only to those natural forces far beyond his control but to a traditional *ethos,* acknowledging both his relatedness and his obligation to his kind (Ahab cannot endure obligation: "Cursed be . . . mortal inter-indebtedness . . ."). Encountering the raw power of physical nature, he can maintain his livelihood and his equanimity by ingenuity, patience, submission to necessity, and the fulfilment of his sense of responsibility. But let some traumatic experience or historical upheaval upset his sense of cosmic and social proportion, his humanity, and his proper respect toward immensity and careless omnipotence; above all, let him then indulge in vindictiveness toward that which is incapable of charity, justice, and premeditated animosity alike, and he is lost. His presumption ("I'd strike the sun if it insulted me"), violating a law of his own nature, will ignite a conflict in his soul so abrasive that he will gradually wear away a lung and half a heart (yet possibly become great in the process—". . . all mortal greatness is but disease," says Melville; the trauma is perhaps the grain which stings the pearl into being); he will become an unconsciously eager victim of a catastrophe which will seem to him in his phantasm the working of a purposeful external vengeance.

So with Ahab. In him nature's mold has cracked, and so the universe seems to have turned against him. As in the opening of *King Lear*, the loyal and wholly human man (Kent, Starbuck) is impotent; the runaway fragment holds mad sway. What such a desperate man, who would be whole and reign within himself, has then to contend with is something in the nature of an autonomous complex: Ahab's "purpose, by its own sheer inveteracy of will, forced itself against gods and devils into a kind of self-assumed, independent being of its own." Now, the conflict between Ahab and Starbuck is the direct reflection of this conflict within Ahab; Starbuck submits to an *ethos,* a job, and an emotional responsibility to his family, accepting any disproportion "between his just deserts and what he gets"; Ahab, on the other hand, profoundly sensitive enough to have been hurt by life, identifying his whole being with an injured part that will not heal, and rationalizing his consequent derangement, sets himself up above the *ethos,* denies his obligations and his human feeling, and opposes his personal conscious will to destiny. And this, of course, is the *hubris;* oversimplified, it is the sin of pride. Here is a basic thematic interpretation.

But again, "the little lower layer." More than the pride of a particular man is involved, both initially and ultimately, and more than trauma. Melville's intention was not nearly so simple, and part of the novel's durable fascination is the fact that the *hubris* is less readily apparent, in its precise nature, than the nemesis. In fact, it is both deeply subtle and extremely complex.

Mankind itself (all races and important nationalities are represented in the crew of the *Pequod*) is fatefully embarked on a pursuit which is, as we have seen, a titanically malicious attack on nature itself. (Ahab's malice is partly intellectual—more of that anon—while the crew's is blindly instinctive.) Now, while it is of course fitting, or at least traditional, that hazardous expeditions are for men, the absence of women and their influence from the crew and, generally speaking, from the story, may be taken as symbolic. For not merely humanity (the moral quality) is left ashore, but the specific feminine principle of relatedness, of nurturing, of instinctive affection, is implicitly and expressly denied. Even the comradeship of Ishmael and Queequeg, so intimate in the early chapters, is dropped. Pip, the most defenseless and lovable creature imaginable, is deranged by being abandoned in the water and is later agonized by the crew's denial of the security which he needs and which, paradoxically, it becomes Ahab's particular joy to give him. Ahab cancels his ties with his new wife and babe. Masculinity is isolated; life is unbalanced. Only Starbuck, among the active characters, remains whole, despite his limitations, and truly human —that is, both masculine and potentially feminine.

The denouement is thus made psychologically inevitable, since self-mutilation can result only in disaster; Melville hints at it many times in advance. The sexless, inhuman symbol Fedallah (identified with the devil, for he casts no shadow) is an early harbinger of what is to come. From the moment of embarkation at Nantucket there is an insidious presence and a tension on board, manifested in all sorts of external omens and symbols; these are a sort of ground bass for the gradual revelation of the core of evil in Ahab's soliloquies, colloquies, and actions.

Vast destructive powers are loosed as Ahab and the opposing forces converge; despite the integrity and sanity and (in normal human measure) the considerable strength of Starbuck, despite his protests to the captain, despite Ahab's intense struggle with himself and his long surviving ability to feel sympathy and pain, the captain totally rejects his instincts, casts off his humanity, even the tool of his craft of navigation; he resolves on his own destruction. As his mania gathers the support of all his faculties, his fervor and his will catch up all the other men (but Starbuck) in a great bonfire of destructive energy. All values are inverted—note Ishmael's sense of psychic inversion in "The Try-Works"; there are no laws to hold to when man sets himself to wreak vengeance on the nameless phantom life itself, on the universe, on himself. And, inevitably, all is lost in the grand debacle of such a paranoiac orgy.

Justice poetic enough, and righteous enough even for the orthodox Christian of Melville's day. The sins of pride and self-mutilation are fittingly punished. May we not now sum up the theme and extend it to a universal moral? Ahab's intellectual presumption, his denial of humanity, his identification of his entire personality with his injured pride and towering conscious will, is in every one of us who seeks knowledge of all mysteries, who seeks total power over circumstance, and who would refuse submission to the law of personal integration, who would reject that which is greater than personality and beyond the human. This it is to be a renegade. The dramatization of the issue is, of course, out of all proportion to our individual variant experiences; but that is precisely why it so affects us. It is as if one of our own little inward battles against super-personal necessity were projected on a screen in dimensions and social ramifications a thousand times beyond the scope of our insignificance. *Moby-Dick* is a huge nightmare of ourselves at war with fate and the universe, one which we would do well to contemplate—Americans particularly, who have yet, in all their scientific plundering and tinkering, to learn respect for nature and the cosmos, for life and death, and for themselves.

But, once more, the situation is not so simple. There is another "lower layer." For Ahab voluntarily and deliberately places himself outside the pale of Christendom; *and yet he dies a hero of a sort.* Renegade though he is, it is he, not Starbuck, who excites our admiration and our vicarious participation, and is meant to. Starbuck is by contrast simply too human, too normally proportioned. ("Thou art but too good a fellow, Starbuck," says Ahab.) Let us consider Ahab as a hero, and let us see the way in which Melville presents him to us.

Just as Hawthorne's too masculine Ethan Brand embodies the destructive aspect of the pride of knowledge, Ahab, in our initial oversimplification, embodies the pride of will. He must overcome destiny. But he is presented far more effectively than Hawthorne's character, with far more of revelation, for Melville is magnanimous and daring enough to force us to admire Ahab and to pity him, to make us feel the pull of his electric leadership, to have us see for ourselves what it is to become exalted and then overwhelmed in the identification with maimed and self-maimed, vengeful masculinity ("I, Ishmael, was one of that crew; my shouts had gone up with the rest . . ."). In the Hawthorne tale (as in many of his others) it is hard for us to embed the author's implied judgment very deep in our feeling, however much we may intellectually agree, for the protagonist is too black and furtive, too repugnant, too pitiless toward himself, for us to see readily in him a reflection of any part of ourselves. But Ahab, figurehead of the independent mind, scorning to reconcile himself to a fate he can neither control nor avoid, much less understand; Prometheus-like refusing (in Elizabethan rhetoric!) to acknowledge the everlasting superiority of the cosmic forces concentrated against his brittleness like an immense, careless army; above all, knowing his own madness, his pain, and his humanity: this is irresistible. Though we quit and condemn his presumptuous folly at last, even as Ishmael escapes the wreck of the *Pequod,* we do so with intimate knowledge and with profit; for Melville, instead of reading us a homily, has made us participants. If nothing else in the book will do it, the titanic pathos of the "Sunset" chapter, or the heartrending gibberish of Pip (Lear's fool's descendant), or the tremendous climactic antiphony of "The Symphony," will implicate us in pity for the part of ourselves that has been wrenched from us in the magnificently demented Ahab. Perhaps not even Lear, who cracks too easily and whose fault is so much more trivial, can stir us so.

For Ahab is tragic, not just pathetic or grotesque. He has the courage to face what he fears, the inner nemesis he knows he has prepared for himself; and he finds he must constantly fight his own humanity to keep that courage. The sacrifice is not easy. This is made especially convincing in the two chapters last named above. At the same time that he misdirects his great spiritual energies to a suicidal as well as homicidal end, he becomes fully, painfully aware of what he has sacrificed in himself and in others. (His ordering Starbuck to keep to the ship at the end is profoundly humane as well as self-propitiatory.) If he is not finally master of himself or of the situation he finds himself in, not able to balance values and create himself anew at his death, he at least has the courage and far exceeds the vision of Milton's Satan, who has been more than sufficiently admired as a "tragic hero." And if, like Conrad's Kurtz, he dies unreconstructed despite his at times prayerful awareness of the moral and psychic horror in which he has become involved, he has the decency to outlive his moment of pause and to die unself-forgiving and with harness on his back. Satan's end is repulsive, Kurtz's pathetic; Ahab's, though like the others' morally repugnant, is paradoxically magnificent. The ambivalence, as in *Macbeth*, makes this a doubly stirring, if disconcerting, denouement for modern readers.

Now, the nature of the theme on this sixth layer will become evident if we examine the situation which calls forth heroic action. This tragedy is neither Aristotelian nor, in the Elizabethan sense, personally or politically ethical, nor, in the Thomas Hardy sense, psychologically deterministic. Ahab's downfall carries with it far more than the undoing of one man and his accomplices. The tone of the ending, to take one of the many indications, is epically grand and out of all proportion to Ahab's immediate significance as a mere individual. It does indeed, in spite of Melville's scornful disclaimer, suggest an allegory of man in a historical predicament.

The plain fact is that Melville, in dealing with the problem of fate, is doing so completely outside the Christian frame of reference. "I have written a wicked book, and feel spotless as a lamb," he wrote Hawthorne after finishing *Moby-Dick*. His depiction of a *universe both godless and purposeless*, was, and he knew it, in effect a blasphemy from the point of view of orthodoxy and transcendentalism alike. The shock upon his contemporary public (if they had widely understood) could be compared to the effect that Robinson Jeffers' theology might have had upon Queen Victoria.

Now we see why Melville left his hero unredeemed and apparently uncondemned (note the final helplessness of the godly Starbuck), dying in a black destructive fury of pride and negation—yet, paradoxically, still heroic. For Ahab's tragic predicament is the result of his own heroic temper and special personality *plus* this philosophical or theological condition: the removal of God and Providence from the universe. If the universe is ethically ungoverned and purposeless, the apparent corollary is the absence of any principle of fatal justice, and so the stultification of human ethical norms and social laws. No wonder Ahab sought his own death and met it with a curse! No wonder Melville felt socially "guilty," for he was cutting himself loose from all the bulwarks of ethical and theological thought familiar and normal in his day. He was heading into a dangerous open sea, and he knew it.

Interestingly enough, the process seems to have begun during the writing of the book. In the early chapters, before Ishmael and Queequeg reach Nantucket, there are no eschatological undertones, and the frame of reference is specifically Protestant: both Father Mapple's austere but genuine kindliness and evangelism, and the brotherly rapport between the self-respecting New Englander and the pagan harpooneer embody this. All is black and white. But these are points of departure only, for we soon move on into an already senile, partly blasphemous world of Quaker commercialism at Nantucket, which in its decadence is threatened by Elijah's prophecy and the mysterious embarkation of the apostate Ahab's boat crew. Next Bulkington, the unaffiliated man of pure, unquestioning spirituality, is swept overboard at the start of the voyage (how isolated he would have been among the *Pequod's* crew!). Then the comradeship of Ishmael and Queequeg is quietly dropped, as Ishmael becomes less a character and more a device; and the whole focus of the book ("WHALING VOYAGE BY ONE ISHMAEL"?) seems to change as Melville becomes caught up in an immense superpersonal theme.

Ultimately, in *Moby-Dick,* we find ourselves involved in a sort of apocalypse: "This is the way the world ends." (At least there's a bang to it in nineteenth-century America!) This, Melville's prophetic intuition seems to tell him, is the only at-present-conceivable result of the collision between the wayward spirit and intellect of man (with all his inherited ideals of justice) and the un-Providential, unjudicial, uncaring universe empty of God. Note that Melville wastes no love upon his steadfast Christian, Starbuck: the mate is, in the moral climate of the story, an anachronism: he lives on, secure and unshakable, in a world whose illusions are irreparably shattered for Ahab. When Starbuck at the height of the typhoon says, "God, God is against thee, old man, . . ." and the superstitious crew falter before the corposants, we can only laugh, not at the fear but at the terms in which it is articulated by the mate; for the poetry has converted us already to Ahab's fierce animism, as our identification with him (so carefully and gradually developed by Melville) had previously made us atheists. Though we cannot but respect Starbuck's uprightness, his humanitarian goodness, his steadfastness, we can only scorn his prosaic mildness beside the splendid vigor of Ahab.

True, Ahab is a fated loser; even at his most admirable, when he is struggling most awarely and more feelingly to preside over his own experience and salvage his soul, he is damned. Melville never lets us forget or doubt this. He carries his personal doom with him, and loves it, for in a collapsing moral creation its grandeur is all he has left. But, *natural* laws are still in operation: Ahab, by the nature of his reaction to the void with which his time, his misfortune, and his personal disposition confront him, seals his own fate. Hate still does not, cannot, triumph over nature, but over the hater at last; Moby Dick goes free, immortal, and essentially invulnerable, while Captain Ahab and his accomplices are unmercifully drowned. As Lewis Mumford has said, Ahab "becomes the image of the thing he hates; he has lost his humanity in the very act of vindicating it."

If he is heroic, it is because of his intellectual and spiritual fortitude as a mere human being in confronting chaos—physical, ethical, metaphysical chaos, the long displaced but never extinguished old deity of the myths. How, indeed, when God and the comforting concepts of Providence, divine justice, and salvation are lost, does man reconcile himself to his fate? Ahab, born into the story scarred and godless, most nakedly exposed to the apparent nihilism of the universe, faces this challenge alone. The others do not see it; he is their superior. The fact that from the outset he takes a course which dooms him to frustration and madness makes him no less heroic, and no less pitiable. Finding in the cosmos indifference, injustice, even (apparently) total depravity, he determines to make it bow to his personal need for revenge—an attempt at restoration of order —or know the reason why. It is a blind, typically human reaction, stirring because of the preterhuman stature and intellectual power of the man who embodies it, and because of his abiding sense of alternatives. The fact that his personality is still inadequate to embrace a resolution that is not self-destructive suggests Melville's, the prophet's, terror before the looming problem—and his courage in revealing its direct and present threat.

Having progressed through so many levels of interpretation to this exposition of a theological allegory, we might think we had reached the full depth, the quintessence, of Melville's "mighty theme." This, indeed, is as mighty as the story of Job himself: the confrontation of chaos by man—Chaos, the old god of the Mediterranean, so frighteningly depicted by Milton as waiting, though in abeyance, outside the framework of the created universe, where he waits still, no doubt, for modern man, beyond the crumbling pale of the Christian citadel and the evaporating heavenly city of rationalism, close beneath the flimsy suburban scaffolding of scientific relativism. But, "Hark ye yet again . . ."—there is more.

The chaos, says Melville, is not merely around man; it is in him. For, after the dissipation of the Christian theology, the heart of man is still found to be literally writhing with evil. In fact, the evil in man is the cause of the apparent outer chaos ("Moby Dick seeks thee not . . ."). Perhaps our author would have liked to be a humanist; but his insight into human nature would not let him! For, in one telling passage (buttressed by many others), he indisputably objectifies and points up for us the eternal problem of human evil and man's bewilderment before it as the basis of Ahab's preoccupation and therefore as the inmost core of the book's theme:

> *The White Whale swam before him as the monomaniac incarnation of all those malicious agencies which some deep men feel eating in them. . . . That intangible malignity which has been from the beginning . . . deliriously transferring its idea to the abhorred white whale, he pitted himself, all mutilated, against it. . . . all the subtle demonisms of life and thought; all evil, to crazy Ahab, were visibly personified and made practically assailable in Moby Dick. He piled upon the whale's white hump the sum of all the general rage and hate felt by his whole race from Adam down; and then, as if his chest had been a mortar, he burst his hot heart's shell upon it.*

Moby-Dick, then, is ultimately a study of evil. But what sort of evil? What is Melville's notion of evil? Evil's first apparent manifestation (or so it is interpreted by Ahab) is the White Whale's mutilation of his leg. But the *Pequod* meets an English whaler whose captain has had his arm torn off by the same whale; this man is not maddened, nor does he regard the event as more than a perfectly natural, though fearful, accident incurred in the routine business of whaling. His sensible conclusion is that, as far as he and his men are concerned, this particular whale is best let alone. Now, Ahab, a deeper man by far, is obsessed not only with what seems the injustice of the excruciating treatment accorded him (he was delirious for days after the accident, and convalescent for months); he is obsessed too, as we have seen, with the notion of hidden forces in the universe. More than this, he is a sinisterly marked man, with a long, livid, probably congenital scar (an emblem, surely, of original sin); with a record of blasphemy and certain peculiar, darkly violent deeds; with a series of evil prophecies hanging over him; and with the given name of an idolatrous and savage king.

All this is fittingly suggestive preparation for the complete deliverance of Ahab's soul to evil through obsession and revenge. But his motive for revenge is not simple, not merely wicked. His quest for Moby Dick is in part a metaphysical one, for he is *in revolt against the existence of evil itself.* His vindictiveness, blind as it is, and motivated by personal hurt, is nevertheless against the eternal fact of evil. He thinks "the invisible spheres were formed in fright," feels his burden is that of all mankind (". . . as though I were Adam, staggering beneath the piled centuries since Paradise"), thinks the White Whale either the "principal" or the agent of all evil. He, Ahab, is evil, Melville seems to say (through Starbuck and Ahab both), because he seeks to overthrow the established order of dualistic human creation; and yet he is admirable, for he has gone over to evil not merely, like Faustus, for purposes of self-gratification, but in angry and misguided protest against its existence and its ravages in him.

What inevitably happens is that, in casting himself as the race-hero opposing the existence of the principle of evil, he but projects his own evil outward ("deliriously transferring its idea to the abhorred white whale") and so becomes all the more its avatar and its prey. He would "strike through the mask" of the visible object (the agent of evil), hoping there to find the key to the riddle. His occasional suspicion ("Sometimes I think there's naught beyond") that this will not result in any discovery whatsoever, and so not in an effective revenge, deters him not at all, though it drives him ever in upon himself as his fatal hour approaches, till, near the end, he does see the working of evil in himself—and yet dies its avowed agent. For he is mad; he is "madness maddened," quite conscious of his own derangement, and obsessed with it. The final, terrifying chaos, then, is that which he discovers within himself as his vestigial sanity contemplates his madness and its futility, as he admits his incomprehension of the thing that has driven him to irreparable folly and has lost him his very identity ("Is Ahab, Ahab?"):

> *"What is it, what nameless, inscrutable, unearthly thing is it* [the very language used earlier to describe evil]; *what cozening, hidden lord and master, and cruel, remorseless emperor commands me; that against all natural lovings and longings, I so keep pushing, and crowding, and jamming myself on all the time? . . ."*

Here is raised even the question of whether man, this proud and splendid aristocrat of the spirit, is indeed a free agent; Ahab, having at other times defied all the gods and called them cricket players, having assumed and never doubted that he could have made himself lord of creation, now turns (in "The Symphony") from Edmund's flouting, free-will cynicism to Gloucester's craven determinism: "By heaven, man, we are turned round and round in this world, like yonder windlass, and Fate is the handspike." He is not captain of his soul after all.

Ahab knows, then, everything about his predicament except its cause in himself—and so its solution. He feels the cause to be an immemorial curse visited upon all men. An exile from Christendom, he yet perceives and abhors the existence of evil. Worse still, he resists it; he will not come to terms with it. He wishes it could simply be swept away, or covered over: "Man, in the ideal, is so noble and so sparkling, such a grand and glowing creature, that over any ignominious blemish in him all his fellows should run to throw their costliest robes." But the dark side (which cannot be concealed) cannot be explained or avoided, either. And the most maddening thing of all about it—this is a constant refrain throughout the book—is the deceptive way it lurks beneath a smiling and lovely exterior. ("These temporary apprehensions, so vague but so awful, derived a wondrous potency from the contrasting serenity of the weather . . ." ". . . Fate is the handspike. And all the time, lo! that smiling sky, and this unsounded sea!" And on the very morning of the last terrible day of The Chase—

> *"What a lovely day again! were it a new-made world, and made for a summer-house to the angels, and this morning the first of its throwing open to them, a fairer day could not dawn upon that world."*)

Ahab's tragedy (and, on this final level, the book's theme) is, then, his inability to locate and objectify evil in himself, or to accept it and deal with it prudently as part of the entire created world, and so to *grow* despite it and because of it; it is his own fated indenture to evil while he seeks to destroy it, and his more and more precise knowledge of what is happening to him. It is the magnificence and yet the futility of his attempt. "I know that of me, which thou knowest not of thyself, oh, thou omnipotent," he cries to the great impersonal spirit of fire which he acknowledges as his maker and which, as its individualized creation, he defies. He defies his paternal maker, light, because, discovering his own dual nature (he says he never knew his mother), he has revolted and leagued himself now with darkness (the unrecognized mother-symbol, standing here for a regressive identification, which is of course what supplies the destructive energy). Then, "I am darkness leaping out of light," and "cursed be all the things that cast man's eyes aloft to that heaven, whose live vividness but scorches him. . . ." "So far gone am I in the dark side of earth, that its other side, the theoretic bright one, seems but uncertain twilight to me." And at his death, the magnificent line—as great and moving in its utter verbal simplicity, and yet as fraught with complex resignation as Edgar's "Ripeness is all": "I turn my body from the sun"—a line whose full and exact significance has been specifically constellated in advance by his own apostrophe to the dying whale in Chapter CXVI.

Ahab is no Faustus. He always has a choice. Many are the times he backslides; the tension between humanity and will is constantly active. Pip, the piteous embodiment of warmly instinctive human nature, of all that Ahab must tread on in himself, acts several times as the unwitting touchstone of that humanity. "Hands off from that holiness!" But, "There is that in thee, poor lad, which I feel too curing to my malady . . . and for this hunt, my malady becomes my most desired health." Starbuck too again and again is the foil and the polar opposite; and once Ahab even finds it good to feel dependence on human aid, for when the White Whale has crushed his ivory leg in the "Second Day," he exclaims while half hanging on the shoulder of his chief mate, "Aye, aye, Starbuck, 'tis sweet to lean sometimes . . . and would old Ahab had leaned oftener than he has." And just once, in "The Symphony," "Ahab dropped a tear into the sea; nor did all the Pacific contain such wealth as that one wee drop."

He must remain, for the brooding Melville apparently and for us, a symbol of that independent spirit and will which, scorning all "lovely leewardings," pushes off from the haven of all creeds to confront an ultimate chaos in the human soul; admirable, perhaps, beyond all flawed heroes (Bulkington was too simple an embodiment—pure essence, he was fit only for deification) in his energy and his courage, but condemned to split at last on the rock of evil, the very thing he willed out of existence; fated—and magnificently, agonizingly willing—to become the pawn (no, the prince, the king) of evil in consequence of his misguided revolt, to lose his identity in the end because he sought to exalt it against the immutable principles of its creation.

Here is our many-layered theme—a Protean archetype indeed! The physical adventure, the spiritual exaltation of hazardous voyaging, the interaction of husbandmen and nature, are there as fresh and valid as ever. The pride and retribution thesis still stands, and the nemesis of self-mutilation through the exalting of will at the expense of instinct. On the meta-physical level, however, chaos, even if thought of only as externally cosmic, is an old, old image of man's, the adversary of all enshrined deities; its confrontation by man is fit matter for grand tragedy. But as an internal moral and emotional predicament the chaos of evil and idealism and madness in the individual is certainly the most compelling phase of the archetype, and the one which evokes more and deeper echoes than any other.

For Melville's grand implication seems to be that all attempts to resist or deny evil, no matter how they are rationalized, are maddeningly futile. Christianity may be gone, he says in effect, but evil is here to stay; no use trying to idealize it out of existence, or conceal it with "costliest robes" or annihilate it by main strength of will and resentment. It will abide and elude; and it must be reckoned with. It is in us, even the deepest of us. Melville cites no text; he preaches no sermon on this head; he merely enunciates as best he can the critical moral predicament which his prophetic imagination apprehends.

Part of the extendibility of Melville's theme on this final level, of course, is due to the fact that he was truly prophetic, both in the sense of apprehending an incipient but suppressed conflict and dilemma of his own day (which only Hawthorne among his American contemporaries honestly confronted in his writings), and in the sense that historically the full reckoning with the problem was yet to come—*and just such an ill-starred solution was to be attempted* by modern man, who has tried philosophically and pragmatically to dismiss the notion of evil.

The problem has been with us now so long that there are many who have lost the capacity to be terrified by it; if an ever richer general response to this tragic novel can help us today or tomorrow to grasp and hold the reality of evil in our imagination, the book will have served as high a human purpose as any less "wicked" book in a time of more stable values. And if Ahab is to be the last of the race of great literary heroes (fittingly embodying the evil of evils and the highest spiritual splendor of man), why, even in the decline of our culture our pleasure in reading *Moby-Dick*, mixed with pain in a true purgation, will come in large part from our sense of participation in the magnificence and the richly deserved doom.

How it could be avoided, Melville does not tell us. Could we tell him?

The Tragic Meaning of Moby-Dick*
by Henry Alonzo Myers

Inspired by the infinite worth of the individual Melville set out to explore the final mysteries of equality. He created the story of Ahab and the white whale in order to prove that men are equal in their fate. *Moby Dick* is more than a strange melodrama of vengeance. For Captain Ahab the last voyage of the *Pequod* was a quest for certainty that ended in a great discovery. In losing his life Ahab discovered its meaning.

Like all great heroes, Ahab is enough like other men to make his fate representative of their own: he is also unusual enough to excite and hold their interest. His unusual trait is his unyielding will to do or die, his fierce intentness of purpose, from which no one, not even the gods, may swerve him.

All men have purposes. Ahab's purpose is to destroy the white whale, Moby Dick, which in a previous encounter had wounded him severely in body and in spirit. Melville calls Ahab a monomaniac, but by a monomaniac he means not a madman, in the ordinary sense of the word, but a man whose singleness of purpose and intensity of will distinguish him from his fellows. In order to make his meaning clear Melville has carefully arranged a hierarchy of intensities: Ahab, Starbuck the mate, the whalers, and ordinary men. Starbuck and the whalers are close enough to Ahab in spirit to be carried away at first by his wild will; it is not too mad to attract them, and when their own wills weaken, it keeps them true to his fixed course. Ahab's voyage is not distinguished from ordinary whaling by its hazards. Starbuck, a resolute and sensible officer, would never turn back because of the loss of a life or of a boat; for him Ahab's madness lies in wasting on a single whale the pertinacity needed in the pursuit of all whales. And to the whalers Ahab's madness lies in wasting effort on a chase without material reward. Their own sanity, in the face of their daily risk of life and limb, is guaranteed to the reader only by their interest in profit, a profit often so small that they were fortunate at the end of a long cruise if they were not actually in debt to the owners.

The point of Ahab's monomania is that the same intensity which brought him to the top of his profession could make terrible the consequences of his mistake. His resolve to destroy the white whale depended on his mistaken identification of evil with a single cause external to his own nature. Since this is an almost universal form of monomania, Ahab's case is remarkable only for its intensity. Men commonly ascribe good fortune to some idea, person, or talisman, to a variety of causes ranging from lucky numbers to divine providence. Even more regularly they ascribe misfortune to fate, to chance, to the malice of gods or men. Part of the meaning of

* Henry Alonzo Myers, *Are Men Equal?* New York: G. P. Putnam's Sons (1945), pp. 51–56.

Moby Dick lies in the tracing back of fortune and misfortune to their true cause in the character of man himself.

Every earnest reformer of the nineteenth century should have recognized himself in Ahab the monomaniac. For the one error of judgment of the otherwise good and capable captain—an error compatible with his intense nature—was his assumption that he could by a single heroic act stamp out all evil. Once he had identified the whale as the cause of evil, his fierce, proud spirit refused to accept the necessity of defeat and suffering. The consciousness of his own powers led him to believe that he could trace all sorrows to a single cause, pursue that cause to the ends of the earth, and in one last, Titanic struggle rid the universe of evil. So it has been for two hundred years; the pursuit of the white whales—ignorance, clericalism, slavery, alcohol, capitalism, war—has busied many an Ahab. *Moby Dick* is well suited to be the tragedy of an age. The whole romantic world has made Ahab's mistake again and again, but in life only an occasional John Brown can match his intensity and devotion to the iron way of heroes.

Ahab's purpose was not only to kill the whale but also to find the ultimate meaning of life. For this reason his final victory, coming at the moment of the loss of his ship and his life, is a victory of insight as well as of will. "Oh, now I feel my topmost greatness lies in my topmost grief. . . . Towards thee I roll, thou all-destroying but unconquering whale . . ." So at last came the answer to Ahab's quest. The moment of insight in which he sees that his grief and his greatness are but the two sides of his nature, one impossible without the other, is Ahab's great discovery and the key to the tragic meaning of *Moby Dick*.

The central meaning of *Moby Dick*, like that of every tragedy, lies in the influence of character upon event. Ahab, a man with a Catskill eagle in his soul, possesses the unyielding will which leads to the iron way of heroes, a capacity for feeling far beyond the ordinary, and a large share of intellectual curiosity. Convinced by a striking misfortune that the evil in his life is identified with Moby Dick, he determines to pursue the white whale to the ends of the earth. His monomania is close enough to the ordinary pursuits of men to draw the whalers into the chase. The final meeting between man and whale results in the loss of Ahab's ship and of his life. Yet his spirit is unbroken, and at the end he has his flash of insight, the discovery that his topmost greatness lies in his topmost grief, that his unconquerable spirit and his unyielding will are meaningless without the suffering which brings them out and gives them significance. His own nature is the cause of both the heights of his fortune and the depths of his misfortune. For only he can feel the fierce exultation of a purpose grooved in iron who can also feel the utmost agony of defeat.

Ahab's state of mind before his discovery is partly that of a Calvinist, partly that of a romanticist. In so far as he gloomily views nature as fundamentally evil, he follows the Calvinist tradition. In so far as he resolves to rid nature of the principle of evil, as though evil were an accident in the universe, he is the child of romanticism. But Ahab is never a free and romantic spirit. He feels at all times as though predestined to play his part like Fate's lieutenant. Further, he feels himself damned by his very resolve, as though his attempt to rid the world of evil were diabolical. This is the cause of the terrible inner struggle which convulses him. Possessed by his one idea of striking through Moby Dick to the source of evil, he nevertheless feels that he is acting against the will of God. Feeling that his central impulse comes from the devil, he proposes to be the devil's child, not serenely, if it must be so, as Emerson suggested, but with a delirious bravado. Ahab's is the struggle of a man with a romantic purpose and a Calvinist conscience.

Had Ahab been granted opportunity to live on in the light of his final insight, he would have seen the world as neither Calvinist nor romanticist sees it, for his discovery was that good and evil derive their meaning from one another. The all-destroying whale was the proof of the unconquerable Ahab, and the sorrow which gnawed at his vitals was the counterpart of the pride and resolution which carried him on. Whether or not in his last moment Ahab thought himself accursed, he accepted his fate, for he grasped the high principle of tragic morality, the principle that men pay for what they get. The price of intensity is intensity. In that one flash of insight Ahab was ready and willing to pay the price for his skyhawk spirit. Time for further reflection would have shown him that his purpose to destroy evil was impossible, not diabolical, and that it was, after all, merely one way of coming to the destiny foreordained by his character.

What light does Ahab's discovery throw on the question of equality? In the last analysis we can generalize from the story of one man only if some universal law governs the fortunes of all. *Moby Dick,* like all tragedies, stresses the inevitability with which fate flows from character and by which the lot of the individual is governed by fixed conditions and not by chance. These conditions, if we judge by Ahab, are rooted in human nature: chief among them is the principle whereby man is equal to himself. Ahab is, first of all, the equal of Ahab. Not until the moment of his final discovery does he realize this truth. Then in the feeling that his greatness lies in his grief, he discovers that the compensations for his fate are to be found in himself, in the nature that is capable of an exaltation exactly equal to his grief. Ahab, who is different from other men in the degree of his intensity, is like all other men in that he is equal to himself. Ahab's victory equals his defeat, his joy equals his sorrow.

If Ahab's discovery that his joys and sorrows are equal in intensity can be applied to others, then Ahab is a representative man because his story is a dramatic revelation of the bedrock law of human nature. If it cannot be applied to others, then each man lives in a private world of chance fortunes and misfortunes, and universal significance in *Moby Dick,* or in any tragedy, or in life itself, is merely illusion.

Obviously Melville believed that the universality of the tragic hero, his importance as a representative man, depends upon the just law of equality which apportions triumph and disaster in equal degrees to every human being. . . . Although some men have a greater capacity for feeling than others, a universal law of intensity balances sorrows and joys in the life of every individual. By virtue of this law meanest mariners and renegades are the equals of captains and kings.

Ishmael*
by R. E. Watters

Whereas Ahab's interpretations of the white whale have received much attention, Ishmael's have been almost equally neglected. But before Ahab reveals his problem and his purpose of hunting the white whale, Ishmael has already told us that "the problem of the universe" was revolving in him. When Ahab binds the crew with an oath to hunt Moby Dick to his death, the occasion produced in Ishmael "a wild, mystical, sympathetical feeling"; as he says, "Ahab's quenchless feud seemed mine." He gave himself "up to the abandonment of the time and the place; but while yet all a-rush to encounter the whale, could see naught in that brute but the deadliest ill."

Ishmael, however, is a thoughtful man—a Melville. And the problem of the universe and/or the whale went on revolving in him. He devotes an entire chapter to the attempt to say "what the white whale . . . at times . . . was to me." He begins with these words: "Aside from those more obvious considerations touching Moby Dick, which could not but occasionally awaken in any man's soul some alarm, there was another thought, or rather vague, nameless horror concerning him, which at times by its intensity completely overpowered all the rest; and yet so mystical and well nigh ineffable was it, that I almost despair of putting it in a comprehensible form. It was the whiteness of the whale that above all things appalled me. But how can I hope to explain myself here; and yet, in some dim, random way, *explain myself I must, else all these chapters might be naught"* (my italics). The rest of this famous

   * From R. E. Watters, "The Meanings of the White Whale." Toronto: *University of Toronto Quarterly* (XX, Jan., 1951), 155–168.

chapter on the whiteness of the whale discusses *this* meaning—
and it is surely significant that *no one else, not even Ahab,* appears
to be troubled by this aspect of Moby Dick. To Ahab and the others
the whiteness is merely a useful but fortuitous aid in identifying
a particular whale; only to Ishmael has the whiteness any further
meaning at all.

Ishmael recognizes that there are innumerable "sweet, and hon-
ourable, and sublime" associations with whiteness, that, indeed,
"whiteness . . . is at once the most meaning symbol of spiritual
things, nay, the very veil of the Christian's Deity; and yet . . . it
is the intensifying agent in things the most appalling to mankind."
The root of the horror inspired in him by whiteness, Ishmael con-
cludes, seems to be that whiteness symbolizes the "indefiniteness,"
the "heartless voids and immensities," the "dumb blankness" of
the universe. Later, on reading about the "most wondrous phenomenon which the secret seas have hitherto revealed to mankind," the great squid, which appeared as a silent "great white
mass . . . like a snow slide . . . no perceptible face or front . . .
no conceivable token of either sensation or instinct; but . . . an
unearthly, formless, chancelike apparition of life," we are reminded
of these phrases in Ishmael's conclusion. But in the chapter on "The
Whiteness of the Whale" Ishmael goes on to interpret the whiteness as a symbol that the universe is a formless, indefinite blank,
and that beauty and meaning are "but subtile deceits, not actually
inherent in substances, but only laid on from without" by the observer. Here we quite obviously have again the idea of "I look, you
look, he looks. . . ." The universe, this "rounder globe" is like the
doubloon, and both are like the white whale—a blank existence
upon which form or meaning is projected by the observer. Ishmael
goes farther, to consider that light itself "remains white or colourless
in itself" and requires a "medium" (presumably the "eyes" of some
observer) if any colour is to be seen by the light. Even Ahab himself, when his "tormented spirit" was for a time dissociated from
his monomaniac purpose, becomes a meaningless being. Melville
employs the same metaphor of light to express this point, in the
chapter entitled "The Chart," which explains how sometimes there
would be a spontaneous rebellion of Ahab's "living principle or
soul" against "the characterizing mind, which at other times employed it for its outer vehicle or agent. . . . Therefore, the tormented spirit that glared out of bodily eyes, when *what seemed
Ahab* rushed from his room, was for a time but a vacated thing,
a formless somnambulistic being, a ray of living light, to be sure,
but without an object to colour, and therefore a blankness in itself"
(my italics).

The meaning Ishmael finds in the white whale is obviously very
different from any of Ahab's—and the difference is perhaps most
briefly suggested by saying that to Ahab the white whale was a
personification, a "pasteboard mask," or perhaps an effigy, of something otherwise unknown and unassailable; whereas to Ishmael the

whale is merely a symbol. If afflicted with a monomania such as Ahab's, one can feel like assaulting and destroying a personification or effigy; but the only thing to do with a symbol is to understand it. Ishmael, therefore, saw the white whale as a symbol of what might be called a metaphysical hypothesis, and throughout the rest of the book he shows himself endeavouring to study the evidence for and against that hypothesis. He seeks not to destroy the whale for vengeance, profit, or pleasure, but simply to understand it, to comprehend it, to reduce the unknown to intelligibility. And this, he insists, is not a project to be pursued in a quiet study, ruminating over the partial and unreliable reports of other men (as provided in fragmentary books or faulty paintings of whales). As he puts it: "Only in the heart of quickest perils; only when within the eddyings of his angry flukes; only on the profound unbounded sea, can the fully invested whale be truly and livingly found out."

The fact has been strangely overlooked that Ishmael, as well as Ahab, deliberately embarked in quest of the white whale. The others aboard the *Pequod* were pursuing other ends when they were irresistibly drawn into Ahab's wake. But Ishmael tells us in the first chapter that "chief among these motives" which induced him into going a-whaling "was the overwhelming idea of the great whale himself. Such a portentous and mysterious monster roused all my curiosity. . . . the great floodgates of the wonder-world swung open, and in the wild conceits that swayed me to my purpose, two and two there floated into my inmost soul, endless processions of the whale, and, mid most of them all, one grand hooded phantom, like a snow hill in the air."

This curiosity, or passion to comprehend, explains why it is Ishmael (not Ahab, Starbuck, or anyone else) who is shown as being interested in every detail about whales, both species and individuals—the whales that appear in books, pictures, and door-knockers; that contribute food, oil, and corset stays; that are detected in mountain ridges and stars; that have been fossilized, worshipped, hunted, and scientifically studied; that have been dissected, analysed, and described to exhibit every possible characteristic. Understandably enough, he often feels that complete comprehension is impossible—"there is no earthly way of finding out precisely what the whale really looks like"; "the mystic-marked whale remains undecipherable" and "dissect him how I may . . . I know him not, and never will." Nevertheless, he must continue to make the attempt "to approve myself omnisciently exhaustive in the enterprise," to pursue his "thoughts of this Leviathan" wherever they lead, through "the whole circle of the sciences, and all the generations of whales, and men, and mastodons, past, present, and to come, with all the revolving panoramas of empire on earth, and throughout the whole universe."

This necessity to learn and include everything in order to comprehend the essential principle is the true artistic justification of Ishmael's compiling the mass of whaling details given in *Moby*

Dick. He is attempting to see the whale not partially, as a personified malignancy, a natural peril, a challenge, or a monetary value, but omnisciently, as a possibly intelligible microcosm in a possibly intelligible cosmos. The meaning of the white whale, for Ishmael, seems to be either the totality or essential of all meanings—in a word, attainable only by omniscience.

Although Ishmael's details and measurements tell us much about the species to which the white whale belongs, knowledge of Moby Dick himself is provided before the final encounter by the several ships hailed by the *Pequod*. What information might have been given by the long-seasoned veteran whalers aboard the spectral and forlorn *Goney* was lost when her captain dropped his speaking trumpet in the very act of answering. Two of the others—the *Jungfrau* and the *Rosebud*—had never even heard of the white whale. The rolling *Bachelor* has heard of him but in its rollicking prosperity chooses not to believe in him. The *Town-Ho* regarded the white whale as an instrument of God's judgment and justice, and the *Jeroboam* went so far as to consider him "the Shaker God incarnated." The *Samuel Enderby* had once encountered him, and her captain now wore a white whalebone arm as the price of his present wisdom; though he has seen him twice since, and recognizes that there would be both profit and glory in killing him, "he's best let alone." The *Rachel* has lost a whole boat's crew, including the captain's twelve-year-old son. The *Delight* is burying the only body recovered of "five stout men" lost the previous day. For each ship Moby Dick has acquired a different meaning.

It is worth remembering that none of these ships sought the white whale; they came upon him (those that did) only by chance while they were hunting other whales, and each time (as in Ahab's own first encounter) Moby Dick was acting as the protector of those hunted whales. Only the *Pequod* deliberately sought out the white whale himself, and whereas on the other encounters he was shepherding other whales, he was a solitary when the *Pequod* came upon him. Moreover, only Ahab is able to "raise" the white whale on each of the three days of the chase. As he boasts: "I only; none of ye could have raised the White Whale first." He is quite right: it is Ahab's whale they have been persuaded into chasing, and it is Ahab's whale they have found.

Indeed, it is not until the *third* day of the chase that the qualities perceived by Ahab in the whale become really apparent to the others aboard the *Pequod*. Ishmael gives us a careful description of Moby Dick when he is overtaken on the first day:

> *A gentle joyousness—a mighty mildness of repose in swiftness, invested the gliding whale. Not the white bull Jupiter swimming away with ravished Europa . . . not Jove, not that great majesty Supreme! did surpass the glorified White Whale as he so divinely swam. . . .*
>
> *. . . No wonder there had been some among the hunters*

*who namelessly transported and allured by all this serenity, had
ventured to assail it; but had fatally found that quietude but
the vesture of tornadoes. Yet calm, enticing calm, oh, whale!
thou glidest on, to all who for the first time eye thee. . . .*

*And thus, through the serene tranquillities of the tropical
sea, among waves whose hand-clappings were suspended by
exceeding rapture, Moby Dick moved on, still withholding
from sight the full terrors of his submerged trunk, entirely
hiding the wrenched hideousness of his jaw. But soon the fore
part of him slowly rose from the water; for an instant . . .
and warningly waving his bannered flukes in the air, the grand
god revealed himself . . . .*

That first day the white whale treated all his pursuers as gently,
if as warningly, as a patient mother might her wilfully erring children. And the second day he took away simultaneously both Ahab's
"evil shadow," Fedallah, and Ahab's ivory leg—not even his remaining human one. No wonder Starbuck believed that "all good
angels" were mobbing Ahab with warnings. "Oh, oh,—Impiety and
blasphemy to hunt him more!"

The third day ended the drama—except for the epilogue about
Ishmael. Now it is certain that Ishmael is saved not for the technical reason that a narrator must be left alive to tell the story—
for when throughout the book has Melville ever allowed himself
to be cramped by the exigencies of technique? No. Ishmael was
saved because he alone had learned anything from all their experiences, because he had, in effect, solved *his* problem, had tri-
umphed over the symbolic white whale and the universe. He had,
I think, proved his hypothesis—to his own satisfaction at least—
and *the very means of his salvation* symbolizes the truth, for him,
of *his* meaning of the white whale.

That marvellous concluding paragraph of the book contains
words which can almost be taken as a summary description of
Ishmael's role throughout the entire story:

*So, floating on the margin of the ensuing scene, and in full
sight of it, when the half-spent suction of the sunk ship reached
me, I was then, but slowly, drawn towards the closing vortex.
When I reached it, it had subsided to a creamy pool. Round
and round, then, and ever contracting towards the button-like
black bubble at the axis of that slowly wheeling circle, like
another Ixion I did revolve. Till, gaining that vital centre, the
black bubble upward burst; and now, liberated by reason of
its cunning spring, and, owing to its great buoyancy, rising
with great force, the coffin lifebuoy shot lengthwise from the
sea, fell over, and floated by my side. Buoyed up by that coffin,
for almost one whole day and night, I floated on a soft and
dirge-like main. The unharming sharks, they glided by as if
with padlocks on their mouths; the savage sea-hawks sailed*

*with sheathed beaks. On the second day, a sail drew near,
nearer, and picked me up at last. It was the devious-cruising
Rachel, that in her retracing search after her missing children,
only found another orphan.*

From **Herman Melville's Moby-Dick***
by D. H. Lawrence

Moby-Dick, *or the White Whale.*

A hunt. The last great hunt.

For what?

For Moby-Dick, the huge white sperm whale: who is old, hoary,
monstrous, and swims alone; who is unspeakably terrible in his
wrath, having so often been attacked; and snow-white.

Of course he is a symbol.

Of what?

I doubt if even Melville knew exactly. That's the best of it.

He is warm-blooded, he is loveable. He is lonely Leviathan, not
a Hobbes sort. Or is he?

But he is warm-blooded and loveable. The South Sea Islanders,
and Polynesians, and Malays, who worship shark, or crocodile,
or weave endless frigate-bird distortions, why did they never worship the whale? So big!

Because the whale is not wicked. He doesn't bite. And their
gods had to bite.

He's not a dragon. He is Leviathan. He never coils like the
Chinese dragon of the sun. He's not a serpent of the waters. He is
warm-blooded, a mammal. And hunted, hunted down.

It is a great book.

At first you are put off by the style. It reads like journalism.
It seems spurious. You feel Melville is trying to put something
over you. It won't do.

And Melville really is a bit sententious: aware of himself, self-
conscious, putting something over even himself. But then it's not
easy to get into the swing of a piece of deep mysticism when you
just set out with a story.

Nobody can be more clownish, more clumsy and sententiously
in bad taste, than Herman Melville, even in a great book like
Moby-Dick. He preaches and holds forth because he's not sure of
himself. And he holds forth, often, so amateurishly.

The artist was so *much* greater than the man. The man is rather
a tiresome New Englander of the ethical mystical-transcendentalist

* From D. H. Lawrence, *Studies in Classic American Literature.*
New York: The Viking Press (1964).

sort: Emerson, Longfellow, Hawthorne, etc. So unrelieved, the solemn ass even in humour. So hopelessly *au grand sérieux*, you feel like saying: Good God, what does it matter? If life is a tragedy, or a farce, or a disaster, or anything else, what do I care! Let life be what it likes. Give me a drink, that's what I want just now.

For my part, life is so many things I don't care what it is. It's not my affair to sum it up. Just now it's a cup of tea. This morning it was wormwood and gall. Hand me the sugar.

. One wearies of the *grand sérieux*. There's something false about it. And that's Melville. Oh dear, when the solemn ass brays! brays! brays!

But he was a deep, great artist, even if he was rather a sententious man. He was a real American in that he always felt his audience in front of him. But when he ceases to be American, when he forgets all audience, and gives us his sheer apprehension of the world, then he is wonderful, his book commands a stillness in the soul, an awe.

In his "human" self, Melville is almost dead. That is, he hardly reacts to human contacts any more; or only ideally: or just for a moment. His human-emotional self is almost played out. He is abstract, self-analytical and abstracted. And he is more spell-bound by the strange slidings and collidings of Matter than by the things men do. In this he is like Dana. It is the material elements he really has to do with. His drama is with them. He was a futurist long before futurism found paint. The sheer naked slidings of the elements. And the human soul experiencing it all. So often, it is almost over the border: psychiatry. Almost spurious. Yet so great.

It is the same old thing as in all Americans. They keep their old-fashioned ideal frock-coat on, and an old-fashioned silk hat, while they do the most impossible things. There you are: you see Melville hugged in bed by a huge tattooed South Sea Islander, and solemnly offering burnt offering to this savage's little idol, and his ideal frock-coat just hides his shirt-tails and prevents us from seeing his bare posterior as he salaams, while his ethical silk hat sits correctly over his brow the while. That is so typically American: doing the most impossible things without taking off their spiritual get-up. Their ideals are like armour which has rusted in, and will never more come off. And meanwhile in Melville his bodily knowledge moves naked, a living quick among the stark elements. For with sheer physical vibrational sensitiveness, like a marvellous wireless-station, he registers the effects of the outer world. And he records also, almost beyond pain or pleasure, the extreme transitions of the isolated, far-driven soul, the soul which is now alone, without any real human contact.

The first days in New Bedford introduce the only human being who really enters into the book, namely, Ishmael, the "I" of the book. And then the moment's heart's-brother, Queequeg, the tattooed, powerful South Sea harpooner, whom Melville loves as Dana loves "Hope." The advent of Ishmael's bedmate is amusing and unforgettable. But later the two swear "marriage," in the language of the savages. For Queequeg has opened again the floodgates of love and human connexion in Ishmael.

"As I sat there in that now lonely room, the fire burning low, in that mild stage when, after its first intensity has warmed the air, it then only glows to be looked at; the evening shades and phantoms gathering round the casements, and peering in upon us silent, solitary twain: I began to be sensible of strange feelings. I felt a melting in me. No more my splintered heart and maddened hand were turned against the wolfish world. This soothing savage had redeemed it. There he sat, his very indifference speaking a nature in which there lurked no civilized hypocrisies and bland deceits. Wild he was; a very sight of sights to see; yet I began to feel myself mysteriously drawn towards him."—So they smoked together, and are clasped in each other's arms. The friendship is finally sealed when Ishmael offers sacrifice to Queequeg's little idol, Gogo.

"I was a good Christian, born and bred in the bosom of the infallible Presbyterian Church. How then could I unite with the idolater in worshipping his piece of wood? But what is worship? —to do the will of God—*that* is worship. And what is the will of God?—to do to my fellow man what I would have my fellow man do to me—*that* is the will of God."—Which sounds like Benjamin Franklin, and is hopelessly bad theology. But it is real American logic. "Now Queequeg is my fellow man. And what do I wish that this Queequeg would do to me? Why, unite with me in my particular Presbyterian form of worship. Consequently, I must unite with him; ergo, I must turn idolater. So I kindled the shavings; helped prop up the innocent little idol; offered him burnt biscuit with Queequeg; salaamed before him twice or thrice; kissed his nose; and that done, we undressed and went to bed, at peace with our own consciences and all the world. But we did not go to sleep without some little chat. How it is I know not; but there is no place like bed for confidential disclosures between friends. Man and wife, they say, open the very bottom of their souls to each other; and some old couples often lie and chat over old times till nearly morning. Thus, then, lay I and Queequeg—a cosy, loving pair——"

You would think this relation with Queequeg meant something to Ishmael. But no. Queequeg is forgotten like yesterday's newspaper. Human things are only momentary excitements or amusements to the American Ishmael. Ishmael, the hunted. But much more Ishmael the hunter. What's a Queequeg? What's a wife? The white whale must be hunted down. Queequeg must be just "KNOWN," then dropped into oblivion.

And what in the name of fortune is the white whale?

Elsewhere Ishmael says he loved Queequeg's eyes: "large, deep eyes, fiery black and bold." No doubt like Poe, he wanted to get the "clue" to them. That was all.

The two men go over from New Bedford to Nantucket, and there sign on to the Quaker whaling ship, the *Pequod*. It is all strangely fantastic, phantasmagoric. The voyage of the soul. Yet curiously a real whaling voyage, too. We pass on into the midst of the sea with this strange ship and its incredible crew. The Argonauts were mild lambs in comparison. And Ulysses went *defeating* the Circes and overcoming the wicked hussies of the isles. But the *Pequod's* crew is a collection of maniacs fanatically hunting down a lonely, harmless white whale.

As a soul history, it makes one angry. As a sea yarn, it is marvellous: there is always something a bit over the mark, in sea yarns. Should be. Then again the masking up of actual seaman's experience with sonorous mysticism sometimes gets on one's nerves. And again, as a revelation of destiny the book is too deep even for sorrow. Profound beyond feeling.

You are some time before you are allowed to see the captain, Ahab: the mysterious Quaker. Oh, it is a God-fearing Quaker ship.

Ahab, the captain. The captain of the soul.

> *"I am the master of my fate,*
> *I am the captain of my soul!"*

Ahab!

"Oh, captain, my captain, our fearful trip is done."

The gaunt Ahab, Quaker, mysterious person, only shows himself after some days at sea. There's a secret about him! What?

Oh, he's a portentous person. He stumps about on an ivory stump, made from sea-ivory. Moby-Dick, the great white whale, tore off Ahab's leg at the knee, when Ahab was attacking him.

Quite right, too. Should have torn off both his legs, and a bit more besides.

But Ahab doesn't think so. Ahab is now a monomaniac. Moby-Dick is his monomania. Moby-Dick must DIE, or Ahab can't live any longer. Ahab is atheist by this.

All right.

This *Pequod,* ship of the American soul, has three mates.

1. Starbuck: Quaker, Nantucketer, a good responsible man of reason, forethought, intrepidity, what is called a dependable man. At the bottom, *afraid.*

2. Stubb: "Fearless as fire, and as mechanical." Insists on being reckless and jolly on every occasion. Must be afraid too, really.

3. Flask: Stubborn, obstinate, without imagination. To him "the wondrous whale was but a species of magnified mouse or water-rat——"

There you have them: a maniac captain and his three mates, three splendid seamen, admirable whalemen, first-class men at their job.

America!

It is rather like Mr. Wilson and his admirable, "efficient" crew, at the Peace Conference. Except that none of the Pequodders took their wives along.

A maniac captain of the soul, and three eminently practical mates.
America!

Then such a crew. Renegades, castaways, cannibals: Ishmael,
Quakers.

America!

Three giant harpooners, to spear the great white whale.

1. Queequeg, the South Sea Islander, all tattooed, big and powerful.

2. Tashtego, the Red Indian of the sea-coast, where the Indian
meets the sea.

3. Daggoo, the huge black negro.

There you have them, three savage races, under the American
flag, the maniac captain, with their great keen harpoons, ready
to spear the white whale.

And only after many days at sea does Ahab's own boat-crew
appear on deck. Strange, silent, secret, black-garbed Malays, fire-
worshipping Parsees. These are to man Ahab's boat, when it leaps
in pursuit of that whale.

What do you think of the ship *Pequod,* the ship of the soul of
an American?

Many races, many peoples, many nations, under the Stars and
Stripes. Beaten with many stripes.

Seeing stars sometimes.

And in a mad ship, under a mad captain, in a mad, fanatic's
hunt.

For what?

For Moby-Dick, the great white whale.

But splendidly handled. Three splendid mates. The whole thing
practical, eminently practical in its working. American industry!

And all this practicality in the service of a mad, mad chase.

Melville manages to keep it a real whaling ship, on a real cruise,
in spite of all fantastics. A wonderful, wonderful voyage. And a
beauty that is so surpassing only because of the author's awful
flounderings in mystical waters. He wanted to get metaphysically
deep. And he got deeper than metaphysics. It is a surpassingly
beautiful book, with an awful meaning, and bad jolts. . . .

The fight with the whale is too wonderful, and too awful, to be
quoted apart from the book. It lasted three days. The fearful sight,
on the third day, of the torn body of the Parse harpooner, lost
on the previous day, now seen lashed on to the flanks of the white
whale by the tangle of harpoon lines, has a mystic dream-horror.
The awful and infuriated whale turns upon the ship, symbol of this
civilized world of ours. He smites her with a fearful shock. And
a few minutes later, from the last of the fighting whale-boats comes
the cry: " 'The ship! Great God, where is the ship?' Soon they,
through dim, bewildering mediums, saw her sidelong fading phantom, as in the gaseous Fata Morgana; only the uppermost masts
out of the water; while fixed by infatuation, or fidelity, or fate, to
their once lofty perches, the pagan harpooners still maintained their

sinking lookouts on the sea. And now concentric circles seized the lone boat itself, and all its crew, and each floating oar, and every lance-pole, and spinning, animate and inanimate, all round and round in one vortex, carried the smallest chip of the *Pequod* out of sight——"

The bird of heaven, the eagle, St. John's bird, the Red Indian bird, the American, goes down with the ship, nailed by Tashtego's hammer, the hammer of the American Indian. The eagle of the spirit. Sunk!

"Now small fowls flew screaming over the yet yawning gulf; a sullen white surf beat against its steep sides; then all collapsed; and the great shroud of the sea rolled on as it rolled five thousand years ago."

So ends one of the strangest and most wonderful books in the world, closing up its mystery and its tortured symbolism. It is an epic of the sea such as no man has equalled; and it is a book of esoteric symbolism of profound significance, and of considerable tiresomeness.

But it is a great book, a very great book, the greatest book of the sea ever written. It moves awe in the soul.

The terrible fatality.

Fatality.

Doom.

Doom! Doom! Doom! Something seems to whisper it in the very dark trees of America. Doom!

Doom of what?

Doom of our white day. We are doomed, doomed. And the doom is in America. The doom of our white day.

Ah, well, if my day is doomed, and I am doomed with my day, it is something greater than I which dooms me, so I accept my doom as a sign of the greatness which is more than I am.

Melville knew. He knew his race was doomed. His white soul, doomed. His great white epoch, doomed. Himself, doomed. The idealist, doomed. The spirit, doomed.

The reversion. "Not so much bound to any haven ahead, as rushing from all havens astern."

That great horror of ours! It is our civilization rushing from all havens astern.

The last ghastly hunt. The White Whale.

What then is Moby-Dick? He is the deepest blood-being of the white race; he is our deepest blood-nature.

And he is hunted, hunted, hunted by the maniacal fanaticism of our white mental consciousness. We want to hunt him down. To subject him to our will. And in this maniacal conscious hunt of ourselves we get dark races and pale to help us, red, yellow, and black, east and west, Quaker and fire-worshipper, we get them all to help us in this ghastly maniacal hunt which is our doom and our suicide.

The last phallic being of the white man. Hunted into the death of upper consciousness and the ideal will. Our blood-self subjected to our will. Our blood-consciousness sapped by a parasitic mental or ideal consciousness.

Hot-blooded sea-born Moby-Dick. Hunted by monomaniacs of the idea.

Oh God, oh God, what next, when the *Pequod* has sunk?

She sank in the war, and we are all flotsam.

Now what next?

Who knows? *Quien sabe? Quien sabe, señor?*

Neither Spanish nor Saxon America has any answer.

The *Pequod* went down. And the *Pequod* was the ship of the white American soul. She sank, taking with her negro and Indian and Polynesian, Asiatic and Quaker and good, businesslike Yankees and Ishmael: she sank all the lot of them.

Boom! as Vachel Lindsay would say.

To use the words of Jesus, IT IS FINISHED.

Consummatum est!

But *Moby-Dick* was first published in 1851. If the Great White Whale sank the ship of the Great White Soul in 1851, what's been happening ever since?

Post-mortem effects, presumably.

Because, in the first centuries, Jesus was Cetus, the Whale. And the Christians were the little fishes. Jesus, the Redeemer, was Cetus, Leviathan. And all the Christians all his little fishes.

The Fire Symbolism in Moby-Dick*
by Charles Child Walcutt

A critical passage in *Moby-Dick* occurs toward the end of the story, when Ahab grasps the links of the lightning chain, places his foot upon the kneeling body of Fedallah, and addresses the corpusants (St. Elmo's fire) burning from the tips of the spars:

> *Oh! thou clear spirit of clear fire, whom on these seas I as Persian once did worship, till in the sacramental act so burned by thee, that to this hour I bear the scar; I now know thee, thou clear spirit, and I now know that thy right worship is defiance. To neither love nor reverence wilt thou be kind; and e'en for hate thou canst but kill; and all are killed. No fearless fool now fronts thee. I own thy speechless, placeless power; but to the last gasp of my earthquake life will dispute its unconditional, unintegral mastery in me. (Ch.* CXIX.)

* Charles Child Walcutt, "The Fire Symbolism in *Moby-Dick*." *Modern Language Notes* (May, 1944).

The first sentence, which contains the only explanation in the book of the scar described upon Ahab's first appearance,[1] appears not only mystifying, inadequate, and irrelevant, but even Gothic and ridiculous. There is more than a little melodramatic paraphernalia in *Moby-Dick*, and the idea of Ahab's practising a Persian cult of fire-worship on a whaling vessel might appear to head the list of such monstrosities. Yet this sentence is not irrelevant; nor is it merely designed to magnify Ahab by mystifying the reader;[2] it is the key which explains many paradoxical and confusing references to fire and enables us to relate the fire symbolism to the final, central meaning of the book.

Hints too numerous to mention throughout the story question the orthodox Christian and Transcendental belief in the essential goodness of the universe and in the idea of progress. The sea symbolizes the evil in man which reflects a corresponding evil in reality.[3] It is not surprising that such speculations should take Melville to Zoroastrianism, which divides the universe between Ahmazd, the god of light, who is good, and Ahriman, the god of darkness, who is evil—two equal forces in ceaseless conflict. This conception of reality leads to the introduction of the ambiguous harpooner, Fedallah, who acts as an alter ego of Ahab, his evil self;[4] as Mephistopheles luring Ahab Faust to sell his soul for aid in his vengeance against the white whale; and, finally, as a Parsee—a Zoroastrian fireworshipper. Clearly the presence of Fedallah the Parsee suggests that Ahab has practiced Zoroastrian rites, assisted by him. Since fire represents Ahmazd, the good, to the Zoroastrians, it is difficult to understand how it can also symbolize evil, as it does constantly,[5] and finally, in the scene of the corpusants, be virtually identified with the malign element in nature that Ahab is opposing. Nor can this paradox be resolved by blending Fedallah's roles of

---

[1] "Threading its way out from among his grey hairs, and continuing right down one side of his tawny scorched face and neck, till it disappeared in his clothing, you saw a slender rod-like mark, lividly whitish. It resembled that perpendicular seam sometimes made in the straight, lofty trunk of a great tree, when the upper lightning tearingly darts down it, and without wrenching a single twig, peels and grooves out the bark from top to bottom ere running off into the soil, leaving the tree still greenly alive, but branded." (Ch. XXVIII.)

[2] For example, Melville's indebtedness to the style of Sir Thomas Browne, notable in the final paragraphs of chapters L, LVII, LXXXV, XCVIII, CIV, CV, etc., is revealed in imaginative flights that would justify such an explanation if no more reasonable one could be found.

[3] See especially Ch. LVIII.

[4] See Ch. CXXX, and LXXIII, CXXXII.

[5] As in Ch. XCVI, "The Try-Works": "Look not too long in the face of the fire, O Man! Never dream with thy hand on the helm! . . . believe not the artificial fire, when its redness makes all things look ghastly."

Parsee and Mephistopheles.[6] It demands rather an understanding of Ahab's spiritual development through his quest into the nature of things.

Before the opening of *Moby-Dick*, Ahab must be assumed to have accepted the Christian belief in the goodness and omnipotence of God. Speculation (or experience—the book moves on both levels) led him to recognize the presence of ubiquitous evil. Still on the side of the good, Ahab ranged himself against evil and even attempted to eradicate it. At this point, when searching out evil, he was smitten, not by evil but by what he had considered the element of good. When Moby-Dick severed his leg, when lightning struck him,[7] when speculation revealed a preponderance of evil in the grand scheme of being—the story presents itself on all these levels of meaning—Ahab turned from a believer in good-menaced-by-evil to the desperate conviction that evil lay at the heart of reality. From a quester he turned to a hater, madly seeking to find and destroy the "unknown but still reasoning thing," with "outrageous strength" and "inscrutable malice sinewing it" that had injured him.[8]

But Ahab's development does not stop there. The story of *Moby-Dick* is not merely the carrying through of this insane purpose to inevitable self-destruction. On another level Ahab continues to

[6] F. O. Matthiessen, *American Renaissance* (New York, 1941), p. 441, finds a confusion in the symbols which "involves reversals of values that are not always easy to understand. . . . As an instance of the way he made his shifts, you find him first numbering among the sacred associations of whiteness, 'the white forked flame . . . held the holiest on the altar . . . by the Persian fire-worshippers.' Yet when he came to treat the relations between Ahab and Fedallah, he was thinking in terms of a Yankee *Faust*, and the Parsee's power had therefore to be made diabolic. Consequently, fire-worship became a sinister act that had left Ahab scarred for life." I do not think there is any confusion of symbols or reversal of values here, but rather an organic use of them in the dramatic movement of the story, as will be demonstrated.

[7] Upon Ahab's first appearance, he is described as looking "like a man cut away from the stake, when the fire has overrunningly wasted all the limbs without consuming them. . . ." (Ch. XXVIII.) This description, which appears purely metaphorical on first reading, must also be taken literally.

[8] Ch. XXXVI. Also Ch. XLI: "No turbaned Turk, no hired Venetian or Malay, could have smote him with more seeming malice. Small reason was there to doubt, then, that ever since that almost fatal encounter, Ahab had cherished a wild vindictiveness against the whale, all the more fell for that in his frantic morbidness he at last came to identify with him, not only all his bodily woes, but all his intellectual and spiritual exasperations. The White Whale swam before him as the monomaniac incarnation of all those malicious agencies which some deep men feel eating in them, till they are left living on with half a heart and half a lung."

speculate and to develop until he comes finally to the higher wisdom of knowing that man's fate must be tragic,[9] that opposition brings out whatever greatness is his, and that, on the contrary, in a "perfect" world man would be no different from the animals. Speaking of the pull toward love that Pip exerts on him, Ahab says, "My malady becomes my more desired health." (Ch. CXXIX.) With this realization the conflict between "good" and "evil" disappears, for these once alien principles are fused in a conception of a Reality that requires and indeed embodies both.[10]

The fire symbolism in *Moby-Dick* is in complete harmony with these ideas. Ahab first worshipped fire as the destroyer of evil, in the authentic Zoroastrian manner, considering it the principle of light. When doing so he was struck by lightning: fire burned him.[11] The burning was the counterpart of his being maimed by Moby-Dick, although we must assume that it happened before his fated encounter with the Whale (previously a source of nature's bounty) and that the latter spurred him on from disillusion to indignation and madness. Such an order of events is in keeping with the development of the theme of the book; nor do Ahab's actions after being "dismasted" allow for an interlude of fire-worship. His being burned is the revelation—not yet understood by Ahab—that "evil" and "good" are not separate but One. After this experience Ahab hates the fire as he hates Moby-Dick because he considers it essential evil, alien to man and maliciously destructive. As the voyage proceeds and Ahab grows wiser through speculation, he brings his two polar attitudes toward fire together. Ad-

---

[9] This interpretation has been admirably presented by H. A. Myers, "Captain Ahab's Discovery: The Tragic Meaning of *Moby-Dick*," *New England Quarterly*, Spring, 1942,—an article to which I am greatly indebted.

[10] Ishmael touches this idea in the Try-Works chapter: "The sun hides not the ocean, which is the dark side of this earth, and which is two thirds of this earth. So, therefore, that mortal man who hath more of joy than sorrow in him, that mortal man cannot be true—not true, or undeveloped." (Ch. XCVI.) Ahab skirts it in his address to the fire of the corpusants and expresses it explicitly in the last chapter, when he is at the point of death: "Oh lonely death on lonely life! Oh, now I feel my topmost greatness lies in my topmost grief." See Myers, *op. cit.*

[11] In this connection we may note the symbolism of Ahab's words uttered when he is destroying the quadrant: "Cursed be all things that cast man's eyes aloft to that heaven, whose live vividness but scorches him, as these old eyes are even now scorched with thy light, O sun!" (Ch. CXVIII.) It seems probable that Melville intended this fire-worship to have been practiced under the direction of Fedallah, on a previous voyage; but the dramatic requirement of having Ahab smuggle Fedallah aboard, plus the fact of Fedallah's Mephistophelean role and the fact that the mates would have recognized him and thereby lessened his mysteriousness, made it impossible for Melville to be explicit on this point.

dressing the corpusants, he calls fire a "clear spirit" and thus seems to be calling it good; yet in the same speech he says it is unmoved by love or reverence, that it can only kill, and that it is indifferent to man. Yet he worships it now, even though he proclaims that its "right worship is defiance." This attitude is a great development from his earlier insane hatred of Moby-Dick,—a hatred which, curiously enough, must be preserved for the concluding action even though Ahab has in some senses outgrown it.

Ahab, in short, realizes that evil (Emerson would say Fate) cannot be destroyed but that man rises to greatness in struggling with it. More strictly, he realizes the necessity of what he has found to be the nature of being, and he also knows that he is a part of this order, with all its qualities. He indicates the fusion of opposites in the One by saying, "Come in thy lowest form of love, and I will kneel and kiss thee; but at thy highest, come as mere supernal power; and though thou launchest navies of full-freighted worlds, there's that in here that still remains indifferent." And in the next sentence he asserts his affinity with this reality by identifying himself with fire: "Oh, thou clear spirit, of thy fire thou madest me, and like a true child of fire, I breathe it back to thee."[12]

It would have been incongruous for Ahab, at the moment of recognition, to have identified himself with the whale; for this conception the fire is a more expressive symbol. Faced, also, with the dramatic requirements of the chase and the rising tempo of the action which permitted less digression and philosophical extension as the climax approached, Melville set up the accompanying fire-symbol as another string to his bow; with it he could foreshadow, even forestate, his conclusions in a different set of terms, in order to prepare his reader for the implications of the climax. Fire as destroyer and purifier, as in the Phoenix myth, was an obvious complementary symbol to the whale.

Although the fire symbolism greatly enriches the texture of Moby-Dick and particularly adds depth and force to the idea that emerges at the climax, the corpusants scene may seem to raise a formidable question; namely, why, with the wisdom evinced there, did Ahab have to go on to his destruction? Why could he not profit by his tragic insight? How could he ignore his knowledge that good and evil were not separable? The obvious answer—that the tremendous dynamic impetus of the action had to be carried through to its tragic conclusion—merely underlines the question of its probability, even though all aesthetic considerations demand such an outcome. The impetus of the action, however, is such that this

---

[12] Ch. CXIX. Not content with this, Melville goes a step further and describes an ultimate power beyond even the fire: "There is some unsuffusing thing beyond thee, thou clear spirit, to whom all thy eternity is but time, all thy creativeness mechanical. Through thee, thy flaming self, my scorched eyes do dimly see it. Oh, thou foundling fire, thou hermit immemorial, thou too hast thy incommunicable riddle, thy unparticipated grief."

scene, occurring some sixty pages from the end, actually participates in the rush toward the climax. It is turning water moving in from the edge of the maelstrom. More important is the fact that Ahab's tragic wisdom cannot fulfill itself merely as wisdom. Conceiving an alien reality in the Fire, Ahab must, like the Phoenix, experience its destruction in order to experience its purification. He attains through action what cannot be merely reasoned; or, if the word "action" has unwholesome connotations, we might say that experience must be concrete or personal to be true experience.[18] Ahab's glory appears in his tragedy, as he is driven forward by the exasperating knowledge that the inscrutable Other which "heaps" and "tasks" him is indifferent to love and hate alike. Ahab's constant introspection makes him, more than other tragic heroes, a sort of spectator, experiencing catharsis at his own tragedy.

Although the role of fire is thus explained, the role of Fedallah becomes more ambiguous toward the end of the story. On the Faust level he is given an important chapter of prophesies by which he reassures Ahab in his hellish pursuit.[14] This level underlies the final action and climax. But on the higher level of Ahab's growing insight into reality, Fedallah must be cast off, and he is; his part becomes less significant and Ahab's more imposing. These struggling roles of Fedallah are revealed in the following passage, where the attempt to reconcile them is obviously unsuccessful:

And yet, somehow, did Ahab—in his own proper self as daily, hourly, and every instant, commandingly revealed to his subordinates.—Ahab seemed an independent lord; the Parsee but his slave. Still again both seemed yoked together, and an unseen tyrant driving them; the lean shade siding the solid rib. For be this Parsee what he may, all rib and keel was solid Ahab. (Ch. CXXX.)

[18] Melville's recognition that his tragic hero was not caught in the usual net of circumstances from which, after the first fatal step, there was no possible escape, is indicated by his efforts to add another strand to the web of necessity by playing upon the notion that the whole action is *fated*, as in the following passage: "Ahab is for ever Ahab, man. This whole act's immutably decreed. 'Twas rehearsed by thee and me a billion years before this ocean rolled. Fool! I am the Fates' lieutenant; I act under orders. Look thou, underling! that thou obeyest mine.—Stand round me, men. Ye see an old man cut down to the stump; leaning on a shivered lance; propped up on a lonely foot. 'Tis Ahab—his body's part; but Ahab's soul's a centipede, that moves upon a hundred legs. I feel strained, half-stranded, as ropes that tow dismasted frigates in a gale; and I may look so. But ere I break, ye'll hear me crack; and till ye hear *that*, know that Ahab's hawser tows his purpose yet." (Ch. CXXXIV.)

[14] Ch. CXVII. Also Chap. CXXX: "Even as Ahab's eyes so awed the crew's, the inscrutable Parsee's glance awed his."

But perhaps it is not necessary to reconcile them: Fedallah is not a personality, has no revealed consciousness or point of view; he merely serves as part of the stage-setting in the drama of Ahab's quest.

A LIST OF RECOMMENDED READINGS

ARVIN, NEWTON, *Herman Melville*, New York, 1950.

BERTHOFF, WARNER, *The Example of Melville*, Princeton, 1962.

CHASE, RICHARD, *Herman Melville*, New York, 1949.

DAVIS, M. R. and GILMAN, W. H., *The Letters of Herman Melville*, New Haven, 1960.

HILLWAY, TYRUS, *Herman Melville*, New York, 1963.

———, and MANSFIELD, LUTHER S., eds., *Moby-Dick Centennial Essays*, Dallas, 1953.

LEYDA, JAY, *The Melville Log*, 2 vols., New York, 1951.

MATTHIESSEN, F. O., *American Renaissance*, New York, 1941.

METCALF, ELEANOR MELVILLE, *Herman Melville: Cycle and Epicycle*, Cambridge, 1953.

MILLER, PERRY, *The Raven and the Whale*, New York, 1956.

MYERS, H. A., *Are Men Equal?* New York, 1945.

OLSON, CHARLES, *Call Me Ishmael*, Chicago, 1947.

PERCIVAL, M. O., *A Reading of Moby-Dick*, Chicago, 1950.

ROSENBERRY, E., *Melville and the Comic Spirit*, Cambridge, 1955.

SEALTS, MERTON M., JR., *Melville as Lecturer*, Cambridge, 1957.

SEDGWICK, W. E., *Herman Melville: The Tragedy of Mind*, Cambridge, 1944.

STERN, MILTON R., *The Fine Hammered Steel of Herman Melville*, Urbana, Ill., 1957.

THOMPSON, LAWRANCE, *Melville's Quarrel with God*, Princeton, 1952.

THORP, WILLARD, ed., *Herman Melville*, New York, 1938.

VINCENT, HOWARD P., *The Trying-Out of Moby-Dick*, Boston, 1949.

WALCUTT, CHARLES C., *Man's Changing Mask*, Minneapolis, 1966.

WRIGHT, NATHALIA, *Melville's Use of the Bible*, Durham, N. C., 1949.